W9-CAO-643

EVERYMAN'S LIBRARY

EVERYMAN,
I WILL GO WITH THEE,
AND BE THY GUIDE,
IN THY MOST NEED
TO GO BY THY SIDE

R.K. NARAYAN

SWAMI AND FRIENDS, THE BACHELOR OF ARTS, THE DARK ROOM, THE ENGLISH TEACHER

WITH AN INTRODUCTION
BY ALEXANDER MCCALL SMITH

EVERYMAN'S LIBRARY
Alfred A. Knopf New York London Toronto

293

THIS IS A BORZOI BOOK
PUBLISHED BY ALFRED A. KNOPF

First included in Everyman's Library, 2006
First published in Great Britain in 1935 by Hamish Hamilton.
Swami and Friends – © R. K. Narayan, 1935
First published in Great Britain in 1937 by Thomas Nelson & Sons Ltd.
The Bachelor of Arts – © R. K. Narayan, 1937
First published in Great Britain in 1938 by Macmillan & Company Ltd.
The Dark Room – © R. K. Narayan, 1938
First published in Great Britain in 1945 by Eyre & Spottiswoode Ltd.
The English Teacher – © R. K. Narayan, 1945

Introduction Copyright © 2006 by Alexander McCall Smith
Bibliography and Chronology Copyright © 2006 by Everyman's Library
Typography by Peter B. Willberg

All rights reserved under International and Pan-American Copyright Conventions. Published in the United States by Alfred A. Knopf, a division of Random House, Inc., New York, and simultaneously in Canada by Random House of Canada Limited, Toronto. Distributed by Random House, Inc., New York. Published in the United Kingdom by Everyman's Library, Northburgh House, 10 Northburgh Street, London EC1V 0AT, and distributed by Random House (UK) Ltd.

US website: www.randomhouse.com/everymans

ISBN: 0-4000-4476-6 (US)
1-85715-293-X (UK)

A CIP catalogue reference for this book is available from the British Library

Book design by Barbara de Wilde and Carol Devine Carson

Printed and bound in Germany by GGP Media GmbH, Pössneck

CONTENTS

INTRODUCTION

A novelist of all humanity

R. K. Narayan's novels are like a box of Indian sweets: a highly-coloured container conceals a range of delectable treats, all different in a subtle way, but each one clearly from the same place. There are fourteen novels in the oeuvre – enough to create a world. Enthusiasts of his work will read them all and return to them time and again. The busy, or the less committed, may open the box and take out one at random – it does not really matter which order one reads them in. But be warned: the consumption of one leads to a strong craving for more.

Narayan's life spanned the twentieth century, which meant that he belonged both to an old world and a new. At the time of his birth in 1906, the British Raj, that astonishing imperial conceit, was firmly in place, as were those iron-clad notions of caste that were to prove so difficult to shrug off. The British presence in India had brought with it a large civil service, an educational system, and railways – to all of which institutions the people of the subcontinent took with enthusiasm. But it had also brought with it a language, and the literature which that language created, and it is this which proved a most productive legacy. The British took English to India and the Indians gave back a literary tradition which continues to delight and enrich us to this day. Contemporary writers such as Vikram Seth, Rohinton Mistry, or Anita Desai, whose novels have given such pleasure to readers in Europe and North America, stand rooted in a tradition which R. K. Narayan, as one of the earlier Indian novelists to write in English, did a great deal to establish.

Although Narayan did not draw attention to his personal life, he did write a memoir, *My Days*, which tells us a great deal about his boyhood years and the inception and development of his literary career. His childhood was fairly typical of that of a middle-class boy of the time. His father was the headmaster of a school, a somewhat stern figure in his professional life, and this connection with the world of education is very much apparent in the earlier novels, where schools, colleges, and the whole business of becoming educated play a major role. His father's job required mobility, and Narayan spent a number of childhood years living with his grandmother in Madras. Eventually, though, he joined his parents in Mysore, where he attended the school presided over by his father.

He became a voracious reader, wading through the books and magazines which arrived on his father's desk for the school library. As he wrote in *My Days*:

> My father did not mind our taking away whatever we wanted to read – provided we put them back on his desk without spoiling them, as they had to be placed on the school's reading-room table on Monday morning. So our week-end reading was full and varied. We could dream over the advertisement pages in the *Boys' Own Paper* or the *Strand Magazine*. Through the *Strand* we made the acquaintance of all English writers: Conan Doyle, Wodehouse, W.W. Jacobs, Arnold Bennett, and every English fiction writer worth the name . . . Through *Harper's* and the *Atlantic*, and *American Mercury* we attained glimpses of the New World and its writers.

This sense of distance, of being a participant in a culture and yet not being of it, is a familiar feature of the literature of what is now the British Commonwealth and it is vividly portrayed in Narayan's novels. Colonialism hurt and damaged those subjected to it, but it would be inaccurate to portray the process as being a simple matter of subjugation and humiliation; it was far more complex than that. The writer in the colonized country tended to soak up the culture of the colonial power and feel a familiarity and some affection for it, even though the experience of colonialism may have demoralized and destabilized his own colonized culture. This damage, although it may later be seen for what it is, is passed over: in his mind he is a member-in-waiting of a broader community of letters. His aspirations, though, are likely to be dashed; his yearning unfulfilled. Although he may not realize it, the metropolitan culture is largely indifferent to him and his world: the literary circles after which he yearns are distant, impossibly out of reach. Of course, the conquest is feasible, and literary doors may open. Narayan himself made it, as did others, although some did so by leaving the culture in which they had been brought up. Narayan remained in India – an Indian writer who was happy to be read by those outside India but who remained firmly within the world into which he had been born.

The young Narayan was not a great scholar. Having failed his university entrance examinations, he spent a year reading and writing before he eventually succeeded in being admitted to the BA course at Maharaja's College. During this year he acquired a copy of a book called *How to Sell your Manuscripts* and started to send his literary efforts off to magazines in London. He met with no success, encountering for the first time those pieces of paper so familiar, and yet so devastating, to the aspiring writer – the printed rejection slip. In due course he completed his studies and graduated as a Bachelor of Arts. There then followed various attempts by his father and others to secure him a position. These were mostly unsuccessful, although they eventually bore fruit in the shape of a teaching post where he was immediately required to teach Tennyson's *Morte d'Arthur* to a class of burly and uncooperative boys who had no interest in poetry. His teaching career was a dismal failure and shortly afterwards he walked out of the school and returned home. That was that: he would become a writer.

How many have made that decision, and how many have failed. And how many aspiring writers have written their first novel in the belief that it is fiction, only to discover that it is really about them, and, quite commonly, about their childhood. *Swami and Friends*, Narayan's first novel, is a novel of boyhood which draws heavily on his own experiences. Narayan sent the typescript to a series of publishers in London and became accustomed to having it returned at regular intervals. He experienced similar rejection with the short stories which he was now writing, although he eventually succeeded in his ambition to get into print abroad when a piece he wrote for *Punch* magazine in London was accepted and produced a handsome fee of six guineas.

Narayan was to use this small measure of success to persuade his future father-in-law that the financial prospects of a writer were not entirely gloomy. But he needed more than this: the unsuitability of his horoscope was seen by his intended bride's family as being a major drawback to a possible match, and it was only after lengthy discussions that the marriage was able to go ahead. Narayan's personal experience of the vagaries of matrimonial astrology was later reflected in the highly amusing account of astrological discussions in his second novel, *The Bachelor of Arts.*

Now married, Narayan began to earn a living as a journalist. *Swami and Friends* was still doing the rounds in London, with no success, and in desperation he wrote to a friend in Oxford, advising him that if the manuscript were to be returned to him from the publisher who was then considering it, he should weigh it down with a stone and throw it in the Thames. Fortunately the friend ignored this instruction and continued to show the manuscript to prospective publishers. Eventually he showed it to Graham Greene, who was then living in Oxford, and asked him to read it. It sat on Greene's desk for some weeks and then eventually, in one of those moments of great good fortune which occur from time to time in literary history, Greene was sufficiently excited by the book to recommend and secure its publication in October 1935.

The publication of a first novel is one thing, security in the literary world is another. *Swami and Friends* was well-reviewed, but was not a commercial success. In the years that followed, Narayan had to seek a variety of different publishers, and it was to be some time before his reputation was secured amongst a wide international audience. His personal circumstances were also sometimes difficult. In 1939 his wife, Rajam, died of typhoid. Narayan was devastated. In *My Days* he wrote:

> I have described this part of my experience of her sickness and death in *The English Teacher* so fully that I do not, and perhaps cannot, go over it again. More than any other book, *The English Teacher* is autobiographical in content, very little part of it being fiction . . . The toll that typhoid took and all the desolation that followed, with a child to look after, and the psychic adjustments, are based on my own experience.

After the publication of his fourth novel, *The English Teacher*, in 1945, Narayan's writing entered a period of greater maturity and confidence. The autobiographical element which had been so obvious in his earlier writing became less prominent, allowing him to develop his characters more freely. With the growing critical success of his novels in the West, he began to lead the life of the successful literary figure both in India and abroad. He travelled widely and, in time, was showered with honours. He did not leave his accustomed milieu, though, which was Mysore, where he built himself a house, went for rambling and talkative walks, and savoured the quotidian pursuits of life, including agriculture, which he studied with interest. In 1989 he was appointed to membership of the Rajya Sabha, the Upper House of the Indian Parliament. His inaugural speech there was on the subject of Indian children. Children, he said, were being deprived of time to play or to look at birds and trees. In 2001 he died. His mind was clear to the end, and on his death-bed he spoke of his desire to write another novel. This was the man who had confessed to friends: 'I have become lazy since I entered my nineties.'

Narayan's novels are sometimes described as simple. The prose is indeed limpid, the descriptions clear, and the emphasis is on direct and intelligible storytelling, invoking a cast of vivid characters. To the modern reader, accustomed to artifice and allusion, this may give the books a slightly dated feel, and yet it is this quality of simplicity and directness which makes them such fine works of art. Narayan is a storyteller first and foremost, a characteristic which puts him in the company of the great nineteenth-century novelists as well as those twentieth-century writers, such as Somerset Maugham, who believed that the novelist's business is to narrate. His storytelling, though, sometimes has a somewhat rambling flavour, with plots that can wander and which sometimes betray an absence of resolution. But this is not necessarily a flaw: real lives are often aimless and unresolved, and when we read of such lives in literature we are quick to recognize their authenticity. There is nothing false in the world which Narayan creates – quite the opposite, in fact: these novels convey the taste and texture of India with a vividness which strikes the reader as utterly true. Even those who have no first-hand experience of India will feel that what they experience in reading these books is a taste of the real place.

The favoured setting of Narayan's novels is Malgudi, an imaginary town which he describes as having 'swum into view' when he sat down to write *Swami and Friends.* Malgudi provides the strong sense of place which suffuses these books. This is India distilled – an urban India, but one in which a hinterland of jungle, of small villages, of wide plains is still present. When we read about Malgudi we feel we are there, and this powerful impression is created not by detailed descriptions of the countryside or buildings, but by the characters themselves and the suggestive nature of their thought and their speech. It is the voice which is distinctive here. It is a voice which is rooted in a world-view quite different from that which we will encounter in, say, a modern novel located in North America or Western Europe. This voice is sensitive to a distinctive tradition in which the accumulated beliefs and social practices of centuries inform the smallest act. It is a wholly different way of looking at the world.

The four novels in this volume form the first phase of Narayan's career as a novelist. In them we see the author working through a number of concerns which, as a young man, were very much on his mind. These include boyhood (*Swami and Friends*), education and the finding of a role in life (*The Bachelor of Arts*), and marriage (*The Dark Room* and *The English Teacher*). In these early novels, we also see the development of Narayan as a writer, as he makes his way to the more mature and confident vision of the later novels. *Swami and Friends* is episodic in nature, which is exactly what the life of a young boy tends to be. Boys on the whole do not to have a long-term plan; they live for the moment, act on impulse, they pursue new enthusiasms and abandon old. Boyhood friendships, though, can persist, even if they may be tempestuous and competitive. The portrayal of Swami's relationship with Rajam, the son of a senior police officer, reveals how posturing and social embarrassment can loom large in the dealings a boy has with his friends. So many of us can remember the strength of that childhood feeling that our friends have more impressive parents, houses, cars, than we do. Narayan paints a deft picture of that particular anxiety.

In *Swami and Friends* we are given an early sight of the humour which runs through Narayan's novels. One of the features of British colonialism was the export of cricket, a game which strikes North Americans as being opaque and slow-moving. But at the time that *Swami* was written, cricket was more than just a sport – it stood, quite absurdly, for the whole ethos of an empire. Thus although we see Swami raised to heights of indignation by a political orator who laments the passivity of his countrymen which has allowed them to be dominated by an alien power, when it comes to cricket the boy is sufficiently enthusiastic to spend some time trying to explain what the game is all about to his aged grandmother. This comic scene, like so much of Narayan's humour, has a strong poignancy to it. The grandmother represents the old India, a world in which cricket is not played. Her ignorance of the rules is a vivid metaphor for the extent to which the old and the new India are different worlds. The cricket episode also allows Narayan to portray the naive aspirations of the boys. This is a familiar theme in many of his works, where so many of the characters are striving for something which is often just beyond their grasp.

Narayan's second novel, *The Bachelor of Arts*, again contains autobiographical elements but is much more satisfying in its structure than *Swami*. Chandran, the protagonist of this novel, is a typical Narayan hero – he is modest, slightly at odds with his surroundings, and engaged in a search. The search in this case is for freedom, and it takes place in the face of all the constraints which the Hindu family and wider Indian society can place in the way of a young man eager to find himself. It is in this novel that we see one of Narayan's main preoccupations come to the fore. This is marriage, and the complexities that Indian marriage involved and, indeed, still involves. Contemporary Westerners are sometimes astounded by the sheer fuss involved in an Indian marriage. In particular, the elaborate negotiations and the very large sums of money spent on celebrations impress outsiders, especially those who are accustomed to relatively informal weddings. The traditional

Hindu marriage, however, is an altogether different thing from the typical arrangements of a Western couple: it involves the families on both sides, who are strongly interested in the suitability of the other side for a union. This means that the young man or young woman who nurtures hopes of a love-match, detached from considerations of social position or caste, may be heading for a major confrontation with family members who have very different ideas.

The Bachelor of Arts tells of a young man whose views of life, including marriage, are more 'modern' than those of his family. His relatives are immersed in the traditional beliefs of their religion: marriage is not a matter of personal choice, but something that is divinely ordained. As Chandran's mother points out to her son: 'It is all a matter of fate ... You can marry only the person whom you are destined to marry and at the appointed time. When the time comes, let her be the ugliest girl, she will look all right to the destined eye.' And in a letter which he writes to Chandran's father, the intended bride's own father says: '... we can only propose. He on the Thirupathi Hills alone knows what is best for us.' When Chandran's horoscope is found to involve incompatibilities with that of the girl whom he wishes to marry, the full force of this fatalistic view of human affairs comes home to him. What can a young man do in such circumstances other than give in or defy the convictions of everybody about him? And the prospect of revolt defeats Chandran, who is ultimately drawn back into the world of family and tradition, even although he does succeed in negotiating for himself a certain freedom. This process of self-exploration, challenge, and finally reconciliation is a familiar theme in Narayan's fiction. In a sense it mirrors Narayan's own life as a man whose vision and understanding transported him beyond the rigid beliefs and practices of his society but never took him away from that society. And that central message – that we can be ourselves to an extent but that we all need to be anchored in society – is really a very attractive feature of these novels. Ultimately we feel comfortable and secure in reading Narayan because we detect in his work a resolution, an acceptance that we ourselves need in our own lives.

If there is a great deal of light and freedom in these two

charming early novels, then in his third novel, *The Dark Room*, we enter graver, more disturbing territory. Marriage is the common theme of three of the novels in this collection, and in *The Dark Room*, which Narayan was to describe as an early women's liberation novel, we see how the traditional Hindu marriage could trap women in complete subservience. Savitri is married to a tin-god husband, Ramani, a man who runs a branch office of an insurance agency, who is prosperous enough to drive a car (remember that this novel was published in 1938), and who expects in his home-life to be danced attendance upon by his wife. The portrait of this domestic tyrant is a compelling one, and we are also appalled, but fascinated, by the coquettish Shanta Bai, with whom he starts an affair. The conduct of this affair is beautifully described as Narayan directs his gaze at the shoddiness and deception of the office romance. At the end of the day the patient Savitri, driven to an attempt at suicide as the only way out of her intolerable situation, returns to the matrimonial home and her unapologetic husband, defeated by centuries of custom. Hers is an awful fate, and although the position of women in traditional societies has improved, we might leave this book remembering that there are many women for whom this story would still ring very true.

Marriage again plays a central role in *The English Teacher*. Narayan lost his wife to typhoid, and that is what happens to the central character, Krishna, in this novel. It is very sad, and very painful – just as it must have been for him in real life. The grief here is described with great tenderness, in passages that are quite haunting in their simplicity. The prose is like a funeral bell: solemn and resonant. As in the earlier novels, the idea of acceptance looms large: ultimately the hero, Krishna, has to accept the fact of the loss of his wife and the loneliness that follows. He has fought against this brute fact by attempting to communicate with her through paranormal means, but this leads nowhere, in the same way as all the smoke and mirrors of the various mystic figures who parade through Malgudi seem ultimately to lead nowhere.

R. K. Narayan is a much beloved novelist, and for very good reason. Although the books in this volume were all written more than half a century ago, they are the freshest, the most sparkling of gems. The struggle of the characters against social restrictions, their struggle to be something other than that which social destiny appears to be forcing them to be, are struggles with which we can all identify to a greater or lesser extent. As Samuel Johnson observed, many people waste part of their lives trying to be something they are not. Eventually, of course, they may come to realize what they really are, and if that happens to be a citizen of a small town, rather like Narayan's Malgudi, bound up with neighbours and their concerns, sewn into a family and a nation, then there are very much worse fates than that.

Alexander McCall Smith

Alexander McCall Smith is a professor of medical law at Edinburgh University. He was born in what is now known as Zimbabwe and taught law at the University of Botswana. He is the author of over fifty books on a wide range of subjects, including the internationally bestselling novels of the No. 1 Ladies Detective Agency series and the Sunday Philosophy Club series. He lives in Scotland.

SELECT BIBLIOGRAPHY

R. K. NARAYAN, *My Days: A Memoir*, Viking, New York, 1974, Chatto & Windus, London, 1975.

SUSAN RAM and N. RAM, *R. K. Narayan: The Early Years*, 1906–1945, Viking, New Delhi, 1996.

RANGA RAO, *R. K. Narayan* ('Makers of Indian Literature' series), Sahitya Akademi, New Delhi, 2004.

WILLIAM WALSH, *R. K. Narayan: A Critical Appreciation*, William Heinemann Ltd., London, 1982, University of Chicago Press, Chicago, 1982.

CHRONOLOGY

DATE	AUTHOR'S LIFE	LITERARY CONTEXT
1906	Rasipuram Krishnaswami Narayanaswami is born in Madras on 10 October at 1 Vellala Street in the Purasawalkam, district. He is one of several children in a middle-class family. His mother is frail and his father, a headmaster in the government educational service, moves frequently, so the boy is brought up by his grandmother.	Kipling: *Puck of Pook's Hill.* Galsworthy: *The Man of Property* (vol. 1 of *The Forsyte Saga*).
1907		Conrad: *The Secret Agent.* Kipling first English Nobel laureate for literature.
1909		Wells: *Ann Veronica*; *Tono-Bungay.*
1910		Forster: *Howards End.* Wells: *The History of Mr Polly.*
1911		Conrad: *Under Western Eyes.* Bennett: *Clayhanger.* Chesterton: *The Innocence of Father Brown.*
1912	Attends a severe Lutheran missionary school where, as the only Brahmin boy in the class, he is often mocked by the teachers. Begins to learn English (his native language is Tamil). Dissatisfied with his schooling, his grandmother coaches him every evening.	Mann: *Death in Venice.* Tagore: *Gitanjali: Song Offerings.*
1913		Tagore: *The Crescent Moon.* Tagore awarded Nobel Prize for Literature.
1914		Tagore: *The King of the Dark Chamber*; *The Post Office.* Joyce: *Dubliners.* W. W. Jacobs: *Night Watches.*

HISTORICAL EVENTS

Foundation of Muslim League, first Muslim political party in India. Simla deputation to British Viceroy, Lord Minto, asking for separate electorates for Muslim community.

Asiatic Registration Act becomes law in the province of Transvaal, South Africa.

Minto-Morley Reforms: Indians given more power in legislative affairs; creation of separate Muslim electorates. Blériot flies across the English Channel.
Dalai Lama flees from the Chinese and takes refuge in India.

George V recognized as King-Emperor in Delhi (during a hunting trip in Nepal the King bags 21 tigers, 8 rhinos, and a bear). Transfer of capital to Delhi announced.

Sinking of *Titanic*.

Gandhi arrested as he leads a march of Indian miners in South Africa.

Beginning of World War I (to 1918); large numbers of Indians, Hindu and Muslim, rally to the British cause. General Smuts begins negotiations with Gandhi to eradicate many of the racist laws imposed on South African Indians.

DATE	AUTHOR'S LIFE	LITERARY CONTEXT
1915		Buchan: *The Thirty-nine Steps.* Lawrence: *The Rainbow.* Maugham: *Of Human Bondage.*
1916		Tagore: *Fruit Gathering.* Joyce: *A Portrait of the Artist as a Young Man.*
1917		Kipling: *A Diversity of Creatures.*
1918	Joins Besant Scouts of India, vowing to serve 'God, Freedom, and India'.	
1919		Woolf: *Night and Day.* Wodehouse: *My Man Jeeves.* Saki: *The Toys of Peace.*
1920	Begins attending CRC High School, 'a school with no particular quality of good or evil about it'.	Mansfield: *Bliss.* Wharton: *The Age of Innocence.*
1921		Maugham: *The Trembling of a Leaf.*
1922	Admitted to Christian College High School.	Eliot: *The Waste Land.* Joyce: *Ulysses.* Mansfield: *The Garden Party.*
1924	Sent to Mysore, where his father has been appointed headmaster of Maharaja's Collegiate High School; begins studies at this school.	Ford: *Parade's End.* Forster: *A Passage to India.*
1925	Fails university entrance exams; is left free for a year to read what he pleases. Starts to write, 'in the style of any writer who was uppermost in my mind at the time', and begins sending off manuscripts.	Tagore: *Red Oleanders*; *Broken Ties and Other Stories.* Hemingway: *In Our Time.* Eliot: *Poems 1909–25.* Fitzgerald: *The Great Gatsby.* Kafka: *The Trial.*
1926	Enters Maharaja's College, Mysore, studying for a BA.	Ghose: *Songs of Love and Death.* Kafka: *The Castle.*
1927		Gandhi: *My Experiments with Truth.* Proust: *A la recherche du temps perdu.* Woolf: *To the Lighthouse.*
1929		Tagore: *Farewell, My Friend.* Faulkner: *The Sound and the Fury.* Hemingway: *A Farewell to Arms.* Graves: *Goodbye to All That.*

CHRONOLOGY

HISTORICAL EVENTS

Mahatma Gandhi returns to India from South Africa.

Muslim League and Congress Party agree to work together to campaign for self-government.

Bolshevik Revolution in Russia.
End of World War I.

Versailles peace conference. Montague-Chelmsford Reforms (Government of India Act): reorganizes central legislature but falls short of Indian expectations. Demonstrations against British rule become widespread; massacre of peaceful protesters by armed British troops at Amritsar. Non-cooperation movement launched by Gandhi. League of Nations created.

Opening of the Victoria Memorial in Calcutta.

Gandhi sentenced to six years' imprisonment for civil disobedience – he is released after serving two years. Establishment of USSR. Stalin beomes General Secretary of Communist Party.
Gateway of India monument in Delhi is completed. Gandhi undertakes a fast to end Hindu–Muslim rioting. Death of Lenin.

Commuter rail service introduced in Bombay.

Germany admitted to League of Nations.

Lindbergh makes first solo flight over Atlantic.

Gandhi nominates Jawaharlal Nehru to succeed him as leader of the Congress movement. Wall Street Crash. Period of worldwide depression begins. First non-stop flight from England to India.

DATE	AUTHOR'S LIFE	LITERARY CONTEXT
1930	Graduates from Maharaja's College. Begins work on *Swami and Friends* while staying with his grandmother in Bangalore. After abortive attempts to become a railway officer and bank official he takes up teaching at a government school in Chennapatna.	Faulkner: *As I Lay Dying*. Pritchett: *The Spanish Virgin and Other Stories*.
1931	Gives up teaching and resolves to become a full-time writer, which he is able to do with the support of his family. Stays in Madras where he pursues editors of newspapers and magazines; one book review and an article published. His friend Kittu Purna leaves for Oxford, promising to find a publisher for *Swami and Friends*.	Premchand: 'Deliverance'. Woolf: *The Waves*. Walpole: *Judith Paris*. Hammett: *The Glass Key*.
1932	Receives 18 rupees for the publication of a short story in *The Hindu*.	Tagore: *Sheaves, Poems and Songs*. Premchand: *Arena of Action*. Huxley: *Brave New World*. Waugh: *Black Mischief*.
1933	Publication of a children's story brings in 30 rupees. A short piece, 'How to Write an Indian Novel', lampooning Western writers, is accepted by *Punch*. In July, while staying with his sister in Coimbatore, sees a young girl drawing water from a street-tap and falls in love with her. Befriends her father, a headmaster, and asks for her hand in marriage. After some difficulties, the wedding takes place a few months later, and Rajam joins her husband's household. Takes a job as Mysore correspondent for *The Justice*, a Madras newspaper.	Maugham: *Ah King*. Wodehouse: *Mulliner Nights*; *Heavy Weather*. Hemingway: *Winner Take Nothing*.
1934	His father becomes bed-ridden after a severe stroke. Purna approaches Graham Greene, who is living in Oxford, and gives him the manuscript of *Swami and Friends*.	Fitzgerald: *Tender is the Night*. Waugh: *A Handful of Dust*; *Ninety-two Days*.

CHRONOLOGY

HISTORICAL EVENTS

Mahatma Gandhi sets off on famous salt march, sparking off a wave of anti-British demonstrations and boycotts. Chandrasekhara Raman wins Nobel Prize for Physics.

Inauguration of New Delhi as India's capital. Series of Round Table Conferences in London to discuss the future of India (to 1933).

Clampdown on demonstrators in India; 60,000 Congress activists are imprisoned. Gandhi's hunger strike against the treatment of untouchables. Election of Roosevelt in US.

Gandhi's hunger strike to protest against British oppression in India. Hitler becomes German Chancellor. Roosevelt announces 'New Deal'.

Gandhi resigns from Congress Party.

DATE	AUTHOR'S LIFE	LITERARY CONTEXT
1935	Shortens his name to R. K. Narayan on Graham Greene's suggestion. With the help of Greene, his first novel *Swami and Friends*, set in the fictional town of Malgudi, is published in the UK by Hamish Hamilton. The book receives enthusiastic reviews though sales are disappointing. Gives up his job on *The Justice*.	Anand: *Untouchable*. Isherwood: *Mr Norris Changes Trains*.
1936	Birth of his daughter, Hemavati.	Anand: *Coolie*. Premchand: *The Gift of a Cow*. Orwell: *Keep the Aspidistra Flying*
1937	*The Bachelor of Arts* is published by Nelson, thanks again to Graham Greene's recommendation. Death of his father. Money is short and Narayan works as a hack journalist to make ends meet.	Anand: *Two Leaves and a Bud*. Kumar: *Tyagapatra* (The Resignation). Steinbeck: *Of Mice and Men*.
1938	*The Dark Room* is published by Macmillan and receives enthusiastic reviews.	Rao: *Kanthapura*. Greene: *Brighton Rock*. Bowen: *The Death of the Heart*.
1939	Narayan's wife, Rajam, dies of typhoid. He elects to bring up his daughter himself. Endures a period of depression, during which time he attempts to contact his wife through spiritual mediums. Publishes *Mysore*, a travel book. Begins a regular Sunday column for *The Hindu*.	Anand: *The Village*. Joyce: *Finnegans Wake*. Steinbeck: *The Grapes of Wrath*.
1940		Anand: *Across the Black Waters*. Greene: *The Power and the Glory*. Hemingway: *For Whom the Bell Tolls*.
1941	Begins publishing his own quarterly journal, *Indian Thought*. Abandons it after three issues due to disappointing sales.	
1942		Anand: *The Sword and the Sickle*. Camus: *The Stranger*. Eliot: *Four Quartets*.

CHRONOLOGY

HISTORICAL EVENTS

Government of India Act creates a central legislature; provincial government handed over to elected Indian representatives. Burma separated from India. In Germany Nuremberg laws deprive Jews of citizenship and rights.

Outbreak of Spanish Civil War (to 1939). Hitler and Mussolini form Rome–Berlin Axis. Stalin's 'Great Purge' of the Communist Party (to 1938).

Japanese invasion of China.

Germany annexes Austria; Munich crisis.

Hitler invades Poland; outbreak of World War II. Gandhi calls on the world to disarm. The Indian subcontinent contributes the largest volunteer army in history (some 2.5 million servicemen and women) to the Allied cause.

Italy enters war as German ally. Fall of France. Battle of Britain. Muslim League adopt the Pakistan Resolution, which demands an independent state for Muslims.

Japanese attack Pearl Harbor; US enters war. Japanese invasion of Burma begins. Hitler invades USSR. India's population is 389 million.

Sir Stafford Cripps visits India with British government's offer of complete self-government after the war: described by Gandhi as 'a post-dated cheque on a failing bank', it is rejected by Hindus and Muslims alike. Gandhi calls on British to 'Quit India' but the movement to eject the British is quickly suppressed. Japanese troops capture Rangoon and consolidate their position in Burma.

DATE	AUTHOR'S LIFE	LITERARY CONTEXT
1943	*Malgudi Days* published by Indian Thought Publications, which also publishes *Dodu and Other Stories* the same year.	
1944		
1945	*The English Teacher* published by Eyre & Spottiswoode, where Greene is a director. *Cyclone and Other Stories* published by Indian Thought Publications, Mysore, and Rock House & Sons, Madras.	Borges: *Fictions*. Orwell: *Animal Farm*. Waugh: *Brideshead Revisited*.
1946		
1947	*An Astrologer's Day and Other Stories*.	Rao: *The Cow of the Barricades*. Maugham: *Creatures of Circumstance*. C. P. Snow: *The Light and the Dark*.
1948	Begins building his own house on a plot of land outside Mysore.	Desani: *All About H. Hatterr*. Greene: *The Heart of the Matter*.
1949	*Mr Sampath*.	Orwell: *Nineteen Eighty-Four*. Bowen: *The Heat of the Day*.
1950		Powell: *A Question of Upbringing* (vol. 1 of *A Dance to the Music of Time*).
1951		Ruskin Bond: *The Room on the Roof*. Chaudhuri: *Autobiography of an Unknown Indian*. Salinger: *The Catcher in the Rye*.
1952	*The Financial Expert* published in the UK by Methuen. The following year it becomes the first of Narayan's works to be published in the US (by Michigan State College Press).	Beckett: *Waiting for Godot*. Waugh: *Men at Arms* (vol. 1 of *The Sword of Honour Trilogy*). Ezekiel: *A Time to Change* (poems).

CHRONOLOGY

HISTORICAL EVENTS

Major famine in Bengal leaves three million people dead. Allied invasion of Italy. Fall of Mussolini.

D-Day: Normandy landings. Japanese troops driven out of Burma.
Fall of Berlin and suicide of Hitler. Unconditional surrender of Germany. Atomic bombs dropped on Hiroshima and Nagasaki. End of World War II. Foundation of the United Nations. Truman US President. Labour Party comes to power in Britain, with Attlee as Prime Minister.

Cabinet Mission: three British ministers led by Lord Pethwick-Lawrence visit India to negotiate terms for Indian independence. They refuse to accept Muslim claims for partition and their proposals are rejected by both Congress and the Muslim League. Riots between Hindus and Muslims; 5,000 lose their lives in Calcutta. USSR extends influence in Eastern Europe. Beginning of Cold War.
In February, British government resolves to hand over power in June 1948 regardless of whether or not a new Indian constitution is in place. Newly appointed viceroy Lord Mountbatten, persuaded that partition is the only way forward, puts pressure on the Congress leaders to agree. Indian Independence Act is hurried through and on 15 August India is partitioned into two Dominions; India (Hindu) and Pakistan (Muslim). Jawaharal Nehru Prime Minister of India.
Assassination of Mahatma Gandhi. Campaign of violence by Communists in India crushed by new government. The last British troops leave India. Jewish state of Israel comes into existence. Soviet blockade of West Berlin. Apartheid introduced in South Africa.
Chinese Revolution. North Atlantic Treaty signed.

Beginning of Korean War. Mother Teresa founds the Missionaries of Charity in Calcutta.

India declares itself a Republic within the British Commonwealth; first national general election confirms India's status as world's largest democracy; Congress Party is dominant. First Five-Year Plan in India sets in motion huge number of irrigation projects.

Eisenhower elected US President. Accession of Elizabeth II in UK.

DATE	AUTHOR'S LIFE	LITERARY CONTEXT
1953	*The English Teacher* published in the US by Michigan State College Press under the title *Grateful to Life and Death.* Narayan's new house at Yadavagiri being finally ready for occupation, he uses it as a retreat for writing, continuing to live with his extended family at their home in the Laxmipuram district.	Anand: *Private Life of an Indian Prince.* Hartley: *The Go-Between.*
1954		Markandaya: *Nectar in the Sieve.* Masters: *Bhowani Junction.* K. Amis: *Lucky Jim.*
1955	*Waiting for the Mahatma.*	Ezekiel: *Sixty Poems.* Nabokov: *Lolita.*
1956	Marriage of Hema with her cousin Chandru. Although their home is 120 miles from Mysore, Narayan visits them frequently over the years and plays an important role in the life of his two grandchildren. *Lawley Road and Other Stories* and *Next Sunday: Sketches and Essays.* Leaves for the United States.	Pillai: *Chemmeen* ('Shrimps'). Mishima: *The Temple of the Golden Pavilion.* Mahfouz: *The Cairo Trilogy* (to 1957).
1957		Dom Moraes: *A Beginning* (poems). Kerouac: *On the Road.* Pasternak: *Doctor Zhivago.*
1958	*The Guide* (written while travelling in America), the first of Narayan's novels to be published by Viking in the US.	Jhabvala: *Esmond in India.* Achebe: *Things Fall Apart.* Lampedusa: *The Leopard.*
1959		Chaudhuri: *A Passage to England.* Bellow: *Henderson the Rain King.* Burroughs: *Naked Lunch.* Grass: *The Tin Drum.*
1960	Narayan wins the Sahitya Akademi (India's National Academy of Letters) Award for *The Guide.*	Malgonkar: *Distant Drum.* Moraes: *Poems.* Rao: *The Serpent and the Rope.* Updike: *Rabbit, Run* (vol. 1 of *Rabbit* tetralogy).

HISTORICAL EVENTS

Death of Stalin. European Court of Human Rights set up in Strasbourg. Korean War ends.

Indo-Chinese Treaty. Vietnam War begins.

India establishes a policy that bars foreign print media from publishing within the country. India's parliament accepts Hindu divorce.
Second Five Year Plan in India aims to increase national income by 25 per cent. Soviets invade Hungary. Suez crisis.

European Economic Community founded.

India begins designing and buying equipment for a plutonium reprocessing plant at Trombay.

Castro seizes power in Cuba.

Union of Kashmir with India. Bombay state split into Gujarat and Maharashtra states.

DATE	AUTHOR'S LIFE	LITERARY CONTEXT
1961	*The Man-Eater of Malgudi.*	Markandaya: *A Silence of Desire.* Naipaul: *A House for Mr Biswas.* Heller: *Catch-22.* Spark: *The Prime of Miss Jean Brodie.*
1962		Malgonkar: *Combat of Shadows.* Nabokov: *Pale Fire.* Solzhenitsyn: *One Day in the Life of Ivan Denisovich.*
1963		Malgonkar: *The Princes.* Markandaya: *Possession.*
1964	*My Dateless Diary: An American Journey* (travel book). *Gods, Demons and Others* (retelling of stories from the Sanskrit religious epics). Meets Graham Greene briefly while visiting London.	Malgonkar: *A Bend in the Ganges.* Naipaul: *An Area of Darkness.* Bellow: *Herzog.*
1965	Opening of *Survival,* the film based on *The Guide.*	Jnanpith Award, Indian literary prize, established. Das: *Summer in Calcutta* (poems). Moraes: *John Nobody* (poems). Rao: *Cat and Shakespeare.* Scott: *Raj Quartet* (to 1975). Tagore: *The Housewarming.*
1966		Markandaya: *A Handful of Rice.* Bulgakov: *The Master and Margarita.*
1967	*The Vendor of Sweets.*	Das: *The Descendants.* Márquez: *One Hundred Years of Solitude.*
1968	Play version of *The Guide,* by Patricia Rinehart and Harvey Breit, opens on Broadway on 6 March and closes within a week.	Solzhenitsyn: *Cancer Ward.*
1969		Markandaya: *The Coffer Dams.*
1970	*A Horse and Two Goats* (short stories).	
1971		Tagore: *The Broken Nest.*
1972	*The Ramayana* (shortened modern prose version of the Indian epic).	Malgonkar: *The Devil's Wind.*

CHRONOLOGY

HISTORICAL EVENTS

Third Five Year Plan in India propels the country into the ranks of the ten most industrialized nations; India's population rises to 434 million. Goa liberated from Portuguese rule. John F. Kennedy elected US President. Erection of Berlin Wall. Yuri Gagarin becomes first man in space.

Sino-Indian border clashes lead to threats of Chinese invasion. Cuban missile crisis.

Assassination of John F. Kennedy.

Death of Nehru; succeeded by Shastri. Khrushchev deposed and replaced by Brezhnev.

Indo-Pakistan War. Tamil riots against Hindi language; English confirmed as official language of India.

Mrs Indira Gandhi, daughter of Nehru, becomes Prime Minister of India.

Arab–Israeli Six-Day War. Population of India reaches 500 million.

Student unrest in US and throughout Europe. Soviet-led invasion of Czechoslovakia. Assassination of Martin Luther King. Nixon US President. India refuses to sign Nuclear Non-Proliferation Treaty. The *Beatles* arrive in India for transcendental meditation with the Maharishi Mahesh Yogi.

Americans land first man on the moon.
The shooting of tigers is banned in India.

Revolt in East Pakistan, state of emergency, formation of Bangladesh. Indira Gandhi strips Indian princes of their titles and abolishes privy purses. Pakistan leaves the Commonwealth. President Amin expels Ugandan Asians.

DATE	AUTHOR'S LIFE	LITERARY CONTEXT
1973		Das: *The Old Playhouse and Other Poems.* Markandaya: *Two Virgins.* Jhabvala: *A New Dominion.* Pynchon: *Gravity's Rainbow.* Solzhenitsyn: *The Gulag Archipelago* (to 1975).
1974	*My Days: A Memoir. Reluctant Guru* (essays).	Das: *My Story* (autobiography). Bellow: *Humboldt's Gift.*
1975		Das: *Manas* (novel). Jhabvala: *Heat and Dust.* Singh: *Train to Pakistan.* Rushdie: *Grimus.* Levi: *The Periodic Table.*
1976	*The Painter of Signs.*	Das: *Alphabet of Lust* (novel). Rao: *Comrade Kirillov.*
1977	*The Emerald Route* (travel book).	Desai: *Fire on the Mountain.* Morrison: *Song of Solomon.*
1978	*The Mahabharata* (shortened modern prose version).	Pillai: *Kayar* (The Rope). Greene: *The Human Factor.* P. Fitzgerald: *The Bookshop.*
1979		Desai: *Games at Twilight.* Naipaul: *A Bend in the River; India: A Wounded Civilization.* Calvino: *If on a winter's night a traveler.*
1980	Made an Honorary Member of the American Academy and Institute of Arts and Letters. Awarded the A. C. Benson award by the Royal Society of Literature.	Desai: *Clear Light of Day.*
1981		Naipaul: *Among the Believers: an Islamic Journey.* Rushdie: *Midnight's Children.*
1982	*Malgudi Days* (short stories).	Levi: *If not Now, When?*
1983	*A Tiger for Malgudi.*	Rushdie: *Shame.*
1984		Brookner: *Hotel du Lac.* Barnes: *Flaubert's Parrot.*
1985	*Under the Banyan Tree and Other Stories.*	Márquez: *Love in the Time of Cholera.*

HISTORICAL EVENTS

Arab–Israeli War. Rising prices and downturn in Indian economy. India establishes a network of tiger reserves.

Resignation of Nixon following Watergate scandal. Strikes and demonstrations against Indira Gandhi. India explodes its first nuclear device.
State of emergency declared in India because of growing strikes and unrest (to 1977). First Indian satellite launched into space, on a Soviet rocket. End of Vietnam War. Civil war between Christians and Moslems in Lebanon.

Death of Mao Tse-Tung. Soweto massacre in South Africa.

First defeat of Congress Party in India since Independence. Morarji Desai becomes Prime Minister. Zulfiqar Ali Bhutto, Prime Minister of Pakistan since 1971, overthrown by the military, and later hanged (1979). Carter US President.
P. W. Botha comes to power in South Africa.

Margaret Thatcher first woman Prime Minister in UK. Carter and Brezhnev sign SALT-2 arms limitation treaty. Soviet occupation of Afghanistan. Mother Teresa is awarded the Nobel Peace Prize.

Indira Gandhi wins election and returns to power. Sanjay Gandhi killed in plane crash. Lech Walesa leads strikes in Gdansk, Poland. Iran–Iraq War (to 1988).

Ronald Reagan becomes US President.

Falklands War.
Emergency rule invoked in Punjab to suppress Sikh terrorism.
Indira Gandhi assassinated by Sikh bodyguard; her son, Rajiv, becomes Prime Minister (to 1989). Bhopal gas leak kills 2,000. Indian troops storm the Sikh Golden Temple in Amritsar. Famine in Ethiopia.
Heavy fighting in Kashmir. India files suit against Union Carbide over Bhopal disaster. Riots in South Africa. Gorbachev General Secretary in USSR.

DATE	AUTHOR'S LIFE	LITERARY CONTEXT
1986	*Talkative Man.*	Seth: *The Golden Gate.*
1987		Rushdie: *The Jaguar Smile: A Nicaraguan Journey.* Morrison: *Beloved.*
1988	*A Writer's Nightmare: Selected Essays 1958–1988.*	Chatterjee: *An English August.* Desai: *Baumgartner's Bombay.* Ghosh: *The Shadow Lines.* Rao: *The Chessmaster and His Moves.* Rushdie: *The Satanic Verses.*
1989	Made a member of the Rajya Sabha (the non-elective House of Parliament in India). His inaugural speech is on the plight of Indian children. Visiting professor for the fall semester at the University of Texas at Austin. *A Story-Teller's World* (essays).	Ezekiel: *Collected Poems.* Tharoor: *The Great Indian Novel.*
1990	*The World of Nagaraj.*	Naipaul: *India: A Million Mutinies Now.* Rushdie: *Haroun and the Sea of Stories.* P. Fitzgerald: *The Gate of Angels.* Trevor: *Two Lives.*
1991		Mistry: *Such a Long Journey.* Kanga: *Heaven on Walls.* Okri: *Songs of Enchantment.*
1992	*Malgudi Landscapes: The Best of R. K. Narayan.* Leaves his home in Yadavagiri, Mysore, and settles down in Madras, closer to his grandchildren.	Das: *Padmavati the Harlot and Other Stories.* Ghosh: *In an Antique Land.* Ondaatje: *The English Patient.*
1993	*The Grandmother's Tale* (three novellas: 'The Grandmother's Tale', 'Guru' and 'Salt and Sawdust') published by Heinemann in the UK. *Salt and Sawdust: Stories and Tabletalk* published by Penguin in India.	Seth: *A Suitable Boy.*
1994	*The Grandmother's Tale and Selected Stories* published by Viking in the US. Narayan's daughter, Hema, dies of cancer. Narayan is looked after by Hema's husband Chandru for the remainder of his life.	Gunesekera: *Reef.*

CHRONOLOGY

HISTORICAL EVENTS

Benazir Bhutto returns to Pakistan. Gorbachev–Reagan summit. Nuclear explosion at Chernobyl.
Seventy-two people killed by Sikh extremists.

Benazir Bhutto Prime Minister of Pakistan. George Bush elected US President. Gorbachev announces big troop reductions suggesting end of Cold War.

Pakistan rejoins the Commonwealth. V. P. Rao becomes Prime Minister of India. De Klerk becomes South African President. USSR loses control of Eastern Europe; fall of Berlin Wall.

V. P. Singh forms coalition government.

First Gulf War. Yeltsin President of Russia. USSR disbanded. Rajiv Gandhi assassinated during Indian election campaign by Tamil suicide bomber; Narashima Rao becomes Prime Minister in tenth general election. Destruction of the Mosque of Babur at Ayodhya by Hindus leads to Hindu–Muslim rioting in several Indian cities. Bill Clinton elected US President. Civil war in former Yugoslavia.

Israel hands over West Bank and Jericho to the Palestinians.

Mandela and ANC sweept to victory in South African elections. Rwandan massacres. Russian military action against the Chechen republic.

DATE	AUTHOR'S LIFE	LITERARY CONTEXT
1995		Desai: *Journey to Ithaca.* Kesavan: *Looking Through Glass.* Rushdie: *The Moor's Last Sigh.*
1996	*Tales from Malgudi.*	Mistry: *A Fine Balance.*
1997		
1998		Arundhati Roy becomes first Indian-based writer to win Booker Prize for her novel *The God of Small Things.* Rao: *Great Indian Way: A Life of Mahatma Gandhi.*
1999		Seth: *An Equal Music.* Desai: *Feasting, Fasting.*
2000		Desai: *Diamond Dust.*
2001	Narayan dies aged 94 in a private hospital in Chennai (formerly Madras) on 13 May.	

HISTORICAL EVENTS

Bharatha Janata Party (BJP) government collapses after a matter of days.
Bombay becomes Mumbai, Madras becomes Chennai.
Fiftieth anniversary of Indian Independence. Death of Mother Teresa.
India declares itself a nuclear weapons state. BJP form coalition government. Amartya Sen wins the Nobel Prize for Economics.

Pakistani troops cross India-Kashmir border leading to fierce fighting in Kargil–Drass region. Thirteenth general election; BJP government.
India's population reaches 1 billion. Sonia Gandhi becomes President of Congress Party. Vishvanath Anand wins World Chess Championship.
Twin towers of World Trade Center in New York collapse after terrorist attack. Earthquake in northern Gujarat leaves 20,000 dead and an estimated 100,000 trapped in the debris. Terrorist attack on Indian parliament.

SWAMI AND FRIENDS

To my parents

CONTENTS

CHAPTER ONE

MONDAY MORNING

It was Monday morning. Swaminathan was reluctant to open his eyes. He considered Monday specially unpleasant in the calendar. After the delicious freedom of Saturday and Sunday, it was difficult to get into the Monday mood of work and discipline. He shuddered at the very thought of school: that dismal yellow building; the fire-eyed Vedanayagam, his class-teacher; and the headmaster with his thin long cane ...

By eight he was at his desk in his 'room', which was only a corner in his father's dressing-room. He had a table on which all his things, his coat, cap, slate, ink-bottle, and books, were thrown in a confused heap. He sat on his stool and shut his eyes to recollect what work he had for the day: first of course there was arithmetic – those five puzzles in profit and loss; then there was English – he had to copy down a page from his Eighth Lesson, and write dictionary meanings of difficult words; and then there was geography.

And only two hours before him to do all this heap of work and get ready for the school!

Fire-eyed Vedanayagam was presiding over the class with his back to the long window. Through its bars one saw a bit of the drill ground and a corner of the veranda of the Infant Standards. There were huge windows on the left showing vast open grounds bound at the other extreme by the railway embankment.

To Swaminathan existence in the classroom was possible only because he could watch the toddlers of the Infant Standards falling over one another, and through the windows on the left see the 12.30 mail gliding over the embankment, booming and rattling while passing over the Sarayu Bridge.

The first hour passed off quietly. The second they had arithmetic. Vedanayagam went out and returned in a few minutes in the role of an arithmetic teacher. He droned on monotonously. Swaminathan was terribly bored. His teacher's voice was beginning to get on his nerves. He felt sleepy.

The teacher called for home exercises. Swaminathan left his seat, jumped on the platform, and placed his notebook on the table. While the teacher was scrutinizing the sums, Swaminathan was gazing on his face, which seemed so tame at close quarters. His criticism of the teacher's face was that his eyes were too near each other, that there was more hair on his chin than one saw from the bench, and that he was very very bad-looking.

His reverie was disturbed. He felt a terrible pain in the soft flesh above his left elbow. The teacher was pinching him with one hand, and with the other crossing out all the sums. He wrote 'Very Bad' at the bottom of the page, flung the notebook in Swaminathan's face, and drove him back to his seat.

Next period they had history. The boys looked forward to it eagerly. It was taken by D. Pillai, who had earned a name in the school for kindness and good humour. He was reputed to have never frowned or sworn at the boys at any time. His method of teaching history conformed to no canon of education. He told the boys with a wealth of detail the private histories of Vasco da Gama, Clive, Hastings, and others. When he described the various fights in history, one heard the clash of arms and the groans of the slain. He was the despair of the headmaster whenever the latter stole along the corridor with noiseless steps on his rounds of inspection.

The scripture period was the last in the morning. It was not such a dull hour after all. There were moments in it that brought stirring pictures before one: the Red Sea cleaving and making way for the Israelites; the physical feats of Samson; Jesus rising from the grave; and so on. The only trouble was that the scripture master, Mr Ebenezar, was a fanatic.

'Oh, wretched idiots!' the teacher said, clenching his fists. 'Why do you worship dirty, lifeless, wooden idols and stone images? Can they talk? No. Can they see? No. Can they bless you? No. Can they take you to heaven? No. Why? Because they have no life. What did your gods do when Muhammad of Gazni smashed them to pieces, trod upon them, and constructed out of them steps for his lavatory? If those idols and images had life, why did they not parry Muhammad's onslaughts?'

He then turned to Christianity. 'Now see our Lord Jesus. He could cure the sick, relieve the poor, and take us to heaven. He was a real God. Trust him and he will take you to heaven; the kingdom of heaven is within us.' Tears rolled down Ebenezar's cheeks when he pictured Jesus before him. Next moment his face became purple with rage as he thought of Sri Krishna: 'Did our Jesus go gadding about with dancing girls like your Krishna? Did our Jesus go about stealing butter like that arch-scoundrel Krishna? Did our Jesus practise dark tricks on those around him?'

He paused for breath. The teacher was intolerable today. Swaminathan's blood boiled. He got up and asked, 'If he did not, why was he crucified?' The teacher told him that he might come to him at the end of the period and learn it in private. Emboldened by this mild reply, Swaminathan put to him another question, 'If he was a god, why did he eat flesh and fish and drink wine?' As a brahmin boy it was inconceivable to him that a god should be a non-vegetarian. In answer to this, Ebenezar left his seat, advanced slowly towards Swaminathan, and tried to wrench his left ear off.

Next day Swaminathan was at school early. There was still half an hour before the bell. He usually spent such an interval in running round the school or in playing the Digging Game under the huge tamarind tree. But today he sat apart, sunk in thought. He had a thick letter in his pocket. He felt guilty when he touched its edge with his fingers.

He called himself an utter idiot for having told his father about Ebenezar the night before during the meal.

As soon as the bell rang, he walked into the headmaster's room and handed him a letter. The headmaster's face became serious when he read:

SIR,

I beg to inform you that my son Swaminathan of the First Form, A section, was assaulted by his scripture master yesterday in a fanatical rage. I hear that he is always most insulting and provoking in his references to the Hindu religion. It is bound to have a bad effect upon the boys. This is not the place for me to dwell upon the necessity for toleration in these matters.

I am also informed that when my son got up to have a few doubts cleared, he was roughly handled by the same teacher. His ears were still red when he came home last evening.

The one conclusion that I can come to is that you do not want non-Christian boys in your school. If it is so, you may kindly inform us as we are quite willing to withdraw our boys and send them elsewhere. I may remind you that Albert Mission School is not the only school that this town, Malgudi, possesses. I hope you will be kind enough to inquire into the matter and favour me with a reply. If not, I regret to inform you, I shall be constrained to draw the attention of higher authorities to these unchristian practices.

I have the honour to be,

Sir,

Your most obedient servant,

W. T. SRINIVASAN.

When Swaminathan came out of the room, the whole school crowded round him and hung on his lips. But he treated inquisitive questions with haughty indifference.

He honoured only four persons with his confidence. Those were the four that he liked and admired most in his class. The first was Somu, the monitor, who carried himself with such an easy air. He set about his business, whatever it was, with absolute confidence and calmness. He was known to be chummy even with the teachers. No teacher ever put to him a question in the class. It could not be said that he shone brilliantly as a student. It was believed that only the headmaster could reprimand him. He was more or less the uncle of the class.

Then there was Mani, the Mighty Good-For-Nothing. He towered above all the other boys of the class. He seldom brought any books to the class, and never bothered about homework. He came to the class, monopolized the last bench, and slept bravely. No teacher ever tried to prod him. It was said that a new teacher who once tried it very nearly lost his life. Mani bullied all strangers that came his way, be they big or small. People usually slunk aside when he passed. Wearing his cap at an angle, with a Tamil novel under his arm, he had been coming to the school ever since the old school peon could remember. In most of the classes he stayed longer than his friends did. Swaminathan was proud of his friendship. While others crouched in awe, he could address him as 'Mani' with gusto and pat him on the back familiarly. Swaminathan admiringly asked whence Mani derived his power. Mani replied that he had a pair of wooden clubs at home with which he would break the backs of those that dared to tamper with him.

Then there was Sankar, the most brilliant boy of the class. He solved any problem that was given to him in five minutes, and always managed to border on ninety per cent. There was a belief among a section of the boys that if only he started cross-examining the teachers, the teachers would be nowhere. Another section asserted that Sankar was a dud and that he learnt all the problems and their solution in advance by his sycophancy. He was said to receive his ninety per cent as a result of washing clothes for his masters. He could speak to the teachers in English in the open class. He knew all the rivers, mountains, and countries in the world. He could repeat history in his sleep. Grammar was child's play to him. His face was radiant with intelligence, though his nose was almost always damp, and though he came to the class with his hair braided and with flowers in it, Swaminathan looked on him as a marvel. He was very happy when he made Mani see eye to eye with him and admit Sankar to their company. Mani liked him in his own way and brought down his heavy fist on Sankar's back whenever he felt inclined to demonstrate his affection. He would scratch his head and ask where the blithering fool of a scraggy youngster got all that brain from and why he should not part with a little of it.

The fourth friend was Samuel, known as 'the Pea' on account of his size. There was nothing outstanding about him. He was just ordinary, no outstanding virtue of muscle or intellect. He was as bad in arithmetic as Swaminathan was. He was as apprehensive, weak, and nervous about things as Swaminathan was.

The bond between them was laughter. They were able to see together the same absurdities and incongruities in things. The most trivial and unnoticeable thing to others would tickle them to death.

When Swaminathan told them what action his father had taken in the scripture master affair, there was a murmur of approval. Somu was the first to express it, by bestowing on his admirer a broad grin. Sankar looked serious and said, 'Whatever others might say, you did right in setting your father to the job.' The mighty Mani half closed his eyes and grunted an approval of sorts. He was only sorry that the matter should have been handled by elders. He saw no sense in it. Things of this kind should not be allowed to go beyond the four walls of the classroom. If he were Swaminathan, he would have closed the whole incident at the beginning by hurling an ink-bottle, if nothing bigger was available, at the teacher. Well, there was no harm in what Swaminathan had done; he would have done infinitely worse by keeping quiet. However, let the scripture master look out: Mani had decided to wring his neck and break his back.

Samuel the Pea found himself in an acutely embarrassing position. On the one hand, he felt constrained to utter some remark. On the other, he was a Christian and saw nothing wrong in Ebenezar's observations, which seemed to be only an amplification of one of the Commandments. He felt that his right place was on Ebenezar's side. He managed to escape by making scathing comments on Ebenezar's dress and appearance and leaving it at that.

The class had got wind of the affair. When the scripture period arrived there was a general expectation of some dramatic *dénouement*. But nothing happened. Ebenezar went on as merrily as ever. He had taken the trouble that day to plod through Bhagavadgita, and this generous piece of writing lends itself to any interpretation. In Ebenezar's hand it served as a weapon against Hinduism.

His tone was as vigorous as ever, but in his denunciation there was more scholarship. He pulled Bhagavadgita to pieces, after raising Hinduism on its base. Step by step he was reaching the sublime heights of rhetoric. The class Bible lay uncared for on the table.

The headmaster glided in.

Ebenezar halted, pushing back his chair, and rose, greatly flurried. He looked questioningly at the headmaster. The headmaster grimly asked him to go on. Ebenezar had meanwhile stealthily inserted a finger into the pages of the closed Bible. On the word of command from the headmaster, he tried to look sweet and relaxed his brow, which was knit in fury. He then opened his book where the finger marked and began to read at random. It happened to be the Nativity of Christ. The great event had occurred. There the divine occupant was in the manger. The Wise Men of the East were faithfully following the Star.

The boys attended in their usual abstracted way. It made little difference to them whether Ebenezar was making a study of Hinduism in the light of Bhagavadgita or was merely describing the Nativity of Christ.

The headmaster listened for a while and, in an undertone, demanded an explanation. They were nearing the terminal examination and Ebenezar had still not gone beyond the Nativity. When would he reach the Crucifixion and Resurrection, and begin to revise? Ebenezar was flabbergasted. He could not think of anything to say. He made a bare escape by hinting that that particular day of the week he usually devoted to a rambling revision. Oh, no! He was not as far behind as that. He was in the proximity of the Last Supper.

At the end of the day Swaminathan was summoned to the headmaster's room. As soon as he received the note, he had an impulse to run home. And when he expressed it, Mani took him in his hands, propelled him through to the headmaster's room, and gave him a gentle push in. Swaminathan staggered before the headmaster.

Ebenezar was sitting on a stool, looking sheepish. The headmaster said: 'What is the trouble, Swaminathan?'

'Oh – nothing, sir,' Swaminathan replied.

'If it is nothing, why this letter?'

'Oh!' Swaminathan ejaculated uncertainly.

Ebenezar attempted to smile. Swaminathan wished to be well out of the whole affair. He felt he would not mind if a hundred Ebenezars said a thousand times worse things about the gods.

'You know why I am here?' asked the headmaster.

Swaminathan searched for an answer: the headmaster might be there to receive letters from boys' parents; he might be there to flay Ebenezars alive; he might be there to deliver six cuts with his cane every Monday at twelve o'clock. And above all why this question?

'I don't know, sir,' Swaminathan replied innocently.

'I am here to look after you,' said the headmaster.

Swaminathan was relieved to find that the question had such a simple answer.

'And so,' continued the headmaster, 'you must come to me if you want any help, before you go to your father.' Swaminathan furtively glanced at Ebenezar, who writhed in his chair.

'I am sorry,' said the headmaster, 'that you should have been so foolish as to go to your father about this simple matter. I shall look into it. Take this letter to your father.'

Swaminathan took the letter and shot out of the room with great relief.

CHAPTER TWO

RAJAM AND MANI

River Sarayu was the pride of Malgudi. It was some ten minutes' walk from Ellaman Street, the last street of the town, chiefly occupied by oilmongers. Its sandbanks were the evening resort of all the people of the town. The Municipal President took any distinguished visitor to the top of the town hall and proudly pointed to him Sarayu in moonlight, glistening like a silver belt across the north.

The usual evening crowd was on the sand. Swaminathan and Mani sat aloof on a river-step, with their legs dangling in water. The *peepul* branches overhanging the river rustled pleasantly. A light breeze played about the boughs and scattered stray leaves on the gliding stream below. Birds filled the air with their cries. Far away, near Nallappa's Mango Grove, a little downstream, a herd of cattle was crossing the river. And then a country cart drawn by bullocks passed, the cart-man humming a low tune. It was some fifteen minutes past sunset and there was a soft red in the west.

'The water runs very deep here, doesn't it?' Mani asked.

'Yes, why?'

'I am going to bring Rajam here, bundle him up, and throw him into the river.'

Rajam was a fresh arrival in the First A. He had sauntered into the class on the reopening day of the second term, walked up to the last bench, sat beside Mani, and felt very comfortable indeed till Mani gave him a jab in the ribs, which he returned. He had impressed the whole class on the very first day. He was a newcomer; he dressed very well – he was the only boy in the class who wore socks and shoes, fur cap and tie, and a wonderful coat and knickers. He came to the school in a car. As well as all this, he proved to be a very good student too. There were vague rumours that he had come from some English boys' school somewhere in Madras. He spoke very good English, 'exactly like a "European" '; which meant that few in the school could make out what he said. Many of his class-mates could not trust themselves to speak to him, their fund of broken English being small. Only Sankar, the genius of the class, had the courage to face him, though his English sounded halting and weak before that of Rajam.

This Rajam was a rival to Mani. In his manner to Mani he assumed a certain nonchalance to which Mani was not accustomed. If Mani jabbed, Rajam jabbed; if Mani clouted, he clouted; if Mani kicked, he kicked. If Mani was the overlord of the class, Rajam seemed to be nothing less. And add to all this the fact that Rajam was a regular seventy-percenter, second only to Sankar. There were sure indications that Rajam was the new power in the class. Day by day as Mani looked on, it was becoming increasingly clear that a new menace had appeared in his life.

All this lay behind his decision on the river-step to bundle up Rajam and throw him into the river. Swaminathan expressed a slight fear: 'You forget that his father is the Police Superintendent.' Mani remained silent for a while and said, 'What do I care? Some night I am going to crack his shoulders with my clubs.'

'If I were you, I would keep out of the way of policemen. They are an awful lot,' said Swaminathan.

'If you were me! Huh! But thank God I am not you, a milk-toothed coward like you.'

Swaminathan bit his lips and sighed.

'And that reminds me,' said the other, 'you are in need of a little warning. I find you hanging about that Rajam a bit too much. Well, have a care for your limbs. That is all I can say.'

Swaminathan broke into loud protestations. Did Mani think that Swaminathan could respect anyone but him, Mani the dear old friend and guide? What made him think so? As far as Swaminathan could remember, he had never been within three yards of Rajam. Oh, how he hated him! That vile upstart! When had Mani seen him with Rajam? Oh, yes, it must have been during the drawing period on Monday. It was Rajam who had come and talked to him in spite of the cold face that Swaminathan had turned to him. That ass had wanted a pencil-sharpener, which he did not get, as he was promptly directed to go to a shop and buy it if he needed it so urgently. Oh, there was no comparison between Rajam and Mani.

This pleased Mani greatly. For the first time that evening he laughed, and laughed heartily too. He shook Swaminathan and gave such an affectionate twist to his ear that Swaminathan gave a long howl. And then he suddenly asked, 'Did you bring the thing that I wanted?'

'Oh, Mani! I beg a hundred pardons of you. My mother was all the time in the kitchen. I could not get it.' ('It' referred to lime pickles.)

'You are a nasty little coward – Oh, this river-bank and the fine evening. How splendid it would have been!'

Swaminathan was to act as a cord of communication between Rajam and Mani. They were sitting on the last bench with their backs against the yellow wall. Swaminathan sat between Rajam and Mani. Their books were before them on the desks; but their minds were busy.

Mani wrote on a piece of paper 'Are you a man?' and gave it to Swaminathan, who pushed it across to Rajam, putting on as offensive a look as possible. Rajam read it, crumpled it, and threw it away. At which Mani wrote another note repeating the question, with the addition 'You are the son of a dog if you don't answer this,' and pushed it across. Rajam hissed into Swaminathan's face, 'You scoundrel, don't disturb me,' and crumpled the letter.

Further progress was stopped.

'Swaminathan, stand up,' said the teacher. Swaminathan stood up faithfully.

'What is Lisbon famous for?' asked the teacher.

Swaminathan hesitated and ventured, 'For being the capital of Spain.'

The teacher bit his moustache and fired a second question, 'What do you know about the Indian climate?'

'It is hot in summer and cold in winter.'

'Stand up on the bench!' roared the teacher. And Swaminathan stood up without a protest. He was glad that he was given this supposedly degrading punishment instead of the cane.

The teacher resumed his lessons: Africa was a land of forests. Nile was the most important river there. Did they understand? What did he say? He selected someone from the first bench to answer this question. (Nile was the most important river in Africa, the boy answered promptly, and the teacher was satisfied.) What was Nile? (The most important river in Africa, a boy answered with alacrity and was instantly snubbed for it, for he had to learn not to answer before he was asked to.) Silence. Silence. Why was there such a lot of noise in the class? Let them go on making a noise and they would get a clean, big zero in the examination. He would see to that ...

Swaminathan paid no attention to the rest of the lessons. His mind began to wander. Standing on the bench, he stood well over the whole class. He could see so many heads, and he classified them according to the caps: there were four red caps, twenty-five Gandhi caps, ten fur caps, and so on.

When the work for the day was over, Swaminathan, Mani, and Rajam adjourned to a secluded spot to say what was in their minds. Swaminathan stood between them and acted as the medium of communication. They were so close that they could have heard each other even if they had spoken in whispers. But it was a matter of form between enemies to communicate through a medium. Mani faced Swaminathan steadily and asked, 'Are you a man?' Swaminathan turned to Rajam and repeated, 'Are you a man?' Rajam flared up and shouted, 'Which dog doubts it?' Swaminathan turned to Mani and said ferociously, 'Which dirty dog doubts it?'

'Have you the courage to prove that you are a man?' asked Mani.

Swaminathan turned to Rajam and repeated it.

'How?'

'How?' repeated Swaminathan to Mani.

'Meet me at the river, near Nallappa's Grove, tomorrow evening.'

' – Near Nallappa's Grove,' Swaminathan was pleased to echo.

'What for?' asked Rajam.

'To see if you can break my head.'

'Oh, to pieces,' said Rajam.

Swaminathan's services were dispensed with. They gave him no time to repeat their words. Rajam shouted in one ear, and Mani in the other.

'So we may expect you at the river tomorrow,' said Swaminathan.

'Yes,' Rajam assured them.

Mani wanted to know if the other would come with guards. No, he would not. And Mani voiced another doubt: 'If anything happens to you, will you promise to keep it out of your father's knowledge?' Rajam promised, after repudiating the very suggestion that he might act otherwise.

Nallappa's Grove stood a few yards before them. It was past six and the traffic for the day between the banks was over. The usual evening crowd was far behind them. Swaminathan and Mani were squatting on the sand. They were silent. Mani was staring at the ground, with a small wooden club under his arm. He was thinking: he was going to break Rajam's head in a short while and throw his body into the river. But if it should be recovered? But then how could they know that he had done it? But if Rajam should come and trouble him at night as a spirit? Since his grandfather's death, he was sleeping alone. What if Rajam should come and pull his hair at night? After all it would be better not to kill him. He would content himself with breaking his limbs and leaving him to his fate. If he should batter his head, who was going to find it out? Unless of course – He cast a sly look at Swaminathan, who was blinking innocently ... Unless of course Swaminathan informed the police.

At the sound of the creaking of boots, they turned and found that Rajam had come. He was dressed in khaki, and carried under his arm an airgun that was given to him a couple of months ago on his birthday. He stood very stiff and said: 'Here I am, ready.'

'You are late.'

'Yes.'

'We will start.'

Rajam shouldered his gun and fired a shot in the air. Mani was startled. He stood still, his club down.

'You heard the shot?' asked Rajam. 'The next is going to be into your body, if you are keen upon a fight.'

'But this is unfair. I have no gun while you have ... It was to be a hand-to-hand fight.'

'Then why have you brought your club? You never said anything about it yesterday.'

Mani hung down his head.

'What have I done to offend you?' asked Rajam.

'You called me a sneak before someone.'

'That is a lie.'

There was an awkward pause. 'If this is all the cause of your anger, forget it. I won't mind being friends.'

'Nor I,' said Mani.

Swaminathan gasped with astonishment. In spite of his posing before Mani he admired Rajam intensely, and longed to be his friend. Now this was the happiest conclusion to all the unwanted trouble. He danced with joy. Rajam lowered his gun, and Mani dropped his club. To show his goodwill, Rajam pulled out of his pocket half a dozen biscuits.

The river's mild rumble, the rustling of the *peepul* leaves, the half-light of the late evening, and the three friends eating, and glowing with new friendship – Swaminathan felt at perfect peace with the world.

CHAPTER THREE

SWAMI'S GRANDMOTHER

In the ill-ventilated dark passage between the front hall and the dining-room, Swaminathan's grandmother lived with all her belongings, which consisted of an elaborate bed made of five carpets, three bed sheets, and five pillows, a square box made of jute fibre, and a small wooden box containing copper coins, cardamoms, cloves, and areca nut.

After the night meal, with his head on his granny's lap, nestling close to her, Swaminathan felt very snug and safe in the faint atmosphere of cardamom and cloves.

'Oh, Granny!' he cried ecstatically. 'You don't know what a great fellow Rajam is.' He told her the story of the first enmity between Rajam and Mani and the subsequent friendship.

'You know, he has a real police dress,' said Swaminathan.

'Is it? What does he want a police dress for?' asked Granny.

'His father is the Police Superintendent. He is the master of every policeman here.' Granny was impressed. She said that it must be a tremendous office indeed. She then recounted the days when her husband, Swaminathan's grandfather, was a powerful submagistrate, in which office he made the police force tremble before him, and the fiercest dacoits of the place flee. Swaminathan waited impatiently for her to finish the story. But she went on, rambled, confused, mixed up various incidents that took place at different times.

'That will do, Granny,' he said ungraciously. 'Let me tell you something about Rajam. Do you know how many marks he gets in arithmetic?'

'He gets all the marks, does he, child?' asked Granny.

'No, silly. He gets ninety marks out of one hundred.'

'Good. But you must also try and get marks like him ... You know, Swami, your grandfather used to frighten the examiners with his answers sometimes. When he answered a question, he did it in a tenth of the time that others took to do it. And then, his answers would be so powerful that his teachers would give him two hundred marks sometimes ... When he passed his F.A. he got such a big medal! I wore it as a pendant for years till – when did I remove it? Yes, when your aunt was born ... No, it wasn't your aunt ... It was when your father was born ... I remember on the tenth day of confinement ... No, no. I was right. It was when your aunt was born. Where is that medal now? I gave it away to your aunt – and she melted it and made four bangles out of it. The fool! And such flimsy bangles too! I have always maintained that she is the worst fool in our family ...'

'Oh, enough, Granny! You go on bothering about old unnecessary stories. Won't you listen to Rajam?'

'Yes, dear, yes.'

'Granny, when Rajam was a small boy, he killed a tiger.'

'Indeed! The brave little boy!'

'You are saying it just to please me. You don't believe it.'

Swaminathan started the story enthusiastically: Rajam's father was camping in a forest. He had his son with him. Two tigers came upon them suddenly, one knocking down the father from behind. The other began chasing Rajam, who took shelter behind a bush and shot it dead with his gun. 'Granny, are you asleep?' Swaminathan asked at the end of the story.

'No, dear, I am listening.'

'Let me see. How many tigers came upon how many?'

'About two tigers on Rajam,' said Granny.

Swaminathan became indignant at his grandmother's inaccuracy. 'Here I am going hoarse telling you important things and you fall asleep and imagine all sorts of nonsense. I am not going to tell you anything more. I know why you are so indifferent. You hate Rajam.'

'No, no, he is a lovely little boy,' Granny said with conviction, though she had never seen Rajam. Swaminathan was pleased. Next moment a new doubt assailed him. 'Granny, probably you don't believe the tiger incident.'

'Oh, I believe every word of it,' Granny said soothingly. Swaminathan was pleased, but added as a warning: 'He would shoot anyone that called him a liar.'

Granny expressed her approval of this attitude and then begged leave to start the story of Harichandra, who, just to be true to his word, lost his throne, wife, and child, and got them all back in the end. She was halfway through it when Swaminathan's rhythmic snoring punctuated her narration, and she lay down to sleep.

Saturday afternoon. Since Saturday and Sunday came so rarely, to Swaminathan it seemed absurd to waste them at home, gossiping with Granny and Mother or doing sums. It was his father's definite orders that Swaminathan should not start loafing in the afternoon and that he should stay at home and do school work. But this order was seldom obeyed.

Swaminathan sat impatiently in his 'study', trying to wrest the meaning out of a poem in his *English Reader*. His father stood before the mirror, winding a turban round his head. He had put on his silk coat. Now only his spectacles remained. Swaminathan watched his progress keenly. Even the spectacles were on. All that now remained was the watch.

Swaminathan felt glad. This was the last item and after that Father would leave for the court. Mother came in with a tumbler of water in one hand and a plate of betel leaves and nuts in the other. Father drank the water and held out his hand. She gave him a little areca nut and half a dozen neatly-rolled betel leaves. He put them all into his mouth, chewing them with great contentment. Swaminathan read at the top of his voice the poem about a woolly sheep. His father fussed about a little for his tiny silver snuff-box and the spotted kerchief, which was the most unwashed thing in that house. He hooked his umbrella on his arm. This was really the last signal for starting. Swaminathan had almost closed the book and risen. His father had almost gone out of the room. But – Swaminathan stamped his foot under the table. Mother stopped Father and said: 'By the way, I want some change. The tailor is coming today. He has been pestering me for the last four days.'

'Ask him to come tomorrow,' Father said. Mother was insistent. Father returned to his bureau, searched for the keys, opened it, took out a purse, and gave her the change. 'I don't know how I am going to manage things for the rest of the month,' he said, peering into the purse. He locked the bureau, and adjusted his turban before the mirror. He took a heavy pinch of snuff and, wiping his nose with his kerchief, walked out. Swaminathan heaved a sigh of relief.

'Bolt the door,' came Father's voice from the street door. Swaminathan heard the clicking of the bolts. He sat at the window, watched his father turn the corner, and then left his post.

His mother was in the kitchen giving instructions to the cook about the afternoon coffee. Granny was sitting up in her bed. 'Come here, boy,' she cried as soon as she saw him.

'I can't. No time now.'

'Please. I will give you three paise,' she cried.

Swaminathan ignored the offer and dashed away.

'Where are you going?' Mother asked.

'I have got to go,' Swaminathan said with a serious face.

'Are you going to loaf about in the sun?'

'Certainly not,' he replied curtly.

'Wander about recklessly and catch fever? ...'

'No, Mother, I am not going to wander about.'

'Has your father not asked you to stay at home on holidays?'

'Yes, but my drawing master has asked me to see him. I suppose even then I should not go.' He added bitterly: 'If I fail in the drawing examination I think you will be pleased.'

Swaminathan ran down Grove Street, turned to his right, threaded his way through Abu Lane, stood before a low-roofed, dingy house, and gave a low whistle. He waited for a second and repeated it. The door-chain clanked, the door opened a little, and Mani's head appeared and said: 'Fool! My aunt is here, don't come in. Go away and wait for me there.'

Swaminathan moved away and waited under a tree. The sun was beating down fiercely. The street was almost deserted. A donkey was standing near a gutter, patiently watching its sharp shadow. A cow was munching a broad, green, plantain leaf. Presently Mani sneaked out of his house.

Rajam's father lived in Lawley Extension (named after the mighty engineer Sir Frederick Lawley, who was at one time the Superintending Engineer for Malgudi Circle), which consisted of about fifty neat bungalows, mostly occupied by government officials. The trunk road to Trichinopoly passed a few yards in front of these houses.

Swaminathan and Mani were nervously walking up the short drive leading to Rajam's house. A policeman in uniform cried to them to stop and came running towards them. Swaminathan felt like turning and fleeing. He appealed to Mani to speak to the policeman. The policeman asked what they were doing there. Mani said in a tone in which overdone carelessness was a trifle obvious: 'If Rajam is in the house, we are here to see him. He asked us to come.' The policeman at once became astonishingly amiable and took them along to Rajam's room.

To Mani and Swaminathan the room looked large. There were chairs in it, actually chairs, and a good big table with Rajam's books arranged neatly on it. What impressed them most was a timepiece on the table. Such a young fellow to own a timepiece! His father seemed to be an extraordinary man.

Presently Rajam entered. He had known that his friends were waiting for him, but he liked to keep them waiting for a few minutes, because he had seen his father doing it. So he stood for a few minutes in the adjoining room, biting his nails. When he could keep away no longer, he burst in upon his friends.

'Sit down, boys, sit down,' he cried when he saw them standing.

In a few minutes they were chatting about odds and ends, discussing their teachers and schoolmates, their parents, toys, and games.

Rajam took them to a cupboard and threw it open. They beheld astounding things in it, miniature trains and motors, mechanical marvels, and a magic lantern with slides, a good many large picture-books, and a hundred other things. What interested Mani most was a grim airgun that stood in a corner. Rajam gave them permission to handle anything they pleased. In a short while Swaminathan was running an engine all over the room. Mani was shooting arrow after arrow from a bow, at the opposite wall. When he tired of it, he took up the gun and devastated the furniture around with lead balls.

'Are you fellows, any of you, hungry?' Rajam asked.

'No,' they said half-heartedly.

'Hey,' Rajam cried. A policeman entered.

'Go and ask the cook to bring some coffee and tiffin for three.' The ease and authority with which he addressed the policeman filled his friends with wonder and admiration.

The cook entered with a big plateful of eatables. He set down the plate on the table. Rajam felt that he must display his authority.

'Remove it from the table, you – ' he roared at the cook. The cook removed it and placed it on a chair.

'You dirty ass, take it away, don't put it there.'

'Where am I to put it, Raju?' asked the cook.

Rajam burst out: 'You rascal, you scoundrel, you talk back to me?'

The cook made a wry face and muttered something.

'Put it on the table,' Rajam commanded. The cook obeyed, mumbling: 'If you are rude, I am going to tell your mother.'

'Go and tell her, I don't care,' Rajam retorted.

He peered into a cup and cursed the cook for bringing it so dirty. The cook looked up for a moment, quietly lifted the plate, and saying, 'Come and eat in the kitchen if you want food,' went away with it.

This was a great disappointment to Swaminathan and Mani, who were waiting with watering mouths. To Rajam it was a terrible moment. To be outdone by his servant before his friends! He sat still for a few minutes and then said with a forced laugh: 'The scoundrel, that cook is a buffoon ... Wait a minute.' He went out.

After a while he returned, carrying the plate himself. His friends were a bit astonished at this sign of defeat. Obviously he could not subdue the cook. Swaminathan puzzled his head to find out why Rajam did not shoot the cook dead, and Mani wanted to ask if he could be allowed to have his own way with the cook for a few minutes. But Rajam set their minds at rest by explaining to them: 'I had to bring this myself. I went in and gave the cook such a kick for his impertinence that he is lying unconscious in the kitchen.'

CHAPTER FOUR

'WHAT IS A TAIL?'

The geography master was absent, and the boys of the First A had leisure between three and three forty-five on Wednesday.

Somehow Swaminathan had missed his friends and found himself alone. He wandered along the corridor of the Infant Standards. To Swaminathan, who did not really stand over four feet, the children of the Infant Standards seemed ridiculously tiny. He felt vastly superior and old. He was filled with contempt when he saw them dabbling in wet clay, trying to shape models. It seemed such a meaningless thing to do at school! Why, they could as well do those things resembling elephants, mangoes, and whatnots, in the backyards of their houses. Why did they come all the way to a school to do this sort of thing? Schools were meant for more serious things like geography, arithmetic, Bible, and English.

In one room he found all the children engaged in repeating simultaneously the first two letters of the Tamil alphabet. He covered his ears and wondered how the teacher was able to stand it. He passed on. In another room he found an ill-clad, noisy crowd of children. The noise that they made, sitting on their benches and swinging their legs, got on his nerves. He wrinkled his brow and twisted his mouth in the hope of making the teacher feel his resentment; but unfortunately the teacher was sitting with his back to Swaminathan.

He paused at the foot of the staircase leading to the senior classes – the second and the third forms. He wanted to go up and inspect those classes which he eagerly looked forward to joining. He took two or three steps up and changed his mind. The headmaster might be up there, he always handled those classes. The teachers too were formidable, not to speak of the boys themselves, who were snobs and bullies. He heard the creak-creak of sandals far off and recognized the footsteps of the headmaster. He did not want to be caught there – that would mean a lot of unsatisfactory explanations.

It was with pleasant surprise that he stumbled into his own set, which he had thought was not at school. Except Rajam and Mani all the rest were there. Under the huge tamarind tree they were playing some game. Swaminathan joined them with a low, ecstatic cry. The response disappointed him. They turned their faces to him with a faint smile, and returned to their game. What surprised Swaminathan most was that even the genial Somu was grim. Something seemed to be wrong somewhere. Swaminathan assumed an easy tone and shouted: 'Boys, what about a little place for me in the game?' Nobody answered this. Swaminathan paused and announced that he was waiting for a place in the game.

'It is a pity, we can't take more,' Sankar said curtly.

'There are people who can be very efficient as tails,' said the Pea. The rest laughed at this.

'You said tail, didn't you?' asked Sankar. 'What makes you talk of tail now?'

'It is just my pleasure. What do *you* care? It doesn't apply to you anyway,' said the Pea.

'I am glad to hear it, but does it apply to anyone here?' asked Sankar.

'It may.'

'What is a tail?'

'A long thing that attaches itself to an ass or a dog.'

Swaminathan could comprehend very little except that the remark contained some unpleasant references to himself. His cheeks grew hot. He wanted to cry.

The bell rang and they ran to their class. Swaminathan slunk to his seat with a red face.

It was the English period presided over by Vedanayagam. He was reading the story of the old man who planted trees for posterity and was paid ten rupees by a king. Not a word reached Swaminathan's brain, in which there was only dull pain and vacuity. If he had been questioned he would have blundered and would have had to spend the rest of the hour standing on the bench. But his luck was good.

The period was over. He was walking home alone, rather slowly, with a troubled heart. Somu was going a few yards in front of him. Swaminathan cried out: 'Somu, Somu ... Somu, won't you stop?' Somu, stopped till the other came up.

After a brief silence Swaminathan quavered: 'What is the matter with you fellows?'

'Nothing very particular,' replied Somu. 'By the way, may I inform you that you have earned a new name? The Tail – Rajam's Tail, to be more precise. We aren't good enough for you, I believe. But how can everyone be a son of a police superintendent?' With that he was off.

This was probably Swaminathan's first shock in life. It paralysed all his mental process. When his mind started working again, he faintly wondered if he had been dreaming. The staid Somu, the genial Somu, the uncle Somu, was it the same Somu that had talked to him a few minutes ago? What was wrong in liking and going about with Rajam? Why did it make them so angry?

He went home, flung his coat and cap and books on the table, gulped down the cold coffee that was waiting for him, and sat on the *pyol*, vacantly gazing into the dark intricacies of the gutter that adorned Vinayaka Mudali Street. A dark volume of water was rushing along. Odd pieces of paper, leaves, and sticks floated by. A small piece of tin was gently skimming along. Swaminathan had an impulse to plunge his hand in and pick it up. But he let it go. His mind was inert. He watched the shining bit float away. It was now at the end of the compound wall; now it had passed under the tree. Swaminathan was slightly irritated when a brick obstructed the progress of the tin. He said that the brick must either move along or stand aside without interfering with the traffic. The piece of tin released itself and dashed along furiously, disappearing round a bend at the end of the street. Swaminathan ran in, got a sheet of paper, and made a boat. He saw a small ant moving about aimlessly. He carefully caught it, placed it in the boat, and lowered the boat into the stream. He watched in rapture its quick motion. He held his breath when the boat with its cargo neared a danger zone formed by stuck-up bits of straw and other odds and ends. The boat made a beautiful swerve to the right and avoided destruction. It went on and on. It neared a fatal spot where the waters were swirling round and round in eddies. Swaminathan was certain that his boat was nearing its last moment. He had no doubt that it was going to be drawn right to the bottom of the circling eddies. The boat whirled madly round, shaking and swaying and quivering. Providentially a fresh supply of water from the kitchen in the neighbour's house pushed it from behind out of danger. But it rushed on at a fearful speed, and Swaminathan felt that it was going to turn turtle. Presently it calmed, and resumed a normal speed. But when it passed under a tree, a thick dry leaf fell down and upset it. Swaminathan ran frantically to the spot to see if he could save at least the ant. He peered long into the water, but there was no sign of the ant. The boat and its cargo were wrecked beyond recovery. He took a pinch of earth, uttered a prayer for the soul of the ant, and dropped it into the gutter.

In a few days Swaminathan got accustomed to his position as the enemy of Somu and company.

All the same, now and then he had an irresistible desire to talk to his old friends. When the scripture master pursed his lips and scratched his nose, Swaminathan had a wild impulse to stamp on the Pea's leg and laugh, for that was a joke that they had never failed to enjoy day after day for many years past. But now Swaminathan smothered the impulse and chuckled at it himself, alone. And again, when the boy with the red cap nodded in his seat and woke up with a start every time his head sank down, Swaminathan wanted to whisper into the Pea's ear: 'Look at that fellow, third on the first bench, red cap – now he is falling off again – ' and giggle; but he merely bit his lips and kept quiet.

Somu was looking in his direction. Swaminathan thought that there was friendliness in his look. He felt a momentary ecstasy as he realized that Somu was willing to be friendly again. They stared at each other for a while, and just as Swaminathan was beginning to put on a sweet friendly look, Somu's expression hardened and he turned away.

Swaminathan was loitering in the compound. He heard familiar voices behind, turned round, and saw Somu, Sankar, and the

Pea following him. Swaminathan wondered whether to stop and join them, or wait till they had passed and then go in the opposite direction. For it was awkward to be conscious of the stare of three pairs of hostile eyes behind one's ears. He believed that every minute movement of his body was being watched and commented on by the three followers. He felt that his gait was showing unfavourably in their eyes. He felt they were laughing at the way in which he carried his books. There was a slight itching on his nape; his hand almost rose, but he checked it, feeling that the scratching would be studiously watched by the six keen eyes.

He wanted to turn to his right and enter the school hall. But that would be construed as cowardice; they would certainly think that he was doing it to escape from them. He wanted to run away, but that would be no better. He wanted to turn back and get away in the opposite direction, but that would mean meeting them square in the face. So his only recourse was to keep on walking as best he could, not showing that he was conscious of his followers. The same fellows ten days ago, what they were! Now what formidable creatures they had turned out to be! Swaminathan was wonder-struck at the change.

It was becoming unendurable. He felt that his legs were taking a circular motion, and were twining round each other when he walked. It was too late to turn and dash into the school hall. He had passed it. Now he had only one way of escape. He must run. It was imperative. He tried a trick. He paused suddenly, turned this way and that, as if looking for something, and then cried aloud: 'Oh, I have left my notebook somewhere,' raised his hand and was off from the spot like a stag.

CHAPTER FIVE

'FATHER'S' ROOM

It was Saturday and Rajam had promised to come in the afternoon. Swaminathan was greatly excited. Where was he to entertain him? Probably in his own 'room'; but his father often came in to dress and undress. No, he would be at court, Swaminathan reminded himself with relief. He cleaned his table and arranged his books so neatly that his father was surprised and had a good word to say about it. Swaminathan went to his grandmother. 'Granny,' he said, 'I haved talked to you about Rajam, haven't I?'

'Yes. That boy who is very strong but never passes his examination.'

'No. No. That is Mani.'

'Oh, now I remember, it is a boy who is called the Gramme or something, that witty little boy.'

Swaminathan made a gesture of despair. 'Look here Granny, you are again mistaking the Pea for him. I mean Rajam, who has killed tigers, whose father is the Police Superintendent, and who is great.'

'Oh,' Granny cried, 'that boy, is he coming here? I am so glad.'

'H'm ... But I have got to tell you – '

'Will you bring him to me? I want to see him.'

'Let us see,' Swaminathan said vaguely. 'I can't promise. But I have got to tell you, when he is with me you must not call me or come to my room.'

'Why so?' asked Granny.

'The fact is, you are – well, you are too old,' said Swaminathan with brutal candour. Granny accepted her lot cheerfully.

That he must give his friend something very nice to eat, haunted his mind. He went to his mother, who was squatting before a cutter with a bundle of plantain leaves beside her. He sat before her, nervously crushing a piece of leaf this way and that, and tearing it to minute bits.

'Don't throw all those bits on the floor. I simply can't sweep the floor any more,' she said.

'Mother, what are you preparing for the afternoon tiffin?'

'Time enough to think of it,' said Mother.

'You had better prepare something very nice, something fine and sweet. Rajam is coming this afternoon. Don't make the sort of coffee that you usually give me. It must be very good and hot.' He remembered how in Rajam's house everything was brought to the room by the cook. 'Mother, would you mind if I don't come here for coffee and tiffin? Can you send it to my room?' He turned to the cook and said: 'Look here, you can't come to my room in that dhoti. You will have to wear a clean, white dhoti and shirt.' After a while he said: 'Mother, can you ask Father to lend me his room for just an hour or two?' She said that she could not as she was very busy. Why could he himself not go and ask?

'Oh, he will give more readily if you ask,' said Swaminathan.

He went to his father and said: 'Father, I want to ask you something.' Father looked up from the papers over which he was bent.

'Father, I want your room.'

'What for?'

'I have to receive a friend,' Swaminathan replied.

'You have your own room,' Father said.

'I can't show it to Rajam.'

'Who is this Rajam, such a big man?'

'He is the Police Superintendent's son. He is – he is not ordinary.'

'I see. Oh! Yes, you can have my room, but be sure not to mess up the things on the table.'

'Oh, I will be very careful. You are a nice father, Father.'

Father guffawed and said: 'Now run in, boy, and sit at your books.'

Rajam's visit went off much more smoothly than Swaminathan had anticipated. Father had left his room open; Mother had prepared some marvel with wheat, plum, and sugar. Coffee was really good. Granny had kept her promise and did not show her senile self to Rajam. Swaminathan was only sorry that the cook did not change his dhoti.

Swaminathan seated Rajam in his father's revolving chair. It was nearly three hours since he had come. They had talked out all subjects – Mani, Ebenezar, trains, tiger-hunting, police, and ghosts.

'Which is your room?' Rajam asked.

Swaminathan replied with a grave face: 'This is my room, why?'

Rajam took time to swallow this. 'Do you read such books?' he asked, eyeing the big gilt-edged law books on the table. Swaminathan was embarrassed.

Rajam made matters worse with another question. 'But where are your books?' There was just a flicker of a smile on his lips.

'The fact is,' said Swaminathan, 'this table belongs to my father. When I am out, he meets his clients in this room.'

'But where do you keep your books?'

Swaminathan made desperate attempts to change the topic. 'You have seen my grandmother, Rajam?'

'No. Will you show her to me? I should love to see her,' replied Rajam.

'Wait a minute then,' said Swaminathan and ran out. He had one last hope that his granny might be asleep. It was infinitely safer to show one's friends a sleeping granny.

He saw her sitting on her bed complacently. He was disappointed. He stood staring at her, lost in thought.

'What is it, boy?' Granny asked. 'Do you want anything?'

'No. Aren't you asleep? Granny,' he said a few minutes later, 'I have brought Rajam to see you.'

'Have you?' cried Granny. 'Come nearer, Rajam. I can't see your face well. You know I am old and blind.'

Swaminathan was furious and muttered under his breath that his granny had no business to talk all this drivel to Rajam.

Rajam sat on her bed. Granny stroked his hair and said that he had fine soft hair, though it was really short and prickly. Granny asked what his mother's name was, and how many children she had. She then asked if she had many jewels. Rajam replied that his mother had a black trunk filled with jewels, and a green one containing gold and silver vessels. Rajam then described to her Madras, its lighthouse, its sea, its trams and buses, and its cinemas. Every item made Granny gasp with wonder.

When Swaminathan entered the class, a giggle went round the benches. He walked to his seat hoping that he might not be the cause of the giggling. But it continued. He looked about. His eyes travelled up to the blackboard. His face burnt red. On the board was written in huge letters TAIL. Swaminathan walked to the blackboard and rubbed it off with his hands. He turned and saw Sankar's head bent over his notebook, and the Pea was busy unpacking his satchel. Without a word Swaminathan approached the Pea and gave him a fierce slap on his cheek. The Pea burst into tears and swore that he did not do it. He cast a sly look at Sankar, who was absorbed in some work. Swaminathan turned to him and slapped his face also.

Soon there was pandemonium: Sankar, Swaminathan, and the Pea rolling over, tearing, scratching, and kicking one another. The teacher came in and stood aghast. He could do little more than look on and ejaculate. He was the old Tamil pundit, the most helpless teacher in the school.

Somu and Mani parted the fighters. The teacher ascended the platform and took his seat. The class settled down.

Somu got up and said: 'Sir, please let us go out. We do not want to disturb the class.'

The teacher demurred; but already Mani had gone out, pushing Swaminathan and the Pea before him. Somu followed him with Sankar.

They came to a lonely spot in the field adjoining the school. There was tense silence for a while, and Mani broke it: 'What is wrong with you, you little rogues?'

Three started to speak at once. Swaminathan's voice was the loudest: 'He – the Pea – wrote TAIL – Big Tail – on the blackboard – big – '

'No – I didn't, you – ' screamed the Pea.

'The other too wrote it,' cried Swaminathan pointing at Sankar.

'Rascal! Did you see me?' howled Sankar.

Mani covered their mouths with his hands. 'What is a tail, anyway?' he asked, not having been told anything about it till then.

'They call me Rajam's tail,' sobbed Swaminathan.

A frozen expression came over Mani's face, and he asked, 'And who dares to talk of Rajam here?'

'Oh, dare!' repeated Somu.

'If any of you fellows have done it – ' growled Mani looking at the trembling Sankar and the Pea.

'If they have, what can you do?' asked Somu with a contemptuous smile.

'What do you mean, Somu, what do you mean?'

'Look here, Mani,' Somu cried, 'for a long time I have been waiting to tell you this: you think too much of yourself and your powers.'

Mani swung his hand and brought it down on Somu's nape. Somu pushed it away with a heavy blow. Mani aimed a kick at Somu, which would send him rolling. Somu stepped aside and delivered one himself, which nearly bent the other.

The three youngsters could hardly believe their eyes. Somu and Mani fighting! They lost their heads. They thought that Somu and Mani were killing each other. They looked accusingly at one another, and then ran towards the school.

They burst in upon the headmaster, who gathered from them with difficulty that in the adjacent field two murders were being committed at that very moment. He was disposed to laugh at first. But the excitement and seriousness on the boys' faces made him check his laughter and scratch his chin. He called a peon and with him set off to the field.

The fighters, rolling and rolling, were everywhere in the field. The headmaster and the peon easily picked them apart, much to the astonishment of Swaminathan, who had thought till then that the strength that Somu or Mani possessed was not possessed by anyone else in the world.

CHAPTER SIX

A FRIEND IN NEED

One afternoon three weeks later, Swaminathan stood before Mani's house and gave a low whistle. Mani joined him. They started for Rajam's house, speculating on the way about the surprise which Rajam had said he would give them if they saw him that afternoon.

'I think,' said Swaminathan, 'Rajam is merely joking. It is merely a trick to get us to his house.' He was very nearly pushed into a gutter for this doubt.

'Probably he has brought a monkey or something,' Swaminathan ventured again. Mani was gracious enough to admit that it might be so. They thought of all possible subjects that might surprise them, and gave up the attempt in the end.

Their thoughts turned to their enemies. 'You know what I am going to do?' Mani asked. 'I am going to break Somu's waist. I know where he lives. He lives in Kabir Street behind the market. I have often seen him coming out at nights to a shop in the market for betel leaves. I shall first fling a stone at the municipal lamp and put it out. You have no idea how dark Kabir Street is ... I shall wait with my club, and as soon as he appears – He will sprawl in the dust with broken bones ...' Swaminathan shuddered at the thought. 'And that is not all,' said Mani, 'I am going to get that Pea under my heel and press him to the earth. And Sankar is going to hang by his tuft over Sarayu, from a *peepul* branch ...'

They stopped talking when they reached Rajam's house. The gate was bolted, and they got up the wall and jumped in. A servant came running towards them. He asked, 'Why did you climb the wall?'

'Is the wall your property?' Mani asked and burst into laughter.

'But if you had broken your ribs – ' the servant began.

'What is that to you? Your ribs are safe, are they not?' Swaminathan asked ungraciously and laughed.

'And just a word more,' Mani said, 'do you happen to be by any chance the Police Superintendent's son?'

'No, no,' replied the servant.

'Very well then,' replied Mani, 'we have come to see and talk to the Police Superintendent's son.' The servant beat a hasty retreat.

They banged their fists on Rajam's door. They heard the clicking of the latch and hid themselves behind the pillar. Rajam peeped out and shut the door again.

They came out, stood before the door, and wondered what to do. Swaminathan applied his mouth to the keyhole and mewed like a cat. Mani pulled him away and putting his mouth to the hole barked like a dog. The latch clicked again, and the door slightly opened. Mani whispered to Swaminathan, 'You are a blind kitten, I will be a blind puppy.'

Mani fell down on his knees and hands, shut his eyes tight, pushed the door with his head, and entered Rajam's room in the role of a blind puppy. Swaminathan crawled behind him with shut eyes, mewing for all he was worth. They moved round and round the room, Rajam adding to the interest of the game by mewing and barking in answer every few seconds. The blind puppy brushed its side against a leg, and thinking that it belonged to Rajam softly bit the calf muscle. Imagine its confusion when it opened its eyes and saw that it was biting its enemy, Somu! The blind kitten nestled close to a leg and scratched it with its paw. Opening its eyes it found that it was fondling a leg that belonged to its enemy, Sankar.

Mani remained stunned for a moment, and then scrambled to his feet. He looked around, his face twitching with shame and rage. He saw the Pea sitting in a corner, his eyes twinkling with mischief, and felt impelled to take him by the throat. He turned round and saw Rajam regarding him steadily, his mouth still quivering with a smothered grin.

As for Swaminathan, he felt that the best place for himself would be the darkness and obscurity under a table or a chair.

'What do you mean by this, Rajam?' Mani asked.

'Why are you so wild?'

'It was your fault,' said Mani vehemently, 'I didn't know –' He looked round.

'Well, well. I didn't ask you to crawl and bark, did I?'

Somu and company laughed. Mani glared round, 'I am going away, Rajam. This is not the place for me.'

Rajam replied, 'You may go away, if you don't want me to see you or speak to you any more.'

Mani fidgeted uneasily. Rajam took him aside and soothed him. Rajam then turned to Swaminathan, who was lost in bottomless misery. He comforted and flattered him by saying that it was the best imitation of a cat and dog that he had ever witnessed in his life. He admitted that for a few minutes he wondered whether he was watching a real cat and a dog. They would get prizes if they did it in fairs. If Swaminathan and Mani would be good enough to repeat the fun, he would be delighted, and even ask his father to come and watch.

This was soothing. Swaminathan and Mani felt proud of themselves. And after the round of eating that followed, they were perfectly happy, except when they thought of the other three in the room.

They were in this state of mind when Rajam began a lecture on friendship. He said impressive things about friendship, quoting from his book the story of the dying old man and the faggots, which proved that union was strength. A friend in need was a friend indeed. He then started giving hair-raising accounts of what hell had in store for persons who fostered enmity. According to Rajam, it was written in the Vedas that a person who fostered enmity should be locked up in a small room, after his death. He would be made to stand, stark naked, on a pedestal of red-hot iron. There were beehives all around with bees as big as lemons. If the sinner stepped down from the pedestal, he would have to put his foot on immense scorpions and centipedes that crawled about the room in hundreds ...

A shudder went through the company.

... The sinner would have to stand thus for a month, without food or sleep. At the end of a month he would be transferred to another place, a very narrow bridge over a lake of boiling oil. The bridge was so narrow that he would be able to keep only one foot on it at a time. Even on the narrow bridge there were plenty of wasp nests and cactus, and he would be goaded from behind to move on. He would have to balance on one foot and then on another, for ages and ages, to keep himself from falling into the steaming lake below, and move on indefinitely ...

The company was greatly impressed. Rajam then invited everyone to come forward and say that they would have no more enemies. If Sankar said it, he would get a bound notebook; if Swaminathan said it, he would get a clockwork engine; if Somu said it, he would get a belt; and if Mani said it, he would get a nice pocket-knife; and the Pea would get a marvellous little pen.

He threw open the cupboard and displayed the prizes. There was silence for some time as each sat gnawing his nails. Rajam was sweating with his peace-making efforts.

The Pea was the first to rise. He stood before the cupboard and said, 'Let me see the fountain-pen'. Rajam gave it to him. The Pea turned it round and round and gave it back without any comment. 'Why, don't you like it?' Rajam asked. The Pea kept staring into the cupboard and said, 'Can I have that box?' He pointed at a tiny box with a lot of yellow and black designs on it and a miniature Taj Mahal on its lid. Rajam said, 'I can't give you that. I want it.' He paused. He had two more boxes like that in his trunk. He changed his mind. 'No. I don't want it. You can take the box if you like.'

In a short while, Mani was sharpening a knife on his palm; Somu was trying a belt on; Sankar was fingering a thick bound notebook; and Swaminathan was jealously clasping a green engine to his bosom.

CHAPTER SEVEN

A NEW ARRIVAL

Mother had been abed for two days past. Swaminathan missed her very much in the kitchen, and felt uncomfortable without her attentions. He was taken to her room, where he saw her lying dishevelled and pale on her bed. She asked him to come nearer. She asked him why he was looking emaciated and if he was not eating and sleeping well. Swaminathan kept staring at her blankly. Here seemed to be a different Mother. He was cold and reserved when he spoke to her. Her appearance depressed him. He wriggled himself from her grasp and ran out.

His granny told him that he was going to have a brother. He received the news without enthusiasm.

That night he was allowed to sleep on Granny's bed. The lights kept burning all night. Whenever he opened his eyes, he was conscious of busy feet scurrying along the passage. Late at night Swaminathan woke up and saw a lady doctor in the hall. She behaved as if the house belonged to her. She entered Mother's room, and presently out of the room came a mingled noise of whispers and stifled moans. She came out of the room with a serious face and ordered everybody about. She commanded even Father to do something. He vanished for a moment and reappeared with a small bottle in his hand. He hovered about uncertainly. The hushed voices, hurry, seriousness, agitation, hot water, and medicine – preparations for ushering a new person into the world – were too bewildering for Swaminathan's comprehension. Meanwhile Granny kept asking something of everybody that passed by, and no one troubled to answer her.

What did it matter? The five carpets in Granny's bed were cosy; her five pillows were snug; and Granny's presence nearby was reassuring; and above all, his eyelids were becoming heavy. What more did he want? He fell asleep.

* * *

The Tamil pundit, with his unshaven face and the silver-rimmed spectacles set askew on his nose, was guiding the class through the intricacies of Tamil grammar. The guide was more enthusiastic than his followers. A continual buzz filled the air. Boys had formed themselves into small groups and carried on private conversations. The pundit made faint attempts to silence the class by rapping his palms on the table. After a while, he gave up the attempt and went on with his lecture. His voice was scarcely audible.

Sankar and a few others sat on the first bench with cocked-up ears and busy pencils.

Swaminathan and the Pea sat on the last bench.

'I say, Pea,' said Swaminathan, 'I got a new brother this morning.'

The Pea was interested. 'How do you like him?'

'Oh, like him! He is hardly anything. Such a funny-looking creature!' said Swaminathan and gave what he thought was an imitation of his little brother: he shut his eyes, compressed his lips, folded his hands on his chest, protruded his tongue, and tilted his head from side to side. The Pea laughed uncontrollably. 'But,' Swaminathan said, 'this thing has a wonderful pair of hands, so small and plump, you know! But I tell you, his face is awful, red, red like chilli.'

They listened to the teacher's lecture for a few minutes. 'I say, Swami,' said the Pea, 'these things grow up soon. I have seen a baby that was just what your brother is. But you know, when I saw it again during Michaelmas I could hardly recognize it.'

CHAPTER EIGHT

BEFORE THE EXAMINATIONS

In April, just two weeks before the examinations, Swaminathan realized that his father was changing – for the worse. He was becoming fussy and difficult. He seemed all of a sudden to have made up his mind to harass his son. If the latter was seen chatting with his granny, he was told sourly, 'Remember, boy, there is an examination. Your granny can wait, not your examination.' If he was seen wandering behind his mother, he was hunted down and sent to his desk. If his voice was heard anywhere after the Taluk Office gong had struck nine, a command would come from his father's room, 'Swami, why haven't you gone to bed yet? You must get up early and study a bit.' This was a trying period in Swaminathan's life. One day he was piqued enough to retort, 'Why are you so nervous about my examination?'

'Suppose you fail?'

'I won't.'

'Of course you won't if you study hard and answer well ... Suppose you fail and all your class-mates go up, leaving you behind? You can start doing just what you like on the very day your examination closes.'

Swaminathan reflected: suppose the Pea, Mani, Rajam and Sankar deserted him and occupied Second A? His father was right. And then his father drove home the point. 'Suppose all your juniors in the Fifth Standard become your class-mates?'

Swaminathan sat at decimals for half an hour.

At school everybody seemed to be overwhelmed by the thought of the examinations. It was weeks since anybody had seen a smile on Sankar's face. Somu had become brisk and businesslike. The Pea took time to grasp jokes, and seldom gave out any. And as for Rajam, he came to the school at the stroke of the first bell, took down everything the teacher said, and left at the stroke of the last bell, hardly uttering a dozen words to anybody. Mani was beginning to look worried and took every opportunity to take Sankar aside so as to clear the doubts that arose from time to time as he plodded through his texts. He dogged the steps of the school clerk. There was a general belief in the school that the clerk was omniscient and knew all the question papers of all the classes.

One day Mani went to the clerk's house and laid a neat bundle containing fresh brinjals at his feet. The clerk was pleased and took Mani in and seated him on a stool.

The clerk looked extremely amiable and Mani felt that he could ask anything at that moment and get it. The clerk was murmuring something about his cat, a lank ill-fed thing, that was nestling close to him. Most of what he was saying did not enter Mani's head. He was waiting feverishly to open the topic of question papers. The clerk had meanwhile passed from cats to eye-flies; but it made little difference to Mani, who was waiting for the other to pause for breath to launch his attack. 'You must never let these eye-flies buzz near your eyes. All cases of eyesore can be traced to it. When you get eyesore the only thing you can do is to take a slice of raw onion ...'

Mani realized that the other would not stop, and butted in. 'There is only a week more for the examinations, sir ...'

The clerk was slightly puzzled: 'Yes, indeed, a week more ... You must take care to choose only the juicy variety, the large juicy variety, not the small onion ...'

'Sir,' Mani interrupted, ignoring the juicy variety, 'I am much worried about my examination.' He tried to look pathetic.

'I am glad. If you read well, you will pass,' said the Oracle.

'You see, sir, I am so worried, I don't sleep at nights, thinking of the examination ... If you could possibly tell me something important ... I have such a lot to study – don't want to study unnecessary things that may not be necessary for the examination.' He meandered thus. The clerk understood what he was driving at, but said, 'Just read all your portions and you will pass.' Mani realized that diplomacy was not his line. He asked bluntly, 'Please tell me, sir, what questions we are getting for our examination.'

The clerk denied having any knowledge of the question papers. Mani flattered him by asking, if he did not know the questions, who else would. By just a little more of the same judicious flattery the clerk was moved to give what Mani believed to be valuable hints. In spite of the fact that he did not know what the First Form texts were, the clerk ventured to advise, 'You must pay particular attention to geography. Maybe you will have to practise map-drawing a lot. And in arithmetic make it a point to solve at least five problems every day, and you will be able to tackle arithmetic as easily as you swallow plantains.'

'And what about English?'

'Oh, don't worry about that. Have you read all your lessons?'

'Yes, sir,' Mani replied without conviction.

'It is all right then. You must read all the important lessons again, and if you have time, yet again, and that will be ample.'

These answers satisfied Mani greatly. On his way home, he smiled to himself and said that the four annas he had invested on brinjals was not after all a waste.

Mani felt important. He secretly pitied his class-mates, who had to do work coolly without valuable hints to lighten their labour. He felt he ought to share his good secret with Swaminathan without divulging the source.

They were going home from the school. They stopped for a while at the junction of Vinayak Mudali and Grove Streets before parting ways. Mani said, 'Young man, have you any idea what we are getting for the examination?'

'Nothing outside the covers of the textbooks.'

Mani ignored the humour. 'Now listen to me carefully: last night from seven to ten, do you know what I did?'

'Munched ground-nuts?'

'Idiot, don't joke. I made two maps of India, two of Africa, and one map of Europe.'

'Say all the maps in the atlas.'

'Maybe,' Mani said, not quite liking the remark, 'but I do it with some definite purpose ... It may be that I know one or two questions. But don't let the other fellows know anything about it. I may get into trouble.' Swaminathan was taken in by the other's seriousness and inferred a moral.

* * *

Reaching home, Swaminathan felt rather dull. His mother was not at home. Granny was not in a talking mood. He related to her some exciting incidents of the day: 'Granny, guess what happened in our school today. A boy in First C stabbed another in the forearm with a penknife.'

'What for?' asked Granny mechanically.

'They were enemies.' Finding that it fell flat, he brought out the big event of the day. 'Granny, Granny, here is another thing. The headmaster knocked his toe against a door-post and oh! there was such a lot of blood! He went limping about the school the whole day. He couldn't take the Third Form and so they had leave, the lucky fellows!'

'Is it?' asked Granny.

Swaminathan perceived, to his intense disgust, that his granny was in one of her dull sleepy moods.

He strayed near the swing-cradle of his little brother. Though at first he had been sceptical of his brother's attractions and possibilities, now day by day he was finding him more interesting. This little one was now six months old and was charming. His attainments were: he made shrill noises whenever he saw anybody; thrust his fists into his mouth and damped his round arms up to the elbow; vigorously kicked the air; and frequently displayed his bare red gums in a smile. Swaminathan loved every inch of him. He would spend hours balancing himself on the edge of the cradle and trying to make him say 'Swaminathan'. The little one would gurgle, and Swaminathan would shriek, pretending that it was the other's futile version of his name.

Now he peered in and was disappointed to find the baby asleep. He cleared his throat aloud and coughed in the hope of waking him. But the baby slept. He waited for a moment, and tiptoed away, reminding himself that it was best to leave the other alone, as he had a knack of throwing the house in turmoil for the first half-hour whenever he awoke from sleep.

Staying at home in the evenings was extremely irksome. He sighed at the thought of the sandbanks of Sarayu and Mani's company. But his father had forbidden him to go out till the examinations were over. He often felt he ought to tell his father what he thought of him. But somehow when one came near doing it, one failed. He would have to endure it after all only for a week ... The thought that he would have to put up with his travails only for a week at worst gave him fresh energy.

He sat at his table and took out his atlas. He opened the political map of Europe and sat gazing at it. It puzzled him how people managed to live in such a crooked country as Europe. He wondered what the shape of the people might be who lived in places where the outline narrowed as in a cape, and how they managed to escape being strangled by the contour of their land. And then another favourite problem began to tease him: how did those map-makers find out what the shape of a country was? How did they find out that Europe was like a camel's head? Probably they stood on high towers and copied what they saw below. He wondered if he would be able to see India as it looked in the map, if he stood on the top of the town hall. He had never been there nor ever did he wish to go there. Though he was incredulous, tailor Ranga persistently informed him that there was a torture chamber in the top storey of the town hall to which Pathans decoyed young people.

He shook himself from his brown study and copied the map of Europe. He kept the original and his own copy side by side and congratulated himself on his ability to draw, though his outline looked like some strange animal that had part bull's face and part camel's.

It was past seven by now and his father came home. He was greatly pleased to see his son at work. 'That is right, boy,' he said looking at the map. Swaminathan felt that that moment was worth all his suffering. He turned over the pages and opened out the map of Africa.

Two days before his examination he sat down to draw up a list of his needs. On a piece of paper he wrote:

Unruled white paper	20 sheets
Nibs	6
Ink	2 bottles
Clips	
Pins	

He nibbled his pencil and reread the list. The list was disappointing. He had never known that his wants were so few. When he first sat down to draw the list he had hoped to fill two or three imposing pages. But now the cold lines on the paper numbered only five. He scrutinized the list again: 'Unruled white paper 20 sheets.' He asked himself why he was so particular about the paper's being unruled. It was a well-known fact that, try as he would, his lines had a tendency to curl up towards the right-hand corner of the paper. That would not do for examinations. He had better keep a stock of ruled paper. And then 'Nibs'. He wondered how many nibs one would need for an examination. One? Two? Five? ... And then the Ink column worried him. How much of it did one buy? After that he had trouble with clips and pins. He not only had not the faintest idea of the quantity of each that he would need but was totally ignorant of the unit of purchase also. Could one go to a shop and demand six pins and six clips without offending the shopman?

At the end the list was corrected to:

Unruled white paper	20 sheets
Ruled white paper	10 sheets
Black ink	1 bottle
Clips	3̸–6̸–12
Pins	6̸–12

The list was not satisfactory even now. After pondering over it, he added 'Cardboard Pad One' and 'One Rupee For Additional Expenses'.

His father was busy in his office. Swaminathan stood before him with the list in his hand. Father was absorbed in his work and did not know that Swaminathan was there. Swaminathan suddenly realized that it would be better to approach his father at some other time. He could be sure of a better reception if he opened the question after food. He tiptoed out. When he was just outside the door, his father called out, 'Who is that?' There was no friendliness in the tone. 'Who is that I say?' roared Father again and was at his side with a scowling face before Swaminathan could decide whether to sneak out or stop and answer.

'Was it you?'

'Yes.'

'You idiot, why couldn't you answer instead of driving me hoarse calling out "Who is that? Who is that?"... A man can't have peace in this house even for a second. Here I am at work – and every fifth second somebody or other pops in with some fool question or other. How am I to go on? Go and tell your mother that she can't come to my room for the rest of the day. I don't care if the whole battalion of oilmongers and vegetable women come and clamour for money. Let her drive them out. Your mother seems to think – what is that paper in your hand?'

'Nothing, Father,' Swaminathan answered, thrusting the paper into his pocket.

'What is that?' Father shouted, snatching the list. Reading it with a terrific scowl, he went back to his chair. 'What is this thing?'

Swaminathan had to cough twice to find his voice. 'It is – my – examination list.'

'What examination list?'

'My examinations begin the day after tomorrow, you know.'

'And yet you are wandering about the house like an unleashed donkey! What preposterous list is this? Do you think rupees, annas and paise drop from the sky?'

Swaminathan did not think so, but something nearly so.

Father pulled out a drawer and peering into it said: 'You can take from me anything you want. I haven't got clips. You don't need them. And then the pad, why do you want a pad? Are there no desks in your rooms? In our day slates were good enough for us. But now you want pen, paper, ink, and pad to keep under the paper ...'

He took out an awful red pencil and scored out the 'Pad' from the list. It almost gashed the list. He flung it back at Swaminathan, who looked at it sadly. How deliciously he had been dreaming of going to Ameer Mart, jingling with coins, and buying things!

He was just going out when Father called him back and said: 'Here, boy, as you go, for goodness' sake, remove the baby from the hall. I can't stand his idiotic cry ... What is the matter with him? ... Is your mother deaf or callous? The child may cry till he has fits, for aught she cares ...'

CHAPTER NINE

SCHOOL BREAKS UP

With dry lips, parched throat, and ink-stained fingers, and exhaustion on one side and exaltation on the other, Swaminathan strode out of the examination hall on the last day.

Standing in the veranda, he turned back and looked into the hall and felt slightly uneasy. He would have felt more comfortable if all the boys had given their papers as he had done, twenty minutes before time. With his left shoulder resting against the wall, Sankar was lost to the world. Rajam, sitting under the second ventilator, between two third-form boys, had become a writing-machine. Mani was still gazing at the rafters, scratching his chin with the pen. The Pea was leaning back in his seat, revising his answers. One supervisor was drowsing in his chair; another was pacing up and down with an abstracted look in his eyes. The scratchy noise of active nibs, the rustle of papers, and the clearing of the throats, came through the brooding silence of the hall.

Swaminathan suddenly wished that he had not come out so soon. But how could he have stayed in the hall longer? The Tamil paper was set to go on till five o'clock. He had found himself writing the last line of the last question at four-thirty. Out of the six questions set, he had answered the first question to his satisfaction, the second was doubtful, the third was satisfactory, the fourth he knew was clearly wrong (but then, he did not know the correct answer).

The sixth answer was the best of the lot. It took only a minute to answer it. He had read the question at two minutes to four-thirty, started answering a minute later, and finished it at four-thirty. The question was: 'What moral do you infer from the story of the Brahmin and the Tiger?' (A brahmin was passing along the edge of a pond. A tiger hailed him from the other bank and offered him a gold bangle. The brahmin at first declined the offer, but when the tiger protested its innocence and sincerity and insisted upon his taking the bangle, he waded through the water. Before he could hold out his hand for the bangle, he was inside the tiger.)

Swaminathan had never thought that this story contained a moral. But now he felt that it must have one since the question paper mentioned it. He took a minute to decide whether the moral was: 'We must never accept a gold bangle when it is offered by a tiger' or 'Love of gold bangle cost one one's life'. He saw more logic in the latter and wrote it down. After writing, he had looked at the big hall clock. Half an hour more! What had he to do for half an hour? But he felt awkward to be the first to go out. Why could not the others be as quick and precise as he?

He had found it hard to kill time. Why wasn't the paper set for two and a half hours instead of three? He had looked wistfully at the veranda outside. If only he could pluck up enough courage to hand in the paper and go out – he would have no more examination for a long time to come – he could do what he pleased – roam about the town in the evenings and afternoons and mornings – throw away the books – command Granny to tell endless tales.

He had seen a supervisor observing him, and had at once pretended to be busy with the answer paper. He thought that while he was about it, he might as well do a little revision. He read a few lines of the first question and was bored. He turned over the leaves and kept gazing at the last answer. He had to pretend that he was revising. He kept gazing at the moral of the tiger story till it lost all its meaning. He set his pen to work. He went on improving the little dash under the last line indicating the end, till it became an elaborate complicated pattern.

He had looked at the clock again, thinking that it must be nearly five now. It was only ten minutes past four-thirty. He saw two or three boys giving up their papers and going out, and felt happy. He briskly folded the paper and wrote on the flap the elaborate inscription:

Tamil Tamil
W. S. Swaminathan
1st Form A section

Albert Mission School
Malgudi
South India
Asia.

The bell rang. In twos and threes boys came out of the hall. It was a thorough contrast to the preceding three hours. There was the din of excited chatter.

'What have you written for the last question?' Swaminathan asked a class-mate.

'Which? The moral question? ... Don't you remember what the teacher said in the class? ..."Love of gold cost the brahmin his life." '

'Where was gold there?' Swaminathan objected. 'There was only a gold bangle. How much have you written for the question?'

'One page,' said the class-mate.

Swaminathan did not like this answer. He had written only a line. 'What! You should not have written so much.'

A little later he found Rajam and Sankar. 'Well, boys, how did you find the paper?'

'How did you find it?' Sankar asked.

'Not bad,' Swaminathan said.

'I was afraid only of Tamil,' said Rajam, 'now I think I am safe. I think I may get passing marks.'

'No. Certainly more. A class,' Sankar said.

'Look here,' Swaminathan said, 'some fools have written a page for that moral question.'

'I wrote only three-quarters of a page,' Rajam said.

'And I only a little more than half,' said Sankar, who was an authority on these matters.

'I too wrote about that length, about half a page,' lied Swaminathan as a salve to his conscience, and believed it for the moment.

'Boys, do you remember that we have no school from tomorrow?'

'Oh, I forgot all about it,' Rajam said.

'Well, what are you going to do with yourselves?' somebody asked.

'I am going to use my books as fuel in the kitchen,' Swaminathan said.

'My father has bought a lot of books for me to read during the vacation, *Sinbad the Sailor*, *Alibaba*, and so on,' said Sankar.

Mani came throwing up his arms and wailing: 'Time absolutely insufficient. I could have dashed off the last question.'

The Pea appeared from somewhere with a huge streak of ink on his left cheek. 'Hallo Sankar, first class?'

'No. May hardly get thirty-five.'

'You rascal, you are lying. If you get a first class, may I cut off your tuft?' Mani asked.

The bell rang again fifteen minutes later. The whole school crowded into the hall. There was joy in every face and good fellowship in every word. Even the teachers tried to be familiar and pleasant. Ebenezar, when he saw Mani, asked: 'Hallo, blockhead, how are you going to waste your vacation?'

'I am going to sleep, sir,' Mani said, winking at his friends.

'Are you likely to improve your head by the time you return to the school?'

'How is it possible, sir, unless you cut off Sankar's head and present it to me?'

A great roar of laughter followed this. There would have been roars of laughter at anything; the mood was such. In sheer joy the drawing master was bringing down his cane on a row of feet because, he said, he saw some toes growing to an abnormal length.

The headmaster appeared on the platform, and after waiting for the noise to subside, began a short speech in which he said that the school would remain closed till the nineteenth of June and open again on the twentieth. He hoped that the boys would not waste their time but read story-books and keep glancing through the books prescribed for their next classes, to which, he hoped, most of them were going to be promoted. And now a minute more, there would be a prayer, after which the boys might disperse and go home.

At the end of the prayer the storm burst. With the loudest, lustiest cries, the gathering flooded out of the hall in one body. All through this vigorous confusion and disorder, Swaminathan kept close to Mani. For there was a general belief in the school that enemies stabbed each other on the last day. Swaminathan had no enemy as far as he could remember. But who could say? The school was a bad place.

Mani did some brisk work at the school gate, snatching from all sorts of people ink-bottles and pens, and destroying them. Around him was a crowd seething with excitement and joy. Ecstatic shrieks went up as each article of stationery was destroyed. One or two little boys feebly protested. But Mani wrenched the ink-bottles from their hands, tore their caps, and poured ink over their clothes. He had a small band of assistants, among whom Swaminathan was prominent. Overcome by the mood of the hour, he had spontaneously emptied his ink-bottle over his own head and had drawn frightful dark circles under his eyes with the dripping ink.

A policeman passed in the road. Mani shouted: 'Oh, policeman, policeman! Arrest these boys!' A triumphant cry from a hundred throats rent the air. A few more ink-bottles exploded on the ground and a few more pens were broken. In the midst of it Mani cried: 'Who will bring me Singaram's turban? I shall dye it for him.'

Singaram, the school peon, was the only person who was not affected by the spirit of liberty that was abroad, and as soon as the offer to dye his turban reached his ears, he rushed into the crowd with a big stick and dispersed the revellers.

CHAPTER TEN

THE COACHMAN'S SON

Swaminathan had two different attachments: one to Somu, Sankar, and the Pea – a purely scholastic one, which automatically ceased when the school gates closed; his other attachment was more human, to Rajam and Mani. Now that they had no school, they were free from the shackles of time and were almost always together, and arranged for themselves a hectic vacation.

Swaminathan's one consuming passion in life now was to get a hoop. He dreamt of it day and night. He feasted on visions of an ex-cycle wheel without spokes or tyre. You had only to press a stick into the groove and the thing would fly. Oh, what joy to see it climb small obstacles, and how gently it took curves! When running it made a steady hum, which was music to the ear. Swaminathan thought that anybody in Malgudi would understand that he was coming, even a mile away, by that hum. He sometimes kept awake till ten-thirty in the night, thinking of this hoop. He begged everyone that he came across, from his father's friends to a municipal sweeper that he knew, to give him a cycle wheel. Now he could not set his eyes on a decent bicycle without his imagination running riot over its wheels. He dreamt one night that he crossed the Sarayu near Nallappa's Grove 'on' his wheel. It was a vivid dream: the steel wheel crunched on the sandy bed of the river as it struggled and heaved across. It became a sort of horse when it reached the other bank. It went back home in one leap, took him to the kitchen, and then to his bed, and lay down beside him. This was fantastic; but the early part of the dream was real enough. It nearly maddened him to wake to a hoopless morning.

In sheer despair he opened his heart to a coachman – a casual acquaintance of his. The coachman was very sympathetic. He agreed that existence was difficult without a hoop. He said that he would be able to give Swaminathan one in a few hours if the latter could give him five rupees. This was an immense sum, which Swaminathan hoped to possess in some distant future when he should become as tall as his father. He said so. At which the coachman gave a convincing talk on how to get it. He wanted only six paise to start with; in a short time he would make it six annas, and after that convert it to six rupees. And Swaminathan could spend the five out of the six rupees on the hoop and the balance of one rupee just as he pleased. Swaminathan declared that nothing would give him greater happiness than giving that extra rupee to the coachman. If any doubts arose in Swaminathan's mind, they were swept away by the other's rhetoric. The coachman's process of minting higher currency was this: he had a special metal pot at home in which he kept all base copper coins together with some mysterious herb (whose name he would not reveal even if he were threatened with torture). He kept the whole thing, he said, buried in the ground, he squatted on the spot at dead of night and performed some yoga, and lo when the time came, all the copper was silver. He could make even gold, but to get the herbs for it, he would have to walk two hundred and fifty miles across strange places, and he did not consider it worth all that exertion.

Swaminathan asked him when he might see him again as he had to think out and execute a plan to get six paise. The coachman said that if the other did not get the money immediately he would not be available for weeks to come as his master was going away and he would have to go away too. Swaminathan cringed and begged him to grant him six hours and ran home.

He first tried Granny. She almost shed tears that she had no money, and held her wooden box upside down to prove how hard up she was.

'I know, Granny, you have a lot of coins under your pillows.'

'No, boy. You can search if you like.'

Swaminathan ordered Granny to leave the bed and made a thorough search under the pillows and the carpets.

'Why do you want money now?' Granny asked.

'If you have what I want, have the goodness to oblige me. If not, why ask futile questions?'

Granny cried to Mother: 'If you have money, give this boy six paise.' But nobody was prepared to oblige Swaminathan. Father dismissed the request in less than a second, which made Swaminathan wonder what he did with all the money that he took from his clients.

He now tried a last desperate chance. He fell on his hands and knees and, resting his cheek on the cold cement floor, peered into the dark space under his father's heavy wardrobe. He had a wild notion that he might find a few coins scattered there. He thrust his hand under the wardrobe and moved it in all directions. All that he was able to collect was a disused envelope musty with cobweb and dust, a cockroach, and pinches of fine dust.

He sometimes believed that he could perform magic, if only he set about it with sufficient earnestness. He also remembered Ebenezar's saying in the class that God would readily help those that prayed to him.

He secured a small cardboard box, placed in it a couple of pebbles, and covered them with fine sand and leaves. He carried the box to the *pooja* room and placed it in a corner. It was a small room in which a few framed pictures of gods hung on the wall, and a few bronze and brass idols kept staring at Swaminathan from a small carved wooden pedestal. A permanent smell of flowers, camphor, and incense hung in the air.

Swaminathan stood before the gods and with great piety informed them of the box and its contents, how he expected them to convert the two pebbles into two three-paise coins, and why he needed money so urgently. He promised that if the gods helped him, he would give up biting his thumb. He closed his eyes and muttered: 'Oh, Sri Rama! Thou hast slain Ravana though he had ten heads, can't you give me six paise? ... If I give you the six paise now, when will you give me the hoop? I wish you would tell me what that herb is ... Mani, shall I tell you the secret of getting a hoop? Oh, Rama! Give me six paise and I will give up biting my thumb for a year ...'

He wandered aimlessly in the backyard persuading himself that in a few minutes he could return to the *pooja* room and take his money – transmuted pebbles. He fixed a time-limit of half an hour.

Ten minutes later he entered the *pooja* room, prostrated himself before the gods, rose, and snatching his box, ran to a secluded place in the backyard. With a fluttering heart he opened the box. He emptied it on the ground, ran his fingers through the mass of sand and leaves, and picked up the two pebbles. As he gazed at the cardboard box, the scattered leaves, sand, and the unconverted pebbles, he was filled with rage. The indifference of the gods infuriated him and brought tears to his eyes. He wanted to abuse the gods, but was afraid to. Instead, he vented all his rage on the cardboard box, and kicked it from place to place and stamped upon the leaves and sand. He paused and doubted if the gods would approve of even this. He was afraid that it might offend them. He might get on without money, but it was dangerous to incur the wrath of gods; they might make him fail in his examinations, or kill Father, Mother, Granny, or the baby. He picked up the box again and put back into it the sand, the leaves, and the pebbles that were crushed, crumpled, and kicked a minute ago. He dug a small pit at the root of a banana tree and buried the box reverently.

Ten minutes later he stood in Abu Lane, before Mani's house, and whistled twice or thrice. Mani did not appear. Swaminathan climbed the steps and knocked on the door. As the door-chain clanked inside, he stood in suspense. He was afraid he might not be able to explain his presence if anyone other than Mani should open the door. The door opened, and his heart sank. A big man with bushy eyebrows stood before him. 'Who are you?' he asked.

'Who are you? Where is Mani?' Swaminathan asked. This was intended to convey that he had come to see Mani but was quite surprised to meet this other person, and would like to know who it was whom he had the pleasure of seeing before him. But in his confusion he could not put this sentiment in better form.

'You ask me who I am in my own house?' bellowed the Bushy-Eyebrows. Swaminathan turned and jumped down the steps to flee. But the Bushy-Eyebrows ordered: 'Come here, little man.' It was impossible to disobey this command. Swaminathan slowly advanced up the steps, his eyes bulging with terror. The Bushy-Eyebrows said: 'Why do you run away? If you have come to see Mani, why don't you see him?' This was logic absolute.

'Never mind,' Swaminathan said irrelevantly.

'Go in and see him, little man.'

Swaminathan meekly entered the house. Mani was standing behind the door, tame and unimpressive in his domestic setting. He and Swaminathan stood staring at each other, neither of them uttering a single word. The Bushy-Eyebrows was standing in the doorway with his back to them, watching the street. Swaminathan pointed a timid finger and jerked his head questioningly. Mani whispered: 'uncle.' The uncle suddenly turned round and said: 'Why do you stand staring at each other? Did you come for that? Wag your tongues, boys.' After this advice he stepped into the street to drive away two dogs that came and rolled in front of the house, locked in a terrible fight. He was now out of earshot.

Swaminathan said: 'Your uncle? I never knew. I say, Mani, can't you come out now? ... No? ... I came on urgent business. Give me – urgent – six paise – got to have it – coachman goes away for weeks – may not get the chance again – don't know what to do without hoop ...'

He paused. Mani's uncle was circling round the dogs, swearing at them and madly searching for stones. Swaminathan continued: 'My life depends on it. If you don't give it, I am undone. Quick, get the money.'

'I have no money, nobody gives me money,' Mani replied.

Swaminathan felt lost. 'Where does your uncle keep his money? Look into that box ...'

'I don't know.'

'Mani, come here,' his uncle cried from the street, 'drive away these devils. Get me a stone.'

'Rajam, can you lend me a policeman?' Swaminathan asked two weeks later.

'Policeman! Why?'

'There is a rascal in this town who has robbed me.' He related to Rajam his dealings with the coachman. 'And now,' he said, continuing his tale of woe, 'whenever he sees me, he pretends not to recognize me. If I go to his house I am told he is not at home, though I can hear him cursing somebody inside. If I persist, he sends word that he will unchain his dog and kill me.'

'Has he a dog?' asked Rajam.

'Not any that I could see.'

'Then why not rush into his house and kick him?'

'It is all very well to say that. I tremble whenever I go to see him. There is no knowing what coachmen have in their houses ... He may set his horse on me.'

'Let him, it isn't going to eat you,' said Mani.

'Isn't it? I am glad to know it. You come with me one day to tailor Ranga and hear what he has to say about horses. They are sometimes more dangerous than even tigers,' Swaminathan said earnestly.

'Suppose you wait one day and catch him at the gate?' Rajam suggested.

'I have tried it. But whenever he comes out, he is on his coach. And as soon as he sees me, he takes out his long whip. I get out of his reach and shout. But what is the use? That horse simply flies! And to think that he has duped me of two annas!'

'It was six paise, wasn't it?'

'But he took from me twice again, six paise each time ...'

'Then it is only an anna and a half,' Rajam said.

'No, Rajam. It is two annas.'

'My dear boy, twelve paise make an anna, and you have paid thrice, six paise each time; that is eighteen paise in all, one anna and a half.'

'It is a useless discussion. Who cares how many paise make an anna?' Swaminathan said.

'But in money matters, you must be precise – very well, go on, Swami.'

'The coachman first took from me six paise, promising me the silver coins in two days. He dodged me for four days and demanded six more paise, saying that he had collected herbs for twelve paise. He put me off again and took from me another six paise, saying that without it the whole process would fail. And after that, every time I went to him he put me off with some excuse or other; he often complained that owing to the weather the process was going on rather slowly. And two days ago he told me that he did not know me or anything about my money. And now you know how he behaves – I don't mind the money, but I hate his boy – that dark rascal. He makes faces at me whenever he sees me, and he has threatened to empty a bucketful of drain-water on my head. One day he held up an open penknife. I want to thrash him; that will make his father give me back my two annas.'

Next day Swaminathan and Mani started for the coachman's house. Swaminathan was beginning to regret that he had ever opened the subject before his friends. The affair was growing beyond his control. And considering the interest that Rajam and Mani displayed in the affair, one could not foresee where it was going to take them all.

Rajam had formed a little plan to decoy and kidnap the coachman's son. Mani was his executive. He was to befriend the coachman's son. Swaminathan had very little part to play in the preliminary stages. His duty would cease with pointing out the coachman's house to Mani.

The coachman lived a mile from Swaminathan's house, westward in Keelacheri, which consisted of about a dozen thatched huts and dingy hovels, smoke-tinted and evil-smelling, clustering together irregularly.

They were now within a few yards of the place. Swaminathan tried a last desperate chance to stop the wheel of vengeance.

'Mani, I think the coachman's son has returned the money.'

'What!'

'I think ...'

'You think so, do you? Can you show it to me?'

Swaminathan pleaded: 'Leave him alone, Mani. You don't know what troubles we shall get into by tampering with that boy ...'

'Shut up or I will wring your neck.'

'Oh, Mani – the police – or the boy himself – he is frightful, capable of anything.' He had in his heart a great dread of the boy. And sometimes in the night would float before him a face dark, dirty and cruel, and make him shiver. It was the face of the coachman's son.

'He lives in the third house,' Swaminathan pointed out.

At the last moment Mani changed his plan and insisted upon Swaminathan's following him to the coachman's house. Swaminathan sat down in the road as a protest. But Mani was stubborn. He dragged Swaminathan along till they came before the coachman's house, and then started shouting at him.

'Mani, Mani, what is the matter?'

'You son of a donkey,' Mani roared at Swaminathan and swung his hand to strike him.

Swaminathan began to cry. Mani attempted to strangle him. A motley crowd gathered round them, urchins with prodigious bellies, women of dark aspect, and their men. Scurvy chickens cackled and ran hither and thither. The sun was unsparing. Two or three mongrels lay in the shade of a tree and snored. A general malodour of hencoop and unwashed clothes pervaded the place.

And now from the hovel that Swaminathan had pointed out as the coachman's, emerged a little man of three feet or so, ill clad and unwashed. He pushed his way through the crowd and, securing a fine place, sucked his thumb and watched the fight in rapture. Mani addressed the crowd indignantly, pointed at Swaminathan: 'This urchin, I don't know who he is, all of a sudden demands two annas from me. I have never seen him before. He says I owe him that money.'

Mani continued in this strain for fifteen minutes. At the end of it, the coachman's son took the thumb out of his mouth and remarked: 'He must be sent to the gaol.' At this Mani bestowed an approving smile upon him and asked: 'Will you help me to carry him to the police station?'

'No,' said the coachman's son, being afraid of police stations himself.

Mani asked: 'How do you know that he must be taken to the police station?'

'I know it.'

'Does he ever trouble you similarly?' asked Mani.

'No,' said the boy.

'Where is the two annas that your father took from me?' asked Swaminathan, turning to the boy his tear-drenched face. The crowd had meanwhile melted, after making half-hearted attempts to bring peace. Mani asked the boy suddenly: 'Do you want this top?' He held a shining red top. The boy put out his hand for the top.

Mani said: 'I can't give you this. If you come with me, I will give you a bigger one. Let us become friends.'

The boy had no objection. 'Won't you let me see it?' he asked. Mani gave it to him. The boy turned it in his hand twice or thrice and in the twinkling of an eye disappeared from the place. Mani took time to grasp the situation. When he did grasp it, he saw the boy entering a hovel far off. He started after him.

When Mani reached the hovel, the door was closed. Mani knocked a dozen times, before a surly man appeared and said that the boy was not there. The door was shut again. Mani started knocking again. Two or three menacing neighbours came round and threatened to bury him alive if he dared to trouble them in their own locality. Swaminathan was desperately appealing to Mani to come away. But it took a great deal more to move him. He went on knocking.

The neighbours took up their positions a few yards off, with handfuls of stones, and woke the dogs sleeping under the tree.

It was only when the dogs came bouncing towards them that Mani shouted: 'Run,' to Swaminathan, and set an example himself.

A couple of stones hit Swaminathan on the back. One or two hit Mani also. A sharp stone skinned Mani's right heel. They became blind and insensible to everything except the stretch of road before them.

CHAPTER ELEVEN

IN FATHER'S PRESENCE

During summer Malgudi was one of the most detested towns in South India. Sometimes the heat went above a hundred and ten in the shade, and between twelve and three any day in summer the dusty blanched roads were deserted. Even donkeys and dogs, the most vagrant of animals, preferred to move to the edge of the street, where catwalks and minor projections from buildings cast a sparse strip of shade, when the fierce sun tilted towards the west.

But there is this peculiarity about heat: it appears to affect only those that think of it. Swaminathan, Mani and Rajam would have been surprised if anybody had taken the trouble to prove to them that the Malgudi sun was unbearable. They found the noon and the afternoon the most fascinating part of the day. The same sun that beat down on the head of Mr Hentel, the mill manager, and drove him to Kodaikanal, or on the turban of Mr Krishnan, the Executive Engineer, and made him complain that his profession was one of the hardest, compelling him to wander in sun and storm, beat down on Swaminathan's curly head, Mani's tough matted hair, and Rajam's short wiry crop, and left them unmoved. The same sun that baked the earth so much that even Mr Retty, the most Indianized of the 'Europeans', who owned a rice mill in the deserted bungalow outside the town (he was, by the way, the mystery man of the place: nobody could say who he was or where he had come from; he swore at his boy and at his customers in perfect Tamil and always moved about in shirt, shorts, and sandalled feet), screamed one day when he forgetfully took a step or two barefoot – the same sun made the three friends loath to remain under a roof.

They were sitting on a short culvert, half a mile outside the municipal limits, on the trunk road. A streak of water ran under the culvert on a short stretch of sand, and mingled with Sarayu farther down. There was no tree where they sat, and the sun struck their heads directly. On the sides of the road there were paddy-fields; but now all that remained was scorched stubble, vast stretches of stubble, relieved here and there by clustering groves of mango or coconut. The trunk road was deserted but for an occasional country cart lumbering along.

'I wish you had done just what I had asked you to do and nothing more,' said Rajam to Mani.

Swaminathan complained: 'Yes, Rajam. I just showed him the coachman's son and was about to leave him, just as we had planned, when all of a sudden he tried to murder me ...' He shot an angry glance at Mani.

Mani was forlorn. 'Boys, I admit that I am an idiot. I thought I could do it all by the plan that came to my head on the spot. If I had only held the top firmly, I could have decoyed him, and by now he would have been howling in a lonely shed.' There was regret in his tone.

Swaminathan said, nursing his nape: 'It is still paining here.' After the incident at Keelacheri, it took three hours of continuous argument for Mani to convince Swaminathan that the attack on him was only sham.

'You needn't have been so brutal to Swami,' said Rajam.

'Sirs,' Mani said, folding his hands, 'I shall stand on my head for ten minutes, if you want me to do it as a punishment. I only pretended to scratch Swami to show the coachman's boy that I was his enemy.'

A jingling was now heard. A close mat-covered cart drawn by a white bullock was coming down the road. When it had come within a yard of the culvert, they rose, advanced, stood in a row, and shouted: 'Pull up the animal, will you?'

The cart driver was a little village boy.

'Stop the cart, you fool,' cried Rajam.

'If he does not stop, we shall arrest him and confiscate his cart.' This was Swaminathan.

The cart driver said: 'Boys, why do you stop me?'

'Don't talk,' Mani commanded, and with a serious face went round the cart and examined the wheels; he bent down and scrutinized the bottom of the cart. 'Hey, cart man, get down.'

'Boys, I must go,' pleaded the driver.

'Whom do you address as "boys"?' asked Rajam menacingly. 'Don't you know who we are?'

'We are the Government Police out to catch humbugs like you,' added Swaminathan.

'I shall shoot you if you say a word,' said Rajam to the young driver. Though the driver was incredulous, he felt that there must be something in what they said.

Mani tapped a wheel and said: 'The culvert is weak, we can't let you go over it unless you show us the pass.'

The cart driver jabbered: 'Please, sirs, let me – I have to be there.'

'Shut up,' Rajam commanded.

Swaminathan examined the animal and said: 'Come here.'

The cart driver was loath to get down. Mani dragged him from his seat and gave him a push towards Swaminathan.

Swaminathan scowled at him, and pointing at the sides of the animal asked: 'Why have you not washed the animal, you block-head?'

The villager replied timidly: 'I have washed the animal, sir.'

'But why is this here?' Swaminathan asked, pointing at a brown patch.

'Oh, that! The animal has had it since its birth, sir.'

'Birth? Are you trying to teach me?' Swaminathan shouted and raised his leg to kick the cart driver.

They showed signs of relenting.

'Give the rascal a pass, and be done with him,' Rajam conceded graciously. Swaminathan took out a pencil stub and a grubby pocket-book that he always carried about him on principle. It was his habit to note down all sorts of things: the number of cycles that passed him, the number of people going barefoot, the number going with sandals or shoes on, and so forth.

He held the paper and pencil ready. Mani took hold of the rope of the bullock, pushed it back, and turned it the other way round. The cart driver protested. But Mani said: 'Don't worry. It has got to stand here. This is the boundary.'

'I have to go this way, sir.'

'You can turn it round and go.'

'What is your name?' asked Rajam.

'Karuppan,' answered the boy.

Swaminathan took it down.

'Age?'

'I don't know, sir.'

'You don't know? Swami, write a hundred,' said Rajam.

'No sir, no sir, I am not a hundred.'

'Mind your business and hold your tongue. You are a hundred. I will kill you if you say no. What is your bullock's name?'

'I don't know, sir.'

'Swami, write "Karuppan" again.'

'Sir, that is my name, not the bullock's.'

They ignored this and Swaminathan wrote 'Karuppan' against the name of the bullock.

'Where are you going?'

'Sethur.'

Swaminathan wrote it down.

'How long will you stay there?'

'It is my place, sir.'

'If that is so, what brought you here?'

'Our headman sent ten bags of coconut to the railway shed.'

Swaminathan entered every word in his notebook. Then all the three signed the page, tore it off, gave it to the cart driver, and permitted him to start.

Much to Swaminathan's displeasure, his father's courts closed in the second week of May and Father began to spend the afternoons at home. Swaminathan feared that it might interfere with his afternoon rambles with Rajam and Mani. And it did. On the very third day of his vacation, Father commanded Swaminathan, just as he was stepping out of the house: 'Swami, come here.'

Father was standing in the small courtyard, wearing a dhoti and a banian, the dress which, for its very homeliness, Swaminathan detested to see him in; it indicated that he did not intend going out in the near future.

'Where are you going?'

'Nowhere.'

'Where were you yesterday at this time?'

'Here.'

'You are lying. You were not here yesterday. And you are not going out now.'

'That is right,' Mother added, just appearing from somewhere, 'there is no limit to his loafing in the sun. He will die of sunstroke if he keeps on like this.'

Father would have gone on even without Mother's encouragement. But now her words spurred him to action. Swaminathan was asked to follow him to his 'room' in his father's dressing-room.

'How many days is it since you have touched your books?' Father asked as he blew off the fine layer of dust on Swaminathan's books, and cleared the web that an industrious spider was weaving between a corner of the table and the pile of books.

Swaminathan viewed this question as a gross breach of promise.

'Should I read even when I have no school?'

'Do you think you have passed the B.A.?' Father asked.

'I mean, Father, when the school is closed, when there is no examination, even then should I read?'

'What a question! You must read.'

'But Father, you said before the examinations that I needn't read after they were over. Even Rajam does not read.' As he uttered the last sentence, he tried to believe it; he clearly remembered Rajam's complaining bitterly of a home tutor who came and pestered him for two hours a day thrice a week.

Father was apparently deaf to Swaminathan's remarks. He stood over Swaminathan and set him to dust his books and clean his table. Swaminathan vigorously started blowing off the dust from the book covers. He caught the spider carefully, and took it to the window to throw it out. He held it outside the window and watched it for a while. It was swinging from a strand that gleamed in a hundred delicate tints.

'Look sharp! Do you want a whole day to throw out the spider?' Father asked. Swaminathan suddenly realized that he might have the spider as his pet and that it would be a criminal waste to throw it out. He secretly slipped it into his pocket and, after shaking an empty hand outside the window, returned to his duty at the desk.

'Look at the way you have kept your English text! Are you not ashamed of yourself?' Swaminathan picked up the oily red-bound *Fourth Reader*, opened it, and banged together the covers in order to shake off the dust, and then rubbed violently the oily covers with his palm.

'Get a piece of cloth, boy. That is not the way to clean things. Get a piece of cloth, Swami,' Father said, half kindly and half impatiently.

Swaminathan looked about and complained, 'I can't find any here, Father.'

'Run and see.'

This was a welcome suggestion. Swaminathan hurried out. He first went to his grandmother.

'Granny, get me a piece of cloth, quick.'

'Where am I to go for a piece of cloth?'

'Where am *I* to go?' he asked peevishly, and added quite irrelevantly, 'If one has got to read even during holidays, I don't see why holidays are given at all.'

'What is the matter?'

This was his opportunity to earn some sympathy. He almost wept as he said: 'I don't know what Rajam and Mani will think, waiting for me there, if I keep on fooling here. Granny, if Father cannot find any work to do, why shouldn't he go and sleep?'

Father shouted across the hall: 'Did you find the cloth?'

Swaminathan answered: 'Granny hasn't got it. I shall see if Mother has.' His mother was sitting in the back corridor on a mat, with the baby sleeping on her lap. Swaminathan glared at her. Her advice to her husband a few minutes ago rankled in his heart. 'You are a fine lady, Mother,' he said in an undertone, 'why don't you leave us poor folk alone?'

'What?' she asked, unconscious of the sarcasm, and having forgotten what she had said to her husband a few minutes ago.

'You needn't have gone and carried tales against me. I don't know what I have done to you.' He would have enjoyed prolonging this talk, but Father was waiting for the duster.

'Can you give me a piece of cloth?' he asked, coming to business.

'What cloth?'

'What cloth! How should I know? It seems I have got to tidy up those – those books of mine. A fine way of spending the holidays!'

'I can't get any now.'

'H'm. You can't, can't you?' He looked about. There was a piece of cloth under the baby. In a flash, he stooped, rolled the baby over, pulled out the cloth, and was off. He held his mother responsible for all his troubles, and disturbing the baby and snatching its cloth gave him great relief.

With a fierce satisfaction he tilted the table and tipped all the things on it over the floor, and then picked them up one by one, and arranged them on the table.

Father watched him. 'Is this how you arrange things? You have kept all the light things at the bottom and the heavy ones on top. Take out those notebooks. Keep the atlas at the bottom.'

Mother came in with the baby in her arms and complained to Father, 'Look at that boy, he has taken the baby's cloth. Is there nobody to control him, in this house? I wonder how long his school is going to be kept closed.'

Swaminathan continued his work with concentrated interest. Father was pleased to ignore Mother's complaint; he merely pinched the sleeping baby's cheeks, at which Mother was annoyed and left the room.

Half an hour later Swaminathan sat in his father's room in a chair, with a slate in his hand and pencil ready. Father held the arithmetic book open and dictated: ' "Rama has ten mangoes with which he wants to earn fifteen annas. Krishna wants only four mangoes. How much will Krishna have to pay?" '

Swaminathan gazed and gazed at this sum, and every time he read it, it seemed to acquire a new meaning. He had the feeling of having stepped into a fearful maze ...

His mouth began to water at the thought of mangoes. He wondered what made Rama fix fifteen annas for ten mangoes. What kind of a man was Rama? Probably he was like Sankar. Somehow one couldn't help feeling that he must have been like Sankar, with his ten mangoes and his iron determination to get fifteen annas. If Rama was like Sankar, Krishna must have been like the Pea. Here, Swaminathan felt an unaccountable sympathy for Krishna.

'Have you done the sum?' Father asked, looking over the newspaper he was reading.

'Father, will you tell me if the mangoes were ripe?'

Father regarded him for a while and smothering a smile remarked: 'Do the sum first. I will tell you whether the fruits were ripe or not, afterwards.'

Swaminathan felt utterly helpless. If only Father would tell him whether Rama was trying to sell ripe fruits or unripe ones! Of what avail would it be to tell him afterwards? He felt strongly that the answer to this question contained the key to the whole problem. It would be scandalous to expect fifteen annas for ten unripe mangoes. But even if he did, it wouldn't be unlike Rama, whom Swaminathan was steadily beginning to hate and invest with the darkest qualities.

'Father, I cannot do the sum,' Swaminathan said, pushing away the slate.

'What is the matter with you? You can't solve a simple problem in Simple Proportion?'

'We are not taught this kind of thing in our school.'

'Get the slate here. I will make you give the answer now.' Swaminathan waited with interest for the miracle to happen. Father studied the sum for a second and asked: 'What is the price of ten mangoes?'

Swaminathan looked over the sum to find out which part of the sum contained an answer to this question. 'I don't know.'

'You seem to be an extraordinary idiot. Now read the sum. Come on. How much does Rama expect for ten mangoes?'

'Fifteen annas of course,' Swaminathan thought, but how could that be its price, just price? It was very well for Rama to expect it in his avarice. But was it the right price? And then there was the obscure point whether the mangoes were ripe or not. If they were ripe, fifteen annas might not be an improbable price. If only he could get more light on this point!

'How much does Rama want for his mangoes?'

'Fifteen annas,' replied Swaminathan without conviction.

'Very good. How many mangoes does Krishna want?'

'Four.'

'What is the price of four?'

Father seemed to delight in torturing him. How could he know? How could he know what that fool Krishna would pay?

'Look here, boy. I have half a mind to thrash you. What have you in your head? Ten mangoes cost fifteen annas. What is the price of one? Come on. If you don't say it –'

His hand took Swaminathan's ear and gently twisted it. Swaminathan could not open his mouth because he could not decide whether the solution lay in the realm of addition, subtraction, multiplication, or division. The longer he hesitated, the more violent the twist was becoming. In the end when Father was waiting with a scowl for an answer, he received only a squeal from his son. 'I am not going to leave you till you tell me how much a single mango costs at fifteen annas for ten.'

What was the matter with Father? Swaminathan kept blinking. Where was the urgency to know its price? Anyway, if Father wanted so badly to know, instead of harassing him, let him go to the market and find it out. The whole brood of Ramas and Krishnas, with their endless transactions with odd quantities of mangoes and fractions of money, were getting disgusting.

Father admitted defeat by declaring: 'One mango costs fifteen over ten annas. Simplify it.'

Here he was being led to the most hideous regions of arithmetic – fractions. 'Give me the slate, Father. I will find it out.' He worked and found at the end of fifteen minutes: 'The price of one mango is three over two annas.'

He expected to be contradicted any moment. But Father said: 'Very good, simplify it further.'

It was plain sailing after that. Swaminathan announced at the end of half an hour's agony: 'Krishna must pay six annas,' and burst into tears.

At five o'clock when he was ready to start for the club, Swaminathan's father felt sorry for having worried his son all the afternoon. 'Would you like to come with me to the club, boy?' he asked when he saw Swaminathan sulking behind a pillar with a woebegone face. Swaminathan answered by disappearing for a minute and reappearing dressed in his coat and cap. Father surveyed him from head to foot and remarked: 'Why can't you be a little more tidy?' Swaminathan writhed awkwardly.

'Lakshmi,' Father called, and said to Mother when she came: 'There must be a clean dress for the boy in the box. Give him something clean.'

'Please don't worry about it now,' said Mother. 'He is all right. Who is to open the box? The keys are somewhere ... I have just mixed milk for the baby –'

'What has happened to all his dresses?'

'What dresses? You haven't bought a square inch of cloth since last summer.'

'What do you mean? What has happened to all the pieces of twill I bought a few months ago?' he demanded vaguely, making a mental note at the same time, to take the boy to the tailor on Wednesday evening. Swaminathan was relieved to find his mother reluctant to get him a fresh dress, since he had an obscure dread that his father would leave him behind and go away if he went in to change.

A car hooted in front of the house. Father snatched his tennis racket from a table and rushed out followed by Swaminathan. A gentleman, wearing a blazer that appealed to Swaminathan, sat at the wheel, and said: 'Good evening,' with a grin. Swaminathan was at first afraid that this person might refuse to take him in the car. But his fears were dispelled by the gentleman's saying amiably: 'Hallo, Srinivasan, are you bringing your boy to the club? Righto!' Swaminathan sat in the back seat while his father and his friend occupied the front.

The car whizzed along. Swaminathan was elated and wished that some of his friends could see him then. The car slid into a gate and came to a stop amidst half a dozen other cars.

He watched his father playing tennis, and came to the conclusion that he was the best player in all the three courts that were laid side by side. Swaminathan found that whenever his father hit the ball, his opponents were unable to receive it and so let it go and strike the screen. He also found that the picker's life was one of grave risks.

Swaminathan fell into a pleasant state of mind. The very fact that he was allowed to be present there and watch the play gave him a sense of importance. He would have something to say to his friends tomorrow. He slowly moved and stood near the screen behind his father. Before stationing himself there, he wondered for a moment if the little fellow in khaki dress might not object. But the little fellow was busy picking up balls and throwing them at the players. Swaminathan stayed there for about ten minutes. His father's actions were clearer to watch from behind, and the twang of his racket when hitting the ball was very pleasing to the ear.

For a change Swaminathan stood looking at the boy in khaki dress. As he gazed, his expression changed. He blinked fast as if he disbelieved his eyes. It was the coachman's son, only slightly transformed by the khaki dress! Now the boy had turned and seen him. He grinned maliciously and hastily took out of his pocket a penknife, and held it up. Swaminathan was seized with cold fear. He moved away fast unobtrusively, to his former place, which was at a safe distance from his enemy.

After the set when his father walked towards the building, Swaminathan took care to walk a little in front of him and not behind, as he feared that he might get a stab any minute in his back.

'Swami, don't go in front. You are getting under my feet.' Swaminathan obeyed with a reluctant heart. He kept shooting glances sideways and behind. He stooped and picked up a stone, a sharp stone, and held it ready for use if any emergency should arise. The distance from the tennis court to the building was about a dozen yards, but to Swaminathan it seemed to be a mile and a half.

He felt safe when he sat in a chair beside his father in the card-room. A thick cloud of smoke floated in the air. Father was shuffling and throwing cards with great zest. This was the safest place on earth. There was Father and any number of his friends, and let the coachman's son try a hand if he liked. A little later Swaminathan looked out of the window and felt disturbed at the sight of the stars. It would be darker still by the time the card game finished and Father rose to go home.

An hour later Father rose from the table. Swaminathan was in a highly nervous state when he got down the last steps of the building. There were unknown dangers lurking in the darkness around. He was no doubt secure between Father and his friend. That thought was encouraging. But Swaminathan felt at the same time that it would have been better if all the persons in the card-room had escorted him to the car. He needed all the guarding he could get, and some more. Probably by this time the boy had gone out and brought a huge gang of assassins and was waiting for him. He could not walk in front as, in addition to getting under his father's feet, he had no idea which way they had to go for the car. Following his father was out of the question, as he might not reach the car at all. He walked in a peculiar side-step which enabled him to see before him and behind him simultaneously. The distance was interminable. He decided to explain the danger to Father and seek his protection.

'Father.'

'Well, boy?'

Swaminathan suddenly decided that his father had better not know anything about the coachman's son, however serious the situation might be.

'What do you want, boy?' Father asked again.

'Father, are we going home now?'

'Yes.'

'Walking?'

'No. The car is there, near the gate.'

When they came to the car, Swaminathan got in first and occupied the centre of the back seat. He was still in suspense. Father's friend was taking time to start the car. Swaminathan was sitting all alone in the back seat, very far behind Father and his friend. Even now, the coachman's son and his gang could easily pull him out and finish him.

The car started. When its engine rumbled, it sounded to Swaminathan's ears like the voice of a saviour. The car was outside the gate now and picked up speed. Swaminathan lifted a corner of his dhoti and mopped his brow.

CHAPTER TWELVE

BROKEN PANES

On the 15th of August 1930, about two thousand citizens of Malgudi assembled on the right bank of Sarayu to protest against the arrest of Gauri Sankar, a prominent political worker of Bombay. An earnest-looking man clad in khaddar stood on a wooden platform and addressed the gathering. In a high, piercing voice, he sketched the life and achievements of Gauri Sankar; and after that passed on to generalities: 'We are slaves today,' he shrieked, 'worse slaves than we have ever been before. Let us remember our heritage. Have we forgotten the glorious periods of Ramyana and Mahabharata? This is the country that has given the world a Kalidasa, a Buddha, a Sankara. Our ships sailed the high seas and we had reached the height of civilization when the Englishman ate raw flesh and wandered in the jungles, nude. But now what are we?' He paused and said on the inspiration of the moment, without troubling to verify the meaning: 'We are slaves of slaves.' To Swaminathan, as to Mani, this part of the speech was incomprehensible. But five minutes later the speaker said something that seemed practicable: 'Just think for a while. We are three hundred and thirty-six millions, and our land is as big as Europe minus Russia. England is no bigger than our Madras Presidency and is inhabited by a handful of white rogues and is thousands of miles away. Yet we bow in homage before the Englishman! Why are we become, through no fault of our own, docile and timid? It is the bureaucracy that has made us so, by intimidation and starvation. You need not do more. Let every Indian spit on England, and the quantity of saliva will be enough to drown England ...'

'Gandhi ki Jai,' shouted Swaminathan involuntarily, deeply stirred by the speaker's eloquence at this point. He received a fierce dig from Mani, who whispered: 'Fool! Why can't you hold your tongue?'

Swaminathan asked: 'Is it true?'

'Which?'

'Spitting and drowning the Europeans.'

'Must be, otherwise do you think that fellow would suggest it?'

'Then why not do it? It is easy.'

'Europeans will shoot us, they have no heart,' said Mani. This seemed a satisfactory answer, and Swaminathan was about to clear up another doubt when one or two persons sitting around frowned at him.

For the rest of the evening Swaminathan was caught in the lecturer's eloquence; so was Mani. With the lecturer they wept over the plight of the Indian peasant; resolved to boycott English goods, especially Lancashire and Manchester cloth, as the owners of those mills had cut off the thumbs of the weavers of Dacca muslin, for which India was famous at one time. What muslin it was, a whole piece of forty yards could be folded and kept in a snuff-box! The persons who cut off the thumbs of such weavers deserved the worst punishment possible. And Swaminathan was going to mete it out by wearing only a khaddar, the rough homespun. He looked at the dress he was just then wearing, in chagrin. 'Mani,' he said in a low voice, 'have you any idea what I am wearing?'

Mani examined Swaminathan's coat and declared: 'It is Lancashire cloth.'

'How do you know it?'

Mani glared at him in answer.

'What are you wearing?' asked Swaminathan.

'Of course khaddar. Do you think I will pay a paisa to those Lancashire devils? No. They won't get it out of me.'

Swaminathan had his own doubts over this statement. But he preferred to keep quiet, and wished that he had come out nude rather than in what he believed to be Lancashire cloth.

A great cry burst from the crowd: 'Bharat Matha ki Jai!' And then there were cries of 'Gandhi ki Jai!' After that came a kind of mournful 'national' song. The evening's programme closed with a bonfire of foreign cloth. It was already dark. Suddenly the darkness was lit up by a red glare. A fire was lighted. A couple of boys wearing Gandhi caps went round begging people to burn their foreign cloth. Coats and caps and upper cloth came whizzing through the air and fell with a thud into the fire, which purred and crackled and rose high, thickening the air with smoke and a burnt smell. People moved about like dim shadows in the red glare. Swaminathan was watching the scene with little shivers of joy going down his spine. Somebody asked him: 'Young man, do you want our country to remain in eternal slavery?'

'No, no,' Swaminathan replied.

'But you are wearing a foreign cap.'

Swaminathan quailed with shame. 'Oh, I didn't notice,' he said, and removing his cap flung it into the fire with a feeling that he was saving the country.

Early next morning as Swaminathan lay in bed watching a dusty beam of sunlight falling a few yards off his bed, his mind, which was just emerging from sleep, became conscious of a vague worry. Swaminathan asked himself what that worry was. It must be something connected with school. Homework? No. Matters were all right in that direction. It was something connected with dress. Bonfire, bonfire of clothes. Yes. It now dawned upon him with an oppressive clearness that he had thrown his cap into the patriotic bonfire of the previous evening; and of course his father knew nothing about it.

What was he going to wear for school today? Telling his father and asking for a new cap was not practicable. He could not go to school bareheaded.

He started for the school in a mood of fatalistic abandon, with only a coat and no cap on. And the fates were certainly kind to him. At least Swaminathan believed that he saw the hand of God in it when he reached the school and found the boys gathered in the road in front of the school in a noisy irregular mob.

Swaminathan passed through the crowd unnoticed till he reached the school gate. A perfect stranger belonging to the Third Form stopped him and asked: 'Where are you going?' Swaminathan hesitated for a moment to discover if there was any trap in this question and said: 'Why – er ... of course ...'

'No school today,' declared the stranger with emphasis, and added passionately, 'one of the greatest sons of the motherland has been sent to gaol.'

'I won't go to school,' Swaminathan said, greatly relieved at this unexpected solution to his cap problem.

The headmaster and the teachers were standing in the front veranda of the school. The headmaster looked care-worn. Ebenezar was swinging his cane and pacing up and down. For once, the boys saw D. Pillai, the history teacher, serious, and gnawing his close-clipped moustache in great agitation. The crowd in the road had become brisker and noisier, and the school looked forlorn. At five minutes to ten the first bell rang, hardly heard by anyone except those standing near the gate. A conference was going on between the teachers and the headmaster. The headmaster's hand trembled as he pulled out his watch and gave orders for the second bell. The bell that at other times gave out a clear rich note now sounded weak and inarticulate. The headmaster and the teacher were seen coming towards the gate, and a lull came upon the mob.

The headmaster appealed to the boys to behave and get back to their classes quietly. The boys stood firm. The teachers, including D. Pillai, tried and failed. After uttering a warning that the punishment to follow would be severe, the headmaster withdrew. Thundering shouts of 'Bharat Matha ki Jai!' 'Gandhi ki Jai!' and 'Gaura Sankar ki Jai!' followed him.

There were gradual unnoticed additions of all sorts of people to the original student mob. Now zestful adult voices could be detected in the frequent cries of 'Gandhi ki Jai!'

Half a dozen persons appointed themselves leaders, and ran about crying: 'Remember, this is a hartal. This is a day of mourning. Observe it in the proper spirit of sorrow and silence.'

Swaminathan was an unobserved atom in the crowd. Another unobserved atom was busily piling up small stones before him, and flinging them with admirable aim at the panes in the front part of the school building. Swaminathan could hardly help following his example. He picked up a handful of stones and searched the building with his eyes. He was disappointed to find at least seventy per cent of the panes already attended to.

He uttered a sharp cry of joy as he discovered a whole ventilator, consisting of small square glasses, in the headmaster's room, intact! He sent a stone at it and waited with cocked-up ears for the splintering noise as the stone hit the glass, and the final shivering noise, a fraction of a second later, as the piece crashed on the floor. It was thrilling.

A puny man came running into the crowd announcing excitedly, 'Work is going on in the Board High School.'

This horrible piece of news set the crowd in motion. A movement began towards the Board High School, which was situated at the tail-end of Market Road.

When they reached the Board High School, the self-appointed leaders held up their hands, requested the crowd to remain outside and be peaceful, and entered the school themselves. Within fifteen minutes, trickling in by twos and threes, the crowd was in the school hall.

A spokesman of the crowd said to the headmaster, 'Sir, we are not here to create a disturbance. We only want you to close the school. It is imperative. Our leader is in gaol. Our motherland is in the throes of war.'

The headmaster, a wizened owl-like man, screamed, 'With whose permission did you enter the building? Kindly go out. Or I shall send for the police.'

This was received with howling, jeering, and hooting. And following it, tables and benches were overturned and broken, and window-panes were smashed. Most of the Board School boys merged with the crowd. A few, however, stood apart. They were first invited to come out; but when they showed reluctance, they were dragged out.

Swaminathan's part in all this was by no means negligible. It was he who shouted 'We will spit on the police' (though it was drowned in the din), when the headmaster mentioned the police. The mention of the police had sent his blood boiling. What brazenness, what shamelessness, to talk of police – the nefarious agents of the Lancashire thumb-cutters! When the pandemonium started, he was behind no one in destroying the school furniture. With tremendous joy he discovered that there were many glass panes untouched yet. His craving to break them could not be fully satisfied in his own school. He ran round collecting ink-bottles and flung them one by one at every pane that caught his eye. When the Board School boys were dragged out, he felt that he could not do much in that line, most of the boys being as big as himself. On the flash of a bright idea, he wriggled through the crowd and looked for the Infant Standards. There he found little children huddled together and shivering with fright. He charged into this crowd with such ferocity that the children scattered about, stumbling and falling. One unfortunate child who shuffled and moved awkwardly received individual attention. Swaminathan pounced upon him, pulled out his cap, threw it down and stamped on it, swearing at him all the time. He pushed him and dragged him this way and that and then gave him a blow on the head and left him to his fate.

Having successfully paralysed work in the Board School, the crowd moved on in a procession along Market Road. The air vibrated with the songs and slogans uttered in a hundred keys by a hundred voices. Swaminathan found himself wedged in among a lot of unknown people, in one of the last ranks. The glare from the blanched treeless Market Road was blinding. The white dust stirred up by the procession hung like thin mist in the air and choked him. He could see before him nothing but moving backs and shoulders and occasionally odd parts of some building. His throat was dry with shouting, and he was beginning to feel hungry. He was pondering whether he could just slip out and go home, when the procession came to a sudden halt. In a minute the rear ranks surged forward to see what the matter was.

The crowd was now in the centre of Market Road, before the fountain in the square. On the other side of the fountain were drawn up about fifty constables armed with *lathis*. About a dozen of them held up the procession. A big man, with a cane in his hand and a revolver slung from his belt, advanced towards the procession. His leather straps and belts and the highly-polished boots and hose made him imposing in Swaminathan's eyes. When he turned his head Swaminathan saw to his horror that it was Rajam's father! Swaminathan could not help feeling sorry that it should be Rajam's father. Rajam's father! Rajam's father to be at the head of those traitors!

The Deputy Superintendent of Police fixed his eyes on his wrist-watch and said, 'I declare this assembly unlawful. I give it five minutes to disperse.' At the end of five minutes he looked up and uttered in a hollow voice the word, 'Charge.'

In the confusion that followed Swaminathan was very nearly trampled upon and killed. The policemen rushed into the crowd, pushing and beating everybody. Swaminathan had joined a small group of panic-stricken runners. The policemen came towards them with upraised *lathis*. Swaminathan shrieked to them, 'Don't kill me. I know nothing.' He then heard a series of dull noises as the *lathis* descended on the bodies of his neighbours. Swaminathan saw blood streaming from the forehead of one. Down came the *lathis* again. Another runner fell down with a groan. On the back of a third the *lathis* fell again and again.

Swaminathan felt giddy with fear. He was running as fast as his legs would carry him. But the policemen kept pace with him; one of them held him up by his hair and asked, 'What business have you here?'

'I don't know anything, leave me, sirs,' Swaminathan pleaded.

'Doing nothing! Mischievous monkey!' said the grim, hideous policeman – how hideous policemen were at close quarters! – and delivering him a light tap on the head with the *lathi*, ordered him to run before he was kicked.

Swaminathan's original intention had been to avoid that day's topic before his father. But as soon as Father came home, even before taking off his coat, he called Mother and gave her a summary of the day's events. He spoke with a good deal of warmth. 'The Deputy Superintendent is a butcher,' he said as he went in to change. Swaminathan was disposed to agree that the Deputy Superintendent was a butcher, as he recollected the picture of Rajam's father looking at his watch, grimly ticking off seconds before giving orders for massacre.

Father came out of the dressing-room before undoing his tie, to declare: 'Fifty persons have been taken to the hospital with dangerous contusions. One or two are also believed to be killed.' Turning to Swaminathan he said, 'I heard that schoolboys have given a lot of trouble, what did you do?'

'There was a strike ...' replied Swaminathan and discovered here an opportunity to get his cap problem solved. He added, 'Oh, the confusion! You know, somebody pulled off the cap that I was wearing and tore it to bits ... I want a cap before I start for school tomorrow.'

'Who was he?' Father asked.

'I don't know, some bully in the crowd.'

'Why did he do it?'

'Because it was foreign ...'

'Who said so? I paid two rupees and got it from the Khaddar Stores. It is a black khaddar cap. Why do you presume that you know what is what?'

'I didn't do anything. I was very nearly assaulted when I resisted.'

'You should have knocked him down. I bought the cap and the cloth for your coat on the same day in the Khaddar Stores. If any man says that they are not khaddar, he must be blind.'

'People say that it was made in Lancashire.'

'Nonsense. You can ask them to mind their own business. And if you allow your clothes to be torn by people who think this and that, you will have to go about naked, that is all. And you may also tell them that I won't have a paisa of mine sent to foreign countries. I know my duty. Whatever it is, why do not you urchins leave politics alone and mind your business? We have enough troubles in our country without you brats messing up things ...'

Swaminathan lay wide awake in bed for a long time. As the hours advanced, and one by one as the lights in the house disappeared, his body compelled him to take stock of the various injuries done to it during the day. His elbows and knees had their own tales to tell: they brought back to his mind the three or four falls that he had had that day. One was – when? – yes, when Rajam got down from his car and came to the school, and Swaminathan had wanted to hide himself, and in the hurry stumbled on a heap of stones, and there the knees were badly skinned. And again when the policemen charged, he ran and fell flat before a shop, and some monster ran over him, pinning him with one foot to the ground.

Now as he turned there was a pang about his hips. And then he felt as if a load had been hung from his thighs. And again as he thought of it, he felt a heavy monotonous pain in the head – the merciless rascals! The policeman's *lathi* was none too gentle. And he had been called a monkey! He would – he would see – to call him a monkey! He was no monkey. Only they – the policemen – looked like monkeys, and they behaved like monkeys too.

The headmaster entered the class with a slightly flushed face and a hard ominous look in his eyes. Swaminathan wished that he had been anywhere but there at that moment. The headmaster surveyed the class for a few minutes and asked, 'Are you not ashamed to come and sit there after what you did yesterday?' Just as a special honour to them, he read out the names of a dozen or so that had attended the class. After that he read out the names of those that had kept away, and asked them to stand on their benches. He felt that that punishment was not enough and asked them to stand on their desks. Swaminathan was among them and felt humiliated at that eminence.

Then they were lectured. When it was over, they were asked to offer explanations one by one. One said that he had had an attack of headache and therefore could not come to school. He was asked to bring a medical certificate. The second said that while he had been coming to school on the previous day, someone had told him that there would be no school, and he had gone back home. The headmaster replied that if he was going to listen to every loafer who said there would be no school, he deserved to be flogged. Anyway, why did he not come to the school and verify? No answer. The punishment was pronounced: ten days' attendance cancelled, two rupees fine, and the whole day to be spent on the desk. The third said that he had had an attack of headache. The fourth said that he had had stomach-ache. The fifth said that his grandmother died suddenly just as he was starting for the school. The headmaster asked him if he could bring a letter from his father. No. He had no father. Then, who was his guardian? His grandmother. But the grandmother was dead, was she not? No. It was another grandmother. The headmaster asked how many grandmothers can a person have. No answer. Could he bring a letter from his neighbours? No, he could not. None of his neighbours could read or write, because he lived in one of the more illiterate parts of Ellaman Street. Then the headmaster offered to send a teacher to this illiterate locality to ascertain from the boy's neighbours if the death of the grandmother was a fact. A pause, some perspiration and then the answer that the neighbours could not possibly know anything about it, since the grandmother died in the village. The headmaster hit him on the knuckles with his cane, called him a street dog, and pronounced the punishment: fifteen days' suspension.

When Swaminathan's turn came, he looked around helplessly. Rajam sat on the third bench in front, and resolutely looked away. He was gazing at the blackboard intently. But yet the back of his head and the pink ears were visible to Swaminathan. It was an intolerable sight. Swaminathan was in acute suspense lest that head should turn and fix its eyes on his; he felt that he would drop from the desk to the floor, if that happened. The pink ears three benches off made him incapable of speech. If only somebody would put a blackboard between his eyes and those pink ears!

He was deaf to the question that the headmaster was putting to him. A rap on his body from the headmaster's cane brought him to himself.

'Why did you keep away yesterday?' asked the headmaster, looking up.

Swaminathan's first impulse was to protest that he had never been absent. But the attendance register was there. 'No – no – I was stoned. I tried to come, but they took away my cap and burnt it. Many strong men held me down when I tried to come ... When a great man is sent to gaol ... I am surprised to see you a slave of the Englishmen ... Didn't they cut off – Dacca muslin – slaves of slaves ...' These were some of the disjointed explanations which streamed into his head, and which, even at that moment, he was discreet enough not to express. He had wanted to mention a headache, but he found to his distress that others beside him had done.

The headmaster shouted, 'Won't you open your mouth?' He brought the cane sharply down on Swaminathan's right shoulder.

Swaminathan kept staring at the headmaster with tearful eyes, massaging with his left hand the spot where the cane was laid. 'I will kill you if you keep on staring without answering my question,' cried the headmaster.

'I – I – couldn't come,' stammered Swaminathan.

'Is that so?' asked the headmaster, and turning to a boy said, 'Bring the peon.'

Swaminathan thought: 'What, is he going to ask the peon to thrash me? If he does any such thing, I will bite everybody dead.' The peon came. The headmaster said to him, 'Now say what you know about this rascal on the desk.'

The peon eyed Swaminathan with a sinister look, grunted and demanded, 'Didn't I see you break the panes ...?'

'Of the ventilators in my room?' added the headmaster with zest.

Here there was no chance of escape. Swaminathan kept staring foolishly till he received another whack on the back. The headmaster demanded what the young brigand had to say about it. The brigand had nothing to say. It was a fact that he had broken the panes. They had seen it. There was nothing more to it. He had unconsciously become defiant and did not care to deny the charge. When another whack came on his back, he ejaculated, 'Don't beat me, sir. It pains.'

This was an invitation to the headmaster to bring down the cane four times again. He said, 'Keep standing here, on this desk, staring like an idiot, till I announce your dismissal.'

Every pore in Swaminathan's body burnt with the touch of the cane. He had a sudden flood of courage, the courage that comes of desperation. He restrained the tears that were threatening to rush out, jumped down, and, grasping his books, rushed out muttering, 'I don't care for your dirty school.'

CHAPTER THIRTEEN

THE 'M.C.C.'

Six weeks later Rajam came to Swaminathan's house to announce that he forgave him all his sins – starting with his political activities, to his new acquisition, the Board High School air – by which was meant a certain slowness and stupidity engendered by mental decay.

After making his exit from Albert Mission School in that theatrical manner on the day following the strike, Swaminathan became so consistently stubborn that a few days later his father took him to the Board School and admitted him there. At first Swaminathan was rather uncertain of his happiness in the new school. But he excited the curiosity that all newcomers do, and found himself to his great satisfaction the centre of attraction in Second C. All his new class-mates, remarkably new faces, often clustered round him to see him and hear him talk. He had not yet picked the few that he would have liked to call his chums. He still believed that his Albert Mission set was intact, though since the reopening in June the set was not what it had been before. Sankar disappeared, and people said that his father had been transferred; Somu, was not promoted, and that meant he was automatically excluded from the group, the law being inexorable in that respect; the Pea was promoted, but he returned to the class exactly three months late, and he was quite full up with medical certificates, explanations, and exemptions. He was a man of a hundred worries now, and passed his old friends like a stranger. Only Rajam and Mani were still intact as far as Swaminathan was concerned. Mani saw him every day. But Rajam had not spoken to him since the day when his political doings became known.

And now this afternoon Swaminathan was sitting in a dark corner of the house trying to make a camera with a cardboard box and a spectacle lens. In his effort to fix the lens in the hole that was one round too large, he was on the point of losing his temper, when he heard a familiar voice calling him. He ran to the door.

'Hallo! Hallo! Rajam,' he cried, 'why didn't you tell me you were coming?'

'What is the thing in your hand?' Rajam asked.

'Oh,' Swaminathan said, blushing.

'Come, come, let us have a look at it.'

'Oh, it is nothing,' Swaminathan said, giving him the box.

As Rajam kept gazing at the world through the hole in the cardboard box, Swaminathan said, 'Akbar Ali of our class has made a marvellous camera.'

'Has he? What does he do with it?'

'He has taken a lot of photos with it.'

'Indeed! Photos of what?'

'He hasn't yet shown them to me, but they are probably photos of houses, people, and trees.'

Rajam sat down on the doorstep and asked, 'And who is this Akbar Ali?'

'He is a nice Muhammadan, belongs to our class.'

'In the Board High School?' There was just a suspicion of a sneer in his tone.

Swaminathan preferred to ignore this question and continued, 'He has a bicycle. He is a very fine Muhammadan, calls Muhammad of Gazni and Aurangazeb rascals.'

'What makes you think that they were that?'

'Didn't they destroy our temples and torture the Hindus? Have you forgotten the Somnathpur God?'

'We brahmins deserve that and more,' said Rajam. 'In our house my father does not care for New-Moon days and there are no annual ceremonies for the dead.' He was in a debating mood, and Swaminathan realized it and remained silent. Rajam said, 'I tell you what, it is your Board High School that has given you this mentality.'

Swaminathan felt that the safest course would be to agree with him. 'You are right in a way. I don't like the Board High School.'

'Then why did you go and join it?'

'I could not help it. You saw how beastly our master was. If you had been in my place, you would have kicked him in the face.'

This piece of flattery did not soothe Rajam. 'If I were you I would have kept clear of all your dirty politics and strikes.' His father was a government servant, and hence his family was anti-political.

Swaminathan said, 'You are right. I should have remained at home on the day of the strike.'

This example of absolute submissiveness touched Rajam. He said promptly that he was prepared to forgive Swaminathan his past sins and would not mind his belonging to the Board School. They were to be friends as of old. 'What would you say to a cricket team?' Rajam asked.

Swaminathan had not thought of cricket as something that he himself could play. He was, of course, familiar with Hobbs, Bradman, and Duleep, and vainly tried to carry their scores in his head, as Rajam did. He filched pictures of cricket players, as Rajam did, and pasted them in an album, though he secretly did not very much care for those pictures – there was something monotonous about them. He sometimes though that the same picture was pasted in every page of the album.

'No, Rajam, I don't think I can play. I don't know how to play.'

'That is what everybody thinks,' said Rajam. 'I don't know myself, though I collect pictures and scores.'

This was very pleasing to hear. Probably Hobbs too was shy and sceptical before he took the bat and swung it.

'We can challenge a lot of teams, including our school eleven. They think they can't be beaten,' said Swaminathan.

'What! The Board School mugs think that! We shall thrash them. Oh, yes.'

'What shall we call it?'

'Don't you know? It is the M.C.C.,' said Rajam.

'That is Hobbs's team, isn't it? They may drag us before a court if we take their name.'

'Who says that? If we get into any trouble, I shall declare before the judge that M.C.C. stands for Malgudi Cricket Club.'

Swaminathan was a little disappointed. Though as M.C.C. it sounded imposing, the name was really a bit tame. 'I think we had better try some other name, Rajam.'

'What would you suggest?'

'Well – I am for "Friends Eleven".'

'Friends Eleven?'

'Or, say, "Jumping Stars"?' said Swaminathan.

'Oh, that is not bad, not bad, you know.'

'I do think it would be glorious to call ourselves "Jumping Stars"!'

Rajam instantly had a vision of a newspaper report: 'The Jumping Stars soundly thrashed the Board High School Eleven.' 'It is a beauty, I think,' he cried, moved by the vision. He pulled out a piece of paper and a pencil, and said, 'Come on, Swami, repeat the names that come to your head. It would be better to have a long list to select from. We shall underline "Jumping Stars" and "M.C.C." and give them special consideration. Come on.'

Swaminathan remained thoughtful and started, ' "Friends Eleven"..."Jumping Stars"..."Friends Union"...'

'I have "Friends Union" already here,' Rajam said pointing to the list.

Swaminathan went on: ' "Excelsiors"...'

'I have got it.'

' "Excelsior Union"..."Champion Eleven"...' A long pause.

'Are you dried up?' Rajam asked.

'No, if Mani were here, he would have suggested a few more names ..."Champion Eleven".'

'You have just said it.'

' "Victory Union Eleven"...'

'That is very good. I think it is very very good. People would be afraid of us.' He held the list before him and read the names with great satisfaction. He had struggled hard on the previous night to get a few names. But only 'Friends Union' and 'Excelsiors' kept coming till he felt fatigued. But what a lot of names Swaminathan was able to reel off. 'Can you meet me tomorrow evening, Swami? I shall get Mani down. Let us select a name.'

After a while Swaminathan asked, 'Look here, do you think we shall have to pay tax or something to the Government when we start the team?'

'The Government seems to tax everything in this world. My father's pay is about five hundred. But nearly two hundred and over is demanded by the Government. Anyway, what makes you think that we shall have to pay tax?'

'I mean – if we don't pay tax, the Government may not recognize our team or its name and a hundred other teams may take the same name. It might lead to all sorts of complications.'

'Suppose we have two names?' asked Rajam.

'It is not done.'

'I know a lot of teams that have two names. When I was in Bishop Waller's, we had a cricket team that we called – I don't remember the name now. I think we called it "Cricket Eleven" and "Waller's Cricket Eleven". You see, one name is for ordinary use and the other is for matches.'

'It is all very well for a rich team like your Waller's. But suppose the Government demands two taxes from us?'

Rajam realized at this point that the starting of a cricket team was the most complicated problem on earth. He had simply expected to gather a dozen fellows on the *maidan* next to his compound and play, and challenge the world. But here were endless troubles, starting with the name that must be unique, Government taxes, and so on. The Government did not seem to know where it ought to interfere and where not. He had a momentary sympathy for Gandhi; no wonder he was dead against the Government.

Swaminathan seemed to be an expert in thinking out difficulties. He said, 'Even if we want to pay, whom are we to pay the taxes to?' Certainly not to His Majesty or the Viceroy. Who was the Government? What if somebody should take the money and defraud them, somebody pretending to be the Government? Probably they would have to send the taxes by Money Order to the Governor! Well, that might be treason. And then what was the amount to be paid?

They sat round Rajam's table in his room. Mani held before him a catalogue of Messrs Binns, the Shop for Sports Goods. He read, ' "Junior Willard Bats, Seven Eight, made of finest seasoned wood, used by Cambridge Junior Boys' Eleven".'

'Let me have a look at it ...' said Rajam. He bent over the table and said, 'Seems to be a fine bat. Have a look at it, Swami.'

Swaminathan craned his neck and agreed that it was a fine bat, but he was indiscreet enough to say, 'It looks like any other bat in the catalogue.'

Mani's left hand shot out and held his neck and pressed his face close to the picture of the bat: 'Why do you pretend to be a cricket player if you cannot see the difference between Junior Willard and other bats? You are not fit to be even a sweeper in our team.' After this admonition the hold was relaxed.

Rajam asked, 'Swami, do you know what the catalogue man calls the Junior Willard? It seems it is the Rolls-Royce among the junior bats. Don't you know the difference between the Rolls-Royce and other cars?'

Swaminathan replied haughtily, 'I never said I saw no difference between the Rolls-Royce and other cars.'

'What is the difference?' urged Rajam.

Mani laughed and teased, 'Come on. If you really know the difference, why don't you say it?'

Swaminathan said, 'The Rolls costs a lakh of rupees, while other cars cost about ten thousand; a Rolls has engines made of silver, while other cars have iron engines.'

'Oh, oh!' jeered Rajam.

'A Rolls never gives trouble, while other cars always give trouble; a Rolls engine never stops; a Rolls-Royce never makes a noise, while other cars always make a noise.'

'Why not deliver a lecture on the Rolls-Royce?' asked Mani.

'Swami, I am glad you know so much about the Rolls-Royce. I am at the same time ashamed to find you knowing so little about Willard Junior. We had about a dozen Willard Juniors when I was in Bishop Waller's. Oh! what bats! There are actual springs inside the bat, so that when you touch the ball it flies. There is fine silk cord wound round the handle. You don't know anything, and yet you talk! Show me another bat which has silk cord and springs like the Willard.'

There was a pause, and after that Rajam said, 'Note it down, Swami.' Swaminathan noted down on a paper, 'Vilord june-ear bat.' And looking up asked, 'How many?'

'Say three. Will that do, Mani?'

'Why waste money on three bats? Two will do ...'

'But suppose one breaks in the middle of a match?' Rajam asked.

'Do you suppose we are going to supply bats to our opponents? They will have to come provided with bats. We must make it clear.'

'Even then, if our bat breaks we may have to stop playing.'

'Two will do, Rajam, unless you want to waste money.'

Rajam's enthusiasm was great. He left his chair and sat on the arm of Mani's chair, gloating over the pictures of cricket goods in the catalogue. Swaminathan, though he was considered to be a bit of a heretic, caught the enthusiasm and perched on the other arm of the chair. All the three devoured with their eyes the glossy pictures of cricket balls, bats, and nets.

In about an hour they selected from the catalogue their team's requirements. And then came the most difficult part of the whole affair – a letter to Messrs Binns, ordering goods. Bare courtesy made Rajam offer the authorship of the letter to Mani, who declined it. Swaminathan was forced to accept it in spite of his protests, and he sat for a long time chewing his pencil without producing a word; he had infinite trouble with spelling, and the more he tried to be correct the more muddled he was becoming; in the end he sat so long thinking of spelling that even such words as 'the' and 'and' became doubtful. Rajam took up the task himself. Half an hour later he placed on the table a letter:

From

M.C.C. (And Victory Union Eleven),
Malgudi.

To

Messrs Binns,
Sportsmen,
Mount Road,
Madras.

DEAR SIR,

Please send to our team two junior willard bats, six balls, wickets and other things quick. It is very urgent. We shall send you money afterwards. Don't fear. Please be urgent.

Yours obediently,
Captain Rajam (Captain).

This letter received Swaminathan's benedictions. But Mani expressed certain doubts. He wanted to know whether 'Dear' could stand at the beginning of a letter to a perfect stranger. 'How can you call Binns "Dear Sir"? You must say "Sir".'

Rajam's explanation was: 'I am not Binns's clerk. I don't care to address him as "Sir".'

So this letter went as it was.

After this exacting work they were resting, with a feeling of relief, when the postman came in with a card for Rajam. Rajam read it and cried, 'Guess who has written this?'

'Binns.'

'Silly. It must be our headmaster.'

'Somebody.'

'J. B. Hobbs.'

'It is from Sankar,' Rajam announced joyfully.

'Sankar! We had almost forgotten that old thief.' Swaminathan and Mani tore the card from Rajam's hand and read:

> MY DEAR FRIEND,
>
> I am studying here because my father came here. My mother is also here. All of us are here. And we will be only here. I am doing well. I hope you are doing well. It is very hot here. I had fever for three days and drank medicine. I hope I will read well and pass the examination. Is Swami and Mani doing well! It is very hot here. I am playing cricket now. I can't write more.
>
> With regards,
> your dearest friend,
> SANKAR.
>
> P.S. Don't forget me.
> S.

They were profoundly moved by this letter, and decided to reply at once.

Three letters were ready in an hour. Mani copied Sankar's letter verbatim. Swaminathan and Rajam wrote nearly similar letters: they said they were doing well by the grace of God; they hoped that Sankar would pass and also that he was doing well; then they said a lot about their cricket team and hoped that Sankar would become a member; they also said that Sankar's team might challenge them to a match.

The letters were put into a stamped envelope, and the flap was pasted. It was only then that they felt the need of knowing Sankar's address. They searched all parts of Sankar's card. Not a word anywhere, not even the name of the town he was writing from. They tried to get this out of the postmark. But a dark curved smudge on the stamp cannot be very illuminating.

The M.C.C. and its organizers had solid proof that they were persons of count when a letter from Binns came addressed to the Captain, M.C.C., Malgudi. It was a joy, touching that beautiful envelope and turning it over in the hand. Binns were the first to recognize the M.C.C., and Rajam took a vow that he would buy every bit that his team needed from that great firm. There were three implications in this letter that filled Rajam and his friends with rapture: (1) that His Majesty's Post Office recognized their team was proved by the fact that the letter addressed to the captain was promptly delivered to him; (2) that they were really recognized by such a magnificent firm as Binns of Madras was proved by the fact that Binns cared to reply in a full letter and not on a card, and actually typed the letter! (3) Binns sent under another cover carrying four annas postage a huge catalogue. What a tribute!

The letter informed the captain that Messrs Binns thanked him for his letter and would be much obliged to him if he would kindly remit 25 per cent with the order and the balance could be paid against the V.P.P. of the railway receipt.

Three heads buzzed over the meaning of this letter. The trouble was that they could not understand whether Binns were going to send the goods or not. Mani promised to unravel the letter if somebody would tell him what 'obliged' meant. When they turned the pages of a dictionary and offered him the meaning, he was none the wiser. He felt that it was a meaningless word in that place.

'One thing is clear,' said Rajam, 'Binns thanks us for our letter. So I don't think this letter could mean a refusal to supply us goods.'

Swaminathan agreed with him, 'That is right. If he did not wish to supply you with things, would he thank you? He would have abused you.' He scrutinized the letter again to make sure that there was no mistake about the thanks.

'Why has the fool used this word?' Mani asked, referring to 'obliged' which he could not pronounce. 'It has no meaning. Is he trying to make fun of us?'

'He says something about twenty-five per cent. I wish I knew what it was,' said Rajam.

Swaminathan could hardly contain himself, 'I say, Rajam, I am surprised you cannot understand this letter; you got sixty per cent in the last examination.'

'Have you any sense in you? What has that to do with this? Even a B.A. cannot understand this letter.'

In the end they came to the conclusion that the letter was sent to them by mistake. As far as they could see, the M.C.C. had written nothing in their previous letter to warrant such expressions as 'obliged', 'remit', and '25 per cent'. It could not be that the great firm of Binns were trying to make fun of them. Swaminathan pointed out 'To the Captain, M.C.C.' at the beginning of the letter. But he was told that it was also part of the mistake.

This letter was put in a cover with a covering letter and dispatched. The covering letter said:

> We are very sorry that you sent me somebody's letter. We are returning this somebody's letter. Please send our things immediately.

The M.C.C. were an optimistic lot. Though they were still unhonoured with a reply to their second letter, they expected the goods to arrive with every post. After ten days they thought they would start playing with whatever was available till they got the real bats, et cetera. The bottom of a dealwood case provided them with three good bats, and Rajam managed to get three used tennis balls from his father's club. The Pea was there, offering four real stumps that he believed he had somewhere in his house. A neat slip of ground adjoining Rajam's bungalow was to be the pitch. Everything was ready. Even if Binns took a month more to manufacture the goods specially for the M.C.C. (as they faintly thought probable), there need be no delay in starting practice. By the time the real bats and the balls arrived, they would be in form to play matches.

Rajam had chosen from his class a few who, he thought, deserved to become members of the M.C.C.

At five o'clock on the opening day, the M.C.C. had assembled, all except the Pea, for whom Rajam was waiting anxiously. He had promised to bring the real stumps. It was half an hour past time and yet he was not to be seen anywhere.

At last his puny figure was discovered in the distance. There was a catch in Rajam's heart when he saw him. He strained his eyes to find out if the Pea had the things about him. But since the latter was coming from the west, he was seen in the blaze of the evening sun. All the twelve assembled in the field shaded their eyes and looked. Some said that he was carrying a bundle, while some thought that he was swinging his hands freely.

When he arrived, Rajam asked, 'Why didn't you tell us that you hadn't the stumps?'

'I have still got them,' protested the Pea, 'I shall bring them tomorrow. I am sure my father knows where they are kept.'

'You kept us waiting till now. Why did you not come earlier and tell us that you could not find them?'

'I tell you, I have been spending hours looking for them everywhere. How could I come here and tell you and at the same time search?'

A cloud descended upon the gathering. For over twenty hours every one among them had been dreaming of swinging a bat and throwing a ball. And they could have realized the dream but for the Pea's wickedness. Everybody looked at him sourly. He was isolated. Rajam felt like crying when he saw the dealwood planks and the tennis balls lying useless on the ground. What a glorious evening they could have had if only the stumps had been brought!

Amidst all this gloom somebody cast a ray of light by suggesting that they might use the compound wall of Rajam's bungalow as a temporary wicket.

A portion of the wall was marked off with a piece of charcoal, and the captain arranged the field and opened the batting himself. Swaminathan took up the bowling. He held a tennis ball in his hand, took a few paces, and threw it over. Rajam swung the bat but missed it. The ball hit the wall right under the charcoal mark. Rajam was bowled out with the very first ball! There was a great shout of joy. The players pressed round Swaminathan to shake him and pat him on the back, and he was given on the very spot the title, 'Tate'.

CHAPTER FOURTEEN

GRANNY SHOWS HER IGNORANCE

Work was rather heavy in the Board High School. The amount of homework given at the Albert Mission was nothing compared to the heap given at the Board. Every teacher thought that his was the only subject that the boys had to study. Six sums in arithmetic, four pages of 'handwriting copy', dictionary meanings of scores of tough words, two maps, and five stanzas in Tamil poetry, were the average homework every day. Swaminathan sometimes wished that he had not left his old school. The teachers here were ruthless beings: not to speak of the drill three evenings a week, there were scout classes, compulsory games, et cetera, after the regular hours every day; and missing a single class meant half a dozen cane-cuts on the following day. The wizened spectacled man was a repulsive creature, with his screeching voice; the Head of the Albert Mission had a majestic air about him in spite of all his defects.

All this rigour and discipline resulted in a life with little scope for leisure. Swaminathan got up pretty early, rushed through all his homework, and rose just in time to finish the meal and reach the school as the first bell rang. Every day, as he passed the cloth shop at the end of Market Road, the first bell reached his ears. And just as he panted into the class, the second bell would go off. The bell lacked the rich note of the Albert Mission gong; there was something mean and nasal about it. But he soon got accustomed to it.

Except for an hour in the afternoon, he had to be glued to his seat right on till four-thirty in the evening. He had lost the last-bench habit (it might be because he no longer had Mani's company in the classroom). He sat in the second row, and no dawdling easy-going nonsense was tolerated there; you sat right under the teacher's nose. When the four-thirty bell rang, Swaminathan slipped his pencil into his pocket and stretched his cramped aching fingers.

The four-thirty bell held no special thrill. You could not just dash out of the class with a howl of joy. You had to go to the drill ground and stand in a solemn line, and for three-quarters of an hour the drill master treated you as if you were his dog. He drove you to march left and right, stand attention, and swing the arms, or climb the horizontal or parallel bars, whether you liked it or not, whether you knew the thing or not. For aught the drill master cared, you might lose your balance on the horizontal bars and crack your skull.

At the end of this you ran home to drink coffee, throw down the books, and rush off to the cricket field which was a long way off. You covered the distance half running, half walking, moved by the vision of a dun field sparsely covered with scorched grass, lit into a glaze by the slant rays of the evening sun, enveloped in a flimsy cloud of dust, alive with the shouts of players stamping about. What music there was in the thud of the bat hitting the ball! Just as you took the turn leading to Lawley Extension, you looked at the sun, which stood poised like a red-hot coin on the horizon. You hoped it would not sink. But by the time you arrived at the field the sun went down, leaving only a splash of colour and light in the sky. The shadows already crept out, and one or two municipal lanterns twinkled here and there. You still hoped you would be in time for a good game. But from about half a furlong away you saw the team squatting carelessly round the field. Somebody was wielding the bat rather languidly, bowled and fielded by a handful who were equally languid – the languor that comes at the end of a strenuous evening in the sun.

In addition to the misery of disappointment, you found Rajam a bit sore. He never understood the difficulties of a man. 'Oh, Swami, why are you late again?'

'Wretched drill class.'

'Oh damn your drill classes and scout classes! Why don't you come early?'

'What can I do, Rajam? I can't help it.'

'Well, well. I don't care. You are always ready with excuses. Since the new bats, balls and things arrived, you have hardly played four times.'

Others being too tired to play, eventually you persuaded the youngest member of the team (a promising, obedient boy of the Fifth Standard, who was admitted because he cringed and begged Rajam perseveringly) to bowl while you batted. And when you tired of it, you asked him to hold the bat and started bowling, and since you were the Tate of the team, the youngster was rather nervous. And again you took up batting, and then bowling, and so on. It went on till it became difficult to find the ball in the semi-darkness and the picker ran after small dark objects on the ground, instead of after the ball. At this stage a rumour started that the ball was lost and caused quite a stir. The figures squatting and reposing got busy, and the ball was retrieved. After this the captain passed an order forbidding further play, and the stumps were drawn for the day, and soon all the players melted in the darkness. You stayed behind with Rajam and Mani, perched upon Rajam's compound wall, and discussed the day's game and the players, noting the improvement, stagnation, or degeneration of each player, till it became quite dark and a peon came to inform Rajam that his tutor had come.

One evening, returning from the cricket field, after parting from Mani at the Grove Street junction, Swaminathan's conscience began to trouble him. A slight incident had happened during the early evening when he had gone home from the school to throw down the books and start for the cricket field. He had just thrown down the books and was running towards the kitchen when Granny cried, 'Swami, Swami. Oh, boy, come here.'

'No,' he said as usual and was in a moment out of her sight, in the kitchen, violently sucking coffee out of a tumbler. He could still hear her shaky querulous voice calling him. There was something appealing in that weak voice, and he had a fit of pity for her sitting and calling people who paid no heed to her. As soon as he had drunk the coffee, he went to her and asked, 'What do you want?'

She looked up and asked him to sit down. At that he lost his temper and all the tenderness he had felt for her a moment back. He raved, 'If you are going to, say what you have to say as quickly as possible ... If not, don't think I am a silly fool ...'

She said, 'I shall give you six paise. You can take three paise and bring me a lemon for three paise.' She had wanted to open this question slowly and diplomatically, because she knew what to expect from her grandson. And when she asked him to sit down, she did it as the first diplomatic move.

Without condescending to say yes or no, Swaminathan held out his hand for the coins and took them. Granny said, 'You must come before I count ten.' This imposition of a time-limit irritated him. He threw down the coins and said, 'If you want it so urgently, you had better go and get it yourself.' It was nearing five-thirty and he wanted to be in the field before sunset. He stood frowning at her as if giving her the choice of his getting the lemon late when he returned from the field, or not at all. She said, 'I have a terrible pain in my stomach. Please run out and come back, boy.' He did not stay there to hear more.

But now, all the excitement and exhilaration of the play being over, and having bidden the last 'good night', he stood in the Grove and Vinayaka Mudali Street junction, as it were face to face with his soul. He thought of his grandmother with pain at that very moment. It stung his heart as he remembered her pathetic upturned face and watery eyes. He called himself a sneak, a thief, an ingrate, and a hard-hearted villain.

In this mood of self-reproach he reached home. He softly sat beside Granny and kept looking at her. It was contrary to his custom. Every evening as soon as he reached home he would dash straight into the kitchen and worry the cook. But now he felt that his hunger did not matter.

Granny's passage had no light. It had only a shaft falling from the lamp in the hall. In the half-darkness, he could not see her face clearly. She lay still. Swaminathan was seized with a horrible passing doubt whether she might not be dead – of stomach-ache. He controlled his voice and asked, 'Granny, how is your pain?'

Granny stirred, opened her eyes, and said, 'Swami, you have come! Have you had your food?'

'Not yet. How is your stomach-ache, Granny?'

'Oh, it is all right. It is all right.'

It cost him all his mental powers to ask without flinching, 'Did you get the lemon?' He wanted to know it. He had been feeling genuinely anxious about it. Granny answered this question at once, but to Swaminathan it seemed an age – a terrible stretch of time during which anything might happen, she might say anything, scold him, disown him, swear that she would have nothing more to do with him, or say reproachfully that if only he had cared to go and purchase the lemon in time he might have saved her, and that she was going to die in a few minutes. But she simply said, 'You did right in not going. Your mother had kept a dozen in the kitchen.'

Swaminathan was overjoyed to hear this good news. And he expressed his mood of joy in: 'You know what my new name is? I am Tate.'

'What?'

'Tate.'

'What is Tate?' she asked innocently. Swaminathan's disappointment was twofold: she had not known anything of his new title, and failed to understand its rich significance even when told. At other times he would have shouted at her. But now he was a fresh penitent, and so asked her kindly, 'Do you mean to say that you don't know Tate?'

'I don't know what you mean.'

'Tate, the great cricket player, the greatest bowler on earth. I hope you know what cricket is.'

'What is that?' Granny asked. Swaminathan was aghast at this piece of illiteracy. 'Do you mean to say, Granny, that you don't know what cricket is, or are you fooling me?'

'I don't know what you mean.'

'Don't keep on saying "I don't know what you mean". I wonder what the boys and men of your days did in the evenings! I think they spent all the twenty-four hours in doing holy things.'

He considered for a second. Here was his granny stagnating in appalling ignorance; and he felt it his duty to save her. He delivered a short speech setting forth principles, ideals, and the philosophy of the game of cricket, mentioning the radiant gods of that world. He asked her every few seconds if she understood, and she nodded her head, though she caught only three per cent of what he said. He concluded the speech with a sketch of the history and the prospects of the M.C.C. 'But for Rajam,

Granny,' he said, 'I don't know where we should have been. He has spent hundreds of rupees on this team. Buying bats and balls is no joke. He has plenty of money in his box. Our team is known even to the Government. If you like, you may write a letter to the M.C.C. and it will be delivered to us promptly. You will see us winning all the cups in Malgudi, and in course of time we shall show even the Madras fellows what cricket is.' He added a very important note: 'Don't imagine all sorts of fellows can become players in our team.'

His father stood behind him, with the baby in his arms. He asked, 'What are you lecturing about, young man?'

Swaminathan had not noticed his father's presence, and now writhed awkwardly as he answered, 'Nothing ... Oh, nothing, Father.'

'Come on. Let me know it too.'

'It is nothing – Granny wanted to know something about cricket and I was explaining it to her.'

'Indeed! I never knew Mother was a sportswoman. Mother, I hope Swami has filled you with cricket-wisdom.'

Granny said, 'Don't tease the boy. The child is so fond of me. Poor thing! He has been trying to tell me all sorts of things. You are not in the habit of explaining things to me. You are all big men ...'

Father replied, pointing at the baby, 'Just wait a few days and this little fellow will teach you all the philosophy and the politics in the world.' He gently clouted the baby's fat cheeks, and the baby gurgled and chirped joyfully. 'He has already started lecturing. Listen attentively, Mother.' Granny held up her arms for the baby. But Father clung to him tight and said, 'No. No. I came home early only for this fellow's sake. I can't. Come on, Swami, I think we had better sit down for food. Where is your mother?'

The captain sternly disapproved Swaminathan's ways. 'Swami, I must warn you. You are neglecting the game. You are not having any practice at all.'

'It is this wretched Board School work.'

'Who asked you to go and join it? They never came and invited you. Never mind. But let me tell you. Even Bradman,

Tate, and everybody spends four to five hours on the pitch every day, practising, practising. Do you think you are greater than they?'

'Captain, listen to me. I do my best to arrive at the field before five. But this wretched Board High School timetable is peculiar.'

A way out had to be found. The captain suggested, 'You must see your headmaster and ask him to exempt you from extra work till the match is over.' It was more easily said than done and Swaminathan said so, conjuring up before his mind a picture of the wizened face and the small dingy spectacles of his headmaster.

'I am afraid to ask that monster,' Swaminathan said. 'He may detain me in Second Form for ages.'

'Indeed! Are you telling me that you are in such terror of your headmaster? Suppose I see him?'

'Oh, please don't, captain. I beg you. You don't know what a vicious being he is. He may not treat you well. Even if he behaves well before you, he is sure to kill me when you are gone.'

'What is the matter with you, Swami? Your head is full of nonsense. How are we to go on? It is two months since we started the team, and you have not played even for ten days ...'

Mani, who had stretched himself on the compound wall, now broke in: 'Let us see what your headmaster can do. Let him say yes or no. If he kills you I will pulp him. My clubs have had no work for a long time.'

There was no stopping Rajam. The next day he insisted that he would see the headmaster at the school. He would not mind losing a couple of periods of his own class. Mani offered to go with him but was advised to mind his business.

Next morning at nine-thirty Swaminathan spent five minutes rubbing his eyes red, and then complained of headache. His father felt his temples and said that he would be all right if he dashed a little cold water on his forehead.

'Yes, Father,' Swaminathan said and went out. He stood outside Father's room and decided that if cold water was a cure for headache he would avoid it, since he was praying for that malady just then. Rajam was coming to see the headmaster, and it would be unwise to go to school that morning. He went in and asked, 'Father, did you say cold water?'

'Yes.'

'But don't you think it will give me pneumonia or something? I am also feeling feverish.'

Father felt his pulse and said, 'Now run to school and you will be all right.' It was easier to squeeze milk out of a stone than to get permission from Father to keep away from school.

He whispered into his granny's ear, 'Granny, even if I die, I am sure Father will insist on sending my corpse to the school.' Granny protested vehemently against this sentiment.

'Granny, a terrible fever is raging within me and my head is splitting with headache. But yet, I mustn't keep away from school.'

Granny said, 'Don't go to school.' She then called Mother and said, 'This child has fever. Why should he go to school?'

'Has he?' Mother asked anxiously, and fussed over him. She felt his body and said that he certainly had a temperature. Swaminathan said pathetically, 'Give me milk or something, Mother. It is getting late for school.' Mother vetoed this virtuous proposal. Swaminathan faintly said, 'But Father may not like it.' She asked him to lie down on a bed and hurried along to Father's room. She stepped into the room with the declaration, 'Swami has fever, and he can't go to school.'

'Did you take his temperature?'

'Not yet. It doesn't matter if he misses school for a day.'

'Anyway, take his temperature,' he said. He feared that his wife might detect the sarcasm in his suggestion, and added as a palliative, 'That we may know whether a doctor is necessary.'

A thermometer stuck out of Swaminathan's mouth for half a minute and indicated normal. Mother looked at it and thrust it back into his mouth. It again showed normal. She took it to Father, and he said, 'Well, it is normal,' itching to add, 'I knew it.' Mother insisted, 'Something has gone wrong with the thermometer. The boy has fever. There is no better thermometer than my hand. I can swear that he has 100.2 now.'

'Quite likely,' Father said.

And Swaminathan, when he ought to have been at school, was lying peacefully, with closed eyes, on his bed. He heard a footstep near his bed and opened his eyes. Father stood over him and said in an undertone, 'You are a lucky fellow. What a lot of champions you have in this house when you don't want to go to school!' Swaminathan felt that this was a sudden and unprovoked attack from behind. He shut his eyes and turned towards the wall with a feeble groan.

By the afternoon he was already bedsore. He dreaded the prospect of staying in bed through the evening. Moreover, Rajam would have already come to the school in the morning and gone.

He went to his mother and informed her that he was starting for the school. There was a violent protest at once. She felt him all over and said that he was certainly better but in no condition to go to school. Swaminathan said, 'I am feeling quite fit, Mother. Don't get fussy.'

On the way to the school he met Rajam and Mani. Mani had his club under his arm. Swaminathan feared that these two had done something serious.

Rajam said, 'You are a fine fellow! Where were you this morning?'

'Did you see the headmaster, Rajam?'

'Not yet. I found that you had not come, and did not see him. I want you to be with me when I see him. After all it is your business.'

When Swaminathan emerged from the emotional chaos which followed Rajam's words, he asked, 'What is Mani doing here?'

'I don't know,' Rajam said, 'I found him outside your school with his club, when he ought to have been in his class.'

'Mani, what about your class?'

'It is all right,' Mani replied, 'I didn't attend it today.'

'And why your club?' Swaminathan asked.

'Oh! I simply brought it along.'

Rajam asked, 'Weren't you told yesterday to attend your class and mind your business?'

'I don't remember. You asked me to mind my business only when I offered to accompany you. I am not accompanying you. I just came this way, and you have also come this way. This is a public road.' Mani's jest was lost on them. Their minds were too busy with plans for the impending interview.

'Don't worry, young men,' Mani said, 'I shall see you through your troubles. I will talk to the headmaster, if you like.'

'If you step into his room, he will call the police,' Swaminathan said.

When they reached the school Mani was asked to go away, or at worst wait in the road. Rajam went in, and Swaminathan was compelled to accompany him to the headmaster's room.

The headmaster was sleeping with his head between his hands and his elbows resting on the table. It was a small stuffy room with only one window opening on the weather-beaten side wall of a shop; it was cluttered with dust-laden rolls of maps, globes, and geometrical squares. The headmaster's white cane lay on the table across two ink-bottles and some pads. The sun came in a hot dusty beam and fell on the headmaster's nose and the table. He was gently snoring. This was a possibility that Rajam had not thought of.

'What shall we do?' Swaminathan asked in a rasping whisper.

'Wait,' Rajam ordered.

They waited for ten minutes and then began to make gentle noises with their feet. The headmaster opened his eyes and without taking his head from his hands, kept staring at them vacantly, without showing any sign of recognition. He rubbed his eyes, raised his eyebrows three times, yawned, and asked in a voice thick with sleep, 'Have you fellows no class?' He fumbled for his spectacles and put them on. Now the picture was complete – wizened face and dingy spectacles calculated to strike terror into the hearts of Swaminathans. He asked again, 'To what class do you fellows belong? Have you no class?'

'I don't belong to your school,' Rajam said defiantly.

'Ah, then which heaven do you drop from?'

Rajam said, 'I am the captain of the M.C.C. and have come to see you on business.'

'What is that?'

'This is my friend W. S. Swaminathan of Second C studying in your school ...'

'I am honoured to meet you,' said the headmaster turning to Swaminathan. Rajam felt at that moment that he had found out where the Board High School got its reputation from.

'I am the captain of the M.C.C.'

'Equally honoured ...'

'He is in my team. He is a good bowler ...'

'Are you?' said the headmaster, turning to Swaminathan.

'May I come to the point?' Rajam asked.

'Do, do,' said the headmaster, 'for heaven's sake, do.'

'It is this,' Rajam said, 'he is a good bowler and he needs some practice. He can't come to the field early enough because he is kept in the school every day after four-thirty.'

'What do you want me to do?'

'Sir, can't you permit him to go home after four-thirty?'

The headmaster sank back in his chair and remained silent.

Rajam asked again, 'What do you say, sir, won't you do it?'

'Are you the headmaster of this school or am I?'

'Of course you are the headmaster, sir. In Albert Mission they don't keep us a minute longer than four-thirty. And we are exempted from drill if we play games.'

'Here I am not prepared to listen to your rhapsodies on that parish school. Get out.'

Mani, who had been waiting outside, finding his friends gone too long, and having his own fears, now came into the headmaster's room.

'Who is this?' asked the headmaster, looking at Mani sourly. 'What do you want?'

'Nothing,' Mani replied and quietly stood in a corner.

'I can't understand why every fellow who finds nothing to do comes and stands in my room.'

'I am the Police Superintendent's son,' Rajam said abruptly.

'Is that so? Find out from your father what he was doing on the day a gang of little rascals came in and smashed these windows ... What is the thing that fellow has in his hand?'

'My wooden club,' Mani answered.

Rajam added, 'He breaks skulls with it. Come out, Mani, come on, Swami. There is nothing doing with this – this madcap.'

CHAPTER FIFTEEN

BEFORE THE MATCH

The M.C.C.'s challenge to a 'friendly' match was accepted by the Young Men's Union, who kept themselves in form by indefatigable practice on the vacant site behind the Reading Room, or when the owner of the site objected, right in the middle of Kulam Street. The match was friendly in nought but name. The challenge sent by the M.C.C. was couched in terms of defiance and threat.

There were some terrifying conditions attached to the challenge. The first condition was that the players should be in the field promptly at eleven o'clock. The second was that they should carry their own bats, while the stumps would be graciously supplied by the M.C.C. The third was not so much a plain condition as a firm hint that they would do well to bring and keep in stock a couple of their own balls. The reason for this was given in the pithy statement 'that your batsmen might hit your own balls and not break ours'. The next was the inhospitable suggestion that they had better look out for themselves in regard to lunch, if they cared to have any at all. The last condition was perhaps the most complicated of the lot, over which some argument and negotiation ensued: 'You shall pay for breaking bats, balls, wickets, and other damages.'

The Y.M.U. captain was rather puzzled by this. He felt that it was irrelevant in view of the fact that there were conditions 2 and 3, and if they broke any bats and balls at all, it would be their own property and the M.C.C.'s anxiety to have the damage made good was unwarranted. He was told that the stumps belonged to the M.C.C. anyway, and there was also the Y.M.U.'s overlooking clauses 2 and 3. At which the Y.M.U. captain became extremely indignant and asked why if the M.C.C. was so impoverished, it should not come and play in their (Y.M.U.'s) own pitch and save them the trouble of carrying their team about. The stinging rejoinder occurred to the indignant Rajam exactly twenty minutes after the other captain had left, that it could not be done as the M.C.C. did not think much of a match played in the middle of Kulam Street, if the owner of the vacant site behind the Reading Room should take it into his head to object to the match. Before he left, the Y.M.U. captain demanded to be told what 'other damages' in the last clause meant. Rajam paused, looked about, and pointed to the windows and tiles of a house adjoining the M.C.C. field.

The match was to be played on Sunday two weeks later.

Rajam lost all peace of mind. He felt confident that his team could thrash the Y.M.U. He himself could be depended upon not to let down the team. Mani was steady if unimpressive. He could be depended upon to stop with his head, if necessary, any ball. His batting was not bad. He had a peculiar style. With his bat he stopped all reasonable approaches to the wicket and brought the best bowlers to a fainting condition. Rajam did not consider it worth while to think of the other players of the team. There was only one player who caused him the deepest anxiety day and night. He was a dark horse. On him rested a great task, a mighty responsibility. He was the Tate of the team. But he looked uncertain. Even with the match only a fortnight off, he did not seem to care for practice. He stuck to his old habit of arriving at the field when darkness had fallen on the earth. 'Swami,' Rajam pleaded, 'please do try to have at least an hour's practice in the evenings.'

'Certainly Rajam, if you can suggest a way ...'

'Why not tell your headmaster that ...'

'Oh, no, no,' Swaminathan cried, 'I am grateful to you for your suggestion. But let us not think of that man. He has not forgotten your last visit yet.'

'I don't care. What I want is that you should have good practice. If you keep any batsman standing for more than five minutes, I will never see your face again. You needn't concern yourself with the score. You can leave it to us ...'

Just seven days before the match, Swaminathan realized that his evenings were more precious than ever. As soon as the evening bell rang, he lined up with the rest in the drill ground. But contrary to the custom, he had not taken off his coat and cap. All the others were in their shirts, with their dhotis tucked up. The drill master, a square man with protruding chest, a big moustache sharpened at the ends, and a silk turban wound in military style, stood as if he posed before a camera, and surveyed his pupils with a disdainful side-glance. The monitor called out the names from the greasy register placed on the vaulting-horse. The attendance after an interminable time was over and the drill master gave up his pose, came near the file, and walked from one end to the other, surveying each boy sternly. Swaminathan being short came towards the end of the file. The drill master stopped before him, looked him up and down and passed on muttering: 'You won't get leave. Coat and cap off.'

Swaminathan became desperate and pursued him: 'Sir, I am in a terrible state of health. I can't attend drill today. I shall die if I do. Sir, I think I shall – ' He was prancing behind the drill master.

The drill master had come to the last boy and yet Swaminathan was dogging him. He turned round on Swaminathan with a fierce oath: 'What is the matter with you?'

'Sir, you don't understand my troubles. You don't even care to ask me what I am suffering from.'

'Yes, yes, what exactly is ailing you now?'

Swaminathan had first thought of complaining of headache, but now he saw the drill master was in a mood to slight even the most serious of headaches. He had an inspiration and said: 'Sir, the whole of last night I was delirious.'

The drill master was stunned by this piece of news. 'You were delirious! Are you mad?'

'No, sir. I didn't sleep a wink last night. I was delirious. Our doctor said so. He has asked me not to attend drill for a week to come. He said that I should die if I attended drill.'

'Get away, young swine, before I am tempted to throttle you. I don't believe a word. But you are a persevering swine. Get out.'

The intervening period, about half an hour, between leaving the drill ground and reaching the cricket field, was a blur of hurry and breathlessness. Everybody at the field was happy to see him so early. Rajam jumped with joy.

On the whole everything was satisfactory. The only unpleasant element in all this was an obsession that the drill master might spy him out. So that, when they dispersed for the evening, Swaminathan stayed in Rajam's house till it was completely dark and then skulked home, carefully avoiding the lights falling in the street from shop-fronts.

The next morning he formed a plan to be free all the evenings of the week. He was at his desk with the *Manual of Grammar* open before him. It was seven-thirty in the morning, and he had still two and a half hours before him for the school.

He did a little cautious reconnoitring: Mother was in the baby's room, for the rhythmic creaking of the cradle came to his ears. Father's voice was coming from the front room; he was busy with his clients. Swaminathan quietly slipped out of the house.

He stood before a shop in front of which hung the board: 'Doctor T. Kesavan, L. M. & S. Sri Krishna Dispensary.' The doctor was sitting at a long table facing the street. Swaminathan found that the doctor was alone and free, and entered the shop.

'Hallo, Swaminathan, what is the matter?'

'Nothing, sir. I have come on a little business.'

'All well at home?'

'Quite. Doctor, I have got to have a doctor's certificate immediately.'

'What is the matter with you?'

'I will tell you the truth, doctor. I have to play a match next week against the Young Men's Union. And I must have some practice. And yet every evening there is a drill class, scouting, some dirty period or other. If you could give me a certificate asking them to let me off at four-thirty, it would help the M.C.C. to win the match.'

'Well, I could do it. But is there anything wrong with you?'

Swaminathan took half a second to find an answer: 'Certainly, I am beginning to feel of late that I have delirium.'

'What did you say?' asked the doctor anxiously.

Swaminathan was pleased to find the doctor so much impressed, and repeated that he was having the most violent type of delirium.

'Boy, did you say delirium? What exactly do you mean by delirium?'

Swaminathan did not consider it the correct time for cross-examination. But he had to have the doctor's favour. He answered: 'I have got it. I can't say exactly. But it isn't some, some kind of stomach-ache?'

The doctor laughed till a great fit of coughing threatened to choke him. After that he looked Swaminathan under the eye, examined his tongue, tapped his chest, and declared him to be in the pink of health, and told him he would do well to stick to his drill if he wanted to get rid of delirium. Swaminathan again explained to him how important it was for him to have his evenings free. But the doctor said: 'It is all very well. But I should be prosecuted if I gave you any such certificate.'

'Who is going to find out, doctor? Do you want our M.C.C. to lose the match?'

'I wish you all success. Don't worry. I can't give you a certificate. But I shall talk to your headmaster about you and request him to let you off after four-thirty.'

'That will do. You are very kind to me, doctor.'

At four-thirty that evening, without so much as thinking of the scouting class in the quadrangle of the school, Swaminathan went home and then to the cricket field. Next day he had drill class, and he did not give it a thought. He was having plenty of practice. Rajam said: 'Swami, you are wonderful! All that you needed was a little practice. What have you done about your evening classes?'

'It is a slight brainwave, my boy. Our doctor has told the headmaster that I should die if I stayed in the school after four-thirty. I got him to do it. What do you think of it?'

Mani dug him in the ribs and cried: 'You are the brainiest fellow I have ever seen.' Rajam agreed with him, and then was suddenly seized with worry: 'Oh, I don't know if we shall win the match. I will die if we lose.'

Mani said: 'Here, Rajam, I am sick of your talks of defeat. Do you think those monkey-faced fools can stand up to us?'

'I shall write to the papers if we win,' said Rajam.

'Will they print our photos?' Tate asked.

'Without doubt.'

It was during the geography hour on Friday that the headmaster came to the class, cane in hand. The geography master, Mr Rama Rao, a mild elderly person, rose respectfully. The headmaster gave the full benefit of his wizened face to the class. His owl-like eyes were fixed upon Swaminathan, and he said: 'Get up.'

Swaminathan got up.

'Come here.'

Swaminathan 'came' there promptly.

'Show your shameless face to the class fully.'

Swaminathan now tried to hide his face. The headmaster threw out his arm and twisted Swaminathan's neck to make him face the class, and said: 'This great man is too busy to bother about such trivial matters as drill and scouting, and has not honoured these classes with his presence since last Monday.' His lips twisted in a wry smile. The class considered it safer to take the cue, and gently giggle. Even on the geography master's face there appeared a polite smile.

'Sir, have you any explanation to give?' the headmaster asked.

With difficulty Swaminathan found his voice and answered: 'It was the doctor – didn't the doctor talk to you about me, sir?'

'What doctor talk about what?'

'He said he would,' faintly answered Swaminathan.

'If you talk in enigmas I shall strip you before the class and thrash you.'

'Dr Kesavan said – '

'What about Dr Kesavan?'

'He said he would talk to you about me and get me exemption from drill and other extra periods. He said that I should die if I attended drill for some days to come.'

'And pray what is your trouble?'

'He thinks it is some – some kind – of – delirium you know.' He had determined to avoid this word since he met the doctor last, but at this critical moment he blundered into it by sheer habit.

The headmaster turned to the teacher and raised his brow. He waited for some time and said: 'I am waiting to hear what other words of truth and wisdom are going to drop from your mouth.'

'Sir, I thought he had talked to you. He said he would ...'

'I don't care to have every street mongrel come and tell me what to do in my school with my boys. It is a good thing that this surgeon-general did not come. If he had, I would have asked the peon to bash his head on the table.'

Swaminathan realized that the doctor had deceived him. He remembered the genial smile with which the doctor had said that he would see the headmaster. Swaminathan shuddered as he realized what a deep-dyed villain Dr Kesavan was behind that genial smile. He would teach that villain a lesson, put a snake into his table-drawer; he would not allow that villain to feel his pulse even if he (Swaminathan) should be dying of fever.

Further plans of revenge were stopped by a flick of the cane on his knuckles. The headmaster held the cane ready and cried: 'Hold out your hand. Six on each hand for each day of absence, and the whole of the next lesson on the bench. Monitor, you had better see to it. And remember, W. S. Swaminathan, if you miss a single class again, I shall strip you in the school hall and ask the peon to cane you. You can't frighten me with your superintendents of police, their sons, grandsons, or grandfathers. I don't care even if you complain to His Majesty.' He released Swaminathan's neck and raised the cane.

Another moment and that vicious snake-like cane, quivering as if with life, would have descended on Swaminathan's palm. A flood of emotion swept him off his feet, a mixture of fear, resentment, and rage. He hardly knew what he was doing. His arm shot out, plucked the cane from the headmaster's hand, and flung it out of the window. Then he dashed to his desk, snatched his books, and ran out of the room. He crossed the hall and the veranda in a run, climbed the school gate because the bolt was too heavy for him, and jumped into the end of Market Road.

He sat under a tree on the roadside to collect his thoughts. He had left the school to which he would never go back as long as that tyrant was there. If his father should hear of it, he would do heaven knew what. He would force him to go back, which would be impossible ... He had got out of two schools in this fashion. There were no more schools in Malgudi. His father would have to send him to Trichinopoly or Madras. But probably the Board High School headmaster would write to all the schools, telling them who Swaminathan was. He would not be admitted to any school. So he would have to work and earn ... He might get some rupees – and he could go to hotels and buy coffee and tiffin as often as he pleased. What divine sweets the Bombay Anand Bhavan made! There was some green slab on the top left of the stall, with almonds stuck on it. He had always wanted to eat it, but lacked the courage to ask the hotel man, as he believed it to be very costly ... His father would not allow him to remain in the house if he did not go to school. He might beat him. He would not go home that day nor on any other day. He could not face his father. He wondered at the same time where he could go. Anywhere. If he kept walking along Market Road where would it lead him? Probably to Madras. Could he reach Bombay and England if he went further? He could work in any one of those places, earn money and do what he pleased. If he should go by train ... But what to do for money? There might not be much trouble about that. The station-master was an amiable man and Swaminathan knew him.

The school bell rang, and Swaminathan rose to hurry away. The boys might come out, stand around and watch him as if he were something funny.

He hurried along Market Road, turned to his right, along Smith Street, and taking a short cut through some intricate lanes, stood before his old school, the Albert Mission. The sight of the deep yellow building with its top storey filled him with a nostalgia for old times. He wished he had not left it. How majestic everything now seemed! The headmaster, so dignified in his lace-turban, so unlike the grubby wretch of the Board. Vednayagam, Ebenezar – even Ebenezar. D. P. Pillai, how cosy and homely his history classes were! Swaminathan almost wept at the memory of Somu and Pea ... All his friends were there, Rajam, Somu, Mani, and the Pea, happy, dignified, and honoured within the walls of the august Albert Mission School. He alone was out of it, isolated, as if he were a leper. He was an outcast, an outcast. He was filled with a sudden self-disgust. Oh, what would he not give to be back in the old school! Only, they would not take him in. It was no use. He had no more schools to go to in Malgudi. He must run away to Madras and work. But he had better see Rajam and Mani before going away.

He lingered outside the school gate. He had not the courage to enter it. He was the enemy of the school. The peon Singaram might assault him and drive him out if he saw him. He discreetly edged close to the massive concrete gatepost which screened him from a direct view of the school. He had to meet Rajam and Mani. But how? He stood still for a few minutes and formed a plan.

He went round behind the school. It was a part of the building that nobody frequented. It was a portion of the fallow field adjoining the school and terminating in the distant railway embankment. Swaminathan had not seen this place even once in all the six or seven years that he had spent at the school. Here the school compound wall was half covered with moss, and the rear view of the school was rather interesting. From here Swaminathan could see only the top half of the building, but even that presented a curious appearance. For instance, he could not at once point out where his old Second A was situated. He rolled up a stone to the foot of the wall, and stood on it. He could just see the school compound now. It was about twelve, the busiest hour in the school, and there was not a single person in the compound. He waited. It was tedious waiting. After a short time, a very small person came out of the First Standard, to blow his nose. The three sections of the First Standard were in a block not a dozen yards from Swaminathan.

Swaminathan whistled softly, and the very small person did not hear. Swaminathan repeated the whistling, and the very small person turned and started as if he saw an apparition. Swaminathan beckoned to him. The small person took just a second to decide whether to obey the call of that apparition or to run back to the class. Swaminathan called him again. And the very small man drew towards him as if in a hypnotic state, staring wildly.

Swaminathan said: 'Would you like to have an almond peppermint?'

The small man could hardly believe his ears. Here was a man actually offering almond peppermints! It could not be true. There was probably some fraud in it. Swaminathan repeated the offer and the small man replied rather cautiously that he would like to have the peppermint.

'Well, then,' Swaminathan said, 'you can't have it just now. You will have to earn it. Just go to Second Form A and tell M. Rajam that somebody from his house wants him urgently and bring him over here, and then hold out your hand for the peppermint. Maybe you will be given two.'

The small man stood silent, assimilating every detail of the question and then with a puckered brow asked: 'Where is Second Form A?'

'Upstairs.'

'Oh!' the boy ejaculated with a note of despair, and stood ruminating.

'What do you say?' Swaminathan asked, and added: 'Answer me before I count to ten. Otherwise the offer is off. One, two, three – '

'You say it is upstairs?' the boy asked.

'Of course I do.'

'But I have never gone there.'

'You will have to now.'

'I don't know the way.'

'Just climb the stairs.'

'They may – they may beat me if I am seen there.'

'If you care for the almond peppermint you will have to risk it. Say at once whether you will go or not.'

'All right. Wait for me.' The very small man was off.

Ten minutes later he returned, followed by Rajam. Rajam was astonished to see Swaminathan's head over the wall. 'What are you doing here?'

'Jump over the wall. I want you very urgently, Rajam.'

'I have got a class. I can't come now.'

'Don't be absurd. Come on. I have something very urgent to say.'

Rajam jumped over the wall and was by his side.

Swaminathan's head disappeared from view. A pathetic small voice asked over the wall: 'Where is my peppermint?'

'Oh, I forgot you, little one,' Swaminathan said, reappearing, 'come on, catch this.' He tossed a three-paisa coin at the other.

'You said an almond peppermint,' the boy reminded.

'I may say a thousand things,' Swaminathan answered brusquely, 'but isn't a three-paisa coin sufficient? You can buy an almond peppermint if you want.'

'But you said two almond peppermints.'

'Now be off, young man. Don't haggle with me like a brinjal seller. Learn contentment,' said Swaminathan and jumped down from the stone.

'Rajam, do you know what has happened in the school today? I have fought with the headmaster. I am dismissed. I have no more schools or classes.'

'You fought with the headmaster?'

'Yes, he came to assault me about the drill attendance, and I wrenched his hand, and snatched the cane ... I don't believe I shall ever go back to the school. I expect there will be a lot of trouble if I do.'

'What a boy you are!' exclaimed Rajam. 'You are always in some trouble or other wherever you go. Always, always –'

'It was hardly my fault, Rajam,' Swaminathan said, and tried to vindicate himself by explaining to him Dr Kesavan's villainy.

'You have no sense, Swami. You are a peculiar fellow.'

'What else could I do to get the evenings off for practice? The Y.M.U. are no joke.'

'You are right, Swami. I watched the fellows at practice this morning. They have morning practice too. They are not bad players. There is one Mohideen, a dark fellow, oh, you know – you will have to keep an eye on him. He bats like Bradman. You will have to watch him. There is another fellow, Shanmugam. He is a dangerous bowler. But there is one weakness in Mohideen. He is not so steady on the leg side ... Swami, don't worry about anything for some time to come. You must come in the morning too tomorrow. We have got to beat those fellows.'

Swaminathan had really called Rajam to bid him goodbye, but now he changed his mind. Rajam would stop him if he came to know of his adventurous plans. He wasn't going to tell Rajam or anybody about it, not even Mani. If he was stopped, he would have no place to stay in. The match was still two days off. He would go away without telling anyone, somehow practise on the way, come back for a few hours on the day of the match, disappear once again, and never come back to Malgudi – a place which contained his father, a stern stubborn father, and that tyrant of a headmaster ... And no amount of argument on his part could ever make his father see eye to eye with him. If he went home, Father might beat him, thrash him, or kill him, to make him return to the Board High School. Father was a tough man ... He would have to come back on the day of the match, without anybody's knowledge. Perhaps it would not be necessary. He asked suddenly: 'Rajam, do you think I am so necessary for the match?'

Rajam regarded him suspiciously and said: 'Don't ask such questions.' He added presently: 'We can't do without you, Swami. No. We depend upon you. You are the best bowler we have. We have got to give those fellows a beating. I shall commit suicide if we lose. Oh, Swami, what a mess you have made of things! What are you going to do without a school?'

'I shall have to join a workshop or some such thing.'

'What will your father say when he hears of it?'

'Oh, nothing. He will say it is all right. He won't trouble me,' Swaminathan said.

'Swami, I must get back to the class. It is late.' Rajam rose and sprinted towards the school, crying: 'Come to the field early. Come very soon, now that you are free ...'

CHAPTER SIXTEEN

SWAMI DISAPPEARS

Swaminathan's father felt ashamed of himself as he approached Ellaman Street, the last street of the town, which turned into a rough track for about a hundred yards and disappeared into the sands of the Sarayu River. He hesitated for a second at the end of Market Road, which was bright with the lights of a couple of late shops and a street gas-lamp, before he turned to plunge into the darkness and silence of Ellaman Street. A shaft of greenish light from the gas-lamp fell athwart Ellaman Street, illuminating only a few yards of the street and leaving the rest in deep gloom. A couple of municipal lanterns smouldered in their wicks, emphasizing the darkness around.

Swaminathan's father felt ashamed of himself. He was going to cross the street, plod through the sand, and gaze in the Sarayu – for the body of his son! His son, Swami, to be looked for in the Sarayu! It seemed to him a ridiculous thing to do. But what could he do? He dared not return home without some definite news of his son, good or bad. The house had worn a funeral appearance since nine o'clock. His wife and his old mother were more or less dazed and demented. She – his wife – had remained cheerful till the Taluk Office gong struck ten, when, her face turning white, she had asked him to go and find out from Swaminathan's friends and teachers what had happened to him.

He did not know where Swaminathan's headmaster lived. He had gone to the Board School and asked the watchman, who had misdirected him and made him wander over half the town without purpose. He could not find Mani's house. He had gone to Rajam's house, but the house was dark, everybody had gone to bed, and he felt that it would be absurd to wake up the household of a stranger to ask if they had seen his son. From what he could get out of the servant sleeping in the veranda, he understood that Swaminathan had not been seen in Rajam's house that evening. He had then vaguely wandered in the streets. He was doing it to please his wife and mother. He had not shared in the least his wife's nervousness. He had felt all along that the boy must have gone out somewhere and would return, and then he would treat him with some firmness and nip this tendency in the bud. He had spent nearly an hour thus and gone home. Even his mother had left her bed and was hobbling agitatedly about the house, praying to the God of the Thirupathi Hills and promising him rich offerings if he should restore Swaminathan to her safe and sound. His wife stood like a stone image, looking down the street. The only tranquil being in the house was the youngest member of the family, whose soft breathings came from the cradle, defying the gloom and heaviness in the house.

When Swaminathan's father gave his wife the news – or no news – that he had gathered from his wanderings, he had assumed a heavy aggressive cheerfulness. It had lasted for a while, but gradually the anxiety and the nervousness of the two women infected him. He had begun to feel that something must have happened to his son – a kidnapping or an accident. He was trying to reason out these fears when his wife asked in a trembling voice: 'Did you search in the hospital?' and broke into a hysterical cry. He received this question with apparent disdain, while his mind was conjuring up a vision of his son lying in a pulp in the hospital. He was struggling to erase this picture from his mind when his mother made matters worse with the question: 'Tell me – tell me – where could the boy have gone? Were you severe with him for anything this morning?'

He was indignant at this question. Everybody seemed to be holding him responsible for Swaminathan's disappearance. Since nine o'clock he had been enduring the sly references and the suspicious glances. But this upset him, and he sharply asked his mother to return to her bed and not to let her brain concoct silly questions. He had after that reviewed his behaviour with his son since the morning, and discovered with surprise and relief that he had not seen him the whole day. The boy had risen from bed, studied, and gone to school, while he had shut himself up in his room with his clients. He then wondered if he had done anything in the past two or three days. He was not certain of his memory, but he felt that his conduct was blameless. As far as he could remember there had not been any word or act of his that could have embittered the boy and made him do – do – wild things.

It was nearing twelve and he found his wife still sobbing. He tried to console her and rose to go out saying, again with a certain loud cheerfulness: 'I am going out to look for him. If he comes before I return, for heaven's sake don't let him know what I am out for. I don't care to appear a fool in his eyes.'

He had walked rather briskly up Hospital Road, but had turned back after staring at the tall iron gates of the hospital. He told himself that it was unnecessary to enter the hospital, but in fact knew that he lacked the courage. That very window in which a soft dim light appeared might have behind it the cot containing Swaminathan all pulped and bandaged. He briskly moved out of Hospital Road and wandered about rather aimlessly through a few dark lanes around the place. With each hour, his heart became heavier. He had slunk past Market Road, and now entered Ellaman Street.

He swiftly passed through Ellaman Street and crossed the rough footpath leading to the river. His pace slackened as he approached the river. He tried to convince himself that he was about to do a piece of work which was a farce. But if the body of his son, sodden and bloated, should be stuck up among the reeds, and rocking gently on the ripples ... He shut his eyes and prayed: 'Oh, God, help me.'

He looked far up and down the river which was gliding along with gentle music. The massive *peepul* trees overhanging the river sighed to the night. He started violently at the sight of the flimsy shadow of some branch on the water; and again as some float kept tilting against the moss-covered parapet with muffled thuds.

And then, still calling himself a fool, he went to the Malgudi Railway Station and walked a mile or so along the railway line, keenly examining the iron rails and the sleepers. The ceaseless hum and the shrill whistle of night insects, the whirring of bats, and the croaking of frogs, came through the awful loneliness of the night. He once stooped with a shudder to put his finger on some wet patch on the rails. As he held up the finger and examined it in the starlight and found that it was only water and not blood, he heaved a sigh of relief and thanked God.

CHAPTER SEVENTEEN

THE DAY OF THE MATCH

A narrow road branching to the left of the trunk road attracted Swaminathan because it was shaded by trees bearing fruits. The white ball-like wood-apple, green figs, and the deep purple eugenia peeped out of thick green foliage. He walked a mile and did not like the road. It was utterly deserted and silent. He wished to be back in the trunk road in which there was some life and traffic, though few and far between: some country cart lumbering along; or an occasional motor-car with trunks and bedding strapped behind, whizzing past and disappearing in a cloud of dust; or groups of peasants moving on the edge of the road. But this branch road oppressed him with its stillness. Moreover, he had been wandering for many hours away from home, and now longed to be back there. He became desperate at the thought of home. What fine things the cook prepared! And how Mother always insisted upon serving ghee and curds herself! Oh! how he would sit before his leaf and watch Mother open the cupboard and bring out the aluminium curd-pot, and how soft and white it was as it noiselessly fell on the heap of rice on the leaf and enveloped it! A fierce hunger now raged within him. His thighs were heavy and there was pain around his hips. He did not notice it, but the sun's rays were coming obliquely from the west and the birds were on their homeward flight.

When hunger became unbearable, he plucked and ate fruits. There was a clean pond nearby.

He rested for some time and then started to go back home. The only important thing now was home, and all the rest seemed trivial beside it. The Board School affair appeared inconsequent. He marvelled at himself for having taken it seriously and rushed into all this trouble. What a fool he had been! He wished with all his heart that he had held out his hand when the headmaster raised his cane. Even if he had not done it, he wished he had gone home and told his father everything. Father would have scolded him a little (in case he went too far, Granny and Mother could always be depended upon to come to his rescue). All this scolding and frowning would have been worth while, because Father could be depended upon to get him out of any trouble. People were afraid of him. And what foolishness to forgo practice with the match only two days ahead! If the match was lost, there was no knowing what Rajam would do.

Meanwhile, Swaminathan was going back towards the trunk road. He thought he would be presently back in it, and then he had only to go straight and it would take him right into Market Road, and from there he could reach home blindfold. His parents might get angry with him if he went home so late. But he could tell them that he had lost his way. Or would that be too mild? Suppose he said that he had been kidnapped by Pathans and had to escape from them with great difficulty ...

He felt he had been walking long enough. He ought to have reached the trunk road long ago, but as he stopped and looked about, he found that he was still going along the thick avenue of figs and wood-apple. The ground was strewn with discoloured, disfigured fruits, and leaves. The road seemed to be longer now that he was going back. The fact was that he had unconsciously followed a gentle imperceptible curve, as the road cunningly branched and joined the Mempi Forest Road. Some seventy miles further it split into a number of rough irregular tracks disappearing into the thick belt of Mempi Forests. If he had just avoided this deceptive curve, he would have reached the trunk road long ago.

Night fell suddenly, and his heart beat fast. His throat went dry as he realized that he had not reached the trunk road. The trees were still thick and the road was still narrow. The trunk road was broader, and there the sky was not screened by branches. But here one could hardly see the sky; the stars gleamed through occasional gaps overhead. He quickened his pace though he was tired. He ran a little distance, his feet falling on the leaf-covered ground with a sharp rustling noise. The birds in the branches overhead started at this noise and fluttered their wings. In that deep darkness and stillness the noise of fluttering wings had an uncanny ghostly quality. Swaminathan was frightened and stood still. He must reach the trunk road and thence find his way home. He would not mind even if it were twelve o'clock when he reached the trunk road. There was something reassuring in its spaciousness and in the sparseness of vegetation. But here the closeness of the tree-trunks and their branches intertwining at the top gave the road the appearance of a black, bleak cavern with an evil spirit brooding over it.

The noise of the disturbed birds subsided. He started on again. He trod warily so as not to make a noise and disturb the birds again, though he felt an urge to run, run with all his might and reach the trunk road and home. The conflict between the impulse to run and the caution that counselled him not to run was fierce. As he walked noiselessly, slowly, suppressing the impulse to run on madly, his nerves quivered with the strain. It was as if he had been rope-walking in a gale.

His ears became abnormally sensitive. They caught every noise his feet made, with the slightest variations. His feet came down on the ground with a light tick or a subdued crackle or a gentle swish, according to the object on the ground: small dry twigs, half-green leaves, or a thick layer of dry withered leaves. There were occasional patches of bare uncovered ground, and there the noise was a light thud, or pit-pat; pit-pat-pit-pat in monotonous repetition. Every noise entered Swaminathan's ears. For some time he was conscious of nothing else. His feet said pish – pish – pat – pit – pat – swish and crackled. These noises streamed into his head, monotonously, endlessly. They were like sinister whispers, calling him to a dreadful sacrifice. He clearly heard his name whispered. There was no doubt about it. 'Swami ... Swami ... Swami ... Swami ... Swami ...' the voice said, and then the dreadful suggestion of a sacrifice. It was some devil, coming behind him noiselessly, and saying the same thing over and over again, deep into his ears. He stopped and looked about. There the immense monster crouched, with its immense black legs wide apart, and its shadowy arms joined over its head. It now swayed a little. He dared not take his eyes off it for fear that it might pounce upon him. He stood frozen to the ground and stared at this monster. Why did it cease its horrid whispers the moment he turned back? He stood staring. He might have spent about five minutes thus. And when the first thrill of fear subsided, he saw a little more clearly and found that the monster consisted of massive tree-trunks and their top branches.

He continued his journey. He was perhaps within a yard of the trunk road, and afterwards he would sing as he sauntered home. He asked himself whether he would rest a while on the trunk road or go, without stopping, home. His legs felt as if they had been made of stone. He decided that he would sit down for some time when he reached the trunk road. It did not matter. The trunk road was safe and secure even at twelve o'clock. If he took a rest, he would probably be able to run home ...

He came to a clearing. The stars were visible above. The road wound faintly in front of him. No brooding darkness, no clustering crowded avenue here. He felt a momentary ecstasy as he realized that he had come to the trunk road. It bore all the characteristics of the trunk road. The sight of the stars above, clear and uninterrupted, revived him. As he paused and watched the million twinkling bodies, he felt like bursting into music out of sheer relief. He had left behind the horrid, narrow, branch-roofed road. At this realization his strength came back to him. He decided not to waste time in resting. He felt fit to go forward. But presently he felt uneasy. He remembered clearly that the branch road began at right angles to the trunk road. But here it continued straight. He stood bewildered for a moment and then told himself that it was probably a continuation of the branch road, a continuation that he had not noticed before. Whatever it was, the trunk road must surely cut this at right angles, and if he turned to his right and went forward he would reach home. He looked to his right and left, but there was not the faintest trace of a road anywhere. He soon explained to himself that he was probably not able to see the trunk road because of the night. The road must be there all right. He turned to his right, took a step or two, and went knee-deep in quagmire. He waded through it and went forward. Long spiked grass tickled his face and in some places he was lost in undergrowth. He turned back and reached the road.

* * *

Presently he realized his position. He was on an unknown distant road at a ghostly hour. Till now the hope that he was moving towards the familiar trunk road sustained him. But now even the false hope being gone, he became faint with fear. When he understood that the trunk road was an unreal distant dream, his legs refused to support him. All the same he kept tottering onwards, knowing well that it was a meaningless, aimless march. He walked like one half-stunned. The strangeness of the hour, so silent indeed that even the drop of a leaf resounded through the place, oppressed him with a sense of inhumanity. Its remoteness gave him a feeling that he was walking into a world of horrors, subhuman and supernatural.

He collapsed like an empty bag, and wept bitterly. He called to his father, mother, granny, Rajam, and Mani. His shrill, loud cry went through the night past those half-distinct black shapes looming far ahead, which might be trees or devils or gateposts of Inferno. Now he prayed to all the gods that he knew to take him out of that place. He promised them offerings: two coconuts every Saturday to the elephant-faced Ganapathi; a vow to roll bare-bodied in dust, beg, and take the alms to the Lord of Thirupathi. He paused as if to give the gods time to consider his offer and descend from their heights to rescue him.

Now his head was full of wild imaginings. He heard heavy footfalls behind, turned and saw a huge lump of darkness coming towards him. It was too late, it had seen him. Its immense tusks showed faintly white. It came roaring, on the way putting its long trunk around a tree and plucking it out by the roots and dashing it on the ground. He could see its small eyes, red with anger, its tusks lowered, and the trunk lifted and poised ready. He just rolled to one side and narrowly escaped. He lay panting for a while, his clothes wet with sweat. He heard stealthy footsteps and a fierce growl, and before he could turn to see what it was, heavy jaws snapped behind his ears, puffing out foul hot breath on his nape. He had the presence of mind to lower his head and lie flat, and the huge yellow-and-black tiger missed him. Now a leopard, now a lion, even a whale, now a huge crowd, a mixed crowd of wild elephants, tigers, lions, and demons, surrounded him. The demons lifted him by his ears, plucked every hair on his head, and peeled off his skin from head to foot. Now what was this, coiling round his legs, cold and slimy? He shrank in horror from a scorpion that was advancing with its sting in the air. No, this was no place for a human being. The cobra and the scorpion were within an inch of him. He shrieked, scrambled to his feet, and ran. He kept looking back, the scorpion was moving as fast as he, there was no escaping it; he held his breath and with the last ounce of strength doubled his pace –

He had touched the other wicket and returned. Two runs. He stood with the bat. The captain of the Y.M.U. bowled, and he hit a sixer. The cheers were deafening. Rajam ran round the field in joy, jumped up the wall and down thrice. The next ball was bowled. Instead of hitting it, Swaminathan flung the bat aside and received it on his head. The ball rebounded and speeded back towards the bowler – the Board High School headmaster; but Swaminathan ran after the ball, overtook it half-way, caught it, and raising his arm, let it go with terrific force towards the captain's head, which was presently hit and shattered. The M.C.C. had won, and their victory was marked by chasing the Y.M.U. out of the field, with bricks and wickets, bats and balls; and Swaminathan laughed and laughed till he collapsed with exhaustion.

Ranga, the cart man, was returning to his village five miles on this side of Mempi Forests, early on Saturday morning. He had left Malgudi at two in the morning, so as to be in his village by noon. He had turned the long stretch of the Mempi Forest Road, tied the bullock-rope to the cart, and lain down. The soft tinkling of the bells and the gentle steady pace of the bullock sent him to sleep at once.

Suddenly the bullock stopped with a jerk. Ranga woke up and uttered the series of oaths and driving cries that usually gave the bullock speed, and violently tugged the rope. The bullock merely tossed its head with a tremendous jingle of its bells, but did not move. Ranga, exasperated by its conduct, got down to let the animal know and feel what he thought of it. In the dim morning light, he saw a human form across the way. He shouted. 'Hi! Get up, lazy lubber. A nice place you have found to sleep in!

Be up and doing. Do you follow me?' When the sleeper was not awakened by this advice, Ranga went forward to throw him out of the way.

'Ah, a little fellow! Why is he sleeping here?' he said, and bending closer still, exclaimed, 'Oh, Siva, he is dead!' The legs and arms, the exposed portions of the body, were damp with the slight early dew. He tore the boy's shirt and plunged his hand in and was greatly relieved to find the warmth of life still there. His simple mind tortured itself with the mystery of the whole situation. Here was a little boy from the town, his dress and appearance proclaimed, alone in this distant highway, lying nearly dead across the road. Who was he? Where did he come from? Why was he there? Ranga's brain throbbed with these questions. Devils were known to carry away human beings and leave them in distant places. It might be, or might not be. He gave up the attempt to solve the problem himself, feeling that he had better leave such things to learned people like the *sircar* officer who was staying in the Travellers' Bungalow three stones on this side of the forests. His (Ranga's) business would be nothing more than taking the boy to the officer. He gently lifted the boy and carried him to the cart.

He sat in his seat, took the ropes in his hand, raised a foot and kicked the bullock in the stomach, and loosened the rope with the advice to his animal that if it did not for once give up its usual dawdling ways, he would poke a red-hot pike into its side. Intelligently appreciating the spirit of this advice, the bullock shook itself and set off at a trot that it reserved for important occasions.

Swaminathan stared blankly before him. He could not comprehend his situation. At first he had believed he was where he had been day after day for so many years – at home. Then gradually, as his mind cleared, he remembered several remote incidents in a confused jumble. He blinked fast. He put out his arm and fumbled about. He studied the objects before him more keenly. It was an immense struggle to keep the mind alert. He fixed his eyes on a picture on the wall – or was it a calendar? – to find out if it was the same thing that hung before his bed at home. He was understanding its details little by little when all of a sudden his mind collapsed with exhaustion, and confusion began. Was there an object there at all on the wall? He was exasperated by the pranks of the mind ... He vaguely perceived a human figure in a chair nearby. The figure drew the chair nearer and said, 'That is right, boy. Are you all right now?'... These words fell on ears that had not yet awakened to life. Swaminathan was puzzled to see his father there. He wanted to know why he was doing such an extraordinary thing as sitting by his side.

'Father,' he cried, looking at the figure.

'You will see your father presently. Don't worry,' said the figure and put to him a few questions which would occur to any man with normal curiosity. Swaminathan took such a long time to answer each question and then it was all so incoherent and irrelevant that the stranger was first amused, then irritated, and in the end gave up asking questions. Swaminathan was considerably weakened by the number of problems that beset him: Who was this man? Was he Father? If he was not, why was he there? Even if he was, why was he there? Who was he? What was he saying? Why could he not utter his words louder and clearer?

This Father-and-not-Father person then left the room. He was Mr M. P. S. Nair, the District Forest Officer, just then camping near Mempi Forests. He had been out in the forest the whole day and returned to the Travellers' Bungalow only at seven in the evening. He had hardly rolled off his puttees and taken off his heavy boots when he was told about the boy. After hours of effort with food and medicine, the boy was revived. But what was the use? He was not in a fit condition to give an account of himself. If the boy's words were to be believed, he seemed to belong to some strange unpronounceable place unknown to geographers.

Early next morning Mr Nair found the boy already up and very active. In the compound, the boy stood a few yards from a tree with a heap of stones at his feet. He stopped, picked up a stone, backed a few yards, took a few quick steps, stopped abruptly, and let the stone go at a particular point on the tree-trunk. He repeated this like clockwork with stone after stone.

'Good morning, young man,' Mr Nair said. 'How are you now?'

'I am grateful to you, sir, you have saved me from great trouble.'

'Oh, yes ... You are busy?'

'I am taking practice, sir. We are playing a match against the Y.M.U. and Rajam is depending upon me for bowling. They call me Tate. I have not had practice at all – for – for a long time. I did a foolish thing in starting out and missing practice with the match coming off on – what day is this, sir?'

'Why do you want to know?'

'Please tell me, sir. I want to know how many days more we have for the match.'

'This is Sunday.'

'What? What?' Swaminathan stood petrified. Sunday! Sunday! He gazed dully at the heap of stones at his feet.

'What is the matter?'

'The match is on Sunday,' Swaminathan stammered.

'What if it is? You have still a day before you. This is only Saturday.'

'You said it was Sunday, sir.'

'No. No. This is Saturday. See the calendar if you like.'

'But you said it was Sunday.'

'Probably a slip of the tongue.'

'Sir, will you see that I am somehow at the field before Sunday?'

'Certainly, this very evening. But you must tell me which your place is and whose son you are.'

CHAPTER EIGHTEEN

THE RETURN

It was three-thirty on Sunday afternoon. The match between the M.C.C. and the Y.M.U. was still in progress. The Y.M.U. had won the toss, and were all out for eighty-six at two o'clock. The captain's was the top score, thirty-two. The M.C.C. had none to bowl him out, and he stood there like an automaton, hitting right and left, tiring out all the bowlers. He kept on for hours, and the next batsman was as formidable, though not a scorer. He exhausted the M.C.C. of the little strength that was left, and Rajam felt keenly the lack of a clever bowler.

After the interval the game started again at two-thirty, and for the hour that the M.C.C. batted the score stood at the unimpressive figure of eight with three out in quick succession. Rajam and Mani had not batted. Rajam watched the game with the blackest heart and cursed heartily everybody concerned. The match would positively close at five-thirty: just two hours more, and would the remaining eight make up at least seventy-eight and draw the match? It was a remote possibility. In his despair he felt that at least six more would follow suit without raising the score to twenty. And then he and Mani would be left. And he had a wild momentary hope that each might be able to get forty with a few judicious sixers and boundaries.

He was squatting along with his players on the ground in the shade of the compound wall.

'Raju, a minute, come here,' came a voice from above. Rajam looked up and saw his father's head over the wall. 'Father, is it very urgent?'

'It is. I won't detain you for more than a minute.'

When he hopped over the wall and was at his father's side, he was given a letter. He glanced through it, gave it back to his father, and said casually, 'So he is safe and sound. I wonder what he is doing there.' He ruminated for a second and turned to go.

'I am sending this letter to Swaminathan's father. He is sure to get a car and rush to the place. I shall have to go with him. Would you like to come?'

Rajam remained silent for a minute and said emphatically, 'No.'

'Don't you want to see your friend and bring him back?'

'I don't care,' Rajam said briefly, and joined his friends. He went back to his seat in the shade of the wall. The fourth player was promising. Rajam whispered to Mani, 'I say, that boy is not bad. Six runs already! Good, good.'

'If these fellows make at least fifty we can manage the rest.'

Rajam nodded an assent, but an unnoticed corner of his mind began to be busy with something other than the match. His father's news had stirred in him a mixture of feelings. He felt an urgent desire to tell Mani what he had just heard. 'Mani, you know Swami – ' he said and stopped short because he remembered that he was not interested in Swaminathan. Mani sprang up and asked, 'What about Swami? What about him? Tell me, Rajam. Has he been found?'

'I don't know.'

'Oh, Rajam, Rajam, you were about to say something about him.'

'Nothing. I don't care.'

Swaminathan had a sense of supreme well-being and security. He was flattered by the number of visitors that were coming to see him. His granny and mother were hovering round him ceaselessly, and it was with a sneaking satisfaction that he saw his little brother crowing unheeded in the cradle, for once overlooked and abandoned by everybody.

Many of his father's friends came to see him and behaved more or less alike. They stared at him with amusement and said how relieved they were to have him back, and asked some stereotyped questions and went away after uttering one or two funny remarks. Father went out with one of his friends. Before going, he said, 'Swami, I hope I shall not have to look for you when I come back.' Swaminathan was hurt by this remark. He felt it to be cruel and inconsiderate.

After his father left he felt more free, free to lord over a mixed gathering consisting of Mother's and Granny's friends and some old men who were known to the family long before Swaminathan's father was born.

Everybody gazed at Swaminathan and uttered loud remarks to his face. Through all this crowd Swaminathan espied the cook and bestowed a smile over him. Over the babble the cook uttered some irrelevant, happy remark, which concluded with the hope that now Father, Mother and Granny might resume the practice of taking food. Swaminathan was about to shout something in reply when his attention was diverted by the statement of a widow, who, rolling her eyes and pointing heavenward, said that He alone had saved the boy, and who could have foreseen that the Forest Officer would be there to save the boy from the jaws of wild beasts? Granny said that she would have to set about fulfilling the great promises of offerings made to the Lord of the Seven Hills to whom alone she owed the safe return of the child.

Mother had meanwhile disappeared into the kitchen and now came out with a tumbler of hot coffee with plenty of sugar in it, and some steaming tiffin on a plate. Swaminathan, quickly and with great relish, disposed of both. A mixed fragrance, delicate and evocative, came from the kitchen.

Swaminathan cast his mind and felt ashamed of himself for his conduct with the Forest Officer, when that harassed gentleman was waiting for a reply from the Deputy Superintendent of Police, which took the form of a taxi drawing up before the Travellers' Bungalow, disgorging Father, Mother, Rajam's father, and an inspector of police. What a scene his mother created when she saw him! He had at first feared that Rajam's father and the inspector were going to handcuff him. What a fine man Rajam's father was! And how extraordinarily kind his own father was! So much so that, five minutes after meeting him, Swaminathan blurted out the whole story, from his evasion of drill classes to his disappearance, without concealing a single detail. What was there so funny in his narration? Everybody laughed uproariously, and Mother covered her face with the end of her *sari* and wiped her eyes at the end of every fit of laughter ... This retrospect was spoiled by one memory. He had forgotten to take leave of the Forest Officer, though that gentleman opened the door of the car and stood near it. Swaminathan's conscience scorched him at the recollection of it. A gulp came to his throat at the thought of the kindly District Forest Officer, looking after the car speeding away from him, thoroughly broken-hearted by the fact that a person whose life he had saved should be so wicked as to go away without saying goodbye.

His further reflections on the subject and the quiet discussion among the visitors about the possible dangers that might have befallen Swaminathan, were all disturbed – destroyed, would be more accurate – by a tornado-like personality sweeping into their midst with the tremendous shout, 'What! Oh! Swami!' The visitors were only conscious of some mingled shoutings and brisk movements and after that both Swaminathan and Mani disappeared from the hall.

As they came to a secluded spot in the backyard Mani said, 'I thought you were dead or some such thing.'

'I was, nearly.'

'What a fool you were to get frightened of that Headmaster and run away like that! Rajam told me everything. I wanted to break your shoulders for not calling me when you had come to our school and called Rajam ...'

'I had no time, Mani.'

'Oh, Swami. I am so glad to see you alive. I was – I was very much troubled about you. Where were you all along?'

'I – I – I really can't say. I don't know where I was. Somewhere – ' He recounted in this style his night of terrors and the subsequent events.

'Have I not always said that you were the worst coward I have ever known? You would have got safely back home if you had kept your head cool and followed the straight road. You imagined all sorts of things.'

Swaminathan took this submissively and said, 'But I can't believe that I was picked up by that cart man. I don't remember it at all.'

Mani advised, 'If he happens to come to your place during Deepavali or Pongal festival, don't behave like a niggard. He deserves a bag of gold. If he had not cared to pick you up, you might have been eaten by a tiger.'

'And I have done another nasty thing,' Swaminathan said, 'I didn't think and say goodbye to the Forest Officer before I came away. He was standing near the car all the time.'

'If he was so near why did you seal your mouth?'

'I didn't think of it till the car had come half-way.'

'You are a – a very careless fellow. You ought to have thanked him.'

'Now what shall I do? Shall I write to him?'

'Do. But do you know his address?'

'My father probably does.'

'What will you write?'

'Just tell him – I don't know. I shall have to ask Father about it. Some nice letter, you know. I owe him so much for bringing me back in time for the match.'

'What are you saying?' Mani asked.

'Are you deaf? I was saying that I must ask Father to write a nice letter, that is all.'

'Not that. I heard something about the match. What is it?'

'Yes?'

'Are you mad to think that you are in time for the match?' asked Mani. He then related to Swaminathan the day's encounter with the Y.M.U. and the depressing results, liberally explaining what Swaminathan's share was in the collapse of the M.C.C.

'Why did you have it today?' Swaminathan asked weakly.

'Why not?'

'But this is only Saturday.'

'Who said that?'

'The Forest Officer said that this was only Saturday.'

'You may go and tell him that he is a blockhead,' Mani retorted.

Swaminathan persisted that it could not be Sunday till Mani threatened to throw him down, sit on his body, and press his entrails out. Swaminathan remained in silence, and then said, 'I won't write him that letter. He has deceived me.'

'Who?'

'The Forest Officer ... And what does Rajam say about me?'

'Rajam says a lot, which I don't wish to repeat. But I will tell you one thing. Never appear before him. He will never speak to you. He may even shoot you on sight.'

'What have I done?' asked Swaminathan.

'You have ruined the M.C.C. You need not have promised us, if you had wanted to funk. At least you could have told us you were going away. Why did you hide it from Rajam when you saw him at our school? That is what Rajam wants to know.'

Swaminathan quietly wept, and begged Mani to pacify Rajam and convey to him Swaminathan's love and explanations. Mani refused to interfere. 'You don't know Rajam. He is a gem. But it is difficult to get on with him.'

With a forced optimism in his tone Swaminathan said, 'He will be all right when he sees me. I shall see him tomorrow morning.'

Mani wanted to change the topic, and asked: 'Are you going back to school?'

'Yes, next week. My father has already seen the headmaster, and it seems things will be all right in the school. He seems to have known everything about the Board School business.'

'Yes, I and Rajam told him everything.'

'After all, I shall have to go back to the Board High School. Father says I can't change my school now.'

CHAPTER NINETEEN

PARTING PRESENT

On Tuesday morning, ten days later, Swaminathan rose from bed with a great effort of will at five o'clock. There was still half an hour for the train to arrive at the Malgudi Station and leave it four minutes later, carrying away Rajam for ever.

Swaminathan had not known that this was to happen till Mani came and told him, on the previous night at about ten, that Rajam's father was transferred to Trichinopoly and the whole family would be leaving Malgudi on the following morning. Mani said that he had known it for about a week, but Rajam had strictly forbidden him to say anything about it to Swaminathan. But at the last moment Mani could not contain himself and had violated Rajam's ban.

A great sense of desolation seized Swaminathan at once. The world seemed to have become blank all of a sudden. The thought of Lawley Extension without Rajam appalled him with its emptiness. He swore that he would never go there again. He raved at Mani. And Mani bore it patiently. Swaminathan could not think of a world without Rajam. What was he to do in the evenings? How was he to spend the holiday afternoons? Whom was he to think of as his friend? At the same time he was filled with a sense of guilt: he had not gone and seen Rajam even once after his return. Fear, shame, a feeling of uncertainty, had made him postpone his visit to Rajam day after day. Twice he had gone up to the gate of Rajam's house but had turned back, his courage and determination giving way at the last moment. He was in this state, hoping to see Rajam every tomorrow, when Mani came to him with the shattering news. Swaminathan wanted to rush up to Rajam's house that very second and claim him once again. But – but – he felt awkward and shirked. Tomorrow morning at the station. The training was leaving at six. He would go to the station at five.

'Mani, will you call me at five tomorrow morning?'

'No. I am going to sleep in Rajam's house, and go with him to the station.'

For a moment Swaminathan was filled with the darkest jealousy. Mani to sleep in Rajam's house, keep him company till the last moment, talk and laugh till midnight, and he to be excluded! He wanted to cling to Mani desperately and stop his going.

When Mani left, Swaminathan went in, opened his dealwood box, and stood gazing into it. He wanted to pick out something that could be presented to Rajam on the following morning. The contents of the box were a confused heap of odds and ends of all metals and materials. Here a cardboard box that had once touched Swaminathan's fancy, and there a toy watch, a catalogue, some picture-books, nuts and bolts, disused insignificant parts of defunct machinery, and so on to the brim. He rummaged in it for half an hour, but there seemed to be nothing worth taking to Rajam. The only decent object in it was a green engine given to him over a year ago by Rajam. The sight of it, now dented and chipped in a couple of places and lying between an empty thread-reel and a broken porcelain vase, stirred in him vivid memories. He became maudlin ... He wondered if he would have to return that engine to Rajam now that they were no longer friends. He picked it up to take it with him to the station and return it to Rajam. On second thoughts he put it back, partly because he loved the engine very much, partly because he told himself it might be an insult to reject a present after such a long time ... Rajam was a good reader, and Swaminathan decided to give him a book. He could not obviously give him any of the textbooks. He took out the only book that he respected (as the fact of his separating it from the textbooks on his desk and giving it a place in the dealwood box showed). It was a neat tiny volume of Andersen's *Fairy Tales* that his father had bought in Madras years ago for him. He could never get through the book to his satisfaction. There were too many unknown, unpronounceable English words in it. He would give this book to Rajam. He went to his desk and wrote on the fly-leaf 'To my dearest friend Rajam.'

* * *

Malgudi Station was half dark when Swaminathan reached it with the tiny volume of Andersen's *Fairy Tales* in his hand. The station-master was just out of bed and was working at the table with a kerosene light, not minding in the least the telegraph keys that were tapping away endless messages to the dawn.

A car drew up outside. Swaminathan saw Rajam, his father, mother, someone he did not know, and Mani, getting down. Swaminathan shrank at the sight of Rajam. All his determination oozed out as he saw the captain approach the platform, dressed like a 'European boy'. His very dress and tidiness made Swaminathan feel inferior and small. He shrank back and tried to make himself inconspicuous.

Almost immediately, the platform began to fill with police officers and policemen. Rajam was unapproachable. He was standing with his father in the middle of a cluster of people in uniform. All that Swaminathan could see of Rajam was his left leg, through a gap between two policemen. Even that was obstructed when the policemen drew closer. Swaminathan went round, in search of further gaps.

The train was sighted. There was at once a great bustle. The train hissed and boomed into the platform. The hustle and activity increased. Rajam and his party moved to the edge of the platform. Things were dragged and pushed into a Second Class compartment with desperate haste by a dozen policemen. Rajam's mother got in. Rajam and his father were standing outside the compartment. The police officers now barricaded them completely, bidding them farewell and garlanding them. There was a momentary glimpse of Rajam with a huge rose garland round his neck.

Swaminathan looked for and found Mani. 'Mani, Rajam is going away.'

'Yes, Swami, he is going away.'

'Mani, will Rajam speak to me?'

'Oh, yes. Why not?' asked Mani.

Now Rajam and his father had got into the compartment. The door was closed and the door-handle turned.

'Mani, this book must be given to Rajam,' Swaminathan said. Mani saw that there was no time to lose. The bell rang. They desperately pushed their way through the crowd and stood under a window. Swaminathan could hardly see anything above. His head hardly came up to the door-handle. The crowd pressed from behind. Mani shouted into the compartment: 'Here is Swami to bid you goodbye.' Swaminathan stood on his toes. A head leaned over the window and said: 'Goodbye, my Mani. Don't forget me. Write to me.'

'Goodbye, friend ... Here is Swami,' Mani said.

Rajam craned his neck. Swaminathan's upturned eyes met his. At the sight of the familiar face Swaminathan lost control of himself and cried: 'Oh, Rajam, Rajam, you are going away, away. When will you come back?'

Rajam kept looking at him without a word and then (as it seemed to Swaminathan) opened his mouth to say something, when everything was disturbed by the guard's blast and the hoarse whistle of the engine. There was a slight rattling of chains, a tremendous hissing, and the train began to move. Rajam's face, with the words still unuttered on his lips, receded.

Swaminathan became desperate and blurted: 'Oh, Mani! This book must be given to him,' and pressed the book into Mani's hand.

Mani ran along the platform with the train and shouted over the noise of the train: 'Goodbye, Rajam. Swami gives you this book.' Rajam held out his hand for the book, and took it, and waved a farewell. Swaminathan waved back frantically.

Swaminathan and Mani stood as if glued where they were, and watched the train. The small red lamp of the last van could be seen for a long time, it diminished in size every minute, and disappeared around a bend. All the jarring, rattling, clanking, spurting, and hissing of the moving train softened in the distance into something that was half a sob and half a sigh. Swaminathan said: 'Mani, I am glad he has taken the book. Mani, he waved to me. He was about to say something when the train started. Mani, he did wave to me and to me alone. Don't deny it.'

'Yes, yes,' Mani agreed.

Swaminathan broke down and sobbed.

Mani said: 'Don't be foolish, Swami.'

'Does he ever think of me now?' Swaminathan asked hysterically.

'Oh, yes,' said Mani. He paused and added: 'Don't worry. If he has not talked to you, he will write to you.'

'What do you mean?'

'He told me so,' Mani said.

'But he does not know my address.'

'He asked me, and I have given it,' said Mani.

'No. No. It is a lie. Come on, tell me, what is my address?'

'It is – it is – never mind what ... I have given it to Rajam.'

Swaminathan looked up and gazed on Mani's face to find out whether Mani was joking or was in earnest. But for once Mani's face had become inscrutable.

THE BACHELOR OF ARTS

PART ONE

CHAPTER ONE

Chandran was just climbing the steps of the College Union when Natesan, the secretary, sprang on him and said, 'You are just the person I was looking for. You remember your old promise?'

'No,' said Chandran promptly, to be on the safe side.

'You promised that I could count on you for a debate any time I was hard pressed for a speaker. You must help me now. I can't get a Prime Mover for the debate tomorrow evening. The subject is that in the opinion of this house historians should be slaughtered first. You are the Prime Mover. At five tomorrow evening.' He tried to be off, but Chandran caught his hand and held him: 'I am a history student. I can't move the subject. What a subject! My professor will eat me up.'

'Don't worry. I won't invite your professor.'

'But why not some other subject?'

'We can't change the Union Calendar now.'

Chandran pleaded, 'Any other day, any other subject.'

'Impossible,' said the secretary, and shook himself free.

'At least make me the Prime Opposer,' pleaded Chandran.

'You are a brilliant Mover. The notices will be out in an hour. Tomorrow evening at five ...'

Chandran went home and all night had dreams of picking up a hatchet and attacking his history professor, Ragavachar. He sat down next morning to prepare for the debate. He took out a piece of paper and wrote:

'His'ians to be slaughtered first. Who should come second? Scientists or carpenters? Who will make knife-handles if carpenters are killed first? In any case why kill anybody? Must introduce one or two humorous stories. There was once a his'ian who dug in his garden and unearthed two ancient coins, which supplied the missing link of some period or other; but lo! they were not ancient coins after all but only two old buttons ... Oh, a most miserable story. Idiotic. What am I to do? Where can I get a book full of jokes of a historical nature? A query in some newspaper. Sir, will you or any of your numerous readers kindly let me know where I can get historical humours?' It was quite an hour before Chandran woke up and his pen ceased. He looked through the jottings that were supposed to be notes for his evening speech. He suddenly realized that his mind wandered when he held pen over paper, but he could concentrate intensely when he walked about with bent head. He considered this a very important piece of self-realization.

He pushed his chair back, put on his coat, and went out. After about two hours of wandering he returned home, having thought of only one argument for killing historians first, namely, that they might not be there to misrepresent the facts when scientists, poets, and statesmen were being killed in their turn. It appeared to him a very brilliant argument. He could see before him a whole house rocking with laughter....

Chandran spent a useful half-hour gazing at the college notice board. He saw his name in a notice announcing the evening's debate. He marched along the corridor, with a preoccupied look, to his class. With difficulty he listened to the lecture and took down notes. When the hour closed and the lecturer left the class, Chandran sat back, put the cap on his pen, and let his mind dwell on the subject of historians. He had just begun a short analysis of the subject when Ramu, sitting three benches down the gallery, shouted to him: 'Shall we go out for a moment till Brown comes in?'

'No.'

'Why not?'

Chandran was irritated. 'You can go if you like.'

'Certainly. And you can just stay there and mope,' said Ramu, and walked down the gallery. Chandran felt relieved at his exit, and was settling down to further meditations on historians when somebody asked him to lend his notes of the lecture in the previous hour; somebody else wanted something else. It went on like that till Professor Brown, principal of the college, entered the class with a pile of books under his arm. This was an important hour, Greek Drama. Chandran had once again to switch his mind off the debate.

At the end of the hour Chandran went to the library and looked through the catalogue. He opened several shelves and examined the books. He could not get the slightest help or guidance. The subject of the debate seemed to be unique. There was any quantity of literature in support of history, but not one on the extermination of historians.

He went home at three. He had still two hours before the debate. He said to his mother, 'I am speaking in a debate this evening. I am now going to my room to prepare. Nobody must knock on my door or shout near my window.'

He came out of his room at four-thirty, ran up and down the hall, banged his fists on the bathroom door, splashed cold water on his head, and ran back to his room. He combed and brushed his crop, put on his chocolate-coloured tweed coat, which was reserved for special occasions, and hurried out of the house.

Natesan, the secretary, who was waiting with a perspiring face on the Union veranda, led Chandran into the hall and pushed him into his seat – the first of the four cushioned chairs arranged below the platform for the main debaters. Chandran mopped his face with his handkerchief and looked about. The gallery, built to accommodate about a thousand members of the Union, was certainly not filled to overflowing. There were about fifty from the junior classes and a score from the Final Year classes. Natesan bent over Chandran's shoulder and whispered, 'Good house, isn't it?' It was quite a big gathering for a Union debate.

A car stopped outside with a roar. The secretary dashed across the hall and returned in a moment, walking sideways, with a feeble official smile on his face, followed by Professor Brown. He led the professor to the high-backed chair on the platform, and whispered to him that he might open the proceedings. Professor Brown rose and announced, 'I call upon Mr H. V. Chandran to move the proposition ...' and sat down.

The audience clapped their hands. Chandran rose, looked fixedly at the paperweight on the table, and began, 'Mr Speaker, I am certain that this house, so well known for its sanity and common sense, is going to back me solidly when I say that historians should be slaughtered first. I am a student of History and I ought to know...'

He went on thus for about twenty minutes, inspired by the applause with which the audience received many of his cynicisms.

After that the Prime Opposer held the attention of the audience for about twenty minutes. Chandran noted with slight displeasure that the audience received his speech with equal enthusiasm. And then the seconders of the prime speakers droned on for about ten minutes, each almost repeating what their principals had said. When the speakers in the gallery rose there was an uproar, and Professor Brown had to ring the bell and shout 'Order, order.' Chandran felt very bored. Now that he had delivered his speech he felt that the speeches of the others in the hall were both unnecessary and inferior. His eyes wandered about the hall. He looked at the Speaker on the platform. He kept gazing at Professor Brown's pink face. Here he is, Chandran thought, pretending to press the bell and listen to the speeches, but really his thoughts are at the tennis court and the card table in the English Club. He is here not out of love for us, but merely to keep up appearances. All Europeans are like this. They will take their thousand or more a month, but won't do the slightest service to Indians with a sincere heart. They must be paid this heavy amount for spending their time in the English Club. Why should not these fellows admit Indians to their clubs? Sheer colour arrogance. If ever I get into power I shall see that Englishmen attend clubs along with Indians and are not so exclusive. Why not give the poor devils – so far away from their home – a chance to club together at least for a few hours at the end of a day's work? Anyway who invited them here?

Into this solo discussion Professor Brown's voice impinged: 'Members from the House having expressed their views, and the Prime Opposer having summed up, I call upon Mr Chandran to speak before putting the proposition to the vote.'

Chandran hurriedly made one or two scratches on a sheet of paper, rose, and began: 'Mr Speaker and the Honourable House, I have followed with keen excitement the views expressed by the honourable members of this House. It has considerably lightened my task as the Prime Mover. I have no doubt what the verdict of this House will be on this proposition...' He spun out sentences till the Speaker rang the bell to stop him. Before sitting down he threw in his anecdote about the professor who dug up brass buttons in his garden.

When the division was taken the House, by an overwhelming majority, voted for an early annihilation of historians. Chandran felt victorious. He dramatically stretched his arm across the table and shook hands with the Prime Opposer.

Professor Brown rose and said that technically he ought not to speak, and then explained for five minutes why historians should be slaughtered and for five minutes why they should be deified. He complimented the movers on their vigorous arguments for the proposition, and the opposers on the able stand they had taken.

As soon as he sat down, the secretary jumped on to the platform and mumbled a vote of thanks. By the time the vote of thanks was over the hall had become empty and silent.

Chandran lingered in the doorway as the lights were dimmed, and the secretary, in a very exhausted condition, supervised the removal of the paperweights and table-cloth to the store-room.

'You are coming my way?' Chandran asked.

'Yes.'

'Well, the meeting is over,' said the secretary as they descended the Union steps. Chandran hoped that the secretary would tell him something about his speech. But the secretary was busy with his own thoughts. 'I am sorry I ever took up this business,' he said. 'Hardly any time is left over for my studies. We are already in the middle of August and I don't know what Political Philosophy is.'

Chandran was not interested in the travails of a secretary. He wanted him to say something about his own speech in the debate. So he said, 'Nobody invited you to become the secretary. You forget that you begged, borrowed, and stole votes at the Union elections.'

'I agree with you,' the secretary said. 'But what is to be done about it now?'

'Resign,' said Chandran. He resented the secretary's superficial interest in Chandran's speech. He had cringed for Chandran's help before the debate, and immediately the thing was over did not trouble to make the slightest reference to the speech.

'I will tell you a secret,' the secretary said. 'If I had kept clear of the Union elections, I should have saved nearly seventy rupees.'

'What do you mean?'

'Every vote was purchased with coffee and tiffin, and, in the election month, the restaurant bill came to seventy. My father wrote to me from the village asking if I thought that rupees lay scattered in our village street.'

Chandran felt sympathy for him, but was still disappointed that he made no reference to his speech. There was no use waiting for him to open the subject. He was a born grumbler. Settle all his debts and give him all the comforts in the world, he would still have something to grumble about.

'I have not paid the restaurant bill yet ...' began the secretary. Chandran ignored this and asked abruptly:

'What do you think of the Boss's speech?'

'As humorous as ever,' said the secretary.

'It is an idiotic belief you fellows have that everything he says is humorous. He has only to move his lips for you to hold your sides and laugh.'

'Why are you so cynical?'

'I admit he has genuine flashes of humour, but ...'

'You can't deny that Brown is a fine principal. He has never turned down any request to preside at meetings.'

'That is all you seem to care for in a man. Presiding over meetings! It proves nothing.'

'No. No. I only mean that he is a very pleasant man.'

'He is a humbug, take it from me,' said Chandran. 'He gets his thousand a month, and no wonder he is pleasant. Remember that he is a scoundrel at heart.'

They had now covered half the length of Market Road. As they passed the fountain in the Square, Chandran realized that he was wasting much time and energy in a futile discussion. A few paces more and they would be at the mouth of Kabir Street. A few more moments of that futile discussion and the other would turn and vanish in the darkness. Chandran resolved to act while there was still time: 'Secretary, how did you like my speech today?'

The secretary stopped, gripped Chandran's hand and said, 'It was a wonderful speech. You should have seen Brown's face as he watched you. He would certainly have clapped his hands, but for the fact that he was the Speaker ... I say, I really liked your story about the professor and his buttons. Such a thing is quite possible, you know. Fine speech, fine speech. So few are really gifted with eloquence.'

When they came to Kabir Street, Chandran asked sympathetically, 'You live here?'

'Yes.'

'With your people?'

'They are in the village. I have taken a room in a house where a family lives. I pay a rent of about three rupees. It is a small room.'

'Boarding?'

'I go to a hotel. The whole thing comes to about fifteen rupees. Wretched food, and the room is none too good. But what can I do? After the elections my father cut my allowance, and I had to quit the college hostel. Why don't you come to my room some day?'

'Certainly, with pleasure,' said Chandran.

'Good-night.'

The secretary had gone a few yards down Kabir Street, when Chandran called suddenly, 'Here, secretary!' The other came back. Chandran said, 'I did not mean that thing about your resignation seriously. Just for fun.'

'Oh, it is all right,' said the secretary.

'Another thing,' said Chandran. 'Don't for a moment think that I dislike Brown. I agree with you entirely when you say he is a man with a pleasant manner. He has a first-rate sense of humour. He is a great scholar. It is really a treat to be taught Drama by him. I was only trying to suggest that people saw humour even where he was serious. So please don't mistake me.'

'Not at all,' said the secretary, and melted in the darkness of Kabir Street.

Chandran had still a quarter of Market Road to walk. A few dim Municipal lamps, and the gas-lamps of the roadside shops, lit the way. Chandran walked, thinking of the secretary. The poor idiot! Seemed to be always in trouble and always grumbling. Probably borrowed a lot. Must be taking things on credit everywhere, in addition to living in a dingy room and eating bad food. What with a miserly father in the village and the secretary's work and one thing and another, how was he to pass his examination? Not a bad sort. Seemed to be a sensible fellow.

His feet had mechanically led him to Lawley Extension. His was the last bungalow in the Second Cross Road of the Extension. As he came before the house that was the last but one, he stopped and shouted from the road, 'Ramu!'

'Coming!' a voice answered from inside.

Ramu came out. 'Didn't you come to the debate?' Chandran asked.

'I tried to be there, but my mother wanted me to escort her to the market. How did it go off?'

'Quite well, I think. The proposition was carried.'

'Really!' Ramu exclaimed, and shook Chandran's hand.

They were as excited as if it were the Finance Bill before the Legislative Assembly in Delhi.

'My speech was not bad,' said Chandran. 'Brown presided. I was told that he liked it immensely ...'

'Good crowd?'

'Fairly good. Two rows of the gallery were full. I am really sorry you were not there.'

'How did the others speak?'

'The voting ought to indicate. Brown really made a splendid speech in the end. It was full of the most uproarious humour.'

Chandran asked, 'Would you care to see a picture tonight?'

'It's nearly nine.'

'It doesn't matter. You've finished your dinner. I won't take even five minutes. Put on your coat and come.'

Ramu asked, 'I hope you are paying for both of us?'

'Of course,' said Chandran.

As Chandran came to his gate, he saw his father in the veranda, pacing up and down. Late-coming was one of the few things that upset him. Chandran hesitated for a moment before lifting the gate chain. He opened the gate a little, slipped in, and put the chain back on its hook noiselessly. His usual move after this would be to slip round to the back-door and enter the house without his father's knowledge. But now he had a surge of self-respect. He realized that what he usually did was a piece of evasive cowardice worthy of an adolescent. He was not eighteen but twenty-one. At twenty-one to be afraid of one's parents and adopt sneaky ways! He would be a graduate very soon and he was already a remarkable orator!

This impulse to sneak in was very boyish. He felt very sorry for it and remedied it by unnecessarily lifting the gate chain and letting it noisily down. The slightest noise at the gate excited an alert watchfulness in his father. And as his father stood looking towards the gate, Chandran swaggered along the drive with an independent air, but within he had a feeling that he should have chosen some other day for demonstrating his independence. Here he was, later than ever, with a cinema programme before him, and his father would certainly stop him and ask a lot of questions. He mounted the veranda steps. His father said, 'It is nine.'

'I spoke in a debate, Father. It was late when it closed.'

'How did you fare in the debate?'

Chandran gave him an account of it, all the time bothered about the night show. Father never encouraged anyone to attend a night show.

'Very good,' Father said. 'Now get in and have your food. Your mother is waiting.'

Chandran, about to go in, said casually, 'Father, Ramu will be here in a moment; please ask him to wait.'

'All right.'

'We are going to a cinema tonight ... We are in a rather festive mood after the debate.'

'H'm. But I wouldn't advise you to make it a habit. Late shows are very bad for the health.'

He was in the dining-room in a moment, sitting before his leaf and shouting to the cook to hurry up.

The cook said, 'Please call your mother. She is waiting for you.'

'All right. Bring me first rice and curd.'

He then gave a shout, 'Mother!' which reached her as she sat in the back veranda, turning the prayer beads in her hand, looking at the coconut trees at the far end of the compound. As she turned the beads, her lips uttered the holy name of Sri Rama, part of her mind busied itself with thoughts of her husband, home, children, and relatives, and her eyes took in the delicate beauty of coconut trees waving against a starlit sky.

By the time she reached the dining-room Chandran had finished his dinner. She slowly walked to the *pooja* room, hung the string of beads on a nail, prostrated before the gods, and then came to her leaf. By that time Chandran was gone. Mother sat before her leaf and asked the cook, 'Didn't he eat well?'

'No. He took only rice and curd. He bolted it down.'

She called Chandran.

'What, Mother?'

'Why are you in such a hurry?'

'I am going to the cinema.'

'I had that potato sauce prepared specially for you, and you have eaten only curd and rice! Fine boy!'

'Mother, give me a rupee.'

She took out her key bunch and threw it at him. 'Take it from the drawer. Bring the key back.'

They walked to the cinema. Chandran stopped at a shop to buy some betel leaves and a packet of cigarettes. Attending a night show was not an ordinary affair. Chandran was none of your business-like automatons who go to a cinema, sit there, and return home. It was an aesthetic experience to be approached with due preparation. You must chew the betel leaves and nut, chew gently, until the heart was stimulated and threw out delicate beads of perspiration and caused a fine tingling sensation behind the ears; on top of that you must light a cigarette, inhale the fumes, and with the night breeze blowing on your perspiring forehead, go to the cinema, smoke more cigarettes there, see the picture, and from there go on to an hotel nearby for hot coffee at midnight, take some more betel leaves and cigarettes, and go home and sleep. This was the ideal way to set about a night show.

Chandran squeezed the maximum aesthetic delight out of the experience, and Ramu's company was most important to him. It was his presence that gave a sense of completion to things. He too smoked, chewed, drank coffee, laughed (he was the greatest laugher in the world), admired Chandran, ragged him, quarrelled with him, breathed delicious scandal over the names of his professors and friends and unknown people.

The show seemed to have already started, because there was no crowd outside the Select Picture House. It was the only theatre that the town possessed, a long hall roofed with corrugated iron sheets. At the small ticket-window Chandran inquired, 'Has the show begun?'

'Yes, just,' said the ticket man, giving the stock reply.

You might be three-quarters of an hour late, yet the man at the ticket-window would always say, 'Yes, just.'

'Hurry up, Ramu,' Chandran cried as Ramu slackened his pace to admire a giant poster in the narrow passage leading to the four-annas entrance.

The hall was dark; the ticket collector at the entrance took their tickets and held apart the curtains. Ramu and Chandran looked in, seeking by the glare of the picture on the screen for vacant seats. There were two seats at the farthest end. They pushed their way across the knees of the people already seated. 'Head down!' somebody shouted from a back seat, as two heads obstructed the screen. Ramu and Chandran stooped into their seats.

It was the last five minutes of a comic in which Jas Jim was featured. That fat genius, wearing a ridiculous cap, was just struggling out of a paint barrel.

Chandran clicked his tongue in despair: 'What a pity. I didn't know there was a Jas two-reeler with the picture. We ought to have come earlier.'

Ramu sat rapt. He exploded with laughter. 'What a genius he is!' Chandran murmured as Jas got on his feet, wearing the barrel around his waist like a kilt. He walked away from Chandran, but turned once to throw a wink at the spectators, and, taking a step back, stumbled and fell, and rolled off, and the picture ended. A central light was switched on. Chandran and Ramu raised themselves in their seats, craned their necks, and surveyed the hall.

The light went out again, the projector whirred. Scores of voices read aloud in a chorus, 'Godfrey T. Memel presents Vivian Troilet and Georgie Lomb in *Lightguns of Lauro...*' and then came much unwanted information about the people who wrote the story, adapted it, designed the dresses, cut the film to its proper length, and so on. Then the lyrical opening: 'Nestling in the heart of the Mid-West, Lauro city owed its tranquillity to the eagle-eyed sheriff –'; then a scene showing a country girl (Vivian Troilet) wearing a check skirt, going up a country lane. Thus started, though with a deceptive quietness, it moved at a breathless pace, supplying love, valour, villainy, intrigue, and battle in enormous quantities for a whole hour. The notice 'Interval' on the screen, and the lights going up, brought Chandran and Ramu down to the ordinary plane. The air was thick with tobacco smoke. Ramu yawned, stood up, and gazed at the people occupying the more expensive seats behind them. 'Chandar, Brown is here with some girl in the First Class.'

'May be his wife,' Chandran commented without turning.

'It is not his wife.'

'Must be some other girl, then. The white fellows are born to enjoy life. Our people really don't know how to live. If a person is seen with a girl by his side, a hundred eyes stare at him and a hundred tongues comment, whereas no European ever goes out without taking a girl with him.'

'This is a wretched country,' Ramu said with feeling.

At this point Chandran had a fit of politeness. He pulled Ramu down, saying that it was very bad manners to stand up and stare at the people in the back seats.

Lights out again. Some slide advertisements, each lasting a second.

'Good fellow, he gets through these inflictions quickly,' said Chandran.

'For each advertisement he gets twenty rupees a month.'

'No, it is only fifteen.'

'But somebody said that it was twenty.'

'It is fifteen rupees. You can take it from me,' Chandran said.

'Even then, what a fraud! Not one stays long enough. I hardly take in the full name of that baby's nourishing food, when they tell me what I ought to smoke. Idiots. I hate advertisements.'

The advertisements ended and the story started again from where it had been left off. The hero smelt the ambush ten yards ahead. He took a short cut, climbed a rock, and scared the ruffians from behind. And so on and on it went, through fire and water, and in the end the good man Lomb always came out triumphant; he was an upright man, a courageous man, a handsome man, and a strong man, and he had to win in the end. Who could not foresee it? And yet every day at every show the happy end was awaited with breathless suspense. Even the old sheriff (all along opposed to the union of Vivian with Georgie) was suddenly transformed, and with tears in his eyes he placed her hands on his. There was a happy moment before the end, when the lovers' heads were shown on an immense scale, their lips welded in a kiss. Good-night.

Lights on. People poured out of the exits, sleepy, yawning, rubbing their smarting eyes. This was the worst part of the evening, this trudge back home, all the way from the Select Picture House to Lawley Extension. Two or three cars sounded their horns and started from the theatre.

'Lucky rascals. They will be in their beds in five minutes. When I start earning I shall buy a car first of all. Nothing like it. You can just see the picture and go straight to bed.'

'Coffee?' Chandran asked, when they passed a brightly lit coffee hotel.

'I don't much care.'

'Nor do I.'

They walked in silence for the most part, occasionally exchanging some very dull, languid jokes.

As soon as his house was reached, Ramu muttered, 'Good-night. See you tomorrow,' and slipped through his gate.

Chandran walked on alone, opened the gate silently, woke up his younger brother sleeping in the hall, had the hall door opened, and fumbled his way to his room. He removed his coat in the dark, flung it on a chair, kicked a roll of bedding on the floor, and dropped down on it and closed his eyes even before the bed had spread out.

CHAPTER TWO

July, August, September, and October were months that glided past without touching the conscience. One got up in the morning, studied a bit, attended the classes, promenaded the banks of Sarayu River in the evenings, returned home at about eight-thirty, talked a little about things in general with the people at home, and then went to bed. It did not matter whether all the books were on the table or whether the notes of lectures were up-to-date. Day after day was squandered thus till one fine morning the young men opened their eyes and found themselves face to face with November. The first of November was to a young man of normal indifference the first reminder of the final trial – the examination. He now realized that half the college year was already spent. What one ought to do in a full year must now be done in just half the time.

On November the first Chandran left his bed at 5 a.m., bathed in cold water, and sat at his study table, before even his mother, the earliest riser in the house, was up. He sat there strengthening himself with several resolutions. One was that he would get up every day at the same hour, bathe in cold water, and get through three hours of solid work before starting for the college. The second resolution was that he would be back home before eight in the evenings and study till eleven-thirty. He also resolved not to smoke because it was bad for the heart, and a very sound heart was necessary for the examination.

He took out a sheet of paper and noted down all his subjects. He calculated the total number of preparation hours that were available from November the first to March. He had before him over a thousand hours, including the twelve-hour preparations on holidays. Of these thousand hours a just allotment of so many hundred hours was to be made for Modern History, Ancient History, Political Theories, Greek Drama, Eighteenth-Century

Prose, and Shakespeare. He then drew up a very complicated time-table, which would enable one to pay equal attention to all subjects. Balance in preparation was everything. What was the use of being able to score a hundred per cent in Modern European History if Shakespeare was going to drag you in the mire?

Out of the daily six hours, three were to be devoted to the Optional Subjects and three to the Compulsory. In the morning the compulsory subjects, and Literature at night. European History needed all the freshness and sharpness of the morning brain, while it would be a real pleasure to read Literature in the evenings.

He put down for that day *Othello* and the Modern Period in Indian History. He would finish these two in about forty-eight hours and then take up Milton and Greek History.

And he settled down to this programme with a scowl on his face.

The Modern Period in Indian History, which he had to take up immediately, presented innumerable difficulties. The texts on the subject were many, the notes of class lectures very bulky. Moreover, if he went on studying the Modern Period, what was to happen to the Mediaeval Period and the Ancient? He could not afford to neglect those two important sections of Indian History. Could he now start at the beginning, with the arrival of the Aryans in India, and at a stretch go on to Lord Curzon's Viceroyalty? That would mean, reckoning on Godstone's three volumes, the mastication of over a thousand pages. It was a noble ambition, no doubt, but hardly a sound one, because the university would not recognize your work and grant you a degree if you got a hundred per cent in History and one per cent in the other subjects. Chandran sat for nearly half an hour lost in this problem.

The household was up by this time. His father was in the garden, minutely examining the plants for evidence of any miracle that might have happened overnight. When he passed before Chandran's window he said, 'You have got up very early today.'

'I shall get up before five every day hereafter,' said Chandran.

'Very good.'

'This is November the first. My examinations are on the eighteenth of March. How many days is it from now?'

'About one hundred and thirty-eight –'

'About that,' said Chandran. 'It must be less because February, which comes before the examination month, has only twenty-eight days unless the leap year gives it a day more. So it must be less than one hundred and twenty-eight by three days. Do you know the total number of pages I have to read? Roughly about five thousand pages, four times over, not to speak of class lecture notes. About twenty thousand pages in one hundred and twenty days. That is the reason why I have to get up so early in the morning. I shall probably have to get up earlier still in course of time. I have drawn up a programme of work. Won't you step in and have a look at it?'

Father came in and gazed at the sheet of paper on Chandran's table. He could not make anything of it. What he saw before him was a very intricate document, as complicated as a railway time-table. He honestly made an attempt to understand it and then said, 'I don't follow this quite clearly.' Chandran took the trouble to explain it to him. He also explained to him the problems that harassed him in studying History, and sought his advice. 'I want to know if it would be safe to read only the Modern Period in Godstone and study the rest in notes.' His father had studied science for his B.A. This consultation on an historical point puzzled him. He said, 'I feel you ought not to take such risks.'

Chandran felt disappointed. He had hoped that his father would agree with him in supplementing Godstone with the class notes. This advice irritated him. After all, Father had never been a history student.

'Father, you have no idea what splendid lectures Ragavachar gives in the class. His lectures are the essence of all the books on the subject. If one reads his notes, one can pass even the I.C.S. examination.'

'You know best,' said Father. As he started back for the garden, he said, 'Chandar, if you go to the market will you buy some wire-netting? Somebody is regularly stealing the jasmine from the creeper near the compound wall. I want to put up some kind of obstruction that side.'

'That will spoil the appearance of the house, Father.'

'But what are we to do? Somebody comes in even before dawn and steals the flowers.'

'After all, only flowers,' said Chandran, and Father went out muttering something.

Chandran returned to his work, having definitely made up his mind to study only the Modern Period in Godstone. He pulled out the book from the shelf, blew off the dust, and began at the Mogul Invasion. It was a heavy book with close print and shining pages, interspersed with smudgy pictures of kings dead and gone.

At nine he closed the book, having read five pages. He felt an immense satisfaction at having made a beginning.

While going in to breakfast he saw his younger brother, Seenu, standing in the courtyard and looking at the crows on an areca-nut tree far off. He was just eight years old, and was studying in the Third Class in Albert Mission School. Chandran said to him, 'Why do you waste the morning gazing at the sky?'

'I am waiting to bathe. Somebody is in the bathroom.'

'It is only nine. What is the hurry for your bath? Do you want to spend the whole day before the bathroom? Go back to your desk. You will be called when the bathroom is vacant. Let me not catch you like this again!'

Seenu vanished from the spot. Chandran was indignant. In his days in the Albert Mission he had studied for at least two hours every morning. The boys in these days had absolutely no sense of responsibility.

His mother appeared from somewhere with the flower-basket in her hand. She was full of grievances: 'Somebody takes away all the flowers in the garden. Is there no way of stopping this nuisance? Nobody seems to care for anything in this house.' She was in a fault-finding mood. Not unusual at this hour. She had a variety of work to do in the mornings – tackling the milkman, the vegetable-seller, the oilmonger, and other tradespeople; directing the work of the cook and of the servants; gathering flowers for the daily worship; and attending to all the eccentricities and wants of her husband and children.

Chandran knew that the worst one could do at that time was to argue with her. So he said soothingly, 'We will lock the gate at night, and try to put up some wire-netting on the wall.'

She replied, 'Wire-netting! It will make the house hideous! Has your father been suggesting it again?'

'No, no,' Chandran said, 'he just mentioned it as a last measure if nothing else is possible.'

'I won't have it,' Mother said decisively; 'something else has got to be done.' Chandran said that steps should be taken, and asked himself what could be done short of digging a moat around the house and putting crocodiles in it. Mother, however, was appeased by this assurance. She explained mildly, 'Your father spends nearly twenty-five rupees on the garden and nearly ten rupees on a gardener. What is the use of all this expense if we can't have a handful of flowers in the morning, for throwing on the gods in the *Pooja* room?'

That afternoon, while crossing the quadrangle, Chandran met Ragavachar, the Professor of History. He was about to pass him, paying the usual tribute of a meek salute, when Ragavachar called, 'Chandran!'

'Yes, sir,' answered Chandran, much puzzled, having never been addressed by any professor outside the class. In a big college the professors could know personally only the most sycophantic or the most brilliant. Chandran was neither.

'What hour do you finish your work today?'

'At four-thirty, sir.'

'See me in my room at four-thirty.'

'Yes, sir.'

When told of this meeting Ramu asked, 'Did you try to plant a bomb or anything in his house?' Chandran retorted hotly that he didn't appreciate the joke. Ramu said that he was disappointed to hear this, and asked what Chandran wanted him to do. Chandran said, 'Will you please shut up and try not to explain anything?' They were sitting on the steps outside the lecture hall. Ramu got up and said, 'If you want me, I shall be in the Union reading-room till five.'

'We have *Othello* at three-thirty.'

'I am not attending it,' said Ramu, and was gone.

Chandran sat alone, worrying. Why had Ragavachar called him? He hadn't misbehaved; no library book overdue; there were one or two tests he hadn't attended, but Ragavachar never corrected any test paper. Or could it be that he had suddenly gone through all the test papers and found out that Chandran had not attended some of the tests? If it was only a reprimand, the professor would do it in the open class. Would any professor waive such an opportunity and do it in his room? For that matter, Ramu had not attended a single test in his life. Why was he not called? What did Ramu mean by going away in a temper? 'Not attending it!' Seemed to be taking things easy.

The bell rang. Chandran rose and went in. He climbed the gallery steps and reached his seat. He opened the pages of *Othello*, placed a sheet of paper on the page, and took out his pen.

It was the Assistant Professor's subject. The Assistant Professor of English was Mr Gajapathi, a frail man with a meagre moustache and heavy spectacles. He earned the hatred of the students by his teaching and of his colleagues by his conceit. He said everywhere that not ten persons in the world had understood Shakespeare; he asserted that there were serious errors even in Fowler's *Modern English Usage*; he corrected everybody's English; he said that no Indian could ever write English; this statement hurt all his colleagues, who prepared their lectures in English and wished to think that they wrote well. When he valued test or examination papers, he never gave anybody more than forty per cent; he constituted himself an authority on punctuation, and deducted half a mark per misplaced comma or semicolon in the papers that he corrected.

He entered the hall at a trot, jumped on the platform, opened his book, and began to read a scene in *Othello*. He read Shakespeare in a sing-song fashion, and with a vernacular twang. He stopped now and then to criticize other critics. Though Dowden had said so and so, Mr Gajapathi was not prepared to be browbeaten by a big name. No doubt Bradley and others had done a certain amount of research in Shakespeare, but one couldn't accept all that they said as gospel truth. Gajapathi proved in endless instances how wrong others were.

Chandran attempted to take down notes, but they threatened to shape into something like the Sayings of Gajapathi. Chandran screwed the cap on his pen and sat back. Gajapathi never liked to see people sitting back and looking at him. He probably felt nervous when two hundred pairs of eyes stared at him. It was his habit to say, 'Heads down and pencils busy, gentlemen,' and 'Listen to me with your pencils, gentlemen.'

In due course he said, 'Chandran, I see you taking a rest.'

'Yes, sir.'

'Don't say "yes". Keep your pen busy.'

'Yes, sir.' Chandran, with his head bent, began to scribble on the sheet of paper before him: 'Oh, Gajapathi, Gajapathi! When will you shut up? Do you think that your lecture is very interesting and valuable? In these two lines Shakespeare reveals the innermost core of Iago. *Gaja*, in Sanskrit, means elephant; *pathy* is probably master. A fine name for you, you Elephant Master.' And here followed the sketch of an elephant with spectacles on.

'Chandran, do I understand you are taking down notes?'

'Yes, sir.'

The bell rang. Gajapathi intended to continue the lecture even after the bell; but two hundred copies of Verity's *Othello* shut with a loud report like the cracking of a rifle. The class was on its feet.

When he came down the gallery, Gajapathi said, 'A moment, Chandran.' Chandran stopped near the platform as the others streamed past him. Everybody seemed to want him today.

Gajapathi said, 'I should like to see your lecture notes.'

Chandran was nonplussed for a moment. If he remembered aright he had scribbled an elephant. The other things he did not clearly recollect; but he knew that they were not meant for Gajapathi's scrutiny. He wondered for a moment whether he should escape with a lie, but felt that Gajapathi did not deserve that honour. He said, 'Honestly, I have not taken down anything, sir. If you will excuse me, I must go now. I have to see Professor Ragavachar.'

As he came near the Professor's room, Chandran felt very nervous. He adjusted his coat and buttoned it up. He hesitated for a moment before the door. He suddenly pulled himself up. Why this cowardice? Why should he be afraid of Ragavachar or anybody? Human being to human being. Remove those spectacles, the turban, and the long coat, and let Ragavachar appear only in a loin-cloth, and Mr Ragavachar would lose three-quarters of his appearance. Where was the sense in feeling nervous before a pair of spectacles, a turban, and a black long coat?

'Good-evening, sir,' said Chandran, stepping in.

Ragavachar looked up from a bulky red book that he was reading. He took time to switch his mind off his studies and comprehend the present.

'Well?' he said, looking at Chandran.

'You asked me to see you at four-thirty, sir.'

'Yes, yes. Sit down.'

Chandran lowered himself to the edge of a chair. Ragavachar leaned back and spent some time looking at the ceiling. Chandran felt a slight thirsty sensation, but he recollected his vision of Ragavachar in a loin-cloth, and regained his self-confidence.

'My purpose in calling you now is to ascertain your views on the question of starting an Historical Association in the college.'

Saved! Chandran sat revelling in the sense of relief he now felt.

'What do you think of it?'

'I think it is a good plan, sir,' and he wondered why he was chosen for this consultation.

'What I want you to do,' went on the commanding voice, 'is to arrange for an inaugural meeting on the fifteenth instant. We shall decide the programme afterwards.'

'Very well, sir,' said Chandran.

'You will be the Secretary of the Association. I shall be its President. The meeting must be held on the fifteenth.'

'Don't you think, sir ...' Chandran began.

'What don't I think?' asked the Professor.

'Nothing, sir.'

'I hate these sneaky half-syllables,' the Professor said. 'You were about to say something. I won't proceed till I know what you were saying.'

Chandran cleared his throat and said, 'Nothing, sir. I was only going to say that someone else might do better as a secretary.'

'I suppose you can leave that to my judgement.'

'Yes, sir.'

'I hope you don't question the need for starting the association.'

'Certainly not, sir.'

'Very good. I for one feel that the amount of ignorance on historical matters is appalling. The only way in which we can combat it is to start an association and hold meetings and read papers.'

'I quite understand, sir.'

'Yet you ask me why we should have this association!'

'No, I did not doubt it.'

'H'm. You talk the matter over with one or two of your friends, and see me again with some definite programme for the Inaugural Meeting.'

Chandran rose.

'You seem to be in a hurry to go,' growled the tiger.

'No, sir,' said Chandran, and sat down again.

'If you are in a hurry to go, I can't stop you because it is past four-thirty, and you are free to leave the college premises. On the other hand, if you are not in a hurry, I have some more details to discuss with you.'

'Yes, sir.'

'There is no use repeating "Yes, sir; yes, sir." You don't come forward with any constructive suggestion.'

'I will talk it over with some friends and come later, sir.'

'Good-evening. You may go now.'

Chandran emerged from the Professor's room with his head bowed in thought. He felt a slight distaste for himself as a secretary. He felt that he was on the verge of losing his personality. Now he would have to be like Natesan, the Union Secretary. One's head would be full of nothing but meetings to be arranged! He was now condemned to go about with a fixed idea, namely, the Inaugural Meeting. The Inaugural Meeting by itself was probably not a bad thing, if it were also the final meeting; but they would expect him to arrange at least half a dozen meetings before March: readings of papers on mock subjects, heavy lectures by paunchy hags, secretary's votes of thanks, and endless other things. He hated the whole business. He would have to sit through the lectures, wait till the lights were put out and the doors locked, and go out into the night with a headache, forgoing the walk by the river with Ramu. Ah, Ramu; that fellow behaved rather queerly in the afternoon, going off in a temper like that.

Chandran went to the reading-room in the Union. None of the half a dozen heads bent over the illustrated journals belonged to Ramu. Chandran had a hope that Ramu might be in the chess-room. He was not the sort to play chess, but he occasionally might be found in the company that stood around and watched a game of chess, shutting out light and air from the players. But today the game of chess seemed to be going on without Ramu's supervision; nor was he to be found in the ping-pong room. Chandran descended the Union steps in thorough discontent.

He turned his steps to the river, which was a stone's throw from the college. He walked along the sand. The usual crowd was there – girls with jasmine in their hair, children at play, students loafing about, and elderly persons at their constitutionals. Chandran enjoyed immensely an evening on the river bank: he stared at the girls, pretended to be interested in the children, guffawed at friends, perambulated about twice or thrice, and then walked to the lonely Nallapa's Grove and smoked a cigarette there. Ramu's company and his running commentary lent vitality to the whole experience.

But today his mind was clogged, and Ramu was absent. Chandran was beginning to feel bored. He started homeward.

It was a little past seven when he turned into the Second Cross road in Lawley Extension. He stood before Ramu's gate and shouted, 'Ramu!' Ramu came out.

'Why were you not in the reading-room?'

'I waited, and thought that you would be late and came away.'

'You were not by the river.'

'I returned home and went for a walk along the Trunk Road.'

'What did you mean by going away like that to the reading-room, so abruptly?'

'I wanted to read the magazines.'

'I don't believe it. You went away in a temper. I wonder why you are so lacking in patience!'

'What about your temper? You meet Ragavachar and are worried, and a fellow says something lightly and you flare up!'

Chandran ignored the charge. He seized upon the subject of Ragavachar. He gave a full account of the amazing interview. They stood on the road, talking the matter over and over again, for nearly two hours.

When Chandran went home his father said, 'Nine o'clock.' Later, when he was about to go to bed, Father asked, 'Your plan of study not come into force yet?' That question hurt Chandran's conscience. He went to his table and stood looking at the programme he had sketched out in the morning. Not much of it was clear now. He went to bed and his conscience gnawed at him in the dark till about eleven. He had spent the morning in drawing plans and the rest of the day somehow. First of November gone, irrevocably gone, and wasted; six of the forty-eight hours for *Othello* and Godstone thrown on the scrap-heap.

The Inaugural Meeting troubled Chandran day and night, and he was unable to make any progress in *Othello* and Godstone. His notions as to what one did on the day of the meeting were very vague. He faintly thought that at such a meeting people sat around, drank tea, shook hands with each other, and felt inaugural.

Five mornings before the meeting, in a fit of desperation, he flung aside his Godstone, and started for Natesan's room. If ever there was a man to guide another in these matters, it was Natesan. He had been twice the Secretary of the Sanskrit Association, once its Vice-President, Secretary of the Philosophy Association, of a Social Service League, and now of the Union. Heaven knew what other things he was going to be. He must have conducted nearly a hundred meetings in his college life. Though Chandran had sometimes dreaded meeting this man, now he felt happy when he knocked on his door and found him in. It was a very narrow room with a small window opening on the twisting Kabir Street, and half-filled with a sleeping cot, and the remaining space given over to the four legs of a very big table, on which books were heaped. One opened the door and stepped on the cot. Natesan was reclining on a roll of bedding and studying. He was very pleased to see Chandran, and invited him to take a seat on the cot.

Chandran poured out his troubles. 'What does one do on the inaugural day?'

'A lengthy address is delivered, and then the chairman thanks the lecturer, and the secretary thanks the lecturer and the chairman, and the audience rise to go home.'

'No tea or anything?'

'Oh, no. Nothing of the sort. Who is to pay for the tea?'

And then hearing of Chandran's vagueness and difficulties, Natesan suggested the Principal for the address, and Professor Ragavachar for the chair. After his interview with Natesan, Chandran realized that a secretary's life was a tormented one. He was now in a position to appreciate the services of not only Natesan, but also of Alam, the Secretary of the Literary Association, of Rajan, the Philosophy Association Secretary, of Moorty, the Secretary of the Economics Association, the people who were responsible for all the meetings in the college. Chandran realized that there was more in these meetings than met the eye or entered the ear. Each meeting was a supreme example of human endeavour, or selfless service. For what did a secretary after all gain by sweating? No special honours from the authorities nor extra marks in the examinations. Far from it. More often ridicule from class-mates and frowns from professors, if something went wrong. The bothers of a secretary were: a clash with other secretaries over the date of a meeting; finding a speaker; finding a subject for the speaker; and getting an audience for the subject.

That day Chandran skipped nearly two periods in order to see the Principal. The peon squatting before the Principal's room would not let him in. Chandran pleaded and begged. The peon spoke in whispers, and commanded Chandran to talk in whispers. Chandran whispered that he had to see the Principal, whispered a threat, whispered an admonition, in whispers cringed and begged, but the peon was adamant.

'I have orders not to let anybody in,' said the peon. He was an old man, grown grey in college service, that is in squatting before the Principal's office door. His name was Aziz.

'Look here, Aziz,' Chandran said in a soothing tone, 'why can't anybody see him now?'

'It is not for me to ask. I won't let anybody in. He is very busy.'

'Busy with what?'

'What do you care?' Aziz asked haughtily.

'Is he given his thousand a month to sit behind that door and refuse to see people?'

At this the servant lost his temper, and asked, 'Who are you to question it?' Chandran gave some stinging answer to this. It was a great strain to carry on the conversation, the whole thing having to be conducted in whispers. Chandran realized that it was no use losing one's temper. He tried strategy now. He said, 'Aziz, I have an old coat at home; not a tear in it. Will you come for it tomorrow morning?'

'What time?'

'Any time you please. I live in Lawley Extension.'

'Yes, I know. I will find out your house.'

'Give me a slip of paper.'

Aziz tore out a slip from a bundle hung on the door. Chandran wrote his name on it and sent it in. Aziz came out of the room in a few minutes and said that Chandran might go in. Chandran adjusted his coat and entered.

'Good-morning, sir.'

'Good-morning.'

Chandran delivered a short preamble on the Historical Association, and stated his request. The Principal took out a small black diary, turned over its pages, and said, 'The fifteenth evening is free. All right.'

'Thank you, sir,' said Chandran, and remained standing for a few minutes. He himself could not say what he was waiting there for. His business had been completed too rapidly. He didn't know whether he ought to say something more or leave the room abruptly. The Principal took out a cigarette and lighted it. 'Well?'

'We are ... We are very grateful to you, sir, for your great kindness.'

'Oh, it's all right. Don't mention it.'

'May I take my leave?'

'Yes.'

'Thank you, sir. Good-morning.' Chandran marched out of the room. When he passed Aziz he said, 'What a bad fellow you are, you wouldn't let me in!'

'Master, I do my duty and get a bad name. What am I to do? Can I see you tomorrow morning?'

'I shall ask the peon at our gate not to let you in.'

'Oh, master, I am a poor old fellow, always shivering with cold. Don't disappoint me. If you give me a coat, I shall always remember you as my saviour.'

'All right. Come tomorrow,' whispered Chandran, and passed on.

He went to Ragavachar's room and announced that the Principal had consented to deliver the inaugural address. Ragavachar did not appear excited by the news. He growled, after some rumination, 'I am not sure if his address will be suitable for an Historical Association.'

'I think, sir, he can adjust himself.'

'One hopes so.'

'You must take the chair, sir.'

'I suppose ... H'm.' Nothing further was said. Having moved with him closely for ten days Chandran understood it to mean consent.

'May I go, sir?'

'Yes.'

CHAPTER THREE

The fifteenth of November was a busy day for Chandran. He spent a great part of the morning in making arrangements for the meeting in the evening.

Two days before, he had issued printed notices over his signature to all the members of the staff, and to all the important lawyers, doctors, officials, and teachers in the town. From every board in the college his notices invited everyone to be present at the meeting.

As a result of this, on the fifteenth at five in the evening, while Chandran was still arranging the dais and the chairs in the lecture hall of the college, the audience began to arrive.

The college peon, Aziz, lent him a stout hand in making the arrangements. The old coat had done the trick. Aziz personally attended to the arrangement of the chairs in the front row. He arranged the chairs and the table on the dais. He gave a gorgeous setting to the Historical Association. He spread a red cloth on the dais, and a green baize on the table. He illuminated the hall with petrol lamps.

As the guests arrived, Chandran ran to the veranda and received them and conducted them to their seats. At 5.15 almost all the chairs were occupied; all the seats in the gallery were also filled. Students of the college who came late hung on to the banisters.

The Principal and Professor Ragavachar arrived and stopped in the veranda. Chandran flitted about uncertainly, and invited them in. The Principal looked at his watch and said, 'Five minutes more. We shall stay here till five-thirty.'

Ragavachar adjusted his spectacles and murmured, 'Yes, yes.'

Some more guests arrived. Chandran showed them their seats. Ramu was all the time at his side, running errands, helping him, asking questions, and not always receiving an answer.

'What a crowd!' Ramu said.

'You see ...' began Chandran, and saw the Headmaster of the Albert Mission School arriving and ran forward to meet him. Chandran returned after seating the Headmaster in the hall.

Ramu said, 'It looks as if you were giving a dinner-party to the town folk.'

Chandran said, his eyes scanning the drive for visitors, 'Yes, it looks like that. Only flowers, scents, and a dinner missing to complete the picture.'

Ramu asked, 'Shall I wait for you at the end of the lecture?' and was not destined to receive an answer. For, at this moment, Ragavachar looked at his watch and said, 'It is five-thirty, shall we begin?'

'Yes, sir.'

The Secretary led the speaker and the Chairman to their chairs on the dais, and occupied a third chair placed on the edge of the dais.

After the cheering and stamping had subsided, Ragavachar rose, put on his spectacles, and began, 'Ladies and gentlemen, I am not going to presume to introduce to you the lecturer of this evening. I do not propose to stand between you and the lecturer. I shall take only a few minutes, perhaps only a few seconds, to enlighten you on a few facts concerning our association ...' He then filled the hall with his voice for a full forty minutes. The audience gathered from his speech that an Historical Association represented his faith in life; it was a vision which guided him in all his activities. The audience also understood that darkness prevailed in the minds of over ninety per cent of human beings, and that he expected the association to serve the noble end of dispelling this darkness. Great controversial fires were raging over very vital matters in Indian History. And what did they find around them? The public went about their business as if nothing was happening. How could one expect these fires to be extinguished if the great public did not show an intelligent appreciation of the situation and lend a helping hand? To quote an instance: everybody learnt in the secondary school history book that Sirajudowlla locked some of the East Indian Company people in a very small room, and allowed them to die of suffocation. This was the well-known Black Hole of Calcutta. There were super-historians who appeared at a later stage in one's education and said that there had been neither Black nor Hole nor Calcutta. He was not going to indicate his own views on the question. But he only wished to convey to the minds of the audience, to the public at large, to all intelligent humanity in general, what a state of bloody feud existed in the realm of Indian History. True history was neither fiction nor philosophy. It was a hardy science. And to place Indian History there, an Association was indispensable. If he were asked what the country needed most urgently, he would not say Self-Government or Economic Independence, but a clarified, purified Indian History.

After this he repeated that he would not stand between the lecturer and his audience, and, calling upon Professor Brown to deliver the Inaugural Address, sat down.

As Professor Brown got up there was great applause. He looked about, put his right hand in his trouser pocket, held his temples with his left hand, and began. He looked at Chandran and said that he had not bargained for this, a meeting of this dimension and importance, when he acceded to the Secretary's request. Chandran tapped the arms of his chair with his fingers, looked down and smiled, almost feeling that he had played a deep game on the Principal. The lecturer said that he had consented to deliver an address this evening, thinking that he was to be at the opening of a very simple Association. From what Ragavachar said, he understood it to be something that was of national importance. If he had known this, his place now would be in one of the chairs that he saw before him, and he would have left the responsible task to better persons. However, it was too late to do anything now. He hoped that he would have an occasion to settle his score with Chandran.

The audience enjoyed every word of this. People who had awaited Brown's humour were fully satisfied.

Professor Brown traced his relations with History from the earliest times when he was in a private school in Somerset to the day on which he entered Oxford, where he shook History off his person, because he found the subject as treacherous as a bog at night. Thereafter, for his degree, he studied Literature, and regularly spent some hours of private study on History. 'I can now give a fairly coherent account of mankind's "doings", if I may borrow an expression from the composition books that I correct. But don't ask me the date of anything. In all History I remember only 1066.'

He held the audience for about an hour thus, with nothing very serious, nothing profound, but with the revelation of a personality, with delicious reminiscences, touched with humour and occasional irony.

He sat down after throwing at his audience this advice: 'Like Art, History must be studied for its own sake; and so, if you are to have an abiding interest in it, take it up after you leave the university. For outside the university you may read your history in any order; from the middle work back to the beginning of things or in any way you like, and nobody will measure how many facts you have rammed into your poor head. Facts are, after all, a secondary matter in real History.'

Ragavachar inwardly fretted and fumed at the speech. If the lecturer had been anyone else than Brown, the Principal of the college, he would have taken the speech to bits and thrown it to the four winds, and pulled out the tongue of the lecturer and cut it off. At the end of the lecture, he merely rose and thanked the lecturer on behalf of the audience and sat down. When Chandran rose to propose a hearty vote of thanks to the lecturer and to the chairman for their great kindness in consenting to conduct the meeting, it acted as a signal for the audience to rise and go home. A babble broke out. Chandran's voice could hardly be heard except by a select few in the very first row.

CHAPTER FOUR

Chandran put off everything till the Inaugural Meeting was over. He consoled himself with the fact that he had wasted several months so far, and a fortnight more, added to that account, should not matter. He had resolved that the moment the meeting was over he would get up at 4.30 instead of 5 a.m. as decided originally. The time wasted in a fortnight could then be made up by half an hour's earlier rising every day. He would also return home at seven in the evening instead of at seven-thirty. This would give him a clear gain of an hour a day over his previous programme. He hoped to make up the ninety study hours, at six hours a day, lost between the first of November and the fifteenth, in the course of ninety days.

This was a sop to his clamouring conscience. He thought now he would be able to get up at four-thirty on the following morning and begin his whirlwind programme of study. But man can only propose. He was destined to throw away two more mornings. On the night of the big meeting, before going to bed, he spent some time on the carpet in the hall, gossiping with his mother. He announced that he would get up at four-thirty next morning.

Father, who appeared to be reading a newspaper in the veranda, exclaimed, 'So after all!' This remark disturbed Chandran. But he remained silent, hoping that it would discourage his father from uttering further remarks. Father, however, was not to be kept off so easily. The newspaper rustled on the veranda, and five minutes later came the remark, 'Since this is the third time you have made a resolution, it is likely you will stick to it, because every plan must have two trials.' Chandran rose and went on to the veranda. His father was in a puckish, teasing mood. As soon as Chandran came out, he looked at him over his spectacles and asked, 'Don't you agree with me?'

'What, Father?'

'That a plan must have two trials.'

Chandran felt uncomfortable. 'You see, Father, but for this dreadful meeting I should have done ninety hours of study, according to my time-table. I shall still make it up. I shall not be available to anyone from tomorrow.' He gave a glowing account of what he was going to do from the next morning onwards.

Father said that he was quite pleased to hear it. He said, 'If you get up at four-thirty, do wake me up also. I want to wait and catch the scoundrel who steals the flowers in the morning.'

Mother's voice came from the hall, 'So, after all, you are doing something!'

'Hardly my fault that,' Father shouted back. 'I offered to put up wire-fencing over the wall.'

'Why, do you want to give the thief some wire in addition to the flowers?'

Father was greatly affected by this taunt.

Mother added fuel to it by remarking, 'Twenty-five rupees on the garden and not a single petal of any flower for the gods in the *Pooja* room.'

Father was very indignant. He behaved like a mediaeval warrior goaded by his lady-love into slaying a dragon. Father dropped a hint that the flower thief would be placed at her feet next day, alive or dead.

Next morning Chandran was awakened by his alarm clock. He went to his father's room and woke him up. After that he went to the bathroom for a cold bath.

In ten minutes Chandran was at his table. He adjusted the light, drew the chair into position, and pondered over the piece of paper on which he had written a time-table.

His father entered the room, carrying a stout bamboo staff in his hand. Behind him came Seenu, armed with another stick. There was the light of a hunter in Father's eyes, and Seenu was bubbling over with enthusiasm. Chandran was slightly annoyed at this intrusion. But Father whispered an apology, and requested, 'Put out that light. If it is seen in your room, the thief will not come near the house.'

'So much the better. Mother can take the flowers in the morning,' said Chandran.

'He will come some other day.'

'From now on, at least till March, there is no fear of this room ever being without a light at this hour. So the flower thief will be away till March. Let us catch him after that.'

'Oh, that is all far-fetched. I must get him today. It doesn't matter if you lose about an hour. You can make it up later.'

Chandran blew out the lamp and sat in the dark. Father and Seenu went out into the garden. Chandran sat in his chair for some time. He rose and stood looking out of the window. It was very dark in the garden.

Chandran began to wonder what his father and brother were doing, and how far they had progressed with the thief. His curiosity increased. He went into the garden, and moved cautiously along the shadows, and heard hoarse whispers coming from behind a big sprawling croton.

'Oh, it is Chandran,' said a voice.

Father and Seenu were crouching behind the croton.

'Don't make any noise,' Father whispered to Chandran.

Chandran found the tactics weak. He took command. It seemed to him waste to concentrate all the forces in one place. He ordered his father to go a little forward and conceal himself behind a rose bush; and his younger brother to prowl around the backyard, while he himself would be here and there and everywhere, moving with panther-like steps from cover to cover.

There was a slight hitch in the campaign. Seenu objected to the post he was allotted. It was still dark, and the backyard had a mysterious air. Chandran called him a coward and several other things, and asked him why he had left his bed at all if he could not be of some use to people.

In about an hour the sun came out and revealed the jasmine and other plants bare of flowers. Father merely looked at them and said, 'We must get up at four o'clock, not at four-thirty.'

Next day Chandran was out of bed at four, and with his father hunting in the garden. Nothing happened for about ten minutes. Then a slight noise was heard near the gate. Father was behind the rose bush, and Chandran had pressed himself close to the compound wall. A figure heaved itself on to the portion of the wall next to the gate, and jumped into the garden. The stranger looked about for a fraction of a second and went towards the jasmine creeper in a business-like way.

Hardly had he plucked half a dozen flowers when father and son threw themselves on him with war-cries. It was quite a surprise for Chandran to see his father so violent. They dragged the thief into the house, held him down, and shouted to Mother to wake up and light the lamp.

The light showed the thief to be a middle-aged man, bare bodied, with matted hair, wearing only a loin-cloth. The loin-cloth was ochre-coloured, indicating that he was a *sanyasi*, an ascetic. Father relaxed his hold on noticing this.

Mother screamed, 'Oh, hold him, hold him.' She was shaking with excitement. 'Take him away and give him to the police.'

Chandran said to the thief, 'You wear the garb of a *sanyasi*, and yet you do this sort of thing!'

'Is he a *sanyasi*?' Mother asked, and noticed the colour of the thief's loin-cloth. 'Ah, leave him alone, let him go.' She was seized with fear now. The curse of a holy man might fall on the family. 'You can go, sir,' she said respectfully.

Chandran was cynical. 'What, Mother, you are frightened of every long hair and ochre dress you see. If you are really a holy man, why should you do this?'

'What have I done?' asked the thief.

'Jumping in and stealing flowers.'

'If you lock the gate, how else can I get in than by jumping over the wall? As for stealing flowers, flowers are there, God-given. What matters it whether you throw the flowers on the gods, or I do it. It is all the same.'

'But you should ask our permission.'

'You are all asleep at that hour, and I don't wish to disturb you. I can't wait until you get up because my worship is over before sunrise.'

Mother interposed and said, 'You can go now, sir. If you want flowers you can take them. There couldn't be a better way of worship than giving flowers to those who really worship.'

'Truly said, Mother,' said the holy man. 'I should certainly have asked your permission but for the fact that none of you are awake at that hour.'

'I shall be awake,' said Chandran, 'from tomorrow.'

'Do you use these flowers for your worship, Mother?' asked the stranger.

'Certainly, every day. I never let a day go without worship.'

'Ah, I did not know that. I had thought that here, as in many other bungalows, flowers were kept only for ornament. I am happy to hear that they are put to holy use. Hereafter I shall take only a handful and leave the rest for your worship. May I take leave of you now?' He crossed the hall and descended the veranda steps.

Father said to Chandran, 'Take the gate key and open the gate. How can he get out?'

'If you leave him alone, he will jump over the wall and go,' mumbled Chandran sourly as he took the gate key from the nail on the veranda wall.

CHAPTER FIVE

November to March was a very busy period for Chandran. He got up every day at four-thirty in the morning, and did not get to bed until eleven. He practised his iron scheme of study to the letter. By the beginning of March he was well up in every subject. There were still a few inevitable dark corners in his mind: a few hopeless controversies among Shakespearean Scholars, a few impossible periods in History like the muddle that was called the mediaeval South Indian History, early Christianity with warring popes and kings, and feudalism. He allowed the muddle to remain undisturbed in his mind; he got into the habit of postponing the mighty task of clarifying these issues to a distant favourable day. He usually encouraged himself in all this vagueness by saying that even if he lost thirty marks in each paper owing to these doubts he would still be well within the reach of seventy in each, and, out of this, allowing twenty for defective presentation and examiners' eccentricities, he would still get fifty marks in each paper, which would be ten more than was necessary for a pass degree.

He had a few other achievements to his credit. Before March he conducted about eight meetings of the Historical Association. He himself read a paper on 'The Lesser-known Aspects of Mauryan Polity'.

The Historical Association was responsible for two interesting contacts. He came to know Veeraswami, the revolutionary, and Mohan, the poet.

Veeraswami was a dark, stocky person, about twenty-two years old. One day he came to Chandran and offered to read a paper on 'The Aids to British Expansion in India'. Chandran was delighted. He had never met anyone who volunteered to address the Association. On a fateful day, to an audience of thirty-five, Veeraswami read his paper. It was the most violent paper ever read before an association. It pilloried Great Britain before the Association, and ended by hoping that the British would be ousted from India by force. Ragavachar, who was present at the meeting, felt very uncomfortable. Next day he received a note from Brown, the custodian of British prestige, suggesting that in future papers meant to be read before the Association should be first sent to him. This infuriated Chandran so much that he thought of resigning till Ragavachar assured him that he would not get his degree if he tried these antics. Chandran sought Veeraswami and told him of the turmoil that his paper had caused, and consulted him on the ways and means to put an end to Brown's autocracy. Veeraswami suggested that he should be allowed to read a paper on 'The Subtleties of Imperialism', without sending the paper to Brown for his approval. Chandran declined this offer, explaining that he did not wish to be expelled from the college. Veeraswami asked why not, and called Chandran a coward. Chandran had a feeling that he had got into bed with a porcupine. Veeraswami bristled with prejudices and violence. Imperialism was his favourite demon. He believed in smuggling arms into the country, and, on a given day, shooting all the Englishmen. He assured Chandran that he was even then preparing for that great work. His education, sleep, contacts, and everything, were a preparation. He was even then gathering followers. He seemed to have considered this plan in all its aspects. Indians were hopelessly underfed and sickly. He proposed to cure hunger by encouraging the use of coconuts and the fruits of cactus for food. He was shortly going to issue pamphlets in Tamil, Telugu, and English on the subject. In regard to sickness he believed that the British encouraged it in order to provide a permanent market for the British drug manufacturers. He was going to defeat that plan by propagating the nature-cure idea. After thus improving the physique of the masses he would take charge of their minds. He would assume the garb of a village worker, a rural reconstruction maniac, but secretly prepare the mind of the peasantry for revolution.

After that Veeraswami never gave Chandran a moment's peace. In all leisure hours Chandran lived in terror of being caught by Veeraswami, which invariably happened. If Chandran went to the reading-room, Veeraswami was sure to hunt him down; if he went into the ping-pong room, he would be chased even there. So Chandran took to slinking out and going to a secluded spot on the river-bank. This almost led to a misunderstanding with Ramu, who thought that Chandran was avoiding him. In the evenings, too, Veeraswami would catch Chandran and follow him everywhere. Veeraswami would talk all the evening as Ramu and Chandran followed him with the look of a sacrificial goat in their eyes.

The other person whom the Historical Association brought in, Mohan, was less troublesome. He sidled up to Chandran one afternoon as the latter sat over his coffee in the Union Restaurant, and asked if a meeting could be arranged where some poems might be read. Chandran felt quite thrilled to meet a poet in the flesh. He never read poetry for pleasure, but he had a great admiration for poets. Chandran asked the other to take a seat and offered him a cup of coffee.

'Have your poems anything to do with History?'

'I don't understand you.'

'I want to know if they deal with historical facts. Something like a poem on the Mogul Emperors and things of that type. Otherwise it would not be easy to get them read before the Historical Association.'

'I am sorry you are so narrow-minded. You want everything to stay in water-tight compartments. When will you get a synthetic view of things? Why should you think that poetry is different from history?'

Chandran felt that he was being dragged into dangerous zones. He said, 'Please let me know what your subjects are.'

'Why should a poem have any subject? Is it not enough that there it is in itself?'

Chandran was thoroughly mystified. He asked, 'You write in English or in Tamil?'

'Of course in English. It is the language of the world.'

'Why don't you read your poems before the Literary Association?'

'Ah, do you think any such thing is possible with grandmother Brown as its president? As long as he is in this college no original work will ever be possible. He is very jealous, won't tolerate a pinch of original work. Go and read before the Literary Association, for the two-hundredth time, a rehash of his lecture notes on Wordsworth or Eighteenth Century Prose, and he will permit it. He won't stand anything else.'

'I should certainly like to read your poems myself, but I don't see how it will be possible before the Association.'

'If you have properly understood History as a record of human culture and development, you can't fail to see poetry as an integral part of it. If poems are to be read anywhere, it must be before an Historical Association.'

When Chandran asked for permission to arrange this meeting, Ragavachar ruled it out. He said that he did not care to have all sorts of versifiers come and contaminate the Association with their stuff. As he conveyed the refusal to Mohan, Chandran felt a great pity for the poet. He liked the poet. He was fascinated by his obscure statements. He desired to cultivate his friendship. He expressed his willingness to have some of the poems read to him. The only time he could spare was the evening, after the college was over. So the next evening he cancelled his walk and listened to verse. Ramu told Chandran not to expect him to sit down and enjoy that kind of entertainment, and went away before Mohan arrived.

Chandran hated his room in the evenings, but now he resigned himself to suffer in the cause of poetry.

Mohan came, with a bundle of typed sheets under his arm. After giving him a seat, Chandran asked, 'How many poems have you brought?'

'A selection of about twenty-five, that is all.'

'I hope we can finish them before seven,' said Chandran, 'because at seven-thirty I have to sit down to my studies.'

'Oh, yes,' said the poet, and began. He read far into the evening. The poems were on a wide variety of subjects – from a Roadside Grass-seller to the Planet in Its Orbit; from Lines suggested by an Ant to the Dying Musician. All conceivable things seemed to have incited Mohan to anger, gloom, despair, and defiance. Some had rhymes, some had not; some had a beginning, some had no end, some had no middle. But most of the poems mystified Chandran. After a time he gave up all attempt to understand them. He sat passively, listening, as the poet read by the twilight. He sighed with relief when the poet put down the twenty-fifth poem. The clock showed seven-fifteen. Chandran suggested a short stroll.

Chandran had a slight headache. The poet was hoarse with reading. During the stroll Chandran suggested, 'Why don't you try to get some of the poems published in a paper?'

'By every post I receive my poems back,' said the poet. 'For the last five years I have been trying to get my poems accepted. I have tried almost all the papers and magazines in the world – England, America, Canada, South Africa, Australia, and our own country. I must have spent a fortune in postage.'

Chandran expressed his admiration for the other for still writing so much.

'I can no more help writing than I can help breathing,' said the poet. 'I shall go on writing till my fingers are paralysed. Every day I write. I hardly read any of the class texts. I know I shall fail. I don't care. I hope some day I shall come across an editor or publisher who is not stupid.'

'Oh, you will very soon be a famous man,' said Chandran with conviction.

In March Chandran lost about six pounds in weight. He hardly thought of anything, saw anybody, or did anything, except study. The college now existed only for the classroom, and the classroom only for the lectures. Everybody in the college was very serious and purposeful. Even Gajapathi now devoted less of his time to attacks on critics than to lectures that would be useful in the examination.

On the last day of the term there was an air of conclusion about everything. Every professor and lecturer came to the end of his subject and closed his book. Brown shut Sophocles and ended the year with the hope that his pupils' interest in literature would long survive the examination. He left the class amid great cheering and clapping of hands. Gajapathi put away his copy of *Othello* and hoped that he had presented Shakespeare's mind clearly to his class; he also hoped that after the examination they would all be in a position to form independent judgements of their own. The Professor of European History closed the year with the League of Nations. The last period on the last day was Indian History. Ragavachar growled out the full stop with a summary of the Montague-Chelmsford Reforms, and left the class after warning them not to disturb the other classes by cheering and clapping.

They had their Class Socials that evening. A group photo, with the Principal sitting in the centre, was taken. A large lunch was eaten, and coffee drunk. Songs were sung, speeches were made, everybody wished everybody else success in the examination; professors shook hands with the students, and students shook hands with each other. Everybody was soft and sentimental. They did everything short of shedding tears at the parting.

As they dispersed and went home, Chandran was aware that he had passed the very last moment in his college life, which had filled the major portion of his waking hours for the last four years. There would be no more college for him from tomorrow. He would return to it a fortnight hence for the examination and (hoping for the best) pass it, and pass out into the world, for ever out of Albert College. He felt very tender and depressed.

PART TWO

CHAPTER SIX

Within six months of becoming a graduate Chandran began to receive suggestions from relatives and elderly friends of the family as to what he should do with himself. Till this time it had never occurred to him that he ought to be doing anything at all. But now, wherever he went, he was pestered with the question, 'Now what do you propose to do?'

'I have not thought of anything yet.'

'Why don't you go to Madras and study Law?'

There was his uncle in Nellore who wrote to him that he ought to do something and try to settle in life. There was his mother's cousin who advised him to study Law. There was his Madras uncle who said that staying in Malgudi would not lead him anywhere, but that he ought to go to a big city and see people. He had immense faith in seeing people. He himself volunteered to give a letter of introduction to some big man, an auditor in the railways, who could in his turn give a further introduction to someone else, and finally fix up Chandran in the railways. This uncle seemed to live in an endless dream of introductory letters. Several relatives, chiefly women, asked him why he did not sit for the Indian Civil Service or the Indian Audit Service examination. Chandran felt flattered by their faith in him. There were others who said that there was nothing like a business occupation; start on a small capital and open a shop; independence and profit. All sorts of persons advised him to apply for a clerk's post in some Government office. Nothing like Government service, they said; on the first of the month you were sure of your money; security. Chandran had a feeling of persecution. He opened his heart to his father when the latter was trimming the roses early one morning.

'I am sorry, Father, that I ever passed the B.A.'

'Why?'

'Why should everybody talk about my career? Why can't they mind their business?'

'It is the way of the world. You must not let that upset you. It is just a form of courtesy, you see.'

Then they began to talk of Chandran's future. His father gathered that Chandran had a vague desire to go to England and do something there. He did not consider the plan absurd himself.

'What do you propose to do in England?'

'I want to get a doctorate or something and come back, and then some quiet lectureship in some college will suit me wonderfully. Plenty of independence and leisure.'

After that Chandran went about with a free mind. To his persecutors he would say, 'I am going to England next year.' Some demanded why he was not starting immediately. Chandran told them, 'We can't go to England on an impulse, can we?'

And now, without college or studies to fetter him, Chandran was enjoying a freedom he had never experienced in his life before. From his infant class up to B.A., a period of over sixteen years, he had known nothing like this holiday, which stretched over six months. He would have enjoyed this freedom still more if Ramu had been there with him. After the results were announced Ramu disappeared. He went away to Bombay in search of employment, and drifted all over Northern India without securing any. Chandran received only one card informing him that Ramu had joined the law course in Poona.

So Chandran was compelled to organize his life without Ramu. He became a member of the Town Public Library, and read an enormous quantity of fiction and general literature. He discovered Carlyle. He found that after all Shakespeare had written some stirring dramas, and that several poets were not as dull as they were made out to be. There was no scheme or order in his study. He read books just as they came. He read a light humorist and switched on to Carlyle, and from there pounced on Shakespeare, and then wandered to Shaw and Wells. The thing that mattered most to him was that the book should be enjoyable, and he ruthlessly shut books that threatened to bore him.

After spending a large part of the day with books he went out in the evening for long walks, necessarily alone, since most of his friends had gone away. He went on long rambles by the river, returned home late, and sat up for an hour or two chatting with his parents, and then read a little in bed. As he settled down to this routine he got used to it and enjoyed this quiet life. Every day as he went through one item he eagerly looked forward to the next, and then the next, till he looked forward to the delicious surge of sleep as he put away his book for the night.

CHAPTER SEVEN

It was on one of his river ramblings that he met Malathi and thought that he would not have room for anything else in his mind. No one can explain the attraction between two human beings. It happens.

One evening he came to the river, and was loafing along it, when he saw a girl, about fifteen years old, playing with her younger sister on the sands. Chandran had been in the habit of staring at every girl who sat on the sand, but he had never felt before the acute interest he felt in this girl now. He liked the way she sat; he liked the way she played with her sister; he liked the way she dug her hands into the sand and threw it in the air. He paused only for a moment to observe the girl. He would have willingly settled there and spent the rest of his life watching her dig her hands into the sand. But that could not be done. There were a lot of people about.

He passed on. He went forward a few paces and wanted to turn back and take another look at the girl. But that could not be done. He felt that the scores of persons squatting on the sand were all watching him.

He went on his usual walk down to Nallappa's Grove, crossed the river, went up the opposite bank, and away into the fields there; but he caught himself more than once thinking of the girl. How old was she? Probably fourteen. Might be even fifteen or sixteen. If she was more than fourteen she must be married. There was a touch of despair in this thought. What was the use of thinking of a married girl? It would be very improper. He tried to force his mind to think of other things. He tried to engage it in his favourite subject – his trip to England in the coming year. If he was going to England how was he to dress himself? He had better get used to tie and shoes and coat and hat and knife and fork. He would get a first-class degree in England and come back and marry. What was the use of thinking of a married girl? Probably she was not married. Her parents were very likely rational and modern, people who abhorred the custom of rushing a child into marriage. He tried to analyse why he was thinking of her. Why did he think of her so much? Was it her looks? Was she so good-looking as all that? Who could say? He hadn't noticed her before. Then how could he say that she was the most beautiful girl in the world? When did he say that? Didn't he? If not, why was he thinking of her so much? Chandran was puzzled, greatly puzzled by the whole thing.

He wondered next what her name might be. She looked like one with the name of Lakshmi. Quite a beautiful name, the name of the Goddess of Wealth, the spouse of God Vishnu, who was the Protector of Creatures.

That night he went home very preoccupied. It was at five o'clock that he had met her, and at nine he was still thinking of her.

After dinner he did not squat on the carpet in the hall, but preferred to go to his room and remain alone there. He tried to read a little; he was in the middle of Wells's *Tono Bungay*. He had found the book gripping, but now he felt it was obtrusive. He was irritated. He put away the book and sat staring at the wall. He presently realized that darkness would be more soothing. He blew out the lamp and sat in his chair. Suppose, though unmarried, she belonged to some other caste? A marriage would not be tolerated even between sub-sects of the same caste. If India was to attain salvation these water-tight divisions must go – Community, Caste, Sects, Sub-sects, and still further divisions. He felt very indignant. He would set an example himself by marrying this girl whatever her caste or sect might be.

The next day he shaved with great care and paid a great deal of attention to his crop, and awaited the evening. When evening came he put on his chocolate-coloured tweed coat and started out. At five he was on the river-bank, squatting on the sand near the spot where he had seen the girl the previous day. He sat there for over two hours. The girl did not come. Dozens of other townspeople came to the river and sprawled all over the place, but not that girl. Chandran rose and walked along, peering furtively at every group. It was a very keen search, but it brought forth nothing. Why wasn't she there? His heart beat fast at the sight of every figure that approached the river clad in a *sari*. It was seven forty-five when he set his face homeward, feeling that his brilliantine, shave, ironed tweed coat, were all wasted.

The next day he again went to the river and again waited till seven forty-five in the evening, and went home dispirited. He tossed in bed all night. In moments of half-wakefulness he whispered the word 'Lakshmi', 'Lakshmi'. He suddenly pulled himself up and laughed at himself: it looked as if the girl had paid a first and last visit to the river, and it seemed more than likely that she belonged to another caste, and was married. What a fool he was to go on thinking of her night and day for three whole days. It was a ridiculous obsession. His sobriety ought to assert itself now. An idle brain was the devil's workshop. Too true. A brain given rest for over nine months brought one to this state.

He rose in the morning with a haggard face. His mother asked him if he was not well. Chandran felt that some explanation was due and said he had a terrible headache. His mother, standing two inches shorter than he, put out her hands, stroked his temples, gave him special coffee, and advised him to stay at home the whole day. Chandran felt that nothing could be better than that. He decided not to shave or comb his hair or wear a coat and go out. For he feared that if he went out he might be tempted to go on the foolish quest.

He stayed in his room all day. His father came in at midday and kept him company. He sat in the chair and talked of this and that. Chandran all of a sudden realized that he had better leave Malgudi. That would solve the problem.

'Father, will you let me go to Madras?'

'By all means, if you'd like a change.'

'I suppose it will be very hot there?'

'Must be. The saying is that Madras is hot for ten months in the year and hotter for two.'

'Then I don't want to go and fry myself there,' said Chandran.

'Try some other place. You can go to your aunt at Bangalore.'

'No, no. She will keep telling me what jewels she has got for her daughter. I can't stand her.' He decided that he would stay in the best place on earth, home.

Mother came in at about three o'clock to ask how he was feeling. Seenu came in at four-thirty, as soon as school was over, and stood near Chandran's bed, staring at him silently.

'What is it?' Chandran asked.

'Nothing. Why are you in bed?'

'Never mind why. What is the news in the school?'

'We are playing against the Y.M.U. on Saturday. After that we are meeting the Board School Eleven. What we can't understand is why the Captain has left out Mohideen. He is bound to have a lot of trouble over that. People are prepared to take it up to the Headmaster.'

He could not stay in bed beyond six-thirty. He got up, opened all the windows, washed his face, combed his hair, put on a coat (not the tweed one), and went out. What he needed, he told himself, was plenty of fresh air and exercise and things to think about. Since he wanted exercise he decided to avoid the riverside. The place, he persuaded himself, was stale and overcrowded. He wished today to take a walk at the very opposite end of the town, the Trunk Road. He walked a mile along the Trunk Road and turned back. He hurried back across Lawley Extension, Market Road, and the North Street, and reached the river. It was dark and most people had gone home.

Chandran saw her at the river-bank next evening. She was wearing a green *sari*, and playing with her little companion. Chandran saw her from a distance and went towards her as if drawn by a rope. But, on approaching her, his courage failed him, and he walked away in the opposite direction. Presently he stopped and blamed himself for wasting a good opportunity of making his person familiar to her; he turned once again with the intention of passing before her closely, slowly, and deliberately. At a distance he could look at her, but when he came close he felt self-conscious and awkward, and while passing actually in front of her he bent his head, fixed his gaze on the ground, and walked fast. He was away, many yards away, from her in a moment. He checked his pace once again and looked back for a fraction of a second, and was quite thrilled at the sight of the green *sari* in the distance. He did not dare to look longer; for he was obsessed with the feeling that he was being observed by the whole crowd on the bank ... He hoped that she had observed him. He hoped that she had noted his ironed coat. He stood there and debated with himself whether she had seen him or not. One part of him said that she could not have observed him, because he had walked very fast and because there were a lot of people passing and repassing on the sand. Chandran steadily discouraged this sceptical half of his mind, and lent his whole-hearted support to the other half, which was saying that just as he had noticed her in a crowd she was sure to have noticed him. Destiny always worked that way. His well-ironed chocolate tweed was sure to invite notice. He hoped that he didn't walk clumsily in front of her. He again told himself she must have noticed that he was not like the rest of the crowd. And so why should he not now go and occupy a place that would be close to her and in the direct line of her vision? Staring was half the victory in love. His sceptical half now said that by this procedure he might scare her off the river for ever; but, said the other half, tomorrow she may not come to the river at all, and if you don't start an eye friendship immediately, you may not get the opportunity again for a million years ... He was engaged in this internal controversy when he received a slap on the back and saw Veeraswami and Mohan, his old class-mates, behind him.

'How are you, Chandran? It seems years since we met.'

'We met only last March, less than a year, you know,' said Chandran.

Mohan asked, 'Chandran, do you remember the evening we spent in your room, reading poetry?'

'Yes, yes. What have you done with your poems?'

'They are still with me.'

Chandran felt all his courtesy exhausted. He was not keen on reunions just then. He tried to get away. But Veeraswami would not let him go: 'A year since we met. I have been dying to see an old class-mate, and you want to cut me! Won't you come and have a little coffee with us in some restaurant?' He hooked his arm in Chandran's and dragged him along. Chandran tried to resist, and then said, 'Let us go this way. I promised to meet somebody. I must see if he is there ...' He pointed down the river, past the spot of green *sari*. They went in that direction. Mohan inquired three times what Chandran was doing and received no reply; Veeraswami was talking without a pause. Chandran pretended to listen to him, but constantly turned his head to his left and stole glances at something there; he had to do this without being noticed by his friends. Finally, when he passed before her, he looked at her for so short a space of time that she appeared only as a passing green blur ... Before leaving the river-bank he looked back twice only. He heartily disliked his companions.

'What are you doing now, Chandran?' Mohan asked, undefeated.

'Nothing at present. I am going to England in a few months.'

At this Veeraswami started a heated discourse on the value of going to England. 'What have we to learn from the English? I don't know when this craze for going to England will stop. It is a drain on the country's resources. What have we to learn from the English?'

'I may be going there to teach them something,' said Chandran. Even granted that she had not noticed him the first time, she couldn't have helped noticing him when he passed before her again; that was why he didn't look at her fully; he didn't want to embarrass her by meeting her gaze.

'Shall we go to the Welcome?' Veeraswami asked.

They had now left the river and were in North Street.

'Anywhere,' Chandran said mechanically.

'You seem to be worried over something,' Veeraswami said.

'Oh, nothing. I am sorry.' Chandran pulled himself up resolutely.

Here were two fellows eager for his company, and he had no business to be absorbed in distant thoughts.

'Forgive me,' he said again.

They were now before the Welcome Restaurant, a small, smoky building, from which the smell of sweets and burning ghee assailed the nostrils of passers-by in the street.

They sat round an oily table in the dark hall. Serving boys were shouting menus and bills and were dashing hither and thither. A server came and asked, 'What will you have, sir?'

'What shall we have?'

'What will you have?'

'I want only coffee.'

'Have something with it.'

'Impossible. Only coffee.'

'Bring three cups of coffee, good, strong.'

Chandran asked, 'What are you doing, Mohan? Did you get through?'

'No. I failed, and my uncle cut me. I am now the Malgudi correspondent of the *Daily Messenger* of Madras. They have given me the whole district. They pay me three-eight per column of twenty-one inches.'

'Are you making much money?'

'Sometimes fifty, sometimes ten. It all depends on those rascals, mad fellows. Sometimes they cut everything that I send.'

'It is a moderate paper,' Veeraswami said jeeringly.

'I am not concerned with their policy,' Mohan said.

'What are you doing?' Chandran asked, turning to Veeraswami.

'It will take a whole day for me to tell you. I am starting a movement called the Resurrection Brigade. I am touring about a lot on that business.'

'What is the brigade?'

'It is only an attempt to prepare the country for revolution. Montagu-Chelmsford reform, Simon Report, and what not, are all a fraud. Our politicians, including the Congressmen, are playing into the hands of the Imperialists. The Civil Disobedience Movement is a childish business. Our brigade will gain the salvation of our country by an original method. Will you join it? Mohan is already a member.'

Chandran promised to think it over, and asked what they expected Mohan to do for the movement.

'Everything. We want everybody there, poets, philosophers, musicians, sculptors, and swordsmen.'

'What is its strength now?'

'About twenty-five have so far signed the brigade pledge. I expect that in two years we shall have a membership of fifty thousand in South India alone.'

They finished their coffee and rose. They went back to the river, smoked cigarettes, and talked all the evening. Before parting, Chandran promised to see them again and asked them where they lived.

'I am staying with Mohan,' said Veeraswami.

'Where do you live, Mohan?'

'Room 14, Modern Indian Lodge, Mill Street.'

'Right. I shall drop in sometime,' said Chandran.

'I won't be in town after Tuesday. I am going into the country for six months,' said Veeraswami.

Chandran realized that friends and acquaintances were likely to prove a nuisance to him by the river. He decided to cut everyone hereafter. With this resolution he went to the Sarayu bank next evening. He also decided to be very bold, and indifferent to the public's observation and criticism.

She was there with her little companion.

Chandran went straight to a spot just thirty yards from where she sat, and settled down there. He had determined to stare at her this evening. He might even throw in an elegant wink or smile. He was going to stare at her and take in a lot of details regarding her features. He had not made out yet whether she was fair or light brown; whether she had long hair or short, and whether her eyes were round or almond-shaped; and he had also some doubts about her nose.

He sat at this thirty yards' range and kept throwing at her a side glance every fifth second. He noticed that she played a great deal with her little companion. He wanted to go to her and ask whether the little companion was her sister or cousin and how old she was. But he abandoned the idea. A man of twenty-two going up and conversing with a grown-up girl, a perfect stranger, would be affording a very uncommon sight to the public.

This optical communion became a daily habit. His powers of observation and deduction increased tremendously. He gathered several facts about the girl. She wore a dark *sari* and a green *sari* alternately. She came to the river chiefly for the sake of her little companion. She was invariably absent on Fridays and came late on Wednesdays. Chandran concluded from this that the girl went to the temple on Friday evenings, and was delayed by a music master or a stitching master on Wednesdays. He further gathered that she was of a religious disposition, and was accomplished in the art of music or embroidery. From her regularity he concluded that she was a person of very systematic habits. The fact that she played with her young companion showed that she had a loving disposition. He concluded that she had no brothers, since not a single soul escorted her on any evening. Encouraged by this conclusion, he wondered if he should not stop her and talk to her when she rose to go home. He might even accompany her to her house. That might become a beautiful habit. What wonderful things he would have to say to her. When the traffic of the town had died, they could walk together under the moon or in magic starlight. He would stop a few yards from her house. What a parting of sweetness and pain! ... It must be noted that in this dream the young companion did not exist, or, if she did, she came to the river and went home all by herself.

An evening of this optical fulfilment filled him with tranquillity. He left the river and went home late in the evening, meditating on God, and praying to Him with concentration that He would bless this romance with success. All night he repeated her name, 'Lakshmi', and fervently hoped that her soul heard his call through the night.

He had lived for over a month in a state of bliss, notwithstanding his ignorance. He began to feel now that he ought to be up and doing and get a little more practical. He could not go on staring at her on the sands all his life. He must know all about her.

He followed her at a distance of about half a furlong on a dark evening when she returned home from the river. He saw her enter a house in Mill Street. He paced before the house slowly, twice, slowing up to see if there was any board before the house. There was none.

He remembered suddenly that Mohan lived in Mill Street. Room number 14, Modern Indian Lodge, he had said. He went up and down the street in search of the hotel. At last he found it was the building opposite the girl's house. There was a signboard, but that could not be seen in the dark. Room number 14 was half a cubicle on the staircase landing. The cubicle was divided by a high wooden partition into Room 14 and Room 15.

Mohan was delighted to receive Chandran.

'Is Veeraswami gone?' Chandran asked.

'Weeks ago,' replied Mohan.

There was not a single table or chair in the room. Mohan lived on a striped carpet spread on the floor. He sat on it reclining against the wooden partition. There was a yellow trunk in a corner of the room, on which a shining nickel flower vase was kept with some paper flowers in it. The room received its light and ventilation from the single window in Room 15, over the wooden partition. A bright gas-lamp hung over the wooden partition and shed its greenish glare impartially on Room 14 and Room 15.

'Would you believe it? I have never been in this street before?' said Chandran.

'Indeed! But why should you come here? You live at the south end while this is the east end of the town.'

'I like this street,' Chandran said. 'I wonder why this is called Mill Street. Are all the people that live here mill owners?'

'Nothing of the kind. Years ago there were two weaving mills at the end of the street. There are all sorts of people here.'

'Oh. Any particularly important person?'

'None that I can think of.'

It was on Chandran's lips, at this point, to ask who lived in the opposite house. But he merely said that he wished to meet his friend oftener in his room.

'I go out news-hunting at ten in the morning and return at about four, after posting my letters. I do not usually go out after that. You can come any time you please,' said Mohan.

'Have you no holidays?'

'On Sundays we have no paper. And so on Saturday I have a holiday. I spend the whole day in the room. Please do come any time you like, and as often as you like.'

'Thanks, thanks. I have absolutely no company. I shall be delighted to come here frequently.'

CHAPTER EIGHT

Through Mohan's co-operation Chandran learnt that his sweetheart's name was Malathi, that she was unmarried, and that she was the daughter of Mr D. W. Krishna Iyer, Head Clerk in the Executive Engineer's office.

The suffix to the name of the girl's father was a comforting indication that he was of the same caste and sub-caste as Chandran. Chandran shuddered at the thought of all the complications that he would have had to face if the gentleman had been Krishna Iyengar, or Krishna Rao, or Krishna Mudaliar. His father would certainly cast him off if he tried to marry out of caste.

Chandran took it all as a favourable sign, as an answer to his prayers, which were growing intenser every day. In each fact, that Mohan lived in the hotel opposite her house, that she was unmarried, that her father was an 'Iyer'. Chandran felt that God was revealing Himself.

Chandran prayed to God to give him courage, and went to his father to talk to him about his marriage. His courage failed him at the last moment, and he went away after discussing some fatuous subject. The next day he again went to his father with the same resolution and again lapsed into fatuity. He went back to his room and regretted his cowardice. He would be unworthy of Malathi if he was going to be such a spineless worm. Afraid of a father! He was not a baby asking for a toy, but a full-grown adult out on serious business, very serious business. It was very doubtful if a squirming coward would be any good to Malathi as a husband.

He went back to his father, who was on the veranda reading something. Mother had gone out to see some friends; Seenu had gone to school. This was the best time to talk to Father confidentially.

Father put down the book on seeing Chandran, and pulled the spectacles from over his nose. Chandran drew a chair close to Father's easy-chair.

'Have you read this book, Chandar?'

Chandran looked at it – some old novel, Dickens. 'No.' At another time he would have added, 'I hate Dickens's laborious humour,' and involved himself in a debate. But now he merely said, 'I will try to read it later.' He did not want to throw away precious time in literary discussions.

'Father, please don't mistake me. I want to marry D. W. Krishna Iyer's daughter.'

Father put on his spectacles and looked at his son with a frown. He sat up and asked, 'Who is he?'

'Head Clerk in the Executive Engineer's office.'

'Why do you want to marry his daughter?'

'I like her.'

'Do you know the girl?'

'Yes. I have seen her often.'

'Where?'

Chandran told him.

'Have you spoken to each other?'

'No ...'

'Does she know you?'

'I don't know.'

Father laughed, and it cut into Chandran's soul.

Father asked, 'In that case why this girl alone and not any other?'

Chandran said, 'I like her,' and left Father's company abruptly as Father said, 'I don't know anything about these things. I must speak to your mother.'

Later Mother came into Chandran's room and asked, 'What is all this?' Chandran answered with an insolent silence.

'Who is this girl?' There was great anxiety in her voice.

Chandran told her. She was very disappointed. A Head Clerk's daughter was not what she had hoped to get for her son. 'Chandar, why won't you consider any of the dozens of girls that have been proposed to you?'

Chandran rejected this suggestion indignantly.

'But suppose those girls are richer and more beautiful?'

'I don't care. I shall marry this girl and no one else.'

'But how are you sure they are prepared to give their daughter to you?'

'They will have to.'

'Extraordinary! Do you think marriage is a child's game? We don't know anything about them, who they are, what they are, what they are worth, if the stars and the other things about the girl are all right, and above all, whether they are prepared to marry their girl at all ...'

'They will have to. I hear that this season she will be married because she is getting on for sixteen.'

'Sixteen!' Mother screamed. 'They can't be all right if they have kept the girl unmarried till sixteen. She must have attained puberty ages ago. They can't be all right. We have a face to keep in this town. Do you think it is all child's play?' She left the room in a temper.

In a few days this hostility had to be abandoned, because Chandran's parents could not bear for long the sight of an unhappy Chandran. For his sake they were prepared to compromise to this extent: they were prepared to consider the proposal if it came from the other side. Whatever happened they would not take the initiative for the matter; for they belonged to the bridegroom's side, and according to time-honoured practice it was the bride's people who proposed first. Anything done contrary to this would make them the laughing-stock of the community.

Chandran raved: 'To the dust-pot with your silly customs.'

But his mother replied that she at any rate belonged to a generation which was in no way worse than the present one for all its observances; and as long as she lived she would insist on respecting the old customs. Ordinary talk at home was becoming rarer every day. It was always a debate on Custom and Reason. His father usually remained quiet during these debates. One of the major mysteries in life for Chandran at this period was the question as to which side his father favoured. He did not appear to place active obstacles in Chandran's way, but he did little else. He appeared to distrust his own wisdom in these matters and to have handed the full rein to his wife. Chandran once or twice tried to sound him and gain him to his side; but he was evasive and non-committal.

Chandran's only support and consolation at this juncture was Mohan. To his room he went every night after dinner. This visit was not entirely from an unmixed motive. While on his way he could tarry for a while before her house and gladden his heart with a sight of her under the hall-lamp as she passed from one part of the house to another. Probably she was going to bed; blessed be those pillows. Or probably she went in and read; ah, blessed books with the touch of her hands on them. He would often speculate what hour she would go to bed, what hour she would rise, and how she lay down and slept and how her bed looked. Could he not just dash into the house, hide in the passage, steal up to her bed at night, crush her in his arms, and carry her away?

If it happened to be late, and the lights in the house were put out, he would walk distractedly up and down before the house, and then go to Room 14 of the Modern Indian Lodge.

Mohan would put away whatever poem he was writing. But for him Chandran would have been shrivelled up by the heat of hopeless love. Mohan would put away his pad, and clear a space on the carpet for Chandran.

Chandran would give him the latest bulletin from the battle front, and then pass on to a discussion of theories.

'If the girl's father were called something other than a Head Clerk, and given a hundred more to his pay, I am sure your parents would move heaven and earth to secure this alliance,' said the poet.

'Why should we be cudgelled and nose-led by our elders?' Chandran asked indignantly. 'Why can't we be allowed to arrange our lives as we please? Why can't they leave us to rise or sink on our own ideals?'

These were mighty questions; and the poet tackled them in his own way. 'Money is the greatest god in life. Father and mother and brother do not care for anything but your money. Give them money and they will leave you alone. I am just writing a few lines entitled "Moneylove". It is free verse. You must hear it. I have dedicated it to you.' Mohan picked up the pad and read:

'The parents loved you, you thought.
No, no, not you, my dear.
They've loved nothing less for its own sake.
They fed you and petted you and pampered you

Because some day they hope you will bring them money;
Much money, so much and more and still more;
Because some day, they hope, you'll earn a
Bride who'll bring much money, so much and
More and still more ...'

There were two more stanzas in the same strain. It brought the tears to Chandran's eyes. He hated his father and mother. He took this poem with him when he went home.

He gave it to his father next day. Father read through it twice and asked with a dry smile: 'Did you write this?'

'Never mind the authorship,' Chandran said.

'Do you believe what these lines say?'

'I do,' said Chandran, and did not stay there for further talk.

When he was gone Father explained the poem to Mother, who began to cry. Father calmed her and said, 'This is what he seems to feel. I don't know what to do.'

'We have promised to consider it if it is made from that side. What more can we do?'

'I don't know.'

'They seem to be thorough rogues. The marriage season has already begun. Why can't they approach us? They expect Chandran to go to them, touch their feet, and beg them for their girl.'

'They probably do not know that Chandran is available,' said Father.

'Why do you defend them? They can't be ignorant of the existence of a possible bridegroom like Chandran. That man, the girl's father, seems to be a deep man. He is playing a deep game. He is waiting for our boy to go to him, when he can get a good husband for his daughter without giving a dowry and without an expensive wedding ... This boy Chandra is talking nonsense. This is what we get from our children for all our troubles ... I am in a mood to let him do anything he likes ... But what more can we do? I shall drown myself in Sarayu before I allow any proposal to go from here.'

CHAPTER NINE

Chandran's parents sent for Ganapathi Sastrigal, who was matchmaker in general to a few important families in Malgudi. He had a small income from his lands in the village; he was once a third clerk in a Collector's Office, which also gave him now a two-digit pension. After retiring from Government service he settled down as a general adviser, officiating priest at rituals, and a matchmaker. He confined his activities to a few rich families in the town.

He came next day in the hot sun, and went straight into the kitchen, where Chandran's mother was preparing some sweets.

'Oh, come in, come in,' Chandran's mother exclaimed on seeing him. 'Why have you been neglecting us so long? It is over a year since you came to our house.'

'I had to spend some months in the village. There was some dispute about the lands; and also some arrears had to be collected from the tenants. I tell you lands are a curse ...'

'Oh, you are standing,' she cried, and said to the cook, 'Take a sitting-board and give it to him.'

'No, no, no. Don't trouble yourself. I can sit on the floor,' said the old man. He received the proffered sitting-board, but gently put it away and sat on the floor.

'Won't you take a little tiffin and coffee?' Chandran's mother asked.

'Oh, no. Don't trouble yourself. I have just had it all in my house. Don't trouble yourself.'

'Absolutely no trouble,' she said, and set before him a plate of sweets and a tumbler of coffee.

He ate the sweets slowly, and poured the coffee down his throat, holding the tumbler high over his lips. He said, 'I have taken this because you have put it before me, and I don't like to see anything wasted. My digestion is not as good as it was before I had the jaundice. I recently showed myself to a doctor, Doctor

Kesavan. I wonder if you know him? He is the son-in-law of Raju of Trichinopoly, whom I have known since his boyhood. The doctor said that I must give up tamarind and use only lemon in its place ...'

Afterwards he followed her out of the kitchen to the back veranda of the house. Chandran's mother spread a mat before him and requested him to sit on it, and opened the subject.

'Do you know D. W. Krishna Iyer's family?'

The old man sat thinking for a while, and then said, 'D. W. Krishnan; you mean Coimbatore Appaji's nephew, the fellow who is in the Executive Engineer's office? I have known their family for three generations.'

'I am told he has a daughter ready for marriage.'

The old man remained very thoughtful and said, 'Yes, it is true. He has a daughter old enough to have a son, but not yet married.'

'Why is it so? Anything wrong with the family?'

'Absolutely nothing,' replied the old man. He now saw he ought not to be critical in his remarks. He tried to mend his previous statement. 'Absolutely nothing. Anyone that says such a thing will have a rotting tongue. The girl is only well-grown, and I don't think she is as old as she looks. She can't be more than fifteen. This has become the standard age for girls nowadays. Everybody holds advanced views in these days. Even in an ancient and orthodox family like Sadasiva Iyer's they married a girl recently at fifteen!'

This was very comforting to Chandran's mother. She asked, 'Do you think that it is a good family?'

'D. W. Krishnan comes of a very noble family. His father was ...' The Sastrigal went on giving an impressive history of the family, ranging over three generations. 'If Krishnan is now only a Head Clerk it is because when he came into the property his elder brothers had squandered all of it and left only debts and encumbrances. Krishnan was rocked in a golden cradle when he was young, but became the foster-son of Misfortune after his father died. It is all fate. Who can foresee what is going to happen?'

After two hours of talk he left the house on a mission; that was to go to D. W. Krishna Iyer's house and ascertain if they were going to marry their girl this season, and to move them to take the initiative in a proposal for an alliance with Chandran's family. The old man was to give out that he was acting independently, and on his own initiative.

Next day Ganapathi Sastrigal came with good news. As soon as Chandran's mother saw him at the gate she cried, 'Sastrigal has come!'

As soon as he climbed the veranda steps Chandran's father said, 'Ah, come in, come in, Sastriar,' and pushed a chair towards him. The Sastrigal sat on the edge of the chair, wiped the sweat off his nape with his upper cloth, and said to Mother, 'Summer has started very early this year ... Do you cool water in a mud jug?'

'Certainly, otherwise it is impossible to quench our thirst in summer. It is indispensable.'

'If that is so, please ask your cook to bring me a tumbler of jug water.'

'You must drink some coffee.'

'Don't trouble yourself. Water will do.'

'Will you take a little tiffin?'

'No, no. Give me only water. Don't trouble yourself about coffee or tiffin.'

'Absolutely no trouble,' said Mother, and went in and returned with a tumbler of coffee.

'You are putting yourself to great trouble bringing me this coffee,' said the old man, taking the tumbler.

'Have you any news for us?' she asked.

'Plenty, plenty,' said the old man. 'I went to D. W. Krishnan's house this morning; as you may already know, we have known each other for three generations. He was not at home when I went. He had gone to see his officer or on some such work, but his wife was there. She asked her daughter to spread a mat for me, and then sent her in to bring me coffee. I am simply filled with coffee everywhere. I drank the coffee and gave the tumbler back to the girl ... She is a smart girl; stands very tall, and has a good figure. Her skin is fair, may be called fair, though not as fair as that of our lady here; but she is by no means to be classed as a dark girl. Her mother says that the girl has just completed her fourteenth year.' Chandran's mother felt a great load off her mind now. She wouldn't have to marry her son to a girl over sixteen, and incur the comments of the community.

'I knew all along that there couldn't be truth in what people said ...' she said.

'And then we talked of one thing and another,' said the Sastrigal, 'and the subject came to marriage. You can take it from me that they are going to marry their girl this season. She will certainly be married in *Panguni* month. Just as I was thinking of going, Krishnan came in. He is a very good fellow. He showed me the regard due to my age, and due to me for my friendship with his father and uncles. He is very eager to complete the marriage this season. He asked me to help him to secure a bridegroom. I suggested two or three others and then your son. I may tell you that he thinks he will be extraordinarily blessed if he can secure an alliance with your family. He feels you may not stoop to his status.'

'Status! Status!' Chandran's mother exclaimed. 'We have seen with these very eyes people who were rich once, but are in the streets now, and such pranks of fate. What a foolish notion to measure status with money. It is here today and gone tomorrow. What I would personally care for most in any alliance would be character and integrity.'

'That I can guarantee,' said the Sastrigal. 'When I mentioned this family, the lady was greatly elated. She seems to know you all very well. She even said that she and you were related. It seems that your maternal grandfather's first wife and her paternal grandfather were sister and brother, not cousins, but direct sister and brother.'

'Ah, I did not know that. I am so happy to hear it.' She then asked, 'Have you any idea how much they are prepared to spend?'

'Yes. I got it out in a manner; very broadly, of course; but that will do for the present. I think they are prepared to give a cash dowry of about two thousand rupees, silver vessels and presents up to a thousand, and spend about a thousand on the wedding celebrations. These will be in addition to about a thousand worth of diamond and gold on the girl.'

Chandran's mother was slightly disappointed at the figures. 'We can settle all that later.'

'Quite right,' said the old man. 'Tomorrow, if everything is auspicious, they will send you the girl's horoscope. We shall proceed with the other matters after comparing the horoscopes. I am certain that this marriage will take place very soon. Even as I started for their house a man came bearing pots of foaming toddy; it is an excellent omen. I am certain that this alliance will be completed.'

'Why bother with horoscopes?' asked Chandran's father. 'Personally, I have no faith in them.'

'You must not say that,' said the Sastrigal. 'How are we to know whether two persons brought together will have health, happiness, harmony, and long life, if we do not study their horoscopes individually and together?'

Chandran felt very happy that her horoscope was coming. He imagined that the very next thing after the horoscope would be marriage. The very fact that they were willing to send the girl's horoscope for comparison proved that they were not averse to this alliance. They were probably goaded on by the girl. He had every reason to believe that the girl had told her parents she would marry Chandran and no one else. But how could she know him or his name? Girls had a knack of learning of these things by a sort of sixth sense. How splendid of her to speak out her mind like this, brave girl. If her mind matched her form, it must be one of the grandest things in the world ...

The thought of her melted him. He clutched his pillow and cried in the darkness, 'Darling, what are you doing? Do you hear me?'

In these days he met her less often at the river, but he made it up by going to Mill Street and wandering in front of her house until her form passed under the hall light. He put down her absence at the river to her desire to save Chandran's reputation. She felt, Chandran thought, that seeing him every day at the river would give rise to gossip. Such a selfless creature. Would rather sacrifice her evening's outing than subject Chandran to gossip. Chandran had no doubt that she was going to be the most perfect wife a man could ever hope to get.

As he sauntered in front of her house, Chandran would often ask God when His grace would bend low so that Chandran might cease to be a man in the street and stride into the house as a son-in-law. After they were married, he would tell her everything. They would sit in their creeper-covered villa on the hill slope, just those two, and watch the sun set. In the afterglow of the evening he would tell her of his travails, and they would both laugh.

The next day Ganapathi Sastrigal did not come, and Chandran began to think wild things. What was the matter? Had they suddenly backed out?

The horoscope was not sent on the next day either. Chandran asked his mother every half-hour if it had come, and finally suggested that someone should be sent to bring it. When this suggestion reached Father's ears, he asked, 'Why don't you yourself go and ask them for a copy of the girl's horoscope?'

Chandran's mind being in a state of lowered efficiency, he asked eagerly, 'Shall I? I thought I shouldn't do it.'

Father laughed and told it to Mother, who became scared and said, 'Chandra, please don't do it. It would be a very curious procedure. They will send the horoscope themselves.'

Father said to Chandran, 'Look here, you will never be qualified to marry unless you cultivate a lot of patience. It is the only power that you will be allowed to exercise when you are married.'

Mother looked at Father suspiciously and said, 'Will you kindly make your meaning clearer?'

Chandran went to his room in a very distracted state. He tried to read a novel, but his mind kept wandering. Seenu, his younger brother, came in and asked, 'Brother, are you not well?' He could not understand what was wrong with Chandran. He very much missed Chandran's company in the after-dinner chatting group; he very much missed his supervision, though it had always been aggressive. Chandran looked at him without giving any answer. Seenu wanted to ask if his brother was about to be married, but he was too shy to mention a thing like marriage. So he asked if Chandran was unwell. Chandran answered, after the question was repeated, 'I am quite well; why?'

'You don't look well.'

'Quite likely.'

'That is all I wanted to know. Because Mother said that you were going to be married.'

There was no obvious connection between the two, but Seenu felt he had led on to the delicate topic with cunning diplomacy.

Chandran asked, 'Boy, would you like to have a sister-in-law?'

Seenu slunk behind the chair with shame at this question.

Chandran made it worse by asking, 'Would you like a sister-in-law to be called Malathi?'

At this Seenu was so abashed that he ran out of the room, leaving Chandran to the torture of his thoughts and worries.

When the horoscope did not come on the next day, Chandran went to Mohan and asked, 'Why should I not go to Mr Krishna Iyer and ask for it?'

Mohan replied, 'Why have you not done it already?'

'I thought that it might be irregular.'

'Would it be different now?'

Chandran remained silent. His special pride in the conducting of his romance so far was that he had not committed the slightest irregularity at any time. He felt that he could easily have talked to her when she was alone on the sands; he could have tried to write to her; he could have befriended Mr Krishna Iyer and asked him for the hand of his daughter; and he could have done a number of other things, but he didn't, for the sake of his parents; he wanted everything to be done in the correct, orthodox manner.

Mohan said, 'I don't care for orthodoxy and correctness myself. But since you care for those things, at least for the sake of your parents keep it up and don't do anything rashly now.'

But Chandran wailed that they had not sent the horoscope. What could it mean except coldness on their part?

Mohan said, 'Till they show some more solid proof of their coldness we ought not to do anything.'

Chandran rested in gloom for a while and then came out with a bright idea: 'I have got to know the girl's father, and you must help me.'

'How?'

'You are a newspaper correspondent, and you have access everywhere. Why don't you go to his house on some work;

say that you want some news connected with the Engineering Department. People are awfully nice to newspaper correspondents.'

'They are. But where do you come in?'

'You can take me along with you and introduce me to him. You may even say that I am your assistant.'

'How is that going to help you?'

'You had better leave that to me.'

'There is absolutely no excuse for me to go and see him.'

'There is a rumour of a bridge over Sarayu, near Nallappa's Grove. You must know if it is true. Engineering Department.' Mohan realized that love sharpened the wits extraordinarily.

While walking home Chandran formulated a perfect scheme for interviewing Mr D. W. Krishna Iyer. He would do it without Mohan's help. The scheme that he had suggested to Mohan fired his imagination. Chandran decided to go and knock on the door of Krishna Iyer's house. Malathi would open the door. He would ask if her father was in, and tell her he was there in order to know if it was a fact that there was going to be a bridge over Sarayu; he could tell her he would call in again and go away. This would help him to see her at close quarters, and to decide once for all whether her eyes were round or almond-shaped, and whether her complexion was light brown or dusky translucence. He might even carry a small camera with him and take a snapshot of her. For one of the major exercises for his mind at that time was trying to recollect the features of Malathi, which constantly dissolved and tormented him. His latest hobby was scanning the faces of passers-by in the streets to see if anyone resembled her. She had no double in the world. There was a boy in a wayside shop whose arched, dark eyebrows seemed to Chandran to resemble Malathi's; Chandran often went to that shop and bought three-pies' worth of peppermint and gazed at the boy's eyebrows.

There was good news for him at home. Ganapathi Sastrigal came in the evening with the girl's horoscope. He explained the delay was due to the fact that the preceding days were inauspicious. He took Chandran's horoscope with him, to give to the girl's people.

So the first courtesies were exchanged between the families. As Chandran looked at the small piece of paper on which the horoscope was drawn, his heart bubbled over with joy. He noticed that the corners of the paper were touched with saffron – a mark of auspiciousness. So they had fully realized that it was an auspicious undertaking. Did not that fact indicate that they approved of this bridegroom and were anxious to secure him? If they were anxious to secure him, did not that mean that she would soon be his? Chandran read the horoscope a number of times, though he understood very little of it. It dissipated his accumulated gloom in a moment.

Chandran was very happy the whole of the next day; but his mother constantly checked his exuberance: 'Chandra, you must not think that the only thing now to be settled is the date of the marriage. God helping, all the difficulties will be solved, but there are yet a number of preliminaries to be settled. First, our astrologer must tell us if your horoscope can be matched with the girl's; and then I don't know what their astrologer will say. Let us hope for the best. After that, they must come and invite us to see the girl.'

'I have seen the girl, Mother, and I like her.'

'All the same they must invite us, and we must go there formally. After that they must come and ask us if you like the girl. And the terms of the marriage must be discussed and settled ... I don't mean to discourage you, but you must be patient till all this is settled.'

Chandran sat biting his nails: 'But, Mother, you won't create difficulties over the dowry?'

'We shall see. We must not be too exacting, nor can we cheapen ourselves.'

'But suppose you haggle too much?'

'Don't you worry about anything, boy. If they won't give you the girl on reasonable conditions, I shall get you other girls a thousand times more suitable.'

'Don't talk like that, Mother. I shall never forgive you if this marriage does not take place through your bickerings over the dowry and the presents.'

'We have a status and a prestige to keep. We can't lower ourselves unduly.'

'You care more for your status than for the happiness of your son.'

'It doesn't seem proper for you to be speaking like this, Chandra.'

Chandran argued and tried to prove that demanding a cash dowry amounted to extortion. He said that the bridegroom's parents exploited the anxiety of the parents of a girl, who must be married before she attained puberty. This kind of talk always irritated Chandran's mother. She said, 'My father gave seven thousand in cash to your father, and over two thousand in silver vessels, and spent nearly five thousand on wedding celebrations. What was wrong in it? How are we any the worse for it? It is the duty of every father to set some money apart for securing a son-in-law. We can't disregard custom.'

Chandran said that it was all irrational extravagance and that the total expenses for a marriage ought not to exceed a hundred rupees.

'You may go and tell your girl's father that, and finish your marriage and come home. I shall gladly receive you and your wife, but don't expect any of us to attend the wedding. If you want us there, everything must be done in the proper manner.'

'But, Mother,' Chandran pleaded, 'you will be reasonable in your demands, won't you? They are not well-to-do.'

'We shall see; but don't try to play their lawyer already. Time enough for that.'

Father was dressing to go out. Chandran went to him and reported his mother's attitude. Father said, 'Don't be frightened. She doesn't mean you any harm.'

'But suppose she holds to a big dowry and they can't pay. What is to happen?'

'Well, well, there is time to think of that yet. They have taken your horoscope. Let them come and tell us what they think of the horoscopes.'

He took his walking-stick and started out. Chandran followed him to the gate, pleading. He wanted his father to stop and assure him of his support against Mother.

But Father merely said, 'Don't worry,' and went out.

CHAPTER TEN

Three days later a peon from the Engineering Department came with a letter for Father. Father, who was on the veranda, took it, and after reading it, passed it on to Chandran, who was sitting on a chair with a book. The letter read:

> 'Dear and Respected Sir, I am returning herewith the copy of your son's horoscope, which you so kindly sent to me for comparison with my daughter's. Our family astrologer, after careful study and comparison, says that the horoscopes cannot be matched. Since I have great faith in horoscopy, and since I have known from experience that the marriage of couples ill-matched in the stars often leads to misfortune and even tragedy, I have to seek a bridegroom elsewhere. I hope that your honoured self, your wife, and your son will forgive me for the unnecessary trouble I have caused you. No one can have a greater regret at missing an alliance with your family than I. However, we can only propose. He on the Thirupathi Hills alone knows what is best for us.
>
> 'With regards,
> 'Yours sincerely,
> 'D. W. Krishnan.'

Chandran gave the letter back to his father, rose without a word, and went to his room. Father sat tapping the envelope on his left hand, and called his wife.

'Here they have written that the horoscopes don't match.'

'Have they? ... H'm. I knew all along that they were up to some such trick. If there is any flaw in the horoscope it must be in the girl's, not in the boy's. His is a first-class horoscope. They want a cheap bridegroom, somebody who will be content with a dowry of one hundred rupees and a day's celebration of the wedding, and they know that they cannot get Chandra on those terms. They want some excuse to back out now.' She remained silent for a while, and said, 'So much the better. I have always disliked this proposal to tack Chandran on to a hefty, middle-aged girl. There are fifty girls waiting to be married to him.'

Just when Father was dressed and ready to go out, Chandran came out of his room and said in a voice that was thick, 'Father, will you still try and find out if something can't be done?'

Father was about to answer, 'Don't worry about this girl, I shall get you another girl,' but he looked up and saw that Chandran's eyes were red. So he said, 'Don't worry. I shall find out what is wrong and try to set it right.' He went out, and Chandran went back to his room and bolted the door.

Chandran's father wrote next day:

> 'DEAR MR KRISHNAN, I shall be very glad if you will kindly come and see me this evening. I meant to call on you, but I did not know what hour would suit you. Since I am always free, I shall be at your service and await the pleasure of meeting you.'

Mr Krishna Iyer came that evening. After the courtesies of coffee and inane inquiries were over, Chandran's father asked, 'Now, sir, please tell me why the horoscopes don't match.'

'I ought not to be saying it, sir, but there is a flaw in your son's horoscope. Our astrologer has found that the horoscopes cannot be matched. If my girl's horoscope had Moon or Mars in the Seventh House, there couldn't be a better match than your son for her. But as it is ...'

'Are you sure?'

'I know a little of astrology myself. I am prepared to overlook many things in a horoscope. I don't usually concern myself with the factors that indicate prosperity, wealth, progeny, and all that. I usually overlook them. But I do feel that we can't ignore the question of longevity. I know hundreds of cases where the presence of Mars in this house ... I can tell you that ...' He hesitated to say it. 'It kills the wife soon after the marriage,' he said, when pressed by Chandran's father.

Chandran's father was for dropping the question at this point, but when he remembered that Chandran had shut himself in his room, he sent for one Srouthigal, an eminent astrologer and almanac-compiler in the town.

The next day there was a conference over the question of the stars and their potency. After four hours of intricate calculations and the filling of several sheets of paper with figures, Srouthigal said that there was nothing wrong with Chandran's horoscope. D. W. Krishna Iyer was sent for, and he came. Srouthigal looked at Krishna Iyer and said, 'These two horoscopes are well matched.'

'Did you notice the Mars?'

'Yes, but it is powerless now. It is now under the sway of the Sun, which looks at it from the Fifth House.'

'But I doubt it, sir,' Krishna Iyer said.

Srouthigal thrust the papers into Krishna Iyer's hands, and asked, 'How old is the boy?'

'Nearly twenty-three.'

'What is twelve and eight?'

'Twenty.'

'How can the boy be affected by it at twenty-three? If he had married at twenty, he might have had to marry again, but not now. Mars became powerless when the boy was twenty years, three months, and five days old.'

'But I get it differently in my calculations,' said Krishna Iyer. 'The power of Mars lasts till the boy reaches twenty-five years and eight months.'

'Which almanac do you follow?' asked Srouthigal, with a fiery look.

'The *Vakya*,' said Krishna Iyer.

'There you are,' said Srouthigal. 'Why don't you base your calculations on the *Drig* almanac?'

'From time immemorial we have followed only the *Vakya*, and nothing has gone wrong so far. I think it is the only true almanac.'

'You are making a very strange statement,' said the Srouthigal, with a sneer.

When he went home Krishna Iyer took the papers with him, promising to calculate again and reconsider. He wrote to Chandran's father next day: 'I worked all night, till about 4 a.m., on the horoscopes. Our astrologer was also with me. We have not arrived at any substantially different results now. The only change we find is that the Sun's sway comes in the boy's twenty-fifth year and fourth month and not in the eighth month as I stated previously.

'Anyone who is not a fanatic of the *Drig* system will see that the potency of Mars lasts very nearly till the boy's twenty-fifth year. This is not a matter in which we can take risks. It is a question of life and death to a girl. Mars has never been known to spare. He kills.

'I seek your forgiveness for all the trouble I may have caused you in this business. I cannot find adequate words to express how unhappy I am to miss the opportunity of an alliance with your great house. I hope God will bless Mr Chandran with a suitable bride soon ...'

Chandran's mother raved, 'Why can't you leave these creatures alone? A black dot on Chandran's horoscope is what we get for associating with them. If they go on spreading the rumour that Chandran has Mars, a nice chance he will have of ever getting a girl. This is what we get for trying to pick up something from a gutter.'

When she was gone, Chandran suggested to his father, 'Let us grant that Mars lasts till my twenty-fifth year. I am nearly twenty-three now. I shall be twenty-five very soon. Why don't you tell them that I will wait till my twenty-fifth year; let them also wait for two years. Let us come to an understanding with them.'

Chandran's father knew that it would be perfectly useless to reason things with Chandran. Hence he said that he would try to meet Krishna Iyer and suggest this to him.

Thereafter every day Chandran privately asked his father if he had met Krishna Iyer, and Father gave the stock reply that Krishna Iyer could not be found either at home or in his office.

After waiting for a few days Chandran wrote a letter to Malathi. He guarded against making it a love letter. It was, according to Chandran's belief, a simple, matter-of-fact piece of writing. It only contained an account of his love for her. It explained to her the difficulty in the horoscope, and asked her if she was prepared to wait for him for two years. Let her write the single word 'Yes' or 'No' on a piece of paper and post it to him. He enclosed a stamped addressed envelope for a reply.

He took the letter to Mohan and said, 'This is my last chance.'

'What is it?'

'It is a letter to her.'

'Oh God! You can't do that!'

'It is not a love letter. It is a dry, business letter. You must see that it is somehow delivered to her.'

'Have I to wait for a reply?'

'No. She can post a reply. I have arranged for it.'

'They will shoo me out if they see me delivering a letter to a grown-up girl.'

'But you must somehow manage it for my sake. This is my last attempt. I shall wait till I receive a reply ...' said Chandran, and completed the sentence in sobs.

Next morning he went to the post office and asked the Lawley Extension postman if there was any letter for him. This became a daily routine. Day followed day thus. He rarely went to the river now. He avoided going to the Modern Indian Lodge because it was opposite her house.

On an evening, a fortnight later, Chandran started for the Modern Indian Lodge. 'I must grit my teeth and pass before her house, go to the hotel, see Mohan, and ask him why there is no letter yet,' he told himself.

When he came to Mill Street he heard a drum and pipe music. His heart beat fast. When he reached the Modern Indian Lodge he saw that the entrance of the opposite house was decorated with plantain stems and festoons of mango leaves. These were marks of an auspicious event. Chandran's body trembled. The drummer, sitting on the pyol in front of the house, beat the drum with all the vigour in his arms; the piper was working a crescendo in *Kalyani raga*. The music scalded Chandran's ears. He ran up the steps to Mohan's room.

'What are they doing in the opposite house?'

Mohan sprang up, put his arms around Chandran, and soothed him, 'Calm yourself. This won't do.'

Chandran shouted, 'What are they doing in the opposite house? Tell me! Why this pipe, why the mango leaves, who is going to be married in that house?'

'Nobody yet, but presently. They are celebrating the Wedding Notice. I learn that she is to marry her cousin next week.'

'What has happened to my letter?'

'I don't know.'

'Will nobody choke that piper? He is murdering the tune.'

'Sit down, Chandran.'

'Did you deliver that letter?'

'I couldn't get a chance, and I destroyed it this morning when I learnt that she is to be married.'

Chandran threw at him an angry look. He said, 'Goodbye,' turned round, and fled down the stairs.

The opposite house shone in the greenish brilliance of two Kitson lamps. People were coming to the house, women wearing lace-bordered *saris*, and men in well-ironed shirts and upper cloths – guests to the Wedding Notice ceremony. Chandran ran down the street, chased by the *Kalyani raga* and the doom-doom of the drummer.

Chandran had fever that night. He had a high temperature, and he raved. In about ten days, when he was well again, he insisted on being sent to Madras for a change. His father gave him fifty rupees, sent a wire to his brother at Madras to meet Chandran at the Egmore Station, and put Chandran in a train going to Madras. Chandran's mother said at the station that he must return to Malgudi very plump and fat, and without any kind of worry in his head; Father said that he could write for more money if he needed it; Seenu, who had also come to the station, asked, 'Brother, do you know Messrs Binns in Madras?'

'No,' said Chandran.

'It is in Mount Road,' said Seenu, and explained that it was the most magnificent sports goods firm in the country. 'Please go there and ask them to send me that fat catalogue; there are a lot of cricket pictures in it. Please buy a Junior Willard bat for me. Note it down, you may forget the name; it is Binns, Junior Willard,' he cried as the engine lurched, and Mother wiped her eyes, and Father stood looking after the train.

PART THREE

CHAPTER ELEVEN

Next morning, as the train steamed into the Madras Egmore Station, Chandran, watching through the window of his compartment, saw in the crowd on the platform his uncle's son. Chandran understood that the other was there to receive him, and quickly withdrew his head into the compartment. The moment the train halted, Chandran pushed his bag and hold-all into the hands of a porter, and hurried off the platform. Outside a *jutka* driver greeted him and invited him to get into his carriage. Chandran got in and said, 'Drive to the hotel.'

'Which hotel, master?'

'Any hotel you like.'

'Would you like the one opposite to the People's Park?'

'Yes,' said Chandran.

The *jutka* driver whipped his horse and shouted to the pedestrians to keep out of the way.

The *jutka* stopped in front of a red smoky building. Chandran jumped out of the carriage and walked into the hotel, the *jutka* driver following him, carrying the bag and the hold-all.

A man was sitting before a table making entries in a ledger. Chandran stood before him and asked, 'Have you rooms?'

'Yes,' said the man without looking up.

'My fare, sir,' reminded the *jutka* driver at this point.

'How much?' Chandran asked.

'A rupee, master. I have brought you here all the way from the station.'

Chandran took out his purse and gave him a rupee, and the *jutka* driver went away gasping with astonishment. Invariably if he asked for a rupee he would be given only a quarter of it, after endless haggling and argument. Now this fare had flung out a rupee without any question. It was a good beginning for the day;

he always regretted afterwards that it hadn't occurred to him to ask for two rupees at the first shot.

The man at the table pressed a bell; a servant appeared. The man said, 'Room Three, upstairs,' and gave him a key. The servant lifted the hold-all and the bag and disappeared. Chandran stood hesitating, not knowing what he was expected to do.

'The advance,' said the man at the table.

'How much?' Chandran asked, wishing that the people of Madras were more human; they were so mechanical and impersonal; the porter at the station had behaved as if he were blind, deaf, and mute; now this hotel man would not even look at his guest; these fellows simply did not care what happened to you after they had received your money; the *jutka* man had departed promptly after he received the rupee, not uttering a single word ... Chandran had a feeling of being neglected. 'How many days are you staying?' asked the man at the table. Chandran realized that he had not thought of this question; but he was afraid to say so; the other might put his hand on his neck and push him out; anything was possible in this impersonal place.

'Three days,' Chandran said.

'Then a day's advance will do now,' the man said, looking at Chandran for the first time.

'How much?'

'Four rupees. Upstair room four rupees a day, and downstair two-eight a day. I have sent your things to Three upstairs.'

'Thank you very much,' Chandran said, and gave him the advance.

His room was up a winding staircase. It was a small room containing a chair, a table, and an iron bedstead.

Chandran sat on the bedstead and rubbed his eyes. He felt weary. He got up and stood looking out of the window: tramcars were grinding the road; motor-cars, cycles, rickshaws, buses, *jutkas*, and all kinds of vehicles were going up and down in a tremendous hurry in the General Hospital Road below. Electric trains roared behind the hotel building. Chandran could not bear the noise of traffic. He returned to his bedstead and sat on it, holding his head between his hands. Somebody was humming a tune in the next room. The humming faded and then seemed to come nearer. Chandran looked up and saw a stranger, carrying a towel and a soap box, standing in the doorway. He was a dark, whiskered person. He stood for a while there, looking at Chandran unconcernedly and humming a tune.

'Not coming to bathe, friend?' he asked.

'No. I shall bathe later,' replied Chandran.

'When? You won't have water in the tap after nine. Come with me. I will show you the bathroom.'

From that moment the whiskered man, who announced that his name was 'Kailas', took charge of Chandran. He acted as his guide and adviser in every minute detail of personal existence.

They went out together after breakfast. Chandran had absolutely no courage to oppose the other in anything. Kailas had an aggressive hospitality. He never showed the slightest toleration for any amendment or suggestion that Chandran made. Chandran was taken out and was whirled about in all sorts of tramcars and buses all day. They had tiffin in at least four hotels before the evening. Kailas paid for everything, and talked without a pause. Chandran learnt that Kailas had married two wives and loved both of them; had years ago made plenty of money in Malaya, and had now settled down in his old village, which was about a night's journey from Madras, and that he occasionally descended on Madras in order to have a good time. 'I have brought two hundred rupees with me. I shall stay here till this is spent, and then return to my village and sleep between the two wives for the next three months, and then again come here. I don't know how long it is going to last. What do you think my age is?'

'About thirty,' Chandran said, giving out the first number that came to his head.

'Ah, ah, ah! Do you think my hair is dyed?'

'No, no,' Chandran assured him.

'In these days fellows get greying hairs before they are twenty-five. I am fifty-one. I shall be good enough for this kind of life for another twenty years at least. After that it doesn't matter what happens; I shall have lived a man's life. A man must spend forty years in making money and forty years in spending it.'

By the evening Chandran felt very exhausted. To Kailas's inquiry Chandran replied that he was a student in Tanjore come out to Madras on a holiday tour.

At about five o'clock Kailas took Chandran into a building where ferns were kept in pots in the hall.

'What is this?' Chandran asked.

'Hotel Merton. I am going to have a little drink, if you don't mind.'

Kailas led Chandran up a flight of stairs, and selected a table in the upstair veranda. A waiter appeared behind them.

'Have you Tenets?' Kailas asked.

'Yes, master.'

'Bring a bottle and two glasses. You will have a small drink with me?' he asked, turning to Chandran.

'Beer? No, sorry. I don't drink.'

'Come on, be a sport. You must keep me company.'

Chandran's heart palpitated. 'I never take alcohol.'

'Who said that there was alcohol in beer? Less than five per cent. There is less alcohol in beer than in some of the tonics your doctors advise you to take.'

The waiter came with a bottle of beer and two glasses. Kailas argued and debated till some persons sitting at other tables looked at them. Chandran was firm. In his opinion he was being asked to commit the darkest crime.

Kailas said to the waiter, 'Take the beer away, boy. That young master won't drink. Get me a gin and soda. You will have lime juice?'

'Yes.'

'Give that master lime juice.' The waiter departed. 'Why don't you have a little port or something?'

'No, no,' said Chandran.

'Why not even port?'

'Excuse me. I made a vow never to touch alcohol in my life, before my mother,' said Chandran. This affected Kailas profoundly. He remained solemn for a moment and said, 'Then don't. Mother is a sacred object. It is a commodity whose value we don't realize as long as it is with us. One must lose it to know what a precious possession it is. If I had my mother I should have studied in a college and become a respectable person. You wouldn't find me here. After this, where do you think I am going?'

'I don't know.'

'To the house of a prostitute.' He remained reflective for a moment and said with a sigh, 'As long as my mother lived she said every minute "Do this. Don't do that." And I remained a good son to her. The moment she died I changed. It is a rare commodity, sir. Mother is a rare commodity.'

The spree went on till about eight-thirty in the evening, whisky following gin, and gin following whisky. There was a steady traffic between the table and the bar. At about eight-thirty Kailas belched loudly, hiccuped thrice, looked at Chandran with red eyes, and asked if Chandran thought he was drunk; he smiled with great satisfaction when Chandran said that he did not think so.

'There are fellows,' said Kailas in a very heavy voice, 'who will get drunk on two pegs of brandy. I throw out a challenge to anyone. Put fifteen pegs of neat whisky, neat, mind you, into this soul' – he tapped his chest – 'and I will tell you my name, do any multiplication or addition, and repeat numbers from a hundred backwards.'

They left the hotel. Kailas put his arm on Chandran's shoulder for support. They walked down Broadway, this strange pair. Kailas often stopped to roll his eyes foolishly and scratch his whiskers. He was discoursing on a variety of topics. He stopped suddenly in the road and asked, 'Did you have anything to eat?'

'Thanks. Plenty of cakes.'

'Did you drink anything?'

'Gallons of lime juice.'

'Why not a little beer or something? What a selfish rascal I am!'

'No, no,' said Chandran with anxiety. 'I have made a vow to my mother never to touch alcohol.'

'Ah!' said Kailas. He blew his nose and wiped his eyes with his kerchief. 'Mother! Mother!' He remained moody for some time, and said with an air of contentment, 'I know that my mother will be happy to know that I am happy.' He drew in a sharp breath and moved on again resolutely, as if determined not to let his feelings overcome him.

They walked in silence to the end of the road, and Kailas said, 'Why won't you call a taxi?'

'Where am I to find it?'

Kailas gave a short, bitter laugh. 'You ask me! Go and ask that electric post. Has God made you so blind that you can't see that I can't walk owing to a vile corn on the left foot?'

Chandran stood puzzled. He was afraid to cross the road, though the traffic was light now. Kailas appealed to him:

'Don't stand there, gaping open-mouthed at the wonders of the world, my boy. Get brisk and be helpful. Be a true friend. A friend in need is a friend indeed. Haven't you learnt it at school? I wonder what they teach you in schools nowadays!'

A passer-by helped Chandran to find a taxi. Kailas gave Chandran a hug when the taxi came. He got into the taxi and asked the driver, 'Do you know Kokilam's house?'

'No,' replied the driver.

Kailas threw at Chandran an accusing look and said, 'This is the kind of taxi you are pleased to call! Let us get down.'

'Where does she live?' asked the driver.

'Round about Mint Street.'

'Ah!' said the taxi driver, 'don't I know Kokilam's house?' He started the car, and drove it about for half an hour and stopped before a house in a narrow congested road. 'Here it is,' he said.

'Get down,' said Kailas to Chandran. 'How much?'

'The meter shows fifteen rupees, eight annas,' said the driver.

'Take seventeen-eight,' said Kailas, and gave him the money.

The taxi drove away.

'Whose house is this?' asked Chandran.

'My girl's house,' said Kailas. He surveyed the house up and down and said doubtfully, 'It looks different today. Never mind.' He climbed the steps and asked somebody at the door, 'Is this Kokilam's house?'

'What does a name matter? You are welcome to my poor abode, sir.' It was a middle-aged woman.

'You are right,' said Kailas, greatly pleased. He suddenly asked Chandran, 'Did you take the taxi number?'

'No.'

'Funny man! Do you want me to be telling you every moment what you must do? Have you no common sense?'

'I am sorry,' said Chandran. 'The taxi is over there. I will note the number and come back.' He turned round, feeling happy at this brilliant piece of strategy, and jumped down the steps of the house. Kailas muttered, 'Good boy. You are a good friend in need is a friend inde-e-e-ed.'

Chandran fled from Mint Street. He had escaped from Kailas. This was the first time he had been so close to a man in drink; this was the first time he had stood at the portals of a prostitute's house. He was thoroughly terrified.

After leaving Kailas several streets behind, Chandran felt exhausted and sat down on a pavement. He felt very homesick. He wondered if there was any train which would take him back to Malgudi that very night. He felt that he had left home years ago, and not on the previous evening. The thought of Malgudi was very sweet. He would walk to Lawley Extension, to his house, to his room, and sleep on his cot snugly. He lulled his mind with this vision for some time. It was not long before his searching mind put to him the question why he was wandering about the streets of a strange city, leaving his delightful heaven? The answer brought a medley of memories: piper shrieking through his pipe *Kalyani raga*, glare of Kitson lamps, astrologers, horoscopes, and unsympathetic Mother. Ah, even at this moment Malathi was probably crying into her pillow at having to marry a person she did not like. What sort of a person was he? Would he be able to support her, and would he treat her well? Somebody else to be her husband, and he having dreamed for weeks on the evening sands of Sarayu.

Chandran decided never to return to Malgudi. He hated the place. Everything there would remind him of Malathi – the sands on Sarayu bank, the cobbles in Market Road, Mill Street, the little shopkeeper with Malathi's eyebrows. It would be impossible for him to live again in that hell. It was a horrible town, with its preparations for Malathi's wedding ... Suppose even now some epidemic caught her future husband? Such things never happened in real life.

Chandran realized that he had definitely left his home. Now what did it matter where he lived? He was like a *sanyasi*. Why 'like'? He was a *sanyasi*; the simplest solution. Shave the head, dye the clothes in ochre, and you were dead for aught the world cared. The only thing possible; short of committing suicide, there was no other way out. He had done with the gamble of life. He was beaten. He could not go on living, probably for sixty years more, with people and friends and parents, with Malathi married and gone.

He got up. He wandered a little in search of his hotel, and then suddenly realized that it was quite an unnecessary search. What was he going to do after finding the hotel? Pay the bill, take the bag, and clear out somewhere? Why should a *sanyasi* carry a bag? Cast the bag and the hold-all aside, he told himself. As for payment, the hotel man had already been paid an advance, and if he wanted he could take the bag and the hold-all also into possession.

He slept that night on a pavement, rolling close to some wall. A board hung on the wall. He looked at it to make out what place it was; but the board only said 'Bill Stickers Will Be Prosecuted', with its Tamil translation elaborated in meaning, 'Those Who Stick Notices Will Be Handed Over To The Police'. 'Don't worry, I won't stick notices here,' he told the wall, and lay down. The fatigue of the day brought on sleep. Bill Stickers ... He dreamt a number of times that while sleeping close to the wall he was mistaken for a poster, peeled off the wall by policemen, and placed under arrest.

Next morning he was awakened by a sweeper. Chandran sat rubbing his eyes. When his mind emerged from sleep, he resolved to get out of Madras immediately. There was no use remaining in the city any longer. It was so big and confusing that one didn't know even the way out of it. There was, moreover, the danger of being caught again by Kailas.

He found his way to the Central Station, went to a ticket counter, and asked, 'When is the next train leaving?'

'For?'

'For – for,' repeated Chandran; 'wait a minute, please.' He glanced at a big railway map hanging on the wall and said, 'Bezwada.'

'Grand Trunk Express at seven-forty.'

'One third-class, please, for Bezwada.'

He got into the train. The compartment was not crowded. He suddenly felt very unhappy at having to go to Bezwada. He looked at the yellow ticket in his hand, and turned it between his fingers ... He was not going to be tyrannized over by that piece of yellow cardboard into taking a trip to Bezwada. He didn't like the place, a place with the letter 'z' in its name. He was not going to be driven to that place by anything. The first bell rang. He flung the ticket out of the window and jumped out of the train. He was soon out of the station.

He crossed the road, and got into a tram, and settled down comfortably in a seat. The conductor came and said, 'Ticket, please.'

'Where does this go?'

'Mylapore.'

'One ticket, Mylapore. How much?'

For the next half-hour his problems as to where to go were set at rest. When the tram halted at the terminus he got down and walked till he saw the magnificent grey spire of Kapaleeswarar temple against the morning sky.

He entered the temple, went round the holy corridor, and prostrated before every image and sanctuary that he saw.

He saw a barber sitting on the steps of the temple tank waiting for customers. Chandran went to him and asked, 'Will you shave me?'

'Yes, master.' The barber was rather surprised. Young students with crops never showed any trust in him. His only customers were widows who shaved their heads completely and orthodox Brahmins who shaved their heads almost completely. Now here was a man willing to abandon his crop into his hands. Chandran said, 'I will give you a lot of money if you will do me a little service.'

'I can also crop well, master.'

'It is not only that. You must buy a cheap loin-cloth and an upper covering for me, dye them in ochre, and bring them to me. After that you can shave my head, and take these clothes I am wearing and also the purse in my pocket.' He held the purse open before him. The barber saw in it rupees and some notes, wages for six months' work in these days of safety razors and self-shaving.

'But not a word about it to anyone, mind you,' said Chandran.

'Are you becoming a *sanyasi*?'

'Don't ask questions,' commanded Chandran.

'Master, at your age!'

'Will you stop asking questions or shall I get into a bus and go away? I want your help because I don't know where to get these things in this wretched place. What is your name?'

'Ragavan.'

'Ragavan, help me. You will gain my eternal gratitude. You will also profit yourself. My heart is dead, Ragavan. I have lost everybody I love in this world, Ragavan. I will be waiting for you here. Come soon.'

'Master, if you don't mind, why should you not come and wait in my poor hut?'

Chandran went with him to his house, beyond a network of stifling lanes and by-lanes. It was a one-roomed house, with a small bunk attached to it, full of heat and smoke, serving as kitchen. A very tall, stout woman came out of it and asked the barber, 'Why have you come back so soon?' He went near her and whispered something.

He unrolled a mat for Chandran, requested him to make himself comfortable, and went out.

Chandran's mind and spirit had become so deadened that it did not matter to him where he waited, and how long. So, though he had to spend nearly half the day alone in the barber's house, seeing nothing but the barber's oily pillow and a red rug; and a calendar picture, without month or date sheets, showing Brahma, the Creator of the Universe; and an iron-banded teak-wood box, Chandran did not feel the passing of the time.

The barber returned at three o'clock in the afternoon. He brought with him two pieces of cloth dyed in ochre. He brought also a few plantains and a green coconut.

Chandran was hungry, and did not refuse the coconut and fruits. He sent the barber out again for a postcard.

When the postcard was brought, Chandran borrowed a short pencil from the barber, and wrote to his father: 'Reached this place safely. I am staying with a friend I met at the station, and not with uncle. I am leaving this for ... I won't tell you where. I am going to wander about a lot. I am quite happy and cheerful. Don't fear that I am still worried about the marriage. Not at all. I am going to wander a good deal, and so don't run to the police station if you don't hear from me for a long time. You must promise not to make a fuss. My respects to Mother. I shall be all right.' He added a postscript: 'Am going with some friends, old class-mates, whom I met here.'

CHAPTER TWELVE

His dress and appearance, the shaven pate and the ochre loin-cloth, declared him now and henceforth to be a *sanyasi* – one who had renounced the world and was untouched by its joys and sorrows.

He travelled several districts on foot. When he felt tired he stopped a passing country cart and begged for a lift. No one easily refused an obligation to a *sanyasi*. Occasionally he stopped even buses on the highway.

He never cared to know where he was going or where he was staying (except that it was not in the direction of Malgudi). For what did it matter to a *sanyasi* where he was going? One town was very much like another: the same bazaar street, hair-cutting saloons, coffee hotels, tailors squatting before sewing-machines, grocers, Government officials, cycles, cars, and cattle. The difference was only in the name, and why should a *sanyasi* learn a name?

When he felt hungry he tapped at the nearest house and begged for food; or he begged in the bazaar street for a coconut or plantain.

For the first few days his system craved for coffee, to which he was addicted since his childhood. While one part of him suffered acutely, another part derived a satisfaction in watching it writhe and in saying to it, 'Go on: suffer and be miserable. You were not sent into this world to enjoy. Go on: be miserable and perish. You won't get coffee.' Circumstances gradually wore this craving out.

If anybody invited him to sleep under a roof he did it; if not, he slept in the open, or in a public rest-house, where were gathered scores like him. When he was hungry and found none to feed him, he usually dragged himself about in a weak state, and enjoyed the pain of hunger. He said to his stomach, 'Rage as much as you like. Why won't you kill me?'

His cheek bones stood out; the dust of the highway was on him; his limbs had become horny; his complexion had turned from brown to a dark tan. His looks said nothing; they did not even seem to conceal a mystery; they looked dead. His lips rarely smiled.

He shaved once or twice and found that it was easier to allow the hair to grow as it pleased than to keep it down. His hair grew unhindered; in course of time a very young beard and moustache encircled his mouth.

He was different from the usual *sanyasi*. Others may renounce with a spiritual motive or purpose. Renunciation may be to them a means to attain peace or may be peace itself. They are perhaps dead in time, but they do live in eternity. But Chandran's renunciation was not of that kind. It was an alternative to suicide. Suicide he would have committed but for its social stigma. Perhaps he lacked the barest physical courage that was necessary for it. He was a *sanyasi* because it pleased him to mortify his flesh. His renunciation was a revenge on society, circumstances, and perhaps, too, on destiny.

After about eight months of wandering he reached Koopal Village in Sainad District. It was a small village nestling at the foot of the range of mountains that connected the Eastern and the Western Ghats.

On a hot afternoon Chandran arrived in this village, and drank water in the channel that fed the paddy fields. He then went and sat in the shade of a banyan tree. He had been walking since the dawn, and he felt tired. He reclined on a stout root of the banyan and closed his eyes.

When he opened his eyes again he saw some villagers standing around him.

'May we know where our master is coming from?' somebody asked.

Chandran was tired of inventing an answer to this question. On the flash of an idea he touched his mouth and shook his head.

'He is dumb.'

'No, he can hear us. Can you hear us?'

Chandran shook his head in assent.

'Can you talk?'

Chandran shook his head in assent, held up his ten fingers, touched his lips, looked heavenward, and shook his head. They understood. 'He is under a vow of silence of ten years or ten months or ten days.'

A number of villagers stood around Chandran and gaped at him. Chandran felt rather embarrassed at being the target of the stare of a crowd. He closed his eyes. This was taken by the others for meditation.

An important man of the village came forward and asked, 'Won't you come and reside in my poor abode?'

Chandran declined the offer with a gesture, and spent the night under the tree.

Next day, as the villagers passed him on their way to the fields, they saluted him with joined palms. Somebody brought a few plantains and placed them before him; somebody else offered him milk. Chandran accepted the gifts, consumed them, and then rose to go.

Somebody asked him, 'Master, where are you going?'

With a sweep of his hands Chandran indicated a faraway destination.

At this they begged him to stay. 'Master, our village is so unlucky that few come this way. Bless us with your holy presence for some more days, we beg of you.' Chandran shook his head, but they would not let him go. 'Master, your very presence will bless our village. We rarely see holy men here. We beg of you to stay for some days more.'

Chandran was touched by this request. No one had valued his presence so highly till now. He was treated with consideration everywhere, but not with so much of it as he saw here. He felt: 'Poor fellows. Probably no interesting person comes this way, which is God-knows-how-far from everywhere. Why not stay if it is going to give them any pleasure. This is as good a place as another.'

He went back to the banyan seat. There was great rejoicing when he consented to stay. Men, women, and children followed him to the banyan tree.

Soon the news spread from hamlet to hamlet and village to village that a holy man under a vow of silence for ten years had arrived, and that he spent his time in rigorous meditation under a banyan tree.

Next day scores of visitors came from all the surrounding villages, and gathered under the banyan tree. Chandran sat in the correct pose of a man in meditation, cross-legged and with his eyes shut.

It never occurred to them to doubt. They were innocent and unsophisticated in most matters (excepting their factions and fights), and took an ascetic's make-up at its face value.

Late in the evening Chandran opened his eyes and saw only a few villagers standing around him. He signed to them to leave him alone. After this request was repeated twice they left him.

The night had fallen. Somebody had brought and left a lighted lantern beside him. He looked about. They had all brought gifts for him, milk and fruits and food. The sight of the gifts sent a spear through his heart. He felt a cad, a fraud, and a confidence trickster. These were gifts for a counterfeit exchange. He wished that he deserved their faith in him. The sight of the gifts made him unhappy. He ate some fruit and drank a little milk with the greatest self-deprecation.

He moved away from the gifts; still the light shone on them. He even blew out the lantern – he did not deserve the light.

Sitting in the dark, he subjected his soul to a remorseless vivisection. From the moment he had donned the ochre cloth to the present, he had been living on charity, charity given in mistake, given on the face value of a counterfeit. He had been humbugging through life. He told himself that if he were such an ascetic he ought to do without food or perish of starvation. He ought not to feed his miserable stomach with food which he had neither earned nor, by virtue of spiritual worth, deserved.

He sought an answer to the question why he had come to this degradation. He was in no mood for self-deception, and so he found the answer in the words 'Malathi' and 'Love'. The former had brought him to this state. He had deserted his parents, who had spent on him all their love, care, and savings. He told himself that he had surely done this to spite his parents, who probably had died of anxiety by now. This was all his return for their love and for all that they had done for him. The more he reflected on this, the greater became his anger with Malathi. It was a silly infatuation. Little sign did she show of caring for a fellow; she couldn't say that she had no chance. She had plenty of opportunities to show that she noticed him. Where there was a will there was a way. She had only been playing with him, the devil. Women were like that, they enjoyed torturing people. And for the sake of her memory he had come to this. He railed against that memory, against love. There was no such thing; a foolish literary notion. If people didn't read stories they wouldn't know there was such a thing as love. It was a scorching madness. There was no such thing. And driven by a non-existent thing he had become a deserter and a counterfeit.

He wondered if he ought not to stand in the village street, call everybody, and announce to them what he was. They might not believe, or they might think he had gone mad, or they might believe and feel that they were fooled and mob him and beat him to a pulp. He toyed with this vision, a punishment that he would surely deserve.

He rose. He decided to leave the village, as the most decent and practical thing that he could do. He moved out of the banyan shade.

Chandran walked all night, and early in the morning sighted a bus. He stopped it.

'Will you please take me in?'

'Where are you going?'

'In your direction.'

The conductor looked at the seats and grumbled.

'I will get down anywhere you like, any time you get passengers for the full bus.'

The bus was still empty, and the request came from one who wore the ochre garb, and the conductor said, 'Come on.'

The *sanyasi* climbed the bus and said, 'I have walked all night. Put me down in a place where there is a telegraph office.'

The bus conductor thought for a moment and said, 'There is one at Maduram.'

'How far is it from here?'

'About ten miles, but we do not go there. We branch off about two miles from Maduram. This bus goes to Kalki.'

Chandran got down from the bus at the crossroads and walked to Maduram. It was a small town on the banks of Samari River. In the central street there was a post and telegraph office. Chandran tapped on the post office window and said to the postmaster, 'I want to have a word with you. Can I come in?'

After a severe scrutiny of the visitor the postmaster said, 'Yes.'

Chandran went into the small post office. The postmaster looked at Chandran suspiciously. Too many English-speaking *sanyasis* were about the place now, offering to tell the future, and leaving their hosts minus a rupee or two at the end.

'You want to tell me my future, I suppose,' said the postmaster.

'No, sir. I don't know any astrology.'

'Too many *sanyasis* come here nowadays. We simply can't afford to pay for all the astrology that is available.'

'I wish I had at least that to give in exchange,' said Chandran, and then opened his heart to the postmaster. He gave a clear account of his life and troubles.

After hearing his story the postmaster agreed to lend him a rupee and eight annas for sending a telegram to his father for money.

Chandran expressed a desire for a shave and a change of clothing. The postmaster sent for a barber and gave Chandran an old shirt and a white *dhoti*.

Chandran requested the barber to pay special attention to his head, and to use the scissors carefully there. He also requested the barber to shave his face thrice over.

After that he went in for a bath, and came out of the bathroom feeling resurrected. He was dressed in the postmaster's *dhoti* and shirt. He had in his hand his *sanyasi* robes in a bundle. After inviting the postmaster to witness the sight, he flung the bundle over the wall into the adjoining lane.

He asked for a little hair oil and a comb. He rubbed the oil on his head and tried to comb his hair before a mirror.

The feel of a shirt on his body and of a smooth chin, after months of shirtless and prickly existence, gave him an ecstatic sensation.

At about four in the afternoon a message arrived endowing Chandran with fifty rupees, though he had wired for only twenty-five.

The mail train towards Madras passed Maduram station at one o'clock at night. Chandran bought a ticket for Malgudi, changed trains at two junctions, and finally got down at Malgudi station in the morning two days later.

PART FOUR

CHAPTER THIRTEEN

His parents were amazed to see him so transformed.

'I should have come to the station, Chandar,' said his father, 'but I was not sure when you were coming.'

Mother said, 'You are looking like a corpse. How your bones stick out! What sunken cheeks! What were you at all these days?'

Seenu said, 'What about the cricket bat? Where is your coat? Your shirt is a bit loose. You have also spoilt your crop. It is very short. Where is your bag?'

Father and Mother looked very careworn.

Mother asked, 'Why couldn't you write to us at least a card?'

'I did,' said Chandran.

'Only one. You should have written to us at least once after that.'

Father asked, 'Did you travel much? What were the places you visited?'

'Lots of places. Rolled about a great deal,' said Chandran, and stopped at that. His father could never get more than that from him.

'Why didn't you go to your uncle's?'

'I didn't fancy him,' said Chandran. 'Were you all very greatly worried about me?'

'Your mother was. She thought that something terrible had happened to you. Every morning she troubled me to go and inform the police.' He turned to his wife and added, 'Have I not been telling you that you were merely imagining things?'

'Ah,' she said, 'as if you weren't anxious! How many times did you say that an announcement must be made in the papers?'

Father looked abashed.

Chandran asked, 'I hope you haven't told the police or advertised in the papers?'

'No, no,' said Father. 'But I should certainly have done something if I hadn't heard from you for some weeks more. It was only your mother who was very, very worried.'

'As if you weren't,' Mother retorted. 'Why did you go thrice to Madras, and then to Trichinopoly, and write to all sorts of people?'

Seenu said, 'Father and Mother were worried about you, brother. Nobody would talk to me in this house. They were all very ill-tempered and morose all these months. I didn't like our house, brother. No one to talk to in the house except the cook. You ought to have written to us at least once or twice. I hoped that you would go to Binns and bring at least their catalogue.'

Chandran went to his room and there found everything just as he had left it. The books that had been kept on the table were there; the cot in the same position, the bookshelf in the same old place, his old grey coat on the same hook on the coat stand; the table near the window with even the writing-pad in the same position. There was not a speck of dust on anything, nor a single spider's web. In fact the room and all the objects in it were tidier than they had ever been. The sight of things spick and span excited him. Everything excited him now. He ran to his mother and asked, panting, 'Mother, how is it everything is so neat in my room?'

Father replied, 'She swept and cleaned it with great care every day.'

'Why did you take so much trouble, Mother?'

She became red and was embarrassed. 'What better business did I have?'

'How did you manage to keep Seenu out of my room, Mother?'

'Mother used to lock up the room, and never left it open even for an hour,' Seenu replied.

Chandran suddenly asked, 'What has happened to Ramu? Did anybody hear from him?'

'No.'

'No letters from him for me?'

'None,' his mother replied.

'Where are his people? Are they not in the next house?'

'His father was transferred to some Telegu district, and they have cleared out of this place, bag and baggage.'

Chandran realized that this was the last he would hear of Ramu. Ramu was dead as far as Chandran was concerned. Ramu was never in the habit of writing. Except one card he had not written for nearly two years now. His people till now were in the next house, and there was some hope of hearing about him. Now that too was gone. Chandran reflected gloomily, 'I and he are parted now. He won't bother about me any more. Very frivolous minded. Won't bother about a thing that is out of sight.'

Mother said, 'They came here to take leave of us, and they said that Ramu had found an appointment at seventy-five rupees a month in the Bombay railways.'

Chandran felt very hurt on hearing this. Here was a person who didn't care to communicate to a friend such happy news as the securing of a job. That was like Ramu. Friendship was another illusion like Love, though it did not reach the same mad heights. People pretended that they were friends, when the fact was they were brought together by force of circumstances. The classroom or the club or the office created friendships. When the circumstances changed the relations, too, snapped. What did Ramu care for him now, after all the rambles on the river, cigarettes, cinema, and confidences? Friendship – what meaningless expressions had come into use!

'What is the matter, Chandra, you are suddenly moody?' asked Chandran's father.

'Nothing, nothing,' said Chandran. 'I was only thinking of something. Father, have you any idea where your old college friends are now?'

Father tried to recollect. He gave up the attempt. 'I don't know. If I look at the old college group photo I may be able to tell you something.' He turned to his wife and asked, 'Where is that group photo?'

'How should I know?' she replied.

Seenu said, 'I don't know if it is the one you want. I found a large group photo in the junk-room, and I have hung it over my table, but the glass is broken.'

Chandran said, 'I don't mean the whole class. Just some particular friends you had in the college.'

'For the four years I spent in the Christian College I had about three or four intimate friends. We were room-mates and neighbours in the hostel. We were always together ... Sivaraman, he entered the Imperial Service and was in Bihar for some time. It is over thirty years since we wrote to each other. I recently saw in the papers that he retired as Chief something or other in the Railway Board. Gopal Menon, he was in the Civil Service. He died some time ago of heart failure. This, too, I saw only in the papers, and then wrote a condolence letter to his wife. The other, we used to call him Kutti, his full name was something or other. I don't know where he is now. The only old friend who is still in this town is Madhava Rao.'

'You mean the old man who lives near the college?'

'No, that is another person. I am referring to K. T. Madhava Rao, the retired Postal Superintendent. He and I were very intimate friends.'

'Do you meet often now?'

'Once in a way. He doesn't come to the club. Now that you ask me, I remember I went to his house about four years ago, when he was laid up with blood pressure.'

'And you used to spend all your time together in the college?'

'Yes, yes. But you see ... We can't afford to be always together, you know. Each of us has to go his own way.'

To Chandran it was a depressing revelation. Well, probably ages hence he would be saying to his grandson, 'I had a friend called Ramu. It is fifty years since we have written to each other. I don't know if he is still living.' His father at least had a group photo in the junk-room; he hadn't even that – he had simply forgotten to buy his class group. '... this too I saw only in the papers ...' The callousness of Time!

He stepped down into the garden. He found the garden paths overgrown with grass, and plants in various stages of decay. Thick weeds had sprung up everywhere, and were choking a few cretons and roses that were still struggling for life. He had never seen the garden in this state. Ever since he could remember his father had worked morning and evening in the garden. Now what had happened to the gardener? What had happened to Father?

He went in and asked, 'What has happened to the plants?'

Father looked awkward and said, 'I don't know ...'

'What, have you not been gardening?'

'I couldn't attend to the plants,' he said.

'What were you busy with, then?'

'I don't know what account to give of myself.'

Mother said mischievously, 'He was busy searching for a missing son.'

'But I wrote to you, Father, that you wouldn't hear from me for a long time and not to worry.'

'Oh, yes, you did. It wasn't that. Your mother is only joking. Don't take her seriously.'

Chandran went to Mohan's hotel in the evening. Before starting, he said to his mother, 'I may not come back tonight. I shall sleep in Mohan's hotel.'

As he approached Mohan's hotel he could not help recollecting with a grim detachment the state of mind he was in the last time he was here. The detachment was forced, his heart beat fast as he came in front of the Modern Indian Lodge. Suppose she was standing at that very moment at the entrance of the opposite house? Before slipping into the hotel, in spite of his resolve, he turned his head once; but there was no one at the entrance. As he climbed the staircase he reproached himself severely for this. Still a prey to illusions! Was he making for another bout of asceticism and wandering?

He stopped at the landing and found Room 14 locked. On the door some other name was scrawled in pencil. Chandran descended the stairs and asked the manager if Mohan was still in the hotel.

'Room 14,' said the manager.

'But it is locked. Some other name on the door.'

'That is the old Fourteen. The new Fourteen is on the topmost floor.'

Chandran went up and found Mohan in a newly-built small room at the topmost part of the building. It was airy and bright, a thorough contrast to the wooden-partitioned cell on the landing.

There were a table and chair; a few pictures on the wall. Everything tidy.

Mohan was speechless for five minutes, and then he opened his mouth and let out a volley of questions: 'What did you do with yourself? Where were you? Why ...'

'This is really a splendid room!' Chandran said. 'How did you manage to leave the old one?'

'I am prosperous now, you see,' Mohan said happily. 'Tell me about yourself.'

'Mine is a long story. It is like *Ramayanam*. You will hear it presently. Tell me how you are prospering.'

'Quite well, as I told you. The *Daily Messenger* now sells a total of thirty thousand copies a day. They pay me now five rupees a column, and don't cut much because they want to establish a good circulation in these districts. New company running it now. They are very regular in payment. I am making nearly twenty columns a month. Besides this, they publish my poems once a week in their magazine page, and pay me four annas a line.' Mohan looked very healthy and cheerful.

'This is great news,' said Chandran. 'I am glad you have left that old cell.'

'I am paying five rupees more for this room. I insisted on this room being called Fourteen. It is a lucky number. So this is known as the New Fourteen, and the other as the Old Fourteen. This room was built very recently. The hotel proprietor is very prosperous now; he has purchased this building, and has added many rooms. The poor fellow was down in luck for a number of years; but now lots of guests come here, and he is doing very well. I thought of shifting to another hotel, but hadn't the heart to do it. The old man and I have been friends since our bad days. In those days sometimes he would not have a measure of rice in the whole hotel; and I have several times borrowed a rupee or two and given it to him for running the hotel.'

After attempting to smother the question a dozen times Chandran asked, 'Are they still in the opposite house?'

Mohan smiled a little and paused before answering, 'Soon after the marriage they left that house. I don't know where they are now.'

'Who is living in the house now?'

'Some *marwari*, a moneylender, has acquired it.'

Everywhere there seemed to be change. Change, change, everywhere. Chandran hated it. 'Have I been away for only eight months or eighteen years?' Chandran asked himself. 'Mohan, let us go and spend the whole evening and night on Sarayu bank. I have a lot of things to tell you. I want you. Let us eat something at an hotel and go to the river.'

Mohan demurred. His presence was urgently needed at an Adjourned Meeting of the Municipality.

Chandran turned a deaf ear to the call of duty, and insisted on seducing Mohan away from the meeting. Mohan yielded, saying, 'I shall take it from the *Gazette* man tomorrow. I have got to report it to my paper.'

They went to a coffee hotel, and then to the river-bank. Long after the babble of the crowd on the sands had died, and darkness had fallen on the earth, Chandran's voice was heard, in tune with the rumble of the flowing river, narrating to Mohan his wanderings. He then explained his new philosophy, which followed the devastating discovery that Love and Friendship were the veriest illusions. He explained that people married because their sexual appetite had to be satisfied and there must be somebody to manage the house. There was nothing deeper than that in any man and woman relationship.

The Taluk Office gong sounded eleven at night when Chandran said, 'Remember, I have not told anyone that I was a *sanyasi* for eight months. You must keep it all to yourself. I don't want anyone to talk about me.'

They rose and walked back to the hotel through the silent streets.

CHAPTER FOURTEEN

Chandran settled down to a life of quiet and sobriety. He felt that his greatest striving ought to be for a life freed from distracting illusions and hysterics.

He tended the garden a great deal now. Every morning he spent over two hours in the garden. He divided his time between plants and books. In the evening he took his bicycle (a second-hand one that he had bought recently) and went out for long rides on the Trunk Road. Late in the evening he went to Mohan's hotel.

This kind of life was conducive to quiet and, possibly, sobriety. With an iron will he chased away distracting illusions, and conscientiously avoided hysterics, with the care of one walking on a tight-rope. He decided not to give his mind a moment of freedom. All the mischief started there. Whatever he did, he did it with a desperate concentration now. If he dug the garden, the mind was allowed to play about only the soil and the pick. If he read a book, he tried to make the print a complete drug for the mind. The training of the mind was done feverishly and unsparingly.

There were still sights and sounds and hours which breathed, through some association or other, memories of Malathi. But he avoided them. He rarely went to the river before sundown; and never to the old spot. He was glad that the house opposite to the Modern Indian Lodge was now occupied by a moneylender. The sound of pipe music, especially when *Kalyani raga* was played on it, disturbed his equanimity; when going to Mohan's hotel, he carefully avoided the route that took him by the Shiva temple, where there was pipe music every evening. He never looked at the shop in Market Road for fear of encountering the eyebrows of the boy in the shop. Even then something or other was sure to remind him of Malathi and trouble him. At such moments he fumigated his mind with reflections: this is a mischievous disturbance; this is false; these thoughts of Malathi are unreal because Love is only a brain affection; it led me to beg and cheat; to desert my parents; it is responsible for my mother's extra wrinkles and grey hairs, for my father's neglect of the garden; and a poor postmaster is a shirt and a *dhoti* less on account of my love.

However, there was another matter that troubled him, which could not be forced off the mind. It was the question of occupation. He often told himself that he was making arrangements to go to England in the coming year, and that he ought to come back from there with some distinction, and then search for employment. Sometimes this quietened his mind, sometimes not. He was getting on for twenty-four. It was nearly two years since he left college, and he was still leeching on his father. He was so much bothered by this thought one day that he went to his father in the garden and asked, 'Why should I not apply for a Government post?'

Father looked up from the bed of annuals that he was digging. 'Why do you want to do it?'

Chandran mumbled something.

Father understood that something was troubling him and said, 'Well, there is no hurry.'

'But I have wasted a lot of time already, Father. It is nearly two years since I became a graduate, and I have neither studied further nor done anything else.'

'It is no waste,' Father said. 'You have been reading and getting to know people and life and so on. Don't worry. Time enough to apply for jobs after you return from England. It will be really worth while, you see. There is no use in getting a bare forty or fifty as a clerk, though even that would be difficult to secure in these days.'

'But I am nearly twenty-four, Father, not a baby. There are fellows who support a family at my age.'

'Well, you too could have done it if it was necessary. You could have finished your college before you were twenty if I hadn't put you to school late, and if you hadn't been held up by typhoid for a year.'

Chandran admired his father for admitting as causes of wasted time late schooling and typhoid, and leaving out of account the vagrant eight months, but for which he would have been in England already. Chandran comforted himself by saying that he would compensate for all this by doing something really great in England and getting into some really high post in the Education service. His father was constantly writing to his brother at Madras for a lot of preliminary information connected with Chandran's trip to England. These letters gave Chandran a feeling of progress towards an earning life. But there were times when he doubted this too. He wondered if he really ought to put his father to that expense. He wondered if his comfort from the thought of going to England soon was not another illusion, and if it would not be super-parasitic of him. He could not decide the issue himself. He consulted Mohan. Mohan asked why, if he felt so, he should not do something else. Chandran asked what, and Mohan explained, 'Why not the Chief Agency of our paper? They are not satisfied with the present agent, and have given him notice. They have advertised for an agent in this and in a few other districts.'

'What is it likely to bring?'

'It all depends. If you canvas a large circulation, you will make a lot of money.'

Chandran was sceptical. 'Where am I to go and canvas?'

'That is what an agent gets his income for. In six months the daily circulation of the *Messenger* has gone up to thirty thousand, quite a good figure, and it circulates all over the Presidency. It ought to find a sale in this place also. But for the agent the circulation would not have gone above a bare twenty-five. All the same they are publishing my news because they hope that it will ultimately pull up the circulation.'

Chandran was not quite convinced that it was a very useful line to take.

Next day Mohan came out with further information. 'I saw the present agent. He gets a quarter of an anna per paper sold.' Mohan wrote to the office for information, and in due course, when it arrived, passed it on to Chandran. After some more talk and thought, Chandran became quite enthusiastic. He asked his father, 'Will you be disappointed if I don't go to England?'

'What is the matter? I have already written for official information.'

'I feel that going to England will only mean a lot of expense.'

'You need not worry about that.'

'Getting a distinction and coming back and securing a suitable appointment, all these seem to be a gamble.'

Father was silent. He felt nervous when Chandran came and proposed anything. But Chandran went on developing exquisitely the theme of the *Messenger* agency. He saw in it a beautiful vision of an independent life full of profit and leisure. He quoted facts and figures. A quarter of an anna per day per paper sold. With a miserly circulation of 1,000 for the whole district, he would be making 250 annas a day. He would get at that rate about 480 rupees a month, which one couldn't dream of getting in the Government service even after fifteen years of slavery. And there was always the possibility of expanding the business. He gave the area of Malgudi, its population, out of which the English-knowing persons were at least 10,000; out of which number at least 5,000 would be able to spend an anna a day on a newspaper; and it was these who were going to support the *Daily Messenger*.

'For the agency we must give a security of 2,000 rupees, for which they later pay interest. Somebody has written from the office that a number of people have already applied and that there is a keen fight for the agency. They are selecting the agent only on the first. It is a good chance, Father. I think it is better than going to England.'

Father listened in silence.

Mother, who was twisting small cotton bits into wicks for the lamps in God's room, said, 'I think so. Why should he go to England?'

Father replied that the question could not be so easily settled. He was very ignorant of the newspaper business. He wrote a letter to his brother in Madras for enlightenment on the subject. That evening, in the club, he took aside Nanjundiah, a barrister of the town, a public figure, and his particular friend, and asked him, 'Do you read the *Daily Messenger*?'

'Yes.'

'What sort of a paper is it? I saw a copy, but I should like to have your opinion.'

'I don't subscribe for it but get it from a neighbour. It is quite a good paper, non-party and independent.'

'You see,' said Chandran's father, 'my son wants to take up the agency, giving a security of 2,000 rupees. I have absolutely no idea what it is all about, but he seems to think that it will be a good investment.'

'What about his going to England?'

'Seems to be more keen on this. I don't know, that boy gets a new notion every day; but I don't like to stand in his way if it is really a sound proposition.'

He said to Chandran that night: 'I spoke to Nanjundiah about the paper. He thinks well of it, but doesn't know anything else. However, he has promised to find out and tell me.'

Chandran said, 'We can't be wasting time over all these inquiries. There is a rush for the agency. We must look sharp.'

After Chandran had gone to his room, his mother said, 'Why are you tormenting the boy?' Father did not vouchsafe an answer but merely rustled his paper. She repeated the question, and he said, 'Why don't you leave it to me?'

'If the boy wishes to stay here, why won't you let him stay? What is the use of sending him to England? Waste of a lot of money. What do our boys, who go to England, specially achieve? They only learn to smoke cigarettes, drink wine, and dance with white girls.'

'It is my hope that our boy will do something more than that.'

'If there is as much money in the paper as he says, why shouldn't he do that work?'

'If there is; that is what I must know before I let him do it. I can't very well give him a cheque for 2,000 rupees and ask him to invest it, without knowing something about the persons that are running the paper, how long it will last, and other things. There is hardly any sense in letting him in for work which may not last even a year! I have written to my brother. Let me see what he writes.'

'You have to write to your brother about everything,' she said, rising to go in. 'Only I don't want you to drive the boy to desperation.'

Father looked after her for a long time, shifted in his easy-chair a little, and rustled the paper.

Chandran said to himself: 'I have no business to hustle and harass my father. He has every right to wait and delay. If I am destined to get the agency, I shall get it; if not, I shall not get it for all the hustling.'

There was a delay of four or five days before a reply arrived from his uncle. Till then Father went about his business without mentioning the paper, and Chandran too conducted himself as if there was no such thing as the *Daily Messenger*. But every morning he went out at about nine o'clock, met the Lawley Extension postman on the way and asked if there was any letter for Father. At last, one morning, the postman carried a letter in his hand for Father. It bore the Madras postmark. At other times Chandran would have snatched the letter from the postman, taken it to his father, and demanded to be told of its contents. But now he curbed that impulse, asked the postman to carry the letter himself, went to the Town Reading-room, and returned home at midday. He did not go before Father at all, but confined his movements between the kitchen and the dining-hall, till Father himself called Chandran and gave him the letter. Chandran opened the letter and read: '... There is an influential directorate at the head of the paper. J. W. Prabhu, Sir N. M. Rao, and others are on it. An agency would really be worth while, but would not be easy to secure. If you send Chandran over here immediately I shall see if anything can be done through a friend of mine who knows the Managing Director ...'

Chandran read the letter twice, gave it back to his father, and asked as casually as possible, 'What do you think of it?'

'You can go to Madras today. I shall send a wire to your uncle.'

'All right.'

He went to his mother and said, 'I am starting for Madras today.'

She asked anxiously, 'When will you be back?'

'In two or three days, as soon as my work is finished.'

'Are you sure?'

'Oh, don't worry, Mother. I shall positively come back.'

He immediately started packing his trunk. As he sat in his room, with all his clothes lying scattered about, his father frequently came in with something or other for Chandran in hand. He brought half a dozen kerchiefs.

'You may want these in Madras.' He came next with a pair of new *dhoties*. 'I have a lot more in the chest of drawers.' He then brought a woollen scarf and requested Chandran to hand it over to his brother in Madras. Mother came in and asked if Chandran would like to carry anything to eat on the way. She then expressed a desire to send a small basket of vegetables to her sister-in-law. Chandran said that he would not take it with him. But she argued that she wasn't asking him to carry the load on his head. He threatened that if he were given any basket he would throw it out of the train.

At five o'clock he had finished his dinner and was ready to start. His steel trunk and a roll of bedding were brought to the hall. Mother added a small basket to Chandran's luggage. Chandran protested at the sight of the basket. Mother lifted the basket and said, 'See, it is very light; contains only some vegetables for your aunt. You mustn't go with bare hands.'

His father, mother, and Seenu saw Chandran off at the station. Seenu said, 'Don't stay away long. Don't forget Binns this time.'

Next morning as the train steamed into the Madras Egmore station Chandran, peeping out of the window, saw his uncle on the platform.

His uncle was about forty years old, a cheerful plump man with a greying crop, and wearing thick-rimmed spectacles. He was a business man and a general broker, doing a lot of work, and knowing all possible persons in the city.

As Chandran got down from the train, his uncle said, 'I came here myself in order that you might not slip away this time.'

Chandran blushed and said, 'Father has sent you a scarf.'

'So after all he has the strength to part with it. Is it the same or a different one?'

'Deep blue wool.'

'It is the same. He wouldn't give it to me for years.'

A porter carried the things to a car outside. Chandran sat with his uncle in the front seat.

'How do you like this car?' his uncle asked.

'It is quite good.'

'I bought it recently, giving away my old Essex in exchange.'

'Oh,' said Chandran. He felt quite happy that his uncle was speaking to him like an equal, and was not teasing him as he used to do before. Chandran had always avoided his uncle if he could, but now he found him quite tolerable.

His uncle asked why Chandran had dropped the idea of going to England. He chatted incessantly as he drove along, cutting across tramcars, hooting behind pedestrians, and taking turns recklessly.

He lived in a bungalow in the Luz Church Road. Chandran's aunt and cousins (one of his own age, a youngster, and a girl) were standing on the veranda to receive Chandran.

'Ah, how tall Chandra has grown!' said his aunt; and Chandran felt very tall and proud.

'Mother has sent a basket of vegetables for you, Aunt,' he said, and surveyed the cousins. The one of his own age smiled and said, 'I came to the station last time.'

'Oh,' said Chandran, and blushed. When were people going to forget his last trip?

'Raju, take Chandra's things to your room, and then show him the bathroom,' Uncle said to his cousin.

His cousin took him to his room. Chandran removed his coat, and Raju said again, 'I came to the station last time, and searched for you on the platform.'

Chandran paid no attention, but opened his trunk, took out a towel and soap, and sternly said, 'Show me the bathroom.'

The boy seemed to be a half-wit, incapable of talking of any other subject.

When Chandran was combing his hair, his aunt brought in a very small child with curly hair and large eyes, and said, 'Have you seen this girl? She is just up from bed. She simply wouldn't stay in it, but wanted to be taken to you immediately.'

Chandran tapped its cheeks with his fingers. 'What is her name?'

'Kamala,' replied his aunt.

'Ah, Kamal. What, Kamala?' Chandran asked, staring at the child, and raising his hand once again to tap its cheeks. The child looked at him fixedly for a moment and began to cry. Chandran stood still, not knowing what he was expected to do. Aunt took away the child, saying, 'She can't stand new faces. She will be all right when she gets to know you a little more.'

At eleven o'clock, after food, his uncle took him out in the car. The car stopped before a four-storeyed building in Linga Chetty Street.

He followed his uncle up three flights of stairs, past a corridor and a glass door, into an office. Before a table littered with files a man was sitting.

His uncle said, 'Good-morning, Murugesam.'

'Hallo, hallo, come in,' said the man at the table, pushing aside a file that he was reading.

Uncle said, 'This is my nephew whom I spoke to you about. This is Mr S. T. Murugesam, General Manager of Engladia Limited.'

Chandran stretched his hand across the table and said, 'I am glad to meet you, sir.'

'Take a chair,' said Murugesam.

Uncle and Murugesam talked for a while, and then Uncle got up. 'I shall have to be going now. Some railway people are coming to my office at twelve. So you will take this boy and fix him up?'

'I will do my best.'

'That is not enough,' said Uncle. 'You have got to fix him up. He is a graduate, son of a big Government pensioner; he will give any security you want. You must fix him up. He has even cancelled his trip to England for the sake of this paper ... You can keep him here. I shall pick him up on my way back.' He went out.

Murugesam looked at the time and said, 'We shall go out at two o'clock. I hope you won't mind half an hour's wait.'

'Not at all. You can take your own time, sir,' said Chandran, and leant back in his chair. Murugesam signed a heap of papers, pushed them away, gripped the telephone on the table, and said into it, 'Shipping,' and waited for a moment and said, 'Inform Damodars that we can't load *Waterway* before Thursday midnight. Thursday midnight. Bags are still arriving. She is not sailing before Saturday evening ... Right. Thank you.'

Chandran watched him, fascinated. For the first time he was witnessing a business man at work. Chandran felt a great admiration for Murugesam, a slight man, keeping in his hands the strings of mighty activities; probably ships were waiting to sail at a word from him. How did he pick up so much business knowledge? What did he earn? Ten thousand? What did he do with so much money? When would he find time to spend the money and enjoy life with so many demands on his attention? The telephone bell rang. Murugesam took it up and said, 'That is right. Tell them they will get the notice in due course. Thank you,' and put down the receiver. An assistant brought in some letters and put them before him, Murugesam wrote something on them, gave them back to the assistant, and said, 'I am going out, and shall not be back for about half an hour. If there are any urgent calls, you can ring me up at the *Daily Messenger*.'

'Yes, sir.'

'But remember, don't send anyone there. Only very urgent calls.' He rose and picked up his fur cap. Chandran was impressed with the other's simplicity of dress. He was wearing only a *dhoti*, a long silk coat, and a black fur cap.

He led Chandran out of the building, and got into a sedan. They drove in the car for about a quarter of an hour through whirling traffic, and got down before a new, white building in Mount Road, before which stood in huge letters the sign '*Daily Messenger*'. They went up in a lift, through several halls filled with tables and men bent in work, past shining counters and twisting passages. Murugesam pushed a red-curtained door. A man was sitting at a table littered with files. 'Hallo, Murugesam,' he said. He was a pink, bald man, wearing rimless glasses. A fan was whirring over his head.

'I have brought this young man to see you,' Murugesam said.

The bald man looked at Chandran coldly, and said to Murugesam, 'You were not at the club yesterday.'

'I couldn't come. Had to go to the wharf.'

A servant brought in a visiting card. The bald man looked at it critically and said, 'No more interviews today. Tomorrow at one-thirty.'

Murugesam went over to the other side of the table and spoke in whispers to the bald man. Murugesam almost sat on the arm of the bald man's revolving chair. Chandran was not asked to sit, and so he stood, uncertainly, looking at the walls, with his arms locked behind him. The bald man suddenly looked at Chandran and asked, 'Your father is?'

'H. C. Venkatachala Iyer.'

'He was?'

'A District Judge.'

'I see,' said the bald man. He turned to Murugesam and said, 'I have no idea what they are doing in regard to the agencies. I must ask Sankaran. I will let you know afterwards.'

Murugesam made some deprecating noises and said, 'That won't do. Call up Sankaran and tell him what to do. Surely you can dictate.' He left the arm of the chair and went to another chair, saying, 'He is a graduate, comes from a big family, prepared to give any security. He has cancelled his tour to England for the sake of your paper.'

'Why did you want to go to England?' asked the bald man, turning to Chandran.

'Wanted to get a doctorate.'

'At?'

'The London University.'

'In?'

'Economics or Politics,' said Chandran, choosing his subject for the first time.

'Why do you want to work for our paper?'

'Because I like it, sir.'

'Which? The paper or the agency?'

'Both,' said Chandran.

'Are you confident of sending up the circulation if you are given a district?'

'Yes, sir.'

'By how much?'

Chandran quoted 5,000, and explained the figures with reference to the area of Malgudi, its literate population, and the number of people who could spend an anna a day.

'That is a fair offer,' said Murugesam.

The bald man said with a dry smile, 'It is good to be optimistic.'

'Optimistic or not, you must give him a fair trial,' said Murugesam.

The bald man said, 'The trouble is that I don't usually interfere in these details. The managers concerned look to it. I have no idea what they are doing.'

'Well, well, well,' said Murugesam impatiently. 'There is no harm in it. You can break the rule occasionally and dictate. Just for my sake. I have to go back to the office. Hurry up. Send for Sankaran.' Murugesam pressed a bell. A servant came. Murugesam said, 'Tell Mr Sankaran to come up.'

A man with a scowling face came in, nodded, went straight to a chair, sat down, and leaned forward.

The bald man asked, 'Have you any vacancies in the Southern Districts?'

'For correspondents? No.'

'I mean agencies.'

'Yes, a few where we want to change the present agents.'

'Yours is Malgudi, is it not?' asked the bald man, turning to Chandran.

'Yes, sir.'

'I think that is one of the places,' said Sankaran.

The bald man said, 'Please give me some details of the place.'

Sankaran pressed a bell, scribbled something on a bit of paper, and gave it to the servant. 'Take it to Sastri.'

The servant went out and returned in a few minutes followed by an old man, who was carrying a register with him. He placed the register on the table before Sankaran, opened a page, and stood away respectfully.

Murugesam said at this point, 'Sit down, Mr Chandran.'

'Yes, yes, why are you standing?' asked the bald man.

Chandran sat in a chair and looked at the bald man, Sankaran, the turban-wearing Sastri, and Murugesam, and thought: 'My life is in these fellows' hands! Absolute strangers. Decision of my fate in their hands, absolutely! Why is it so?'

Sankaran said, looking at the register, 'Here are the facts, sir. Malgudi Agency: The present man has been there since the old régime. The top circulation 35 till two years ago; since then steady at 25! Eleven applications for the agency up to date; one from the old agent himself promising to turn over a new leaf. Potential circulation in the district, 7,000.'

'Thank you,' said the bald man. 'When are you settling it?'

'I want to wait till the first.'

'Why should there be any delay? If you have no particular objection, give the agency to this gentleman. He promises to give the security immediately and work for the paper.'

Sankaran looked at Chandran and said to the bald man, 'Some more applications may be coming in, sir.'

'File them.'

'Very well, sir,' said Sankaran, and rose. 'Come with me,' he said to Chandran.

Sankaran took Chandran into a hall, where a number of persons were seated at tables, from the edges of which galley proofs streamed down to the floor. They went to the farthest end of the hall and sat down. Sankaran began a short speech on the *Daily Messenger*: 'The *Daily Messenger* is not the old paper that it was a year or two ago. The circulation has gone up from 8,000 to 30,000 in less than a year. That is due both to the circulation and the editorial departments. They have both work to do, just as you need both legs for walking.' He spoke over the din of the office and of the press below for half an hour, winding up with the threat that if Chandran did not show real progress within six months from the date of appointment, the agency would be immediately transferred to another.

CHAPTER FIFTEEN

Chandran returned to Malgudi and plunged himself in work. He took a small room in Market Road for a rent of seven rupees a month, and hung on the doorway an immense sign: '*THE DAILY MESSENGER* (Local Offices)'. He furnished his office with a table, a chair and a long bench.

He sat in his office from eleven till five, preparing a list of possible subscribers in the town. At the lowest estimate there were five hundred. After enlisting them, he would go out into the district and enlist another five hundred; and for six months he would be quite content to stay at a thousand.

He took out a sheet of paper and noted on it the procedure to be followed in canvassing. He often bit the pen and looked at the traffic in Market Road, steeped in thought. After four days of intense thinking and watching of traffic, he was able to sketch out a complete plan of attack. He wrote: 'Bulletin; Specimen; Interview; Advance'. He would first send his bulletin to the persons on his list, then supply free specimen copies for two days, then go and see them in person, and finally take a month's subscription in advance.

Next he planned the Bulletin. It approached a client in four stages: Information; Illumination; Appeal; and Force.

Bulletin One said: 'Mr H. V. Chandran, B.A., requests the pleasure of your company with family and friends at C-96 Market Road, where he has just opened the local offices of the *Daily Messenger* of Madras.' Bulletin Two said: 'Five reasons why you should immediately subscribe to the *Daily Messenger*. Its daily circulation is 30,000 in the Presidency, and 30,000 persons cannot be making a mistake every day. It is auspicious to wake to the thud of a paper dropped on the floor; and we are prepared to provide you with this auspicious start every morning by bringing the *D. M.* to your house and pushing it in through your front window. It has at its command all the news services in the world, so that you will find in it a Municipal Council resolution in Malgudi as well as a political assassination in Iceland, reported accurately and quickly. The mark of culture is wide information; and the *D. M.* will give you politics, economics, sports, literature; and its magazine supplement covers all the other branches of human knowledge. Even in mere bulk you will be getting your anna's worth; if you find the contents uninteresting you can sell away your copy to the grocer at a rupee per *maund*.' Bulletin Three said: 'As a son of the Motherland it is your duty to subscribe to the *D. M.* With every anna that you pay, you support the anaemic child, Indian Industry. You must contribute your mite for the economic and political salvation of our country.' Bulletin Four merely stated: 'To the hesitant. It is never too late. Come at once to C-96 Market Road and take your paper, or shall we send it to your house? Never postpone to a tomorrow what you can do today.'

He gave these for printing to the Truth Printing Works, which was situated in another room like his, four doors off. The Truth Works consisted of a treadle, a typeboard, and a compositor, besides the proprietor.

The printer delivered the bulletins in about a week. Chandran put them in envelopes and addressed them according to the list he had prepared. He had now in his service three small boys for distributing the paper, and he had purchased for them three cheap cycles. He divided the town into three sections and allotted each of them a section, and gave them the envelopes for distribution. He sent the bulletins out in their order, one on each day.

After that he engaged a small party of brass band and street boys, and sent them through the principal streets of the town in a noisy procession, in which huge placards, shrieking out the virtues of the *Daily Messenger*, were carried.

He then distributed a hundred copies of the *Messenger* every day as specimens to the persons to whom he had sent the bulletins.

After all this preparation, he set out every morning on his cycle, neatly shaved and groomed, and dressed in an impeccable check suit, and interviewed his prospects. He took the town ward by ward. He calculated that if he worked from eight in the morning till eight in the evening he would be able to see about thirty-six prospects a day, giving about twenty minutes to each prospect.

He sent his card into every house and said as soon as his prospect appeared, 'Good-morning, sir. How do you like our paper?' Soon he became an adept salesman, and in ten minutes could classify and label the person before him. He now realized that humanity fell into four types: (1) Persons who cared for the latest news and could afford an anna a day. (2) Persons who were satisfied with stale news in old papers which could be borrowed from neighbours. (3) Persons who read newspapers in reading-rooms. (4) Persons who could be coerced by repeated visits.

Chandran talked a great deal to 1 and 4, and never wasted more than a few seconds on 2 and 3.

He visited club secretaries, reading-room secretaries, headmasters of schools, lawyers, doctors, business men, and landowners, and every literate person in the town, at home, office, and club. To some places, when he was hard-pressed for time, he sent Mohan.

In a few weeks he settled down to a routine. Every morning he left his bed at five o'clock and went to the station to meet the train from Madras at five-thirty. He took the bundles of papers and sent them in various directions with the cycle boys. After that he returned home, and went to his office only at eleven o'clock, and stayed there till five in the evening, when Mohan would drop in after posting his news for the day. Often Mohan would set him on the track of new clients: 'I have reported an interesting criminal case today. Full details will appear in tomorrow's paper.' As soon as the report appeared Chandran would go to the parties concerned and show them the news in print and induce them to part with a month's subscription, or if that was not possible, at least manage to sell them some loose copies containing their names. Some persons would be so pleased to see their names in print that they would buy even a dozen copies at a time. These stray sales account for, on an average, half a dozen copies every day. Mohan reported a wide variety of topics:

excise raids, football matches, accidents, 'smart' arrests by police sub-inspectors, suicides, murders, thefts, lectures in Albert College Union, and social events like anniversaries, tea parties, and farewell dinners.

The *D. M.* was responsible for taking him back to his old college after two years. Mohan had secured the Union and college orders. One of the boys came and told Chandran one day, suddenly, 'Sir, the college clerk says that they won't want the paper from tomorrow.'

'Why?'

'I don't know, sir. They said the same thing in the Union too.'

Chandran went to the college in person. The Union clerk recognized him and asked, 'How are you, Mr Chandran?'

'I say, my boy tells me that you have stopped the paper. Have you any idea why?'

'I don't know, sir. It is the President's order.'

'Who is the President this year?'

'History Ragavachar,' said the clerk.

He left the Union and went to the college, to the good old right wing, in which his Professor's room was situated. Ragavachar was holding a small class in his room, and Chandran went back to the Union to wait till the end of the hour. He sat in the gallery of the debating hall, and nobody took any notice of him. One or two boys stared at him and passed. He had been the Prime Mover in this very hall on a score of occasions; he had been the focus of attention. In those days, when he sat like this in the interim periods, how many people would gather round him, how they would all swagger about and shout as if they owned the place, and how they would throw pitying looks at strangers who sometimes came to look at the Union and moved about the place timidly. 'Not one here that belonged to my set, all new faces, all absolute strangers. Probably these were High School boys when we were in the college ... Ramu, Ramu. How often have I come here looking for Ramu. If any class or lecture threatened to be boring Ramu would prefer to come away and spend his time reading a novel here or up in the reading-room. He had been quite a warm friend, but probably people changed. Time passed swiftly in Ramu's company. He would have some comment or other to make on every blessed thing on earth ... If he had real affection for a friend he should have written letters, especially when there was happy news like the securing of a job. Out of sight out of mind, but that is not a quality of friendship. There is no such thing as friendship ...'

Chandran rose from the gallery and stood looking at some group photos hanging on the wall. All your interests, joys, sorrows, hopes, contacts, and experience boiled down to group photos, Chandran thought. You lived in the college, thinking that you were the first and the last of your kind the college would ever see, and you ended as a group photo; the laughing, giggling fellows one saw about the Union now little knew that they would shortly be frozen into group photos ... He stopped before the group representing the 1931 set. He stood on tiptoe to see the faces. Many faces were familiar, but he could not recollect all their names. Where were all these now? He met so few of his class-mates, though they had been two hundred strong for four years. Where were they? Scattered like spray. They were probably merchants, advocates, murderers, police inspectors, clerks, officers, and what not. Some must have gone to England, some married and had children, some turned agriculturists, dead and starving and unemployed, all at grips with life, like a buffalo caught in the coils of a python ...

There was Veeraswami, the revolutionary. He had appeared only once on the sands of Sarayu, like a dead man come to life for an instant. He had talked of some brigade and a revolution and Nature Cure. Where was he? What had he done with himself?... Among the people seated in the front row there was Natesan, the old Union Secretary, always in complications, always grumbling and arranging meetings. Chandran realized that he hadn't heard of Natesan after the examination; didn't know to which part of the country he belonged. He had been a good friend, very helpful and accommodating; but for his help the Historical Association could not have done any work. Where was he? Had he committed suicide? Could an advertisement be inserted in the papers: 'Oh, Natesa, my friend, where are you?'

The bell rang. Chandran hurried out to meet Ragavachar. He saw several students walking in the corridors of the college.

Scores of new faces. 'At any rate they were better built in our days. All these fellows are puny.' He recognized a few that had been the rawest juniors in his days, but were senior students now. They greeted him with smiles, and he felt greatly pleased. He strode into Ragavachar's room. Ragavachar sat in his chair and was just returning his spectacles to their case.

'Good-morning, sir,' said Chandran. The Professor appeared to be slightly loose in the joints now. How he had been terrified of him in those days, Chandran reflected, as the Professor opened his case, put on the spectacles, and surveyed his visitor. There was no recognition in his manner.

'Please sit down,' said the Professor, still trying to place his visitor.

'Don't you recognize me, sir?'

'Were you in this college at any time?'

'Yes, sir, in 1931. I was the first secretary of the Historical Association. My name is H. V. Chandran.'

'H. V. Chandran,' the Professor repeated reflectively. 'Yes, yes. I remember. How are you? What are you doing now? You see, about two hundred persons pass out of the college every year; sometimes it is difficult to recollect, you see.'

Chandran had never thought that Ragavachar could talk so mildly. In those days how his voice silenced whole classes!

'What are you doing, Chandran?'

Chandran told him, and then stated his business.

'Send for the Union clerk,' said the Professor. When the clerk came, he asked, 'Why have you stopped the *Daily Messenger*?'

'There was a President's order to stop some of the papers,' replied the clerk.

'And you chose the *Daily Messenger*, I suppose?' growled Ragavachar. His voice had lost none of its tigerishness. 'Which daily are you getting in the Union?'

'The *Everyday Post*, sir.'

This name set up a slight agitation in Chandran. The *Post* was his deadliest enemy; but for it he would have enlisted a thousand subscribers in a fortnight. He said, 'The *Post*! It isn't served by the Planet News Service, sir.'

'Isn't it?' asked Ragavachar.

'No, sir. It gets only the "C" grade of the B. K. Press Agency.'

'Is there much difference?'

'Absolutely, sir. I am not saying it because I am the agent of the *Messenger*. You can compare the telegrams in the *Messenger* with those in the *Post*, and you will see the difference, sir. B. K. Agency is not half as wide an organization as the Planet, and its "C" grade is its very lowest service, and supplies the minimum news; the "A" and "B" grades are better. Our paper gets the "A" and "B" grades of the B. K. Agency in addition to the First Grade of the Planet Service; so that our paper gives all the news available.'

'Still, a lot of people buy the *Post*,' said Ragavachar.

'No, sir. Quite a lot of people are buying now only the *Messenger*. The circulation of the *Post* has steadily gone down to 2,000. Once upon a time it reigned supreme, when it was the only paper in the South.'

Ragavachar turned to the clerk and commanded, 'Get the *Messenger* from tomorrow. Stop the *Post*.'

When Chandran rose to go, the Professor said, 'I wish you luck. Please keep in touch with us. It ought to be easier for our students to remember us than for us to remember them. So don't forget.'

'Certainly not, sir,' Chandran said, resolving at that moment to visit his Professor at least once a week.

The college library clerk told him that Gajapathi was in charge of the college reading-room. Chandran went to the Common Room and sent his card in and waited, wondering if Gajapathi was going to resume his attacks on Dowden and Bradley.

'Hallo, hallo, Chandran. It is ages since I saw you. What are you doing now?' Gajapathi put his arm round Chandran's shoulders and patted him. Chandran was taken aback by this affability, something they had not thought him capable of. Except for this Gajapathi had not changed. He still wore his discoloured frame spectacles and the drooping moustache.

When Chandran stated his business, Gajapathi said, 'If they are getting the *Messenger* in the Union we can't get it in the college reading-room, because the Principal has passed an order that papers and magazines should not be duplicated in the two reading-rooms.'

'But it is a waste of money to get the *Post*, sir. There is absolutely no news in it. It has a very inadequate service for telegrams, and it hasn't half as many correspondents as the *Messenger* has.'

'Whatever it is, that is the Principal's order.'

'Why don't you subscribe to my paper, sir?'

'Me! I never read any newspaper.'

Chandran was horrified to hear it. 'What do you do for news, sir?'

'I am not interested in any news.'

Evidently this man read only Shakespeare and his critics.

'Well, sir, if you won't consider it a piece of impertinence, I think you ought to get into the newspaper habit. I am sure you will like it. I am sure you wouldn't like to be without it even for a day.'

'Very well then, send it along. What is the subscription?'

'Two-eight a month and the paper is delivered at your door.'

'Here it is, for a month.' Gajapathi took out his purse and gave a month's subscription. 'You can ask your boy to deliver it to me at –'

'Thank you, sir. I shall send the receipt tomorrow.'

'Don't you trouble yourself about it. I only want my old students to do well in life. I am happy when I see it.'

Chandran had never known this fact, and now he was profoundly moved by it.

'You must visit my office some time, sir,' he said.

'Certainly, certainly. Where is it?'

Before parting, Chandran tried to gratify him by saying, 'I have been reading a lot since I left the college, sir.'

'Really very glad to hear it. What have you been reading?'

'A little of Shakespeare; some Victorian essayists. But in fiction I think the present-day writers are really the masters. Don't you think, sir, that Wells, Galsworthy, and Hardy are superior to the old novelists?'

Gajapathi paused before pronouncing an opinion. 'I honestly think that there has not been anything worth reading after the eighteenth century, and for anyone who cares for the real flavour of literature nothing to equal the Elizabethans. All the rest is trash.'

'Galsworthy, sir?'

'I find him tiresome.'

'Wells and Hardy?' gasped Chandran.

'Wells is a social thinker, hardly a literary figure. He is a bit cranky too. Hardy? Much over-rated; some parts of *Tess* good.'

Chandran realized that Time had not touched his fanaticisms. What an unknown, unsuspected enemy Wells, Galsworthy, Hardy, and a host of critics had in Gajapathi, Chandran thought.

'Don't forget to visit my office, sir, some time,' Chandran pleaded before taking his leave.

CHAPTER SIXTEEN

One evening at five o'clock, as Chandran sat in his office signing receipts and putting them in envelopes for distribution next morning, his father walked in. Chandran pushed his chair back and rose, quite surprised, for Father seldom came to the office; he had dropped in on the opening day, and again at another time with a friend, explaining apologetically that the friend wanted to see Chandran. Now this was his third visit.

'Sit down, Chandar, don't disturb yourself,' said Father and tried to sit on the bench. Chandran pushed the chair towards him, entreating him to be seated on it.

Father looked about and asked, 'How is your business?'

'Quite steady, Father. The only trouble is in collection. If I go in person they pay the subscription; if I send the boys they put them off with some excuse or other. I can't be visiting the 350 subscribers in person every morning. I must engage a bill collector. I can just afford one now.'

'Are they pleased with your work in the Head Office?'

'They must be. For six months I have shown a monthly average of over fifty new subscriptions; but they have not written anything, which is a good sign. I don't expect anything better. If work is unsatisfactory our bosses will bark at us; if it is satisfactory they won't say so, but merely keep quiet.'

'You are right. In Government service too it is the same; the best that we can expect from those above us is a very passive appreciation.'

And then the conversation lagged for some time. Father suddenly said, 'I have come on a mission. I was sent by your mother.'

'Mother?'

'Yes. She wants this thing to be made known to you. She is rather nervous to talk to you about it herself. So she has sent me.'

'What is it, Father?'

'But I wish you to understand clearly that I have not done anything behind your back. I have had no hand in this. It is entirely your mother's work.'

'What is it, Father?'

'You see, Mr Jayarama Iyer, who is a leading lawyer in Talapur, sent his daughter's horoscope to us some time ago; and for courtesy's sake yours was sent to them in return. Yesterday they have written to say that the horoscopes match very well, and asking if we have any objection to this alliance. I was for dropping the whole matter there, but your mother is very eager to make it known to you and to leave it to your decision. They have got in touch with us through our Ganapathi Sastrigal.'

Chandran sat looking at the floor. His father paused for a moment and said, 'I hear that the girl is about fifteen. They have sent a photo. She is good-looking. You can have a look at the photo if you like. They have written that she is very fair. They are prepared to give a cash dowry of 3,000 and other presents.'

He waited for Chandran's answer. Chandran looked at him. There were drops of sweat on Father's brow, and his voice slightly quivered. Chandran felt a great pity for his father. What a strain this talk and the preparation for it must have been to him! Father sat silent for a moment and then said, rising, 'I will be going now. I have to go to the club.'

Chandran saw his father off at the door and watched his back as he swung his cane and walked down the road. Chandran suddenly realized that he hadn't said anything in reply, and that his father might interpret silence for consent and live on false hopes. What a dreadful thing. He called his office boy, who was squatting on the steps of a neighbouring shop, asked him to remain in the office, took out his cycle, and pedalled in the direction his father had taken. Father hadn't gone far. Chandran caught up with him.

'You want me?'

'Yes, Father.'

Father slowed down, and Chandran followed him, looking at the ground. 'You have taken the trouble to come so far, Father, but I must tell you that I can't marry, Father.'

'It is all right, Chandar. Don't let that bother you.'

Chandran followed him for a few yards, and said, 'Shall I go back to the office?'

'Yes.'

As Chandran was about to mount his cycle, Father stopped him and said, 'I saw in your office some papers and letters lying loose on your table. They are likely to be blown away by a wind. Remind me, I will give you some paperweights tomorrow.'

He came back to his table and tried to sign a few more receipts. His father's visit opened a lid that had smothered raging flames. It started once again all the old controversies that racked one's soul. It violently shook a poise that was delicate and attained with infinite trouble and discipline.

He could not sign any more receipts. He pushed away the envelopes and the receipt books in order to make room for his elbows, which he rested on the table, and sat with his face in his hands, staring at the opposite wall.

Mohan came at six o'clock. He flung his cap on the table and sat down on the bench before the table, obstructing Chandran's view of the opposite wall.

Chandran asked mechanically, 'What is the latest news?'

'Nothing special. The usual drab nonsense; lectures and sports and suicides. I am seriously thinking of resigning.'

He was very sullen.

'What is wrong now?' asked Chandran.

'Everything. I took up this work as a stop-gap till I should get a footing in the literary world. And now what has happened? Reporting has swallowed me up. From morning to night I roam about the town, noting other people's business, and then go back to the hotel and sleep. I hardly have any inclination to write a single line of poetry. It is four months since I wrote a single line. The stuff you see in the magazine page are my old bits. When I take my pen I can't write anything more soul-stirring than "Judgment was delivered today in a case in which somebody or other stood charged with something or other ..." '

'I am very hungry,' said Chandran. 'Shall we go to a hotel?'

'Yes.'

When they came out of the hotel, Mohan's mood had changed. He now condemned his previous mood. 'If I have not written anything, it is hardly anybody's fault. I ought to plan my time to include it.'

They smoked a few cigarettes and walked along the river. They walked to Nallappa's Grove, crossed over to the opposite bank, walked some distance there, turned back, and sat down on the sands. Mohan went on talking and solacing himself by planning. He even stretched the definition of poetry; he said that there ought to be no special thing called poetry, and that if one was properly constituted one ought to get a poetic thrill out of the composing of even news paragraphs. There ought to be no narrow boundaries. There ought to be a proper synthesis of life.

When Mohan had exhausted his poetic theories, Chandran quietly said, 'My father came to the office at five o'clock with an offer of marriage.' The troubles of a poet instantly eased or were forgotten. He listened in silence to Chandran's narration of his father's visit. And Mohan dared not comment. From the manner in which Chandran spoke Mohan couldn't tell which way he was inclined; there was the usual denunciation of Love, Marriage, and Woman, but at the same time there was a lack of fire in the denunciation. Mohan could not decide whether it was the beginning of a change of attitude or whether it was a state of atrophy, so complete that even fury and fire were dead. Chandran concluded, '... And I ran after my father and told him that it was unthinkable.'

Chandran stopped. Mohan did not offer any comment. For some moments there was only the rustle of the banyan branches on the water's edge.

'I am very sorry for my poor mother, for her wild hope and her fears. I curse myself for having brought her to this state. But what can I do? What other answer could I give to my father?'

'How did he take it?'

'Quite indifferently. He talked of paperweights. My trouble is, I don't know, I don't know. I can't get angry with my mother for busying herself with my marriage again. I have had enough of it once.'

'Then leave it alone. You are under no compulsion to worry about it.'

'But I pity my father and mother. What a frantic attempt. There is something in the whole business that looks very pathetic to me.'

'What I can't understand is,' said Mohan, 'why you are still worrying about it, seeing that you have very politely told your father that it is unthinkable. I can't understand why you still talk about it.'

'You are right. That question is settled. Let us talk of something else.'

'Something else' was not easy to find. There was another interlude of silence.

'Shall we be starting back?' asked Mohan.

'Yes,' said Chandran, but again sat in silence, not making any effort to get up. For nearly a quarter of an hour Mohan sat listening to the voice of the river, and Chandran drew circles in the sand.

'What would you do in my place?' asked Chandran abruptly.

'How can I say? What would you do in mine?' asked Mohan.

Chandran asked directly, 'What would you honestly advise me to do?'

'If the girl is not bad-looking, and if you are getting some money into the bargain, why don't you marry? You will have some money and the benefits of a permanent help-mate.'

Chandran remarked that Mohan had grown very coarse and prosaic. No wonder he could not write any more poetry.

Stung by this Mohan said, 'If one has to marry one must do it for love, if there is such a thing, or for the money and comforts. There is no sense in shutting your eyes to the reality of things. I am beginning to believe in a callous realism.' He liked immensely the expression he had invented. He loved it. He delivered a short speech on Callous Realism. He had not thought of it till now. Now that he had coined the expression he began to believe in it fully. He raised it to the status of a personal philosophy. Before he had expatiated for five minutes on it, he became a fanatic. He challenged all other philosophies, and pleaded for more Callous Realism in all human thought. When he reached the height of intoxication, he said with a great deal of callous realism, 'I don't see why you shouldn't consider this offer with the greatest care and attention. You get a fat three thousand, and get a good-looking companion, who will sew on your buttons, mend your clothes, and dust your furniture while you are distributing newspapers, and who will bring the coffee to your room. In addition to all this, it is always pleasant to have a soft companion near at hand.'

'And on top of it pleasing one's parents,' added Chandran.

'Quite right. Three cheers for Her Majesty the Soft Companion,' cried Mohan.

'Hip, hip, hooray!'

The callous realist now asked, 'Will you kindly answer a few questions I am going to ask?'

'Yes.'

'You must answer my questions honestly and truthfully. They are to search your heart.'

'Right, go on,' said Chandran.

'Are you still thinking of Malathi?'

'I have trained my mind not to. She is another man's wife now.'

'Do you love the memory of her still?'

'I don't believe in love. It doesn't exist in my philosophy. There is no such thing as love. If I am not unkind to my parents it is because of gratitude, and nothing else. If I get a wife I shall not wrench her hand or swear at her, because it would be indecent. That is all the motive for a lot of habitual decent behaviour we see, which we call love. There is no such thing as love.'

'Then it ought not to make any difference to you whether you marry or not; and so why don't you marry when you know that it will please your parents, when you are getting a lot of money, and when you are earning so well?'

There was no answer to this. Chandran chewed these thoughts in silence, and then said, 'Mohan, let us toss and decide.' They rose and walked across the sand to a dim municipal lantern at the end of North Street. The lantern threw a pale yellow circle of light around a central shadow. Chandran took a copper coin from his pocket. Mohan held Chandran's hand and said, 'Put that back. Let us toss with a silver coin. Marriage, you know.' Mohan took out a four-anna silver coin, balanced it on the forefinger of his right hand, and asked, 'Shall I toss?'

'Yes. Heads, marriage.'

'Right.'

Mohan tossed the silver coin. It fell down in the dim circumference of light. Both stooped. Mohan shouted, 'You must keep your word. Heads. Ha! Ha!'

'Is it?' There was a tremor in Chandran's voice. 'Very well, if the girl is good-looking, only if she is good-looking,' said Chandran.

'That goes without saying,' said Mohan, picking up the coin and putting it in his pocket.

CHAPTER SEVENTEEN

Early in the morning, five days later, Chandran, with his mother, was in a train going to Talapur. He was to look at the girl who had been proposed to him, and then give his final word.

He said to his mother for the dozenth time, 'If I don't like the girl, I hope they won't mind.'

'Not at all. Before I married your father, some three or four persons came and looked at me and went away.'

'Why did they not approve of you?' Chandran asked, looking at her.

'It is all a matter of fate,' said Mother. 'You can marry only the person whom you are destined to marry and at the appointed time. When the time comes, let her be the ugliest girl, she will look all right to the destined eye.'

'None of that, Mother,' Chandran protested. 'I won't marry an ugly girl.'

'Ugliness and beauty is all as it strikes one's eye. Everyone has his own vision. How do all the ugly girls in the world get married?'

Chandran became apprehensive. 'Mother, are you suggesting that this girl is ugly?'

'Not at all. Not at all. See her for yourself and decide. You have the photo.'

'She is all right in the photo, but that may be only a trick of the camera.'

'You will have to wait for only a few hours more. You can see her and then give your decision.'

'But, Mother, to go all the way to their house and see the girl, and then to say we can't marry her. That won't be nice.'

'What is there in it? It is the custom. When a girl is ready for marriage her horoscope will be sent in ten directions, and ten different persons will see her and approve or disapprove, or they might be disapproved by the girl herself; and after all only one will marry her. A year before my marriage a certain doctor was eager for an alliance with our family; the horoscopes, too, matched; and his son came to look at me, but I didn't like his appearance, and told my father that I wouldn't marry him. It was after that that your father was proposed, and he liked my appearance, and when my father asked me if I would marry him I didn't say "no". It is all settled already, the husband of every girl and wife of every man. It is in nobody's choice.'

They reached Talapur at 4 p.m. A boy of about eighteen came and peeped into the compartment and asked, 'Are you from Malgudi?'

'Yes,' said Chandran.

'I am Mr Jayarama Iyer's son. Shall I ask my servant to carry your baggage?'

'We have brought nothing. We are going back by the seven o'clock train, you see,' said Chandran. Chandran and his mother exchanged a brief look. 'This is the girl's brother,' the look said. Chandran took another look at the boy and tried to guess the appearance of the girl. If the girl looked anything like her brother ... ! The boy was dark and rugged. Probably that was not her own brother; he might be her first cousin. Chandran opened his mouth, and was about to ask if Jayarama Iyer was his own father, but he checked himself and asked instead, 'Are you Mr Jayarama Iyer's eldest son?'

'I am his second son,' replied the boy. This answer did not throw any light on the appearance of the girl, as, in some absurd manner, Chandran had imagined that it would.

The boy took them to a car outside. They were soon in the Extensions.

They were welcomed into the house by Mr Jayarama Iyer and his wife, both of whom subjected Chandran to a covert examination just as he tried to make out something of his future relatives-in-law. He found Mr Jayarama Iyer to be a middle-aged person with a greying crop and a sensitive face. He was rather dark, but Chandran noted that the mother looked quite fair, and hoped that the girl would have a judicious mixture of the father's sensitive appearance and the mother's complexion.

And to his immense satisfaction he found that it was so, when, about an hour later, she appeared before him. She had to be coaxed and cajoled by her parents to come to the hall. With her eyes fixed on the ground she stepped from an inner room, a few inches into the hall, trembling and uncertain, ready to vanish in a moment.

Chandran's first impulse was to look away from the girl. He spent a few seconds looking at a picture on the wall; but suddenly remembered that he simply could not afford to look at anything else now. With a sudden decision, he turned his head and stared at her. She was dressed in a blue *sari*. A few diamonds glittered in her ear-lobes and neck. His heart gave a wild beat and, as he thought, stopped. 'Her figure is wonderful,' some corner of his mind murmured. 'Her face must also be wonderful, but I can't see it very well, she is looking at the ground.' Could he shriek out to Mr Jayarama Iyer, sitting in the chair on his right and uttering inanities at this holy moment, 'Please ask your daughter to look up, sir. I can't see her face?'

Mr Jayarama Iyer said to his daughter, 'You mustn't be so shy, my girl. Come here. Come here.'

The girl was still hesitating and very nervous. Chandran felt a great sympathy for her. He pleaded, 'Sir, please don't trouble her. Let her stay there.'

'As you please,' said Jayarama Iyer.

At this moment the girl slightly raised her head and stole a glance at Chandran. He saw her face now. It was divine; there was no doubt about it. He secretly compared it with Malathi's, and wondered what he had seen in the latter to drive him so mad ...

Jayarama Iyer said to his daughter, 'Will you play a little song on the *veena*?' Chandran saw that she was still nervous, and once again rushed to her succour. 'Please don't trouble her, sir. I don't mind. She seems to be nervous.'

'She is not nervous,' said the father. 'She plays very well, and also sings.'

'I am happy to hear that, sir, but it must be very difficult for her to sing now. I hope to hear her music some other day.'

Jayarama Iyer looked at him with amusement and said, 'All right.'

It was with a very heavy heart that Chandran allowed himself to be carried away in the car from the bungalow. He could have cried when he said 'Goodbye' to his future brother-in-law, and the train moved out of Talapur station.

His mother asked him in the train, 'Do you like the girl?'

'Yes, Mother,' said Chandran with fervour. 'Did you tell them that?'

'We can't tell them anything till they come and ask us.'

Chandran made a gesture of despair and said, 'Oh, these formalities. I loathe them. All this means unnecessary delay. Why shouldn't we send them a wire tomorrow?'

'Be patient. Be patient. All in its time, Chandra.'

'But supposing they don't ask us?'

'They will. In two or three days they will come to us or write.'

'I ought to have told Mr Jayarama Iyer that I liked his girl,' Chandran said regretfully.

Mother asked apprehensively, 'I hope you have not done any such thing?'

'No, Mother.'

'Patience, Chandra. You must allow things to be done in proper order.'

Chandran leaned back, resigned himself to his fate, and sat looking out of the window sulkily.

He asked, 'Mother, do you like the girl?'

'Yes, she is good-looking.'

'Is her voice all right? Does she talk all right?'

'She talks quite well.'

'Does she talk intelligently?'

'Oh, yes. But she spoke very little before me. She was shy before her future mother-in-law.'

'What class is she reading in, Mother?'

'Sixth Form.'

'Is she a good student?'

'Her mother says that she is very good in her class.'

'Her father says that she plays very well on the *veena*. It seems she can also sing very well ... Mother, her name is?' He knew it very well, but loved to hear it again.

'Susila,' Mother said.

'I know it,' Chandran said, fearing that his Mother might understand him. 'I want to know if she has any other name at home.'

'Her mother called her once or twice before me, and she called her Susila.'

For the rest of the journey the music of the word 'Susila' rang in his ears. Susila, Susila, Susila. Her name, music, figure, face, and everything about her was divine. Susila, Susila – Malathi, not a spot beside Susila; it was a tongue-twister; he wondered why people liked that name.

CHAPTER EIGHTEEN

A fortnight later the ceremony of the Wedding Notice was celebrated. Jayarama Iyer and a party came to Malgudi for that purpose. It was a day of feast and reception in Chandran's house. A large number of guests were invited, and at the auspicious moment Jayarama Iyer stood up and read the saffron-touched paper which announced that, by the blessing of God, Chandran, son of so and so, was to marry Susila, daughter of so and so, on a particular auspicious date, ten days hence.

The days that followed were days of intense activity. They were days of preparation for the wedding, a period in which Chandran felt the *Daily Messenger* a great nuisance. Chandran had an endless round of visits to make every day, to the tailor, to the jewellers, to the silk shops, and to the printer.

The invitation cards, gold-edged and elegantly printed, were sent to over a thousand in Malgudi and outside. It was while sitting in his office and writing down the addresses that Chandran realized once again how far time had removed him from old class-mates and friends. He was very anxious not to miss anyone. But with the utmost difficulty he could remember only a dozen or so that he occasionally met in the town; he could recollect a few more, but couldn't trace their whereabouts. It rent his heart when he realized his helplessness in regard to even Ramu, Veeraswami, and Natesan. While he knew that Ramu was somewhere in Bombay, there was no one who could give him his address. Heaven knew where Natesan was. And Veeraswami? 'Probably he is a political prisoner somewhere, or he may be in Russia now.'

'Or it is more likely that he is a tame clerk in some Government office,' said Mohan.

'What has happened to his brigade?'

'I have no idea; he came to my hotel once or twice some years ago. I didn't see him after that.'

'Probably his brigade has a strength of a million members now, all of whom may be waiting to overthrow the Government,' said Chandran.

'It is more likely that he has a lucrative job as a police informer,' said the cynical poet. He repeated, 'I have no idea where he is. He came and stayed in my hotel twice several months or years ago.'

This started a train of memories in Chandran. Evenings and evenings ago; Chandran, Mohan and Veeraswami, Malathi evenings; mad days ... There was a radiance about Susila that was lacking in Malathi ... No, no. He checked himself this time; he told himself that it was very unfair to compare and decry; it was a very vile thing to do. He told himself that he was doing it only out of spite ... Poor Malathi! For the first time he was able to view her as a sister in a distant town. Poor girl, she had her points. Of course Susila was different.

'What are you thinking?' asked Mohan.

'That postmaster, the Maduram postmaster, we must send him a card. I don't know if he still remembers me.'

While Chandran was away at Talapur for his wedding, Mohan looked after the newspaper.

Chandran returned a new man, his mind full of Susila, the fragrance of jasmine and sandal paste, the smokiness of the Sacred Fire, of brilliant lights, music, gaiety, and laughter.

For nearly a month after that Mohan had to endure monologues from Chandran: 'On the first day she was too shy to talk to me. It was only on the third day that she uttered a few syllables. Before I came away she spoke quite a lot. Shy at first, you know. She is a very sensible girl; talks very intelligently. I asked her what she thought of me; she merely threw at me a mischievous side glance. She has a very mischievous look. She has promised to write to me on alternate days; she writes beautiful English ...'

Thereafter, every day, Chandran spent a large portion of his waking hours in writing letters to her or in receiving her letters. He would have to live on them for nearly a year more. His talks to Mohan were usually on the subject of these letters. 'She has written a wonderful letter to me today, has addressed me as "My Own Darling" for the first time; she has sent me twenty thousand kisses though I sent her only fifteen thousand in my last letter ...' Or 'She likes very much the silk pieces that I sent to her. She says that they are wonderful.' Or, touching his inner pocket, in which more than one of her letters always rested, 'Poor girl! She writes asking me to take very great care of my health. Says that I ought not to get up so early every morning. She has inquired about the business and wishes me more subscribers. She wishes the *Daily Messenger* long life and health. She has a very great sense of humour.'

Two months later, one evening, Chandran was sitting in his office in a very depressed state. Mohan came, sat on the bench, and asked, 'What is wrong?'

Chandran lifted a care-worn face to him, and said, 'No letter even today. This is the sixth day. I don't know what the matter is.'

'Probably she is studying for the examination or something. She will probably write to you tomorrow.'

'I don't think so,' said Chandran. He was in complete despair. 'This is the first time she has not written for so many days.'

Mohan was baffled. He had never been face to face with such a problem before.

Chandran said, 'I shouldn't worry but for the fact that she is unwell. She wrote in her last letter that she had a bad cold. She is probably down with high fever now. Who knows what fever it might be.'

'It may be just malaria,' hazarded Mohan.

'For six days, unintermittently!' Chandran laughed gloomily. 'I dare not name anything now. I don't know if her people will attend to her properly ... I must go in person and see. I shall go home now, and then catch the six o'clock train. I shall be in Talapur tomorrow morning. Till I come back, please look after the office, will you?'

'Yes,' said Mohan to the afflicted man.

'Many thanks. I shall try to be back soon,' said Chandran and rose. He stepped into the road, took out his cycle from its stand, and said to Mohan, 'I have marked two addresses on the tablet. If they don't give the subscription tell the boys not to deliver them the papers tomorrow.'

As he was ready to get on the cycle, Mohan ran to the door, and said, 'Look here, not that I shirk work and don't want to look after the office or anything, but why do you suppose all these terrible things? On the authority of absent letters and the mention of a slight cold?'

Chandran scorned this question, jumped on his cycle without a word, and pedalled away. Mohan stood looking after the cycle for some time, and turned in, throwing up his arms in despair. But then, it is a poet's business only to ask questions; he cannot always expect an answer.

THE DARK ROOM

CHAPTER ONE

At schooltime Babu suddenly felt very ill, and Savitri fussed over him and put him to bed. And in bed he stayed till Ramani came in and asked, 'What is this?'

'Nothing,' said Savitri, and passed into the kitchen. Ramani questioned the patient himself and called 'Savitri!' Before she could answer, he called her twice again, and asked, 'Are you deaf?'

'I was just – '

'What is the matter with Babu?'

'He is not well.'

'You are too ready with your medical certificate. Babu, get up! Don't miss your school on any account.'

Babu turned on his mother a look of appeal. She said, 'Lie down, Babu. You are not going to school today.'

Ramani said, 'Mind your own business, do you hear?'

'The boy has fever.'

'No, he hasn't. Go and do any work you like in the kitchen, but leave the training of a grown-up boy to me. It is none of a woman's business.'

'Can't you see how ill the boy is?'

'All right, all right,' Ramani said contemptuously. 'It is getting late for my office.' He went to the dining-room.

Babu dressed and slunk off to school. Savitri gave him a tumbler of milk and saw him off. She returned to the kitchen. Her husband had already begun his meal, served by the cook.

She asked again, 'Can't you see how ill the boy is?'

Ramani did not deign to hear the question, but asked, 'Who selected the vegetables for this meal?'

'Why?'

'Brinjals, cucumber, radish, and greens, all the twelve months in the year and all the thirty days in the month. I don't know when I shall have a little decent food to eat. I slave all day in the office for this mouthful. No lack of expenses, money for this and money for that. If the cook can't cook properly, do the work yourself. What have you to do better than that?'

Savitri hovered between the cook and her husband, watching every item on his dining-leaf, and instructing the cook to bring a second or a third helping. This was by no means an easy task, for Ramani was eccentric and lawless in his taste. 'Why do you torment me with this cucumber for the dozenth time? Do you think I live on it?' Or he would say, if there was the slightest delay, 'Ah, ah! I suppose I'll have to apply to my office for leave and wait for this salted cucumber! A fine thing. Never knew people could be so niggardly with cucumber, the cheapest trash in the market. Why not have cut up a few more, instead of trying to feed the whole household on a quarter of it? Fine economy. Wish you'd show the same economy in other matters.' Savitri never interrupted this running commentary with an explanation, and her silence sometimes infuriated her husband. 'Saving up your energy by being silent! Saving it up for what purpose? When a man asks you something you could do worse than honour him with a reply.' Sometimes, if she offered an explanation, as occasionally happened, she would be told, 'Shut up. Words won't mend a piece of foul cooking.'

After the meal he hurried away to his room and dressed for his office. This was an elaborate ritual, complicated by haste. Ramani would keep calling the servant Ranga in order to tell him what he was and where he ought to be for not polishing the boots properly, for folding the trousers with a wrong crease, for leaving the coat on the frame with all the pockets bulging out. Savitri, too, would sometimes be told what her husband thought of her for not attending to buttons or sock-holes, and for not keeping an eye on Ranga. Every item of dress infuriated Ramani and incited him to comment, with the exception of ties, which received his personal attention. He kept them carefully pressed between the leaves of three bulky books which he had on his table: a heavy Annandale's Dictionary, a *Complete Works* of Byron, and an odd volume of the *Encyclopaedia Britannica* contained between them all his best ties.

Dressed in a silk suit, and with a sun-hat on, he stood at the street door and called, 'Who is there?' which meant, 'Savitri, come here and see me off.' When Savitri came he said, 'Close this door.'

'I have finished all the change. I shall have to buy some vegetables for the evening.'

'Will a rupee do?' He gave her the money and strode out. For a moment Savitri lingered in the doorway to hear the protests and growls of the old Chevrolet as it was taken out of the garage. When the noise of the engine ceased, a calm fell on the house.

Now Savitri had before her a little business with her god. She went to the worshipping-room, lighted the wicks and incense, threw on the images on the wooden pedestal handfuls of hibiscus, jasmine and nerium, and muttered all the sacred chants she had learnt from her mother years ago. She prostrated herself before the god, rose, picked up a dining-leaf, and sat down in the kitchen. The cook served her with a doleful face. He asked, 'Are the preparations very bad today, madam?' He was very sensitive to criticism and every day he smarted while his master talked at dinner.

'We ought not to have repeated the brinjals today. We had it yesterday,' Savitri said. 'No more of it this week, whatever happens.'

'All right, madam. Are the preparations very bad this morning?'

'Not exactly bad. Perhaps you would have done well to reduce the tamarind in the sauce. Your master doesn't like tamarind very much.'

The cook served her in sullen silence. Every day this happened. He was affected acutely both by criticism and by hunger, and criticism hurt him all the more because he lived in a state of protracted hunger, being the last to eat. Other cooks might have eased the situation by snatching a gulp of milk or curd when the mistress was not looking their way, but not he; Savitri locked up these commodities in the kitchen cupboard and served them out herself.

'I don't know; master is never satisfied. I do my best, and what more can a human being do?'

As this was almost a daily lament as regular as her husband's lecture, Savitri ceased to pay attention to it and ate in silence. Her thoughts reverted to Babu. The boy looked unwell, and perhaps at that moment was very ill in his class. How impotent she was, she thought; she had not the slightest power to do anything at home, and that after fifteen years of married life. Babu did look very ill and she was powerless to keep him in bed; she felt she ought to have asserted herself a little more at the beginning of her married life and then all would have been well. There were girls nowadays who took charge of their husbands the moment they were married; there was her own friend Gangu who had absolutely tethered up her poor man.

After food she went to her bench in the hall and lay down on it, chewing a little areca-nut and a few betel leaves, and browsed over the pages of a Tamil magazine. In half an hour the house became perfectly still. The servant had finished the day's washing and gone to a nearby shop for a smoke; the cook was out for an hour in order to meet his friends at a coffee-house and compare kitchen politics. Odd noises of crows and sparrows in the garden broke the stillness of the hour. Over the pages of the magazine Savitri snatched a brief nap.

The clatter of the one o'clock bell from the Extension Elementary School reached her drowsing mind and woke her up. It was the recess hour and her two daughters, Sumati and Kamala, would be here presently, jumping about in their haste. Savitri went to the kitchen to mix curd and rice for the girls. Just as she was opening the kitchen cupboard she heard footsteps in the hall and almost immediately Kamala, a plump little girl with a springy pigtail, burst into the kitchen and sat down with her plate before her. She was panting for breath.

'How often am I to tell you not to come running in the sun? Where is Sumati?'

'She is coming with her friends.'

'Why couldn't you have come with her?'

'She won't allow me in her company. They are all in the Eighth Class.'

Kamala stuffed a few mouthfuls and tried to rise. Savitri pushed her down in her seat and said, 'You have got to eat the whole of it. I mixed only a little.' Kamala wriggled and protested.

'It is getting late, Mother. I must go. I can't go on eating all day.'

'I will give you three pies. Finish it.'

'All right,' said Kamala, and related to her mother some of the day's events in the school. 'Our teacher caned Sambu today. He is a bad boy, Mother. He threw a big stone at another boy's toes. Every day he threatens to snatch away my notebooks.'

Kamala had picked up her slate and books and was ready to start when her elder sister Sumati came in. 'Are you going back to school already, Kamala?' she asked authoritatively.

'Yes.'

'Mother,' Sumati cried, 'why do you let Kamala go back so early? We have still half an hour.'

Savitri said, 'Here, Kamala, what is the hurry?'

'I have some work. I have to go,' said Kamala, and vanished.

Sumati went to her desk, carefully put away her books of the morning, and took out her afternoon lessons; she arranged her notebooks in a pile and placed on top the yellow cardboard box in which she kept a number of pencils, a rubber and some pieces of coloured thread. She was examining the points of her pencils when Savitri came to her desk and exclaimed, 'So leisurely!'

'Our music teacher said he would come late today – '

'Your rice is ready.'

At the mention of rice Sumati made a wry face. 'I'm not hungry, Mother.'

Savitri glared at her. 'Don't annoy me, madam.'

'I'm tired of eating rice, nothing but rice morning, noon, and night.'

Sumati went to the kitchen and sat down before her plate. Savitri watched her as she ate and wondered why this girl was getting thinner every day. She was eleven years old and still looked as she did three years ago, as if a whiff of wind could push her off her feet, frail and floating. Perhaps nothing wrong in it; must be hereditary, must be taking after her grandmother: every feature, the dusky colour, the small mouth, rather small eyes, and straight hair. 'As my mother must have looked about forty years ago.'

'Mother, I shall want four annas on Monday,' said Sumati.

'What for?'

'I have to buy an embroidery pattern book.'

'All right. By the way, why don't you keep Kamala with you and see that she doesn't come running through the streets?'

'She doesn't listen to me, Mother.'

'But she said you wouldn't allow her in your company.'

'She is such a nuisance to my friends. She keeps asking everyone for pencils and ribbons. It is disgraceful.'

'All the same, keep an eye on the girl.'

After Sumati went back to school Savitri sat down for a moment fretting about the cook. It was two and he hadn't come yet. How often had she to tell him to be back before two o'clock? He never returned before two-thirty and delayed coffee and tiffin till three-thirty – and close on its heels would come the planning of the night dinner, and on and on endlessly. Was there nothing else for one to do than attend to this miserable business of the stomach from morning till night?

The cook walked in at about two-thirty. 'I was about to light the oven for coffee,' said Savitri.

'Why, madam? Not at all necessary.'

'If you can't be back at two o'clock, you can tell me. I will do this tiffin business myself. I do so many things already one more will make no difference. You can come at your leisure and do whatever is left undone.'

The cook went to the kitchen in a rage, muttering, 'One always comes back, one never goes out to be gone for ever. How is one to know whether it is two or two-thirty? No two clocks agree. When the school bell went off at two o'clock, the clock in the hotel showed only one forty-five. If you want me to be punctual, why can't you buy a watch for me?' When Savitri entered the kitchen a little later he told her, 'From tomorrow I propose to stay here in the afternoon and not go out anywhere.' Savitri said, 'I've no objection to your going out, but if you don't come back at two o'clock this miserable business for the stomach will continue the whole day – ' She issued a few instructions in regard to the night dinner and said, 'I'm going out. If the children come from school before I return, give them coffee and tiffin. Babu will come in the evening. He is not quite well. Give him coffee. Don't compel him to take tiffin if he doesn't want it.'

She dressed her hair, washed her face, renewed the vermilion mark on her forehead, looked at her *sari* for a moment, wondering whether she should wear another and dismissing the thought with, 'This is quite good; I'm not going outside the Extension.' She was ready to go out on her afternoon round of visits at three-thirty. She called the cook and told him: 'Tell the children I'll be back very soon. Don't forget about Babu's coffee.'

At eight-thirty Savitri's ears, as ever, were the first to pick up the hoarse hooting of the Chevrolet horn. She shouted to the servant, 'Ranga, open the motor shed!' Ramani as a rule sounded his horn at about a furlong from his gate, two long hoots which were meant to tell the household, 'Ranga, keep the shed door open when I reach there, if you value your life,' while to Savitri it said, 'It is your business to see that Ranga does his work properly. So take warning.' Some days the hooting would be less emphatic, and Savitri's ears were sufficiently attuned to the nuances and she could tell a few minutes in advance what temper her husband was in. Today the hooting was of the milder kind. It might mean that he was bringing home a guest for dinner or that he was in a happy mood, possibly through a victorious evening at the card table in his club. In either case they could await his arrival without apprehension. If he was happy he treated everyone tolerantly, and even with a kind of aggressive kindness; if he had a guest, he attended on him with such persistence and concentration that he would not notice the failings of his family. Savitri had a qualm for a moment, because a guest would mean a great deal of messing about with oil and frying-pan and stove and getting some extra dish ready within the shortest possible time. Ramani was never in the habit of announcing in advance the arrival of a guest or of tolerating any poor show in the dining-room. He just picked up a friend at the club and brought him home for dinner. It made him furious if it was suggested that he should give notice: 'We are not so down-and-out yet as not to afford some extra food without having to issue warnings beforehand.'

'But if we should have a lot of food left over every day?' Savitri had asked once or twice.

'Throw it into the gutter.'

'Or we can give it to the beggars?' Savitri suggested.

'Certainly. By all means. Make it a rule every day to give some food to the beggars. Remember, if I see any beggar turned away from our door, I shall be very wild.'

Savitri, however, had other methods of dealing with sudden guests. She had a genius for making the existing supply elastic and transforming an ordinary evening course, with a few hurriedly fried trimmings, into a feast.

Today, however, the soft hooting was not due to the presence of a guest. Savitri was greatly relieved to see her husband come into the house alone from the shed. Her alternative inference that he was in a happy mood was confirmed by the fact that he did not pass off into the right wing of the house with bent head, but stood at the doorway wiping his shoes on the mat and looking about. Again he did not say to Savitri, 'See if the fellow has locked the garage door,' but merely asked, 'Have the children had their food?' And again, after going to the room he did not shout in the dark, 'Who is trying to save the electric bill by keeping the house as dark as a burial-ground?' but quietly switched on the lights.

Savitri felt relieved; the same relief ran through the children, who were all at their desks in another room, waiting, keyed up. They had now caught the signals. Ah, Father was going to be pleasant. It meant they could just hang about the dining-hall and listen to their elders' talk; otherwise they would have had to keep to their books for some time and then crawl away to their pillows.

After undressing and changing, Ramani came very quickly towards the dining-hall and said to Savitri, 'Hope you have finished your dinner.'

'Not yet.'

'What a dutiful wife! Would rather starve than precede her husband. You are really like some of the women in our ancient books.'

'And you?' Savitri asked. She could take any liberties with him now. She could say anything. She could be recklessly happy and free.

'I? I'm like – you'd have to write a new epic if you wanted anyone like me in an epic.' And he laughed and patted her on the back. She understood what it meant: he would make love to her, a kind of heavy, boisterous love, even before the cook and the children.

While eating he caught sight of Babu lurking behind the door, and said, 'Hallo, you are still alive? The way your mother protected you this morning I thought – '

'My headache left me in the afternoon, Father.'

'Certainly, so that you might not miss the cricket in the evening; isn't it so?' Babu was silent. Ramani persisted in asking till he confessed that he went to cricket in the evening.

'Look here, young fellow. I've been your age and played all these dodges in my time. So you can't trick me,' said Ramani, and turned to Savitri. 'Which of us was right?'

Savitri blushed. 'The boy did have a headache in the morning,' she said, and felt ashamed of herself for her excessive concern.

'Listen,' Ramani said to Savitri. 'Bear this in mind. There is a golden law of headaches. They come in time for school and leave in time for cricket.' He laughed heartily, well pleased with his epigram. Babu tiptoed away. Ramani said to Savitri: 'You have to learn a lot yet. You are still a child, perhaps a precocious child, but a child all the same.'

The beginning of love-making – Savitri understood and changed the subject. 'What happened to Ramaswami? You never told me what you did with him.'

'Oh, him? We disposed of that affair a long time ago. I didn't want to report the fellow to the head office. I called him up and warned him. He has made good the amount.'

'You won't get into trouble for that?'

'Trouble? Isn't it enough if I don't get them in to it? After all, he's only a poor fellow. Some temptation. A small amount. He has a good record of service.'

'But they may not like your disposing of the question so easily?'

'If they don't like it, here is Mr Ramani's resignation, and you can look out for another secretary for your blessed branch.'

'And suppose they accept the resignation?'

'Madam, the Engladia Insurance Company is a big one, I admit, but it is not the only insurance company in the world. Before I took charge, Malgudi District was not giving them even ten rupees' worth of policies a year, and now ten lakhs of business is passing through my hands every year. What do you say to that?'

Savitri's tactics never failed. If she wanted to divert his attention she had only to work him up into a professional mood. He was going on, expatiating on his work, on the offers he received from other companies, and so on. It saved her from his romantic attentions till the two girls came in.

'Ah, dear lady,' Ramani said to Kamala. 'Why have you neglected us?'

'I was doing my lessons.'

'Lessons! Lessons! You are a great woman. Didn't you hear your father come home?'

'Yes, Father.'

'That's all you care for us poor folk,' Ramani said with an elaborate mischievousness. 'What about you, lady?' he said, turning to his first daughter. 'Ah, how serene you look! You already look as if you had grandchildren.' The children giggled and looked at each other and giggled again. Savitri laughed. He would have been hurt if she hadn't. Ramani looked at his daughters benevolently and then looked at his wife and said with a wink, 'I wonder which of them will grow up like you? In any case, if any of them become half so – h'm, h'm! as you are ... I rather like the way you have arranged the jasmine in your hair today.'

Savitri said, rising, 'Get up. Time to go and wash our hands.'

CHAPTER TWO

Though Savitri was on visiting terms with about a score of houses in the South Extension, she had only two real friends – Gangu and Janamma.

Savitri found Gangu fascinating. She had humour, abundant frivolity, and picturesque ambitions. She was the wife of a school teacher, and had four children. It was her ambition to become a film star, though she lacked any striking figure or features or acting ability; she wanted to be a professional musician, though she had no voice; she hoped to be sent some day as Malgudi delegate to the All-India Women's Conference; to be elected to various municipal and legislative bodies; and to become a Congress leader. She spent her days preparing for the fulfilment of one ambition or another. For serving on public bodies she felt she ought to know a little more English than she needed to read fairy tales and write letters to her husband at the beginning of their married life. Hence she engaged a tutor, who made her go through Scott's novels and trained her in conversation by putting inane questions to her in English. She prepared for her film career by attending two Tamil pictures a week and picking up several screen songs, in addition to wearing flimsy crêpe *saris* and wearing her hair and flowers in an eccentric manner. She talked irresponsibly and enjoyed being unpopular in the elderly society of South Extension. She left home when she pleased and went where she liked, moved about without an escort, stared back at people, and talked loudly. Her husband never interfered with her but let her go her own way, and believed himself to be a champion of women's freedom; he believed he was serving the women's cause by constantly talking about votes and divorce.

Gangu was tolerated in the Extension: she was interesting; with all her talk, she was very religious, visiting the temple regularly, and she was not immoral.

Savitri's other friend, Janamma, was a different type altogether. She was rotund, elderly, and rich. Her husband was a Public Prosecutor. She never moved very freely among people. Savitri had a great regard for her, and consulted her whenever she was seriously worried.

Savitri was friendly with both Janamma and Gangu, though the two found each other intolerable. Janamma said of Gangu, 'That restless rat,' and Gangu said of Janamma, referring to her size and deportment, 'That temple chariot.' Janamma asked Savitri, 'Why do you allow that silly pup to worry you with her company?' Gangu often asked Savitri, 'How do you manage to remain alone with that creature? Isn't her face frightening at close quarters? She looks like a headmaster we had when we were at school.'

Between these two implacable enemies Savitri maintained a subtle balance. Only once did she find herself in a very difficult situation – when both of them met in her house. It happened that Gangu was on a visit to Savitri's house and Janamma dropped in later in the evening. Savitri was sitting on the bench in the hall with Gangu by her side. At the sight of Janamma, Gangu lost her voice but was too proud to get up and go away. Janamma stopped short as if a trap had caught her foot. Savitri said, 'Ah, come in, *mami*,' and edged away a little and made space for her on the bench on her other side. The enemies sat one on each side of her. There was an uneasy silence. Savitri made a vacuous remark on the heat during the day. The remark was in danger of extinction without a response. Shuddering at the prospect of having to invent another equally innocuous, Savitri turned to Gangu and asked anxiously, 'Didn't you feel it?'

'Yes, I did,' replied Gangu cheerlessly.

Savitri, fearing that she might appear to be bestowing more attention on one than on the other, quickly turned to Janamma and inquired, 'It's unusually hot for the time of year, isn't it?'

'I suppose so,' said Janamma.

Then once again silence. Savitri felt the whole situation was thoroughly ridiculous – all three sitting on the same bench side by side like school children, and only one being able to talk. Janamma suddenly rose from the bench and sat on the floor, muttering an explanation, 'I always feel more comfortable on the floor.' Savitri found herself in a dilemma: she couldn't sit on the bench herself while an elderly visitor was sitting down on the floor, and she couldn't leave Gangu for the other. Savitri solved the problem by getting up, moving away from the bench, and standing at a spot which wasn't too near to either Gangu or Janamma. Gangu stared fixedly at a picture on the wall and Janamma kept looking at the door, and Savitri stood completely baffled. How was this to be brought to an end? Neither was willing to be the first to leave. Savitri kept on talking as best as she could of that day's menu for breakfast, the price of vegetables, scarcity of good vegetables, the impudence and avarice of some vegetable-vendors, the difficulties of going to the market every day, and all the bother with servants and cooks. She had to talk looking at neither in particular, and standing. She was invited twice to sit down, and twice did she complain of acute discomfort at the knee-joint.

This terrible situation only came to an end by the passage of time. It was nearing seven and Janamma could not stay any longer because it was time for the Public Prosecutor to return home and she would have to be there. When she was gone Gangu said triumphantly, 'Did she think that I would be afraid of her and scramble out of the house?'

CHAPTER THREE

Savitri was in Janamma's house one evening when Kamala came and said, 'Father wants you to come home immediately.'

'Father! Has he come home?'

It was very unusual. Savitri's heart beat fast. Was he terribly ill? Or had anything happened to him or to the house? Why had he not gone to the club? 'Why has he come home so soon, Kamala?'

'I don't know, Mother. I was playing in Kutti's house when he called me up and told me to find you at once. I couldn't stop and talk to Father: he looked so angry.'

Savitri rose, saying to Janamma, 'I must be going.' She almost ran out of the house. Kamala went prancing before her. 'Why don't you walk like a normal female, Kamala? You will break your neck some day.'

'Mother, shall we see which of us can reach home first?'

When she turned into her street, she saw that the car was still parked in the road. 'Didn't he tell you why he wants us so urgently?' she asked, and Kamala shook her head and said, 'He was very angry that Sumati and Babu were not at home.'

'How can the children be at home in the evenings? Doesn't he know that they have to go out and play?'

Savitri's throat went dry at the sight of her husband. He was pacing the front veranda; he had changed his coat and was wearing a blue blazer. He looked fixedly at her as she came up from the gate and said, 'You have made me wait for half an hour.' He added, 'A fellow comes home from the office, dog-tired, and he has only the doors and windows to receive him. Where is everybody gone? Anyone could walk in and walk out with all the things in the house.'

'I left the cook in charge of the house.'

'He is not a watchman. Perhaps you'd like him to put up his oven at the street gate so that he can look after the house and cook at the same time.'

Her suspense had relaxed. He wasn't ill, and nothing else was wrong anywhere. She knew that he was either going to tell her that he was dining out or ask her to go out with him in the car. He said, looking at his watch, 'It is getting late. Are you coming with me to the cinema or not?'

'Now?'

'Immediately.'

'Where is Sumati, Kamala? Babu will be in the field. Send Ranga to fetch them while I dress.'

'The children can go some other day. Not a fly extra now.'

'Oh,' she said unhappily. She knew it would be useless to plead. All the same she could not restrain herself. 'The poor things, let them come, they will enjoy it.' Kamala was already making some indistinct impatient noises.

'It is very bad for the children to be taken out every time their elders go out.'

'At least let Kamala come with us,' said Savitri.

'Father, let me come to the cinema too.'

'You must never ask to be taken out.'

'If I don't ask, nobody will take me out,' said Kamala, and turned to her mother: 'Please let me come too. Sumati and Babu won't mind.'

Ramani was infuriated at the sight of the girl appealing to her mother and thundered, 'Learn not to whimper before your mother.' To Savitri he said, 'Are you coming out at all or shall I go alone? You can stay here and pet the little darling.'

'Let us go some other day,' she said.

'No. I want you to come now. Children some other day. I have not come all the way to be told "Some other day." I am not a vagabond to come in and go out without a purpose. Go and dress quickly. It is already six-fifteen. We can't fool about on the veranda all day.'

Savitri went in. Kamala went behind her, showing symptoms of stamping her feet and crying. Ramani said, 'If I hear you squeal, I will thrash you, remember. Be a good girl.' He shouted a moment later, 'Savitri, I will count sixty. You must dress and come out before that.' Instead of counting sixty he went on talking; 'Women are exasperating. Only a fool would have anything to do with them.

Hours and hours for dressing! Why can't they put on some decent clothes and look presentable at home instead of starting their make-up just when you are in a hurry to be off? Stacks of costly *saris*, all folded and kept inside, to be worn only when going out. Only silly-looking rags to gladden our sight at home. Our business stops with paying the bill. It is only the outsider who has the privilege of seeing a pretty dress.'

Malgudi in 1935 suddenly came into line with the modern age by building a well-equipped theatre – the Palace Talkies – which simply brushed aside the old corrugated-sheet-roofed Variety Hall, which from time immemorial had entertained the citizens of Malgudi with tattered silent films.

Ramani sat in a first-class seat with his wife by his side, very erect. He was very proud of his wife. She had a fair complexion and well-proportioned features, and her sky-blue *sari* gave her a distinguished appearance. He surveyed her slyly, with a sense of satisfaction at possessing her. When people in the theatre threw looks at her, it increased his satisfaction all the more, and he leant over and said, 'They are showing *Kuchela*.'

'Yes. I read the notice while coming up.'

'It is a Tamil film. I thought you would like it.' He spoke to her because he was in a position to do it, and it made him feel important. He enjoyed his rôle of a husband so much that he showed her a lot of courtesy, constantly inquiring if her chair was comfortable, if she could see the screen properly, and if she would like to have a sweet drink.

The hall became dark and the show began. Savitri, like the majority of those in the hall, knew the story, had heard it a number of times since infancy, the old story from the epics, of Krishna and his old class-mate Kuchela, who was too busy with his daily prayers and meditation to work and earn, and hence left to his wife the task of finding food for their twenty-seven children ...

Everything was there: Krishna's boyhood; he and his gawky class-mates waylaying curd-sellers and gorging themselves. A feat it was to consume so many pots of curds. An endless procession of rustic women with pots on their heads passed under the trees, in the branches of which a gang was waiting; the women halted under the trees and nearly asked to be robbed of their pots. How they wrung their hands at the broken pots and chased Krishna. As the curds spread on the ground, 'What a lot of curd wasted!' Savitri could not help thinking. And then Krishna's classroom jokes and the various ways in which he tormented his monitor; nobody was in a mood to question why the monitor, a perfectly timid and harmless man, deserved this treatment. Savitri enjoyed the sight of the troubled monitor and the triumph of the saucy-looking Krishna so much that she laughed aloud and whispered to her husband, 'Babu should have seen this, he would have enjoyed it.'

'Don't keep bothering about Babu, otherwise you won't be able to enjoy the show,' said her husband.

She was enchanted by the picture. It ran for nearly four hours. The film people had shown no hurry: they had a slow, spacious way of handling a story which gave a film-fan three times his money's worth. There were songs which characters sang as long as they liked, there were scenes of 'domestic humour' which threatened to last the whole evening, a procession complete with elephants and pipers and band that took half an hour to pass, a storm which shook the theatre, a court scene with a dancer which was an independent programme by itself; there were irrelevant interludes which nearly made one forget the main story.

Savitri sympathized intensely with the unfortunate woman, Kuchela's wife. 'The poor girl!' she muttered to her husband.

'Note how patient she is, and how uncomplaining,' Ramani remarked.

Savitri was embarrassed by a suggestive conversation between a very fat husband and his wife at bedtime; she was thrilled by the magnificence of the procession; and she was immensely pleased when in the end Krishna heaped on his old friend wealth and honour. The whole picture swept her mind clear of mundane debris and filled it with superhuman splendours. Unnoticed by her passed the fumbling and faltering of the tinsel gods and the rocking of the pasteboard palaces in the studio wind, and all the exaggeration, emphasis, and noise. The picture carried Savitri with it, and when in the end Kuchela stood in his *pooja* room and lighted camphor and incense before the image of God, Savitri brought her palms together and prayed.

The first show ended at ten o'clock.

The switching-on of the lights, the scurry of feet, and a blue-coated husband yawning, had the air of a vulgar anti-climax. 'You must bring the children tomorrow,' she said. The old Chevrolet groaned and started. She loathed the dull drab prospect of changing her *sari*, dining, and sleeping. The night air blew on her face and revived her earthly senses a little. As she sat beside her husband, she felt grateful to him and loved him very much, with his blue coat and the faint aroma of a leather suitcase hanging about him.

When she reached home, she found Ranga and the cook sitting up in the front veranda. Sumati and Babu were there too. Kamala had slept on the hall bench. 'The poor girl has fallen asleep on the bench!' exclaimed Savitri. 'Have the children had their food? Did Kamala cry long after we went? Babu, you must see this picture. It is very good.'

'An Indian film!' sneered Babu.

'You must see the little boy who acts Krishna. How can a small boy act so well! He is wonderful.'

Babu smiled indulgently. 'That shows you have never seen Shirley Temple. They pay her one thousand pounds a week to act. If you see *Curly Top* you will never like any other picture.'

'Mother, he has not seen that picture. He is lying,' said Sumati.

'I never said I saw it. A friend of mine has seen it twice, and he told me all about it.'

'You see this picture and then say. Your father has promised to send you all to it tomorrow.'

'I don't like Indian films, Mother. I would like to be sent to *Frankenstein*, which is coming next week,' Babu said.

'I don't like English films. Let us go to this tomorrow,' Sumati said.

'It is because you don't understand English films,' said Babu.

'As if you were a master of English and understood all that they say in the films! Why do you pretend?' said Sumati.

This threatened to develop into a quarrel, but Savitri stepped between them and said, 'Sh! Don't start fighting.'

CHAPTER FOUR

In the month of September the streets rang with the cries of hawkers selling dolls – the earliest intimation of the coming *Navaratri* festival.

'Mother, aren't we buying some dolls this year for the festival?'

'What's the use of buying them year after year; where are we to keep them?'

'In the next house they have bought for ten rupees a pair of Rama and Seeta, each image as large as a real child.'

'We have as many as we can manage. Why should we buy any more?'

'Mother, you must buy some new dolls.'

'We have already three casks full of dolls and toys.'

A day before the festival the casks were brought into the hall from an obscure storing-place in the house. Ranga had now a lot of work to do. It was an agreeable change for him from the monotony of sweeping, washing clothes, and running errands. He enjoyed this work. He expressed his gay mood by tying a preposterous turban round his head with his towel and tucking up his *dhoti*.

'Oh, look at Ranga's turban!' screamed Kamala.

'Hey, you look like a cow,' added Sumati.

'Do I?' Ranga bellowed like a cow, and sent the children into fits of laughter.

'Don't waste time in playing. Open the casks and take out the dolls,' said Savitri.

Ranga untied the ropes and brought out the dolls in their yellowing newspaper wrappings. 'Handle them carefully, they may break.' In a short while dust and sheets of old newspaper, startled cockroaches and silverfish were all in a heap on one side of Ranga, and, on the other, all the unwrapped dolls. Most of them had been given to Savitri by her mother, and the rest bought by her at various times. There they were – dolls, images, and toys of all colours, sizes, and shapes; soldiers, guards, and fat merchants; birds, beasts, and toys; gods and demons; fruits and cooking utensils; everything of clay, metal, wood, and cloth.

Ranga in his preposterous turban, stooping into the casks and bringing out the dolls, looked like an intoxicated conjurer giving a wild performance. The children waited, breathlessly watching for the next item, and shrieked at his absurd comments: 'Ah, here is my friend the parrot. He pecks at my flesh.' He would suck the blood on his finger and vow to break the parrot's beak before the end of the festival. He would hurriedly take out and put down a merchant or a grass-seller, complaining that they were uttering terrible swear-words and that he couldn't hold them. He would pretend to put the toy foods into his mouth and munch them with great satisfaction. Or he would scream at the sight of a cobra or a tiger. It was pure drama.

Savitri squatted down and wiped the dust off the dolls, and odd memories of her childhood stirred in her. Her eyes fell on a wooden rattle with the colour coming away in flakes, with which she had played when she was just a few months old. So her mother had told her. There was a toy flute into which she had wasted her babyhood breath. Savitri felt a sudden inexplicable self-pity at the thought of herself as an infant. She next felt an intense admiration for her mother, who never let even the slightest toy be lost but preserved everything carefully, and brought it all out for the *Navaratri* display. Savitri had a sudden longing to be back in her mother's house. She charged herself with neglecting her mother and not writing to her for several months now ... How frightfully she (Savitri) and her sister used to quarrel over these dolls and their arrangements! She remembered a particular *Navaratri* which was completely ruined because she and her sister had scratched each other's faces and were not on speaking terms. Poor girl! Who would have dreamt that she would grow into a bulky matron, with a doctor husband and seven children, away from everybody in Burma? That reminded her, she had not answered her letters received a month ago; positively, next Thursday she would write so as to catch the Friday's steamer.

Now Ranga had put down a rosy-cheeked, auburn-haired doll which was eloquent with memories of her father. She remembered the evening when he had awakened her and given her the cardboard box containing this doll. How she adored this cardboard box and the doll and secretly used to thrust cooked rice into its mouth and steal sugar for it! Poor father, so decrepit now! ...

A crash broke this reverie. Ranga had dropped a bluish elephant, as large as an ordinary cat.

'You ass, did you fall asleep?'

'Oh, it is broken!' wailed Sumati.

'Make him buy a new one, Mother. Don't give him his pay,' suggested Kamala.

Savitri felt very unhappy over the broken elephant: it was one of a pair that her mother had got from *her* mother, and it had been given to Savitri with special admonitions, and not to her sister, because she could not be depended upon to be so careful, and Savitri's mother had been very reluctant to separate the pair ...

'I told you to be careful,' Savitri said, 'and yet, you ass –'

Ranga picked up the broken elephant. 'Oh, madam, only its trunk is broken,' he announced gleefully.

'What is left of an elephant when its trunk is gone?' Savitri asked mournfully.

Ranga stood examining the trunkless elephant and said: 'It looks like a buffalo now. Why not have it in the show as a buffalo, madam?'

'Fool, stop your jokes.'

'He doesn't care a bit!' Kamala said, horrified.

Ranga said to Kamala, 'Little madam, I know now how buffaloes are made.'

'How?' asked Kamala, suddenly interested.

'By breaking off the trunks of elephants,' said Ranga. Then he said, 'Allow me to take this home, madam.'

'Impossible,' said Kamala. 'Mother, don't let him take it. Tell him he must pay for it.'

'It is broken. Why do you want it?' Savitri asked.

'My little boy will tie a string round its neck, drag it about, and call it his dog. He has been worrying me to get him a dog for a long time.'

Kamala said, 'You won't get it,' and snatched the elephant from his hand.

Now all the dolls and toys were there, over five hundred of them, all in a jumble, like the creations of an eccentric god who had not yet created a world.

Babu had given definite instructions that the arrangement of the platform for the dolls was to be left entirely to him, and they were to do nothing till he returned from school. The girls were impatient. 'It is not a boy's business. This is entirely our affair. Why should we wait for him?'

Babu burst in at five o'clock and asked, looking about impatiently, 'Have you put up the platforms yet?'

'No, we are waiting for you. There is no hurry. Eat your tiffin and come,' said Savitri.

In two minutes he was ready to do his work. The girls jeered: 'Are you a girl to take a hand in the doll business? Go and play cricket. You are a man.'

'Shut up, or I will break all the dolls,' he said, at which the girls screamed. Babu hectored Ranga and sent him spinning about on errands. With about eight narrow long planks, resting on raised supports at the ends, he constructed graduated step-like platforms. He pulled out of the rolls of bedding in the house all the white bed sheets and spread them on the planks; he disturbed all the objects in the house and confiscated all the kerosene tins and stools, etc., for constructing supports for the planks. He brought in bamboo poles and built a pavilion round the platform. He cut up strips of coloured paper and pasted them round the bamboo poles and covered their nakedness. He filled the whole pavilion with resplendent hangings and decorations. He did his work with concentration, while the two girls sat down and watched him, not daring to make the slightest comment; for at the slightest word Babu barked and menaced the speaker. He gave Ranga no time to regale the company with his jokes, but kept him standing on a high table in order to execute decorations on the pavilion roof.

In a couple of hours a gorgeous setting was ready for the dolls. Babu surveyed his work from a distance and said to his mother, 'You can arrange your knick-knacks now.' He turned to his sisters and said, 'Move carefully within the pavilion. If I find you up to some mischief, tearing the decorations or disturbing the platforms, you will drive me to a desperate act.'

Savitri said to the girls, pointing to the pavilion, 'Could you have made a thing like this? You prated so much when he began the work.' Sumati was a little apologetic and appreciative, but Kamala said, 'If you had given me a little paste and paper I too could have done it. It is not a great feat.' Savitri said, 'Now lift the dolls carefully and arrange them one by one. Sumati, since you are taller than Kamala you will arrange the dolls on the first four platforms, and, Kamala, you will do it on the lower four platforms. Don't break anything, and don't fight.'

In an hour a fantastic world was raised: a world inhabited by all God's creations that the human mind had counted; creatures in all gay colours and absurd proportions and grotesque companies. There were green parrots which stood taller than the elephants beside them; there were horses of yellow and white and green colours dwarfed beside painted brinjals; there was a finger-sized Turkish soldier with not a bit of equipment missing; the fat, round-bellied merchant, wearing a coat on his bare body, squatted there, a picture of contentment, gazing at his cereals before him, unmindful of the company of a curly-tailed dog of porcelain on one side and a grimacing tiger on the other. Here and there out of the company of animals and vegetables and mortals emerged the gods – the great indigo-blue Rama, holding his mighty bow in one hand, and with his spouse, Seeta, by his side, their serenity unaffected by the company about them, consisting of a lacquered wooden spoon, a very tiny celluloid doll clothed in a pink *sari*, a sly fox with a stolen goose in its mouth, and a balancing acrobat in leaf-green breeches; there stood the great Krishna trampling to death the demon serpent Kalinga, undistracted by the leer of a teddy bear which could beat a drum. Mortals and immortals, animals and vegetables, gods and sly foxes, acrobats and bears, warriors and cooking utensils, were all the same here, in this fantastic universe conjured out of coloured paper, wood, and doll-maker's clay.

'It is all very well now, but the trouble will be in putting them all back carefully after nine days in their casks. It is the most tedious work one could think of,' said Savitri.

'Mother, don't dismantle them again. Why can't we let them stay out for ever? It is always so terribly dull when the decorations are torn down and the dolls are returned to the casks.'

Next morning Babu took a look at his work and decided to improve it. It was all very well as far as gum and paper could go, but the lighting was defective. All the illumination that the pavilion got was from the bulb hanging a few yards from it in the hall. He would get his friend Chandru in, and fix up a festoon of ornamental coloured bulbs under the pavilion arch; he would transform the doll pavilion into something unique in the whole of Extension.

He brought Chandru in the afternoon. Chandru was very much his senior, but Babu spent much of his time with him. Chandru was studying in the Intermediate and had a genius for electricity. He had made miniature dynamos, electric bells, and telegraph sets.

Sumati and Kamala were delighted. 'It is going to beat the pavilion in the Police Inspector's house,' they said ecstatically. Chandru worked wonders with a piece of wire and a spanner. In a short while he had created a new circuit with an independent switch. When the switch was put on, a festoon of coloured bulbs twinkled in the archway and two powerful bulbs flooded all the dolls with a bluish light.

'When you switch on in the evening, do it very carefully,' warned Chandru, and left.

It was a great triumph for Babu. He felt very proud of being responsible for the illumination. 'If you like I will ask him to come and add an electric train to the dolls. That will be wonderful,' he said.

At five o'clock the two girls worried Babu to put the lights on. He told them he knew the right time to do it and warned them not to go near the switch. 'Lighting at six,' he said.

'We will be out at six,' they protested, 'inviting people. A lot of our friends will be coming now to invite us to their houses, and we would so love to have the illuminations at once. Please.'

'Will you leave that to me or not? I know when to do it, and I want you to mind your own business now.'

Savitri said to Babu, 'Don't be so strict. You have done everything for their sake, why should you grudge them the light now?'

'All right, at five-thirty,' said Babu.

At five-thirty nearly a dozen visitors had already arrived. Everyone wore bright silks, and sat gazing at the dolls. Finding so many ladies sitting in the hall, Babu hesitated at the door, wondering how he was to reach the switch in the pavilion. He called Sumati and said, 'With the tip of your finger push that small rod to one side, to the left. You must do it very gently.'

Sumati pushed the switch gently, then less gently, and then Babu shed his shyness and dashed to the switch. He rattled it, but nothing happened. Not only were the pavilion lights not on, but the usual hall bulbs had also gone out. Babu looked at Sumati and said, 'I knew that if I let you touch it something or other would happen.' He stood contemplating the new circuit, rattled the switch once more and said that somebody had tampered with it and that he would get at that person soon. Muttering that one couldn't plumb the depth of mischief in girls, he walked out of the hall. Nobody yet realized that anything was wrong because there was good sunlight.

At about seven-thirty the conditions were different. There was no light in the house. Visitors were received in the pale light of a hurricane lantern, and the pavilion was lit by flickering oil-lamps transferred from the *pooja* room. The atmosphere was dim and gloomy. The sisters' rage knew no limits. 'Mother, do you understand now why we did not want any boy to come and interfere in our business? As if it wouldn't have been a pretty sight without those lights. Who wanted them anyway? We never asked him to come and fix the lights.'

Babu was in utter despair. Chandru had gone to the cinema and would not be back till nearly ten. And he had no friend who knew anything about electricity.

'Send someone to the Electric office,' said Savitri.

'Shall I go?' asked Babu.

Savitri hesitated. How could she send him out all alone so late? 'Take Ranga with you.'

And protected by Ranga's company, Babu set out to the Electric office in Market Road – a distance of about two miles.

Babu stood before the entrance to the Electric office and said to someone, 'There is no light in our house in the South Extension.'

'Go in and tell it to the people you will find there.'

Babu went in and was directed to a room in which three fellows were sitting, smoking and talking. One of them asked him, 'Who are you, boy?'

'The lights are out in our house in the South Extension.'

'Put the switches on,' somebody said, and all three laughed.

Babu felt awkward, but the light had to be set right. He pleaded: 'Can't you do something? We have tried the switches.'

'Probably the fuse has gone. Have you seen if the meter fuses are all right?'

'I haven't. There is nobody in the house.'

'Then, why do you want the lights? If the meter fuse is burnt, it is none of our concern. We will come only when the pole fuse is burnt. Go and see if the meter fuse is all right.'

When Babu reached home he found his father had already arrived. He was in a terrible temper. Ranga's absence delayed the opening of the garage door and had infuriated him. In that state he entered the house and found it dark. Now failure of electric current was one of the things which completely upset him. He stood in the doorway and roared, 'What is this?' Savitri let the question wither without an answer. The girls did not dare to answer. 'Is everybody in this house dead?' he asked.

Savitri was angered by this. 'What a thing to say on a day like this, and at this hour! I have seen very few who will swear and curse at auspicious times as you do.'

'Then why couldn't you have opened your precious mouth and said what the matter was?'

'There is nothing the matter. You see that there is no current and that there are no lights, and that's all that's the matter.'

'Has anybody gone to the Electric office?'

'Babu has gone there.'

'Babu, Babu, a very big man to go.'

This irrational pointless cynicism enraged Savitri, but she remained silent.

Ramani passed in to undress, grumbling all the way. Standing in the dark, he cursed the whole household and all humanity. 'Ranga! here, Ranga!' he howled in the dark.

'I told you Ranga had gone to the Electric office with Babu,' Savitri said.

'Why should everybody go to the Electric office? Is Babu to be protected like a girl? Whose arrangement is it?' He raved, 'Bring some light, somebody.'

Savitri sent the hurricane lantern along with Kamala. Kamala set the lamp on the floor while her father looked at her fixedly. 'Here, that's not the place to put the lantern. Do I want illumination for my feet? Bad training, rotten training.' He lifted the lantern and looked about for a place and said, 'Don't you know that when you bring a lantern you have to bring a piece of paper to keep under it? When will you learn all this?'

'Very well, Father,' Kamala said, much intimidated by his manner.

This submissiveness pleased Ramani. He said, 'You must be a good girl, otherwise people won't like you.' He placed the lantern on the window-sill. Kamala turned to go and took a few steps. 'Little girl, don't shuffle your feet while walking,' said Ramani.

'Hereafter I will walk properly, Father.'

He was thoroughly pleased with her. He felt he ought to bestow on her some attention – honour her with a little conversation. 'Have you been in the dark all the evening?'

'No, Father, we had current till six o'clock and then –' She hesitated.

'What happened?'

'Babu's friend put up new bulbs for the dolls, and when Babu pressed a switch something happened, and all the lights went out.'

When Babu returned from the Electric office he found his father standing in the hall and shouting. As soon as he sighted Babu he asked, 'You blackguard, who asked you to tamper with the electric lights?' Babu stood stunned. 'Don't try to escape by being silent. Are you following your mother's example?'

'No, Father.'

'Who asked you to tamper with the electric lights?'

'I didn't touch anything. I brought in Chandru. He knows all about electricity.'

His father moved towards him and twisted his ear, saying, 'How often have I asked you to keep to your books and mind your business?'

'I'll try to set it right, Father, as soon as Chandru comes home.'

'Who asked you to go near the dolls' business? Are you a girl? Tell me, are you a girl?'

This insistent question was accompanied by violent twists of the ear. Babu's body shook under the grip of his father's hot fingers. 'No, Father, I am not a woman.'

'Then why did you go near the dolls?' He twisted the other ear too. 'Will you do a thing like this again? Tell me!'

In helpless anger Babu remained silent. His father slapped him on the cheek. 'Don't beat me, Father,' he said, and Ramani gave him a few more slaps. At this point Savitri dashed forward to protect Babu. She took him aside, glaring at her husband, who said, 'Leave him alone, he doesn't need your petting.' She felt faint with anger. 'Why do you beat him?' was all that she could ask, and then she burst out crying. At the sight of her tears, Babu could not control himself any longer. He sobbed, 'I didn't know ... I didn't know it was wrong to add those lights.'

Ramani left, remarking that he was sick of this sentimental show. He came back after a wash. 'Now to dinner. We will manage with the available lights.' Savitri squatted down, her face covered with her hands. 'I see that you are holding a stage-show. I can't stand here and watch you. Are you coming in for food or not? ... All right, you can please yourself.' He turned and walked to the dining-room calling, 'Has that effeminate boy eaten? Babu, come for your dinner!'

When he was gone, Savitri rose, went to the dark room next to the store, and threw herself on the floor. Later the cook tracked her down there and requested her to take her food, but she refused. The children came to her one by one and tried to coax her. She turned her face to the wall and shut her eyes.

The next morning the cook brought her a tumbler of coffee. She drank it. The cook took back the tumbler from her hand and asked nervously, 'What shall I cook?'

'Don't ask me,' she said.

'There are only a couple of potatoes. We will have to send for some vegetables and also for some mustard.'

'Do the cooking without the vegetables and the mustard or go and ask whoever is keen on having them for money. Don't come and mention them to me.'

The cook went away, his head bent in perplexity. Had anybody heard of cooking without mustard? Presently he got over his despair and began to enjoy the excitement of the situation. A part of his mind said, 'Go on, prepare the sauce and everything without mustard, and with only two potatoes, and if the master raves, tell him I waited long enough and gave sufficient notice.' Another part of him said, 'Look here, this is an opportunity provided by the gods. Show them your worth.' In the backyard Ranga was splitting firewood. The cook said to him, 'When the master and the mistress quarrel it is we that suffer.'

'Not many words passed between them last night,' Ranga said. 'All the same, the situation appears to be very serious.'

'It is no business of a wife's to butt in when the father is dealing with his son. It is a bad habit. Only a battered son will grow into a sound man.'

'My wife is also like that,' admitted Ranga. 'I have only to look at my son and she will pounce on me. Last year when I went to the village my first boy did something or other. He skinned our neighbour's son's forehead with a sharp stone, and what should a father do?'

'You will have to run up to the shop now and bring vegetables,' said the cook.

'Certainly, but listen to this now,' persisted Ranga. 'What should a father do? I merely slapped the boy's cheek and he howled as I have never heard anyone howl before, the humbug. And the wife sprang on me from somewhere and hit me on the head with a brass vessel. I have sworn to leave the children alone even if they should be going down a well. Women are terrible.'

The servant-maid who was washing the vessels under the tap looked up and said, 'Wouldn't you like to say so! What do you know of the fire in a mother's belly when her child is suffering?'

The cook said, 'Only once has my wife tried to interfere, and then I nearly broke her bones. She has learnt to leave me alone now. Women must be taught their place.' With this he dismissed the subject and turned to the immediate business on hand. 'I'm responsible for the running of the house today. I'm going to show these people what I can do. The mistress of the house said, "Do anything, don't ask me," and I could well cook a dinner that a dog wouldn't touch. But is it a proper thing to do, after having been in the house for five years? Ranga, it is eight o'clock. Master will be coming for food in about two hours. Run to the Nair's shop and buy onions for two annas, potatoes for four annas, two lemons, coriander for one pie ...' He knew what his master liked, and he was out to provide it. 'Tell the Nair that he will get the money by and by.'

Kamala went to her mother and asked, 'Mother, are you still angry?' Savitri did not reply.

'Father won't beat Babu again. Please don't go on lying there.' She hated to see her mother in this condition, during the *Navaratri* of all times. 'Mother, what sweets are we preparing for distributing in the evening?'

'We'll see,' said Savitri.

This reminder pained her. She cursed her own depression of spirits, which threatened to spoil the festival. 'I don't like these quarrels,' Kamala said, and left her. She felt indignant. Her school was closed so that they might remain in the doll-land, visit each other, and eat sweets; but Mother went on lying on the floor with her face to the wall. She traced the whole cause of the trouble to Babu, and threw furious looks at him.

Babu went about without so much as looking at the pavilion. His whole manner declared, 'This is what a man gets for helping in women's business. It is your school after all, not mine, that is closed for this silly festival. Please don't call me for anything.' He was troubled in mind about his mother. It was he who had received the slaps, so why should she go on lying there as if a great calamity had befallen the house? Perhaps he ought not to have cried like a girl. The memory of his tears hurt him now. He loathed himself and resolved he would never cry again in his life. Before starting for school he went to the dark room and said to his mother, 'Why do you go on lying there? It was only a slight slap that he gave me after all. You make too much of it. I am going to school now.'

'Have you taken your food?' she asked.

'Yes, get up and go about your business.'

Ramani came in for food at his usual hour, before going to the office. He decided to ignore severely his wife's absence. He was going to show her that sulking would not pay. He demonstrated his calm indifference by humming a little song, whistling loudly, and by talking to his daughters, whom he saw in the hall sitting near the pavilion. He looked at the pavilion with condescending appreciation and said, 'You must not keep them in such a jumble. You must have all the animals in one line, all the human beings in another, and so on. What sweets are you distributing this evening to your friends?'

The girls looked at each other and said, 'We don't know yet.'

'Don't you worry, I will buy sweets for two rupees.' He raised his voice while saying it, which was a message to the dark room: 'Don't imagine that the festival can be spoilt by your sulking.'

He whistled as he entered the dining-hall. He asked the cook with a decided cheerfulness what he had prepared, and said 'Very good' at the end of the list. The cook had prepared the meal very well because he had the run of the kitchen cupboard, and he had made unstinting use of rarities like pure ghee and parched coconut, while Savitri would have allowed him to use only gingelly oil and no coconut. Ramani ate his food with thorough enjoyment. He shouted suddenly to his daughters in the hall, 'Kamala, did you eat plenty of this potato and onion stuff?'

'Yes, Father.'

'Did your sister eat plenty of it?'

'Yes, Father.'

He then asked, 'Aren't the sauce and the plantain chips excellent?' This was meant to convey to whomsoever it might concern that no one was indispensable.

The cook was very happy, which was due not only to his master's compliments but also to the fact that the freedom of the kitchen cupboard had enabled him to check his ten-thirty hunger with a gulp or two of curd.

Before leaving for the office Ramani called the girls and said, 'On my way I shall drop in at the Electric office and send someone from there. You will have lights this evening.'

'Very good, Father. Can those coloured lights remain?'

'All right, if you want them.'

'But Babu said that he would ask Chandru to come and remove them today.'

'Ask him not to. Tell him that I want them there. When the Electric man comes, ask him to see if they are all right.'

Just as the engine started Kamala ran to the car and shouted above its din, 'Don't forget the sweets.'

'Certainly not,' he said, and wished that his engine made less noise so that his words might be heard in the dark room.

At two o'clock the girls began to feel scared. Mother had refused food and was still lying in the dark room. Sumati sat before the pavilion and wondered what to do. Mother's absence gave the house a still and gloomy appearance. Kamala returned to the hall after her tenth visit to the dark room.

'What does she say?' asked Sumati anxiously.

'She wouldn't answer me at all. "What jumper shall I wear this evening?" I asked, but she wouldn't answer.'

'You are a fool,' Sumati said. 'You ask the same question every time.'

'No. I've asked this question only three times. I've already asked her whom to invite this evening, when we are to go out, at what time to switch on the lights, and what sweets we are to have. I can't think of any more questions.'

The children believed that, if their mother could be made to answer some question and get involved in conversation, she could then be persuaded to come out of the dark room. This was a diplomatic step, but Savitri's answers were discouragingly to the point, and when she understood the purpose of the questions she stopped answering them.

'Why don't you go in and try?' suggested Kamala.

'Impossible,' replied Sumati. 'I'm afraid of anyone who lies in a dark room with her face to the wall.' She presently thought out a plan. 'I know how to get Mother out of this fearful state.'

Kamala was delighted, though she did not yet know what Sumati meant to do.

'I may have to go out for a moment,' Sumati said. 'I shall be back very soon. Look after the house and don't tell anyone that I am out.'

The mysterious air which she gave to the whole business thrilled her. Kamala became excited. 'Where are you going?'

Sumati hesitated and asked, 'Will you swear that you won't tell anyone?'

'I never swear. Isn't it enough if I tell you that I will keep the secret?'

'No,' said Sumati, and rose to go.

'I will come with you,' Kamala said.

'No. You will stay here.'

'Then I will go in and tell Mother that you are going out of the house.'

'If you do that, I will not go out and Mother will remain in the dark room for ever.'

Kamala was in despair. 'By our gods I swear I will not tell anyone where you have gone. Now tell me.'

'I am going to Janamma's house to bring her here. Mother will listen to her words.'

Kamala was doubtful. 'But don't you think that family secrets should not be allowed out of the house?'

This was a reasonable objection. Sumati remained thoughtful and said, 'I will merely tell her that she had better come and see Mother at once, and nothing more.'

'Do you think there will be anything wrong in it if you just mention that Babu spoiled the electric lights last night? I don't think if you merely asked her to come she would come.'

Janamma was enjoying a siesta on a mat in the front room of her house. Sumati stood on the edge of the mat silently. She hesitated for a moment whether to wake her up or not; left alone the *mami* would probably sleep till six in the evening. What was to happen to Mother? She leant over and softly called, '*Mami! Mami!*'

'Oh, Sumati! Come on, child, what do you want?'

'*Mami*, you had better come and see Mother at once.'

'What's the matter with her?'

'I don't know.'

'Is she ill?'

'I don't know. Perhaps.'

'What is she doing?'

'She may be sleeping. You must come at once and ask her to get up and bathe and eat.'

'Savitri,' Janamma said, standing over her in the dark room. Savitri opened her eyes. She took a few seconds to identify the visitor.

'Ah, come in, *mami*. Sit down. Bring a mat, Kamala.'

'I don't want a mat. I can sit on the floor. Do you know what the time is? It is past two, yet I see that you have not had your bath or food. What is the matter?'

Savitri said, 'I am not feeling well.'

'Is this where the sick people of your house usually sleep? Look here, child, I am your senior; you can't deceive me. When Sumati came and told me, I knew at once what it was. Don't contradict me.'

'Why did that girl run up to your house and trouble you?'

'What else could the poor thing do? When the elders quarrel it is the children who really suffer.'

'There is no quarrel. I never uttered a single word.'

'That makes it worse. You should either let your words out or feel that everything your husband does is right. As for me, I have never opposed my husband or argued with him at any time in my life. I might have occasionally suggested an alternative, but nothing more. What he does is right. It is a wife's duty to feel so.'

'But suppose, *mami*, he beats the child savagely?' Savitri explained the situation.

'Men are impetuous. One moment they will be all temper and the next all kindness. Men have to bear many worries and burdens, and you must overlook it if they are sometimes unreasonable.'

'I don't mind any treatment personally, but when a child – '

'After all they are better trainers of children than we can be. If they appear sometimes harsh, you may rest assured they will suffer for it later.' Janamma went on in this strain for an hour more, recounting instances of the patience of wives: her own grandmother who slaved cheerfully for her husband who had three concubines at home; her aunt who was beaten every day by her husband and had never uttered a word of protest for fifty years; another friend of her mother's who was prepared to jump into a well if her husband so directed her; and so on, till Savitri gradually began to feel very foolish at the thought of her own resentment, which now seemed very insignificant.

'Get up, Savitri. Bathe, and wear your best *sari* and take your food. You are a sight.'

Savitri murmured something about still being unwell and not wanting food.

'I am not going to leave this place till I see you out of this room,' Janamma said decisively. Savitri needed only a little more persuasion, and when Janamma said, 'What a foolish, inauspicious thing to do on a *Navaratri* day!' she felt guilty of a great crime. And then Janamma said, 'You are spoiling the happiness of these two girls. After all, *Navaratri* only comes once a year.'

Savitri hated herself for her selfish gloom.

'Girls, your mother wants to bathe. See if there is hot water.'

'I'll ask the cook to get it ready in a moment,' Sumati said, and ran out. Kamala ran behind her, almost dancing with joy. She screamed to the cook, 'Hot water! Mother is coming out of the dark room!'

CHAPTER FIVE

In the New Year the Engladia Insurance Company decided to take a few women probationers into its branches, who were to be trained in office and field work, and later assist the Company in securing insurance policies on female lives. The Company advertised its new scheme with the maximum noise, and the response was very satisfying.

A large number of applications poured into Ramani's office. 'We are not anxious to adorn our establishment with so many of the fair sex; we are more anxious to have them in as policy-holders,' he observed with a dry official humour to Pereira, his office manager.

'What shall we do with these applications, sir?'

'Call them up for interview between the fifteenth and twentieth instant. We can fix up the number of interviews per day accordingly.'

'Many of them have to come up from other towns, sir.'

'They must come at their own expense.'

'A nice treat the boss has arranged. You can have your pick for the harem between the fifteenth and the twentieth. Don't miss the office on any account,' he said to Kantaiengar, the Accountant.

'Wouldn't it be enough if I kept my head above water with the family I have?' said Kantaiengar. He strongly disapproved of the new scheme. 'Do they want to convert the Company into a brothel?' he asked.

'A delightful idea,' Pereira remarked.

To Ramani, too, the scheme appeared novel and fantastic, but the Head Office at Madras pursued it with zest, and Ramani had to sit up and interview a lot of women between the fifteenth and twentieth of January. Out of the thirty or forty women he interviewed every day he couldn't find one that seemed to him likely to do any work for the Company. Some of them were just girls, educated up to Matriculation or Intermediate, young and bashful and pitifully trying not to give an impression of being too young or bashful. Some were widows, some were prostitutes out to take up a spare-time occupation. Ramani felt that these women would in no way add to the profits of the Company, though they added considerable colour to the office on the days when they were present. Kantaiengar bent over his accounts more than ever, resenting this intrusion and feeling self-conscious; the other clerks looked intimidated. Pereira made a festival of it. He arranged their accommodation in a spare corner of the office and flirted with them elegantly.

Ramani went through the interviews in a state of boredom, irritated with his Head Office for this infliction. He told the applicants after a number of questions that they would hear from him in due course.

On the very last day the last applicant entered. At the sight of her Ramani pushed his chair back and rose – a thing he had not done for anyone till now. Pereira, who followed the applicant in, delicately whisked his moustache with his little finger, and showed that he noticed this difference.

'Sit down, please,' Ramani said, and resumed his seat only after the visitor had sat down. He cleared his throat and asked, looking at a list before him, 'You are Mrs Shanta Bai?'

'Yes,' she said.

He looked at Pereira who was hovering about, and Pereira gave another delicate whisk to his moustache and made an unobtrusive exit. Outside, he winked at Kantaiengar and whispered, 'Of that *houri* in there we shall see a great deal, and, perhaps, hear also a great deal, yet.'

'Which district do you come from?' asked Ramani.

'I'm from Mangalore,' Shanta Bai said.

'Mangalore?' Ramani echoed, and added as a piece of courtesy, 'Some day I have planned to visit your district.'

'Oh,' she said, 'but it is a pretty dull place. I'm sure you won't like it.'

Ramani felt that he had been snubbed, but presently he appreciated the candour and smartness which had released the snub. He smiled and replied briskly that he was grateful for the timely warning, otherwise he would have wasted some money and time in going to Mangalore. She received the remark without interest. Ramani felt hurt. He suddenly asked himself angrily, 'Who is the master here?' Abruptly he shed all his unofficial humanity and asked severely, 'Do you live with your people there?'

'It is a difficult question, and it will take a lot of answering.'

Ramani once again felt his official manner slowly melting. He gathered himself together and said, 'I see you are married.'

'I am,' she said in a pathetic low voice, and Ramani did not dare put to her further questions about her private life. He said apologetically, 'I'm sorry to trouble you with personal questions, but I have to send a report to the Head Office. If they appoint you they will want to know all about you, whether your family is likely to hinder you in your work – '

'Oh, of that you can assure them. If I had a family to hinder me I shouldn't have come here with my application.'

'I shall want some more details and facts,' implored Ramani. While, till now, all the interviewees had been at his mercy, he found himself, to his distress, at the mercy of this applicant. He liked her pluck. Very seldom, he told himself, did such fair lips utter words without affectation or timidness. He admired her manners very much. She said as if taking pity on him, 'Well, here is my life story. I was born in Mangalore. I was married when I was twelve to a cousin of mine, who was a gambler and a drunkard. When I was eighteen I found he wouldn't change, and so I left him. My parents would not tolerate it and I had to leave home. I had studied up to the Fifth Form, and now I joined a Mission School. After completing my matriculation, with the help of an aunt, I came to Madras and joined the Women's College. I passed my B.A. three years ago. Since then I have been drifting about. I have had odd teaching jobs and I have also been companion to a few rich children. On the whole it has been a very great struggle. It is all nonsense to say that women's salvation lies in education. It doesn't improve their lot a bit; it leaves them as badly unemployed as the men.'

'I am really surprised to hear it,' said Ramani, feeling it was time he said something.

'So must anyone be, most of all we ourselves. We struggle hard, get our B.A., and think that we are the first of our kind; but what happens? We find that there are thousands like us.'

Her tone was soft and pleasing. Ramani wanted to ask her if she could sing well, but restrained himself and said, 'Yours is a very interesting story. Then I suppose you saw our advertisement?'

'Yes, I did. I sent my application to all the branch offices, and I was called up for interview only by you.'

'Where were you at the time?'

'I was in Bangalore, staying with some old college friends and looking for work. Now I am here. If you find me suitable for your office, I will be for ever grateful to you.'

A thrill went through Ramani's being; this beautiful creature grateful to him! He swelled with importance as he said, 'I will do my best for you. Of course you know the final decision rests with the Head Office. I will do my very best for you.'

'Thank you very much,' she said.

'I must also tell you now,' he began in the orthodox style of the senior to the probationer, 'that an insurance career is not at all an easy one. It is one of the most exacting professions in the world. I've been in it for a decade and a half now ...' The banalities and autobiography lasted till Pereira came in with a bundle of papers in his hand.

Ramani learnt that she lived in a hotel. That simply would not do. He called in Pereira next day and asked, 'What are you doing with that room in the passage?'

'Nothing very definite, sir. We have thrown in a few old chairs and records.'

'Can't you transfer that lumber to some other place, and make it habitable? Mrs Shanta Bai is staying in some dirty hotel; why shouldn't we give her that room till she gets settled in this place? There is no harm in it.'

'Oh, none whatever, sir.'

'It must be rather awkward for a lady to live in a hotel, you see.'

'You are right, sir. No decent hotel in the whole town. I will have the lumber turned out and stocked somewhere else. But the records? They are rather important. What about keeping them here?'

'Here?' Ramani didn't like the idea of anything intruding in his room. 'Put them away in some other place.'

'All right, sir. You will want the room ready tomorrow?'

'Yes, as soon as you can attend to it, thank you.'

Outside, Pereira told Kantaiengar, 'I shall have to fix up a nuptial chamber in the office, Iengar.'

'What is he driving at? It is absurd. This will be the talk of the town.'

'I am sure it will bring more people into the office.'

The other members of the staff also resented this feminine intrusion because a lot of lumber was brought into their room; and the old office watchman resented it because the passage room had been for years his home.

Ramani asked at home, 'What happened to the spare cot we had?'

'Krishnier's people borrowed it months ago when he was down with rheumatism, and they have not returned it.'

'Send for it. I want it for the office. We are going to fit up a guest's room.'

'What for?'

'We get a lot of outsiders; some important people come to us on business now and then, and we have to provide them with some decent accommodation.'

'If it is for the office, buy a cot with your office money. Why should we give ours?' She dared to suggest this amendment because it was one of his good-humoured evenings.

'But look here, my girl. If it comes to that, everything in this house, including the grain in the store-room, belongs to the office, bought with the office money, you know.' She argued elaborately that they were not living on the charity of the Company, and declined to lend the cot. He pleaded and cajoled her. He liked to plead and cajole this evening. He said, 'I shall want it only for a time. I will return it as soon as we buy new furniture. There is no time now. An important guest is coming tomorrow. I shall also want your bench, a chair, and one or two vessels.'

'Oh, you want everything we have in the house.' The teak-wood bench was her favourite piece of furniture. 'If you take away the bench, what am I to sleep on in the afternoons?'

'Oh, I will get you velvet couches, my dear,' he said, bringing his hands together in a romantic gesture. 'There is nothing that I wouldn't buy for you. Only say it.' It made her very happy.

The Head Office confirmed her appointment nearly a week later. Ramani's recommendation was so strong that the Head Office had no choice in the matter. Shanta Bai was to be on probation for six months, provided she did personal canvassing worth ten thousand rupees within the first two months (if she failed she was to be sent away and the next applicant on the list called up and given a chance). During the probationary period she was to receive a stipend of sixty rupees a month; after that she was to have a starting salary of a hundred and fifty rupees a month, with commission, and work as the chief woman agent for the branch.

On the day the confirmation came, Ramani sent for Shanta Bai and dramatically pushed the letter before her. He tried to look casual and unconcerned. He went through some papers while she read it. Though pretending to look at the letters he was secretly noting how artistic her chequered jumper was, and awaited eagerly her thanks for all his trouble.

'I am rather disappointed,' she said.

Ramani looked up, startled.

She said, 'I thought the starting salary would be two hundred.' She remained thoughtful for a moment and added, 'I had no business to imagine it because the advertisement never mentioned the amount.'

'What, is this girl going to reject the job for the sake of fifty rupees?' Ramani thought for a harrowing moment, and rushed to console her. 'You seem to overlook the fact that you will be drawing two hundred in two years. Please read carefully that increment clause. Besides, you will be getting your commission over your actual salary.'

'Well, I take your word for it. I will do whatever you advise me to do.'

He was pleased with the importance she gave him, and sat reflecting for a moment. How well a simple voile *sari* sat on her! Why couldn't one's wife dress as attractively?

Shanta Bai said, 'I thought that if I had a start of two hundred I could buy a tiny Baby Austin for myself.' She added with a sentimental sigh, 'But I suppose all one's dreams can never come true.'

'I am sure your commission on your personal work will enable you to have even a big Austin with a driver and all. Shall I wire to the Head Office that you accept the terms and ask them to post the agreement immediately?'

'As you please,' she said.

Such an exquisite complexion came only from Mangalore, Ramani thought; you could see the blood coursing in her veins. He said aloud, 'I will see if the probationary period cannot be cut down, and if the stipend cannot be put up a bit. But that's all by and by. You may rest assured that your interests will have the best support and protection possible.'

'Excellent! When do I start work?'

'Tomorrow. Now you can go "home" if you like.' She rose and went out. Ramani looked after her and meditated. What a delightful perfume even after she was gone! What an impotent, boorish beggar that husband must be who couldn't hold this fair creature! What an innovation it would be to have a beauty on the office staff! The town was sure to talk about it. He hoped her presence wouldn't be too upsetting for the office staff to go on with their usual work: they must get used to it. It was all nonsense to keep men and women separate in water-tight compartments; women were as good as men and must be treated accordingly. He told Pereira, 'The Head Office has confirmed the lady's appointment.'

'It is pleasing news,' Pereira said.

'She is starting work tomorrow. I want you to arrange a table, etcetera, for her somewhere. Where are we to put her up?'

Pereira reflected for a moment and said, 'There is plenty of space in the office. We can make some kind of arrangement, sir.'

He had a vision of Kantaiengar: wouldn't it give him fits if he heard this? Ramani asked, 'Are you sure it wouldn't be an inconvenience?'

'Not at all. We are only a dozen in that large hall.' He paused, gave an elegant whisk to his moustache, and asked, 'Are we to put up a screen?'

'Is it necessary?'

'I do not know, sir, but I thought that the lady might want it.'

'Hm! You can get the screen if you feel that she might be a distraction to the typists.' He laughed as well as his official dignity would permit him.

Outside Pereira said to Kantaiengar, 'Clean up your table and go to that corner. I will give you another table.'

'What do you mean?'

'Orders from the boss. The fairy is taking her seat here. She is to be given the best place, and so you have to quit.'

'This is atrocious. I shall resign.'

'And leave your family in the streets, I suppose?'

'What does he mean by it?'

'Women and children first, my dear fellow. A rugged piece of timber like you can be kept anywhere, but wouldn't a fresh rose need a lot of air, light, and this large table, to keep it alive?'

Kantaiengar was wild. 'Isn't it enough that he has dumped all that lumber here, making the place unsightly and choking, that he should be bringing in this thing now?'

'The two are hardly alike except to your prejudiced mind. And that reminds me, we shall have to cover the lumber-heap with a Persian carpet when madam sits here.'

'What I can't understand is why he is thrusting her here. Why can't he have her in his room, on his lap if he likes?'

'All in due course. Meanwhile, may I tell you that the boss has asked me to arrange your chair to face a wall? He said, "Take care that the accountant does not lose himself in a trance and fail to add and subtract. Let his chair be arranged to face a wall." '

'Does he take me for a woman-hunter like himself? Remember that if only I cared for these things – '

'You could have had a hundred women at your beck and call? Likely too ... Do you very much wish to stay where you are and not to be disturbed?'

'I will resign this job before I move out of this place,' said Kantaiengar furiously.

'We can't afford to lose you. So I will tell the boss not to worry you, if you promise you won't scowl at her when she is here. I don't see why you should be so sour. Personally, I rather welcome her; something to relieve this drabness, you know. But it will be a difficult job, all the same, for me to see that the typists and others do their work. The boss said, "Keep an eye on the typists, and on the Accountant." '

CHAPTER SIX

One evening while returning home from the club Ramani passed his office in Race-Course Road, and had an impulse to stop his car and go in. He told himself that it would be improper, and passed on; but the car had hardly run a few yards when he told himself that he ought to inspect his office periodically at nights. That would make the watchman more alert. He had also to see if the safe and the file-chest were locked properly. One read in the papers of all sorts of thefts and rifling in the offices. By this time his car had nearly reached the junction of the Race-Course Road with Market Road. He turned the car round and drove towards his office.

He found the watchman sleeping soundly at the foot of the staircase. Ramani stood over him, musing indignantly: 'Fast asleep at eight o'clock! I will speak to Pereira about it tomorrow.' He climbed the stairs. He saw a light in the glass ventilator above the door of the room in the passage. He stood gazing at it for a moment and then passed into his office room. He switched on the lights, went over to the file-chest and the safe, and tugged at their locks solemnly. He then wondered what to do. His inspection was over. He pulled out his drawer and idly looked at some of the envelopes in it; he spent some time pulling the pins out of the cushion and pushing them back; he examined the nibs of the pens on the table, went over to the chest and safe, tugged at their locks again, switched off the lights and came out of the room. He descended two steps, saying that he must really be hurrying away: why keep Savitri and the servants waiting unnecessarily? He paused suddenly, went up the two steps again, and gave a couple of gentle knocks on the door of the passage room.

'Who is that?'

Ramani had a momentary confusion as to who he should say he was. He said, 'Oh, don't disturb yourself. On my way home, I just remembered something and dropped in for a moment.'

Shanta Bai recognized his voice and opened the door. 'I was rather terrified, you know. Wondered if someone had come to abduct me.'

'Abduct you?' Ramani gave a slight inept laugh. 'I just began to doubt if I had locked the safe in the evening. Rather worrying, you see, such doubts. It brings to one's mind all the accounts of thefts and safe-breaking that one reads in the papers. A troublesome business having such a responsibility on one's head.'

'It must be awful. If anything goes wrong, I suppose you will be taken to task?'

'I shall be sent to jail. Not a paper must be lost, not an anna must escape the accounts.'

She listened to him with her eyes sparkling in the light of the bulb hanging in the passage. She was dressed in a white *sari*, and had jasmine in her hair. She asked abruptly, 'Why do you stand in the passage? Won't you step in?'

'I thought you might think it a bit unconventional.'

'Oh, I love unconventional things,' she said. 'Otherwise I shouldn't be here, but nursing children and cooking for a husband. Come in, come in, see how I have made a home for myself.'

Ramani stepped in, pleasantly excited, marvelling at Shanta Bai's ability to adapt herself. How meekly she accepted his official aloofness which he was of late practising in the office, and how warmly she now responded to a little friendliness! She had put up a few printed *khaddar* hangings on the doors and windows, a few group photos of her college days on the wall, a flowery counterpane on her bed, and a silk cushion on the chair. The door of an ante-chamber was covered with a curtain. 'She does her toilet and dressing in there,' Ramani thought with an inexplicable thrill. He looked about and exclaimed, 'What a transformation!'

'Please sit down.'

'Not when a lady is standing,' Ramani said.

'All right,' she said, and went over to her cot and sat on her counterpane. He sat down on the teakwood bench. She threw up her arms and stretched them, saying, 'My joints are becoming stiff. I think I am getting old.'

Ramani treated this remark as a great joke and laughed.

'Do you mind if I don't sit erect?' she asked.

'Oh, not at all, make yourself comfortable.'

She reclined on her pillows, stretched her legs, and said, 'I can't sit up. Even in my college days I used to lie in bed and study all night.'

Ramani's eyes followed every minute movement of her limbs. She tossed her head now and then, slightly pouted her lips, and raised her brow. Ramani felt now that his stiff aloofness with her during the office hours was a piece of cruelty and that some explanation was due to her: 'I have just remembered to tell you – if you have found me a little different in the office, please don't be hurt.'

'Oh no. Nothing can hurt me. In the office you are the chief, and now – '

'Your brother, if you will permit me to say so.'

'You have my fullest consent to think of me as your sister.'

'Oh, it is very good of you. In the office I don't want anyone to notice any difference. That's why I try not to give them any impression that my treatment is different – ' He fumbled on elaborately.

After conferring on him the privilege of brotherhood, she grew intimate in her talk. The account of her life with her harsh husband was really moving. Ramani listened for a second time, with absorbing interest, to her account of her struggles after leaving home. He said that men deserved to be whipped when she hinted at a couple of attempts on her honour. He was in complete agreement with her philosophy of life (which cropped up at the end of every ten minutes thus: 'As for me life is ...' something or other, some simple affair like Living Today and Letting Tomorrow Take Care of Itself or Honour being the One Important Possession, and so forth). He had known all these himself, but they had a new value for him when they issued from those fair lips. He assured her of his very best help when she told him what she hoped to achieve in the services of the Company. And bang into all this philosophy, autobiography, and hopes came the office clock's chime.

'It can't be ten!' he exclaimed, pulling out his watch. 'I thought it was just eight-thirty or nine.' He rose with a sigh.

'If I had had the slightest idea you were coming, I would have kept some food for you,' she said. 'It is very wrong of me to have kept you so long and to turn you out now on an empty stomach.'

She went down the stairs, and walked up to the car to see him off. He started the car and suddenly asked, 'Would you like a drive?'

'Now?'

'Yes, why not?'

'Aren't you hungry?'

He made a noise deprecating the idea of hunger, and suggested that a drive around with his sister would be more than food to him.

'No, I will really not trouble you now. I should have loved a drive if you had eaten something.'

He was deeply touched by her consideration and said: 'I had a very heavy tiffin at the club. I don't think I can eat anything tonight.'

'Why have you stopped the engine?'

'The car won't start.'

'Really? What is wrong?'

'It needs another passenger besides myself to make it go,' he said.

She laughed at the joke and asked him if he was going to wait there all night till he could get a passenger. Yes, he said, with fervour, even if it was going to keep him there all night; and added, 'I suggest that we go round Race-Course Road, and then, if you don't mind, to the river. Have you ever seen it at night?'

'Is it a very lovely sight?'

'Come and see it for yourself,' he said.

'You don't mind the trouble?'

'Don't ask ridiculous questions.'

She went up to lock her room. Ramani took out his handkerchief, dusted the seat lightly, got down, and waited for her. She came back to the car, and opened the door of the back seat.

'No, not there,' he said. 'Don't you see that the door is open here?'

'I prefer the back seat,' she said.

'You do, I am sure, but the engine won't start unless there are two passengers in the front seat. You are not afraid of me, are you?'

'Certainly not,' she said, and climbed in. He sat beside her and drove the car. The engine heaved, sputtered, and settled into a steady rattle, and above it she said, 'Aren't the stars in the sky beautiful? How delightful the night air is when it rushes on one's face!' She tossed her head and took a deep breath.

'Yes, yes,' he agreed with her, and asked, 'Are you fond of moonlit nights or dark nights?' feeling that he wanted to express something poetic himself.

At two o'clock he went home. He drove the car into the garage with as little noise as possible, opening the gate and then the garage door himself. He felt rather irritated afterwards, when he walked back into the house from the garage. 'I am not a thief getting into a house,' he said to himself, and loudly knocked on the door, calling 'Savitri, Savitri!' a dozen times before she could get up from her bed and come to the door.

She was still half-asleep as she followed him to his room and asked, 'Have you dined?' He threw an angry look at her drooping, nodding figure and said: 'I suppose you are too sleepy to serve me. You need not have sent the cook away. Sometimes a man may have to return home late. One can't always be rushing back, thinking of the dinner. Why do you send the cook away at night? You give the servants unheard-of privileges.'

Savitri shook off her sleep, went to the kitchen, and switched on the light.

Ramani was beginning to feel worried. Shanta Bai had been in the office now for a month and yet she exhibited no aptitude for canvassing work. The Head Office seemed to be fanatical in regard to the clause laying down the minimum of work to be done in the first two months. They had just sent a reminder. If Shanta Bai did not complete the amount in a month, she would have to be dismissed. Ramani looked down the list and noted that there was a Sharadamma of Gavipuram next to her. Would *she* have to be called up? It was a distasteful thought. When Pereira next came into the room Ramani said, 'Will you please ask the lady probationer to come in a moment?'

Shanta Bai came in. 'Please sit down,' Ramani said. 'You have been here for a month now. Do you feel you will be able to do ten thousand rupees' worth of canvassing in another month?'

'I hope to. Otherwise I suppose I shall be turned out?'

'It is a pretty rotten condition, I agree, but the Head Office sticks to it. Ten thousand rupees for two months is not very high either. I am rather worried because I have just received a reminder. I would advise you to reduce your office work and go about with the chief canvassing agent a little more. I will ask the office to relieve you of some portion of the work you are at present doing. That's all, thank you.'

She went to her table with bent head. Pereira followed her and asked, 'A troublesome interview?'

'A reminder from the H.O.' She told him about it. 'What a horrid business to get the women of this town to insure! They simply won't do it. Either they do it or I walk out of the office.'

'If I may make a humble suggestion, madam, you may succeed better if you see the men themselves and persuade them to insure their wives.'

She turned over a few papers piled upon her table and said, 'Mr Kantaiengar, here are some accounts papers, I am sure brought by mistake. Please take them away.'

'Madam, from today you will try to learn something of the accounts too. Will you kindly check the figures in those papers?'

'I will do nothing of the kind. The boss said he would relieve me of office work for some time.'

'I was instructed yesterday to put you through the accounts. You can do what you please. Those are merely accounts of the daily agency reports. If you care to check the figures, it will be for your own benefit. Otherwise you can send the papers back to me tomorrow, but till tomorrow they will have to be with you whether you look at them or not. I can't disobey the instructions that I have received. Thank you.'

'What a wicked ruffian!' Shanta Bai whispered to Pereira.

* * *

On the way home from the club Ramani halted at the office. This was threatening to become a daily habit. It was almost impossible to go home direct from the club. Even the club clung to him as a habit, perhaps as a necessity too – one had to leave the office premises at the closing of the day. At the club he cut short his bridge a great deal nowadays, and never went near the billiard table. He left the club early, put in a little unofficial attendance at the office, gave Shanta Bai a drive, and went home at ten at night.

Shanta Bai was in a bad mood today. The afternoon's interview had upset her. 'What a riddance it will be for you in a few weeks,' she said as soon as he came in and took a seat. She compressed her lips and jerked her head in the perfect Garbo manner: the temperamental heroine and the impending doom. Ramani had to be the soothing lover. He went near her and patted her shoulder gently. Shanta Bai refused to be comforted. She revelled in the vision of a blasted future. 'I know my fate, and I will not shirk it.' Ramani told her that he would somehow persuade the Head Office to cancel the troublesome clause. 'Don't be absurd,' she said. 'I won't have you do anything special for me.'

She freed herself from his arms and paced the room up and down. 'You shan't make yourself the laughing-stock of the Company,' she said. She was steadily, definitely, methodically working herself up to a breakdown. Ramani knew it. He had already experienced it twice. She would start thus, and then sit with her face on the pillow, slight tremors shaking her back. In a moment she would rise, draw herself up, jerk her head and laugh at herself and at her moods. Such moments were very painful to Ramani. More than the breakdown, the subsequent heroic effort to master it stirred him deeply. He had never seen such things before; his wife's moods were different. She knew only one thing, a crude sulking in the dark room. She never made an effort to conquer her moods; that was why, he felt, women must be educated; it made all the difference. He felt unhappy at thinking disparagingly of his wife. Poor girl, she did her best to keep him happy and the home running. He told himself that he was not criticizing her but only implying that with a little education she might have been even better.

Shanta Bai went through her breakdown act and was just about to jerk her head and laugh at herself; Ramani rushed at her, locked her in his arms, and implored her to be courageous. She released herself from his arms and said: 'Tonight I feel like pacing the whole earth up and down. I won't sleep. I feel like roaming all over the town and the whole length of the river. I will laugh and dance. That's my philosophy of life. Laugh, clown, laugh – it was a film I saw years ago. Laugh, clown, laugh, though your heart be torn,' she said, unable to quote the exact words of the film. She asked suddenly, 'Shall we go to a picture tonight?' This was the first time she had suggested this, and Ramani sat more or less stunned. 'I said shall we go to a picture tonight?' she repeated with emphasis.

'Tonight?' Ramani asked in weak apprehension. There were already rumours abroad, and now to be seen together in public ...

'Tonight. Answer in a word, yes or no.'

'Certainly, certainly,' Ramani said. 'I was just wondering what the picture was and if it was worth a visit. What is the picture tonight?'

'Whatever it is, I must see a picture tonight. If you are not coming with me, I am going alone. If you are coming, I am prepared to share my food with you.' She added, 'Perhaps you don't wish to be seen in public with me; perhaps your wife will object; perhaps – ' All of which suggestions he indignantly repudiated. He asserted with much bravado that he cared not a straw for public opinion, and that his wife was not the sort to question him or dictate to him.

He dallied till nine-thirty, when the picture should have started, so that he might make an unobtrusive entry into a dark hall and take his seat inconspicuously.

When they reached the theatre, she looked at the posters and exclaimed, 'A wretched Indian film! I'd have given my life to see a Garbo or Dietrich now.'

'What shall we do?'

'Anything is better than nothing.' She sat in the dark hall beside him, whispering criticisms of the picture before her: a stirring episode from the *Ramayana*, in which the giant monkey god set fire to Lanka ...

'What rubbish the whole thing is!' she said. 'Our people can't produce a decent film. Bad photography, awful acting, ugly faces. Till our film producers give up mythological nonsense there is no salvation for our films ... Let us get out. I can't stand this any more.'

Ramani followed her out. In the car she asked, 'Shall we go to the river?'

'Yes,' Ramani said.

'It is only ten. Let us sit on the bank and stay there till the dawn,' she said, and laughed as if she had uttered a huge joke.

Ramani laughed faithfully and drove the car towards the river. She sat nestling close to him as he drove, and said suddenly, 'Let us drive round the town once and then go to the river.' Ramani stopped, reversed, and drove the car into the town and about the streets. 'I'm rather mad tonight,' she said. 'I hope you don't mind it.'

'Not at all,' he said.

After driving the car along the principal thoroughfares of the town Ramani asked, 'What shall we do now?'

'To the river, to the river. You have a mad woman beside you tonight.' After about an hour at the river she suggested going back to her room. 'I can't sleep tonight,' she said as soon as she got down at Race-Course Road. 'Would you care to step in? Shall we sit up and chat till dawn?'

'With pleasure,' Ramani said, and followed her into her room.

He returned home at five o'clock next morning. Savitri was in the veranda, watching the milkman milk the cow. When Ramani came up the veranda steps, she said, 'I was very anxious all night.'

'Oh?' he said.

'I wish you had sent word or something. Where have you been?'

'Can't you wait?' he cut in petulantly. 'Do you want me to stand at the street door and shout my explanation?' Savitri stepped aside and let him pass into the house.

She stood looking at the milkman, listening to the sound of milk squirting into the pail. Suddenly the sound ceased: the milkman looked up and asked, 'Master seems to have gone out very early today.' It stirred a disturbance in her mind. She tried to kill the question with her silence, but the milkman would not be silenced. He repeated, 'Master seems – '

Savitri replied, 'Yes. He had to go out very early in the morning to see someone.'

At about eight o'clock she took a tumbler of coffee and made it an excuse to meet her husband in his room. He was just back from a bath and was combing his hair. He saw her in the mirror but pretended not to have seen her. She saw his face in the mirror and doubted if any effort at peace-making would be possible now. She hesitated whether she should place the coffee on the table and go away or should venture to ask a question. For the last few days disturbing doubts and a dull resentment had been gathering in her mind, and she hated herself for it. She felt angry with him and unhappy at being angry. It sapped all her energy. She would have given anything to lighten her mind of its burdens and to be able to think of her husband without suspicion. Just a word from him would do, just an unangry word; even a lie, a soothing lie. Unpleasant thoughts seemed to corrode her soul.

She set the tumbler on the table, threw a glance at the person engaged in hairdressing so intensely, and decided that it would be better to suffer in silence than to venture a question. She started out, turned once again at the threshold, caught him looking at her with a side glance. 'Shall I go out?' she asked, turning to him. Ramani pretended to be absorbed in his own thoughts. She said, 'I have put the tumbler on the table,' and went out. She saw the maidservant standing uncertainly about. 'Why are you idling there?' Savitri asked. 'Perhaps you are manœuvring to ask for something or other, that you want the afternoon off and so on. If you want to absent yourself in the afternoon you had better absent yourself for ever. I can get scores of persons like you.'

'Why do you shout at me, my lady? What have I done?'

'I will shout as I please. You are not the person to question me. If you don't like it, you had better get out.'

'Madam knows only one thing, and that is saying "Get out" for everything. I was only waiting to ask if I may go home.'

'So soon! Have you done all your work?'

'Yes, madam.'

'Scrubbed the backyard?'

'Yes, madam.'

'Swept the whole house? Washed all the vessels? Have you removed the cowdung near the gate?'

'Yes, madam, I have done everything.'

'Why are you in such a hurry to finish your work and go home? Home, home; always dying to return home. Dust and grime everywhere, at every corner. Now listen to this. You shall not go home before ten from now on, whether you have work or not. Understand me? If you don't like it, you can get out this moment.'

The servant was an old woman who had done a few years of service in the house and so knew her mistress's moods. Savitri went in and found everything in the kitchen irritating. 'Is this how you have been taught to slice brinjal?' she asked, throwing a fiery glance at the cook.

'The brinjals were rather large – ' began the cook.

'Shut up, and don't try to invent an excuse for every blunder you commit! A set of useless, blundering, wasteful parasites in this house!'

Savitri went and sat on a carpet in the hall. Sumati came out of her little study. 'Why are you sitting down, Mother?' she asked.

'Why not? When there was the bench I could just rest on it for a moment when I felt tired; and now I have to squat down on the floor every time. The bench is gone. Nothing remains in this house. Everything has to be sent away to the office. Go and tell your father that I want the bench back immediately. He is in his room. Go and tell him.'

Sumati stood hesitating, and suggested weakly, 'Why don't you tell him that yourself, Mother? I'm afraid ...'

'Afraid! Everybody is afraid of him.'

When he sat down for his dinner before going to the office she hovered about, attending mechanically. He ate very quietly, fixedly looking down at the rice on his leaf. She felt a sudden pity for him; there was something pathetic in the quietness with which he had accepted the ill-cut brinjals. Possibly Gangu might have lied. It might be nothing more than a scandal. The poor man was perhaps poring over account-books all night, and now without a moment's rest he would have to be rushing back once again in the hot day after heavy food. All for whose sake? She despised herself for listening to gossip. After all these years of life together, this was not the way to judge him. She was not going to let her foul mind spoil their life. She resolved not to ask him about the bench. She resolved to re-establish peace. She asked: 'Wouldn't you like a little more rice for the curd?'

'No,' he said.

She said, 'Babu has scored sixty marks out of one hundred in arithmetic. He stands fourth in his class this term.'

He displayed no enthusiasm over this news. She said again: 'I had a letter from my sister in Rangoon yesterday. All are well there. It seems her husband's appointment was recently confirmed. And what do you think? My sister says that she is expecting her eighth child in a few months.'

'So your sister has gone far ahead of you?' he remarked hollowly.

Savitri succeeded in making a few sounds like laughter. Though her bitterness was now gone, she felt still a little uneasy. What would she not have given to be coaxed and cajoled a little now! All the same it was not so bad as it had been a few moments before.

When he was ready for the office she met him at the veranda steps. How well he looked in his silk suit! It was sheer envy that must have made Gangu and the rest talk scandal about him, they with their husbands all crooked and paunchy. She mustered up all her strength and asked, 'Will you be late tonight too?' He frowned at her without a reply. She at once said apologetically, 'I didn't mean to ...'

'I can't be answering idiotic questions. You think I am just as old as Babu?' He strode furiously towards the garage.

* * *

Gangu flitted in in the afternoon. Savitri was lying on the carpet in the hall reading her magazine.

'What has happened to the bench which used to be here all these days? You are lying on the floor,' asked Gangu, and unwittingly started once again the very thoughts that Savitri had been at pains to smother since the morning.

'Something or other has happened to it,' Savitri said, discouraging all further reference to the subject.

Gangu said, 'I just asked because the hall looks so bare without it. I felt perfectly disgusted with the home, and so threw everything up and came out. Sometimes I do get into such a mood, you know.'

'I suppose you have finished the tiffin for the afternoon?'

'That's just what I haven't done. I said to my husband when he started for the school, "Don't expect any tiffin this evening when you come back from school. I would advise you to fill your stomach in a hotel." '

'What about the rest at home?'

'If he does not bring a packet for me and the children I will drive him out once again. He knows it.'

'Well, what is the news in the town?' asked Savitri.

'Nothing very special. Did you see the Tamil picture they are showing at the Palace? There are some good songs in it, but I could have played that heroine better. I will do it some day. Just wait ... I think your husband went to the picture.'

'What!'

'He was sitting two or three chairs off mine.'

'So it was not the account-books that he had been poring over all night,' Savitri thought.

'Didn't you know?' Gangu asked.

'I don't usually bother him with questions as to his whereabouts.'

'But didn't he tell you that he had been to the picture?'

'He doesn't tell me anything unless I ask him; and he was so terribly busy the whole morning that I couldn't get a word with him.'

Savitri wanted all further talk about her husband to cease now, and switched on to, 'I heard that you were about to make records of some of your songs.'

'Yes, one of my husband's friends knows a person who knows some of the gramophone people in Madras. It is well under way. But it is all a secret yet.'

Savitri thought: So he had not been poring over accounts all night. Perhaps he had to go out and meet someone in the theatre. Gangu said unasked, 'Don't think I am gossiping, but there was another person with him; perhaps it is that person about whom people are talking all this nonsense. I didn't want to tell you, but I thought you might as well know, because what harm is there?'

Savitri sat gazing on the floor; she couldn't speak; she felt feverish. Gangu apologized. 'You mustn't let it affect you so much. I wouldn't have mentioned it if I had known you would be so foolish.'

Savitri still said nothing. The silence, to a person unaccustomed to it like Gangu, was very uncomfortable. She made a feeble effort to divert Savitri's thoughts by talking about the picture, its merits and demerits. Savitri did not lift her eyes from the floor. It was a monologue for Gangu. Savitri asked suddenly, 'What was she like?'

'Who? the heroine? They should have ...'

'Not your heroine of the picture, but the real one.'

'Forget her. Don't brood over it like a fool. There can't be anything in it.'

'I must know what she was like. I never asked you to tell me about her. You have done it. Tell me everything. I must know!'

'There is nothing for you to know, that's all.'

'What was she like?'

'She is an old woman, very ugly, and no man would go near her.'

Savitri broke down. 'I know you are lying. She can't be old. Perhaps I am old and ugly. How can I help it? I have borne children and slaved for the house.'

'No, no, you are a darling. You are beautiful. You aren't old.'

Savitri said, 'I am middle-aged, old-fashioned, plain. How can I help it? She must be young and pretty. He has not been coming home before midnight for weeks. And yesterday he didn't come home at all; came only in the morning, and wouldn't talk to me.' She said, blowing her nose, 'He is indifferent even to the children. Tell me everything!'

Gangu wept a little herself and said, clearing her throat: 'I won't hide anything from you. They didn't stay very long in the theatre. She said something and both of them went out at ten o'clock.'

'And he couldn't come back home before the morning,' added Savitri.

She asked, 'Were they sitting very close to each other?'

'Yes.'

'Is she not young and better-looking than I am?'

'Her skin is white, but who cannot make herself up to look younger?'

Savitri saw herself in the mirror in the evening. Her eyes were swollen, her nose was red. The girls came home from school. Kamala cried, 'Mother, your eyes are very red. Have you been crying?'

'No. Why should I cry? I must have touched my eyes with the fingers I used for picking chillies, and I have a bad cold too.'

'Oh, I thought you had been crying, and I was so terrified, you know. I thought Father must have scolded you or something like that. I do hate Father scolding you, because you become so unhappy.'

'Why should your father scold me? He is so good. He only scolds when I do something wrong. How can one teach what is right without scolding?'

'That's what our teacher says. If she raps us on the knuckles when the arithmetic goes wrong and we cry out, she says nothing can be corrected without punishment. I am sure it is all a lie. Can't a sum be set right without a rap on the knuckles?'

'Mother, she gets thrashed every day at school,' said Sumati.

'It's a lie. It is she that gets thrashed every day. Today our teacher sent me out to fetch a piece of chalk, and I saw Sumati in her class standing, and somebody said that her teacher had made her stand the whole period.'

'It is a lie, Mother!' screamed Sumati. 'I was standing because our teacher had asked me to give a dictation to the class. I'm not like you,' she said, turning to Kamala.

They settled their differences very soon and went out to play. Babu came in from school. 'Mother, I won't touch the tiffin unless you promise to give me my cricket fee tomorrow. I must give four annas to the captain.'

'All right. I will give you the money.'

'And I want a rough notebook tomorrow.'

'You bought one only four days ago.'

'Yes. It is all filled. Can't we buy even rough notebooks liberally? There is my friend Gopal. His people buy him one dozen notebooks every month, and here you grumble at buying even two.'

After Babu left for the cricket-ground, Savitri went to the mirror and scrutinized herself in it once again. The swelling of the eyes had subsided a little now. She smoothed out her hair with her fingers, turned her head, and looked at herself sideways. 'What is she like?' she asked herself. 'I'm not very bad, am I? Perhaps she is very good-looking. What is wrong with my face? These strumpets with their powder and paint! Has she as clear a skin as mine without her paints?' She remembered her husband's figure in the morning as he was dressed for the office. 'Perhaps I'm not good enough for him. Let me admit my complexion has become rather sooty, and these dark rings under the eyes. I am getting careless about my hair, and braid it anyhow; it's hardly his fault if he can't like my appearance very much.'

She applied a little scented oil to her hair, and combed it with great care. She braided and coiled it very neatly. She washed her face with soap and water, and applied very lightly a little face-powder. She had given up using face-powder and scented oil years ago. She stood before the mirror, applied a little perfumed paste between her eyebrows and pressed a very elegant pinch of vermilion on it, and trimmed its edges with her little finger to make it perfectly round. He always liked the forehead marking to be a little large. She stood close to the mirror, with her nose almost touching the glass. She was more or less satisfied with her appearance, except for two stray strands of grey hair which she had just discovered; she smoothed them out and tucked them cunningly into an under-layer. The glass clouded with the moisture of her breath; she wiped the moisture and saw herself once again. Perhaps the other one's cheeks were rosy, and her hair thicker and longer. 'My cheeks, too, were rosy and my hair came down to my hips before I had my two miscarriages and three childbirths ...' She went out into the garden and plucked some jasmine and red flowers, strung them together, and placed them in a curve on the coil at the back of her head – he always liked the red flowers to be interspersed with the white jasmine, and always admired the curved arrangement.

She wondered for a moment if she should dress herself in a new *sari* from the box; he always liked to see her in the blue one. But that might be too much. She felt a little shy to dress so well for the home.

The children had finished their dinner. They stood round and admired her and asked if she had been to a marriage-house. 'You smell lovely, Mother,' Kamala said.

'I don't like scents,' Babu said.

'Won't you coil my hair on my head like yours?' Kamala asked.

'I don't like this tight coiling,' Babu said, 'it makes the neck very ugly. I like the hair to fall on the ears a little.'

'You can ask your wife to braid her hair loose,' Savitri said.

'Don't talk rubbish, Mother. I am never going to marry.'

When the children went away for their study and sleep, Savitri sat up, her heart in a flutter: would he come back tonight? It would be impossible to bear it if he kept away again; the perfume and flowers to be wasted! She wrung her hands. She went to the mirror, stole another look at herself, and thought that if he saw her now he would certainly like her. Love her as boisterously as he had loved her in the first week of their marriage ... 'No, no,' she told herself. 'He will not keep away tonight, not after I have asked him. He has great consideration for my feelings though he may appear rough outside. What did he say? – "can't be answering idiotic questions"; of course he couldn't answer a question like that. Where was any sense in asking a man if he would return home? That was why he wouldn't waste his breath in answering such a question.'

She sat up quite late into the night. When overcome by fatigue she lay down, keeping her head lightly on the pillow for fear that she might crush the flowers or rumple the hair. He might come any time and she wanted to meet him fresh as she was in the evening; there was nothing more unsightly than rumpled hair and crushed flowers on one's head ... She dreamt that her husband came home, held her in his arms, and swore that he had been carrying about only a coloured parasol, and silly people said that he had been going about with a woman ...

And morning came. It was a Sunday and the children had no school. Their presence in the house was a check on Savitri's gloom. When she was alone and when the children's voices were not heard, her mind reverted to its obsession: he hasn't come, he hasn't come, he doesn't care for me now (before the mirror), perhaps she is better than I am.

At about midday Kamala asked, 'Mother, what has happened to Father?'

'He has gone out on business. He has so much work to do at the office.'

'Wouldn't he want to eat anything, or sleep?'

'No. When men have work they forget food, sleep, and home.'

Babu said, 'When I become a big man I will be a big officer, and I won't leave the office, but stay there night and day and do my work. I like being there so much.'

'What about your wife and children?' asked Savitri. Babu bared his teeth in disgust and said, 'Why do you always talk about marriage? I hate it. I am not going to marry even if it is going to cost me my life.'

'Very well, but what about me?' she asked. 'Shall I have to be at home all alone while you are away?'

'You! Oh!'

'You had forgotten me. Everybody forgets me. When you become a big man perhaps you won't even recognize your mother if you see her anywhere.'

Babu swore that he would always be at his mother's side, which comforted Savitri a great deal.

Ramani's car snorted and hooted at the gate at about nine that night. The children were already in their beds; the servant had dropped into a sleep in some part of the house. Savitri went to the garage and opened the door herself. Ramani came in and quietly went away to his room. The house had assumed a gloomy silence after the children had gone to bed. Savitri went about with a flush on her face. She decided not to open her mouth till he should finish his dinner. She hovered about him when he ate, and attended on him, while the sleepy cook served the food. Half-way through the dinner he seemed to notice suddenly that she was before him. 'Have you had your dinner?'

'Yes,' she said. 'You want me to sit up and wait for you, do you?' She was astonished at her own manner. Ramani looked up for a moment but said nothing.

When the cook had gone for the day, and she had shut the front door and put out the lights, she went to the bedroom, cleared her throat and said, 'This sort of thing has to stop, understand?' He was already in bed, with a novel shielding his face. He lowered the novel and scowled at her. 'Don't talk. Go and lie on your bed.'

'I'm not going to, till you promise to come to your senses.' She stood firmly beside his cot.

'Hush, don't talk so loudly. You will wake up the children and the neighbours,' he said.

'Ah, how considerate you are for the children!' she said.

He sat up, understood the terrific force that a woman about to be hysterical could muster, and tried to take her hands and draw her nearer. She pushed away his hand, crying, 'Don't touch me.'

'No, no! What's the matter with you, my pet? This is strange. What is wrong with you?'

He tried once again to hold her hands, and she shook her hands free, violently. 'I'm a human being,' she said, through her heavy breathing. 'You men will never grant that. For you we are playthings when you feel like hugging, and slaves at other times. Don't think that you can fondle us when you like and kick us when you choose.'

He tried to treat it as a joke and laugh it off. 'Very well, my dear. I grant here and now that you are a human being who can feel and think. All right. Now go to bed. I am sleepy.'

His endearing tone for a moment won her; his acquiescence momentarily satisfied her; and she was pleased that he had tried to fondle her. She burst into tears and allowed herself to be drawn to his side. She sat on the edge of his bed sobbing, and when he said, 'Now, now, be a good girl, don't! Lie down, my pet,' she felt that all her troubles had ceased, and blamed herself for exaggerating a little mistake that he might have committed.

She remained thus for a little while and, encouraged by his endearments, asked, 'Now, will you promise not to go near her again?' The first surprise was over, he had exhausted the little accommodation his nature was capable of, and he was once again his old self. He was irritated by the question and said, 'I don't want you to dictate to me.' She repeated her question and he said, 'Don't be a silly fool.' She understood the menace in his tone, drew herself away from him, and said, 'So you refuse?'

'Yes.'

'You won't give up this harlot?'

'Mind how you speak!' His head throbbed with anger.

'You are not having me and her at the same time, understand? I go out of this house this minute.'

'You can please yourself. Put out the light. I want to sleep.' He turned towards the wall.

He heard the banging of the door, turned, and found that she had gone out of the room. A terrific indignation welled up in him: so she was trying to nose-lead him with threats of leaving, like a damned servant! She could please herself, the ingrate. All the kindness and consideration wasted on her. When his bank balance was low he had somehow bought her that gold-laced *sari* and jumper because she desired it, and the diamond studs on her nose ... the ingrate! He rose from bed and went out of the room. He found her waking up the three children sleeping in the hall. They sat rubbing their eyes, their minds in a whirl of confusion.

'Why have you disturbed them?'

'I'm taking them with me ....'

'Shut up! Leave them alone! Are you mad?' Kamala began to cry. This was too much for him; he dragged Savitri away from the children, at which all three of them started crying. 'This is a fine scene!' he said. He thundered, 'Now keep quiet. Here, Kamala, if I hear your voice I will peel the skin off your back. Babu, Sumati, lie down and shut your eyes, and shut your mouths. Sleep at once! Obey!'

The children fell down, put their heads on their pillows, and shut their eyes fast, a sob occasionally bursting from one or the other.

Ramani turned to Savitri and said, 'Savitri, you are trying my patience. What madness is this? Go to bed. For the last time I tell you, go to bed.' He tried to take her by the hand and lead her to her bed.

'Don't touch me!' she cried, moving away from him. 'You are dirty, you are impure. Even if I burn my skin I can't cleanse myself of the impurity of your touch.' He clenched his teeth and raised his hands. She said, 'All right, strike me. I am not afraid.' He lowered his hands and said, 'Woman, get away now.'

'Do you think I am going to stay here? We are responsible for our position: we accept food, shelter, and comforts that you give, and are what we are. Do you think that I will stay in your house, breathe the air of your property, drink the water here, and eat food you buy with your money? No, I'll starve and die in the open, under the sky, a roof for which we need be obliged to no man.'

'Very well. Take your things and get out this moment.'

'Things? I don't possess anything in this world. What possession can a woman call her own except her body? Everything else that she has is her father's, her husband's, or her son's. So take these too ...' She removed her diamond earrings, the diamond studs on her nose, her necklace, gold bangles and rings, and threw them at him. 'Now, come on, children, get up! Let us get out.' She tried to go near the children. He barred her way. 'Don't touch them or talk to them. Go yourself, if you want. They are my children.' She hesitated for a moment and then said, 'Yes, you are right. They are yours, absolutely. You paid the midwife and the nurse. You pay for their clothes and teachers.

You are right. Didn't I say that a woman owns nothing?' She broke down, staring at their fidgeting forms on the beds. 'What will they do without me?'

'They will get on splendidly without you, don't you worry. No one is indispensable in this world.'

The diamonds and the gold lay at his feet on the floor. He picked them up. 'This ring and this necklace and this stud were not given by me. They are your father's.'

She shrunk from them. 'Take them away. They are also a man's gift.'

Ramani said, 'I'm very sleepy. I'm waiting to bolt the street door and go to bed; that is, if you decide to go out.'

She threw a look at the children, at him, turned round and walked out, softly closing the door behind her.

Before she reached the gate she heard the sound of the bolting of the front door. She opened the gate a little, let herself out, and saw the light in the front hall put out. 'Will the children sleep there in the dark without me?' She stood for a moment watching the light in her husband's room, and moved on when it was also put out. It was very nearly midnight. She walked down the silent street.

CHAPTER SEVEN

She walked all the way to the north end of the town and reached the river an hour later. Sarayu was flowing in the dark, with a subdued rumble. Summer was still a few weeks ahead, and now the water was fairly deep in some places, though in a few weeks' time the river would shrink to a thin streak of water furrowing the broiling sands.

Her mind was numb. Otherwise she could not have walked through the town at midnight. Nothing seemed to matter now, not even one's children. They were after all a husband's ... Couldn't she just go to the office, drag the other woman out, gash her face with her finger-nails? Wouldn't it be interesting to wait and see if he would still grovel at the feet of that slut whose face was gashed and whose hair was torn out?

Savitri sat on the last step with her feet in the dark moving water. 'This is the end,' she said to herself, and felt very strange. So strange indeed did this statement sound to her that she asked herself: 'Am I the same old Savitri or am I someone else? Perhaps this is just a dream. And I must be someone else posing as Savitri because I couldn't have had the courage to talk back to my husband. I have never done it in my life. I couldn't have had the courage to walk through the streets at midnight. I am afraid to go even a hundred yards from the house unescorted; yes, afraid, afraid of everything. One definite thing in life is Fear. Fear, from the cradle to the funeral pyre, and even beyond that, fear of torture in the other world. Afraid of a husband's displeasures, and of the discomforts that might be caused to him, morning to night and all night too. How many nights have I slept on the bed on one side, growing numb by the unchanged position, afraid lest any slight movement should disturb his sleep and cause him discomfort.' Afraid of one's father, teachers and everybody in early life, afraid of one's husband, children, and neighbours in later life – fear, fear, in one's heart till the funeral pyre was lit, and then fear of being sentenced by Yama to be held down in a cauldron of boiling oil ... 'How many sins have I not committed? ... Not many, I have always performed my daily *pooja* without fail. I've never lied in my life, except a few uttered in childhood. Didn't I and my sister finish off the honey in the bottle and then swear we didn't know what had happened to it? And then that scuffle after which I said that my brother had flung the ball at the glass chimney. Poor fellow, bearing patiently all our anger and vileness and never lifting his hand on us because we were girls. What ages since I saw him, never been the same man since he married that girl from Tayur, a vicious slattern. Far away there from everybody, in Hyderabad, led about by a nose-rope like a bullock. Years since he has written a line to anyone at home; perhaps he has forgotten all his sisters; must have quite a dozen children by now.'

Savitri felt an intense longing to see her brother and her parents. Wouldn't it be better to go round once, see everybody, and then die? Who was so dear to one, after all, as one's parents, one's brothers and sisters, really loving and affectionate? not a husband but one's parents – theirs was the true affection, not even one's children's ... Babu would perhaps not come home at all but spend his time in the office and not think of her; Sumati and Kamala would marry and go away and get wrapped up in their own family bothers and give their mother a thought once in a way when there was nothing else to think about ...

'Must go and see my sister in Rangoon too. Perhaps I can see everybody, see her last, and jump into the sea while returning from Rangoon. What a happy couple those two are, never irritating each other, beautifully balanced. She has always been the luckier since childhood. She was the one to escape thrashing, to be given the first sweets and pencils, to be called up and petted by Father's friends; and no wonder the same luck persists in marriage too. Perhaps one gets the husband one deserves.' She now thought of her husband. Poor man, she said; not so bad by himself, only poisoned in mind now by that slut (was she such a heavenly creature that one should lose all one's senses?). Hadn't he said when they talked to each other for the first time, on the fifth day of marriage, up in the lonely upstairs room, that the moment he saw her he decided to marry her, and that he would have taken his life if he hadn't got her? How he had written to her in all the early letters that he hadn't met anyone with a skin as fair as hers, or with her eyes or hair or cheeks. She wished she had those letters with her now. She would throw them at him and say ... 'The woman in the office might be really good-looking. I'm not the Savitri that I was when he wrote those letters. Give the other one, too, three children and two miscarriages and see what she will come to; no one except me could have retained even so much of my early looks. Day before yesterday the mirror didn't depress me. I looked quite the same as I did before my nuptials, but it was his fault, he should have come home and seen me. All the flowers and trouble absolutely wasted. Not my fault, he came only a day after I looked my best.'

The Taluk office gong was being struck, and its notes came clearly through the still air. Savitri counted, one, two, three .... 'I've never seen this hour before, always been asleep. Not always, when Babu had the chickenpox and Sumati had typhoid I've counted the gong at this hour on several nights. And also when he had his headache. How many nights have I sat up all night, yes, even at three o'clock, and held his throbbing head. Would the other one do it for an hour if he should have any pain now? Why do men have such a bad memory? He said, "Get out, I want to sleep." '

Three o'clock now, in an hour it would be four, then five, and six, and people would come and drag her back home or lock her up as being mad. What was the use of sitting on the river-step with a wandering mind and wasting one's time? No one who could not live by herself should be allowed to exist. 'If I take the train and go to my parents, I shall feed on my father's pension; if I go back home, I shall be living on my husband's earnings, and later, on Babu. What can I do by myself? Unfit to earn a handful of rice except by begging. If I had gone to a college and studied, I might have become a teacher or something. It was very foolish of me not to have gone on with my education. Sumati and Kamala must study up to the B.A. and not depend for their salvation on marriage. What is the difference between a prostitute and a married woman? – the prostitute changes her men, but a married woman doesn't; that's all, but both earn their food and shelter in the same manner. Yes, Kamala and Sumati must take their University course and become independent.' She laughed at herself for planning for her daughters. Who were they? His daughters, not hers. He had said that he had paid for their coming into the world and for their upkeep here.

No one who couldn't live by herself had a right to exist. It was three, in an hour it would be four, and then five ... people would come and drag her away.

She rose and stepped down. There was still one step, the very last submerged under water, very slippery with moss; and then one felt the sand under one's feet; water reached up to one's hips, and as one went further down, to one's breasts; and now the running water tripped up one's legs from behind. She stood in the water and prayed to her God on the Hill to protect the children .... 'In Yama's world the cauldron must be ready for me for the sin of talking back to a husband and disobeying him, but what could I do? What could I do ... no, no, I can't die. I must go back home. I won't, I won't.' The last sensation that she felt was a sharp sting as the water shot up her nostrils, and something took hold of her feet and toppled her over.

CHAPTER EIGHT

Burglary was only a side occupation for Mari. He was the locksmith, umbrella-repairer, and blacksmith of Sukkur village, which was a couple of miles from the other bank of the river. He was a burglar for various reasons; there was a predatory strain in his nature, perhaps handed down to him by his ancestors, which made him love the excitement of breaking into a house; he also valued the profits of the adventure; and he did it to please his wife. He was intensely devoted to her, and her one ambition in life was to fill a small brass pot with coins and precious metal and bury it at the root of a coconut tree which shot up from the back-yard of their little home. Tinkering at iron things gave one a steady income but a small one; and if you put up your rates you might drive your customers to the next village; if you didn't put up your rates you had an inadequate income – which made a wife unhappy and quarrelsome. Mari cared a great deal for his wife, although he chased her about and threw things at her when he was drunk.

He sallied forth once a month or so across the river into Malgudi town, crying 'Locks repaired, sirs, umbrellas repaired!' in the streets. During these journeys, if any locked house caught his eye, he let himself into it at midnight and picked up any silverware or precious trifle that might be there.

On this day he was in town. It was a miserable day. He cried 'Locks repaired, sirs, umbrellas repaired!' till he felt as if a file were working inside his Adam's apple, and yet his only customer was a miser at the market, who wouldn't give even an anna for a new rib to his umbrella; he wanted it to be done for six pies. Mari needed the six pies badly, and he did the work; and something else too: before handing back the umbrella, with a deft twist of the pliers somewhere he assured himself that it would be crippled at the next gust of wind; and then the heir of a miser could thank himself for the six pies saved!

What galled him most was that the wife at home expected a man to return laden with money. Time was when a man could earn at least a rupee in the town, but nowadays it was a mystery what people did with their broken umbrellas. Gone were the days when locks and keys were a luxury; now if a key was lost another with a lock (made in Japan) could be bought for an anna and a half!

Mari turned his steps from the crowded Market Road, Vinayak Mudali and Grove Streets, and with a last hope moved towards Lawley Extension. Here were rich bungalows; and people who never carried umbrellas but went about in cars. All the same occasionally there was a demand for a repairer, and payment was excellent ...

His voice rang through the broad silent streets of Lawley Extension. He shouted louder here than anywhere else because every house had a compound, and the message had to get through the gates and reach the people living yards away from the road. This also proved to be a profitless excursion. Mari coughed and said to himself that he might cry till he spat blood but nobody would give him a pie.

He was in the Fourth Cross Road, cursing his luck, when he saw a locked house. He slackened his pace, observed the house more fully, paced the street up and down, and went away.

He sang as he walked back to Market Road. It seemed immaterial to him if his purse contained only half an anna.

There was an old woman squatting on the narrow pavement at the market gateway selling fried groundnut, coloured edibles, and cucumber slices, arranged on a gunny-sack spread on the ground. Mari put down his small bundle of tools and sat down before the gunny-sack.

'Get out of the way,' the old woman cried.

'Ah, mother, you are really becoming blind,' Mari said, moving nearer. 'I am Mari.'

The old woman laughed and said: 'I can't see who is who at this hour. But what a nuisance the whole day, people coming and sitting down there every other minute! I am hoarse calling out ...'

She struck a match and lit the wick peeping out of a tin container. She placed the container on an inverted basket and brightened the surroundings with the wavering flare. 'I can see better now, can't I? When did you come to town, and why have you come so late, my son?'

'Have I not to earn some money before I come and spend it here? Would you give me a little pinch of anything unless I paid for it at once?'

'I am a poor wretch who has to add pie on pie; what can I do?'

'You have the cunning of a fox! You must have made a fortune by now, which you are salting and pickling somewhere, I know. Your days are nearly over, and yet your avarice has not ended; why should you not give your money to poor folk like me?' After these pleasantries Mari proceeded to business. He bought, after much haggling, groundnut for three pies, a curved slice of cucumber for a pie, and some fried stuff for two pies, and munched them with deliberate care and attention. 'A firelike hunger inside me and this is just a pinch in some corner,' he said at the end of the meal.

'Then buy some more. I have some nice things in this basket ...'

'You tempt me. All right, but will you take the money tomorrow?'

'Credit day after tomorrow,' the old woman said.

Mari walked over to the fountain in the Market Square, took water in his hands, and drank it. 'Now it is better,' he said, coming back to the old woman. 'Oh, sister, give me a little tobacco and betel leaf. God will take you to Heaven for it. I have given you all my money. I have no more. I shall go raving mad if I don't get a little piece of tobacco now.'

The old woman took out her greasy cloth purse, peered into it by the light of the smoky flare, picked up a piece of tobacco and a crumpled betel leaf, and flung them at Mari, grumbling, 'You are the biggest scoundrel God ever made. You spend half an anna but take goods for three-quarters of an anna.'

'Let me be smitten with leprosy if I have a pie more about me,' said Mari, receiving the gift and putting it in his mouth. He took his tool-bag and walked away. He crossed the road, went into the spacious rest-house before the market, and lay down in the veranda. Chewing the betel leaf and tobacco, he had a great sense of well-being; he shut his eyes and revelled in it for some time, and fell asleep.

He got up at midnight. The Market Road was silent; only the lights of a few late shops illuminated the road here and there. The last cinema shows were over and there was no traffic. Mari looked round; a number of others, travellers, adventurers, and mendicants, were lying about fast asleep; some were talking from unseen corners; and one or two were sitting and sucking at an enchanted clay pipe filled with opium leaf, the pipe glowing in the dark.

Mari moved down the road cautiously. He abandoned the main thoroughfare at the earliest possible moment, stole along by-ways and lanes, and reached Lawley Extension.

Not for him now the broad paved roads of the Extension. Here in this locality of Government and Police officials the constables went round with thoroughness on their beats. Mari slipped into an ill-lit conservancy lane, his ears cocked to catch the creaking of police boots. When he heard footsteps he flattened himself against a wall and stood still. The policeman appeared on the edge of the road, looking down the lane, lightly breathing through his whistle, and moved away after shouting, 'Stop, who are you? Don't run, stop! ...'

Mari stood at the gate of the bungalow in the Fourth Cross Road, looked up and down, and vaulted over the compound wall. He closely examined the lock on the front door and squatted down so that he might not be seen from the road. He opened his tool-bag, took out a possible key, ran his file over it, and tried it on the lock. After filing it four or five times he was able to fit it into the lock. He never believed in breaking a lock open, it made things conspicuous. Opening a lock in the correct manner, and locking a house again when leaving it, was, Mari felt, a piece of courtesy which a man owed the absent householders.

Mari let himself into the house, shut the door again, and looked about by the light of a match. He was in a large furnished room. He saw a tray on a stool with betel leaves and areca-nut in it. The leaves were stiff and dry, from which Mari concluded the family must have been away for at least three days. Mari transferred the leaves and nut to his tool-bag, and examined the tray: it looked like plated nickel. He put it down – it wasn't worth the risk a man ran in carrying it about.

He opened the shelves and cupboards. Some of them were empty, and some contained only books, clothes, and other useless stuff. So these people either possessed no silver or were the sneaky sort who kept it in iron safes!

He drifted towards the *pooja* room; there at least one could pick up odd bits of silver – tiny images of gods, incense-holders, and such things. On the way he peeped into the kitchen safe. All the vessels were empty; only a little buttermilk, acrid and fermented, at the bottom of a vessel. He also found, wrapped in a piece of paper, a quarter loaf of bread, stiff as cardboard. Mari felt happy at the sight of it; so he needn't go away with an empty stomach. A handful of groundnut vended by that stingy hag was no food for a hungering stomach. He tried to bite the loaf of bread, but it scratched his gums and hurt the roof of his mouth; he then soaked it in the sour buttermilk and thrust it into his mouth.

He felt contented and hoped that presently in the *pooja* room he might find at least a half-inch-high god, not worth more than a rupee and eight annas, but better than nothing, some keepsake for the wife. These householders were cunning people all the world over: if they had large images and valuable pieces for worship they took care not to leave them about, the cunning hypocrites! Was there any true piety in a person who locked up the gods?

At this moment a noise like that of a terraced roof crashing down came through the darkness. Mari stood stock-still, not daring even to munch his bread. And then he heard groans, and a weak voice calling someone; and again another cascade of falling bricks, groans, and further sounds of choking.

Mari realized it was none of his business to find out what it was, but to clear out immediately if he didn't want to end in jail. While moving towards the exit Mari saw a light through a window. Somebody was living in the back portion of the house. A young boy was administering medicine to an old man who was sitting up, choking and wheezing. 'Never thought for a moment you were all here, friends,' Mari said softly under his breath. 'Your cough will burst you soon, don't worry.'

He was out of the house very soon. His cheeks bulging with the dry bread, he threaded his way through dark alleys and was soon at Ellaman Street. In this part of the town a man could go about freely because the policemen slept on the pyols of houses or under the awnings of shop-fronts and got up only in the morning.

He approached the river, very much depressed. He wished he had brought away at least the tray. Now to be going home empty-handed after a full day out – his wife would spit in his face if she should see what he had brought from the town – a few withered betel leaves. He had better not show her the leaves but chew them off, as soon as he could take a mouthful of water from the river and wash down that terrible bit of bread and rid himself of the hiccups which had been torturing him at regular intervals all along: he had been afraid that in the still night his hiccups might stir up the town or awaken the policemen in Ellaman and North Streets.

He crossed the sands towards the steps; swimming across here saved distance, otherwise one would have to trudge all the way to Nallapa's Grove and cross the river ...

The Taluk office gong struck three. Mari counted it and reckoned that he could be home at four: only a few strokes across the river and then two milestones.

Just as he reached the steps he saw, down below at the water's edge, an apparition. He stood petrified. Surely, this was Mohini, the Temptress Devil, who waylaid lonely wayfarers and sucked their blood ... He watched it in fascination and horror, and presently the Mohini rose and walked into the river. 'Ah, the Devil can walk on water; at what inauspicious moment did I leave home today? She hasn't seen me yet. I dare not move ...' By this time the apparition was in deep water and let out a cry: 'No, no, I can't die: I must go back home ...' And then there was silence. Mari had by now got over his first fright, and said to himself, 'The Devil can't talk, and the Devil can't drown.' He ran down the steps.

He rescued Savitri before she had taken in too much water. Already the currents had carried her to the middle of the river and a little way down. Mari took hold of her hair and dragged her to the opposite bank. He rolled her over and very nearly jumped on her stomach. She opened her eyes and mumbled something.

Mari asked, 'What language are you speaking?'

She asked, 'When will you be back home?'

Mari replied, 'I should have been nearly there now but for you. I am sorry I ever left the village today.'

'Has Babu gone out to play? Did he drink the coffee?'

'I can't say. He might have. Can you get up?'

'Is it morning? Has the milkman come?'

'It is nearly morning, but I can't see the milkman anywhere.'

'What is the matter with him?'

'How can I tell? You didn't expect to find him in the river, did you?' With this Mari shook her, rolled her, twisted her limbs. Savitri stared at the dark face bending over her and screamed, 'Alas! Somebody help me! Thief, thief!' Mari said to himself, 'She has found me out. I am undone. This woman is uncanny,' and left her and broke into a run. He cursed her as he ran: 'This woman will see me in jail for my trouble. I should have let her drown herself ten times over ...'

Savitri awoke next morning with a throbbing head and stiff aching limbs. She realized her position now. All the old bitterness and pain revived in her. On her right, beyond the stretch of water and sand, the Town Hall tower peeped over a cluster of roofs. Savitri gazed on it and reflected that, under some roof in the cluster, *he* must be with the woman; let him be. She must go on with her back to that cluster of roofs and never turn again towards them, never, unless he abandoned the woman and begged for pardon. She was an individual with pride and with a soul, and she wasn't going to submit to everything hereafter. Would *he* be searching for her now? It was more likely he had brought the other one and kept her in the house. Would she be ill-treating the children? Savitri wished that she had asked

Janamma or Gangu to keep an eye on the children. But ... children? Let them alone. They were his; he paid the midwife, and it was his duty to look after them. Hadn't he said that they would get on splendidly without her? 'Now what shall I do with myself? Shall I starve to death?'

A dark hefty man and a woman appeared before her. The woman asked, 'Are you all right now?'

'Who are you?'

'I am of Sukkur village and people call me Ponni. My husband is a blacksmith. While he was returning home from – never mind where or why he had gone there, men have to go out and work, you know – he saw you in the river and he says that he saved your life and left you on the bank.'

'You should have left me alone,' Savitri said.

'Why do you say that? When he told me where he had left you, I shouted to him, "You can't leave a woman helpless, all alone there. Go there this minute and see if she is all right." But when he started someone came along to have a wheel-band set right; when it was over and just as we were starting someone else came along with a battered lock. Oh, it is a nasty profession without any rest, but we are poor people. We can't afford to say to anyone "Come later." We have to live on their goodwill, you know.'

'You are right,' Savitri said.

'I am so happy to see you alive. You are so fair, and you look rich. I can't understand how you came to be here. Why did you jump into the river?'

'Is this your husband?'

'Yes.'

'Do you like him very much?'

At this Ponni looked shy and smiled. Savitri said, 'Suppose he took another woman and neglected you, what would you do?'

Ponni threw a suspicious glance at her husband and asked, 'Have you been up to any such trick?'

'No, no,' Mari said, and asked, turning to Savitri, 'What do you mean by this, madam?' Savitri explained to Ponni, 'I don't say he has done it. Imagine for a moment ...'

Mari asked indignantly, 'Why should she imagine such a thing?'

Savitri persisted, 'If he did such a thing, what would you do?'

Ponni said, 'Let him try. Then he will know what he will get.'

'But that was all that I could do,' Savitri said, pointing at the river. 'I have slaved for him all these years. We have children. And now he is ensnared by a – by a – by some woman. He doesn't want me.'

Ponni said, 'Sister, remember this. Keep the men under the rod, and they will be all right. Show them that you care for them and they will tie you up and treat you like a dog.'

'What do you mean?' Mari protested. 'When have I treated you like a dog?'

'Don't talk now,' Ponni commanded. 'Don't butt in when women are talking. Stay under that tree. I will call you when I want you.' Mari hesitated to go. Ponni said: 'Look here. It is no use your standing here. We are not going to talk to you. You have walked two stones. Rest under that tree. You will hear soon enough when you are wanted.' Mari faded out of the scene. Ponni said to Savitri, 'You see, that is the way to manage them. He is a splendid boy, but sometimes he goes out with bad friends, who force him to drink, and then he will come home and try to break all the pots and beat me. But when I know that he has been drinking, the moment he comes home, I trip him up from behind and push him down, and sit on his back for a little while; he will wriggle a little, swear at me, and then sleep, and wake up in the morning quiet as a lamb. I can't believe any husband is unmanageable in this universe ... Sister, I can't let you sit here all day, the sun is getting warm. Where would you like to go now?'

'Nowhere. I will stay here.'

'Shall I send my husband to the town and ask him to bring your people?'

Savitri shuddered at the suggestion.

'Or come with me to my house. My home is humble, but I will gladly clear a corner for you.' Savitri declined the offer.

Ponni said, 'I see you are a Brahmin and won't stay with us. I will ask someone of your own caste to receive you.'

'No. Leave me alone.'

'Or stay in our house. I will clear a part for you and never come there. I will buy a new pot for you, and rice, and you can cook your own food. I will never come that way. I will never cook anything in our house which may be repulsive to you. Please come with me.'

'No. I won't come anywhere.'

'Our village is only two stones from here. Let us walk slowly.'

'Please go away. Leave me alone.'

At this stubbornness Ponni lost her temper: 'I don't know what you are planning. You want to be neither here nor there. I don't know where you really want to go. A very fine person to deal with!'

'Why do you trouble yourself about me?'

'Why not? See here, my dear lady, either you will come with me to the village or go back to the town. I won't let you stay here. If you persist in moving neither way, I will send my husband to the town and bring someone from there to carry you back home.'

Savitri imagined someone coming from that cluster of roofs, tying her hand and foot, and carrying her back to the South Extension. She asked, 'Which way do we go?' in order to assure herself that it was away from the roofs and not towards them.

'I will come with you,' she said, 'on condition that you don't trouble me to come under your roof or any other roof. I will remain only under the sky.'

CHAPTER NINE

Ramani got up from bed after a night of disturbed sleep. With all his bravado before his wife, he was very much shaken by her manner. Such a thing had never happened to him at any time for fifteen years. She had always been docile and obedient, and the fire inside her was a revelation to him now. Though he had invited her to walk out of the house last night, he had not expected her to do it. He had expected she would go into the dark room and sulk for a few days, a few days more than usual; then she was bound to come to her senses and accept things as they were. He felt irritated when people made any fuss. A man had a right to a little fun now and then, provided it didn't affect his conduct at home. No doubt it took him home rather late, but that could have been rectified by a little persistent persuasion on her part; all this sullenness and dictation was not the right way to set about it; he expected to be coaxed and requested; he told himself that people could get anything from him if only they knew the proper way of approaching him. It would be a very bold person indeed who tried to dictate to him. He had never tolerated any advice from anyone – not even from his father, who, a few years before his death, when Ramani passed his Matriculation, had advised him to continue his studies and was told, 'I know better what I must do.'

Ramani was self-made. He hadn't waited for anybody's help or advice. If he had waited for other people to tell him what to do he might have earned a B.A. and become now a clerk in an office or a lawyer with a miserable practice. As it was, through his own, very own, effort and enterprise he was making a clear five hundred a month, in salary alone, and persons with double or treble degrees constantly applied to him for jobs worth fifty or sixty under him! (This last gave him a certain compensating satisfaction at being without a University degree. He sometimes regretted it because he had often seen B.A.s giving themselves airs, though they could not earn a hundred rupees a year, the ridiculous beings! He occasionally longed for a degree simply in order that he might snub the graduates a little more thoroughly, on their own ground.)

He was entirely self-made, and that proved one was right and needed no advice from others, and least at all from a wife. Of course, he granted, there was some sense in the Women's Movement: let them by all means read English novels, play tennis, have their All-India Conference, and go to pictures occasionally; but that should not blind them to their primary duties of being wives and mothers; they mustn't attempt to ape the Western women, all of whom, according to Ramani's belief, lived in a chaos of promiscuity and divorce. He held that India owed its spiritual eminence to the fact that the people here realized that a woman's primary duty (also a divine privilege) was being a wife and a mother, and what woman retained the right of being called a wife who disobeyed her husband? Didn't all the ancient epics and Scriptures enjoin upon woman the strictest identification with her husband? He remembered all the heroines of the epics whose one dominant quality was a blind stubborn following of their husbands, like the shadow following the substance.

'Will you promise not to go near her again?' and what else? 'You are not having me and her at the same time.' A fine way to talk to a husband. Threatened to walk out like a servant. All the kindness and consideration entirely wasted. How could she forget the six-sovereign necklace he had bought for her at the beginning of his career, when he had not a bank account and was subsisting on insurance canvassing? How could she forget the misery and anxiety he suffered when she had labour pains and the rest? Like a servant threatening to leave, unless something or other was done! No one had any right to object to his friendship with Shanta Bai – that splendid creature with her understanding heart and cultured outlook. Savitri ought not to behave as if her husband was like some low-class fellow who kept a mistress ...

He was decidedly not going to worry about her or search for her. She had walked out of her own will; she would have to face the consequences, of course; old enough to know what she was doing. Firmness was everything in life; that was the secret of success with women. If they found a man squeamish they would drive him about with a whip. He was certain she would return and apologize when her madness passed. This was only a different version of the sulking in the dark room. She might now be sulking in a dark corner of some friend's house. After all, where could she go? He was going to show that *he* wasn't the loser anyway.

In the morning the children sat up rather dazed. They were bewildered and unhappy. They huddled together in a corner of the hall. Sumati took upon herself the task of playing the mother. She went to the cook and said, 'You must give us coffee.'

'Where is your mother?' asked the cook.

Sumati, not being able to answer, said 'Wait a moment,' and came to the hall to consult her brother. 'Babu, the cook asks where is Mother. What shall I tell him?'

'What will you tell him?'

'I don't know.'

'Tell him that it is none of his business.'

Kamala said, 'Perhaps he knows where she is: he might have seen her somewhere last night,' and burst into tears.

Ramani came that way. He now felt that all the responsibility of running the household had descended on him. He was going to prove that no one was indispensable in this world. He also felt that this was his opportunity to introduce certain reforms and economies which he had been suggesting for years to a deaf wife. (He was going to abolish the cooking of brinjals in the house, tell the cook to stay at night, have tea instead of coffee in the afternoons, cut the milk bill by half, and so on.)

He pinched Kamala's cheeks, rumpled Babu's hair, and patted Sumati's back. Decidedly, he was going to make them happy. They were not to miss their mother. 'Have you all had your coffee?' he asked with his brightest smile. His unusual affability comforted the children. 'Now, babies,' he said, 'come to my room.'

'All of us?' Babu asked, surprised. Admission to Father's room was a rare privilege, and only Kamala had it occasionally.

He seated them in a row on the floor, squatted before them like a village school-master, and worked himself up to his best canvassing technique – a gift which made him net a lakh's worth of policies a year in the early days. 'Now, babies, you must not be miserable because your mother is not here.'

'Where is she?' Kamala asked.

'She has only gone to Talapur. Her father was suddenly taken ill. I had a telegram from Talapur at my office yesterday.'

The children listened to this story without enthusiasm, and Ramani asked, 'Why are you all silent?' Babu, being the eldest, believed the story the least. He wanted to ask several questions: why she had gone at midnight, why she had removed the jewels before going, why there had been so much of argument and tears; but he dared not put questions to his father. Kamala asked, 'Why didn't anyone go with her to the station?'

'There was no one to go with her. I couldn't, because you were all alone here.'

Sumati asked, 'Was a carriage brought to take her to the station?'

'Yes. It was waiting in the street.'

'But we didn't see it.'

'I thought, Father,' Kamala ventured, 'that you and Mother had a big quarrel because she cried so much when she went out.'

Ramani said, 'She wanted to take you all with her. I said "No." She became cross. You have school, you know.'

'Why did she cry so much, Father?'

'Her father was very ill. Wouldn't you cry very much if I should be very ill?' He looked at Babu and said, 'Why are you blinking? Do you want to ask anything?'

Babu felt obliged to ask, 'When will Mother be back?'

Ramani replied that it would depend on her father's health. 'Have you all bathed?'

'It is very difficult to make Kamala bathe,' said Sumati. 'Every day Mother had such a bother to make her bathe!'

Ramani looked at Kamala and said, 'No, no. You aren't like that, are you? You are a nice girl. Sumati will give you a bath. Now, will you be a nice little girl?'

'Yes, Father.'

Ramani changed his mind. 'Sumati, I think you had better leave her alone. She will bathe herself. Kamala, you are five years old; you must become self-reliant.'

'Yes, Father.'

Just when the children were starting for school he said, 'What do you do for tiffin?' The girls told him that they came home in the afternoons. Ramani said: 'I will tell the cook to stay. Come in the afternoon and see that he serves you properly. You must all learn to attend to your affairs yourselves. Self-reliance is the first thing you must learn in life. Do you also come home in the afternoon, Babu?'

'No, Father, I come home only in the evening.'

'Do you mean to tell me that you starve till the evening? It won't do.' What did she mean by letting Babu starve till the evening? 'You must carry a small tiffin packet for the afternoon, Babu.' Babu felt his father's attentions irksome. To him there was something shameful and degrading in carrying a packet and eating it in the school. His mother had given up the attempt as hopeless. Now Father was suggesting it. Why could not Father leave people alone?

'I will manage somehow today,' Babu said.

'What will you do? You can't starve,' said Ramani, and called the cook and told him, 'Make a tiffin packet for Babu.'

'The tiffin is not ready yet,' said the cook.

Ramani scowled at the cook. 'What do you mean by it? Don't you know that this boy is to have something for the afternoon? Wonderful work you are doing, to be sure. Let me not catch you at this sort of thing again. As soon as you prepare the tiffin, make a packet of it and take it to his school.' Babu was horrified at the prospect. His schoolfellows would surely stand round and grin at him and his cook as he swallowed the tiffin. It was simply not done. He protested mildly, but Father would not hear of it. 'I know what is best for you. Don't contradict your elders.' Babu accepted his fate with gloomy resignation. It was no use arguing with Father. Life was becoming messy and rotten. 'Now you may all go. Wait for me in the evening. I will take you all to a cinema.'

Sumati and Kamala clapped their hands in joy, but Babu asked, 'In the evening?'

'Yes, sir.'

'I have to play cricket, Father.'

'Not when your father wants you to go to the pictures with him.'

'We are playing against the Y.M.U. next week, and our captain will be very angry if I miss practice.'

'Look here, Babu, you are a very – ' He was irritated and was about to begin a long analysis of Babu's character, but he checked himself as he remembered that he had to be very kind to the children. 'You must learn to be a nice boy, Babu. You must think of your sisters. They can't enjoy a picture without your company, can they? Don't refuse them that pleasure. You must also think of others; you must not be selfish.'

'I like pictures, Father, but I have to practise for a match. I said – '

'Well, well, well! Don't go on saying the same thing over and over again. Your match can wait.' Before going to the office he called the cook and told him, 'Make tea for everybody in the afternoon. Coffee only in the mornings.'

Ramani left the office at five o'clock in the evening. On the way he stopped before a restaurant and bought some sweets. The moment he came home he asked if they had all had their afternoon curd and rice and tiffin and tea correctly, and particularly if Babu had his tiffin at school. Kamala said, 'I don't like the smell of tea, and so I drank only half a tumbler.'

'No, that won't do. You must learn to like tea. It is a very good drink.'

'All right, Father. From tomorrow I will try to like tea.'

Ramani was greatly pleased. He had not known till now that his children were so manageable. 'Did you like your tea, Sumati?' he asked, turning to the other. She said 'Yes,' and added that it didn't make any difference to her whether it was tea or coffee.

He gave the packet of sweets to Sumati and said, 'Share it among yourselves.'

He had bought rather a large quantity of the sweets, and so, though the children started enthusiastically, they couldn't eat more than half of what they took. Ramani shook his head disapprovingly: 'You mustn't get into the habit of wasting things. Babu, you have left the largest quantity; that won't do. You are a sportsman. You must eat a lot and grow strong. Polish it off, otherwise I will never call you a cricket player. Go on.' Babu had been the first to arrive at the stage of retching, but now he grabbed the stuff on the plate, gulped it down, and looked at his father for approval. 'Great boy,' Ramani said. 'You will be in the India Eleven some day.' Babu was tremendously pleased though the sweets turned in his stomach.

He took them to the Palace Talkies, which was showing a Laurel and Hardy film. The children sat completely absorbed. They forgot this world, its troubles, and the absence of a mother, while they watched the antics of the comedians.

Ramani got up in the middle of the show, whispering to them: 'Stay here till I come back and pick you up. Don't leave the theatre even if I am delayed a bit.'

'I will look after them,' Babu said.

'Father, what shall we do if somebody comes and orders us out of the theatre?' Kamala asked.

'Life is one continuous boredom,' Shanta Bai said, locking her arms behind her head and leaning back on the pillow. 'I started out in life wanting to do things, but here I am vegetating. All day long I listen to Pereira's humour and to Kantaiengar's rudeness, and then come here and lie down on the couch. "As wind along the waste – " Have you read Omar Khayyám?'

'Who is he?' Shanta Bai's literary allusions distressed him.

'The Persian poet.'

'I don't know the Mahommedan language,' Ramani said innocently, and Shanta Bai began to lecture him on Omar Khayyám and FitzGerald.

'I can't exist without a copy of *The Rubá'iyát*; you will always find it under my pillow or in my bag. His philosophy appeals to me. Dead yesterday and unborn tomorrow. "What, without asking whither hurried hence" and so on. The cup of life must be filled to the brim and drained; another and another cup to drown the impertinence of this memory. In this world Khayyám is the only person who would have understood the secret of my soul. No one tries to understand me; that is the tragedy of my life. Khayyám says: Into this Universe and why not knowing, etcetera. I am as wind along the waste.'

Ramani went over to the edge of her cot, sat down there, and tried to hold her hands. Shanta Bai took away her hands and pleaded: 'Please leave me alone. I am in no mood now.'

'Are you sure?'

'Absolutely. You may sit here if you like, but please don't touch me.'

Ramani folded his arms across his chest. Shanta Bai hummed a little tune to herself and said, tossing her head, 'I am so unhappy that I have not brought my violin with me. I am in a mood to play.'

'What a pity that I didn't know it!'

'Have you a violin at home?'

'No. I would have bought one for you.'

'Oh, you are so good to me. I don't know how I am ever going to repay your kindness.'

Ramani's heart thrilled at these words. 'I have told you not to talk of repayment. When I know I like a person, I like the person, that is all, and I will do anything for the person. Please don't talk of repayment on any account.'

Presently she said, 'Pereira told me that there is a Laurel and Hardy comic at the Palace. Shall we go there tonight?'

'I am so sorry, not tonight. I have to be with my children. My wife has gone to her parents.'

'Oh,' Shanta Bai said with resignation. 'H'm, just my luck, that is all. I would have so loved a picture tonight! Just my luck, that is all.'

'Don't mistake me, dear,' Ramani begged.

'Not at all. Your family duties first. I was only cursing my luck.' She dismissed the pictures with a sigh. She hummed a few tunes and Ramani said that she sang divinely. She said, 'Would you mind putting out the light? I feel that darkness would be more soothing to my soul now ... I do so hate these electric bulbs ...'

Ramani put out the light.

The Taluk office gong struck nine. Ramani counted it and jumped up, muttering: 'Goodness! I never thought it was nine. The children will be waiting: the poor things must be very hungry and sleepy.'

CHAPTER TEN

As soon as they entered the village Savitri asked, 'Have we arrived?'

'Yes.'

'I will stay here. You may go to your house.'

'Here? On the roadside? You are not talking sensibly, if you will forgive me for saying so.'

'There is nothing wrong in it. Or I will go over to that field and stay there.'

'And get bitten by a cobra? You can't stay anywhere in the open. You are not the kind of person who ought to risk it. You will gather a crowd round you, and you will be suffocated by the crowd if nothing worse happens. Don't be foolish, madam. Come with me to our house and stay there just for this day. We will see if anything is possible tomorrow. God is great. He will show us a way.'

Savitri allowed herself to be taken to the house. She was too dazed and faint to persist.

Sukkur village consisted of about a hundred houses and six streets. Around the village there were immense stretches of paddy-fields. Ponni lived in a hovel, with an extension of thatched shed abutting the crooked street, which served as Mari's workshop.

By this time they had gathered a small crowd of shepherds, urchins, and idlers behind them. People came out of their houses and stared at Savitri. One or two shouted to Ponni, 'Who is this lady?' Ponni passed on without replying.

Ponni said, as soon as they reached her house, 'You come from the town. Perhaps you live in a palatial house there. I don't know if you will find my hut tolerable.' Mari had come running in advance and opened the door. He hurriedly pushed away odds and ends and metal junk, which cluttered their small windowless front room. Ponni entered the house, picked up a broom, and swept the floor. She took out her best mat (which had a coloured pattern of a Japanese girl holding an umbrella), unrolled it, and requested Savitri to sit down on it. Savitri declined the mat and sat on the floor. Ponni said, 'That is what I don't like about you, madam.' She turned to her husband and said, 'Come with me.' Mari followed her. They stood in the backyard where a tall coconut tree shot up into the sky. She asked: 'Have you any money? None, of course, I know.'

'What could I do?'

'You will see me in the streets before we have done with each other,' she said. 'Here is the lady. We shall have to give her something that she will accept from us. How do you propose to get it?' Mari blinked desperately and looked away. She said, 'Now get up this tree and pluck a couple of coconuts. We will beg her to drink at least the water in them.' Mari hugged the tree and pulled himself up. 'Mind you don't throw them on the tiles. Keep them ready. I will be back soon,' she said, and went out. She hurried down the street and went to a shop where a miscellany of goods were sold. Ranganna, the shopman, was squatting amidst his articles. He asked, 'What can I give you, good woman?'

'I hope I see you well. How are your children?'

'They are quite well.'

'Is your wife all right now?'

'Yes, yes, as well as she could be; that is all I can say. What can I give you?'

'If you have plantains, please give me the four ripest ones.'

'With pleasure,' said the shopman, and held his hand for the money.

Ponni looked hurt. 'Why should you be so suspicious? Will I run away with your money?'

'Did I say so? I was just wondering if the fruits were ripe enough for you.'

'I will see for myself,' said Ponni, and hopped up a platform before the shop. She pulled up a bunch of plantains which was hanging by a string. 'These are excellent,' she said. She selected four, plucked them out, and jumped down the platform. She asked, 'How much?'

'Eight pies,' said the shopman.

'Too dear, too dear,' said Ponni, shaking her head disapprovingly. 'How many fruits do you want at a quarter of an anna for six? I will give you four pies, or, say, five pies for your sake. I will bring the money tomorrow.'

'I can't give you anything on credit,' said the shopman; but Ponni was off. 'I don't know what to do with this frightful woman,' said the shopman.

Ponni set the coconut and the plantains before Savitri. Savitri said, 'I don't need these.'

'Only fruits and coconut. I knew that you wouldn't take anything else touched by me, so I have brought only fruits and coconut.'

'I am not hungry,' Savitri said.

Ponni persisted and argued, and there was no escape. And so Savitri had to confess, though she felt very awkward while doing it, 'I am resolved never to accept food or shelter which I have not earned.'

'A nice thing you are saying, my lady! What can you do, with your soft hands? I should be dragged to hell if I made you do any work for me ...'

'It is a foolish thing to say. If you don't want me to starve, give me some work. I can cook, scrub, sew. I know a little gardening too. I had a beautiful garden once. I can look after children. Have you no children?'

'Ah, cursed me! We have been married for twenty years and I have promised offerings to all our gods, but I am not blessed yet.'

'What a pity! I have three children. My son is just thirteen. He is very intelligent and knows a lot of things about electricity. My two girls are reading in a school; very intelligent creatures.'

'You are a blessed being, my lady. God will protect you. The difficulty that has risen before you like a mountain will soon vanish like the dew ... Please take this coconut, sister. It rends my heart to see you starve. You have been in the water a long time.'

'I am not hungry,' Savitri said.

Ponni sought her husband out in his workshop. He had just done a little riveting job on a barrow and was arguing his terms with some heat. Ponni called him aside and asked, 'Do you want a halter round your neck?'

'No.'

'Then do something about that lady in there. She has been starving since the morning, and if she dies the police will come on you for murder; and they will be right because you are going about as if she were none of your business but only mine. You were the person who found her, remember.'

'She is a lady, and so I thought I needn't come to that side.'

'Ah, a virtuous man indeed! You wouldn't speak to a lady, would you? Find out something for that lady to do so that she may take her food and live.'

'Let her come and work these bellows. It will be a good piece of work.'

'Wouldn't you like it? A fine high-caste lady to touch these worm-eaten bellows! Think of something else before I come again.' She turned to go. She added, 'If she dies I will tell the police that you killed her, and they will believe it, be sure.'

When she was gone Mari beat his brow and said to his customer, 'I sometimes think that it would be better to let the police take me and hang me than be married to that woman.'

'Why should the police hang you?'

'There is a mad woman in there who won't touch food unless she is given work. Hard enough for men to get work in these days.'

'What sort of woman is she?'

'Go and see her for yourself.'

The customer went in and saw Savitri. He came out and remarked, 'She is an eyeful. Won't somebody marry her? Or I will give her money.' And he made a ribald suggestion.

Mari, after disposing of the customer, went in and told his wife, 'I will go and see if there is anything for this lady, but what are the things she can do?'

'She can cook, sew, and scrub. What more does a woman need to know? She also says that she knows a little gardening.'

Mari went out.

He left the house briskly enough, but as soon as he came to the street he stopped, not having the faintest idea of what he should do. He didn't know how anyone set about getting a job, much less how a woman did it. He had inherited his foundry from his father, and had never applied to anyone for work; and now to go and beg for the sake of that woman ... He resented the idea. For a moment he reflected how free he would have been now if he had let her float down the river: if her fate was good she would have survived it somehow, and if she had been destined to die she would have died in spite of any rescue, and he told himself that he would not have been particularly responsible for her death if he had left her alone. He felt angry with his wife for her fussing. Why couldn't she leave the woman alone? If she didn't want food it was entirely her business. This was what came of allowing too much liberty to women; they ought to be kept under proper control and then all would be well. He felt irritated with himself at his own helplessness before his wife ...

'Did you start out only to stand in the street and meditate?' asked Ponni, peeping out of the house. Mari moved down the road without turning his head. 'You have started walking. Where do you intend to go?' she asked.

'You can leave it to me, and go in,' he shouted back, and felt a great relief at having said something of his own after all. He went down the street and stopped before Ranganna's shop. He occasionally enjoyed sitting on the platform before the shop and chatting with Ranganna and his customers; he had also a hope now that Ranganna might be able to suggest something.

Ranganna received Mari coldly. Mari did not notice it, but moved on to his favourite seat on the platform, and said, 'Well, well, well, how are you, brother?'

'If you let your wife come this way again I will call the police,' said Ranganna.

'That is a big word you are uttering. What has she done?'

'You already owe me an anna, which I don't know when you are going to pay. And that woman walks in as if she owned the shop ...'

Mari saw that it was no time for companionship. He rose to his feet, saying: 'You talk too much. I fear you may suffer from sore throat tonight. You have not the guts to stop a woman from snatching a thing in your shop. Why do you come and complain to me?'

He crossed some of the lanes and cross-paths and went into the Brahmin street. She was a Brahmin lady and somebody might take her in. He stood at the beginning of the street, reflectively looking at the houses, wondering who was most likely to be useful to him. There was the big landlord in whose house Ponni had, during certain seasons, done odd jobs; there was the teacher with whom Mari was familiar, having repaired the pulley over his well a number of times and soldered a leaky pot an equal number of times; then there was the other landlord, the young man with a violent temper; and his brother-in-law in the opposite house; and the police inspector; and the man who had married the big landlord's second daughter; and then the village accountant.

He drew blank here. In the big landlord's house they wouldn't have anything to do with an adventuress, the teacher was too poor to burden himself with a guest or a servant, the young landlord was tight-fisted, and on the threshold of the police inspector's house Mari changed his mind. 'Keep out of his way,' his instinct told him.

Mari tramped the village streets up and down, spoke to all sorts of people about the woman, but received no help from anyone. Everyone was interested, curious, and even excited. They offered to go to his house and have a look at her, but none could give her work, though all offered her their charity.

Mari started back home, completely depressed. He resolved to suggest once again bellows-blowing for the lady. While passing before the old village temple, he stopped and fervently prayed for a way out. And an idea flashed on him.

The priest of the temple lived in the same street. The old man was sitting on the pyol of his house with a couple of his grandchildren playing about him. Mari stood before him and said, 'My salutations to you, my noble master.'

'Who are you?' asked the old man, half closing his eyes in his effort to catch the identity of his visitor.

'I am Mari, my master, your humble slave.'

'Mari, you are a vile hypocrite,' said the old man.

'What sin have I committed to deserve these harsh words?'

'I sent my boy thrice to your place, and thrice have you postponed and lied. It was after all for a petty, insignificant repair that I sent for you.'

'Nobody came and called me, master. I swear I would have dropped everything and come running if only the lightest whisper had reached me. Whom did you send?'

'Why should I send anyone? After all, some petty repair – I thought I might have a word with you about it if you came to the temple; but you are a godless creature; no wonder your wife is barren. How can you hope to prosper without the grace of Muruga?'

'Yours are words of wisdom. I promise that hereafter I will come to the temple twice a week and bring him a coconut once a month. Now, here I am awaiting your command.'

The old man was appeased by this submission and said, 'It is not ten minutes' work for a workman like you. Wait a minute.'

'I obey your command,' said Mari.

The old man got down from the pyol, looked at Mari, shading his eyes with his webbed, shrunken hands, and said, 'You don't look too well, not a quarter of what you were before.' It was only in the old man's eyes that Mari looked pulled down, but, for the sake of politeness, Mari felt obliged to agree. 'I too am growing old. All kinds of ills and bothers ...'

The old man went in and returned half an hour later carrying three old umbrellas in his hands; behind him followed a youngster – employed in the house for cleaning the cow-shed – carrying on his head a basket filled with junk. With difficulty the old man unfurled the umbrellas, and said: 'These are practically new, will be good enough to use for another ten years, if only a little rib or two is fixed up. I have been telling the boys to take these to you for ages, and they have all been postponing and lying. Everyone is a vile hypocrite.'

'I will make these brand-new,' Mari said. He examined them, reflecting gloomily on the hours he would have to spend over these wretched things; and the old man was a miser.

The old man took out of the basket a bunch of grappling-hooks, four brass locks, a zinc bucket, and a blunt scythe, all of which needed very badly Mari's healing touch. Mari reflected, 'Two days of profitless labour,' and said, 'I will make these brand-new for you, master.'

'What will you charge me for the whole lot?'

'I will take anything you give. What I value most is your blessing.'

'How long will you take to repair these?'

'Three days, master.'

'Can't you do it in a day?'

'I will try,' said Mari, and then opened the subject. 'Would you not like somebody to sweep the gods' shrine, scrub it, and tend the garden?'

'No,' said the old man. 'What am I here for?'

'Ah,' began Mari, his wit sharpened by desperation, 'you have nobler work to do, my master,' and told him about Savitri.

'What have you to do with her?' asked the old man.

'Nothing, master, except that I have given her shelter in our humble home.'

'Why have you done it?'

'How can I say? Fate thrusts such troubles on us at times.'

'What do you care for her?'

'I really don't. My wife has taken a liking to her. It is really her doing, and she won't let me rest till I find some work for this woman.'

'If she won't let you rest, thrash her; that is the way to keep women sane. In these days you fellows are impotent mugs, and let your women ride you about.' After this homily the old man said, 'I won't have any woman in the temple. She will start some mischief or other and then the temple will get a bad name.' Mari took upon himself the task of assuring the old man of Savitri's character, but the old man would not accept it. 'There must be something wrong about her if she has no home and has to seek a livelihood outside; her husband must have driven her out. Why will a husband drive a wife out?'

'I know some sorrow has brought her out of her home,' said Mari. He had told everyone that Savitri had been found wandering on the outskirts of the village; he had not told anyone how she had really been found, fearing that it might lead to questions about his nocturnal movements. 'She is resolved to work and earn. It has grown in her as a madness. She has been starving and won't touch even fruit. I am afraid she may die in our house.'

'Drive her out and don't worry about her,' said the old man.

Mari felt desperate. He felt that it might be useful to remind the other of his debt. He said, 'I will repair these things in a day, and do any other work you may want me to do, but please let this woman work in your temple.'

'The iron bands around our grain-barrel are rather loose. Will you fix them up?'

'Yes, master, and you needn't give me an anna for all the work. Only, please employ this woman.'

'I am not unwilling to have a servant, but where am I to find the money to pay her? You fellows nowadays don't bring offerings to the god. In the days of your fathers and grandfathers I could have engaged ten such servants for the temple. Nowadays you fellows want to worship the god free; no offerings, not even a piece of coconut.'

Mari promised to mend his irreligious ways and also undertook to reform some of his friends, and said, 'She won't demand much. Just give her something to live on, and she will be contented. Even rice will do, but please engage her. I will always be grateful to you for this kindness.' He significantly lifted the grappling-hooks and said, 'A little welding may also be necessary for this.' He then looked at the umbrellas fixedly.

The priest said, 'If I give her a half measure of rice and a quarter of an anna a day, will she be prepared to accept it and work?'

'I think she will, master.'

'If so, bring her here. I will have a look at her. If I don't see anything wrong – people can't deceive me, I can measure anyone at a glance – I will engage her. But not a grain more than a half measure.'

Ponni said to Savitri: 'My husband has found some work for you. I don't know if you will like it. I am sure if he had used his intelligence a little more he could have found a better job for you.'

Mari said fervently, 'I swear by all our gods that nothing better could be found. I searched everywhere and asked everyone.'

'Who are you to say what is good enough for this lady?'

'I never said any such thing. I saw everyone from the Headman down.'

'Do you mean to imply that what you have found is the best for the lady?'

Savitri cut into the middle of this discussion: 'Any work which will keep my life in my body, though why it should I can't say, is suitable for me. I don't want to depend on anyone hereafter for the miserable handful of food I need every day.'

'You say hard words, my lady. May God grant that the sorrow which has risen before you like a mountain may soon vanish like the dew! May the God on the Hill dispel the pain in your soul!' With this prelude she told Savitri what work her husband had found for her.

Savitri felt very happy. She saw a new life opening before her. What more fitting life, she thought, could one choose than serving a god in his shrine? A half measure of rice was more than what she deserved, she felt. She could manage very well with it. She would dedicate her life to the service of God, numb her senses and memory, forget the world, and spend the rest of her years thus and die. No husband, home, or children. Ah, children! She would harden herself not to yearn for them. She would pray for them at the shrine night and day, and God would protect them: they could grow, go their ways, and tackle life according as fate had ordained for each of them. What was this foolish yearning for children, this dragging attachment? One ought to do one's duty and then drift away. Did the birds and the animals worry about their young ones after they had learnt to move? Why should she alone think of them night and day? Babu,

Sumati, and Kamala were quite grown-up now; but Kamala gave no end of trouble over bath and food. Suppose she grew dirty and emaciated? Savitri dismissed this fear with a desperate effort. They were his children. He had paid for the midwife and for clothes, and for everything. He had said that she had no right to wake them up. Into this jumble of reflections Ponni intruded with, 'Madam, don't you like this work?'

'I do. I do like it very much. When shall we go there?'

'Tomorrow morning. It is late now ... I beg of you not to fast any longer. Please eat at least two of these plantains and drink a little of the coconut water. Please rest here tonight. You will be making me very proud and happy if you will kindly accept my hospitality for just this night. You can go away tomorrow morning.' Ponni's eyes glistened with tears as she made this request. She added, 'I will prostrate myself at your feet and never rise unless you say "Yes." '

Savitri said, 'All right. I will take something.'

Eating food that was her own had grown into a perfect obsession, and so she needed some excuse for accepting the plantains and the coconut. She comforted her conscience by saying that this was the very last time in her life she would be doing it, and that it was her duty to show a little more regard for Ponni's feelings. She mentioned her hunger as the least urgent of the reasons.

Next morning Mari and his wife escorted Savitri to the priest's house. Savitri went through it all as if in a trance, unconvinced of the reality of things. How could the one now tramping a village street with unknown people, in search of employment, like a boy just out of college, be the old Savitri of South Extension, wife of So-and-so? Gangu, her old friend, could not have done a thing like this!

They stood before the priest's house. Mari shouted, 'Oh, master, master!' A little boy came to the street and said, 'Grandpa is at his prayers and asks you not to shout.'

After some time the old man came out, wrapped in a deep-red shawl. He went to the pyol and sat on it, muttering: 'Couldn't you wait till I finished my prayers? No chance for a man to meditate in this world with blackguards like you about. Why couldn't you have come a little later? Hm, let bygones be bygones. You are of course come about that woman. Am I right?'

'Absolutely right, my master, that is what I have come about.'

The old man laughed, rather pleased with himself at guessing Mari's mission so correctly. He shaded his eyes, looked at Ponni, and asked, 'Is this the woman?' And added, 'What is the matter with you, madam, that you should run away from home?'

'This is my wife, Ponni; she is not the one who wants to work. She has merely accompanied the other lady. This is the lady.' He whispered to Savitri, 'Please move a little to this side, madam, so that he may see you properly.' Savitri shifted her position, feeling awkward at having to exhibit herself. The old man said: 'What is the use of coming all the way if you keep yourself invisible? Come nearer. Let us have a look at you. I never decide without looking at a person, and no one can deceive me. I can measure a person at a glance, understand? Come nearer.' Savitri blushed, hung down her head, and felt very uneasy at having to display herself, with the sun's rays illuminating her on one side ...

The old man looked at her and said he was surprised that a person like her was wandering in the world unattached. He put to her a number of questions which Savitri could not answer. When she opened her lips once or twice to say something, she found herself trembling and unable to say a word. Ponni intervened and said, 'Why should you ask these questions? There are wounds which must not be prodded.' Mari tried to check her. He whispered, 'Keep quiet. You will be irritating him.' To which she replied aloud, 'You can keep quiet if you like. I will talk to my master.' She asked the old man, 'Will you be offended if I talk to you?'

'Who are you? Oh, you are ... I know. Why should I be offended? Anybody may talk to me. I am a servant of God. I am an old man.'

Saying this made him lose the thread of his previous talk with Savitri. Ponni said abruptly, 'Master, I am like a granddaughter to you, and I will talk to you freely. God has not blessed me with an artful tongue. I utter what I have in my soul.'

'True, true. One must utter the strictest truth,' said the old man.

'So will I. I want to ask you plainly whether you are going to engage this lady or not.'

'I am not,' said the old man promptly.

'All right, we will go home. Come on,' said Ponni. Savitri felt dejected. So back again to the life of charity and dependence. Mari apologized to the old man: 'Please don't be offended. She doesn't mean it.'

'I do mean it,' said Ponni. 'You promise one thing and do another. You are not fortunate enough to have a lady like this in your temple, that is all. And I will tell you another thing: send someone to fetch all the broken umbrellas and rubbish you have sent for repairs. If you don't send someone immediately I will throw it all into the manure dump ...'

The mention of the old umbrellas had a good effect. The old man said, 'Woman, you are too impatient. Who said that this person would not be engaged?'

'You. Why do you ask things that are painful?'

'Just to know if I am dealing with the right person.'

'That is not the way, my master. I need not tell you, master, because you are learned and wise, whereas I am a stupid woman. You can see her, and take her in good trust and on our word, and if you find anything wrong with her later, you can dismiss her. There are questions which hurt one, you mustn't ask them.'

'I only want to know why she has run away from home. Without knowing it, how can I have her in the temple? If its reputation suffers ...' Savitri shuddered at the implication of this remark.

Ponni said, 'There are a hundred reasons for a person to leave home. If this man by my side tries any new tricks I will walk out of home, and that will be the last he will see of me, and people who ask why and what, how and when, will get the proper reply from me. You want us to do all sorts of things for you. Why should we do it? Just for the sake of friendship. And yet you won't do us a little good turn for the same friendship.'

'I never said I wouldn't do it, my good woman.'

'Will you engage this lady or not? That is what I want to know.'

'Of course I will. I am getting old. I really want somebody to keep the temple tidy.'

The temple had been built fifty years before by a local philanthropist, and dedicated to Subramanya, the peacock-enthroned god, the young son of Shiva. It was a small structure of brick and mortar, the inner shrine surmounted by a carved turret, now discoloured by time and weather, with an open circular corridor running between the shrine and the high outer wall.

Savitri and her friends waited in the street while the old man fumbled with a bunch of keys and opened the tall doors at the temple portal. Over it stood a mossy, dun-coloured peacock which once upon a time must have been as white as the plaster it was made of. The priest pushed the doors with his chest; they parted with a groan.

'Come in. Don't try to spend the whole day standing there,' the old man said, and walked in.

'Have you no kinder words to say, sir?' Ponni retorted.

'Hush!' Mari said, 'he doesn't mean any harm. You will irritate him if you speak like this.'

Ponni turned on her husband with a hiss. 'Go away and mind your own business, do you understand? We can look after ourselves quite well without you.' Mari hesitated. Ponni cried, 'Now begone! Go and open your tool-shed and earn some money. There may be people waiting for you. Don't waste the morning gaping at us. We can look after ourselves quite well.'

'Can't I wait till the shrine is opened, so that I may prostrate myself at God's feet before I begin the day's work?'

'All right. Sit down there. Don't follow us about with your remarks. Sit down there and wait till the shrine is opened and then disappear. I hope you understand simple words.'

Mari grunted something and sat down at the portal. Ponni said, 'It is no use losing one's temper.' And to Savitri, 'Come on, madam. Don't mind him; he doesn't know how to behave when there are respectable people about.' The priest had gone round the corridor once and was back again at the starting-point. He was furious. 'Do you want me to be telling you "Come on, come on" at every step? I go round thinking you are following me, and talking, and you are still here!'

'It will cost nothing to repeat your words to us again.'

'Here?' asked the old man, horrified. 'What can I tell you here? I was going round showing you where you have to do what, and you are content to stay behind. You people will kill me one day, making me walk round and round this corridor till I am dizzy. I am not in the prime of life now. Keep it in mind.' He hobbled along, tapping his staff on the cobbled pavement. Savitri and Ponni followed him. He pointed at various corners saying, 'This is where you will have to do a little tidying.' He stopped at almost every bit of litter, saying, 'This must not be here, do you understand? This is what you will get paid for.' When they came to the portion of the corridor that was overshadowed by the branches of an immense mango tree growing in the field outside, he spent nearly half an hour pointing at every leaf which the tree had shed down. 'I have asked those rascals to do something about their tree and they won't do it. I will lop off these branches one day; let them drag me to a law court if they like. I am ready to spend my entire fortune on the lawyers.'

'Why?' Savitri ventured. 'These branches give very good shade here.'

'Do you like the shade?'

'Yes, very much.'

'Very well then,' said the old man as if Savitri's opinion decided the issue. 'I am glad to hear it, but be certain to keep the ground here clean; that is what you are getting your half measure of rice and a quarter of an anna for. Under this pile of withered leaves there may be cobras, and I don't like our devotees to be bitten to death here; devotees are rare enough without cobras.' Dry leaves on the cobbles crackled under their feet. At this corner there was a shanty created by enclosing the angles of the high wall with corrugated iron sheets and wooden boards. It had a rickety door. The old man unlocked it, saying, 'You have no home, I believe.'

'If she had a home here you would never have seen her,' Ponni said.

'You can live in this if you like,' the old man said. 'Come in and have a look. It is not bad.' Savitri stooped into it. It was very dark, light and air being admitted only by the chinks in the joints of the iron sheets. Rats jumped about, startled, and there was some flapping of wings above, which might be bats or sparrows. In a corner there was a gilded pedestal for carrying the image of God in procession, two or three empty kerosene tins, and some gunny-sacks. There was a blackened mud oven in another corner. Savitri withdrew her head and breathed again. 'You can cook your food there, and shut yourself in when you have no work,' said the old man. 'But bear in mind that it is a special concession, and don't imagine that you can demand it as a right. All that you can demand is your half measure of rice and a quarter of an anna, and not this.'

'Are you giving it to me as a charity?'

'Absolutely. What doubt is there? If you have any doubt ask anyone if anyone was ever given that room.'

Savitri said, 'I will do without the room. I will manage somehow.'

'How will you manage? Do you think I will leave the shrine open and that you can go and live there? I would never do that.'

'I never thought so, but I will manage. This corridor will be home enough for me.'

'Here?' the old man exclaimed, looking up. 'With the wind and sun and rain, not to mention any scoundrel who might think of jumping over the wall ... No, no. It won't do. The temple has a name to maintain. I won't have you here if you refuse to have this room; but don't demand it as a right.'

Ponni said, 'If you don't like this, come to my house when you have no work to do here.'

Charity! Charity! Savitri was appalled by the amount of it that threatened one. 'All right, I will live in this,' she said, choosing the lesser charity.

The old man opened a back door and took them into the garden. A few plants, nerium, jasmine, and one or two nondescripts, grew there. There was a mud-walled well in the middle of the garden.

'I was told that you knew something of gardening. I should like you to prove it,' said the old man. 'Here is the water, any amount of it.'

Ponni protested: 'What do you mean by it, sir? You want her to do the work of four persons. You want her to do this and that endlessly in the temple; all right, we won't grumble about it. But what is this? This is not the temple.'

'This is also a part of the temple. God must have His flowers every day.'

'I know all that, but you can engage someone else to do the gardening; we won't do it.'

'Very well,' said the old man. 'She need not do it; she needn't do anything.'

'What do you take her for? What do you think she is?'

'Whatever she is, we are not concerned with it now; she may be a king's wife or a judge's cousin. What do I care? I am a servant of Subramanya, and I don't care for anyone in this world.'

Finally Savitri intervened and said that she considered tending the garden the most agreeable part of the work. The old man spent nearly an hour in the garden. He stooped over every plant, and had a comment to make on every leaf.

When they came back to the portals he saw Mari squatting on the ground and asked, 'Fellow, why are you moping here?'

'I am waiting to prostrate myself before the god.'

'I am not opening the shrine now. Come in the evening. Don't imagine that I am at the beck and call of every guttersnipe in the place. Come in the evening.'

When they were about to start out Ponni asked, 'What are you doing for food today?'

'No need to think of it now. Time enough for it. I am getting my half measure of rice.'

'You will get it tomorrow,' Ponni said. 'Do you tell me that you are going to starve till tomorrow? You have starved enough, I think.'

'Why should anybody starve?' the old man asked. 'Come to my house. I will give you food.' Savitri declined the offer. Ponni suggested to the old man that he might give a measure of rice in advance. The old man revolved it in his mind and agreed. He added, 'But the quarter of an anna, she will get it only tomorrow. On no account will I give the money in advance.'

'What can she do, sir, with bare rice? She has to buy a little salt and something else to go with the rice.'

The old man covered his ears with his hands. 'Don't talk. I am listening to too much talk. I won't, simply won't, give the money in advance, that is all. Don't stand there and talk till my ears ache.'

Ponni said, 'But, sir, my master, will you give her a little firewood and a small vessel?'

'All right. I never say "No" to a reasonable request.' Savitri was annoyed at the number of petty details that living demanded. Ponni was overjoyed. 'I will procure you a little buttermilk and salt.'

'No,' said Savitri emphatically. 'If you bring anything I will throw it into the well.'

'How are you going to eat plain rice?'

'I can do it. If I have to take buttermilk and salt from you, why should I work for the rice alone? You could give me that too!'

Before midday Savitri had swept the corridor clean not only of the dry leaves thrown down by the mango branches but also of all the coconut shells and faded flowers dropped there by devotees. She dug the plants and watered them. She felt a great thrill when she lighted the oven and cooked a little rice for herself. 'This is my own rice, my very own; and I am not obliged to anyone for this. This is nobody's charity to me.' She felt triumphant, and a great peace descended on her as she drank a little water, came out of the kitchen, and lay down in the shade of the mango tree. She lay with her head on the threshold of the shanty, gazing at the blue sky and at the deep green of the mango foliage. Her satisfaction at having eaten food of her own was slightly spoilt by the memory of the concessions she had to accept. She soothed her mind by telling it that she would forgo a portion of her wage for some days to compensate for the vessel and the firewood. From tomorrow she would go out and gather faggots ...

She felt happy to recollect the firmness with which she had declined Ponni's numerous offers ...

It had been rather hard to swallow bare rice, cooked in water, without adding even salt, but it was worth it because it enhanced one's sense of victory.

The cool air, the mango shade, and the noonday glare induced a drowse. She fell asleep. The sound of a bamboo staff tapping the cobbles awoke her. 'Hey, get up, get up,' the old man cried. Savitri opened her eyes and sat up.

'It is four o'clock and you are still sleeping!'

Savitri got up and noticed that the sun had gone down the other side of the mango tree and was throwing a beam of light on the wall of the shrine.

'You think you are employed to sleep?' asked the old man, and hobbled about, peering closely at the ground. 'You have left the garbage of a week; why haven't you swept this properly?'

Savitri looked along the way he pointed. 'I don't see anything,' she said, determined to overcome her timidity.

'There, there,' the old man said, pointing with his stick. 'Don't tell me that you are blind.'

'I have good sight, but I don't see anything anywhere. I have swept the whole place thoroughly.'

'Have you? I am very glad to hear it. You appear to be a person who knows what to do. I like such persons. I don't like slackers. Come with me.'

He unlocked the door of the shrine. They entered the dark shrine, which smelt of burnt lamp-oil, flowers, incense, and bats. The old man lighted a couple of tall bronze lamps. He asked, 'Where are the flowers?'

'Which flowers?'

'Which flowers!' the old man repeated. 'Flowers in the garden. Don't ask "Which garden?" Have you not gathered the flowers yet?'

Savitri went to the garden and brought a handful of flowers. The old man took the flowers and entered the inner shrine. Savitri brought together her palms and prayed to the idol: 'Protect Sumati, Babu, and Kamala. Let them all eat well and grow.

Please see that they are not unhappy.' The old man said, 'This is the first day and so I don't mind if you are a little slack, but from tomorrow I won't show the same patience. Now take a rag and clean all the lamps and fill them with fresh oil.'

'Where can I find a rag?'

'Create one, young woman. You mustn't ask me where is this and what is that. I don't care if you have to tear a piece out of your *sari*. Work should not suffer, and the good name of the temple must be maintained at any cost. What is the use of having you here if you have got to be plaguing me like this? That blackguard and his wife and everybody comes to plead for you. I don't care for anyone here; be pleased to know that. That woman may have the worst tongue in the village, but I am equal to it.' The old man went on talking as he bent over the idol and picked up the faded flowers on it, polished its ornaments, and decorated it with fresh flowers.

At five o'clock visitors began to arrive. Rumour had gone abroad that a mysterious woman was engaged in the temple, and this brought in more visitors than was usual. Everybody looked about, stared at Savitri, nudged each other, went round the corridor, prostrated before the image, and gave the old man the offerings. So many people kept staring at her that Savitri slipped out and shut herself in the shanty.

When the voices ceased, late in the evening, she came out. In the inner shrine the old man was bundling up the coconuts, fruits, and coins that he had collected. He was very pleased. 'People are once again becoming godly,' he said, his small face creased in a smile, and shining in the light near the idol. He threw a piece of coconut at her and said, 'Take it, it is your share.'

'I don't want it. My share is only a half measure of rice.'

'Take the coconut also. You are a good woman, you deserve it.'

'No. I never eat coconut.'

The old man was about to go home. As she saw him at the door, Savitri felt suddenly desolate. She would have to be all alone in this dark temple, with the dim oil-lamp, and stars, and the massive tree looming over the wall. The old man said, 'If you are afraid to remain here, you may come to my house. You can spend the night with the womenfolk in my house.'

'Of what should I be afraid?' asked Savitri. Was there no escape from fear and charity?

'How can I say?' said the old man.

'I am not afraid of anything,' said Savitri, and added, 'I am living in God's house and He will protect me.'

These brave words did not sustain her long. After the old man departed she regretted she had not accepted his offer. Everything terrified her. The whole air was oppressive; the surrounding objects assumed monstrous shapes in the solitary hour. She fled to her shanty and bolted the door. She lit a cotton wick floating on oil in a little mud pan.

As the hours advanced and the stillness grew deeper, her fears also increased. She was furious with herself at this: 'What despicable creations of God are we that we can't exist without a support. I am like a bamboo pole which cannot stand without a wall to support it ...'

And she grew homesick. A nostalgia for children, home, and accustomed comforts seized her. Lying here on the rough floor, beside the hot flickering lamp, her soul racked with fears, she couldn't help contrasting the comfort, security, and un-loneliness of her home. When she shut the door and put out the lights, how comforting the bed felt and how well one could sleep! Not this terrible state ... And then the children. What a void they created! 'I must see them; I must see Babu, I must see Sumati, and I must see Kamala. Oh ...' But what about the fiery vows, and the coming out at midnight?

The futility, the frustration, and her own inescapable weakness made her cry and sob. 'A wretched fate wouldn't let me drown first time. I can't go near the water again. This is defeat. I accept it. I am no good for this fight. I am a bamboo pole ... Perhaps Sumati and Kamala have not had their hair combed for ages now ...'

In the morning Savitri went over to the old man's house and told him, 'I am leaving.'

'What has happened?'

'I can't keep away from my children and home.'

'All right. I never asked you to come and work.'

'Here is the vessel I borrowed yesterday, here is the key of the room.'

'Are the things in it safe?'

'Yes. As you see, I am carrying nothing with me.'

'Hm! There is nothing there worth taking.'

They were silent for some time and he asked, 'Why are you standing there? I gave you your yesterday's wage in advance.'

'Yes,' she said, though he had given only the rice and not the money. 'I am only waiting to take leave of you.'

'All right, you can go. God's blessings be on you. Don't leave your children and wander about hereafter.'

She hesitated before Ponni's house for a moment. Her first impulse was to go away without telling her. A defeat needed no proclamation ...

She knocked on the door. Ponni invited her in. 'No. I am going. I have just come to tell you I am going home.'

Ponni was overjoyed to hear it.

'At first I thought of going away without telling you.'

'Ah, how could you?'

'No, I couldn't. I will remember all my life your affection and help. God will reward you for your goodness. May He bless you with a child soon!'

'How are you going to reach the town?'

'Only two or three miles. I will manage; don't worry yourself.'

'Oh no, impossible,' said Ponni, and came out. She shouted to her neighbour: 'Sister, please keep an eye on this house. There is nobody in.'

They walked down the tree-flanked highway. Ponni explained her husband's absence. 'A cart broke down somewhere and people came and pulled the poor man right out of bed, even before dawn. Poor man, he really does work hard.' She stopped every passing bullock-cart to ask, 'Are you going townward? Will you take a passenger?' At last they found a cartman willing to take in a passenger. Ponni disputed with heat the fare the cartman demanded. It took nearly half an hour for a settlement to be reached.

'Now get into the cart, I will walk back home,' Ponni said. 'Go with a cheerful face. Don't look so sad. Remember: men are good creatures, but you must never give way to them. Be firm and they will behave.'

'All right,' Savitri said. 'I will remember it.' She was about to ask Ponni and her husband to visit her at South Extension, but checked herself. 'Who am I to invite a guest?'

'Murugan's blessings on you. He will protect you and your children. Mari occasionally comes to the town to earn an extra anna. I will ask him to see you,' said Ponni. She wiped her eyes and stood in the middle of the road, watching, till the cart was out of sight.

CHAPTER ELEVEN

The children sat round under the hall bulb.

Babu said, 'I don't like the look of things. We must do something. I don't believe Father.'

Kamala said, 'Father has told us that she has gone to see grandfather.'

'I don't believe it, because if she has ... You are still children. You may believe what he says, but I don't. Don't ask why.' At this Kamala showed signs of bursting into tears. Sumati put her arms around her and frowned at Babu. 'Why do you frighten the child by talking in this mysterious manner?'

Babu said, 'I was only joking. Don't cry. Mother has gone to see Grandpa, she will be back soon. Don't cry, little one. I will take you to Chandru's house tomorrow and show you the electric tram he has made.'

Kamala lifted her tear-filled eyes to him and asked, 'Is it a promise?'

'Yes.'

'Will you swear that you won't break it?'

'I never swear. If you don't believe me, don't believe me, that is all.'

'If you do, I will cry,' said Kamala, and showed signs of fulfilling the threat. Babu said, 'You mustn't cry. If you do, you will never be able to read your lessons, pass your exams, and become a doctor.'

'I don't want to be a doctor,' said Kamala petulantly.

'What else do you want to be? You said that when you were grown-up you wished to be a doctor like our lady doctor.'

'What do you care what I am going to be? It is none of your business.'

'Don't be impertinent. Learn to behave before your elders,' Babu said hotly, at which Kamala threatened to break down once again.

Sumati said, 'Now, will you leave us alone or not? I will call the cook.' She called the cook and told him, 'Babu is teasing me and Kamala, and won't leave us alone.'

The cook held up a finger and warned Babu: 'I will tell Father as soon as he comes home. Leave them alone, and go and read your books.'

'Mind your own business. Who are you to command me?'

The cook sat down on the carpet cross-legged and said, 'Look me in the eyes and say it.' He looked fixedly at Babu. Babu said, 'All right, I will. I am not afraid of your powers of magic.' The girls screamed and covered Babu's eyes with their hands, and also his mouth, in order to stop it from uttering further blasphemies.

'Take away your hands,' the cook said, looking wild.

'No, no. Forgive him for our sake. He won't say such things again. Please take your eyes off him.' The belief was that a person who looked into the cook's eyes at certain moments would be turned to stone. They had been told that many of the furlong and mile stones in the place were once human beings who had dared to look into the cook's eyes; after they became stones the Government people came along, chiselled them into shape, and carved miles and furlongs on them.

The girls very nearly threw Babu down and held him away from the cook's visual range. Babu was gasping for breath. Ranga came in from somewhere at the moment, and the cook appealed to him to decide whether Babu was to be petrified or not. Ranga, after a moment's thought, said, 'Leave him alone. He is more or less motherless now.' He then passed on to scandal: 'What is this that people are saying? I thought things looked rather queer ...' He related how a friend of his working in the Engineer's house overheard the Engineer's wife saying that a certain lady's departure seemed to be rather abrupt, and as far as she knew (she also belonged to Talapur and received letters from there) there was nothing the matter with the old man; and then Ranga's friend had heard something about a new person in the office and complications at home.

The cook said, 'It may be true or it may not be. Why do you waste your time listening to gossip? Our business is to do our business. We don't care what happens to anybody. There was some talk about it this evening at the coffee-house, and I said that the departure was rather abrupt and as far as we knew there was neither letter nor telegram about the old man's health, and if that is so how could anyone be compelled to believe the story? It is no use compelling people to believe this or that, and I told them the truth, namely, that So-and-so has not been coming home punctually of late. Was there anything wrong in what I said?'

'No, none,' said Ranga. 'You spoke only the truth, didn't you?'

Kamala asked, 'Are you talking about Mother?'

'Why?'

'Because if it is about Mother we want to know what you are saying.'

'No. It is about someone else,' the cook said. 'Why should we talk about your mother? You were talking about someone else, weren't you, Ranga?'

'Yes, yes.'

'It was about my uncle in the town who has a lot of money but is not coming home when he should, and so people want to shut him out of the house.'

'Where does he go?'

'He has a number of concubines, and he stays with them.'

'What are concubines?' Kamala asked.

Babu warned Ranga: 'You are uttering bad words before the children. Take care.'

'What is bad about the word? Don't we say "wife"? It is a similar word.'

'Why don't you drop it if it is a bad word?' Sumati asked. Kamala said, 'We don't want to hear any bad word now, so leave it alone. Go on, tell me: if it was about your uncle and not about Mother you were speaking, why did you mention Grandpa in Talapur?'

'My uncle's sister's grandfather is also in Talapur and she went to see him because he was unwell.'

'But you said that no letter or telegram arrived.'

'Yes. No letter or telegram arrived, yet she went off rather abruptly thinking that grandfather was ill ... I will tell you more about it while you eat. Come in for dinner. It is getting late.'

Father came home. He passed straight through to the kitchen, stood on the threshold, and watched the children eat.

'How many runs did you make this evening, Babu?'

'I got only one chance to bat, and I made twenty runs.'

'Is that all? When I was your age I never made anything under fifty. It was because I ate well and was strong. You are puny and won't eat. Look at the rice on your plate! It is a quarter of what I used to eat at your age. Eat well, young man, and you will be able to score more runs. Here, bring some more rice for this boy.'

Father looked at Kamala and said: 'Why is your hair so rumpled? Did you comb and braid it this evening?'

'I forgot to do it, Father,' said Kamala.

Sumati said, 'She gave such a lot of trouble that I couldn't do it. Every day Mother had such a lot of trouble ...'

Ramani looked at Kamala reprovingly and said, 'Is this how you conduct yourself? Your hair is standing on end and you look like a sick person. You must be a good girl now. Sumati, you must attend to her properly. This won't do.' He watched them till they finished their dinner and then went in to change.

After they had washed their hands Babu managed to take Sumati aside, and said, 'Do you know what Janamma told me this evening?'

'No.'

'That Mother has not gone to Talapur. I suspected that there was some such thing.'

'Where is she?'

'Who can say? She might have been carried away by robbers or eaten by lions or tigers.'

Sumati trembled, and put her hands to her eyes. Babu sternly told her, 'None of that. Don't create a scene. If you cry I will never speak to you again.'

'What are we to do about it now?' Sumati asked.

'You leave it to me. I will speak to Father and ask him to search.'

'He may get angry with you.'

'If he gets angry I will do something else.' He had already made up his mind, as a last measure, to inform the police through his friend Chandru.

Babu waited till Kamala went to bed, and tiptoed to his father's room. He stood at the doorway and peeped in. Father was on his rattan lounge with a novel in his hand. Babu could see only Father's back and so was unable to foresee how he would be received. He wished he could get a view of his face, and tiptoed away back to his desk. Though he opened his geography and looked at it, he could not follow a single line. He felt restless. He felt that while he was sniffing at his cursed geography, his mother might be losing the last chance of being saved. He threw down the book and went once again to his father's room. He hesitated for a moment, looking at the back of Father's head ... Suppose Father started beating him the moment Mother was mentioned? If he did, Babu would wrench away, run out of the house, and tell Chandru to tell the police ... But why not wait a little while and try to catch Father some other time? He smothered this suggestion and resolutely walked in and stood before his father.

'Finished your studies for the night?' asked Father, looking over his book.

'Yes.'

'Then go and sleep.'

'All right, Father. But I have come to talk about Mother.'

'What about her?'

'Is she alive?' And saying this he burst into tears. Ramani was slightly frightened. He himself had not been quite easy in mind since the morning. It was three days since she had left, and still there was no sign of her. While the Strong Man in him said that she couldn't have gone far and that she was bound to return when she regained sense, the Weak Man, so long unnoticed by himself, constantly pricked him with the reminder that she had been gone two days and three nights now; and suppose she had done something very rash and foolish or something had happened to her, how was he to answer the children, her people, and everybody? People would talk: 'The wife of the Secretary of the Engladia Insurance Company ...' He shuddered. If anything happened he would have to pack out of Malgudi ... And now this boy.

'Why do you cry?' he asked. Babu sobbed that he had learnt that Mother had not gone to Talapur and he had known that she hadn't gone there. Ramani felt angry. This little boy to come and cause a disturbance with his wild imaginings. 'Look here, I don't like this sort of thing. Don't listen to stupid lies. Go and sleep.' The boy stood still, showed no signs of moving, and his sobbing increased. Ramani looked at him in helpless anger. He felt like slapping him; he would have done it if Savitri had been there. Now he couldn't do it. The boy seemed to have inherited something of his mother's hysteria. He might create a very noisy scene with the other children joining in. He took Babu's hand, drew him nearer, and said, 'Don't cry. Your mother is safe. You are a big boy; you play cricket and all that; how can you cry like a baby if your mother is absent for a little while?'

'It is not that. It is because I suspect things,' Babu said, blowing his nose, considerably mollified by his father's manner. He told his father what he had heard from Janamma. Ramani felt very uncomfortable; he was frightened of the boy; he couldn't stay in his company any longer. He rose from his lounge and said, 'I never knew that you would feel so unhappy. I will go to the post office and send a telegram asking your mother to return at once.'

'Is she really there?'

'Of course. Why do you doubt it?' He dressed hurriedly and started out. 'I have some other business too. I may return late. If you are all afraid to be alone, you can ask the cook to sleep in the hall.'

Babu announced to his sisters, 'Father will be late, and he says the cook may sleep in the hall.' Kamala threw up her pillow for joy. Sumati ran in to inform the cook. Babu followed her and whispered, 'Father has gone to send a telegram to Mother. She will be here very soon. Father wasn't angry with me at all.'

Ramani drove about the streets aimlessly, wondering what steps he should take now. After some time it occurred to him that he might see his friend Naidu, the Police Inspector, and talk things over with him. He might be able to help. He drove the car to the Inspector's quarters behind the Central Police Station in Market Road.

'Hallo, Ramani!' the Inspector said. 'What a rare bird you are nowadays! What brings you here, theft, larceny, or arson? What can I do for you?'

'I just passed this way and thought I might as well drop in,' said Ramani. He stayed with the Inspector for half an hour exchanging town gossip, and left.

He drove the car down Market Road and North Street, and reached the river. 'Why have I come here?' he asked himself. 'How does one search for a lost wife?' He sat in the car, peering across the sands into the darkness as if expecting his wife to rise from the water and come to the car. He stayed for a long time thus. He hated himself for worrying about things. He hated Savitri for bringing him to this pass, and he hated Babu for disturbing his peace. 'Everything is a bother, no peace of mind in this life.' He brooded and speculated and then said, 'I will wait for a day longer.' He felt relieved at having found a way out of the present difficulty, however vague the exit might be. He reversed the car and retraced his way. His heart was lighter now as he drove up the silent Market Road. At the crossing he turned to his left, drove into Race-Course Road, and stopped before his office.

CHAPTER TWELVE

It was over an hour since she had arrived. The children's excitement had subsided. She ventured to ask, 'Where is your father?'

'Last night he went out to send the telegram and he hasn't yet come home. He said that the cook might sleep in the hall. What a fine story the cook told us! He went on till midnight, but Babu wouldn't let him continue ...'

'Why did you interrupt the story, Babu?'

'What nonsense, Mother! Were we to keep awake all night?'

'You could have gone away from us and slept somewhere; you needn't have disturbed us.'

'Mother, he has promised to continue the story tonight. We weren't in the least afraid at being without you. We kept the light on all night.'

'Father took us all to a cinema and bought us such a lot of sweets.'

The car sounded its horn outside. Kamala and Sumati ran to the gate to announce, 'Mother has come!'

'Has she?' Ramani asked, and went into the house. He hesitated for a fraction of a second on the doormat and then passed on to his room. Savitri sat in the passage of the dining-room, trembling. What would he do now? Would he come and turn her out of the house?

An hour later Ramani came towards her. She started up. He threw a brief look at her, noted her ragged appearance, and went into the dining-room. He said to the cook, 'Hurry up, I have to be at the office ...' Savitri stood in the passage for some time. He had started eating. She stepped into the dining-room and stood before him, watching his leaf. She noticed a space in a corner of the leaf.

'Shall I call for some more beans?'

'No,' Ramani said without looking up.

'Curd?' Savitri asked.

'Yes.' Savitri went to the cupboard and took hold of the curd vessel.

At eight-thirty in the evening the children had finished their dinner and were sitting round Savitri, ceaselessly talking, asking questions, and quarrelling. The hooting of the car a furlong off was heard – the long blast and the slight tremolo, which Savitri's accustomed ears picked up and interpreted, 'He is coming home in a sweet mood.' Her habit roused her. She was about to shout to Ranga to run to the garage, fretting and fussing so that the lord's homecoming might be smooth and without annoyance ... She checked herself.

'The car has come,' the children said, jumping up.

'What if it has?' Savitri asked, as the car hooted continuously in front of the garage door.

'As usual Ranga is away somewhere, and the garage door is unopened,' Babu said.

'Find Ranga, or go and open the door yourself,' said Savitri.

Ramani paused on the doormat and threw a genial look around. 'How are we all today?' he asked, and the children made some indistinct sounds in reply. 'What does your mother say?' he asked, and the children giggled. He went in to change.

Later he asked, 'Children finished their dinner?'

'Yes,' said Savitri.

'Haven't you finished yours?'

'No.'

'Waiting for me?'

'Yes.'

'What a dutiful wife you are!' he remarked, and laughed. He was granting her the privilege to laugh and joke and be happy.

'Oh, I should have bought some jasmine for you,' he said, looking at her mischievously. She tried to smile.

He watched her for a moment while she was eating. 'Oh, how poorly you eat!' he exclaimed. 'Have a little more ghee. Eat well, my girl, and grow fat. Don't fear that you will make me a bankrupt by eating.'

She attempted to laugh, and muttered through it, 'If I grow too fat, people may not recognize me.' She knew it was a miserable joke. 'A part of me is dead,' she reflected.

He said, 'I came home early entirely for your sake, and now you won't talk to me properly. What is the matter with you?'

'I don't know. I am all right. I am tired and want to sleep.'

He pleaded with her, later: 'Just a pretty half an hour. You can go to bed at ten-thirty. Just a little talk. I came home early for your sake.'

'I can't even stand. I am very tired. I must sleep.'

'Please yourself,' he said, and went away to his room.

Days later, one afternoon she was lying on her carpet in the hall, half asleep. (The bench was still away at the office.) Her husband had gone to the office, the children had gone to school, the cook on his afternoon rounds, and Ranga was in the backyard washing clothes.

From somewhere came a voice crying, 'Locks repaired, sirs, umbrellas repaired!' Savitri rose from the carpet and sat on the sill of the window facing the street. The voice came nearer, and then she saw Mari passing in the dusty street, with his tool-bag slung over his shoulder and a couple of dilapidated umbrellas under his arm; his dark face was shining with sweat under the hot sun.

Savitri felt excited. She could give him food, water, and a magnificent gift, and inquire about her great friend Ponni; perhaps Ponni had sent him along now. Savitri almost called him through the window, but suddenly checked herself and let him pass. He had now passed the house. She felt unhappy at letting him go; she felt that it was very mean and unjust ...

'Locks repaired, sirs! ...' came from the next street.

The poor fellow's face shone with sweat; perhaps he had been tramping the streets in the hot sun, foodless; perhaps he had not earned a pie yet in the town. How this man and Ponni had begged her to take the coconut and plantain ...

'Very unjust to let him go, but what can I do?' she reflected.

She called Ranga and told him, 'Call that lock-repairer who was crying in the street just now. He must be in the next street.'

'Yes, madam.'

As Ranga was about to step out she changed her mind: 'Let him go, don't call him.' She thought: 'Why should I call him here? What have I?'

'Locks repaired, sirs, umbrellas repaired!' came from four or five streets off.

She sat by the window, haunted by his shining hungry face long after he was gone, and by his 'Locks repaired! ...' long after his cry had faded out in the distance.

THE ENGLISH TEACHER

To My Wife, Rajam

CHAPTER ONE

I was on the whole very pleased with my day – not many conflicts and worries, above all not too much self-criticism. I had done almost all the things I wanted to do, and as a result I felt heroic and satisfied. The urge had been upon me for some days past to take myself in hand. What was wrong with me? I couldn't say, some sort of vague disaffection, a self-rebellion I might call it. The feeling again and again came upon me that as I was nearing thirty I should cease to live like a cow (perhaps, a cow, with justice, might feel hurt at the comparison), eating, working in a manner of speaking, walking, talking, etc. – all done to perfection, I was sure, but always leaving behind a sense of something missing.

I took stock of my daily life. I got up at eight every day, read for the fiftieth time Milton, Carlyle and Shakespeare, looked through compositions, swallowed a meal, dressed, and rushed out of the hostel just when the second bell sounded at college; four hours later I returned to my room; my duty in the interval had been admonishing, cajoling and browbeating a few hundred boys of Albert Mission College so that they might mug up Shakespeare and Milton and secure high marks and save me adverse remarks from my chiefs at the end of the year. For this pain the authorities kindly paid me a hundred rupees on the first of every month and dubbed me a lecturer. One ought, of course, to be thankful and rest content. But such repose was not in my nature, perhaps because I was a poet, and I was constantly nagged by the feeling that I was doing the wrong work. This was responsible for a perpetual self-criticism and all kinds of things aggravated it. For instance what my good chief Brown had said to us that day might be very reasonable, but it irritated and upset me.

We were summoned to his room at the end of the day. Under normal conditions, he would welcome us with a smile, crack a joke or two, talk of nothing in particular for a couple of minutes and then state the actual business. But today we found him dry and sullen. He motioned us to our seats and said, 'Could you imagine a worse shock for me? I came across a student of the English Honours, who did not know till this day that "honours" had to be spelt with a "u"?' He finished his sentence with a sharp, grim laugh. We looked at each other and were at a loss to know what to reply. Our Assistant Professor, Gajapathy, scowled at us as if it were us who had induced the boy to drop the 'u'. Brown cleared his throat as a signal for further speech, and we watched his lips. He began a lecture on the importance of the English language, and the need for preserving its purity. Brown's thirty years in India had not been ill-spent if they had opened the eyes of Indians to the need for speaking and writing correct English! The responsibility of the English department was indeed very great. At this point Gajapathy threw us a further furious look. The chief went on for forty-five minutes; and feeling that it was time to leaven his sermon with a little humour, added: 'It would be a serious enough blunder even from a mathematics honours man!'

When going out I was next to Gajapathy. He looked so heavily concerned that I felt like pricking him so that he might vanish like a bubble leaving no trace behind. But I checked myself. It would be unwise: he was my senior in office, and he might give me an hour of extra work every day, or compel me to teach the history of language, of which I knew nothing. I had to bear with him till we reached the hostel gate. He kept glancing at his own shoulder, swelling with importance. He muttered: 'Disgraceful! I never knew our boys were so bad ... We cannot pretend that we come out of it with flying colours ...' I felt irritated and said, 'Mr Gajapathy, there are blacker sins in this world than a dropped vowel.' He stopped on the road and looked up and down. He was aghast. I didn't care. I drove home the point: 'Let us be fair. Ask Mr Brown if he can say in any of the two hundred Indian languages: "The cat chases the rat". He has spent thirty years in India.'

'It is all irrelevant,' said Gajapathy.

'Why should he think the responsibility for learning is all on our side and none on his? Why does he magnify his own importance?'

'Good-night,' said Gajapathy and was off. I felt angry and insulted, and continued my discussion long after both Gajapathy and Brown were out of my reach. Later when I went for a walk I still continued the debate. But suddenly I saw illumination and checked myself. It showed a weak, uncontrolled mind, this incapacity to switch off. I now subjected myself to a remorseless self-analysis. Why had I become incapable of controlling my own thoughts? I brooded over it. Needless to say it took me nowhere. It left me more exhausted and miserable at the end of the day. I felt a great regret at having spent a fine evening in brooding and self-analysis, and then reached a startlingly simple solution. All this trouble was due to lack of exercise and irregular habits: so forthwith I resolved to be up very early next day, go out along the river on a long walk, run a few yards, bathe in the river and regulate my life thus.

After dinner my friends in the neighbouring rooms in the hostel dropped in as usual for light talk. They were my colleagues. One was Rangappa who taught the boys philosophy, and the other Gopal of the mathematics section. Gopal was sharp as a knife-edge where mathematical matters were concerned, but, poor fellow, he was very dumb and stupid in other matters. As a matter of fact he paid little attention to anything else. We liked him because he was a genius, and in a vague manner we understood that he was doing brilliant things in mathematics. Some day he hoped to contribute a paper on his subject which was going to revolutionize human thought and conceptions. But God knew what it was all about. All that I cared for in him was that he was an agreeable friend, who never contradicted and who patiently listened for hours, though without showing any sign of understanding.

Tonight the talk was all about English spelling and the conference we had with Brown. I was incensed as usual, much to the amazement of Rangappa. 'But my dear fellow, what do you think they pay you for unless it is for dotting the i's and crossing the t's?' Gopal, who had been listening without putting in a word of his own, suddenly became active.

'I don't follow you,' he said.

'I said the English department existed solely for dotting the i's and crossing the t's.'

'Oh!' he said, opening wide his eyes. 'I never thought so. Why should you do it?' His precise literal brain refused to move where it had no concrete facts or figures to grip. Symbols, if they entered his brain at all, entered only as mathematical symbols.

Rangappa answered: 'Look here, Gopal. You have come across the expression "Raining cats and dogs"?'

'Yes.'

'Have you actually seen cats and dogs falling down from the sky?'

'No, no. Why?'

Rangappa would have worried him a little longer, but the college clock struck ten and I said: 'Friends, I must bid you good-night.' 'Good-night,' Gopal repeated mechanically and rose to go. Not so the ever-questioning philosopher. 'What has come over you?' he asked, without moving.

'I want to cultivate new habits ...'

'What's wrong with the present ones?' he asked and I blinked for an answer. It was a long story and could not stand narration. Rangappa did not even stir from his seat; the other stood ready to depart and waited patiently. 'Answer me,' Rangappa persisted.

'I want to be up very early tomorrow,' I said.

'What time?'

'Some time before five.'

'What for?'

'I want to see the sunrise, and get some exercise before I start work.'

'Very good; wake me up too, I shall also go with you – ' said Rangappa rising. I saw them off at the door. I had an alarm clock on which I could sometimes depend for giving the alarm at the set time. I had bought it years before at a junk store in Madras. It had a reddening face, and had been oiled and repaired a score of times. It showed the correct time but was eccentric with regard to its alarm arrangement. It let out a shattering amount of noise, and it sometimes went off by itself and butted into a conversation, or sometimes when I had locked the room and gone out, it started off and went on ringing till exhaustion overcame it. There was no way of stopping it, by pressing a button or a lever. I don't know if it had ever had such an arrangement. At first I did not know about its trouble, so that I suffered a great shock and did not know how to silence it, short of dashing it down. But one day I learnt by some sort of instinctive experiment that if I placed a heavy book like Taine's *History of English Literature* on its crest, it stopped shrieking.

I picked up the clock and sat on my bed looking at it. I believe I almost addressed it: 'Much depends upon you.' I set it at four-thirty and lay down.

At four-thirty it shrieked my sleep away. I switched on the light, picked up Taine hurriedly, and silenced it. I went over to Rangappa's room, stood at the window and called him a dozen times, but there was no answer. As I stood looking at his sleeping figure with considerable disgust and pity, he stirred and asked: 'Who is there?'

'It is nearing five, you wanted to be called out – '

'Why?'

'You said you would come out.'

'Not me – '

'It is about five – ' I said.

'It looks to me like midnight; go back to bed my dear fellow, don't hang about windows pestering people – ' His voice was thick and the last words trailed off into sleep.

I stepped out of the hostel gates. Our college and hostel were not more than a couple of hundred yards from the river. There was a narrow lane to be crossed and at the end of it we were on the sands. As I walked down the lane a couple of municipal lamps were still burning, already showing signs of paling before the coming dawn. The eastern skyline was reddening, and I felt triumphant. I could not understand how people could remain in bed when there was such a glory awaiting them outside. I thought of Rangappa. 'A dry philosopher I suppose – not susceptible to these influences. A hopeless man. In any case not my business ...'

The sand was damp with the morning dew, but as I buried my feet, they felt deep down the warmth of the previous day's sun. In the half-dark dawn I saw some persons already out at work, fording the river, bathing and washing. There were immense banyan trees hanging over the river, and birds stirred and chirped in their nests. I walked on at an even pace, filling my lungs with morning air, and taking great strides. I felt I was really in a new world. I walked nearly four miles down the bank. Before turning back, I selected a clean spot, undressed, and plunged into the water. Coming on shore and rubbing myself with the towel, I felt I had a new lease of life. No doubt in my village home and in this very river I had often bathed, but at no other time could I remember such a glow of joy as filled me now. How could I account for it? There was something in the deliberate effort, and the hour and the air, and surroundings ... Nature, nature, all our poets repeat till they are hoarse. There are subtle, invisible emanations in nature's surroundings: with them the deepest in us merges and harmonizes. I think it is the highest form of joy and peace we can ever comprehend. I decided to rush back to my table and write a poem on nature.

I was going to write of the cold water's touch on the skin, the cold air blowing on chest and face, the rumble of the river, cries of birds, magic of the morning light, all of which created an alchemy of inexplicable joy. I paused for a moment and wondered how this poem would be received in a classroom – the grim tolerance with which boys listen to poetry, the annotator's desperate effort to convey a meaning, and the teacher's doubly desperate effort to wrest a meaning out of the poet and the annotator, the essence of an experience lost in all this handling ...

I returned to my room before seven. I felt very well satisfied indeed with my performance. I told myself: 'I am all right. I am quite sound if I can do this every day. I shall be able to write a hundred lines of poetry, read everything I want to read, in addition to class-work ...' This gave place to a distinct memory of half a dozen similar resolves in the past and the lapses ... I checked this defeatism! 'Don't you see this is entirely different? I am different today ...'

'How?' asked a voice. I ignored the question and it added, 'Why?'

'Shut up,' I cried. 'Don't ask questions.' I myself was not clear as to the 'Why?', except that my conscience perpetually nagged over arrears of work, books from libraries and friends lying in a heap on the table untouched, letters unanswered and accumulating, lines of poetry waiting for months to be put on paper, a picture of my wife meant to be framed and hung on the wall, but for months and months standing on the table leaning against the wall in its cardboard mount, covered with dust, bent by the weight of the books butting into it ...

This table assailed my sight as soon as I entered and I muttered 'Must set all this right', as I sat down on my chair. I called Singaram our servant. He had been a hostel servant for forty years and known all of us as undergraduates and now as teachers – an old man who affected great contempt for all of us, including our senior professors and principal. He spoke to us with habitual rudeness. Somehow he felt that because he had seen all of us as boys, our present stature and age and position were a make-believe, to which he would be no party. 'Singaram,' I called, and he answered from somewhere, 'You will have to wait till I come. If you hurt your throat calling me, don't hold me responsible for it ...' In a few minutes he stood before me, a shrunken old fellow, with angry wrinkles on his face. 'Now what is it this time? Has that sweeper not done her work properly? If she is up to her old tricks ...'

'Tell the cook to bring my coffee ...'

'So late! Why should you dally over your coffee so long, when you ought to be reading at your table ...'

'I went for a bathe in the river, Singaram. I found it very fine ...' He was happy to hear it.

'I'm glad you are ceasing to be the sort who lounges before bathrooms, waiting for a hot bath. A river bath is the real thing for a real man. I am eighty years old, and have never had a day's sickness, and have never bathed in hot water.'

'Nor in cold water, I think,' I said as he went away to send me my coffee.

I made a space on the table by pushing aside all the books; took out a sheet of paper and wrote a poem entitled 'Nature', about fifty lines of verse. I read and reread it, and found it very satisfying. I felt I had discharged a duty assigned to me in some eternal scheme.

I had four hours of teaching to do that day. *Lear* for the Junior B.A. class, a composition period for the Senior Arts; detailed prose and poetry for other classes. Four periods of continuous work and I hadn't prepared even a page of lecture.

I went five minutes late to the class, and I could dawdle over the attendance for a quarter of an hour. I picked out the attendance register and called out the first name.

'Here, sir – ', 'Present', and I marked. Two boys in the front bench got up and suggested 'Sir, take the attendance at the end of the period.'

'Sit down please, can't be done. I can't encroach into the next hour's work ...'

A babble rose in the class, a section demanding that the attendance be taken immediately and another demanding postponement. I banged the table with my fist and shouted over the din: 'Stop this, otherwise I will mark everyone absent.'

'Attendance takes up most of our hours, sir.'

'We can't help it. Your attendance is just as important as anything else. Stop all noise and answer your names; otherwise, I will mark all of you absent ...' At this the boys became quiet, because I out-shouted them. The lion-tamer's touch! In a sober moment perhaps I would reflect on the question of obedience. Born in different households, perhaps petted, pampered, and bullied, by parents, uncles, brothers – all persons known to them and responsible for their growth and welfare. Who was I that they should obey my command? What tie was there between me and them? Did I absorb their personalities as did the old masters and merge them in mine? I was merely a man who had mugged earlier than they the introduction and the notes in the Verity edition of *Lear*, and guided them through the mazes of Elizabethan English. I did not do it out of love for them or for Shakespeare but only out of love for myself. If they paid me the same one hundred rupees for stringing beads together or tearing up paper bits every day for a few hours, I would perhaps be doing it with equal fervour. But such reflections do not mar our peace when we occupy the classroom chair. So that I banged the table – shouted till they were silenced, and went through the attendance; all this tittle-tattle swallowed up half an hour.

I opened my Verity. I had made a pencil mark where I had stopped on the previous day: middle of the first scene in the third act.

I began in a general way: 'You will see that I stopped last time where Lear faces the storm. This is a vital portion of this great tragedy ...' The words rang hollow in my ears. Some part of me was saying: 'These poor boys are now all attention, cowed by your superior force. They are ready to listen to you and write down whatever you may say. What have you to give them in return?' I noticed that some boys were already sitting up alert, ready to note down the pearls dropping from my mouth ... I felt like breaking out into a confession! 'My dear fellows, don't trust me so much. I am merely trying to mark time because I couldn't come sufficiently prepared, because all the morning I have ...' But I caught myself lecturing: 'This is the very heart of the tragedy and I would like you to follow this portion with the greatest attention ...' I stole a look at the watch ... Only fifteen minutes more. 'As usual I shall read through this scene first, and then I shall take it up in detail ...' I looked at the page on the table – 'Enter Lear and Fool. Blow winds and crack your cheeks! Rage! Blow! You cataracts and hurricanes, spout till you have drenched our steeples, drowned the cocks! ...' As I read on I myself was moved by the force and fury of the storm compressed in these lines. The sheer poetry of it carried me on ...

> '... And thou, all-shaking Thunder
> Strike flat the thick rotundity o' the world!'

I forgot all about the time, all about my unpreparedness.

> '... Let the great gods
> That keep this dreadful pother o'er our heads,
> Find out their enemies now.'

I read on. The boys listened attentively. I passed on to the next scene without knowing it. I could not stop.

> 'Poor naked wretches, wheresoe'er you are,
> That hide the pelting of this pitiless storm,
> How shall your houseless heads and unfed sides,
> ... defend you
> From seasons such as these?'

At the thought of helpless humanity I nearly broke down. The bell rang, I shut my book with the greatest relief, and walked out of the class.

I managed the composition hour quite easily. The composition hour is a sort of relaxation for us, where we can sit looking at notebooks and do not demand too much attention from the boys. It was the small gallery room at the end of the southern corridor; I loved this room because the sun came through a ventilator, bringing in a very bright beam of light, and brilliant dust particles floated in it, and the two boys who sat on the second bench looked all aflame. Years and years ago I sat there on the bench as a student, and Gajapathy was then just a junior lecturer and not the big Assistant Professor he was now. I could still see where I used to sit assiduously cultivating correct language and trying to please the lecturer. And to my left would always sit Rangappa, who hated all composition. Little did I dream then that I would be a teacher in the same class.

The boys were making too much noise. I tapped the table lightly and said: 'Ramaswami, here is your notebook. See the corrections on it. There are more corrections on it than on any other paper ...' It was a paraphrase of the poem beginning 'My days among the dead are past ...' He hadn't understood a line of that poem, yet he had written down two pages about it. According to Ramaswami (though not according to Southey) the scholar when he said, 'My days among the dead are past' meant that he was no longer going to worry about his dead relations because wherever his eyes were cast he saw mighty minds of old (he just copies it down from the poem), and so on and on. I enjoyed this paraphrase immensely. I called, 'Ramaswami, come and receive your notebook ...' My comments on the work could not be publicly shown or uttered. When he came near, I opened the notebook and pointed to my remark at the end of the notebook: 'Startling!' I put my finger on this and asked: 'Do you see what I mean?'

'Yes, sir ...' whispered Ramaswami.

'You are very bad in English.'

'I am sorry, sir ...'

'Does this poem make no sense as far as you are concerned?'

'No, sir ...'

'Then why do you write so much about it?'

'I do not know, sir ...'

'All right, go back to your seat ... Come and see me sometime ...'

'Yes, sir, when?'

I couldn't answer this question, because I visualized all my hours so thoroughly allotted for set tasks that I was at a loss to know when I could ask him to see me. So I replied: 'I will tell you, go to your seat.' I spent the rest of the period giving a general analysis of the mistakes I had encountered in this batch of composition – *rather very*, *as such* for *hence*, split infinitives, collective nouns, and all the rest of the traps that the English language sets for foreigners. I then set them an exercise in essay-writing on the epigram 'Man is the master of his own destiny'. 'An idiotic theme,' I felt, 'this abstract and confounded metaphysic,' but I could not help it. I had been ordered to set this subject to the class. I watched with interest how the boys were going to tackle it. As a guidance it was my duty to puff up this theme, and so I wrote on the blackboard – 'Man, what is man? What is destiny? How does he overcome destiny? How does destiny overcome him? What is fate? What is free will?' – a number of headings which reduced man and his destiny and all the rest to a working formula for these tender creatures to handle.

By the afternoon I had finished three hours of lecturing, and was, with a faintly smarting throat, resting in a chair in the common room. There were a dozen other teachers. As each of them sat looking at a book or at the ceiling vacantly, there was a silence which seemed to me oppressive. I never liked it. I had my own technique of breaking it. I remarked to no one in particular: 'We have to decide an important issue before the examinations begin.' The others looked up with bored half-expectancy. 'We will have to call a staff meeting to decide how many marks are to be deducted for spelling honours without the middle u.'

'No, no, I don't think it is necessary,' said Sastri, the logic lecturer, who had a very straightforward, literal mind, looking up for a moment from the four-day-old newspaper which he was reading. Gajapathy looked over his spectacles, and remarked from the farthest end of the room: 'You are joking over yesterday's meeting, I suppose?' I replied, 'I am not joking, I am very serious.'

'What is it all about?' Dr Menon asked. He was Assistant Professor of Philosophy. Gajapathy explained, slowly, like an expert lawyer, what had happened the previous evening.

'No sense of proportion ...' was the philosopher's verdict. Gajapathy removed his spectacles, folded the sides, and put them away as a preparation for dispute. 'How would you treat one of your students if he spelt *Kant*, *Cant*?'

'I wouldn't bother very much if he knew correctly what Kant had or hadn't said,' replied Dr Menon.

'Oh, I won't believe it,' said Gajapathy, 'there is a merit in accuracy, which must be cultivated for its own sake. I believe it wouldn't do to slacken anywhere.'

'Americans spell honours without the u,' I said and this diverted the subject, and deprived Gajapathy of the duel for which he was preparing. 'Americans are saner than their English cousins in most matters,' said Dr Menon, who had obtained his Ph.D. at Columbia University.

'I think the American spelling is foolish buffoonery,' said Gajapathy with his loyalty of a lifetime to English language and literature.

'If we had Americans ruling us, I suppose we would say the same thing of the English people,' I said.

'Politics need not butt in everywhere. There are times when I wish there were no politics in the world and no one knew who was ruling and how,' said Gajapathy. 'This would help a little clearer, freer thinking in all matters. The whole of the West is in a muddle owing to its political consciousness, and what a pity that the East should also follow suit. It is like a weed choking all other human faculties. Shelley in his "Sensitive Plant" ...'

'I am afraid your opinions are at least a thousand years behind the times; it is a one-sided view, Mr Gajapathy,' said Kumar, who lectured on political science to B.A. classes. 'Corporate life marks the beginning of civilized existence and the emergence of its values ...'

'I am sure,' I said, finding the debate dull, 'a tormenting question can be framed for the boys at the next examination. "Corporate existence pulled the cave man out into the open. Discuss." If I have anything to do with the politics paper I'm going to insist on this question and make it compulsory. It will serve the young rascals right ...'

'You haven't yet dropped the frivolous habits of your college days, Krishna,' said Gajapathy. 'You must cultivate a little more seriousness of outlook.'

'I have answered an advertisement I saw in an American paper where someone has offered to take on hand people who lack seriousness and turn them into better citizens. I have filled up the necessary coupon and have every hope you will find me passable ere long ...'

'Don't you believe too much in these ads. In the United States there are any number of them. Once when I was in Chicago ...' began Dr Menon of Columbia University, and the bell rang and all his audience rose to go to their different classes.

I returned to my room. The postman had slipped through the door two letters for me. I knew the pale blue envelope from my wife, who was in the habit of underlining the town three times; she seemed to be always anxious lest the letter should go off to some other town. And then my father's letter, from the village. Letters are very exciting things for me. I don't know why. By the time I open and see the contents, I feel an æon might have passed, and my heart goes thumping against my ribs. I looked through my father's letter first. He still wrote his fine, sharp hand, every letter put down with precision and care but without ornament, written closely on a memo pad of some revenue department. From time immemorial he had written only on those pads. No one knew how many pads he had or how he had come by them – perhaps through the favour of some friend in the Revenue Department. The paper had acquired an elegant tone of brown through years of storing but it was tough as parchment. My father had a steel pen with a fat green wooden handle, with which he had written for years. He had several bottles of ink – his own make from a recipe which was exclusively his and of which he was excessively proud. He would make up his store of ink once a year; and we little ones of the household waited for the event with tremendous enthusiasm – all the servants in the house would be present: a special brick oven was raised in the backyard, with a cauldron sizzling over it all day, and father presiding. The most interesting part, however, would be the trip the previous evening for shopping to Kavadi – our nearest town, fifteen miles off. At three in the afternoon father would yoke the big bulls to the waggon and we were dressed and ready for the expedition – I and my elder brother, and my two sisters. My elder brother would exact obedience and we would have to take our seats in the cart according to his directions. The way he handled us we always expected he would become a commander of an army or a police officer – but the poor fellow settled as auditor in Hyderabad and was nose-led by his wife. He was always full of worries, being a father of ten, and having a haughty nagging wife. He seldom visited us in the village, being so much wrapped up in his own auditing and family.

We reached Kavadi at about two o'clock. Invariably I would fall to sleep lulled by the jingling of the bells around the neck of the bulls.

Kavadi was a wonderful place for one like me from the village – a street full of all sorts of shops, sewing-machines rattling away, coloured ribbons streaming down from shop-fronts. My father had his favourite shop. The shopman would seat us all on the mat; and my father would buy us some edibles from the opposite shop, while the ink-ingredients were being packed. He would buy us each a toy – a ball, a monkey dangling at the end of a rubber-piece, and a doll, and invariably an exercise book and a pencil for my elder brother, declaring that he was past the age of having toys, a reminder which made him smart every time he heard it. The road would be ankle deep in bleached dust and the numerous cattle and country carts passing along stirred it up so much that a cloud always hung over the road, imparting an enchanting haze to the whole place, though, by the time we started back, so much of this dust settled on our skins and hair that our mother had to give us a bath as soon as we reached home.

I don't know why my father took this ink business so very seriously, when we could buy all the ink we wanted in the shop and save ourselves all bother. He would be near his brick kiln the whole of the next day boiling up this potion, and distilling, and straining, and filling up huge mud jugs. He filled small glass pots for our use, and locked up the store in an *almirah*. We wrote our copies and lessons in this ink. It had a greenish tint which we didn't like, and which made us long for the blue or black ink sold in the shop. We never got over the feeling that this ink was not real ink – perhaps because of its pale greenish tinge, but my father seemed to appreciate it for that very reason, declaring that you couldn't buy that elegant shade even if you paid a fortune for it.

My father's letter brought back to me not only the air of the village and all my childhood, but along with it all the facts – home, coconut-garden, harvest, revenue demand. He had devoted nearly a paragraph to my mother's health with a faint suggestion of complaint that she was not looking after herself quite properly – still keeping late hours for food – the last to eat in the house and still reluctant to swallow the medicines given to her ...

And then came a paragraph of more immediate interest to me. 'Your father-in-law has written a letter today. I hear that by God's grace, your wife Susila, and the baby, are keeping well. He suggests that you should take her and the baby and set up a family and not live in a hostel any longer. He has my entire concurrence in this matter, as I think in the best interests of yourself you should set up a family. You have been in the hostel too long and I don't feel you ought to be wasting the best of your life in the hostel as it will affect your health and outlook. Your mother is also of the same view since your father-in-law's place is not a very healthy one for an infant. If you have no serious objection to this, your father-in-law suggests the 10th of next month as the most suitable and auspicious date ...'

He was a B.A. of the olden days brought up on Pater and Carlyle and Scott and Browning; personally looked after by Dr William Miller, Mark Hunter and other eminent professors of Madras College; he was fastidious and precise in handling the English language, though with a very slight pomposity inevitable in the men of those days. After passing his B.A. he refused to enter Government service, as many of his generation did, but went back and settled in his village and looked after his lands and property. I said to myself on reading his letter: 'God, what am I to do with a little child of seven months? ...' This somehow seemed to terrify me. How did one manage these things? I had visited my wife's place three or four times since the baby was born. At the first trip I could hardly take notice of the child, although for my wife's sake I had to pinch its cheeks. I no doubt felt a mild affection for it, but there was nothing compelling or indispensable about it ... During the subsequent interviews I found more interest in the girl and began to feel that it would be nice to have her about the home, cooing and shouting ... But I didn't bargain to accept her guardianship so suddenly. I had seen my sister's children of that age, seven months or eight months old, and they started howling and crying at nights till we felt that they would not survive whatever was afflicting them. But my mother was there, and she could take them in hand expertly: a fomentation, a rub with an oil, some decoction down their throats, and they were quietened.

My father's letter had a postscript: 'To help you set up the family your mother is quite willing to come and stay with you for a few weeks. I have not the slightest objection ...'

I put down my father's letter. There was much food for thought in it.

I smelt my wife's letter before opening it. It carried with it the fragrance of her trunk, in which she always kept her stationery – a mild jasmine smell surrounded her and all her possessions ever since I had known her. I hurriedly glanced through her letter. In her uniform rotund hand, she had written a good deal about the child which made me want to see her at once. The baby was really too intelligent for her age, understood everything that was being said and done in the house. There was every indication that she was going to prove the most astonishingly intelligent person in the family. She crawled on her belly all over the place, and kept a spy-like watch on her mother's movements. Too cunning! She was learning to say 'Appa' (father); and with every look was asking her mother when father proposed to take them home – I liked this, but was not prepared to accept it totally. She then referred to the letter from my father and her father and requested me to set up a house at the earliest moment possible. I felt I was someone whose plans and determinations were of the utmost importance to others ...

I placed the letter on the table, locked the room, and went out for a wash. While crossing the quadrangle my eyes fell on a jasmine bush which completely covered our library wall. I had seen it as a very young sapling years and years ago. When I was a student, I had taken a special interest in its growth, and trained it up a small bamboo bower which I had put up with the help of Singaram the old peon ... Many persons had laughed at me for it. 'Why should we grow a jasmine bush in a boys' hostel?' I was often asked. 'Just to remind us that there are better things in the world, that is all,' I replied. It was a struggle for existence for that plant, all kinds of cows trespassing into the compound and biting off the stalk. It went up and down several times causing me unending anxiety. And then one day I got the idea of entrusting it to Singaram's care with the suggestion that he might take its flowers, if they appeared, to his womenfolk at home and for the god during the celebration of the Vinayaka festival in the hostel. Since then it grew up under his personal care. He dealt severely with persons who went near it; and as a special favour, occasionally left half a dozen buds on the sill of my window. Now as I passed along to the bathroom I looked at it and said: 'I'm about to leave you ... after all these years ... after ten years' – the period I had spent in the hostel, first as student and then as teacher. I sighed as I passed it, the only object of any beauty hereabouts. The rest of the quadrangle was mere mud, scorched by Malgudi sun.

I had to wait in the bathroom passage for some time, all the cubicles were engaged. Behind the doors, to the tune of falling water a couple of boys were humming popular film songs. I paced the passage with the towel round my neck. It was a semi-dark, damp place, with a glass tile giving it its sole lighting. 'I shall soon be rid of this nuisance,' I reflected, 'when I have a home of my own. Hostel bathrooms are hell on earth ... [God said to his assistants, "Take this man away to hell", and they brought him down to the hostel bathroom passage, and God said, "torture him", and they opened the room and pushed him in ... No, no, at this moment the angels said "the room is engaged" ... God waited as long as a god can wait and asked "Have you finished" and they replied "still engaged", and in due course they could not see where their victim was, for grass had grown and covered him up completely while he waited outside the bathroom door. This promises to be a good poem. Must write it some day ...]' At this moment a door opened and someone came out dripping. It was a student of the second-year class. He asked agitatedly: 'Sir, have I kept you waiting long?'

'Yes, my dear fellow, but how could you come out before finishing that masterpiece of a song?' The other held the door ostentatiously open and I passed in.

I was back in my room. I applied a little hair-cream, stood before the small looking glass hanging by the nail on the wall, and tried to comb. The looking glass was in the southern wall and I could hardly see my face. 'Nuisance,' I muttered, picked up the glass, and looked for a place to hang it on – not a place. Light at the window struck me in the face and dazzled. 'The room is full of windows,' I muttered. 'These petty annoyances of life will vanish when I have a home of my own. My dear wife will see that the proper light comes at the proper angle.' I finally put the looking glass down on the table. It had a stand which would not support it. I picked up Taine's *History of Literature* and leaned the glass against it. 'Taine every time,' I muttered and combed my hair back, interrupting the operation for a moment to watch the spray from the comb wet-dotting the covers of books and note-books on the table. I paused for a moment gazing at my face in the glass. 'This is how, I suppose, I appear to that girl and the little one. Yet they have confidence that I shall be able to look after them and run a home!'

I was ready to start out. I picked up the letters, smelt once again my wife's epistle, and sat back in the chair, and read the letter over again, without missing a single word. 'I want to see the baby and her mother very badly. How long am I to be in this wretched hostel?' I said to myself. I leaned back, reflecting. Through my window I could see the college tower and a bit of the sky. I had watched through this window the play of clouds and their mutation for a decade. All that was to be learnt about clouds was learnt by me, sitting in this place, and looking away, while studying for examinations or preparing lectures.

I started out. At the hostel gate I saw Rangappa standing. He was involved in a discussion with Subbaram – an assistant in the Economics Department. I tried to go away pretending not to have seen him.

'Krishna, Krishna! Just a moment,' Rangappa cried on seeing me. He turned to his friend and said: 'Let us refer it to a third party.' I stopped. 'You see,' began Rangappa. 'The point is this ...'

'No, let me first say what it is,' the other interrupted.

'What place would you give to economic values ...' he began.

'It all depends,' I said ironically, without allowing him to finish the sentence.

'No, no, don't put it that way,' interrupted Rangappa.

'I will simplify it for you. Is a hundred per cent materialism compatible with our best traditions?' Just another of our numerous discussions going on night and day among my colleagues, leading God knew where. What pleasure or profit did they get by it? 'I will give the matter deep consideration and tell you in due course,' I said, and moved away. Rangappa cried: 'Wait, I will go with you.'

'I am not going for a walk but to search for a house,' I said, and went away.

'I must have a house,' I told myself, 'which faces south, for its breeze, keeps out the western sun, gets in the eastern, and admits the due measure of northern light that artists so highly value. The house must have a room for each one of us and for a guest or two. It must keep us all together and yet separate us when we would rather not see each other's faces ... We must have helpful people and good people near at hand, but obnoxious neighbours ten miles away. It must be within walking distance of college and yet so far out as to let me enjoy my domestic life free from professional intrusions.'

I spent the entire evening scouring various parts of the town watching for 'To Let' signs.

'The builder of this house must have been dead-drunk while doing the latter portion of the house. This is a house evidently intended for monkeys to live in. This house must have been designed by a tuberculosis expert so that his business may prosper for the next hundred years. This house is ideal for one whose greatest desire in life is to receive constant knocks on his head from door-posts. A house for a twisted pigmy.' Thus, variously, I commented within myself as I inspected the vacant houses in the east, west and south of the town. I scoured South Extension, Fort Area, Race Course Road, and Vinayak Mudali Street. I omitted Lawley Extension because it was expensive, and also the New Extension beyond it, because it was too far out of the way.

The search extended over three or four days. I could think of nothing but houses all the while. The moment I met anyone I asked: 'Can you suggest a good house?' I was becoming a bore, capable of talking of nothing but houses, houses, night and day. I got into the habit of taking aside my students and asking them about it. I was becoming anxious. The day was fast approaching when my wife and child would be arriving. There didn't appear to be a single house fit for their occupation in the whole town. Suppose fifteen days hence I was still in this state and they arrived and had nowhere to go outside the railway station! This vision was a nightmare to me. However I was spared. One of my students knew somebody who knew somebody else who had a house in Sarayu Street, and who was eager to have a good, cultured family as tenants. 'Am I good? Is mine a cultured family?' I asked myself immediately. Sarayu Street was a coveted spot in the town. It fulfilled almost all the conditions that are looked for in a residential locality, cheap houses, refined surroundings, and yet near enough to the market and the offices. I fell into feverish anxiety over this house. The boy promised to take me to the first link in the chain of introductions, on the following morning. I was too impatient to wait till then. I implored him: 'There is no sense in postponing these matters. Somebody else may be there before me. Let us go today.' I visualized the whole town waiting to crowd into the house and fight for it. The boy begged to be let off today since his evening was already committed to some other duty, but I brushed aside all his explanations and clung to him fast. He took me to his house behind the market, and then to someone a mile east of the market, and finally an old man hunched up in a rag-covered cane chair on the veranda of a house in Ellamman Street. It was a very narrow place with the tiles touching one's head, and the chair completely filled the veranda. The old man fussed about on my arrival and compelled me to sit on a stool, which was placed on the edge of the veranda, and I was in constant danger of being tipped off into the street if I moved my limbs a little carelessly. So I sat there holding my breath. He was a very shrunken palsied patriarch. His sight was dim. He strained his eyes to catch a glimpse of me, but did not succeed. A silence fell between us. I broke it by asking: 'Are you the owner of the house?'

'No,' he replied, promptly, in his querulous voice. 'God is the owner and I am his slave.'

'What is the rent?'

'First see the house and tell me if you like it.' I felt rather cowed by his authoritarian manner. I ventured: 'I can't do anything unless I know something about it ...' He shook his head reflectively: 'Do you want the garage or not?'

'Has it a garage?' I asked.

'Don't ask all that now,' said the old man.

'Unless I know first if it has a garage ...' I said.

'You want everything to be told first,' he snapped with disgust, 'before you say anything yourself. Go, go away. I am not prepared to talk to you any more. I don't want to give you my house. I have seen hundreds like you come and ask questions and vanish out of sight.'

'What is the matter with you?' I asked indignantly. He bent close to my face and said: 'I am semi-blind. Till three months ago, I could see clearly, but it came on suddenly. And I can't talk without faltering: that's what paralysis has done for me: speaking is a strain to me. Otherwise I am prepared to sit here a whole day and wag my tongue to your heart's content, not caring whether you are a true tenant or a bogus one who comes and pesters me by the score each day. I will send the boy along with the key. See the house and then come and talk to me.'

'All right,' I said. He called a boy, pressed into his hand a large rusty key and said: 'Show this master the bungalow. Show him every cupboard,' he commanded. I followed the boy out. On the way I tried to engage him in friendly conversation, but he did not want it. He had his pocket filled with fried nuts, and was ceaselessly transferring them to his mouth. He walked ten yards ahead. 'What class are you reading in?' 'I won't read,' he replied. He tossed the key up and caught it in mid-air. He led me through some maze of lanes and took me to Sarayu Street.

Mine was the last house in a particular row. I liked it at first sight. A small wooden gate, ten yards of garden space, and then four steps up to a gabled veranda. There was a small room opening on the veranda detached from the main house. I went in and threw the window open: 'A lovely view of Sarayu Street. When I have nothing else to do,' I told myself, 'I can watch the goings on of Sarayu Street. This room is evidently built for me, where I can study and write without disturbing the household or being disturbed.'

'Why has this been untenanted so long?' I asked the boy, without hoping for a reply as the boy waited for me tossing up the lock and key. But he seemed to have melted towards me; and promptly replied, 'Because grandfather refuses to give it.'

'When was this last occupied?'

'Fifteen days ago,' he said.

'Is that all?' I asked, but he suddenly lapsed into his silent ways once again.

I liked the house very much. It had a central hall, 'where all of us can meet', and a small room at one end of the hall. 'This must be her room and the child's', I told myself. The kitchen and other portions of the house were very satisfactory. There was a coconut tree in the backyard. 'When a monkey goes up that tree, I can show it to the child,' I said, viewing it from the tiny back veranda.

I went back to the old man and said: 'I will take the house. What is the rent?'

'H'm,' he reflected, 'do you want it with or without a garage?' I studiously avoided asking if it had a garage at all and where. I merely said, with a trembling diplomacy: 'What'll be the difference with or without. Suppose I want a garage?'

'Hush!' He made a gesture of utter despair. 'I don't like you to brag about all that unnecessarily. Empty talk! Don't pretend you own a car. You have come walking. Even if I'm blind, do you think I can't notice it?'

'Look here,' I cried, losing all patience. 'If you are letting the house, let it, otherwise don't talk of matters which are not your concern. I'm not here to learn lessons from you. I am myself a teacher: and I teach a thousand boys in that college, mind you!' He was greatly impressed.

'College teacher!' He gave a salute with both hands and said, 'I revere college teachers, our *Gurus*. Meritorious deeds in previous births make them gurus in this life. I'm so happy. I only wanted a good, cultured family.'

'Everybody knows how good we are, and how cultured our family is!' I replied haughtily. This had the desired effect. I added: 'Don't mistake me for an ordinary person!' I drew myself up proudly. He was tremendously impressed. His face beamed with relief: 'Do you know why I want a cultured family?' He whispered as if it were a State secret: 'I'm going away to live with my son after letting the house, and I want someone who will send me the rent without fail ...'

'Depend upon me,' I said. 'What shall I have to pay you?'

'Twenty-five on the fifth of every month. It must reach me on that day at Bellary.'

'Very well. And what about the garage?' I asked haughtily.

'I'll build you one if you want, but ten rupees extra,' he said.

'All right, I will tell you when I need one,' I said.

Four days later my table and trunk and chair were loaded into a bullock-cart, my old room was locked up and the key was handed to Singaram. My hostel friends stood on the veranda and cracked a joke or two. The hostel was a place where people constantly arrived and departed and it was not in anyone's nature there to view these matters pensively. Rangappa and the mathematics man stood on the veranda and said: 'Well, goodbye, friend. Good luck. Don't forget us for the house-warming,' and laughed. Singaram had been very busy the whole day packing up and loading my things. He had attended on me for ten years – sweeping my room, counselling me and running my errands. He walked behind the creaking cart warning the driver: 'When you unload, remove the trunk first and the table last. If I hear that you have broken any leg, I will break your head, remember ...' I walked behind the cart. Singaram had come to the border of his domain – the hostel drive – and stopped. He salaamed me and said, 'Don't forget our hostel, keep visiting us now and then.' He hesitated for a moment and said: 'Now permit this old man to go ...' It was his hint that the time had come for him to receive his reward. He nearly held out his hand for it. I took out my purse and put a rupee on his palm. He looked at me coldly and said: 'Is this all the value you attach to the old man?' 'Yes,' I replied. 'I should have given half that to anyone else ...'

'No, no, don't say so. Don't grudge an honest man his payment. I've been your servant for ten years. Do you know what Professor X gave me when he left this hostel?' 'I don't want all that information,' I said and added a nickel to the rupee. He said: 'Don't grudge an old servant his due. You will perhaps not see me again: I will perhaps be dead; next year I'm retiring and going back to my village. You will never see me again. You will be very sorry when you hear that old Singaram is dead and that you wouldn't give the poor fellow eight annas more ...' I put in his hand an eight-anna coin. He bowed and said: 'God will make you a big professor one day ...' and walked away. I passed out of the hostel gate, following my caravan and goods.

CHAPTER TWO

The next three days I was very busy. My table was placed in the front room of the new house. All my papers and books were arranged neatly. My clothes hung on a peg. The rest of the house was swept and cleaned.

My mother arrived from the village with a sack full of vessels, and helped to make up the house for me. She was stocking the store-room and the kitchen and spent most of her time travelling in a *jutka* to the market and coming back with something or other. She worked far into the night, arranging and rearranging the kitchen and the store. At night she sat down with me on the veranda and talked of her house-keeping philosophy. I liked this veranda very much. We had a cool breeze. I felt immensely satisfied with my choice of the house now. I hoped my wife too would like it. But my mother, the moment she arrived from the village, said, 'What an awful kitchen! so narrow! And the dining-room would have been better if they had added at least a yard in length that side ...'

'We can't have everything our way in a house built by someone else ...' I became rather impatient if anyone criticized this house. She understood it and said: 'I'm not saying it is a bad house ...' She had been used to our large, sprawling home in the village, and everything else seemed to her small and choking. I explained this fact to her and she agreed it was so: 'But do you know how hard it is to keep a huge house like ours clean? It takes me a whole lifetime to keep it tidy, but I don't grudge it. Only I want a little more co-operation. Your father is becoming rather difficult nowadays ...' She explained how impatient he became when he heard the swish of a broom or the noise of scrubbing, and shouted at her to stop it all. As he was growing old, these noises got on his nerves. And so every time she wanted to clean the house, she had to wait till he went away to the fields. 'And do you know, when I delay this, how many other things get out of routine? Unless I have cleaned the house I can't go and bathe. After bathing I've to worship, and only after that can I go near the cows ... And if I fail to look at the cow-shed for half an hour, do you know what happens?' She was completely wrapped up in her duties. House-keeping was a grand affair for her. The essence of her existence consisted in the thrills and pangs and the satisfaction that she derived in running a well-ordered household. She was unsparing and violent where she met slovenliness. 'If a woman can't take charge of a house and run it sensibly, she must be made to get into man's dress and go out in a procession ...' I thought of my wife and shuddered at the fate that might be awaiting her in the few weeks my mother was going to stay and help us run the house. My wife was the last daughter of the family and was greatly petted by her parents, in her own house, where she spent most of her time reading, knitting, embroidering or looking after a garden. In spite of it, after my marriage my mother kept her in the village and trained her up in house-keeping. My wife had picked up many sensible points in cooking and household economy, and her own parents were tremendously impressed with her attainments when she next visited them. They were thrilled beyond words and remarked when I went there, 'We are so happy, Susila has such a fine house for her training. Every girl on earth should be made to pass through your mother's hands ...' which, when I conveyed it to my mother, pleased her. She said: 'I really do not mind doing it for everyone, but there are those who neither know nor learn when taught. I feel like kicking them when I come across that type.' I knew she was referring to her eldest daughter-in-law, my brother's wife, whom she detested heartily. I had half a suspicion that my eldest brother went away to seek his livelihood in Hyderabad solely for this reason, for there used to be very painful scenes at home while the first daughter-in-law was staying in our house, my mother's idiosyncrasy being what it was and the other being of a haughty disposition. She was the daughter of a retired High Court Judge, and would never allow a remark or a look from my mother to pass unchallenged, and as a result great strife existed in the household for a number of years. My mother used to declare when my elder brother was not present, 'Whatever happens, even with a ten-thousand-rupee dowry, I shall never accept a girl from a High Court Judge's family again ...'

It had always been my great anxiety that my wife should not share this fate. My mother seemed to feel that some reference of more immediate interest was due to me and said: 'Susila is a modest girl. She is not obstinate.' I was grateful for that negative compliment. That was at the beginning of our married years. They had constant contact after that, and with every effort Susila came out better burnished than before. And then came a point when my mother declared: 'Susila has learnt how to conduct herself before guests.' At this point they separated; now they were meeting again, with Susila having a home of her own to look after, and my mother ready to teach the obedient pupil her business. It was really this which I secretly dreaded.

On the following Friday, I was pacing the little Malgudi railway station in great agitation. I had never known such suspense before. She was certain to arrive with a lot of luggage, and the little child. How was all this to be transferred from the train to the platform? and the child must not be hurt. I made a mental note, 'Must shout as soon as the train stops: "Be careful with the baby."' This seemed to my fevered imagination the all-important thing to say on arrival, as otherwise I fancied the child's head was sure to be banged against the doorway ... And how many infants were damaged and destroyed by careless mothers in the process of coming out of trains! Why couldn't they make these railway carriages of safer dimensions? It ought to be done in the interests of baby welfare in India. 'Mind the baby and the door.' And then the luggage! Susila was sure to bring with her a huge amount of luggage! She required four trunks for her *saris* alone! Women never understood the importance of travelling light. Why should they? As long as there were men to bear all the anxieties and bother and see them through their travails! It would teach them a lesson to be left to shift for themselves. Then they would know the value of economy in these matters. I wrung my hands in despair. How was she going to get out with the child and all that luggage! The train stopped for just seven minutes. I would help her down first and then throw the things out, and if there were any boxes left over they would have to be lost with the train, that was all. No one could help it. I turned to the gnarled blue-uniformed man behind me. He was known as Number Five and I had known him for several years now. Whatever had to be done on the railway platform was done with his help. I had offered him three times his usual wages to help me today. I turned to him and asked: 'Can you manage even if there is too much luggage?'

'Yes, master, no difficulty. The train stops for seven minutes.' He seemed to have a grand notion of seven minutes; a miserable flash it seemed to me. 'We unload whole waggons within that time.'

'I will tell the pointsman to stop it at the outer signal, if necessary,' he added. It was a very strength-giving statement to me. I felt relieved. But I think I lost my head once again. I believe, in this needless anxiety, I became slightly demented. Otherwise I would not have rushed at the station-master the moment I set eyes on him. I saw him come out of his room and move down the platform to gaze on a far-off signal post. I ran behind him, panting: 'Good-morning station-master!' He bestowed an official smile and moved off to the end of the platform and looked up. I felt I had a lot of doubts to clear on railway matters and asked inanely: 'Looking at the signals?'

'Yes,' he replied, and took his eyes down, and turned to go back to his room. I asked: 'Can't they arrange to stop this train a little longer here?' 'What for? Isn't there enough trouble as it is?' I laughed sympathetically and said: 'I said so because it may not be possible for passengers to unload all their trunks.'

'I should like to see a passenger who carries luggage that will take more than six minutes. I have been here thirty years.'

I said: 'My wife is arriving today with the infant. I thought she would require a lot of time in order to get down carefully. And then she is bound to have numerous boxes. These women, you know,' I said laughing artificially, seeking his indulgence. He was a good man and laughed with me. 'Well, sometimes it has happened that the train was held up for the convenience of a second-class passenger. Are your people travelling second?' 'I can't say,' I said.

I knew well she wouldn't travel second, although I implored her in every letter to do so. She wrote rather diplomatically: 'Yes, don't be anxious, I and the baby will travel down quite safely.' I even wrote to my father-in-law, but that gentleman preserved a discreet silence on the matter. I knew by temperament he disliked the extravagance of travelling second, although he could afford it and in other ways had proved himself no miser. I felt furious at the thought of him and told the station-master. 'Some people are born niggards ... would put up with any trouble rather than ...' But before I could finish my sentence a bell rang inside the station office and the station-master ran in, leaving me to face my travail and anguish alone. I turned and saw my porter standing away from me, borrowing a piece of tobacco from someone. 'Here, Number Five, don't get lost.' A small crowd was gathering unobtrusively on the platform. I feared he might get lost at the critical moment. A bell sounded. People moved about. We heard the distant puffing and whistling. The engine appeared around the bend.

A whirling blur of faces went past me as the train shot in and stopped. People were clambering up and down. Number Five followed me about, munching his tobacco casually. 'Search on that side of the mail van.' I hurried through the crowd, peering into the compartments. I saw my father-in-law struggling to get to the doorway. I ran up to his carriage. Through numerous people getting in and out, I saw her sitting serenely in her seat with the baby lying on her lap. 'Only three minutes more!' I cried. 'Come out!' My father-in-law got down. I and Number Five fought our way up, and in a moment I was beside my wife in the compartment.

'No time to be sitting down; give me the baby,' I said. She merely smiled and said: 'I will carry the baby down. You will get these boxes. That wicker box, bring it down yourself, it contains baby's bottle and milk vessels.' She picked up the child and unconcernedly moved on. She hesitated for a second at the thick of the crowd and said: 'Way please,' and they made way for her. I cried: 'Susila, mind the door and baby.' All the things I wanted to say on this occasion were muddled and gone out of mind. I looked at her apprehensively till she was safely down on the platform, helped by her father. Number Five worked wonders within a split second.

I wouldn't have cared if the train had left now. The mother and child stood beside the trunks piled up on the platform. I gazed on my wife, fresh and beautiful, her hair shining, her dress without a wrinkle on it, and her face fresh, with not a sign of fatigue. She wore her usual indigo-coloured silk *sari*. I looked at her and whispered: 'Once again in this *sari*, still so fond of it,' as my father-in-law went back to the compartment to give a final look round. 'When will she wake up?' I asked pointing at the child, whom I found enchanting, with her pink face and blue shirt.

'Father is coming down,' she said, hinting that I had neglected him and ought to welcome him with a little more ceremony. I obeyed her instantly, went up to my father-in-law and said: 'I am very happy, sir, you have come ...' He smiled and said: 'Your wife and daughter got comfortable places, they slept well.'

'Did they, how, how? I thought there was such a crowd ...' My wife answered: 'What if there are a lot of others in the compartment? Other people must also travel. I didn't mind it.' I knew she was indirectly supporting her father, anticipating my attacks on him for travelling third. 'I only thought you might find it difficult to put the child to sleep,' I said.

'Oh, everybody made way for us, and we got a whole berth to ourselves,' she said, demanding of me by every look and breath that I should be sufficiently grateful to her for it. I turned to him and said: 'I'm so happy you managed it so well, sir.' He was pleased. He said: 'People are ever so good when they see Susila and the baby.'

'I hope you will stop with us for at least a week,' I said, and looked at my wife for approval. But her father declined the invitation with profuse thanks. He was to be back in his town next day and he was returning by the evening train. He said: 'There were three Bombay men, they liked Leela so much that they tried to give her a lot of biscuits. She was only too eager to accept, but I prevented ...'

'Biscuits are bad for the baby,' I said. We moved on. I stretched out my hand: 'Let me carry her,' I said. My wife declined: 'You don't know how to carry a baby yet. You will sprain her.' She clasped her closer, and walked off the platform.

A Victoria carriage waited for us outside. Our trunks were stuffed into it, and we squeezed ourselves in. I shared the narrow seat behind the driver with my father-in-law, leaving the other seat for mother and child. Between us were heaped all the trunks and I caught patches of her face through the gaps in the trunks. She talked incessantly about the habits of the infant, enquired about the plan of our house, and asked the names of buildings and streets that we passed.

My mother came down and welcomed her at the gate. She had decorated the threshold with a festoon of green mango leaves and the floor and the doorway with white flour designs. She was standing at the doorway and as soon as we got down cried: 'Let Susila and the child stay where they are.' She had a pan of vermilion solution ready at hand and circled it before the young mother and child, before allowing them to get down from the carriage. After that she held out her arms, and the baby vanished in her embrace.

A look at my mother, her eagerness as she devoured them with her look, and led them into the house, and I was moved by the extraordinary tenderness which appeared in her face. All my dread of yesterday as to how she would prove as a mother-in-law was suddenly eased.

!My mother was swamped by this little daughter of mine. She found little time to talk or think of anything else. She fussed over the young mother and the child. She felt it her primary duty to keep the young mother happy and free to look after the little one. The child seemed to be their meeting point; and immediately established a great understanding and harmony between them. All day my mother compelled my wife to stay in her own room and spent her entire time in the kitchen preparing food and drink for her and the child. When the child cried at nights, my mother, sleeping in the hall, sprang up and rocked the cradle, before the young mother should be disturbed. The child still drew nourishment from its mother, and so the latter needed all the attention she could get.

My mother stayed with us the maximum time she could spare – two months – and then returned to the village.

* * *

I left the college usually at 4.30 p.m., the moment the last bell rang, and avoiding all interruptions reached home within about twenty minutes. As soon as I turned the street I caught a glimpse of Susila tinkering at her little garden in our compound, or watching our child as she toddled about picking pebbles and mud ... It was not in my wife's nature to be demonstrative, but I knew she waited there for me. So I said: 'I have taken only twenty minutes and already you are out to look for me!' She flushed when I said this, and covered it up with: 'I didn't come out to look for you, but just to play with the child ...' My daughter came up and hugged my knees, and held up her hands for my books. I gave her the books. She went up the steps and put them on the table in my room. I followed her in. I took off my coat and shirt, picked up my towel and went to the bathroom, with the child on my arm, as she pointed at the various articles about the house and explained them to me in her own terms. Most of her expressions were still monosyllables, but she made up a great deal by her vigorous gesticulations. She insisted upon watching me as I put my head under the tap. The sight of it thrilled her and she shrieked as water splashed about. I put her safely away from the spray as I bathed, but she stealthily came nearer step by step and tried to catch some of the drops between her fingers. 'Ay, child, keep off water.' At this she pretended to move off, but the moment I shut my eyes under water and opened them again, she would have come nearer and drenched a corner of her dress, which was a signal for me to turn off the water and dry myself. I rubbed myself, lifted her on my arm, went to my room, and brushed my hair. I did this as a religious duty because I felt myself to be such a contrast to them when I returned in the evening, in my sagging grey cotton suit, with grimy face, and ink-stained fingers, while the mother and daughter looked particularly radiant in the evenings, with their hair dressed and beflowered, faces elegantly powdered.

By the time I reached this stage my wife came out and said: 'Your coffee is getting cold. Won't you come in?'

'Yes, yes,' and we moved off to our little dining-room. An alcove at the end of the dining-room served for a shrine. There on a pedestal she kept a few silver images of gods, and covered them with flowers; two small lamps were lit before them every morning. I often saw her standing there with the light in her face, her eyes closed and her lips lightly moving. I was usually amused to see her thus, and often asked what exactly it was that she repeated before her gods. She never answered this question. To this day I have never learnt what magical words she uttered there with closed eyes. Even when I mildly joked about it, 'Oh! becoming a yogi!' she never tried to defend herself, but merely treated my references with the utmost indifference. She seemed to have a deep secret life. There hung about this alcove a perpetual smell of burnt camphor and faded flowers.

I sat down on the plank facing the shrine, with the child on my lap. A little plate came up with some delicacy or titbit heaped on it – my tiffin. Susila placed this in front of me and waited to see my reaction. I looked up at her standing before me and asked: 'What is this?' She replied: 'Find out for yourself, let us see if you recognize it ...' As I gazed at it wondering what it might be, the child thrust her hand out for it. I put a little into her mouth while the mother protested: 'You are going to spoil her giving her whatever she wants ...'

'No, just a little ...'

'It will make her sick, she has been eating all sorts of things lately. Don't blame me if she gets sick ...'

'Oh, she won't, just a little won't do her any harm ...' As Leela held up her hands for more, her mother cried: 'No, baby, it won't do. Don't trouble father, come away, come away,' and the little one stuck to me fast, avoiding her mother's gaze, and I put my left arm about her and said: 'Don't worry about her, I won't give her any more ...' As I finished what was on the plate Susila asked: 'Do you want some more?' This was always a most embarrassing question for me. As I hesitated she asked, 'Why, is it not good?'

'It is good,' I groaned, 'but ...'

'But smells rather smoky, doesn't it? But for the smell it would be perfect,' she said. And I couldn't but agree with her. 'I prepared such a large quantity thinking you would like it ...' She went in and brought out a little more and pushed it on to my plate and I ate with relish just because she was so desperately eager to get me to appreciate her handiwork!

She gave me coffee. We left the kitchen, and sat down in the hall. The child went over to her box in a corner and rummaged its contents and threw them about and became quite absorbed in this activity. My wife sat in the doorway, leaning against the door and watching the street. We spent an hour or more, sitting there and gossiping. She listened eagerly to all the things I told her about my college, work and life. Though she hadn't met a single person who belonged to that world, she knew the names of most of my colleagues and the boys and all about them. She knew all about Brown and what pleased or displeased him. She took sides with me in all my discussions and partisanships, and hated everyone I hated and respected anyone I respected. She told me a great deal about our neighbours, their hopes and fears, and promises and qualities. This talk went on till darkness crept in, and the lights had to be switched on. At the same time the clattering at the toy box ceased. This was a signal that the child would demand attention. She came towards us whimpering and uttering vague complaints. My wife got up and went in to light the oven and cook the dinner, while I took charge of Leela and tried to keep her engaged till her food was ready.

On the first of every month, I came home, with ten ten-rupee notes bulging in an envelope, my monthly salary, and placed it in her hand. She was my cash-keeper. And what a ruthless accountant she seemed to be. In her hands, a hundred rupees seemed to do the work of two hundred, and all through the month she was able to give me money when I asked. When I handled my finances independently, after making a few routine savings and payments, I simply paid for whatever caught my eyes and paid off anyone who approached me, with the result that after the first ten days, I went about without money. Now it was in the hands of someone who seemed to understand perfectly where every rupee was going or should go, and managed them with a determined hand. She kept the cash in a little lacquer box, locked it up in her *almirah*, and kept a minute account of it in the last pages of a diary, four years old.

We sat down at my table to draw up the monthly budget and list of provisions. She tore off a sheet of notepaper, and wrote down a complete list – from rice down to mustard. 'I have written down the precise quantity, don't change anything as you did once.' This was a reference to a slight change that I once attempted to make in her list. She had written down two seers of Bengal gram, but the National Provision Stores could not supply that quantity, and so the shopman suggested he would give half of it, and to make up the purchase, he doubled the quantity of jaggery. All done with my permission. But when I returned home with these, she saw the alterations and was completely upset. I found that there was an autocratic strain in her nature in these matters, and unsuspected depths of rage. 'Why has he made this alteration?' she had asked, her face going red. 'He didn't have enough of the other stuff,' I replied, tired and fatigued by the shopping and on the point of irritability myself. 'If he hasn't got a simple thing like Bengal gram, what sort of a shop has he?'

'Come and see it for yourself, if you like,' I replied, going into my room. She muttered: 'Why should it make you angry? I wonder!' I lay down on my canvas chair, determined to ignore her, and took out a book. She came presently into my room with a paper screw full of sugar and said: 'This man has given underweight of sugar. He has cheated you.' I lowered the book, frowned at her and asked: 'What do you mean?'

'I fear to speak to you if you get angry,' she said.

'Who is angry?' I asked. 'What is the matter, tell me?'

'I wrote for two measures of sugar, and see this; he has billed for two measures and has actually given a measure and a half. I have measured it just now.' She looked at me victoriously, waiting to hear how I was going to answer this charge. I merely said: 'He wouldn't do such a thing. You must have some extraordinary measure with you at home.'

'Nothing wrong with my measure. Even your mother measured everything with it and said it was correct.' So this was a legacy from her mother-in-law. She had taught the girl even this. She had a bronze tumbler, which she always declared was a correct half measure, and she would never recognize other standards and measures. She insisted upon making all her purchases, ghee or oil or milk or salt, with the aid of this measure, and declared that all other measures, including the Government stamped ones, were incorrect, and were kept maliciously incorrect because some municipal members were business men! She used the same tumbler for weighing too, placing it for weight in the scale pan, declaring that the curious thing about the vessel was that by weight too it was exactly half seer, and she would challenge anyone to disprove it. All tradespeople somehow succumbed to this challenge and allowed her to have her own way. She carried this tumbler about wherever she went, and I now found that she had procured a similar one for her daughter-in-law, and had trained her in the use of it.

'Throw away that tumbler and use an honest measure,' I said. Susila merely looked at me and said: 'Please don't speak so loudly. The child is asleep,' and tried to go out of the room. I called her back and said: 'If you use an honest measure you will find that others have also done so.'

'This National Provisions man is a thief,' she cried, 'the sooner you change the better.' This annoyed me very much. I had known the N.P.S. man for years and liked him. I went all the way to South Extension to patronize his shop, and I liked the man because he was fat and talkative, and Sastri the logic man always said that it was the best shop in the town. I rather prided myself on going to the shop. I liked the fat, thoughtful proprietor. I said: 'There is nothing wrong with him. He is the best shopman known. I won't change him ...' 'I don't know why you should be so fond of him when he is giving undermeasure and rotten stuff ...' she replied. I was by this time very angry: 'Yes, I am fond of him because he is my second cousin,' I said with a venomous grin.

Her hatred of him was not mitigated. She said: 'You would pay cart hire and go all the way to South Extension to be cheated by him rather than go to a nearer shop. And his rates!' She finished the rest of her sentence with a shiver. 'I don't care if he overcharges – I won't drop him,' I declared. 'Hush, remember the child is sleeping,' she said and left the room. I lay in my chair fretting for fifteen minutes and then tried to resume my study, but could read only for five minutes. I got up and went over to the store-room as she was putting away the provisions and articles in their respective tin or glass containers. I stood at the doorway and watched her. I felt a great pity for her; the more because I had not shown very great patience. I asked: 'I will return the jaggery if it is too much. Have you absolutely no use for it?' In answer she pushed before me a glass goblet and said: 'This can hold just half a viss of jaggery and not more; which is more than enough for our monthly use. If it is kept in any other place, ants swarm on it.' I now saw the logic of her indignation, and by the time our next shopping was done, she had induced me to change over to the Co-operative Stores.

Since then every time the monthly list was drawn up she warned me: 'Don't alter anything in it.' I followed her list with strict precision, always feeling that one could never be sure what mess any small change might entail. If there were alterations to be made, I rather erred on the side of omission and went again next day after taking her suggestion.

She was very proud of her list. It was precise. Every quantity was conceived with the correct idea as to how long it should last. There were over two dozen different articles to be indented and she listed them with foresight and calculation. She was immensely proud of this ability. She gave me twenty rupees or more for these purchases. I went out to the Co-operative Stores in the Market Road and returned home three hours later followed by a coolie carrying them all in paper bags and bundles, stuffed into a large basket. She always waited for them at the door with unconcealed enthusiasm. The moment I was at the gate she held out her hand for the bill, and hurriedly ran her eyes down the columns checking the figures and prices. 'Oh! you have got all the things, and the cost didn't go up above 22–8–0 total ... slightly better than it was last month. Which item is cheaper this month?' She was in raptures over it. I loved to see her so pleased, and handed her the change to the last pie. She paid the coolie three annas; she would never alter this figure whatever happened. If anyone had the hardihood to expect more she declared: 'Don't stand there and argue. Be off. Your master has offered you an anna more than you deserve. After all the market is only half a mile away!' She carried the packages to the store-room, and put each in its container, neatly labelled and ranged along a rack. She always needed my assistance to deal with rice. It was the bulkiest bag. It was my set duty on these days to drag the gunny-sack along to the store, lift it and empty it into a zinc drum. I invited her displeasure if I didn't do it carefully. If any rice scattered accidentally on the floor, she said: 'I don't know when you will learn economic ways. You are so wasteful. On the quantity you throw about another family could comfortably live.'

She watched these containers as a sort of barometer, the level of their contents indicating the progress of the month. Each had to be at a particular level on a particular date: and on the last date of the month – just enough for another day, when they would be replenished. She watched these with a keen eye like a technician watching an all-important meter at a power house.

All went very well as long as she was reigning supreme in the kitchen – till my mother sent an old lady from the village to cook for us and assist us.

One evening we were sitting as usual in the front veranda of the house when an old lady stood at our gate, with a small trunk under her arm, and asked: 'Is this teacher Krishnan's house?'

'Yes, who are you, come in ...' I opened the gate for her. She looked at me, wrinkling her eyes and said, 'Kittu ... I have seen you as a baby and a boy. How big you have grown!' She came up to the veranda, peered closely into my wife's face and said: 'You are our daughter-in-law. I am an old friend of Kamu,' she said, referring to my mother by her maiden name. By this time Leela, who had been playing near her box, came out on hearing a new voice. At the sight of her the old lady cried: 'So this is Kamu's grandchild!' She picked her up in her arms and fondled her. Susila's heart melted at the sight of it and she said: 'Come into the house, won't you?' The old lady went in, sat under the lamp and took out of a corner of her *sari* a crumpled letter and gave it to me. It was from my mother: 'I am sending this letter with an old friend of mine, who was assisting me in household work when you were a baby. She then went away to live with her son. He died last year, and she has absolutely no one to support her.

She came to me a few weeks ago in search of work. But I have no need for assistance nowadays. Moreover your father grows rather irritable if he sees any extra person in the house. So I have given her her bus fare and sent her on to you. I have always felt that Susila needed an assistant in the house, the baby demanding all the attention she can give. My friend will cook and look after the child. And you can give her whatever salary you like.'

While the old lady kept fondling the child, sitting on the floor, I read the letter under the hall light and my wife read it over my shoulder. We looked at each other. There was consternation in her look. There were many questions which she was aching to ask me. I adjourned to my room and she followed me.

'What shall we do?' she asked, looking desperate.

'Why do you look so panicky? We will send her back if you do not want her.'

'No, no. How can that be? Your mother has sent her. We have got to have her.'

'I think it will be good to have her. All your time is now spent in the kitchen when you are not tending the baby. I don't like you to spend all your time cooking either tiffin or food.'

'But I like it. What is wrong in it?' she asked.

'You must spend some more time reading or stitching or singing. Man or woman is not born merely to cook and eat,' I said, and added: 'You have neglected your books. Have you finished *Ivanhoe*?' She had been trying to get through *Ivanhoe* for years now, and *Lamb's Tales from Shakespeare*. But she never went beyond the fiftieth page. Her library also contained a book of hymns by a Tamil saint, a few select stanzas of Kamba Ramayana, Palgrave's *Golden Treasury* and a leather-bound Bhagavad-Gita in Sanskrit. I knew how fond she was of books. She was always planning how she was going to devour all the books and become the member of some library. But it never became more than an ambition.

In the earlier years of our married life we often sat together with one or other of the books, in the single top-floor room in her father's house, and tried to read. The first half an hour would be wasted because of an irresponsible mood coming over her, which made her laugh at everything: even the most solemn poem would provoke her, especially such poems as were addressed by a lover. 'My true love hath my heart and I have his.' She would laugh till she became red in the face. 'Why can't each keep his own or her own heart instead of this exchange?' She then put out her hand and searched all my pockets saying: 'In case you should take away mine!'

'Hush, listen to the poem,' I said, and she would listen to me with suppressed mirth and shake her head in disapproval. And then another line that amused her very much was 'Oh, mistress mine, where are you roaming?' She would not allow me to progress a line beyond, saying: 'I shall die of this poem some day. What is the matter with the woman loafing all over the place except where her husband is?'

However much she might understand or not understand, she derived a curious delight in turning over the pages of a book, and the great thing was that I should sit by her side and explain. While she read the Tamil classics and Sanskrit texts without my help, she liked English to be explained by me. If I showed the slightest hesitation, she would declare: 'Perhaps you don't care to explain English unless you are paid a hundred rupees a month for it?'

But all that stopped after the child was born. When the child left her alone, she had to be in the kitchen, and my argument now appealed to her. She said: 'But that will mean an extra expense. What shall we pay her?'

'About eight rupees, just what everyone pays, I think,' I said.

'Oh, too much,' she said. 'I'm sure she will waste another eight rupees' worth of things. This is an unnecessary expense,' she said. I explained: 'Very necessary and we can afford it. In addition to the provident fund, why should we send thirty-five to the savings bank? I think about twenty-five rupees a month for the bank will be more than enough. Many of my friends do not save even five rupees.'

'Why do you want to follow their example? We must live within our means, and save enough.' She often declared: 'When we are old we must never trouble others for help. And remember there is a daughter, for whose marriage we must save.'

'When we bring forth some more daughters and sons ...' I began, and she covered my mouth with her fingers. 'You men! what do you care! You would think differently if God somehow made you share the bothers of bringing forth! Where is your promise?' I often reiterated and confirmed our solemn pact that Leela should be our only child. And anything I said otherwise, even in jest, worried her very much.

With the future so much in mind she planned all our finances. She kept a watch over every rupee as it arrived, and never let it depart lightly, and as far as possible tried to end its career in the savings bank.

But now our savings were affected to the extent of at least ten rupees – as she explained 'Six rupees, old lady's salary' (Susila stubbornly refused more than that for a year) and 'four rupees for all her waste, putting it at a minimum ...' She was disconsolate over it for a long time, till I appeased her by saying: 'Oh, don't worry about it. When I get some money from examination papers I will give you the whole of it for the savings bank.'

In course of time we found that we simply couldn't do without the old lady. She cooked the food for us, tended the child, gave us the necessary courage when the child had fever or stomach-ache and we became distraught; she knew a lot of tricks about children's health, she grew very fond of the child and took her out and kept her very happy. She established herself as a benign elder at home, and for us it meant a great deal. Her devotion to the child enabled me to take my wife twice or thrice a month to a picture, on a walk along the river, or out shopping. My wife grew very fond of her and called her 'Granny', so did Leela. But Susila had a price to pay for this pleasure. She lost her supremacy over the kitchen and the store. The levels in the containers at the store went down in other ways than my wife calculated. Susila protested and fought against it for some time, but the old lady had her own way of brushing aside our objections. And Susila adjusted her own outlook in the matter. 'Didn't I bargain for a waste of four rupees a month? Well, it is not so hard, because she wastes only three rupees ...' Our provision bill fluctuated by only three rupees, and it was a small price to pay for the great company and service of the old lady, who lived on one meal a day, just a handful of cooked rice and buttermilk. It was a wonder how she found the energy for so much activity. My wife often sat down with her in order to induce her to eat well, but it was of no avail.

I sat in my room, at the table. It was Thursday and it was a light day for me at college – only two hours of work in the afternoon, and not much preparation for that either. *Pride and Prejudice* for a senior class, non-detailed study, which meant just reading it to the boys. And a composition class. I sat at my table as usual after morning coffee looking over the books ranged on the table and casually turning over the pages of some exercise books. 'Nothing to do. Why not write poetry? Ages since I wrote anything?' My conscience had a habit of asserting itself once in six months and reminding me that I ought to write poetry. At such moments I opened the bottommost drawer of my table and pulled out a notebook of about five hundred pages, handsomely bound. I had spent nearly a week at a local press getting this done some years ago. Its smooth pages contained my most cherished thoughts on life and nature and humanity. In addition to shorter fragments that I wrote at various times on a miscellany of topics, it contained a long unfinished poem on an epic scale to which I added a few dozen lines whenever my conscience stirred in me. I always fancied that I was born for a poetic career and some day I hoped to take the world by storm with the publication. Some of the pieces were written in English and some in Tamil. (I hadn't yet made up my mind as to which language was to be enriched with my contributions to its literature, but the language was unimportant. The chief thing seemed to be the actual effort.) I turned over the pages looking at my previous writing. The last entry was several months ago, on nature. I felt satisfied with it but felt acute discomfort on realizing that I had hardly done anything more than that. Today I was going to make up for all lost time; I took out my pen, dipped it in ink, and sat hesitating. Everything was ready except a subject. What should I write about?

My wife had come in and was stealthily watching the pages over my shoulder. As I sat biting the end of my pen, she remarked from behind me: 'Oh, the poetry book is out: why are you staring at a blank page?' Her interruption was always welcome. I put away my book, and said: 'Sit down,' dragging a stool nearer. 'No, I'm going away. Write your poetry. I won't disturb you. You may forget what you wanted to write.' 'I have not even thought of what to write,' I said. 'Some day I want to fill all the pages of this book and then it will be published and read all over the world.' At this she turned over the leaves of the notebook briskly and laughed: 'There seem to be over a thousand pages, and you have hardly filled the first ten.'

'The trouble is I have not enough subjects to write on,' I confessed. She drew herself up and asked: 'Let me see if you can write about me.'

'A beautiful idea,' I cried. 'Let me see you.' I sat up very attentively and looked at her keenly and fixedly like an artist or a photographer viewing his subject. I said: 'Just move a little to your left please. Turn your head right. Look at me straight here. That's right ... Now I can write about you. Don't drop your lovely eyelashes so much. You make me forget my task. Ah, now, don't grin please. Very good, stay as you are and see how I write now, steady ...' I drew up the notebook, ran the fountain-pen hurriedly over it and filled a whole page beginning:

'She was a phantom of delight
When first she gleamed upon my sight:
A lovely apparition, sent
To be a moment's ornament.'

I went on for thirty lines, ending:

'And yet a spirit still, and bright
With something of an angel-light.'

I constantly paused to look at her while writing, and said: 'Perfect. Thank you. Now listen.'

'Oh, how fast you write!' she said admiringly.

'You will also find how well I've written. Now listen,' I said, and read as if to my class, slowly and deliberately, pausing to explain now and then.

'I never knew you could write so well.'

'It is a pity that you should have underrated me so long; but now you know better. Keep it up,' I said. 'And if possible don't look at the pages, say roughly between 150 and 200, in the *Golden Treasury*. Because someone called Wordsworth has written similar poems.' This was an invitation for her to run in and fetch her copy of the *Golden Treasury* and turn over precisely the forbidden pages. She scoured every title and first line and at last pitched upon the original. She read it through, and said: 'Aren't you ashamed to copy?'

'No,' I replied. 'Mine is entirely different. He had written about someone entirely different from my subject.'

'I wouldn't do such a thing as copying.'

'I should be ashamed to have your memory,' I said. 'You have had the copy of the *Golden Treasury* for years now, and yet you listened to my reading with gaping wonder! I wouldn't give you even two out of a hundred if you were my student.' At this point our conversation was interrupted by my old clock. It burst in upon us all of a sudden. It purred and bleated and made so much noise that it threw us all into confusion. Susila picked it up and tried to stop it without success, till I snatched Taine and smothered it.

'Now, why did it do it?' she demanded. I shook my head. 'Just for pleasure,' I replied. She gazed on its brown face and said: 'It is not even showing the correct time. It is showing two o'clock, four hours ahead! Why do you keep it on your table?' I had no answer to give. I merely said: 'It has been with me for years, poor darling!'

'I will give it away this afternoon – a man comes to buy all old things.'

'No, no, take care, don't do it ...' I warned. She didn't answer, but merely looked at it and mumbled: 'This is not the first time. When you are away it starts bleating after I have rocked the cradle for hours and made the child sleep, and I don't know how to stop it. It won't do for our house. It is a bother ...'

That evening when I returned home from college the first thing I noticed was that my room looked different. My table had lost its usual quality and looked tidy, with all books dusted and neatly arranged. It looked like a savage, suddenly appearing neatly trimmed and groomed. The usual corner with old newspapers and magazines piled up was clean swept. The pile was gone. So was the clock on the table. The table looked barren without it. For years it had been there. With composition books still under my arm, I searched her out. I found her in the bathroom, washing the child's hands: 'What have you done with my clock?' I asked. She looked up and asked in answer: 'How do you like your room? I have cleaned and tidied it up. What a lot of rubbish you gathered there! Hereafter on every Thursday ...'

'Answer first, where is the clock?' I said.

'Please wait, I will finish the child's business first and then answer.'

I stood at the bathroom doorway and grimly waited. She finished the child's business and came out bearing her on her arm. While passing me she seized the child's hand and tapped me under the chin with it and passed on without a word to her room. She later met me in my room as I sat gloomily gazing at the table.

'Why have you not had your tiffin or wash?' she asked, coming up behind and gently touching my shoulder.

'I don't want any tiffin,' I snapped.

'Why are you so angry?' she asked.

'Who asked you to give away that clock?' I asked.

'I didn't give it away. That man gave me twelve annas for it – a very high price indeed.'

'Now you are a ...' I began. I looked at the paper corner and wailed: 'You have given away those papers too! There were old answer papers there ...'

'Yes, I saw them,' she said. 'They were four years old. Why do you want old papers?' she asked. I was too angry to answer. 'You have no business to tamper with my things,' I said. 'I don't want any tiffin or coffee.' I picked up my coat, put it on and rushed out of the house, without answering her question: 'Where are you going?'

I went straight back to the college. I had no definite plan. There was no one in the college. I peeped into the debating hall, hoping there might be somebody there. But the evening was free from all engagements. I remembered that I hadn't had my coffee. I walked about the empty corridors of the college. I saw the servant and asked him to open our common room. I sent him to fetch me coffee and tiffin from the restaurant. I opened my locker and took out a few composition books. I sat correcting them till late at night. I heard the college clock strike nine. I then got up and retraced my way home. I went about my work with a business-like air. I took off my coat, went at great speed to the bathroom and washed. I first took a peep into my wife's room. I saw her rocking the baby in the cradle. I went into the kitchen and asked the old lady: 'Have the rest dined?'

The old lady answered: 'Susila waited till eight-thirty.'

I was not interested in this. Her name enraged me. I snapped: 'All right, all right, put up my leaf and serve me. I only wanted to know if the child had eaten.' This was to clear any misconception anyone might entertain that I was interested in Susila.

I ate in silence. I heard steps approaching, and told myself: 'Oh, she is coming.' I trembled with anxiety, lest she should be going away elsewhere. I caught a glimpse of her as she came into the dining-room. I bowed my head, and went on with my dinner unconcerned, though fully aware that she was standing before me, dutifully as ever, to see that I was served correctly. She moved off to the kitchen, spoke some words to the old lady, and came out, and softly moved back to her own room. I felt angry: 'Doesn't even care to wait and see me served. She doesn't care. If she cared, would she sell my clock? I must teach her a lesson.'

After dinner I was back in my room and sat down at my table. I had never been so studious at any time in my life. I took out some composition books. I noticed on a corner of my table a small paper packet. I found enclosed in it a few coins. On the paper was written in her handwriting:

Time-piece	12 annas
Old paper	1 rupee
Total	One rupee and twelve annas.

I felt furious at the sight of it. I took the coins and went over to her room. The light was out there. I stood in the doorway and muttered: 'Who cares for this money? I can do without it.' I flung it on her bed and returned to my room.

Later, as I sat in my room working, I heard the silent night punctuated by sobs. I went to her room and saw her lying with her face to the wall, sobbing. I was completely shaken. I didn't bargain for this. I watched her silently for a moment, and collected myself sufficiently to say: 'What is the use of crying, after committing a serious blunder?' Through her sobs, she sputtered: 'What do you care, what use is it or not. If I had known you cared more for a dilapidated clock.' She didn't finish her sentence, but broke down and wept bitterly. I was baffled. I was in an anguish myself. I wanted to take her in my arms and comfort her. But there was a most forbidding pride within me. I merely said: 'If you are going to talk and behave like a normal human being, I can talk to you. I can't stand all this nonsense.'

'You go away to your room. Why do you come and abuse me at midnight?' she said.

'Stop crying, otherwise people will think a couple of lunatics are living in this house ...'

I went back to my room – a very determined man. I lay on a mat, trying to sleep, and spent a miserable and sleepless night.

We treated each other like strangers for the next forty-eight hours – all aloof and bitter. The child looked on this with puzzlement, but made it up by attending to her toys and going to the old lady for company. It was becoming a torture. I could stand no more of it. I had hoped Susila would try to make it up, and that I could immediately accept it. But she confined herself to her room and minded her business with great concentration and never took notice of me. I caught a glimpse of her face occasionally and found that her eyes were swollen. I felt a great pity for her, when I saw her slender neck, as she was going away from the bathroom. I blamed myself for being such a savage. But I couldn't approach her. The child would not help us either; she was too absorbed in her own activities. It came to a point when I simply could not stand any more of it. So the moment I returned home from college next evening I said to her, going to her room:

'Let us go to a picture ...'

'What picture?' she asked.

'*Tarzan* – at Variety Hall. You will like it very much ...'

'Baby?'

'The old lady will look after her. We shall be back at nine. Dress up ...' I was about to say 'Look sharp,' but I checked myself and said: 'There is a lot of time. You needn't hustle yourself.'

'No, I'll be ready in ten minutes ...' she said rising.

By the time we were coming out of the Variety Hall that night we were in such agreement and showed such tender concern for each other's views and feelings that we both wondered how we could have treated each other so cruelly. 'I thought we might buy a new clock, that's why I gave away the old one,' she said.

'You did the best thing possible,' I said. 'Even in the hostel that wretched clock worried everyone near about. I am glad you have rid me of it.'

'They make such beautiful ones nowadays,' she said.

'Yes, yes, right. We will go out and buy one tomorrow evening,' I said. When we reached home we decided that we should avoid quarrelling with each other since, as she put it, 'They say such quarrels affect a child's health.'

CHAPTER THREE

On the occasion of our child's third birthday, my father wrote to say that he would advance me money to buy a house in Malgudi or to build one. He did not think it was very wise to go on living in a rented house. This offer made us very happy. I and my wife sat down and carried on endless discussions to decide which would be better, whether a built house or a site on which to build. 'A room all for myself where I can sit and spin out great poetry,' I said.

'Well, some place where you can be free from my presence?' she asked. 'Why don't you be plain?' 'No, no,' I replied awkwardly.

'I'm not eager to thrust my company on you either,' she said: 'I am as eager to have a separate room.'

'In that case, I don't want one,' I replied. 'Why should both of us have separate rooms?'

'Are you fighting?' the little one asked, gazing at us bewildered. 'You are always scolding mother,' she said looking at me, and I felt unhappy at this thrust.

We agreed to go out on the following Sunday morning to Lawley Extension to choose a house or a site.

We were up with the dawn. The old cook had gone out to see a relation on the previous evening. I had to light the fire and boil the water for coffee while Susila bathed, dressed, and prepared herself for the outing. As I sat struggling with smoke in my eyes and nostrils, she appeared at the kitchen doorway, like a vision, clad in her indigo *sari*, and hair gleaming and jasmine-covered. I looked at her indigo *sari* and smiled to myself. She noticed it and asked, 'Why that?'

'Nothing, nothing,' I said with a cold damp in my nose. My voice was thick. 'What is wrong with this *sari*? It is as good as another!' she said.

'Yes, yes,' I replied. 'That is why I say you should use it more sparingly, otherwise you will wear it out ...' Her eyes sparkled with joy; she spread the fragrance of jasmine more than ever. 'The divine creature!' I reflected within myself, looking at her tall, slim figure.

> 'She was a phantom of delight
> When first she gleamed upon my sight.'

My mind unconsciously quoted – the habit of an English teacher. The water reached boiling point and was lifting and throwing down the lid. All around the kitchen lay scattered faggots and burnt matchsticks and coal. Smoke still hung in the air. I smelt the coffee powder. 'Five spoons of powder and two tumblers of water, am I right?' I asked. She suddenly pushed me aside and said: 'Now, get ready. Let us be off. I will attend to this ...'

I went away, and returned in half an hour ready and dressed. She gave me coffee. The maidservant had come. Susila placed a tumbler of milk on a teapoy outside and told the servant: 'Give this to the baby when she wakes up. Make her drink off the whole of it. Keep her engaged till the old lady returns. She will be back at about eight. Tell her that I will bring her fine toys and biscuits ...'

She threw a look at the sleeping baby, drew a blanket over her, and said: 'Sit by her side, so that when she wakes up she may not cry.'

As we stepped out of the house, she said: 'I hope the child won't cry ...'

'Don't keep bothering about her. She will be all right. You will be spoiling her if you bother so much. She must learn to exist by herself ...' My wife merely smiled at me. 'I'm confident that the old woman will keep her happy, but she must come back in time.'

A fresh morning breeze blew. I took in a deep breath and said: 'Do you know how I used to love the early morning walk along the river when I was in the hostel ... There is a magic in the atmosphere ...' I was highly elated. The fresh sun, morning light, the breeze, and my wife's presence, who looked so lovely – even an unearthly loveliness – her tall form, dusky complexion, and the small diamond ear-rings – Jasmine, Jasmine ... 'I will call you Jasmine, hereafter,' I said. 'I've long waited to tell you that ...'

'Remember, we are in a public road and don't start any of your pranks here,' she warned, throwing at me a laughing glance. Her eyes always laughed – there was a perpetual smile in her eyes. 'The soul laughs through the eyes, it is the body which laughs with lips ...' I remarked. 'What are you saying?' she asked. 'Nothing,' I replied.

'I hope you've not forgotten that we are in a public road?' 'What I say is perfectly innocent, no harm even if repeated on a public platform.' We were now in Market Road. Vehicles were moving about. The market was stirring into activity.

People as they passed threw a glance at us, some students saluted me. I said, 'My boys, good fellows ...' 'Must be, because they salute you,' she said.

We were now passing before Bombay Ananda Bhavan, a restaurant. 'Shall we go in?' she asked. I was only too delighted. I led her in. A number of persons were sitting in the dark hall over their morning coffee. There was a lot of din and clanging of vessels. Everybody turned and stared, the presence of a woman, particularly at that hour, being so very unusual. I felt rather shy. She went ahead, and stood in the middle of the hall not knowing where to go. A waiter appeared. 'Here Mani,' I hailed, knowing this boy, a youngster from Malabar, who had served me tiffin for several years now. I felt very proud of his acquaintance.

Mani said, 'Family room upstairs, follow me.' We followed him. There was a single room upstairs, with a wooden, marble-topped table and four chairs. The walls were lined as usual with fancy, coloured tiles.

'These marbles are so nice,' my wife said, with simple joy, running her fingers over them. 'How smooth!'

'Do you know they are used only in bathrooms in civilized cities; they are called bathroom tiles.'

'They are so nice, why should these be used only for bathrooms?'

'Do you think those bathrooms are like ours?'

'Bathrooms are bathrooms wherever they may be ...' she replied.

'No, no, a bathroom is very much unlike the smoke-ridden, wet, dripping bathing-place we have.'

'I try to keep it as neat as possible, and yet you think it is not good,' she remarked.

'I didn't mean that.'

'I think you did mean it.' I didn't like to spoil a good morning with a debate. So I agreed: 'I am sorry. Forgive and forget.'

'All right,' she said. She stretched her arms back and touched the wall behind her and said, 'I like these tiles, so fine and smooth! When we have a house of our own, won't you have some of them fixed like that on our walls?'

'With pleasure, but not in the hall, they are usually put up only in the bathrooms,' I pleaded.

'What if they are! People who like them for bathrooms may have them there, others if they want them elsewhere ...'

At this moment Mani appeared carrying a tray of eatables. 'How quickly he has brought these!' she remarked: this was her first visit to Bombay Ananda Bhavan. Its magnitude took her breath away. Her eyes sparkled like a child's.

She tried to eat with a spoon. She held it loosely and tipped the thing into her mouth from a distance. I suggested, 'Put it away if you can't manage with it.' She made a wry face at the smell of onion: 'I can't stand it – ' she said. 'I know. I know,' I replied. 'What a pity.' It was careless of me. I knew that she hated onions but had taken no care to see that they were not given to her. I reproached myself: I called for the boy vociferously and commanded: 'Have that removed, bring something without onion.' I behaved as if I were an elaborate, ceremonial host. I wanted to please her. Her helplessness, innocence, and her simplicity moved me very deeply. 'I will give you something nice to eat.' I gave elaborate instructions to the boy. She mentioned her preference, a sweet, coloured drink – like a child's taste once again, I thought. I fussed about her till she said, 'Oh, leave me alone,' with that peculiar light dancing in her eyes. She said, 'Shall we take something for the child?' I didn't like to spoil a good morning with contradictions, but I did not approve of giving hotel stuff to the baby. So I said with considerable diplomacy: 'We will buy her some nice biscuits. She likes them very much.'

Nearly an hour later we came out of the hotel. I proposed that we should engage a *jutka* for going to Lawley Extension, but she preferred to walk. She said that she'd be happy to walk along the river. 'My dear girl,' I said, 'Lawley Extension is south and this river north of the town. We are going to the Extension on business.'

'Please, please,' she pleaded recklessly. 'I must wash my feet in the river today.' I was in the mood to yield completely to her wishes. So I agreed though it meant walking a couple of miles in the opposite direction.

It was a most exhilarating walk down the river. She splashed her feet in the water, rested under the banyan, heaped up sand and kept muttering, 'How the little girl would love it if only she could be brought here! I think she will simply roll in the sand. But we must take care not to let her go near the water.'

I watched her once again ... 'Do you know how I used to spend all my morning here when I was in the hostel ... I used to get up at dawn ...'

'You could continue it even now ... I hope you will not say I'm responsible for your giving up the good habit,' she said. I laughed. 'It doesn't look very important now, that is all; I did it for some time then; no compulsion to repeat the same thing for ever, even if it is good.'

When we were ready to go back I suggested, 'We must go on an all-India tour sometime. I will take you with me.'

'Promise?' she asked.

'Absolutely,' I said. 'I will take you also to England and Europe if I make a lot of money out of the books I am going to write.'

'What about the child?'

'She will be grown up by then,' I replied. 'We can leave her with her grandparents. You must see everything.' I imagined, even as I spoke, how she would touch the marble of Taj, stand astounded before the snow-covered Himalayas, and before the crowd and magnitude of European cities.

* * *

We left the river and went to Lawley Extension in a *jutka*. When we got down there, she looked a little tired. Her face had a slight flush. 'We have to walk a little here,' I warned her. 'Do you think I can't?' she asked, and went forward.

Lawley Extension formed the southernmost portion of the town, and consisted of well-laid-out residential buildings, lining the neat roads and crossroads. It was the very end of the town, beyond which passed the Trichy trunk road, shaded with trees. At one time, only those with very high incomes could have residences there, but about five years ago, under a new scheme, the extension developed farther south; even beyond the trunk road the town was extending. There was a general scramble for these sites and houses, which received an uninterrupted southern breeze blowing across the fields, a most satisfactory outlook aesthetically, the corn fields, which were receding in the face of the buildings, waving in sunlight. 'I shall have to cycle up to the college, but it doesn't matter. We shall have a most enchanting view before us, we won't know that we are in a town.' I became very enthusiastic. A friend of mine, Sastri of the logic section, had promised me his help in choosing a house. He was the moving spirit of this new extension, secretary of the Building and Acquisition Society, and a most energetic 'extender'. No one could have believed that he had so much business capacity – his main occupation being logic. He was a marvellous man – a strange combination of things, at one end 'undistributed middle', 'definition of knowledge', 'syllogisms', and at the other he had the spirit of a pioneer. His was the first building in the New Extension, and then he got together a few persons and formed his company, which was chiefly responsible for the growth of this New Extension.

We reached Sastri's house, a small bungalow in a vast compound overgrown with trees. Sastri – a thin grey-haired man – was sitting under a tree digging its roots.

'Hullo, Sastri!' I cried. 'I am sorry I'm so late. This lady is responsible for it,' I said pointing to my wife. Sastri came up, picking the mud off his hands.

'So glad you have brought your wife, I hear lots of complaints that you don't bring her out,' said Sastri.

'Oh, there is a small child to be looked after,' I replied.

'You could bring her out too.'

'Oh, it is not so easy.' I began to visualize all the difficulties in an instant: the protection, ceaseless attention and all the rest of it. 'Father take me up, I can't walk.' 'Father, put me down, I don't like to be carried.' 'I'm hungry,' and 'I won't eat anything.'

'It is not so easy,' I said.

'Why, why?' asked the logician.

'You see,' I began, but realized how utterly hopeless it would be to explain it all to him – this childless man would not understand the complications. I changed the subject: 'I hope you will take us to see some houses.'

'Come up, come up, we will discuss it.' He took me in and seated me in the veranda, on a discoloured rattan chair, which pricked my back. Sastri said: 'Still interested in houses? Why don't you buy a site and build a good house? I have a beautiful site for you up there.'

'Oh, I can't wait for all the bricks and mortar to take shape. I don't know anything of house building, too much bother.'

'Leave it all to me,' Sastri said. 'I will do it.' He had taken upon himself this task for scores of people, and some uncharitable ones remarked that he made a better living out of it than as a logic lecturer.

'I've no patience to wait, my dear fellow,' I pleaded. 'I can't stand all the nuisance. I want a house at the moment I think of it.'

'Very well, I'll show you some. See how you like them. If you don't like any of them, you may just accept my other suggestion.' He sent his servant to fetch the building contractor: a dark man, with a moustache, and a red vermilion hand. 'Sit down, Swamy, can those houses be seen today?' Sastri asked.

'Yes, yes, I will send the boy to keep them open.' He despatched a boy.

Sastri's wife had given us lemon squash to drink, and refreshed, Susila started out once again with us.

Sastri said: 'We will have to do a little walking. I hope the lady won't feel too fatigued.'

'No, no, not at all. I can walk miles,' Susila replied.

I was walking on between Sastri and the contractor, who were full of house-building talk. A little later I turned and noticed that Susila had fallen back, unable to keep pace with us. I stopped and joined her. Standing beside her I felt like calling her 'Jasmine' once again. I whispered: 'We are going to see some very nice houses, are you pleased?'

'Yes, yes.'

'You must tell me which of them you like best ...'

'Yes,' she replied. I whispered: 'Don't worry about the child, she will be quite happy.'

'If she starts crying for some reason or other, no one can stop her. The old lady will not be able to manage,' she said.

'Oh, don't imagine all those things,' I pleaded. I lowered my voice still further and said, 'Jasmine ...' She suppressed a smile that came on her lips, her eyes flashed a mild reproof.

We came before a row of very small houses – each with a very narrow suffocating veranda, and a front garden, half a dozen monotonously alike.

'Do you like this pattern?' Sastri asked me. I looked at my wife. She said: 'The child will lose her way not knowing which is her house – they are all alike. Why are these so alike?' She shook her head. Sastri added: 'The second house is for sale.' I said: 'Can't we see some other pattern? This is too small.' A young boy held the door open. Sastri said: 'Come in and see the house. No harm in seeing the house.' He was a connoisseur in houses and expected others to be the same. The contractor added: 'Yes, yes, you must see different types before deciding.' 'What an amount of banality surrounds the purchase of a house! How much we have to bear before we are through with it,' I reflected. The contractor commanded the boy: 'Are all the houses open?'

'Yes, master.'

'Don't say "yes"! Keep them open,' he said.

'Yes, master,' he said.

'You are a careless fool,' he added. 'I will pluck off your ear if you aren't careful!' 'Why does this man bully the young fellow unnecessarily?' I reflected. 'Some people are made that way. Perhaps, if a census on this subject were taken, ten thousand persons would be found to be bullying ten thousand others every minute all over the world ...' I wanted the boy to be saved further persecution and so asked the contractor: 'What is the width of this veranda?'

'Forty-four inches ...'

Sastri asked: 'What do you think of it?'

'I don't like it. It is no use having such a small house,' I replied.

'But the price!' Sastri said with a knowing smile. 'The best at twelve hundred!'

'Oh, Sastri, how did this house-salesmanship get into your blood, instead of logic?' I reflected.

At last we came to a house which seemed attractive. It had a wide compound, broad windows, and a general appearance of spaciousness and taste. All the doors and the walls looked fresh with paint. As we turned the street, Susila saw the contractor's boy standing at the gate, and asked with a great thrill: 'Is that also ours?' It was very attractive with two jasmine creepers trained over an arch on the gateway. It was full of flowers. The gates moved on silent hinges. As we were about to go under the arch I lightly touched her arm and pointed at the jasmine creeper. I told the contractor: 'I would love to call this the Jasmine Home, its perfume greets us even as we enter.' The contractor was pleased. 'I hope you will like it inside too,' he said.

A few steps led up to the veranda – a fairly deep and cool veranda, with a short parapet. Susila sat on the parapet. I sat beside her and said: 'Someone with taste has planned it.' Sastri looked greatly pleased that a house of his selection had received such approval. The main door was opened, and we inspected the house room by room. A hall, four rooms, in addition to the kitchen, a pleasing light blue paint on all the walls inside the house. Susila and I were thrilled. We went away by ourselves, lingered in every room, and visualized ourselves as its future occupants.

'What's the price?' she asked.

'Must be within our figure otherwise they would not have brought us here.'

'Plenty of space for the child to play. She can simply run about just as she likes. Those parapets on the veranda are a good idea to prevent her from falling off.'

'There is plenty of space for guests too. The grandparents may also come and stay with us quite comfortably. The small room in the front veranda will be my study. I shall write immense quantities of poetry when I settle here, I think.'

'Sometime my mother must come and stay with us,' she said. 'She has always blamed us for living in a rented house. She will be very happy, I am sure.'

'You must also have the room next to mine as all your own – if you like I will have coloured marble tiles fitted along the walls.'

'So that you may call it the bathroom, I suppose,' she remarked.

We joined the other two sitting on the veranda, and discussed the price and other details: 'It was occupied only for three months after it was built and changed hands.'

'Why?' I asked, trying to appear as a man of great business wisdom. Sastri replied, looking serious, 'I've not enquired. Have you any idea?' The contractor said: 'I built the house for the gentleman, and the family went way and settled in Madras. Rich people don't usually mind these things.'

'I hope it has a clear reputation,' Sastri said.

'Of course, without doubt,' replied the contractor. 'This is at the end of the town, that is the chief reason ...' It was a fact. It was really the very last house, in the last crossroad of the New Extension. Fields of corn stretched away in front of the house, and far beyond it, a cluster of huts of the next village, and beyond it all stood up the blue outlines of Mempi Mountains. It was a lovely prospect. I stood looking at it and said: 'A magnificent view, only a buffalo could be insensible to it.

'Is this a mosquito-ridden place?' I asked.

'Some parts of the year ... The best thing to do is to sleep under a net.'

'I feel suffocated under a mosquito net. I prefer a mosquito bite,' Sastri said.

The contractor said: 'I am sixty-five years old and I have never been under a mosquito net! I've never had malaria even once.'

'Really?' Sastri asked, greatly impressed.

'A fact. You ask my old mother if you like,' replied the contractor. 'I think all this stuff about mosquitoes is nonsense.

As if there were no mosquitoes in the days of our grandfathers.' Susila found the talk boring: 'I'll go and have a look round the compound,' she said. I got up. Susila replied: 'No, you needn't come. I'll just see the compound and backyard, and return.' She started out. I followed her a few paces. 'Why do you want to go?' I asked. 'Shall I follow you?'

'Oh, won't you let me alone even for a few minutes?' she whispered. 'Nobody will carry me off. I can look after myself!' She went away. I returned to my friends, and continued our talk. I promised to write to my father, and complete the transaction at an early date. They fixed the coming Wednesday as a date for further discussions. I took Sastri aside and requested him to settle the price favourably. 'Leave it to me. I will cut down at least five hundred,' Sastri assured me. My mind was in a whirl – I was already tremendously excited. 'We must move in within a month, if possible,' I reflected.

Half an hour passed. 'What is Susila doing with herself so long?' I thought. I jumped down, saying: 'Wait a minute, please,' and ran round to the backyard.

I noticed as I went along what a lot of space there was for making a small manageable garden. The fertility of the surrounding fields had affected this place too and there was a growth of pleasant green grass and one or two uncared-for bushes of leucas – which put forth small, whitish flowers. 'This poor plant is the first to be removed whenever a garden is made, because it grows naturally – but I shall make a point of preserving it.' I stopped and plucked a flower. I wondered what ideas Susila had for the garden, and decided that the bulk of it should be left to her care and management. 'I am sure she is thinking of a very grand kitchen garden in the backyard ...' I told myself. I went on to the backyard, where a few young coconut trees threw a sparse shade around. Susila was not to be seen. I looked for her and called, 'Susila! Susila!' She answered from somewhere. I called again, and she cried: 'Push the door open! I can't open it from this side.' I found that her voice came from the other side of a green-painted lavatory door. I gave it a kick and it flew open. Out she came – red and trembling. I looked at her and felt disturbed.

'What – what were you doing here?' I asked. She was panting with excitement. She was still shivering. I seated her on a stone slab nearby. 'What is the matter? What is the matter?'

'I went in there. The door was so bright and I thought it'd be clean inside ... but oh!' She screwed up her face and I shuddered, unable to bear the disgust that came with recollection. I felt agitated. 'Why did you go there?' I cried. She didn't answer. It was a sad anti-climax to a very pleasing morning. I looked at her feet. 'You went in barefoot?' She nodded.

'Where are your sandals?'

'I forgot them at home.' I shook my head in despair. 'I have told you a hundred times not to come out barefoot. And yet ...' She merely looked at me without replying. Her face was beaded with perspiration. Her cheeks were flushed. She was still trembling. I melted at the sight of it: 'Oh, darling, why did you go there?'

'The door was so bright ...' she replied softly. 'I thought it'd be clean inside too ... but I couldn't come out after I went in – the door shut by itself with a bang. I thought something terrible had happened ... Ah, the flies and other things there!' She was convulsed with disgust. 'Oh, oh ... A fly came and sat on my lip ...' She wouldn't bring her lips together. She kept rubbing them with her fingers in an effort to eradicate the touch of the fly ... I said: 'There is the water tap. Rinse your mouth, and wash your feet, you will be all right. Don't think of it any more.' She jumped up on the stone slab, turned the tap on and washed her hands and feet and mouth, again and again. She rubbed her feet on the stone till they were red and till they smarted. It looked as though she would not stop this operation. I said: 'You'll hurt yourself, or you may catch a cold. Come away. Don't bother about it any more. You are all right.'

We came back to the veranda. Sastri and the contractor were waiting for us. I seated Susila in a clean corner of the veranda and advised her to lean on the wall, and rest. The others observed her flushed face and asked what the matter was. 'She visited that lavatory and found it rather unclean,' I said. 'Oh,' the contractor said: 'I wish the lady had told us, I'd have asked her not to go there. This is one of the curses of the place. It is so far out and so near the field and village that all kinds of people passing this way stop here for shelter, and they foul a lavatory beyond description ... This is not the first time such a complaint has come to us.'

'When the house is occupied?' I asked.

'Oh no, no trouble then, only when it is vacant. It's so difficult to engage a caretaker for every little place, though there is a peon going round to see these things at least once a day.'

After resting for about half an hour Susila got up and said: 'I feel all right.'

Sastri and the contractor went ahead. I kept my wife company, watching her every movement anxiously. When we approached Sastri's house, he suggested: 'Won't you come in for a moment? The lady can have a little coffee. She looks tired.' Susila declined this with a smile.

'Oh no, thanks, we will be going, it is late,' I said. 'We will meet on Wednesday.'

We walked down the crossroad. When the presence of the other two was withdrawn, I grew elaborately fussy – I asked her for the hundredth time if she was feeling all right. As we were passing into the main road, we saw a small, newly-built temple. 'They have built a beautiful temple for this place, so near our house. So thoughtful of them ...' I said. 'We will go in,' she said, 'and see the god.'

'Most certainly.'

There was an old woman sitting on a gunny-sack at the temple gate, selling offerings. 'Buy something for the god,' she entreated.

'What temple is this?' Susila asked.

'*Srinivasa* – the greatest god; you need not visit Thirupathi Hills to see him, if you visit him here – he grants all your boons and blesses all your efforts ...' She held up a coconut, a packet of camphor, plantain, and betel leaves.

'You are both so young and bright. He will bless you with numerous children and may they all be sons ...' said the old lady.

'Hush,' Susila replied: 'We have one and we are satisfied with on ...' she laughed and entered the temple. I was tremendously relieved to see her laugh. We entered the temple hall – a stone pillared hall, smelling of camphor and flowers, cool and shady. There were two bronze lamps burning in the inner sanctuary, illuminating a tall stone image of *Srinivasa*. A priest, wrapped in a shawl, sitting at the foot of the image, rose on seeing us and held up a plate. We placed the offerings on it.

'What a lovely image!' Susila remarked. She brought together her palms and closed her eyes in prayer. I stood watching her. The priest broke the coconut, and placed it and the other things at the feet of the image. He lit the camphor, sounded a bell, and circled the flame around the image. In this flickering light the image acquired strange shadows and seemed to stir, and make a movement to bless – I watched my wife. She opened her eyes for a moment. They caught the light of the camphor flame, and shone with an unearthly brilliance. Her cheeks glowed, the rest of her person was lost in the shadows of the temple hall. Her lips were moving in prayer. I felt transported at the sight of it. I shut my eyes and prayed: 'God bless this child and protect her.' She received the holy water from the priest and touched her lips and eyes, put a vermilion dot on her forehead, and tucked the flower offered to the god in her hair. We stepped out. As we descended the temple steps she muttered: 'Only now do I feel quite well again. We must make it a point to visit this temple as often as we can.'

'You can visit it every evening when we have taken the new house,' I said.

'Yes, yes.' I was greatly relieved to see her happy and fit once again. We hailed a passing *jutka*, climbed into it, and sat snugly close. The *jutka* wheels rattled over the cobbles and it lulled us into a mild drowse. We ceased to pass any remarks or comment and settled in a tranquil silence. I studied her face without her knowledge. A great peace had descended on her. 'It is God's infinite grace that has given me this girl.' The *jutka* was filled with the scent of the jasmine in her hair and the glare of the indigo-coloured *sari*.

As we passed the Market Road, she reminded me, 'You have promised to buy biscuits and a doll for the child.' We stopped the carriage before Novelty House. I dashed in and came out bearing a biscuit packet, a doll and a toy engine.

When we reached home we found the child playing very happily with the cook and a child from the next house. We heard her voice, over and above the rattle of the carriage wheels, when we were still two houses away. As soon as the carriage stopped, Leela came out running. Her mother took her up in her arms immediately, and gave her the doll, train and the biscuits. Leela's friend from the next house was also there. Leela said to her: 'You can go home now, my mother is come.' The friend said: 'All right ...' and hesitated, casting a look on the game they had been playing ... They had raised a building with wooden blocks, and various small utensils filled with water and grains and flowers and leaves were strewn about the small hall – they had been playing 'Home Keeping' and calling on each other.

'Yes, she was a very fine child today. When mother is at home, she gives such a lot of trouble over food! She was my sweet child today,' said the old cook.

'Did she ask where we were?'

'Ah, didn't she? Every few minutes asking and asking why her mother had gone out without telling her. She is a smart child.'

'Why did you go away mother, at night?' the little one asked. 'When I opened my eyes, I didn't see you but her.' The cook shook with laughter: 'What a lot of speech she has learnt! She is going to defeat all the others in your family in speech, madam.'

'Why did you go away, mother?' the little girl asked. Her mother threw herself on the floor, even without changing her dress. 'Too tired for anything now. I won't get up, whatever happens, without resting for another half an hour ...'

'You must eat your food first,' the old cook began.

'No, get up, get up, Susila,' I said. But she begged to be allowed to rest for half an hour.

'Where did you go, mother, without telling me?'

'To buy a house for you.'

'What is it made of?'

'Stone and lime.'

'Is it so high?' She indicated with her hand a yard in height and said: 'I want one which is small and can be put in the trunk.'

'I mean a real big house like this,' said the mother.

'This is our house?' the child asked.

'Another one, more beautiful – Oh! You can play all day with plants.'

'Can I play in mud?'

'Oh, yes, it's very clean and nice ...'

'My friend must also come with me.' She carried on this conversation sitting on her mother, clutching the doll and the train, and eating a biscuit.

I busied myself for half an hour in my room, and came out. I still found my wife lying on the floor: 'Oh, why have you flung yourself down in this manner? Go and change. We will eat ...'

'Leave me alone for a little, please,' she pleaded.

I felt her temples with my fingers: 'If this small excursion exhausts you so much, I don't know what I can do with you when we go on our North Indian travel.'

'I will be all right then.'

'You will be better if you eat a hearty meal at once.'

She begged, 'Please, don't compel me. The thought of food upsets me. Go and finish your food first, and don't wait for me.' I protested at the idea and went away to my room. 'I can also take it later with you. I'm not particularly hungry. I think the hotel stuff has not agreed with you.'

The child snuggled close to her mother and clung to her neck. I said: 'Don't trouble your mother.'

'I'm not troubling her. I'm making her headache go,' replied the child.

I went away to my study and stood for a moment gazing at my table. My wife had given up all attempts at tidying up my room, and it had lapsed into the natural state of my hostel days. Once again all Milton and Shakespeare and Bradley jostled each other in a struggle for existence. There were four library books on my table which had been overdue, accumulating fines and bringing me fierce reminders from the librarian, but which I had not opened even once. There were the latest books on Plato, Swinburne, modern poetry, and others which the librarian had forced on me in one of his hospitable moods. I realized that I used to read better when I was in the hostel and had not become the head of a family. Nor were my hours spent in chatting with my wife or watching the child play or in running about on shopping errands. My conscience troubled me whenever I thought of it. 'I will not waste half an hour, but will get through this stuff on Plato.' I picked up the book and lounged in my canvas chair. 'Plato's idealism ...' I read. 'Sickening fellows. Why won't they leave Plato alone? For the thousandth time someone restating Plato – I don't like this book. I shall return it.' I put it away. The other book too I found unreadable.

I found that I had spent half an hour in these attempted studies. I put away the books. I leaned back in my chair, hoping I should be called. There was no sound in the house. I got up and went to the hall. I saw the mother and the child fast asleep where they lay. My first impulse was to waken Susila. I watched her for a moment. 'Too tired, let her sleep for a while,' I reflected. 'I will dine first, she may wake up and join me.' I went to the dining-room, and sat down before the leaf. The old cook served me. 'Where is ...' she began in her croaking voice. 'Hush, not so loudly. She's asleep,' I said. 'She will wake up presently.' I went through my meal, and tiptoed out to the bathroom, washed my hands, and while I dried them, stood near her and watched. Her lips were slightly parted. 'Is she still reluctant to bring her lips together?' I asked myself. I sat by her side, and gently touched her eyelids with the tip of my finger. She opened her eyes, at once saw the child asleep by her side, clutching her toys, and disengaged herself gently and sat up. I said: 'I've had my food; I felt hungry. Won't you come and eat?'

I led her to the bathroom, and gently splashed a little cold water on her face. I took her to the kitchen, seated her before her leaf, and sat by her side. She obeyed implicitly without saying a word. The old lady muttered, 'You should never delay your food so long. An empty stomach makes poison.' She served some vegetables and dhal. Susila murmured, 'None of these. Only a little rice and buttermilk for me.' After due protests she was allowed to have her choice. She sat gazing at her leaf. After a considerable amount of coaxing, she picked up a tiny quantity of rice between her fingers, put it in her mouth, and retched. 'Biliousness,' I remarked. 'Bring those lime pickles. Now be a good girl and finish off that rice with the help of the pickles. Go on – you can do it.' She sat staring at the leaf. She took another mouthful after a good deal of persuasion and sickened. It was impossible. She rose to her feet declaring, 'I can't. I won't eat any food now. I'll eat at night.' She washed her hands, and went back to the hall, and lay down. I sat beside her worrying myself. She confessed: 'Don't worry, it is nothing, I'll be all right.'

'What is wrong?'

'Shall I say?' she whispered. 'Don't be angry with me. That closet, and those, oh, oh,' she shuddered, 'flies and other things come before me and I can't eat. And that fly which sat here,' she pointed at her lip and finished the rest of the sentence with a shiver.

Three days, four, five, and six days passed and still she did not leave her bed. It was difficult for her to swallow any food or medicine, although she was doing everything in her power to forget the picture of that closet. Luckily for me, the college was closed and I could spend much of my time with the child, who looked forlorn ever since her mother took to bed. Susila lay on her bed, spread on the floor in her room. The grey, vine-patterned bed-spread, green shawl, and that girl lying with her face to the wall, hardly awake for two hours in a day – it shattered my peace.

The old cook was very unhappy. 'Please call a doctor,' she suggested. It hadn't seemed to me necessary; moreover my wife was definitely against showing herself to a doctor. I told the cook, 'She won't allow any doctor to see her.' The cook made a gesture of despair: 'Oh, you young man! Is this the time to consult her wishes!' Her question stirred vague fears in me. So I asked haughtily: 'What is wrong with the time? It is quite a good time, take it from me ...' She ignored my petulance and said: 'She has been in bed for five or six days, what have you done?'

'I have given her medicine.'

'That's not enough, you must ask a doctor to see her.'

'I know my duty,' I replied and went away. I sat by my wife and watched her. It was morning, and she looked fairly well.

'Can you take any solid food today?' I asked solicitously.

'No, no, some milk and gruel will do for me ...'

'I will call a doctor to see you,' I said.

'No, no, please. I don't like doctors,' she pleaded. 'They press the stomach, and here and there, and it hurts. The press given by the doctor before Leela was born still pains.'

'Don't be absurd. You talk like a baby.' She merely looked at me. Her lips were dry. 'Where is the child?' she asked. She was playing in the next house. 'Bring her down. I will comb her hair and change her dress.'

'Don't exert yourself.'

'No, no, I can do it. If I don't, who will do it?' she asked. I went over to the next house. Leela was heaping wet sand on their front step and sticking twigs and flowers on its top. 'This is our temple,' she said. The god was a piece of stone embedded in the mud. She reverently prostrated herself before it. 'She is the temple man,' she pointed to her friend. 'She does the *pooja*.' Her friend came up with a piece of coconut (a castor seed) and flowers (grass tufts) and offered them to me. I said to Leela: 'Your mother wants you.' She brightened: 'Has her fever gone?' she asked, and clutched my hand and ran down with me, leaving the temple and the priest behind.

Her mother sat up. Her hair was dishevelled, and seemed to be all in a knotted mass. Her lips were dry. She still wore the *sari* she had put on the day she came out with me. All the same I felt joyous. She was able to sit up – after all these days. 'Try and change your dress today,' I said. She sent out the child to fetch the coconut oil bottle and the comb from the cupboard in the dining-hall. The child returned hugging the bottle, put it down, and ran out a second time to bring the comb; and sat down before her mother. Susila remarked: 'The poor child looks an orphan without proper attention.' She uncoiled her hair, oiled and combed it, and plaited it, and then said, 'Bring that blue silk frock and shirt.'

'Mother, mother, I hate that blue silk ...'

'You mustn't keep it in the box and outgrow it. It is nice, wear it out.'

'Mother, mother.'

'Which is it?' I asked.

'The one your brother sent from Hyderabad last *Deepavali*,' Susila replied. All my affection for my brother returned immediately. Good fellow – I remembered the bullying he practised on me in that cart whenever we went out together, the wild claims he would make in the afternoon that he had trained a frog (living under a stone near the well) to come out at his call and follow him: remember him helplessly pacing up and down the house when his wife and mother had heated arguments over trifles, and now auditing, henpecked, and with twelve children – a life of worry – so good of him to have thought of me in all this stress ... All this flashed before my mind and I ordered: 'Little one, you must learn to obey your mother in all these matters, without a word ...' The child threw a pained look at me, and went away. I heard her opening the box in the next room – the wicker trunk in which her clothes were kept. My wife said: 'Don't be so harsh with her, poor girl!' The child returned with the blue frock and shirt. I took it in my hand and said: 'How lovely!' The child replied swiftly: 'It is not lovely,' and submitted herself to her mother's handling. Half-way through it her mother said: 'Go and get a little water in a vessel – don't drop it on your toes. I will wash your face ...'

'Here!' I cried. 'You mustn't touch cold water. You may catch a cold.' My wife said: 'I won't catch a cold. Her face is covered with mud.' The child hesitated, and then ran over to the bath-room and fetched a vessel of water and a towel. Her mother rubbed off the mud patches with a wet towel, put a vermilion dot on her forehead, powdered her cheeks, and dressed her in new clothes. Leela looked resplendent. 'Am I all right father?' she asked. I took her in my arms. 'You are beautiful,' I cried.

My wife changed her dress, combed her hair, and ate a little food, though she said it tasted bitter. She looked refreshed. She remade her bed. I was elated. The gloom which had hung on me for these four days lifted, and I hummed a little tune to myself as I went to my room. These exertions, however, tired her, and she lay down and slept. She woke up at five in the evening, and complained of headache. I felt her pulse, and found that she had a temperature. I said, 'Just wait. I will fetch the doctor.'

'Yes,' she agreed. 'Do something and stop this headache.' 'I will give you some Horlicks and go,' I said. I called for boiling water. Horlicks, and a spoon and tumbler, were on a small table in the hall. I made the Horlicks and took it in to her. I found her crying. This was the first day I saw her broken and crying. 'Oh you are hungry!' I cried. I tried to make her drink the Horlicks, but it was at boiling point and wouldn't cool down easily. She lay with her face towards the wall and tears made a wet track all over her face. I lost my head. The cook stood by and advised: 'Give her food first, she is hungry that is all, that is all.'

'But this damned thing is scalding, you can't bring a thing at bearable temperature. I've half a mind to fling away this rubbish.' The child had meanwhile come in and was quietly leaning against the wall and watching us. The cook was averse to seeing her there, and kept muttering: 'Come away, baby,' till I, trying to cool the milk with one hand, and comforting my wife with the other, shouted at her to leave the child alone. Meanwhile my wife's sobbing increased. 'Control yourself, child,' I said. 'Take this, you will be all right.' After all the drink cooled, and she drank it, and smiled at me, I felt relieved. I sat down and caressed her forehead and asked: 'Do you feel all right now? I will fetch the doctor.'

Dr Shankar of Krishna Medical Hall had been introduced to me by Rangappa who swore by him. 'The greatest physician on earth,' he used to say, 'easily the most successful practitioner in the town.' Krishna Medical Hall was in Market Road, and it was a mile's walk from my house. I enjoyed this outing. It suddenly relieved the stress and gloom of the last few days. I met one or two people, and spent a little time in conversation on the way, purchased a packet of cigarettes and smoked. All this seemed to restore the old glow of life – its peace and tranquillity.

The doctor was away. His seat at the central table was vacant, but all around the benches and chairs were filled with patients and patients' relatives waiting for the doctor. An accountant and a clerk sat next to each other at the entrance poring over leather-bound ledgers and making entries.

'Be seated please, the doctor will be in presently,' said the clerk. I felt gratified by the warmth of his welcome and the smile he bestowed on me. I sat in a chair and looked about. The walls were lined with glass shelves loaded with the panacea that drug manufacturers invent – attractive boxes, cellophane wrappings.

The days of bitter drugs were gone. All medicines were good to the taste and even to see. Piles and piles of sterilized cotton in blue packing reached the ceiling. 'How do these people know where they've got the things they want, and when do they take it?' I wondered. The walls were decorated with placards containing coloured pictures of beauties and beasts and skeletons and rosy-cheeked children, benefited by one cellophane-covered nectar or another.

From an ante-chamber issued voices of women and cries of children. Somewhere else a dispenser was jingling his glasses. He came out presently, a business-like man wearing silk trousers, in shirt-sleeves and apron. He held up a bottle wrapped in brown paper: 'Who is Kesav?'

'It is for me,' said a feeble man wrapped in a shawl with a woollen muffler over his ears. The dispenser handed him the bottle with the brief remark: 'Three doses before meals,' and went in. This sufferer had some further question to ask, and opened his mouth to say something, but the dispenser was gone. The man clutched his bottle and looked about helplessly, turned to the clerk and asked: 'Can I take buttermilk?'

'Yes,' replied the clerk.

'Should I take this immediately after or a few minutes before food?'

'Say five minutes before food,' replied the clerk and added: 'Six annas, please.' The patient put down the change with a sad look, still feeling that he hadn't received his money's worth of doctor's advice. He hesitated, looked about and said, 'I would like to ask the doctor himself ...'

'You need not see him till you have taken this mixture for three more days. I will tell him how you are.' The patient felt grateful. 'Please don't forget to say that the pain on the left side still persists.'

'Yes, yes,' replied the clerk, who seemed to be half a doctor. He scattered advice and suggestions liberally. He even examined throats, and suggested remedies for headache.

A car stopped, and there was an agitation in the gathering. The doctor had arrived. Everybody pressed forward to receive him. He looked like a film star being mobbed by admirers. He waved his hand, smiled, and gently pressed all his admirers back to their seats.

His assistant placed some slips of papers and bottles before him and the doctor got down to work. He read out the names on the slips and bottles one by one, examined a throat here, tapped a chest there, listened in to the murmurs of hearts through a tube, and wrote prescriptions at feverish speed. Here he whispered into an ear something private, and there pushed someone into a private room and came out wiping his hand on a towel. He might have been a great machine dispensing health, welfare and happiness. I felt a great admiration for him. At last my turn came: 'What can I do for you, professor?' he asked, mechanically picking up my wrist. For some reason he always called me professor. 'I'm not the patient, doctor,' I said.

I explained to him my wife's symptoms. He asked a few questions, wrote down a prescription, and put it away. He passed on to the next slip and called the next in order. A man from the village stood before him and began: 'Last night ...' The doctor turned to me and asked: 'Have you brought a bottle?'

'No, I didn't expect ...' I began apologetically.

'It is all right,' he said, and on my prescription made a mark, and turned to his next patient. 'Last night ...' the other began and gave a long-winded account of a pain in the back of the head, which travelled all the way down to his ankle and went up again. He might have been a witness deposing before a magistrate. The doctor tapped his back, tingled his ear, looked into the pupils of his eyes, and pinched his knee. He cracked a couple of jokes at the expense of this patient, prescribed the treatment, and disposed of him. In a quarter of an hour the smart dispenser who had swept in the prescriptions a few minutes ago, came out with a few paper-wrapped bottles and called: 'Mrs Krishna ...' I stood up and took my bottle, and looked at the doctor, who was busy writing. The clerk said: 'It is your bottle?' and held his hand out for it. He looked at the label and read: 'A third every four hours before food, and five minutes before each dose one pill. Repeat the mixture for two days and then see the doctor. Diet – rice and buttermilk. Ten annas please.' I was disappointed with the mechanical, red-tape method I found here. I looked at the doctor, he was still busy. I paid down the cash, but returned to my seat. I waited for ten minutes in the hope of catching the doctor's eye. But he was far too busy.

'Doctor,' I butted in.

'Half a moment, please.' He finished the prescription he was writing, leaned back, and said: 'Yes, got your mixture and pills?'

'Yes.' Now that I had his attention I was at a loss to know what to ask. 'When is this to be given?' I asked, guiltily looking at the clerk.

'Didn't he tell you?' he asked pointing at the clerk. 'Yes, yes, he did,' I replied hastily. I now realized the need for this red-tape arrangement – everyone wanted to ask the same set of questions.

'But what I want to know is ... Don't you have to see the patient?'

'Oh, no, it is just malaria. I have fifty cases like this on hand, no need to see her. I'll tell you if it is necessary. You can bring her down sometime if necessary.'

'But she can't move, she is rather weak ...'

'Put her in a *jutka* and bring her along, nothing will happen ... Just peep into that room and see how many persons with fever have come here. It is usually more convenient for me than calling on them.' I really felt it was absurd to have ever thought of asking this great man to visit me.

'No, no, I understand,' I said awkwardly.

'Really no need. She will be all right in a couple of days. She will be all right, don't worry.' He smiled confidently and it cheered me.

'Diet? What can I give her?'

'Buttermilk and rice, anything you like. Don't make it too heavy.' Clutching my bottle I went out.

At the door my daughter met me. 'Mother is very cross, father. She won't look at me at all, but keeps her hand over her eyes and ...'

'Oh, she will be all right. I've brought her the medicines.' My wife looked at me and asked: 'Why've you taken such a long time to get back?' She was still moaning with headache. 'The old lady is cooking and the baby has no one to be with ...'

On hearing my voice the old lady came out of the kitchen. She was overjoyed to see the medicine. 'I pray to the Lord of the

Seven Hills that this medicine may put her on her feet again. I am longing to see her moving about the house. What food is to be given?'

'Buttermilk and rice.' She threw up her hands in horror. 'I have never heard of buttermilk being given for fever!'

'Never mind. The doctor knows better. The days are gone when buttermilk was dreaded,' I said haughtily.

Next day I went to the doctor, reported the patient's condition, and took home the mixture and pills, and then again the next day, and the next. It was becoming difficult to make Susila swallow the pills. It agitated her poor heart so much that she felt suffocated and perspiration left her prostrate. One night she perspired so much that she lay in a faint, and could communicate only by feeble signs. I gave her something hot to drink, and nursed her, but this condition frightened me. It was two o'clock at night. Her feet were cold.

I told the doctor about it when I met him next at his dispensary. He muttered something about idiosyncrasy and declared: 'But we can't stop this pill now. It is the latest anti-malarial compound; it must be effective. It's bound to depress the heart a bit, but don't worry about it. She will be very well again. Don't stop the pills on any account.'

She swallowed the medicine and pills for about a week more. The temperature did not go down.

I went to the doctor's house, and begged him to visit us. He dressed and came along. 'Usually it is unnecessary. All these cases are alike. But I'll do it for your sake, professor ...' He drove down with me by his side to our house. He was most amiable and leisurely – an entirely different man outside the dispensary. He played with my child and gave her a ride on his shoulder, examined all the books on my table, proved to be a great book-lover and student of philosophy, and was delighted that we had similar tastes. He was overjoyed to hear that I also wrote. He had great reverence, he said, for authors as a class. He appreciated one or two pictures I'd hung on the wall. All this established such a harmony between us that when he came to examine my wife he seemed an old friend rather than the medical automaton of Krishna Dispensary.

He took half an hour to examine the patient and declared at the end of it: 'Nothing to worry about ...'

My wife asked him: 'When can I move about again?'

'Very soon. But all your life you will be moving about the house doing this and that, why should you grumble at staying a little while in bed now? Many people take it as an opportunity for a holiday ...' He then narrated his experience at a house (he'd not mention names) where a daughter-in-law fell ill and was in bed for two weeks or so, and put on weight. Her husband came to him privately and said: 'Doctor, please keep her in bed for a fortnight more. It is almost her only chance of being free from the harassment of her mother-in-law.' On hearing this story Susila laughed so much that her face became red and she broke into sweat. He counted her pulse and said: 'She is already shaking off her temperature ... That is a good sign. She will be absolutely well again, in a couple of days unless she wishes to stay in bed like that daughter-in-law,' and he winked at me. 'Take the medicine and pills, madam,' he said and went away. He radiated health and cheer. Susila and I felt more confident and happy after this visit. So that when the child came from the next house she asked: 'Is mother all right?'

The doctor's presence was so beneficial that I requested him to visit her at least once a day. He was very obliging; it was quite a thrill for us to hear the sound of his car every day. We gave him coffee and he stayed for over half an hour talking to us on various matters. In the evening I went to his shop to fetch the medicine. It went on for nearly a week more. Although his visit cheered us it did not help the temperature to go down. It remained unaffected by all the drugs so far administered.

One afternoon the doctor came in, removed his coat briskly, opened his bag, and took out his sterilizer, a syringe and other things. We had never seen him getting down to business in this manner before. 'Will you allow me to take just a little blood, please?' he asked. At this my wife started crying. I pacified her.

'It won't hurt, I assure you,' said the doctor. 'Give me a little blood and I will see what sort of fellow the mischief maker is and throw him out ...'

'That's good, good,' he said, drawing up and sealing. 'Now we will know what stick to beat him with ...'

I was asked to see him next morning at his dispensary. All night I kept awake. 'What is the blood test going to reveal?' I kept asking myself over and over again. My wife asked: 'Why is he taking the blood? Anything serious?'

'Don't be absurd, it is nothing more than malaria. He has taken it only to see what kind of malaria it is. Anyway, why do you worry? He is a good doctor, he will cure you whatever it may be ...'

I sat next to the doctor at his dispensary. He passed me a brown piece of paper with the stamp of the Government Hospital on it. 'I sent the blood for clinical test. This is the report.' I looked at the brown sheet. 'Widol test positive – Typhoid ...' My throat went dry on reading it. 'Doctor, doctor ...' I cried. He was once again in his official seat, and so was an automaton. He said merely: 'Don't worry. It is a mild attack. Take home a tin of glucose, barley and a bottle of Lentol – it is a good disinfectant ... I will drop in on my way home in the afternoon.' I blabbered questions. He merely said: 'Don't get so nervous. I attend a dozen typhoid cases every day: nothing to worry. Here, give this gentleman ...' he gave directions to the dispenser and passed on to other patients.

I entered my house clutching a tin of glucose, some barley, a bottle of Lentol, and broke the news. I said with affected cheerfulness: 'It is a very mild attack; perhaps it is only paratyphoid. If it is, you will be up and doing again in two days.' She merely replied: 'Keep the child away. Write to my father. You must also take something to protect yourself ...'

The doctor came at midday. He seemed cheered that it was typhoid. He beamed on all of us and joked continuously. 'I like typhoid,' he said. 'It is the one fever which goes strictly by its own convention and rules. It follows a time-table and shows a great regard for those who understand its ways! Don't look so miserable, lady. Like a good daughter-in-law, make up your mind to make the most of your stay in bed for the next few weeks ...' Ever since she heard the word typhoid, Susila had become very silent. It was heart-rending to see her in this state.

I tried to speak to her and put a little courage into her, but it was a futile effort. She lay listening to my words with grim unresponsiveness. She felt now that the doctor deserved a remark and muttered: 'I thought it was malaria ...' 'Malaria!' the doctor said. 'I was only dreading lest it should be malaria – the most erratic and temperamental thing on earth. I wouldn't trust it. But typhoid is the king among fevers – it is an aristocrat who observes the rules of the game. I'd rather trust a cobra than a green snake; you can depend upon the cobra to go its way if you understand its habits and moods ...'

My wife's little room was converted into a sick ward.

All the furniture and odds and ends in the room were removed to the hall, where they were dumped in a heap on the floor. I had the room neatly swept. I dragged in an old wooden cot which had been put away somewhere and spread on it the thickest mattress and bed clothes, neatly folded the shawl and kept it at the foot of the bed. I fetched a small table which I used for writing and put it in a corner of the room, spread a white cloth on it and arranged all the bottles and tins on it – the yellow label of the glucose tin, the green of the barley, the pleasing violet-coloured label of Lentol – they were ranged artistically and formed a striking pattern. I looked about me proudly. The doctor nodded his head with approval. And then I brought in another stool and put on it a basin of water with a few drops of Lentol in it. It became a whitish solution and imparted a hospital aroma to the whole house. 'Whenever you touch the patient or her clothes you must dip your hand in it, the best disinfectant on the market ...' There was a slight twinge at my heart at the new designation my wife was given: 'patient'. She would no longer be known as a wife or mother or Susila, but only as a patient! And all this precaution – was she an untouchable? It was a painful line of thinking, but I curbed it by much scientific argument within myself.

Now I gently lifted her and helped her to reach her new bed. 'See how nice,' I said with great pride. 'You will come out of it with a new life ... All your old ailments will be gone. Even the pain at the waist you have been complaining of for so many day ...' The doctor was tremendously pleased with the arrangement: 'It is the most attractive sickroom I've ever come across. You won't get this comfort even in a special ward ...' I brought in a chair, put it beside the cot, and said: 'See, this is where I shall be rooted.'

'Plenty of glucose, barley water and mixture. (And gentle lady, don't ask for lime pickles please.) Temperature once in four hours, and note it down somewhere ... It'll be nice to put up a chart on the wall – you have made it look so perfectly like a special ward ...' I seized on this suggestion with fervour and brought out a piece of paper, and stuck it on the wall. I marked the date on it and her name. There was a morbid pleasure in this thoroughness ... We were setting the stage for a royal illness from which she was going to emerge fresher, stronger ...

The doctor said before he left: 'If my reckoning is correct she is running her second week. So you have to spend less time in bed than you've already done.' It was an exhilarating revelation. I stretched my mind further and further back in order to know if she had been ill longer than we counted.

'For practical purposes let us count it from the day I attended – it leaves us with an outside limit of eleven or twelve days ...' said the doctor.

'No, doctor, it can't be so much ...' I pleaded. I wanted it to be all my own way. The doctor ignored me and said: 'I will see that her fever comes down in eleven days, and it is up to you to see that she doesn't have a relapse ...'

'Oh, I will take great care. You may depend upon us ...'

The following were days of iron routine. I had very little sleep all night. I got up at six o'clock in the morning and took her temperature. It was recorded once in four hours – starting with six a.m. and ending with ten at night. It duly recorded 102 at the first count. As the day progressed the mercury column rose step by step till it reached and passed 104. I watched the mercury column with a beating heart ... When I pulled the thermometer out of its shining case, it was always with a fine hope that the fever was going to be mild. When I stuck it under her tongue and waited, it was like waiting for a verdict – with prayer and trembling. And then taking it against the light and straining to catch its growth from 102 and 104 and the fractions it touched! I began to dread this instrument – it had something irrevocable, stern, like a judge on the bench. I always commented to myself: 'Something wrong with this thermometer. Must break it and get another one.' My wife asked: 'What does it show?' And she was always told a degree or two less. And then the entry on the chart, always ranging between 102 and 104. My vision of a paradise was where all the entries would be confined between normal and 100.

This was a world by itself – this sickroom. The aspirations in this chamber were of a novel kind, different from what they were outside. The chief ambition here was to see a fall in the chart. The height of contentment was reached in observing perfect bodily functions, which at other times would pass unnoticed. 'The patient is hungry!' Ah, very good. 'The patient likes her food.' 'Excellent ...' 'The patient gives sensible answers.' Marvellous. And so on and on. The depth of misery was touched when there was any deviation from these standards. The doctor came in twice a day and radiated good cheer: 'Absolutely normal course. No complications. A perfect typhoid run ...' he used to declare, make a few routine observations, and go away. I sat in that chair watching her sleep, every hour or so pouring into her throat medicine or barley water or glucose. I hardly stirred from the place, and got up only at nine in the evening when my father-in-law or mother-in-law (both of whom had arrived a few days before) took charge of the patient. After ablutions with Lentol, I went in, bathed, changed, and ate my dinner, and took charge of the child, who would not go to bed till she had me to sleep by her side in a corner of the hall.

The child exhibited model behaviour. She came and stood twice or thrice in the course of a day outside the threshold and watched her mother. Susila's eyes lit up when the child came to the door. She would ask if the little one had had her food, and put to her numerous other questions in her feeble voice, to none of which the child would reply. A sort of shyness had seized her. She conducted herself before her mother as if she were a stranger. But though she would speak no word, she liked to stand there and watch. She occasionally put a foot into the room and felt thrilled, as if it were an adventure. She went away and her mother shut her eyes and listened to her footfalls. The child spent all her time with her grandparents and her friend next door. Her grandfather took her out shopping and bought her sweets and toys. At night she waited for me to get free of sickroom duties. The moment I had sufficiently cleansed myself and warded off the poison, she hugged and clung to me, sat on my lap while I ate my dinner, and prattled away about all her day's activities. From the corner where I lay at night, I watched the sickroom, its shaded light, the low voices asking or answering; every time there was a movement in that room I woke up with a start. Once or twice when she snored, I got into a panic and ran to her door, only to see her sleeping peacefully with one of her parents sitting up in the chair. My parents were unable to come. My father was down with his annual rheumatic attack, and my mother was unable to leave his side. They wrote me frantic letters every day, and it was my duty to drop them a card every day. I wrote a number of cards to others too. My brother at Hyderabad, my sister at Vellore, and the other sister at Delhi, wrote me very encouraging letters, and expected me to drop them postcards every day. They wrote, 'Nothing to fear in typhoid. It is only a question of nursing.' Everybody who met me repeated this like a formula, till I began to listen to it mechanically without following its meaning. Numerous people – my friends and colleagues – dropped in all day, some standing aloof fearing infection, and some coming quite close reckless and indifferent.

I lost touch with the calendar. In doing the same set of things in the same place, I lost count of days. Hours flew with rapidity. The mixture once in three hours, food every two hours, but two hours and three hours passed with such rapidity that you never felt there was any appreciable gap between doses.

But I liked it immensely. It kept me so close to my wife that it produced an immense satisfaction in my mind. Throughout I acted as her nurse. This sickness seemed to bind us together more strongly than ever. I sat in the chair and spoke to her of interesting things I saw in the paper. She spoke in whispers as the weeks advanced. She said: 'My father said he would give me five hundred rupees when I got well again ...'

'Very good, very good. Hurry up and claim your reward.'

'Even without it I want to be well again.' There was a deep stillness reigning in the house but for the voice of the child as she argued with her grandparents or sang to herself.

There was an interlude. The contractor and Sastri knocked on my door one day. 'Oh, come in,' I said and took them to my room, but there was no chair or table there. I said apologetically: 'No chair. It is in the other room and also the table, because my wife is down with typhoid.' Sastri said promptly, 'Oh, we will sit on the floor.' They squatted down on the floor.

And then after the preliminaries, Sastri said: 'It is about that house – they are keeping it in abeyance. There is another demand for it ...' I remembered my decision was due long ago. 'I'm afraid I can't think of it. Wait a moment please.' I went up to my wife's bedside and asked: 'Susila, what shall I say about that house?' She took time to understand. 'Do you like it?' she asked.

'Yes, it is a fine house – if we are buying a house.'

'Why not think of it when all this is over?' she said.

'Yes, yes,' I agreed. I ran out and told them: 'I have no time to bother about it now. If it is a loss to you waiting for me ...' As I spoke I disliked the house. I remembered the shock Susila had received in the backyard. They went away. Before going, they said: 'Nursing is everything.'

'Yes, yes, I know,' I said.

The contractor said: 'May I say a word about it?'

'Go on, by all means.'

'Never trust these English doctors. My son had typhoid. The doctors tried to give this and that and forbade him to eat anything; but he never got well though he was in bed for thirty days. Afterwards somebody gave him a herb, and I gave him whatever he wanted to eat, and he got well within two days. The last thing you must heed is their advice. The English doctors always try to starve one to death. Give the patient plenty of things to eat and any fever will go down. That is my principle ...'

Susila's parents suffered quietly. There was a deep attachment between them and their daughter. My mother-in-law was brought up in a social condition where she had to show extreme respect for a son-in-law, and so she never came before me or spoke to me. My father-in-law was more sociable. He was an important landholder in his village, and beside that, he was on the directorate of a number of industrial concerns in Madras. He constantly travelled to and fro and met numerous people and had a very cosmopolitan outlook. So in spite of his age – he was past sixty (my wife being his last issue) – he was rather unorthodox in his speech and habits. He constantly admonished me to be careful not to have a large family: 'One grandchild from this quarter is quite adequate. We are quite satisfied.' He was an extraordinarily merry person for his age. But now he looked intimidated. He was full of anxiety for his daughter's welfare and recovery, but he concealed it under a mask of light-heartedness, for fear that it might frighten me. He sat up with his daughter all night, reading a novel and speaking to her very kindly, but without betraying any excessive sentimentality in his voice. 'Don't trouble me, Susila. The world is a bad enough place without your adding to it by refusing the medicine.' He told me: 'Your mother-in-law is definite that if you hadn't allowed her to go into that lavatory, Susila would not have fallen ill.'

All day he spent unobtrusively in the company of his granddaughter, teaching her lessons, telling her stories, or taking her out shopping. He spoilt her a great deal: 'I believe in spoiling children; who should be spoilt if not children?' he often asked. He undid in a couple of weeks all the elaborate cultivation of character which we imagined we had been practising on the child for over three years now. As a result of his handling Leela spoke like an infant-in-arms (if it could speak) and constantly insisted upon being carried on her grandfather's shoulder, or grandmother's arm. Her grandmother gave her plenty to eat defeating all our regulated dieting. And I was not in a position to protest very effectively.

She was convinced that the Evil Eye had fallen on her daughter and that at the new house a malignant spirit had attacked her. She admonished me: 'You should never step into an unknown house in this manner. You can never be sure. How do you know what happened to the previous tenants or why they left?' She went out in the evening and visited a nearby temple and prayed to the god for her daughter's recovery. She brought in regularly every evening sacred ash and vermilion and smeared it on her daughter's forehead. She helped us run the house and got on well with the cook, who found her a willing help. All through the day, one heard their low voices going on in the kitchen, narrating each other's life and philosophy. My mother-in-law arranged with the help of the cook for an exorcist to visit us. One fine afternoon a man came and knocked on the door. My daughter was the first to see him. My father-in-law was having his afternoon nap in my room, and my mother-in-law was in the kitchen. The little girl had been playing on the front veranda with a doll when she looked up and saw a stranger entering the gate. She let out a cry of fear on seeing him, and she came running in and stood in the doorway of the sickroom, bubbling with excitement. I was just caressing the patient's forehead, because it was the hour when the temperature mounted and she complained of headache.

'What is it, Leela?'

'There is a bad man, a fearful man there!'

I rose and followed her. I saw a man with his forehead ablaze with sacred ash, and a thick rosary around his neck and matted hair, standing at the door. 'Go away,' I said, taking him to be a beggar.

'I am not come to beg,' he said, 'I have been asked to come.'

Meanwhile my mother-in-law came out, saw him, and with great respect brought him in. 'He's come for Susila,' she said, and conducted him to the bedside. He sat in the chair and watched the patient, while Susila who had never seen a bearded man at close quarters gazed on him in panic. Her mother said: 'This *Swamiji* has come for your sake.' I watched it all from the doorway in fury, but I had to be silent because I couldn't argue with my mother-in-law, and I was uncertain how it would be viewed by the *Swamiji*. He felt her pulse. He uttered some *mantras* with closed eyes, took a pinch of sacred ash and rubbed it on her forehead, and tied to her arm a talisman strung in yellow thread. When he came out of the room, my mother-in-law seated him on a mat in the hall, gave him a tumbler of milk to drink and placed before him a tray containing a coconut, betel leaves, and a rupee. Meanwhile, the doctor's car stopped before the house, and I heard his steps approaching. I felt ashamed and wished I could spirit away this mystic. The doctor came in, and saw him and smiled to himself. The mystic sat without noticing him, though looking at him. 'My mother-in-law's idea of treatment,' I said apologetically. 'Ah, no, don't belittle these people,' said the doctor. 'There is a lot in him too, we don't know. When we understand it fully I am sure we doctors will be able to give more complete cures.' He said this with a wink at me. My mother-in-law was greatly pleased and said to the doctor: 'You must allow us old people to have our way now and then.' As I went in with the doctor, the *Swamiji* got up and took his leave, muttering: 'May God help you to see the end of your anxieties.'

The doctor stood at the bedside. He lifted his arm, saw the talisman, and said: 'Now how do you feel after this, lady?' My wife made an effort to smile. She indicated her abdomen and said, 'A lot of pain here.' The doctor pressed his fingers on it. He went over to the temperature chart and scrutinized it: 'You haven't taken the four o'clock temperature yet?' he said.

'No.' He inserted the thermometer, took it out, and washed it. 'How much?' my father-in-law asked, standing at the door, having been disturbed out of his nap by the visitors. 'The usual run,' the doctor answered. My father-in-law asked one or two questions about the patient and moved on. The doctor closely observed the patient and her movements and left the room. I followed him to his car, listening to instructions. At the car he told me, 'Have you an ice bag?'

'No.'

'I will send one. Get some ice and apply it constantly, whenever the temperature is above 102.'

'What is the temperature, doctor?'

'Rather high today, but don't get into a fright: 105, but that is common in this fever. Apply ice.' He went away.

All day I sat pressing down the ice bag on her forehead. The Bombay Ananda Bhavan, where we had our morning tiffin on that Sunday, and perhaps where she had caught her typhoid, had a refrigerator and sold us ice. I purchased a block of ten pounds at a time, covered with sawdust and wrapped in gunny. My father-in-law obliged me by keeping an eye on the ice position and going out and getting it. I loved the smooth crystal appearance as I opened the gunny-sack covering and wiped away the sawdust particles; the cool gust which emanated from it; and then the hammer blow which split it up into lumps just the size to be put into the ice bag. I always took a pride in the fact that the blow I gave was so well calculated that the pieces were neither too large nor too small but of the correct size and slipped into the mouth of the bag ... It was a queer delight for me to see the bag bulging, I liked the feel of it as it acquired the correct weight. I carried it in, sat down, with a towel in hand, and pressed it down to form a cap on her head; when it fitted her head nicely it gave me a profound satisfaction. I sat pressing it down with one hand, while with the towel I wiped off the trickling drops of water condensing on it. My palm froze by this constant contact with ice and her forehead felt like a marble surface on a winter morning. And as the ice inside melted, it made a peculiar gurgling when the bag was shaken, so that by practice and intuition I learnt to gauge how much of the ice inside had melted, without opening the lid. Everything in this sickroom seemed to me profoundly ingenious and full of technical points and pleasures and triumphs. This impressed me so much that one day I wrote a poem about it. With my left hand I was applying the ice on her forehead. She slept and spoke a little in her sleep; I watched her for a while; a coloured bee had drifted in and was droning near the rafters. I had nothing else to do. I left the ice bag balanced on her head, ran in and returned with my writing-pad and a pencil. I placed the pad on my lap and wrote, while she slept and talked in sleep:

The Great Kailas is one Mound of Ice
Where Shiva and Parvathi sport, which catch the
    Gleam of ethereal lights, heavenly Rainbows.
Here for us God has sent a piece of Kailas down
    To subdue the Mercury column ...
And here out of its wood dust it comes,
    Cold mist cloud rises on its crystal face,
And it reflects not mountain light
    But my face ...

And here is a great battle ground,
The great fight goes on
On either side of this red bag.
But so far it is not the fever which cools,
But Ice that melts.

It was a fact. Ice turned into water with great rapidity. I had to hammer out blocks into pieces every twenty minutes.

It was not necessary to keep the ice on at night, but in a couple of days it became indispensable even then. The temperature declined only after midnight. She spoke less clearly now, took time to understand what was being said to her, and she constantly agitated her arms up and down. 'Why do you do it?' I asked.

'Something is running up and down. I won't sleep here unless you make a new bed.' With elaborate difficulty, my father-in-law, mother-in-law and everybody assisting, we rolled her to one side and made a new bed for her. It took us nearly an hour. Changing the sheets was a daily adventure, but now we had to make an entirely new bed for her top to bottom. But the labour was worth it, because she remained quiet, but only for an hour. Again she began to toss her arms and legs. 'You can't do it, child,' I said. 'You will put up your fever.' She merely glared at me and said: 'Don't tell me all that. I know how to look after myself.' I sat down and applied the ice. She tried to seize the ice bag and push it away. 'Oh, I don't want this, please. I am tired of it.' I had to cajole and admonish and keep the bag. She went on grumbling and muttering something. I had to beg her to keep quiet: and when she persisted, I called in her father.

'Do you think I am a child to be frightened?' she asked when her father stood in the doorway.

'Come in, come in, please,' I said to her father. He came over and stood at her bedside. She said: 'Father!' She implored weakly, 'He is worrying me too much. I don't want the ice bag.'

'All right, all right, child, it is good for you. I will apply it.' He sat down in the chair. He took up the ice bag and said to me: 'Why don't you go to your room and rest for a while? It will do you good. You have been sitting up without a break since 6 a.m. I will look after her.'

'No, it will be a bother for you. Not your hour. You'll have to sit up at night too.'

'Oh, it doesn't matter. I do not really mind a little overtime work,' he said. I dipped my hand in Lentol and left the room.

The child was delighted to see me out of the room so early. She clapped her hands in joy and ran towards me. 'Not yet, not yet. Don't touch me. You can speak to me from a distance, that is all. I have not had a wash yet. I'll have it only at night.' She made a wry face: 'All right. I'll go to grandfather.'

'He is with mother.'

She became angry on hearing this. 'Everybody goes into that room. Who is to be with me?'

'Why don't you go to the next house and play with your friend?'

'I don't like her. She beats me whenever she sees me.' This amused me. I knew they were the thickest of friends a second ago. And they would be playing together next minute. So I asked: 'All right, then. Come to my room and see a picture book. You must not sit on my bed but a little way off.'

She agreed to this condition and came to my room. My room served as a guest room for my father-in-law. In a corner there was his canvas hold-all and a trunk, and his coats and clothes hung on the peg. My table was dusty and confused, the books lying in a chaotic jumble, untouched for days and days now. All my waking hours were spent at the bedside, and I seldom visited this room. 'In my happy days this table was a jumble. In my days of anxiety it was no less a jumble. Perhaps a table is meant to be so. No use wasting thought over it ...' I remarked to myself; the habit of wishing to do something or other with the table top, whenever I saw it, had persisted with me for many years now. I kicked up a roll of matting and threw myself down, deciding to relax while the chance was there. 'Let the father and daughter settle it between themselves. I won't go till I am called.' My daughter, who had been standing in the doorway, asked: 'Can I come in, father?'

'Yes, yes, this is not a sickroom,' I said. I had forgotten for a moment I had asked her to follow me in.

She sat down on the edge of the mat, and asked: 'Is this far enough?'

'Yes, you mustn't touch me, that is all, till I have a thorough wash at night.'

'Does mother's fever climb on your hands and stick there?'

'Yes.'

'Won't it get into you?'

'No.'

'Why?'

'Because I am an elder,' I said with a touch of pride in my voice. She was gradually edging nearer to my mat, and now only an inch of space separated us. 'No, no. You are too near me,' I said.

'I'm not touching you,' she argued. I was too fatigued to argue with her, and left her alone, turned over to the other side, and shut my eyes, muttering: 'You are a fine girl. Don't disturb me. I am sleeping.' She agreed to this proposal. But the moment I shut my eyes, she stretched her leg and gently poked my back with her toe.

'Ah, why do you do it?'

'You must not turn away from me. It makes me afraid to be alone.' I turned over to face her and tried to sleep. She called: 'Father.'

'You mustn't disturb me.'

'You said you would give me a picture book.' I groaned, 'Leave me alone, baby. Take the book.' She went over to the table, but could not reach any part of its top. 'It is too high up, father.' I got up and searched among the books on the table. There was not one fit for her perusal – all of them were heavy, academic, and unillustrated. Underneath all these was a catalogue of miscellaneous articles from a mail order firm in Calcutta. It was a stout enough volume. I gave it to her. She was delighted. It was full of small smudgy representations of all kinds of household articles. She kept it on her knee and was soon lost in it, turning the pages. Soothed by the rustling of the pages, I snatched a little sleep, although she constantly tried to get me to explain the pictures.

When I woke up it was about five o'clock. The catalogue was sprawling on the floor. The child was not there. Her voice came from the kitchen. I went in and asked for some coffee.

The child was sitting there on her grandmother's lap, learning a song. On seeing me she stopped her song and asked: 'Can I touch you now?'

'Not yet.'

'You didn't know it when I got up and ran away!' she said with a great triumph in her voice, as if I had kept her in detention and she had managed to escape.

'No, I didn't. You are very cunning,' I replied and it pleased her greatly.

The patient was asleep. My father-in-law rose from his seat on seeing me, dipped his hand in the basin, and came out and whispered: 'Will you take the watch now?'

'Yes.'

'She has managed to sleep after all. Let her sleep quietly. Rather restless today ...' he said and went away.

I resumed my seat, pressing down the ice bag. She woke up. She looked up at me and said: 'Oh, you have come!' She gripped my arms gratefully.

'I am always here. Don't worry, dear.'

'Yes, yes, I'm glad. Do you know what that man did?'

'Who?' I said.

'He was here when you were away.'

'Your father?' I said.

'Know what he did? He tried to remove this necklace.' She lifted her gold neckchain between her fingers and showed it to me. 'But I snatched it back. He wrenched my head. Bad man. You must never leave my side hereafter.'

I agreed. Her fingers lightly ran over the bed clothes as if searching for something, and tugged the edges. She tried to kick away the blanket. She attempted to roll out of bed. When I checked her, she was furious. 'Why do you stop me? I want to go away.'

She held up her arms and asked: 'Where is the baby?'

'In the kitchen,' I explained.

'Oh, who took her there?'

'Your mother,' I said.

'All right. Let them be careful. They must not take away a small baby without telling me. They may drop it.' I understood what she meant. She was imagining herself in childbed. Those memories were confusing her. She still held up her arms for the baby. I gently put them down. After that she started singing. Her faint voice choked with the strain. I couldn't make out the words or the tune. I said: 'Hush, stop it please. You must not sing. You will not get well if you exert yourself.' But she would not stop. I protested, and she said: 'I want to sing, and I will sing. Why should it offend you?'

At night she ceased to sleep peacefully. She talked or sang all night. The doctor examined her more closely every time now. He examined her heart and said: 'She must sleep. It is imperative. This continuous temperature is very taxing. She must rest. I will watch how it goes, and then give a mild hypnotic.'

The ice was melting, we were wearing ourselves out nursing, but the fever would not subside. It never went below 103 in the mornings and rose and hovered about 105 every day. The doctor said: 'The patient is very restless, that's why she has a temperature. If only she could sleep for six hours, you would see a wonderful change.'

The doctor was losing his cheerfulness, and looked harrowed and helpless. Next morning he brought in his car another doctor, a famous Madras physician. Even in our wildest dreams we could never have hoped to get this great physician. His reputation was all over the Presidency and his monthly income was in the neighbourhood of ten thousand. Dr Sankar came in advance and said: 'It's your luck, Doctor – came here for another case. I begged him to see your wife. You are lucky he has agreed. Please ask him in. He is a very good man.' I and my father-in-law rushed out and greeted the great physician effusively, opened the door of the car, and led him in. Dr Sankar looked very nervous in his presence.

The great man spent an hour examining the patient. He tapped her abdomen, scratched a key on it and watched, lifted her arm, flashed a torch into her eyes, and examined the temperature chart. We waited in great suspense. He asked numerous questions. 'Mixture?' he said and held his hand out for it without turning. Dr Sankar jumped up, clutched the medicine bottle, and put it in his hand. The great doctor shook the contents and watched it for a moment: 'If I were you, I'd stop all this and go so far as to administer glucose and brandy every two hours, if possible with five minims of solomine. It is the best stimulant I can think of at the moment.'

'How do you find the patient, sir?' I asked.

'Well ...' the expert drawled. 'Her vitality is not very good, though there are no complications.'

'What can we do? What can we do?' my father-in-law asked in consternation. My mother-in-law stood in the doorway, and behind her the child, looking with wonder on this scene. The doctor did not answer. But my father-in-law writhed: 'Is there anything wanting in our attention? Should we take her to the hospital?'

'Not at all. Everything is quite well done here,' said the physician and we were greatly pleased with the compliment. 'Is there anything special we ought to do now?'

'I will speak to your doctor,' said the big man, with an air of snubbing us.

We poured out our gratitude as he moved to his car, and asked: 'Won't you have a cup of coffee?'

'Thank you, I never drink coffee,' he said.

Our doctor said: 'I'll see you again,' and went away.

The next morning I was jubilant. For the first time the temperature remained at 101. For weeks it had never gone below 102. Now it showed 101. What a joy! We were all jubilant. A ray of sun was breaking through the overcast sky. As soon as our doctor's car drove up at our gate, I ran out to announce, 'Doctor, the temperature has come down.'

'Splendid,' he cried. 'Didn't I tell you it would ...'

'And the patient slept grandly,' I said. 'In fact she is still sleeping ...'

The doctor examined her, but it didn't wake her up. 'Continue the mixture, and diet as usual. No ice bag ... Have a hot water bottle ready. I will come again,' he said and went away. For the first time these weeks my hand did not have to perform the duty of pressing down the ice bag. It lay on a stool untouched. It was a happy sight for me. And also there were still five pounds of ice in the sack. 'Use it for ice cream, if you like,' I told my father-in-law. The atmosphere had suddenly relaxed. The patient had gone into a profound sleep. I had nothing to do in the sickroom. I sat there till afternoon. I disinfected my hands and requested my father-in-law to keep an eye on the patient. I bathed, changed, and took the child upon my shoulder. She was astonished: 'Has mother got well?' she asked. 'Can I go in now?'

'Very soon you will be going in ... but wait. I will take you out for a walk ...' She was elated. She put on her small green coat, clung to my hand and came out. I took her down the road. Her friend was standing at the gate. Leela said: 'Let her also come with us, father. She is so poor!'

'Is she very poor?'

'Yes.'

'What is meant by poor?' I asked.

'Nobody buys her peppermints ...' the child exclaimed.

'Who taught you this?'

'Grandmother,' she replied promptly. So her friend joined us. We then paced down the road. They didn't speak much, but constantly looked at each other and giggled. I took them to a shop at the end of the street, and allowed them to buy whatever they wanted. They chose a few lozenges, and some bright bamboo whistles pasted over with green coloured paper. We returned, both of them blowing through their whistles. All this had taken about an hour, and I had lived in a great peace. Ahead, at our gate I saw the doctor's car standing. 'Let us hurry up,' I said walking fast, and the children trotted behind. At our door the child said: 'I will go and play in the next house, father,' and ran off. I went in. The doctor and my father-in-law were in earnest discussion; the patient was sleeping, breathing noisily.

'The child, the child,' the old man said in a shaking voice the moment he saw me. 'Where is she?'

I didn't understand. 'She has gone to play in the next house,' I said.

'Very well, very well,' he replied. 'Take care of her. You must mind her and keep her.'

I looked at the patient. She had grown a shade whiter, and breathed noisily. There were drops of perspiration on her forehead. I touched it, and found it very cold. 'Doctor, the temperature is coming down.'

'Yes, yes, I knew it would ...' he said, biting his nails. Nothing seemed to be right anywhere. 'Doctor ... tell me ...'

'For heaven's sake, don't ask questions,' he said. He felt the pulse; drew aside the blanket and ran his fingers over her abdomen which appeared slightly distended. He tapped it gently, and said: 'Run to the car and fetch the other bag please, which you will find in the back seat ...'

The doctor opened it. 'Hot water, hot water, please.' He poured turpentine into the boiling water, and applied fomentations to her abdomen. He took out a hypodermic syringe, heated the needle, and pushed it into her arm: at the pressure of the needle she winced. 'Perhaps it hurts her,' I muttered. The doctor looked at me without an answer. He continued the fomentation.

An hour later, he drew up the blanket and packed his bag. I stood and watched in silence. All through this, he wouldn't speak a word to me. I stood like a statue. The only movement the patient showed was the heaving of her bosom. The whole house was silent. The doctor held his bag in one hand, patted my back and pursed his lips. My throat had gone dry and smarted. I croaked through this dryness: 'Don't you have to remain, doctor?' He shook his head: 'What can we do? We have done our best ...' He stood looking at the floor for a few moments, heaved a sigh, patted my back once again, and whispered: 'You may expect change in about two and a half hours.' He turned and walked off. I stood stock still, listening to his shoe creaks going away, the starting of his car; after the car had gone, a stony silence closed in on the house, punctuated by the stentorian breathing, which appeared to me the creaking of the hinges of a prison gate, opening at the command of a soul going into freedom.

Here is an extract from my diary: The child has been cajoled to sleep in the next house. The cook has been sent there to keep her company. Two hours past midnight. We have all exhausted ourselves, so a deep quiet has decended on us (moreover a great restraint is being observed by all of us for the sake of the child in the next house, whom we don't wish to scare). Susila lies there under the window, laid out on the floor. For there is the law that, the body, even if it is an Emperor's must rest only on the floor, on Mother Earth.

We squat on the bare floor around her, her father, mother, and I. We mutter, talk among ourselves, and wail between convulsions of grief; but our bodies are worn out with fatigue. An unearthly chill makes our teeth chatter as we gaze on the inert form and talk about it. Gradually, unknown to ourselves, we recline against the wall and sink into sleep. The dawn finds us all huddled on the cold floor.

The first thing we do is to send for the priest and the bearers ... And then the child's voice is heard in the next house. She is persuaded to have her milk there, dress, and go out with a boy in the house, who promises to keep her engaged and out of our way for at least four hours. She is surprised at the extraordinary enthusiasm with which people are sending her out today. I catch a glimpse of her as she passes on the road in front of our house, wearing her green velvet coat, bright and sparkling.

Neighbours, relations and friends arrive, tears and lamentations, more tears and lamentations, and more and more of it. The priest roams over the house, asking for one thing or other for performing the rites ... The corpse-bearers, grim and subhuman, have arrived with their equipment – bamboo and coir ropes. Near the front step they raise a small fire with cinders and faggots – this is the fire which is to follow us to the cremation ground.

A bamboo stretcher is ready on the ground in front of the house. Some friends are hanging about with red eyes. I am blind, dumb, and dazed.

The parting moment has come. The bearers, after brief and curt preliminaries, walk in, lift her casually without fuss, as if she were an empty sack or a box, lay her on the stretcher, and tie her up with ropes. Her face looks at the sky, bright with the saffron touched on her face, and the vermilion on the forehead, and a string of jasmine somewhere about her head.

The downward curve of her lips gives her face a repressed smile ... Everyone gathers a handful of rice and puts it between her lips – our last offering.

They shoulder the stretcher. I'm given a pot containing the fire and we march out, down our street, Ellamman Street.

Passers-by stand and look for a while. But every face looks blurred to me. The heat of the sun is intense. We cut across the sands, ford the river at Nallappa's Grove, and on to the other bank of the river, and enter the cremation ground by a small door on its southern wall.

The sun is beating down mercilessly, but I don't feel it. I feel nothing, and see nothing. All sensations are blurred and vague.

They find it necessary to put down the stretcher a couple of times on the roadside. Half a dozen flies are dotting her face. Passers-by stand and look on sadly at the smiling face. A madman living in Ellamman Street comes by, looks at her face and breaks down, and follows us on, muttering vile and obscure curses on fate and its ways.

Stretcher on the ground. A deep grove of tamarind trees and mangoes, full of shade and quiet – an extremely tranquil place. Two or three smouldering pyres are ranged about, and bamboos and coirs lie scattered, and another funeral group is at the other end of this grove. 'This is a sort of cloakroom, a place where you leave your body behind,' I reflect as we sit down and wait. Somebody appears carrying a large notebook, and writes down name, age, and disease; collects a fee, issues a receipt, and goes away.

The half a dozen flies are still having their ride. After weeks, I see her face in daylight, in the open, and note the devastation of the weeks of fever – this shrivelling heat has baked her face into a peculiar tinge of pale yellow. The purple cotton *sari* which I bought her on another day is wound round her and going to burn with her.

The priest and the carriers are ceaselessly shouting for someone or other. Basket after basket of dry cowdung fuel is brought and dumped ... Lively discussion over prices and quality goes on. The trappings of trade do not leave us even here. Some hairy man sits under a tree and asks for alms. I am unable to do anything, but quietly watch in numbness ... I'm an imbecile, incapable of doing anything or answering any questions. I'm incapable of doing anything except what our priest orders me to do. Presently I go over, plunge in the river, return, and perform a great many rites and mutter a lot of things which the priest asks me to repeat.

They build up a pyre, place her on it, cover her up with layers of fuel ... Leaving only the face and a part of her chest out, four layers deep down. I pour ghee on and drop the fire.

We are on our homeward march, a silent and benumbed gang. As we cross Nallappa's Grove once again, I cannot resist the impulse to turn and look back. Flames appear over the wall ... It leaves a curiously dull pain at heart. There are no more surprises and shocks in life, so that I watch the flame without agitation. For me the greatest reality is this and nothing else ... Nothing else will worry or interest me in life hereafter.

CHAPTER FOUR

The days had acquired a peculiar blankness and emptiness. The only relief was my child, spick and span and fresh, and mocking by her very carriage the world of elders. I dared not contemplate where I should have been but for her. So much so that I refused to allow her to be taken away by her grandparents and decided to keep her with me. It was a wonder to them how I was going to look after the girl – but our nature adapts itself to circumstances with wonderful speed. In three or four months I could give her a bath with expert hands, braid her hair passably, and wash and look after her clothes, and keep correct count of her jackets and skirts. I slipped into my double role with great expertness. It kept me very much alive to play both father and mother to her at the same time. My one aim in life now was to see that she did not feel the absence of her mother. To this end I concentrated my whole being. From morning till night this kept me busy. I had to keep her cheerful and keep myself cheerful too lest she should feel unhappy.

My mother could come and stay with me only for a couple of weeks occasionally, and whenever she was here, I could well imagine what it meant to my father, who could not get on for a day without her help. Of late he had become utterly helpless, nearly starved, and could not look after himself even for an hour if she was away. He did not know where his clothes were, when to go in for dinner, or what to ask for at dinner. When she came and stayed with me for a week or two at a time, it took months to bring him and his health under control again. My mother was very good and helped me ungrudgingly. But I could not accept her service indefinitely. 'God has given me some novel situations in life. I shall live it out alone, face the problems alone, never drag in another to do the job for me ...' I found a peculiar satisfaction in making this resolve. And next time when my mother had to leave, I did not remonstrate with her as I used to do. She suggested: 'Kittu, send the child with me. Why are you so stubborn?' I was. She grew angry with me when I went to see her off. She sat in the bus. I and the little child stood by waiting for the bus to start. I made it a point to take the child wherever I went, except the college. 'You are unpractical and stubborn,' my mother persisted. 'How are you going to look after her?' 'As if it were a big feat!' I replied with bravado. 'God intends me to learn these things and do them efficiently. I can't shirk it ...' Tears gathered in my mother's eyes. 'That I should be destined to see these scenes in our life – I have never known such things in our family.' I let her quietly have her cry. I was used to such situations and treated them with business-like indifference. Condolences, words of courage, lamentations, or assurances, were all the same. I had become a sort of professional receptacle of condolence and sympathy, and I had received them in such quantity these months that they had ceased to move me or mean anything. Death and its associates, after the initial shock, produce callousness ...

My mother averted her face in order that the child might not observe the tears in her eyes. The child asked: 'When will you be back, mother?' She controlled her voice and gave some vague reply. I didn't want the child to have any illusions about things and be misled. Living without illusions seemed to be the greatest task for me in life now. So I explained, 'She can't come again for a long time, child; she has to look after grandfather ...' That was the stuff to give humanity, nurtured in illusions from beginning to end! The twists and turns of fate would cease to shock if we knew, and expected nothing more than, the barest truths and facts of life. The child accepted my answer with calmness. 'How long will she be away?' This was a point about which I could not be very clear. But it moved my mother and she said, 'I shall try to be back as soon as possible. I only wish your grandfather were more helpful.'

The bus conductor blew his whistle. The driver sat on his seat. An old village woman, with a basket on her knee, sitting next to my mother asked, 'Where are you going?'

'Kamalapuram ... My son is employed here. There you see him with his child ...' She whispered, 'A motherless child and so

I come here often.' At which the village woman clapped her hands and wailed, 'Oh, the poor child! Oh, the poor child!' She insisted upon having the child lifted up and shown to her. She touched the child's cheeks and cracked her fingers on her temple as an antidote for Evil Eye. She cried: 'What a beauty! And a girl!' She sighed deeply, and my mother was once again affected. I wished the bus would move. But the conductor would not allow it to go, he was deeply involved in a controversy with another villager who refused to pay the regular fare but wanted some concession ... The village woman now said: 'When is he marrying again?' I was shocked to hear it, and my mother felt confused. She knew how much such talk upset me ... She did not wish me to overhear it. But the old woman stared at me and said: 'You must marry again, you are so young!' My mother was agitated, and desperately tried to suppress her ... 'Oh, don't speak of all that now.' The old woman could not be suppressed so easily. She said: 'Why not? He is so young! How can he manage the child?'

'That is what I also say,' my mother echoed indiscreetly.

'Men are spoilt if they are without a wife at home,' added the old woman. I looked desperately at the conductor who showed no signs of relenting. I said: 'Conductor, isn't it time to start?'

'Yes, sir, look at this man ...'

'He wants four annas for ...' began the controversialist.

The old woman was saying: 'A man must marry within fifteen days of losing his wife. Otherwise he will be ruined. I was the fourth wife to my husband and he always married within three weeks. All the fourteen children are happy. What is wrong?' she asked in an argumentative manner. The bus roared and started and jerked forward. My daughter sat in my arms, watching the whole scene spellbound. As the bus moved my mother said: 'Don't fail to give her an oil anointment and bath every Friday. Otherwise she will lose all her hair ...'

I was never a sound sleeper at any time in life, but now more than ever I lay awake most of the night, sleeping by fits and starts. My mind kept buzzing with thoughts and memories. In the darkness I often felt an echo of her voice and speech or sometimes her moaning and delirious talk in sickbed. The child lay next to me sleeping soundly. We both slept in my little study on the front veranda. The door of the room in which my wife passed away remained shut. It was opened once a week for sweeping, and then closed again and locked. This had been going on for months now. It was expected that I should leave the house and move to another. It seemed at first a most natural and inevitable thing to do. But after the initial shocks had worn out, it seemed unnecessary and then impossible. At first I put it down to a general disinclination for change and shifting. To remove that chair, and that chaotic table with its contents ... and then another and another ... We had created a few favourite corners in the house, and it seemed impossible to change and settle in a new house. My daughter had played on the edge of that veranda ever since she came to me as a seven-month baby. Yes, at first I put it down to a general disinclination for change, but gradually I realized the experience of life in that house was too precious and that I wouldn't exchange it for anything. There were subtle links with a happy past; they were not merely links but blood channels, which fed the stuff of memory ... Even sad and harrowing memories were cherished by me; for in the contemplation of those sad scenes and hapless hours, I seemed to acquire a new peace, a new outlook; a view of life with a place for everything.

The room which was kept shut had an irresistible fascination for my daughter. She looked at the door with a great deal of puzzlement. On that unhappy day when we had returned from the cremation ground, the child had also just come home. 'Father, why is that door shut?' It threw us into a frenzy. We did not know what to reply. The house at that time was full of guests, all adults – all looking on, suffering, and bewildered by death. Death was puzzling enough, but this question we felt was a maddening conundrum. We looked at each other and stood speechless. My daughter would not allow us to rest there. She repeated authoritatively: 'Why is that door closed?' My father-in-law was deeply moved by this. He tried to change her mind by asking: 'Would you like to have a nice celluloid doll?'

'Yes, where is it?' she asked.

'In the shop. Let us go and buy one.' She picked up her green coat, which she had just discarded, and said: 'All right, let us go, grandfather.' It had been a strenuous morning and we had eaten our food late in the day and were about to rest. He looked forlorn. 'Come on,' she said and he looked at me pathetically. I told my daughter, 'You are a good girl, let your grandfather rest for a little while and then he will take you out ...' She said: 'Why have you had your meal so late?' Another inconvenient question under which we smirked. We were all too fatigued to invent new answers to beguile her mind. She waited for a moment and returned to her original charge. 'Doll – come on grandfather.' He had by this time thrown himself on the floor and was half sunk in sleep. I said: 'Child, you are a nice child. Allow your grandfather to rest. He will take you out and buy two dolls.' She was displeased at this, removed her coat and flung it down. I couldn't check her, as I would have done at other times. She looked at me fixedly and asked: 'Why is that door closed?' At which everyone was once again convulsed and confused and dismayed. She seemed to look on this with a lot of secret pleasure. She waited for an answer with ruthless determination. 'Mother is being given a bath, that is why the door is closed ...' She accepted the explanation with a nod of her head, and then went up to her wooden trunk containing toys, rummaged and picked out a rag book. I went away to my room and reclined on my easy-chair. As I closed my eyes, I heard her footfalls approaching. She thrust the rag book under my nose and demanded: 'Read this story.' I had read that 'story' two hundred times already. The book was dirty with handling. And she always kept it with all the junk in her trunk. It had illustrations in green, and a running commentary of a couple of lines under each. It was really not a story, there was not one in it, but a series of illustrations of tiger, lion, apple, and Sam – each nothing to do with the other. But Leela would never accept the fact that they were disconnected. She maintained that the whole book was one story – and always commanded me to read it; so I fused them all into a whole and gave her a 'story' – 'Sam ate the apple, but the lion and tiger wanted some of it ...' and so on. And she always listened with interest, completely accepting the version. But unfortunately I never repeated the same version and this always mystified her! 'No, father, Sam didn't hit the tiger,' she would correct. So when this book was pressed into my hand today my heart parched at the thought of having to narrate a story ... 'Once upon a time ...' I said, and somehow went on animating the pictures in the book with my narration. She said: 'You are wrong, father, it didn't happen that way. Your story is very wrong ...'

Towards the evening she came up once again and asked: 'The door is still closed, father. Is she bathing still?'

'H'm. If the door is open, she may catch a cold ...'

'Don't you have to go to her?'

'No ...'

'Is she all alone?'

'There is a nurse who looks after her.'

'What is a nurse?'

'A person who tends sick people.'

'You don't have to go and stay with mother any more, ever?'

'No, I will always be with you.' She let out a yell of joy and threw herself on me.

Four days later, she stole into my room one evening, and whispered, with hardly suppressed glee: 'Father, say what I have done?'

'What is it?'

'There was no one there and it wasn't locked; so I pushed the door open and went in. Mother is not there!' She shook with suppressed glee, at the thought of her own escapade.

'God, give me a sensible answer for this child,' I prayed.

'Oh,' I said casually and added, 'the nurse must have taken her away to the hospital.'

'When will she be back?'

'As soon as she is all right again,' I replied.

The first thing that woke me in the morning was the cold hands of my daughter placed on my forehead and the shout 'Appa' (father), or sometimes she just sat, with her elbows on the ground and her chin between her palms, gazing into my face as I lay asleep. Whenever I opened my eyes in the morning, I saw her face close to mine, and her eyes scrutinizing my face. I do not know what she found so fascinating there. Her eyes looked like a pair of dark butterflies dancing with independent life, at such close quarters.

'Oh, father has woken up!' she cried happily. I looked at her with suspicion and asked: 'What have you been trying to do so close to me?' 'I only wanted to watch, that is all. I didn't wake you up.'

'Watch what?'

'I wanted to watch if any ant or fly was going to get into you through your nose, that is all ...'

'Did any get in?'

'No. Because I was watching.' There was a hint in her tone as if a sentry had mounted guard against a formidable enemy.

'What do you do when you sleep, father?' Once again a question that could not be answered by an adult; perhaps only another child could find an answer for it. 'I was saying something close to you and yet you didn't reply.'

'What were you saying?'

'I said: There is a peppermint, open your mouth!'

After these preambles we left the bed. I rolled her about a little on the mattress and then she sat up and picked a book from my table and commanded: 'Read this story.' I had no story-book on my table. She usually picked up some heavy critical work and brought it to me. When I put it back on the table, she brought out her usual catalogue of the Calcutta mail order firm, and asked me to read out of it. This happened almost every morning. I had to put away the book gently and say to her: 'Not now. We must first wash.'

'Why?'

'That is how it must be done.'

'No. We must first read stories,' she corrected me.

'We must first wash, and then read stories,' I persisted.

'Why?'

'Because it is Goddess Saraswathi and we must never touch her without washing.'

'What will she do if we touch her without washing?'

'She will be very unhappy, and she is the Goddess of Learning, you see, and if you please her by washing and being clean, she will make you very learned.'

'Why should I be learned?'

'You can read a lot of stories yourself without my help.'

'Oh! What will you do then?' she asked, as if pitying a man who would lose his only employment in life.

It was as a matter of fact my chief occupation in life. I cared for little else. I felt a thrill of pride whenever I had to work and look after the child. It seemed a noble and exciting occupation – the sole responsibility for a growing creature.

CHAPTER FIVE

The day had been unusually heavy. I had more or less continuous work till three in the afternoon. And at three, when I was looking at the clock, hoping to drop things and go home, I received a note from Gajapathy to say that I was to take Fourth Hons Class, because George of the language section was absent. Some teachers were absent this week, exhausting their leave, and those who were present were saddled with extra work. I implored Gajapathy to spare me this pain since as a student I had found language a torture, and as a teacher I still found it a torture. But he said: 'Just keep the boys engaged. The Principal doesn't want to let the boys off when they have not a teacher for a particular period. In the English department everybody ought to be able to handle any part of it; and I agree with him.' And I had no option but to sit down in the Fourth Hons Class and engage their young minds in tittle-tattle for an hour. Our chief believed in keeping them well-read, and when they had spare time, in spending it over a library book of some consequence. I sent a boy to the library to fetch any book from the English section he liked. He brought down a book of nineteenth-century essays and I sat down to read mechanically through the pages aloud: the boys were busy, with a lot of conversation among themselves. In harmony with this din I read on. Some boys in the front listened. But they found it difficult to hear and complained: 'Can't hear, sir.'

'Ask your friends to shut up and you will hear better,' I said. They turned and stared helplessly at the noise-makers behind them. It was a small class and I could have easily established law and order, but I was too weary to exert myself. I was past that stage of exertion. A terrible fatigue and inertia had come over me these days and it seemed to me all the same whether they listened or made a noise or whether they understood what I said or felt baffled, or even whether they heard it at all or not. My business was to sit in that chair and keep my tongue active – that I did. My mind itself could only vaguely comprehend what was being read ...'This influence became so marked towards the later part of the century that those writers seized on it with avidity. It was a new-found treasure for the literary craftsman, a new weapon for his arsenal, shall we say ...' My voice dully fell on my ears, but my mind refused to maintain pace with its sense. I caught myself constantly reflecting: 'What is it all about? What influence? On whom? Oh, good author, why not say arsenal or whatever you like if you choose?'

Into this pandemonium the most welcome sound impinged – the college bell. It was the end of the hour and of the day. I felt like a schoolboy, genuinely happy that I could go home now to the child waiting for me there, all ready and bubbling with joy; ready to be taken out and ready with a hundred questions on her lips ...

I made my way into the common room, to put away the books in my locker, pick up my umbrella, and go out. As I was closing my locker, the servant came up and said: 'There is someone asking for you, master.' I looked out. He was a stranger, a young boy about fifteen years old. He was standing on the path below the veranda, a thin young man with a tuft behind, and wearing a small cap – a poor boy, I felt, by the look of him; out to ask for a donation for his school fee or something of the kind. 'Father seriously ill, money for his medicines.' One or other of the numerous sad excuses for begging. Of late they were on the increase ... Formerly I used to investigate and preach to them and so on, but now I felt too weary to exert myself and paid out change as far as possible. I saw his hand, bringing out an envelope, and I put my hand in my pocket for my purse. 'The usual typewritten petition addressed to all whom it may concern,' I said to myself.

'What is it?' I asked.

'Are you Krishna of the English section?'

'Yes.'

'Here is a letter for you.'

'From whom?'

'My father has sent it ...'

'Who is your father?'

'You'll find it all in that letter,' he replied. It was a bulky envelope. I tore it open. There was a long sheet of paper, wrapped around which was a small note on which was written:

> 'Dear Sir,
>
> 'I received this message last evening, while I was busy writing something else. I didn't understand what it meant. But the directions, address and name given in it are clear and so I have set my son to find out if the address and name are of a real person, and to deliver it. If this letter reaches you (that is, if you are a real person) please read it, and if it means anything to you keep it. Otherwise you may just tear it up and throw it away; and forgive this intrusion.'

He had given his name and address. I opened the other large sheet. The handwriting on it seemed to be different. It began:

> 'This is a message for Krishna from his wife Susila who recently passed over ... She has been seeking all these months some means of expressing herself to her husband, but the opportunity has occurred only today, when she found the present gentleman a very suitable medium of expression. Through him she is happy to communicate. She wants her husband to know that she is quite happy in another region, and wants him also to eradicate the grief in his mind. We are nearer each other than you understand. And I'm always watching him and the child ...'

It was very baffling. I stared at the boy. I made nothing of it. 'Boy, what is this?' 'I don't know, sir. My father has been trying to send that for a week and could do it only today. I was searching everywhere; and I couldn't get away from my class ...'

'Oh, stop, stop all that, boy. Why has your father sent this letter to me?'

'I don't know, sir.' I stood there and read it again and again and as my head cooled I was seized with elation.

'Take me to your house,' I cried.

'It's far off, sir. In the village Tayur ...' It was on the other side of the river, a couple of miles off.

'No matter, I will come with you. What is your father?'

'He looks after his garden and lands in the village, sir. I read in the Board High School. I had leave today in the last period and so could bring you this letter.'

'Good boy, good boy, take me to your father.' I walked beside him. The child would be waiting at home. 'One minute, will you come with me to my house? I will give you coffee and sweets. We will go ...'

'No, no, sir. I have to go away soon. I have to do some work at ...' I tried to persuade him. But he was adamant. So was I. Finally we agreed upon a compromise. He gave me directions to reach his house. He'd go ahead and wait for me at the crossing and take me to his place. As I saw him go off towards the river, a sudden fear and doubt seized me. Suppose I should never meet him again. It was a horrible thought. 'Boy,' I had to beg him, 'are you sure to wait?'

'Yes, yes. I will stand on the trunk road.'

'If you will wait here a moment, I'll run home, get back and join you,' I said. If it had been any work other than seeing the child ... The boy said: 'I will wait for you at the trunk road positively, even if you are very late.' 'Good boy, good boy,' I cried and raced home. The child was dressed and ready, waiting for me at the door.

As we left the kitchen and came to the hall, I told her: 'Today the little dear will go out with Granny – because father has to go out on business ...' She remained thoughtful and asked: 'What business? Have you to go to college again?'

'No. I've to go and see someone, very important business.'

'When will you come back?'

'As usual. But if you feel sleepy before I come, you just sleep ...'

'I won't do that,' she replied. 'I will go with Granny. She has promised to show me a small doll's house which has electric light. Won't you buy one for me?'

'Well, see it first, we will buy it later.'

'Buy me a small house – this size,' she showed me her thumbnail size, 'with dolls so small.'

'Where can you buy it?'

The old lady answered, 'It is not for sale; it is a small house kept in that medicine shop for decoration ...' I remembered seeing a small plywood doll's house kept in a small medicine seller's shop-front. He sold some home-made pills; it was more or less a quack shop which gave medicine under no known system, but the shop was always crowded. In the centre of his shop he had mounted on a stand a plywood house with electric light ... It was hard to understand what purpose it served there. But perhaps its real purpose was to interest a person like Leela ... I put on a shirt and an upper cloth and rushed out – along Ellamman Street, down river, crossing at Nallappa's Grove. As I passed it I could not help looking at the southern wall of the cremation ground far off. Smoke was climbing over its walls. Jingling bullock-carts, talkative villagers returning home from the town, and a miscellaneous crowd on the dusty path leading to the Tayur Road on the other side. The sun inclined to the west. If I did not reach the crossroad before dusk I'd never be able to spot the boy. I almost ran up the road, and I reached the crossroad, where the boy had promised to wait for me. There I was. The west was ablaze with the sun below the horizon. Dusk would soon fall on us. But there was no sign of the boy. 'Boy, Boy,' I cried; not having asked him his name. Birds twittered on the trees, passers-by moved about, and my voice cried to the evening 'Boy, Boy.' What a fool I was not to have asked his name or precise directions!

'Boy, Boy,' I shouted like a madman and passers-by looked at me curiously. I searched about frantically, and in the end saw the fellow coming up a path across the fields. 'Sorry to be late, excuse me, sir.'

'Good boy,' I cried. 'You are very kind to come.' I liked him. I said to myself that I would do him all the kindness possible when he came my way again. He would get a lot of marks from me when he came to college. I asked him about his school, books, teachers and all sorts of other things as we walked on.

'That's our house.' He pointed at the sloping tiles visible through the dense cluster of trees. A mongrel came and jumped at the boy: 'Oh, keep quiet, Tiger. Go and tell father that a gentleman has come to see him.' Tiger listened with his head tilted and at the mention of father bounced off in the direction of the house, vaulting over the gate of thorns and brambles. By the time we reached the gate, it was opened from the other side and a chubby and cheerful-looking person came towards me extending his hands. He had such good cheer in his face that it melted all the strangeness of the situation. He gripped my hand and said: 'You must forgive the trouble I have given you. You must have thought it was a call from a lunatic asylum!' He laughed, 'Oh, not at all, not at all,' I muttered idiotically. I was too confused. My feelings were all in a mess. I didn't know whether I was happy or unhappy. I was excited and muddled.

He said: 'You see, I would have searched you out, but it seemed too wild, and I thought it was all a fool's errand. I was most surprised to hear there was such a person. I hope you are the person ...'

'I'm the person, name, initials, and address and in regard to the other things ... Have you known my name before ...?'

'Good God, no! You mustn't think so! I sent the letter as a test with the boy. I sent it out just as I got it, including the address ... I sent it out with the boy ... and you could have blown me over with a breath, in spite of my size, when the boy came and told me that he had delivered the letter. I thought the boy was playing a practical joke, but he said you were coming. Are you sure you are yourself?' he asked with a rich quiet laugh. It'd be wrong to say that he laughed ... He hardly made any special sound or noise, but it was there all the time, a permanent background against which all his speech and gestures occurred, something like the melody of a *veena* string from which music arises and ends. 'Come in, come in, we have a lot of things to say to each other,' he said, and took me in through his small gate. The dog followed. He patted its back and said: 'Nice animal, isn't it? I'm very fond of him. I don't much fancy the sentimental cynicism of some dog lovers who say that they prefer dog to man! It's nonsense. A dog is a nice fellow to have around. Though an animate creature, when you don't like him you can put him away, out of sight and hearing. He will obey you cheerfully. He never talks back.'

I looked about. It looked like a green haven. Acres and acres of trees, shrubs and orchards. Far off, casuarina leaves murmured. 'Beyond that casuarina, would you believe it I have a lotus pond, and on its bank a temple, the most lovely ruin that you ever saw! I was in ecstasy when I found that these delightful things were included in the lot.'

'I'd love to see that temple, what temple is it?'

'The Goddess. It is said that *Sankara* when he passed this way built it at night, by merely chanting her name over the earth, and it stood up, because the villagers hereabouts asked for it. The Goddess is known as *Vak Matha*, the mother who came out of a syllable. Would you like to see it? But first rest and refreshment and then the other things of life. This has always been my motto. Shall we sit down here?' We sat down on a stone bench under a spreading mango tree. He pointed at the cottage and said: 'You must also come in and see my home. I've a little library too. Here comes my wife.' He introduced me to her as the unknown man for whom a letter was sent. She looked at me and said: 'We wouldn't believe you really existed. I thought it was some joke of my husband's – won't you have some coffee and fruits?' She went in and brought a tray-load of good things. My host ate heartily, talking all the time; he told me numerous things about himself and the farm. How he purchased these acres eight years ago, and had worked on them night and day. He liked the pond, the temple and the trees, he wanted to be out of town, but near enough to be able to run into it. 'My views have always been that it must be a quiet retreat, but a railway line must be visible from your veranda or at least a trunk road. Now we've both. If you sit here for a while longer, you will see the Madras mail passing over that ridge. I came here, so near the town, but you know for eight years I've hardly moved out of this estate. I'm quite happy where I am. By the way, my wife thinks if I moved up and down a little more into the town, I could occupy less space in my house. As if town-going were a sort of slimming exercise!' I listened to it all with only partial interest. I was very anxious to hear more about that letter and other matters connected with it.

'Shall we go round and see things?' He fetched two staves from a cluster strung on the fork of the mango tree, and gave one to me. He explained: 'When an odd twig catches my eye I cut it off and make a stick. Tree twigs have a sense of humour and adopt funny shapes. I think it is one of Nature's expressions of humour. If only we can see them that way ...' He pointed at his collection: crooked, piked, stunted, awry, all shapes and kinds were there. 'It is better to carry a staff, there are a lot of cobras about. Though I've never killed one in my life. When I see a snake I usually cry for help.'

We wandered about the garden. He spoke incessantly, bursting with mirth, and explaining his garden. All the time he was talking my mind was elsewhere, in a hopeless tension, waiting to hear about the letter. I hoped he would open the subject himself. But he spoke on about all sorts of other things. I tried once or twice to ask him but checked myself and remained quiet. Somehow, I felt too shy to open the topic – like a newly-wed blushing at the mention of his wife.

It was nearly dark when we came to the northern edge of the estate. It was ineffably lovely – a small pond with blue lotus; a row of stone steps leading down to the water. Tall casuarina trees swayed and murmured over the banks. A crescent moon peeped behind the foliage. On the bank on our side stood a small shrine, its concrete walls green with age, and its little dome showing cracks; it had a small portal, and a flagstaff at the entrance.

There was a small platform on the threshold of the temple. The temple was locked. We washed our feet and sat on the platform; it appeared an enchanting place. We squatted on the platform. 'Shall I have the temple opened?' he asked.

'No, don't worry about it now,' I said.

'There is an old priest who occasionally comes here once a month or so ... A very fine man, with whom it is a pleasure to talk. A very learned man. I'm really afraid of him. He is too good for this place; but comes here only out of piety, and he is running some charity institution in the town. He treats this as an opportunity to worship the Goddess ...' He talked, I listened to him in silence. My mind was trembling with eagerness. I listened in tense silence. He asked with a smile: 'You think I'm a bore?'

'Oh, no.'

'Doubtless, you want to know all about that letter ...'

'Of course I'm very eager,' I said, and added with a pathetic foolishness: 'It was so long ago ...' I stopped abruptly not knowing how to finish the sentence.

'Now listen,' he said: 'Of late I have got into the habit of spending more and more of my evenings all alone here on this pyol. This casuarina and the setting sun and the river create a sort of peace to which I've become more and more addicted. I spend long hours here, and desire nothing better than to be left here to this peace. It gives one the feeling that it is a place which belongs to Eternity, and that it will not be touched by time or disease or decay. One day before starting for this place I felt a great urge to bring writing materials with me. Since the morning it had hung on my mind. I felt that an old sin of my undergraduate days of writing prose-poems was returning, but there was no harm in succumbing to it. I slipped a pad and a pencil into my pocket when I started out in the evening on my rounds. I sat down on this pyol with the pencil and pad. For some time I could write nothing; it seemed that a hundred ideas were clamouring to express themselves, crowding into my head. It was a lovely sky. I felt I must write something of this great beauty in my lines. Let me assure you that I'm by no means a poetical-minded fellow. I'm a dead sober farmer ... but what was this thing within? I felt a queer change taking place within me.

'It was dusk when I sat down with the pad and pencil. Before the light should be fully gone I wanted to write down my verse or drama or whatever it was that was troubling me.

'I poised the pencil over the paper. Presently the pencil moved ... I was struck with the ease with which it moved. I was pleased. All the function my fingers had was to hold the pencil, nothing more ... "Thank you" began the page. "Here we are, a band of spirits who've been working to bridge the gulf between life and after-life. We have been looking about for a medium through whom we could communicate. There is hardly any personality on earth who does not obstruct our effort. But we're glad we've found you ... Please, help us, by literally lending us a hand – your hand, and we will do the rest." I replied, "I'm honoured, I will do whatever I can."

" 'You need do nothing more than sit here one or two evenings of the week, relax your mind, and think of us." "The pleasure is mine," I said. And then my hand wrote: "Here is Susila, wife of Krishna, but as yet she is unable to communicate by herself. But by and by she will be an adept in it. Will you kindly send the following as coming from her to her husband." And then I received the message I sent you and they also gave me your name and address!'

Our next meeting was a week later; on the following Wednesday. He brought with him a pad of paper, and a couple of pencils, and a pencil sharpener. 'I don't want to risk a broken pencil,' he remarked. 'There must be no complaint of any omission on my part,' he explained.

The casuarina looked more enchanting than ever. Purple lotus bloomed on the pond surface. Gentle ripples splashed against the bank. The murmur of the casuarina provided the music for the great occasion. We took our seats on the pyol of the little shrine. My friend shut his eyes and prayed: 'Great souls, here we are. You have vouchsafed to us a vision for peace and understanding. Here we are ready to serve in the cause of illumination.' He sat with his eyes shut, and as the dusk gathered around us, utter silence reigned. I too sat, not knowing what we waited for. The casuarina murmured and hushed, the ripples splashed on the shore. A bright star appeared in the sky. I almost held my breath as I waited. There was such a peace in the air that I felt that even if nothing happened this was a rich experience – a glimpse of eternal peace. We sat in silence, not speaking a word to each other. I felt we could spend the rest of our life sitting there thus. He poised his pencil over the pad and waited. Suddenly the pencil began to move. Letters appeared on the paper. The pencil quivered as if with life. It moved at a terrific speed across the paper; it looked as though my friend could not hold it in check. It scratched the paper and tore the lines up into shreds and came through. The scratching it made drowned all other sounds. It seemed to be possessed of tremendous power. My friend said with a smile: 'I think my wrist will be dislocated at this rate, unless I have my wits about me ...' Sheet after sheet was covered thus with scribbling, hardly clear or legible – not a word of it could be deciphered. It looked like the work of a very young child with paper and pencil. By the light of a lantern he tried to make it out and burst into a laugh: 'This writing does me no credit. If I leave it behind, it will be a headache for future epigraphists!' He looked at it again and again and laughed very happily. 'I remember that for writing precisely this sort of thing, my teacher broke my knuckles once.'

He put it away. After a few minutes' interval he took his pencil to the paper again. His hand wrote: 'We are here, trying to express ourselves. Sorry if you find our force too much for you. It is because you are not accustomed to this pressure. Please steady yourself and slow down. You will have better results....'

'I have the feeling of a crow flying in a storm,' my friend muttered to me ... But I ... I suppose I must control myself. I am fat enough ....'

He gripped the pencil as in a vice and steadied himself. 'No, no,' his hand wrote, 'you must relax, you must not set your teeth and get down to it so resolutely.' His hand wrote: 'Relax, slow down, control yourself, even if you feel like rushing off.'

'Rather a difficult combination of things. This relaxed control; till this moment I never imagined such a combination existed,' he muttered. He put away the pencil for a minute, stretched his arm, cracked his fingers and picked up the pencil again and turned over a clean sheet of paper. He said: 'Great souls, I'm ready.' Scrawled-up sheets of paper lay on one side. 'This is better. Go on slowly. Check yourself whenever you feel like running on fast. You will get good results.' His hand steadied, his handwriting improved. The blank sheet was filling up. Letters and words danced their way into existence.

'We are sorry to put you to this trouble. But please understand that this work may revolutionize human ideas, and that you are playing a vital part in it. This is an attempt to turn the other side of the medal of existence, which is called Death ... Please go on for just half an hour today and then stop, or if there are unfinished messages, a maximum of forty minutes. And don't attempt it again for a week more, that is, exactly this same hour, next week this day. We have to warn you that it will take some more sittings before your friend here gets accurate results, but for a start what you are going to receive today will be quite good. Now put away your pencil and then start after five minutes. Your nerves are too much in a tremble, and they must subside ...' My friend put away the pencil, and said to me: 'Are you happy? The next batch of messages may be from your wife.' 'I don't know how to thank you,' I said. We watched the stars on their course for a few minutes; and gazed idly at the pond. Five minutes passed. He picked up his pencil and placed it over the paper. 'Your condition is better. Remember our instructions. Stop in half an hour.' 'I will remember,' he replied and asked aloud, 'Is my friend's wife here?' 'Yes. She is here,' his hand wrote, and the words covered half a page. My friend exercised control over his fingers, checked and presently the writing assumed normal form. His hand wrote: 'Your friend's wife has been here all along. In fact we are at this task mainly for her sake. She is so eager to communicate with her husband.' I looked about. The semi-dark air seemed to glisten with radiant presences – like myriad dewdrops sparkling on the grass on a sunny morning. I strained my eyes and mind to catch a glimpse of these presences.

I told my friend: 'Please ask if my wife will be able to communicate now directly ...' In answer his hand wrote: 'She is very much excited and she is also not able to collect her thoughts easily. At the moment, she finds it easier to tell us ...' I visualized her all a-tremble with excitement as on that day when I went to her place to see and approve the future bride. As I waited in the hall I caught a glimpse of her in another room through a looking glass, agitated and trembling! I had never again seen her so excited. There fell a pause, as my friend's pencil waited. There did not seem to be any need to ask or answer. This was enough. The greatest abiding rapture which could always stay, and not recede or fall into an anti-climax like most mortal joys. After a few moments, I asked, 'Do you remember the name of our child?' The pencil wrote: 'Yes, Radha.' This was disappointing. My child was Leela. I was seized with a hopeless feeling of disappointment. To be unable to recollect the name of the child! What was wrong? Where? My mind buzzed with questions. 'The lady is smiling at the agitation which this name is causing her husband, but assures him that he need not feel so miserable over it. We've warned you that results will not be very accurate today. There are difficulties. We will do our best and gradually all these handicaps will be removed. Meanwhile understand that this is as good as it can be.'

I asked: 'But our child's name? Could this ever escape your mind?'

'No. It can't and it has not. You commit the mistake of thinking that she is responsible for giving that name. As a matter of fact it is a piece of your friend's own mind. You see there are particular difficulties in regard to proper names. We try to get through a particular name, for instance your daughter's ... but since we use the mechanism of your friend's writing, more often than not his mind interferes, bringing up its own selections. This is how you got Radha now.' 'But how is this difficulty to be surmounted?' I asked. 'Is there no hope at all?' I asked. 'Yes, yes, by and by. Even now you may remember we could get through your name and address the other day and he was able to send for you. But it was an exception: he was ideally unselfconscious and his mind was very passive. It will all depend upon our friend's ability to remain passive, and keep his own thoughts out of the field. That's why we have asked him to stop half an hour, which is the maximum time he can hold his ideas in the background.' My friend said: 'No. I can manage a little longer.' 'No. Half an hour will do ... But by and by you may go on even longer ... Please stop after this. The lady wants to say that she is as deeply devoted to her husband and child and the family as ever. She watches over them and prays for their welfare – only she is able to see things far more clearly than when she was on Earth, although you are not aware of my presence at times ... God's blessing be upon you and the child!' The pencil ceased. My friend looked at me as if to say: 'Go on. Get up. It is over.' But I was reluctant. So many questions to ask. My heart choked with the questions still unasked: 'Just a second more,' I pleaded. 'I have just one more question.' I paused. It was not clear to me what the question was. I pondered. 'Can't we have it sooner than next week? ... Please ... Does she remember? ...' It was no use. The pencil stood unmoving. We waited for a moment. And then my friend said. 'They are gone. We will try again next week.'

On the following week we sat there just at the same hour, with the dusk falling about us. They wrote: 'We are here. Conditions are favourable. But remember our instructions and go slowly. Susila, wife of Krishna, is here and will now go on by herself.'

'I have watched you since we met last and seen your mind. I saw the doubts crossing and recrossing your mind regarding identity. Naturally. How can you believe what you can't see? It might be me or someone else; was that not the line of thought going on in your mind? Correct me if I am wrong.'

'You are right, absolutely right,' I answered. It did not require much self-scrutiny to see it. 'And so I decided to clear this doubt first. And all this interval I have been trying to master the art of communication, and our helpers here have been very good to teach me. This is the first step. I hope you like this. I hope I do well for a start.'

'Very well, very well, for a start ....' I replied in Tamil.

'I had not learnt very grammatical Tamil in my days, and if there are any mistakes, don't laugh at me.'

'Oh, you are very good. You wrote beautiful letters,' I said.

'And yet you have destroyed every one of them!' she said. 'You found it possible to destroy every one of them!' she repeated. I was startled. No one knew about it. In the secrecy of night, on that day her condition was declared to be hopeless, I sat in my room, bolted the door, took out of my drawer several bundles of letters she had written to me, tore them up into minute bits and burnt them, and I also did the same with a few diary pages I had kept in the first years of our married life. I remembered saying to myself, gritting my teeth: 'Let life do its worst, this is my answer. Every shred of memory will be destroyed, I will avoid torment thus ....'

'How have you come to know of it?' I asked.

'By watching your mind. I saw you yesterday as you pulled out your table drawer and reflected. I might not have known it at all if you hadn't reflected on it every day. For on the occasion you were performing the deed, I was, you remember, passing over, and in that transition stage one is not aware of things. It takes some time before we are able to know things. You have destroyed not only all that I wrote, but also all the letters you wrote to me. Was that the reason why you demanded them back from me every time I came back to you from my parents?' It was an unwritten law existing between us: whenever we were parted we wrote to each other on alternate days, and when we met again, I took back from her all the letters, bundled them up, and offered to destroy them, but she always protested and I just kept them with me.

'Why did you do it?' she persisted.

'I am very sorry. I thought I might abolish memory!'

'Have you been able to forget? Wasn't it childish to work your temper on those letters?'

'It seemed that memory would torment me.'

'That's how it may appear at first sight; but later, let me tell you that you will have a desire to be surrounded by everything belonging to the departed. Just a turn of the wheel. A man takes to drink to forget sad thoughts, but after a while they return with gathered force. I understand your feelings but can only laugh at the remedy.' I felt really like a child who had misbehaved. 'Please forgive me if I appear to be speaking more than I ought. But I felt very unhappy about it. So this. I hope you will forgive this outburst,' she said.

'You are perfectly right, and entitled to it,' I said. 'God bless you. I felt so vacant yesterday, when I had a longing to see your handwriting and could not find a single letter anywhere,' I confessed.

'The lady is laughing,' the Helpers said. 'She is shaking with laughter. She says don't take anything too tragically – not even this!'

'I accept your advice ....' I said.

'You need not be unduly docile,' she said, 'and strain yourself to be agreeable, just because I'm speaking from this side. Don't hesitate to correct me if I appear silly.'

'Oh, no, no, you are very sensible,' I said.

'You used to be so considerate on the first two days whenever we met after a visit to my parents. You would not contradict anything I said. Here is a piece of news for you. There are about fourteen letters which have been spared ... I don't remember whether they were yours or mine, but I remember tying them up in a bundle; you will find them either in my trunk, or in one of the boxes in my father's place.'

I thought over this and said: 'I'm afraid you are wrong. There is not one letter left. I destroyed every bit that we wrote to each other.'

'I'm sure of these fourteen: I remember the number precisely. I counted them, I tied them up and did not give them to you because you were very busy with something or other. I can't say how long ago; I put them away and then I remember coming across the bundle again and again. What I can't recollect is whether it was in my father's house or in ours. I am certain that the letters are there.' She insisted: 'Will you please make a thorough search once again? – and if you find them please don't repeat your previous act.'

'No, no. I will be very careful,' I said.

'Also, I want you to keep for my sake a sandalwood casket. I have put into it all my knick-knacks.' I cast my mind about. I had looked through all her possessions and I had a knowledge of everything she had.

'I don't think you ever had such a box,' I said. 'Where is it?'

'It is not a very big box, about eight or ten inches long, three inches high and about four inches wide; the lid of the box is not flat but slightly elevated. I kept all my knick-knacks in it. It was given to me by my mother-in-law. Box of ivory and sandalwood. Please find it and keep it. I was fond of it. You may throw away all my other things. They are of no particular value to me.'

'I can't throw out the tiniest speck that belonged to you. I will keep everything, including this box if I find it. But I'm not sure there is such a box.'

At the next meeting she remarked: 'You fret too much about the child. Have no kind of worry about her. When you are away at college, you hardly do your work with a free mind, all the time saying to yourself "What is Leela doing? What is she doing?"

Remember that she is perfectly happy all the afternoon, playing with that friend of hers in the next house, and listening to the stories of the old lady. Just about the time you return, she stands at the door and looks down the street for you. And when you see her you think that she has been there the whole day and feel miserable about it. How you can help it, you never pause to consider. Do you know that she sometimes insists upon being taken to the little children's school, which is nearby? And the old lady, whenever she is free, takes her there and she has become quite a favourite there? Why don't you put her in that school? She will be quite happy there.'

Immediately I contradicted: 'I don't think she is going to a school. She would have told me about it ....'

'She went in casually once or twice, and perhaps forgot it later among other interests. I think she'll tell you when she remembers it. Anyway, if she likes it she may go there ....'

'All right, but is she not too young to be put to school?'

'She'll find it interesting, and it is not regular study. She can go and see other children and come home when she likes ....'

'I have no objection, but the teacher may have some other system.'

'No ... It is a school meant for very small children.'

'How much of the child do you see?' I asked.

'As much as anyone else, perhaps a little more. I have direct access to her heart now: I am always watching her.'

'Does she see you?'

'Perhaps she does. Children are keener-sighted by nature. She sees me, and perhaps takes it naturally, since children spontaneously see only the souls of persons. Children see spirit forms so often that it is natural to their condition and state of mind.'

'If she sees you why doesn't she cry out?'

'It is a natural state to them, and in the depth of their soul they have certain reservations. Perhaps she doesn't speak out as much as she would like because she observes and understands the reserve you are all exercising in her presence about me. She merely saves your feelings by not speaking of me. You must have observed how little she refers to me. Did you think that it was out of forgetfulness? And don't you agree that there is a certain peace about her, which elders lack, although I was no less important to her than to anyone else?'

Nowadays I went about my work with a light heart. I felt as if a dead load had been lifted. The day seemed full of possibilities of surprise and joy. At home I devoted myself to my studies more energetically. The sense of futility was leaving me. I attended to my work earnestly. All the morning I sat preparing my day's lectures. My little daughter watched me curiously. 'Father is reading!' she exclaimed. She drew a chair close to mine and sat up with a book, with any book that caught her fancy, till she saw a squirrel or a sparrow alighting on the roof of the opposite house, and exclaimed: 'Father, the sparrow is come. Do they also read? Do they also go to school?'

'Little girl, just go out near the gate and ask,' I said, with the idea of getting on with my work. Once she had gone out, she slowly got interested in something or other and forgot to come back. When she mentioned school, I pricked up my ears and was on the point of asking her a question, but I restrained myself, because I wanted to watch if the answer would come from her first or from the old lady. That very evening I heard the subject mentioned. When I returned home the child was out. There was only the old lady in the kitchen. I asked: 'Where is Leela?'

'Oh, she has gone to the school,' the old lady replied.

'Which school?' I asked with feigned ignorance.

'That babies' school, in the next street. I took her there once or twice in the afternoon, because she liked to see the other children, and they all like her very much there. Today the teacher said he would bring her back in the evening. She wouldn't come away either: because she is making some animals and other things with clay. They have also given her scissors and coloured paper to cut. She is so happy!'

'Why didn't you tell me before that you had taken her there?'

'I took her out on two days just for a few minutes. When the child in the next house came home in the afternoon and went back to school, Leela also went with her one day,' she said and added, 'Poor thing, it was some way of engaging her mind and keeping her from longing for her mother!'

The child came home half an hour later. Her teacher left her at the gate and went away. 'Father,' she screamed at the gate, 'I've been to school like you.' I went out and picked her up in my arms. The teacher had moved off a few yards.

'Is that your teacher?' I asked.

'Yes.'

'Call him,' I said. At which she shouted: 'Schoolmaster!' and the teacher turned back. 'Come back and speak to my father.'

'You are the headmaster of the school?' I asked.

'Yes.'

'Is there any class to which this girl can be admitted?'

'Oh, yes. She will be happy. We shall be very glad to admit her.'

'Any long hours?' I asked.

'Oh, no, she can come any time and go away when she likes. No restrictions. Please send her. She will be happy with us.'

'May I know your name?'

'Just Headmaster will do ...' he said.

The child was dancing with joy. She was full of descriptions of her school. 'Father, do you know I have made a clay *brinjal*? The teacher said it was nice.' 'All right, all right,' I said, and sat by her side and made her take some tiffin which the old lady had prepared. She was too excited to relish anything. I coaxed her to eat. And then took her to the bathroom. Her face was streaked with the clay she had been handling. I soaked a towel in water and rubbed her cheeks till they glowed. And then I sent her in to the old lady and had her hair combed.

I took her out on her usual walk. I took her through the busy thoroughfare of Market Road. She loved the bustle of Market Road and kept asking questions and I found her view of life enchanting. I bought her some sweets at the stores. She mainly talked about her school. 'Father, at our school, I have a friend. You know her father gives her lots of sweets every day. Why do you always give me only one or two?'

'Children must not eat more than two at a time,' I replied.

'She is a good girl, always plays with me at school,' the child said. 'Shall I also grow tall when I go to school?'

'Yes, certainly.'

'Why do you go to that far-off school, and not to our school, father?' she said. She saw some villagers moving about with turbans on their heads. She asked: 'Do they wear those things on their heads, even when they sleep?' I don't know what idea crossed her mind at such times. I took her to the river-bank. She ran about on the sand. She watched the other children playing. She whispered: 'That girl is in our school.'

'What is her name?'

'Kamala,' she said.

'Is she your friend?'

'She is a very good girl.'

'Go and play with her if you like.' The girl was playing with another group around a circle on the sand. At my suggestion Leela blinked and said with great seriousness: 'She will be very angry if I ask to be taken also.'

'Call her, let me see,' I said.

'Kamala, Kamala,' she called faintly, and then added: 'That is her school name, she doesn't like to be called so when she is not in school.' We passed on. She stood near other girls also and pointed them out to me as her school friends, but she would not go near anyone or call aloud. She seemed to identify her friends in a general way, whatever might be their names and their schools; as far as she was concerned they were all her friends and schoolmates. She was endowing each of them with any character she chose.

Next morning there was great activity. She was to be put to school. I was as excited as if I myself were to be put to school. I did little work at my table that day. I ran about the house in great excitement. I opened her trunk and picked out a shirt and skirt, fresh ones, printed cotton. When she saw them my daughter put them back and insisted upon wearing something in lace and silk. 'Baby, you must not go to school wearing laced clothes. Have you ever seen me going with any lace on?'

'It's because you have no lace skirts, that is all,' she said. 'No, father, I want that for school. Otherwise they will not allow me in.' She threw her clothes about and picked up a deep green, with a resplendent lace three inches wide, and a red skirt studded with stars: the whole thing was too gorgeous for a school. Her mother had selected them for her on a birthday, at the Bombay Cloth Emporium. Two evenings before the birthday we had gone there, and after an hour's search she picked up these bits for the child, who was delighted with the selection. I protested against it and was told, 'Gaudy! There is nothing gaudy where children are concerned, particularly if they are girls. Whom are these for if they are not meant to be worn by children?'

'Go on, go on,' I said cynically. 'Buy yourself two of the same pattern if you are so fond of it.' But the cynicism was lost on her. She disarmed me by taking it literally and said: 'No, no. I don't think they weave *saris* of this pattern? Do they?' she asked turning to the shopman.

The child was excessively fond of this piece and on every occasion attempted to wear it. Today she was so adamant that I had to yield to her. She tried to wear them immediately, but I said: 'After your hair is combed and you have bathed ....' And now as I put her clothes back in the box she grew very impatient and demanded: 'Bathe me, father, bathe me, father.' I turned her over to the old lady's care and arranged the box, carefully folded and kept away her clothes. She had over forty skirts and shirts. Her mother believed in stitching clothes for her whenever she had no other work to do, and all the child's grandparents and uncles and aunts constantly sent her silk pieces and clothes ever since the day she was born. The result was she had accumulated an unmanageable quantity of costly clothes, and it was one of my important occupations in life to keep count of them.

She was ready, dressed in a regalia, and stood before me, a miniature version of her mother. 'Let us go,' she said, and for a moment I was unaware whether the mother or the daughter was speaking – the turn of the head and lips!

'I must carry books,' she insisted.

'No, no, not today ....'

'My teacher will be angry if I don't take my books,' she said, and picked up her usual catalogue. She clasped it to her little bosom, and walked out with me, bubbling with anticipation and joy.

The school was in the next street. A small compound and a few trees and a small brick-red building. The noise those children made reached me as I turned the street. The schoolmaster received us at the gate. As soon as we entered the gate, a few other children surrounded Leela and took her away. She left me without a thought. She behaved as if she had been in that school for years and years.

The headmaster was in raptures over the new arrival. He said: 'Won't you come and have a look round?'

He had partitioned the main hall into a number of rooms. The partition screens could all be seen, filled with glittering alphabets and pictures drawn by children – a look at it seemed to explain the created universe. You could find everything you wanted – men, trees, and animals, skies and rivers. 'All these – work of our children ...' he explained proudly. 'Wonderful creatures! It is wonderful how much they can see and do! I tell you, sir, live in their midst and you will want nothing else in life.' He took me round. In that narrow space he had crammed every conceivable plaything for children, see-saws, swings, sand heaps and ladders. 'These are the classrooms,' he said. 'Not for them. For us elders to learn. Just watch them for a while.' They were digging into the sand, running up the ladder, swinging, sliding down slopes – all so happy. 'This is the meaning of the word joy – in its purest sense. We can learn a great deal watching them and playing with them. When we are qualified we can enter their life ...' he said. The place was dotted with the coloured dresses of these children, bundles of joy and play. 'When I watch them, I get a glimpse of some purpose in existence and creation.' He struck me as an extraordinary man.

'If they are always playing when do they study?'

'Just as they play – I gather them together and talk to them and take them in and show them writing on boards. They learn more that way. Everybody speaks of the game-way in studies but nobody really practises it. It becomes more the subject of a paper in some pompous conference and brings a title or preferment to the educational administrator. Oh, don't allow me to speak too much on this subject as you will find me a terrible bore ....' He was a slight man, who looked scraggy; evidently he didn't care for himself sufficiently. His hair fell on his nape, not because he wanted it to grow that way, but, I was sure, because he neglected to get it cut. His coat was frayed and unpressed. I liked him immensely. I was sure there were many things about him which would fascinate me. I was seized with a desire to know more of him. I asked him: 'Please visit me some day.'

'I will certainly drop in one day when I take a holiday. You see I hate holidays. It is ten or fifteen years since I began this work, and I have not felt the need for a holiday at all. Holidays bore me. And I spend even my Sundays here looking about. This is a nice place; there is a garden too, entirely made by children.' He took me through a bamboo stile to a small plot with tiny lots. He was continually enthusiastic. 'Does he ever sleep?' I asked myself. 'Come to my house on a Sunday instead of coming here,' I said and he agreed. I had a feeling that I was about to make a profound contact in life.

The next sitting was a complete disappointment to me. But perhaps my own frame of mind was somewhat to blame. After the first thrill of discovery subsided, I fell into a questioning mood and asked, the moment my friend was ready with the pencil: 'Do you remember the last day we went out together?'

'Yes, I remember.'

'Can you say where we went and a few incidents of the day and so on?' I asked.

'I remember going out on the last day with you. I feel we visited a temple, bought something for the child, and also visited a painted house. We went out followed by the servant and did a little marketing on the way.'

'Oh!' I said. 'What else do you remember?' The pencil paused for a while and then scratched off: 'We met a scorpion on the way and you nearly put your foot on it. We bought a brass lamp used for worship, and a toy engine.'

'Do you remember what happened in the house we visited?' I asked.

'No,' she replied.

'Absolutely nothing happened?' I asked. In answer to it the Helper wrote: 'The low roof of the kitchen knocked her head, and she is laughing because her husband slipped in the backyard ....'

'To be frank this did not happen. I don't know why she is saying these things,' I said.

'She promises to do better next time,' the Helpers wrote. 'There are some difficulties both in expressing and picking out of memory the exact items. We would advise you to stop now. The lady sends her love and prayers for her husband and child ...' And they were gone. The hand stopped. 'Half an hour over I suppose,' said my friend. I rose to go home very unhappily. Except one or two references, the rest was all too wild .... I grumbled and went home in a most unhappy state of mind. 'To be in this state till next Wednesday.'

But a week passed. I was back there on the following Wednesday. Meanwhile I had scrutinized the pages again and again, and came to the conclusion that after all they were not wild. Each detail was correct, temple, painted house, buying for the child and the lamps. Every time she went to her parents she purchased brass lamps and knick-knacks for someone or other; a toy engine was bought on the last day for the child. As for knocking her head against the kitchen roof, she was rather tall for her age and was very proud of the fact that most doorways were too short for her and that they knocked her on the head, and she always spoke about it. I could not recollect when I had slipped in the backyard, but otherwise each individual item seemed to be after all correct, though chronologically mixed up in utter confusion. I mentioned it to my friend when I met him next and his explanation seemed to be plausible: 'I will ask you a question now at short notice. When did you buy the cloth for this shirt?' I looked at my blue shirt helplessly. 'Was it before or after you purchased the coat you are wearing over it? And on your way home from the shop that day what else did you buy and how much? You see how difficult it is to place these exactly, while you are still living in the midst of these experiences. I can't say for instance what exactly I had for dinner this day last week .... While chronological order and precision in details are so difficult for us, they must be more so to other beings whose surroundings are timeless and entirely different. If my speculation is right their vision of things embraces an experience as a whole rather than events in an order. All memories merge and telescope when the time element between them is removed. I think this is the reason for the apparent confusion. Add to this the possibility of their memory being finer and more selective; there may be a natural law operating by which unpleasant memories and impressions are filtered and left behind with the physical body. If you take all this into consideration, you may view their inaccuracies more charitably.'

At every sitting she urged me on to look for her sandalwood casket and the fourteen letters. I couldn't search very thoroughly because I found it impossible to enter the room and open her trunks. On a holiday afternoon I steeled myself to it. I opened the door and felt a pang at heart when I cast a look around at her trunks, her clothes and possessions. 'For all of us our possessions turn to mementoes. Is there anyone in the whole world who can say his lot is different?' I reflected, as I sat down amidst her trunks. My daughter was thrilled to see me there, and cancelled an appointment she had with her friend and joined me in my search.

I opened Susila's yellow trunk, in which she kept all kinds of toilet sets she had acquired in her lifetime. Three or four different coloured vulcanite cases with mirrors and small bottles. She used to be very fond of these boxes and asked for one whenever she saw them in the shop – green, orange, red, of all colours. I took them out one by one. And then all kinds of cardboard boxes and fancy tin containers stuffed with embroidery thread and woollen bits. The small sweater in yellow – she had been reading about knitting and had become suddenly very enthusiastic. She behaved like a child in her enthusiasm. Every day as I left for college she gave me a commission for a purchase on my way back. It was rarely I was able to pick up the correct colour that she wanted, and I had the task of exchanging it for the correct shade next evening. Finally, exasperated, I arbitrarily forced her to begin work on the yellow sweater for me. She sat down on the veranda step and plied her needles by the evening light, refusing to go out on a walk or do anything else. Night and day she thought and spoke of nothing else. At the end of the day the two shining needles were stuck into the ball and kept on a shelf in the hall. I made all kinds of jokes about it, saying that the sweater seemed to be promised for my hundredth birthday and so on. The back of the sweater was nearly ready and she looked triumphant. The ball of wool was satisfactorily going down in bulk. She proclaimed that the complete sweater would be on my back in eight days; and then our child caught a cold, and she lost all peace of mind and could not knit; thereafter one thing and another intervened and she never took it up again at all. In that condition it was still lying in the box, with the yellow back ready, the needles stuck, as they were on the day, into the ball of wool. 'What is this, father?' the child asked picking it up. I shook my head and said: 'Put it away, girl, you may hurt yourself with the needles.' And then there were fancy borders meant to be stitched into some dress. I had always protested against the purchase of these things and she always waved my protest away with: 'You just see how they look when they are stitched into my jackets and the baby's frocks! You will yourself ransack all the shops for more of them.' But they were still where they had been put the day she bought them. This box contained a couple of fancy lacquer caskets of Burmese origin, which her sister from Rangoon had sent; they were filled with small bottles of scent, which I had given her during the first two years of our married life. I opened their corks one by one and smelt them. Their delicate perfume brought immediately around me other days. Evenings when we went out, and spoke of nothing in particular, first years of married life when I used to be very vehement about my plans for the future. These tiny phials had compressed in them the essence of her personality, the rustle of her dress, her footfalls, laughter, her voice, and the light in her eyes, the perfume of her presence. The bottles were empty now but the lingering scent in them covered for a brief moment the gulf between the present and the past. I shut my eyes and dwelt in that ecstasy: I reflected: 'Of all the senses it is smell which is the subtlest; it takes you back to the core of your experience. Why have they not studied its laws and processes, while they have studied all the other senses? Do these scents mean anything to her in her present state?'

'What are you smelling, father?' asked the child and brought me back to the earth. 'Why are you closing your eyes, father?'

I drew down the lid. There was no trace of the fourteen letters and the sandalwood casket. I opened another trunk in which she had kept her clothes – dozens of *saris* and a hundred and one jackets of all colours and shades; and above all else that glittering gold-woven purple *sari*, in which she was presented to me as a bride on the all-important day. Many of these clothes had not been taken out more than once because she had a dread of spoiling their sheen.

She picked up like a child every soap-box carton and empty container and preserved them in her cupboard and put into them coins and knick-knacks. In a cardboard box I found stuffed a few sheets of paper. I pulled them out. They were embroidery designs copied in pencil, and some recipe for a tooth powder. There was a sheet on which she had even begun a story with childlike simplicity of two brothers, woodcutters, one of whom was good and industrious and the other was lazy and bad. There were my corrections in between the lines. I remembered how on a certain day she sat for hours at my table stroking her lips with the pencil, lost in thought. I do not know what made her want to write a story at all ... But she was filled with shame when I found her out, and was so nervous when I read through it and corrected the grammar; she never proceeded beyond the first page of the story, where the brothers differ and separate ... This seemed to me a precious document now crumpled and stuffed into the box. I carefully smoothed it out, and took it with me to my own table.

The child sat very quietly watching me and derived a great deal of pleasure in arranging the empty tins side by side ... There was still powder in one of the tins, three quarters full, bought a month before she fell ill. I opened the lid and smelt it. 'You are once again shutting your eyes,' remarked my daughter.

At the next meeting, the moment my friend was ready with the pencil, she asked: 'Do you know what a wonderful perfume I have put on! I wish you could smell it ... On second thoughts

I had better not mention it because you will want to smell it and feel disappointed. Perhaps it may look like selfishness for me to be so happy here when there you are so sorrow-filled and unhappy ... It would hardly be right if I produced that impression. If I succeed in making you feel that I am quite happy over here and that you must not be sorry for me, I will be satisfied. Your sorrow hurts us. I hope our joy and happiness will please and soothe you ...'

'Undoubtedly,' I replied. 'But what makes you mention the perfume?' I asked.

'Just to enable you to have the most complete idea of our state of existence, that is all. Moreover, did you not speculate somewhat on those lines a few days ago?'

'How do you spend your time usually?' I asked.

'Time in your sense does not exist for us,' she replied. 'Our life is one of thought and experience. Thought is something which has solidity and power, and as in all existence ours is also a life of aspiration, striving, and joy. A considerable portion of our state is taken up in meditation, and our greatest ecstasy is in feeling the Divine Light flooding us ... We've ample leisure. We are not constrained to spend it in any particular manner. We have no need for exercise as we have no physical bodies. Music is ever with us here, and it transports us to higher planes ... Things here are far more intense than on earth; that means our efforts are far more efficient than yours. If by good fortune we are able to establish a contact with our dear ones who are receptive to our influence, then you say that that person is inspired. And a song or melody can establish a link between our minds, for instance, how sad that you should have neglected your *veena.* If you could take it up once again our minds could more easily join. Why don't you try it?'

It was years since I had put it away. I had a gift for it when I was young. 'I don't know scientific music. I have been after all a self-taught amateur ...'

'Do not worry what anyone will think of your *veena*. For me it will be the most welcome music. I promise that you will feel my presence as you have never felt it yet. It will surely make your heart easier.

'You might have thought I did not very much care for music when on earth, but as a matter of fact I was really intensely interested in it ...' she said. I remembered how quietly she liked music. She never took great pains to learn it although she could sing well. She could never be persuaded to sing; but sometimes unaware of my watching, she would sing to herself while combing her hair or putting the child to sleep. If I showed any signs of listening she would stop. She always listened to music wherever it came from – a gramophone in a house on the way, or a beggar singing; she listened with a silent rapture.

'You think I have become a very learned sort of person and all that kind of stuff?'

'Yes,' I replied. Ever since these communications began I felt, now and then, that she showed a greater wisdom than I had known her to possess. 'You would much rather that I was the same prattling person I was on earth, but let me tell you that the change that takes place when one comes over here is so great and the vision is so cleared that even I, your wife, whose nonsense pleased you so much more, am changed. I'm essentially the same person as far as you and my dear ones are concerned, but the only difference is that I'm without the encumbrance of the physical body and everything is finer and quicker than on earth.

'Between thought and fulfilment there is no interval. Thought is fulfilment, motion and everything. That is the main difference between our physical state and yours. In your state a thought to be realized must always be followed by effort directed towards conquering obstructions and inertia – that is the nature of the material world. But in our condition no such obstruction exists. When I think of you or you of me I am at your side. Music directly transports us. When I think of a garment, it is on me. In our world there is such a fine response for thought. When I come to you I prepare myself every time as befits the occasion. I come to meet my lord and I dress myself as befits the occasion. I think of the subtlest perfume and it already pervades my being; and I think of the garment that will most please you: the wedding *sari*, shimmering purple woven with gold, I have on me at this very moment. You think you saw it in that trunk, how can it be here? What you have seen is its counterpart, the real part of the thing is that which is in thought, and it can never be lost or destroyed or put away.'

Thereafter she mentioned at the close of every evening her appearance. 'Have no shadow of doubt that I'm here. I am wearing a pale orange dress with a clasp of brilliants to hold it in position.'

'What a gorgeous dress!' I exclaimed.

'If only you saw the colour you would not say how gorgeous, you would be speechless. Not even the colours of sunset give you such tints as we have here; to call it pale orange is to give you an idea as inadequate as the idea which a child forms when ...'

I cast a look around. She at once said: 'You look round. I can see you. What a pity you can't see me! Some day let us hope you will see my form. I am at the moment sitting to your left on the floor with my arm resting on your lap, and directing your friend's hand by my thought.' I looked down at my lap. 'No use yet, even if you open your eyes so wide. But by and by, you will hear my bangles clanking and feast your eyes on my dress and form.'

'I think I look the same person as on earth. Only free from all ailments, ills, and cares. You remember I used to have a sort of pain at the waist, even that I do not have now.

'My dress tonight is a shimmering blue interwoven with light and stars. I have done my hair parted on the left. (And what a load of jasmine and other rare flowers I've in my hair for your sake!) I wish a painter could sense me and do a picture for you ...

'Rest assured that I shall always sit in the same place whenever I am here; when you lift your arm you touch me. At the close of this evening when you go home, I will accompany you, stay up with you till you go to bed and fall asleep thinking of me ...

'If you want any evidence of my presence, pluck about ten jasmine buds and keep them near your pillow tonight. Before I go away I will take their scent with me: that I can do. You will see the difference when you smell the flowers in the morning.'

On my way home, through the dark night, across Nallappa's Grove my feet felt lighter, because I knew she was accompanying me. Her presence was unmistakably there. I could sense it. The darkness of the night was not felt by me. The distance and loneliness were nothing to me. She was with me. I quietly enjoyed the fact without stirring the slightest thought. Far off I saw the dark night lit with the fire of a cremation. But it did not disturb me! 'I know more than this ...' I remarked.

CHAPTER SIX

Sunday. I decided to spend the entire day in the company of the child. Of late my college work and the extra activities and the weekly visits to my friend took up so much of my time that I spent less than two hours a day with the child. It was a painful realization. 'Oh, God,' went up my prayer, 'save me from becoming too absorbed in anything to look after the child properly.' And I felt very sorry and guilty when I returned home at nights and found the child asleep.

She had her own plans for the day. As soon as she got up and was ready for the road, she insisted upon being taken to the school. 'This is Sunday, you don't have to go,' I pleaded.

But it was no use. 'You don't know about our school. We have school.' She put on her coat and stepped out. I went out with her. 'Why do you follow me, father?' she asked.

'I too want to see your school today,' I said.

'But my friends are filled with fear if they see you. Don't come with me, father,' she pleaded.

'No, I will take good care not to frighten them,' I assured her. She stood for a moment undecided, looking at me and said to herself: 'Poor father, let him come too,' and smiled patronizingly.

There was no sign at the school to show that it was a Sunday. It was alive with the shouts of children – about twenty of them had already gathered and were running about and playing: the swings and see-saw were all in full use. The headmaster was with them.

'You don't rest even on a Sunday?' I asked the headmaster.

'Rest? This is all right for a rest, what else should I do? They just come in, play, throw the sand about, and go away, and we also do it with them. It is quite good, you know. I feel quite happy. What else should I do on a Sunday?'

'Something to differentiate it from other days ....'

'Quite. We don't do sums today. We just sing, hear stories, and play ....' His eyes were red. He coughed. He did not look as if he had had sleep at night.

'What is the matter with you?' I could not help asking.

'I suffer from sleeplessness, my friend,' he said. 'It is some years since I had anything like sleep. I sleep about an hour. I used to make myself very miserable about it at first. But now I am used to it. I make up stories for children and I hardly feel the time passing. Come in and see.' He took me into his room. It was thatch-roofed. Its floor was covered with clay, and the walls were of bamboo splinters filled in with mud. The floor was uneven and cool, and the whole place smelt of Mother Earth. It was a pleasing smell, and seemed to take us back to some primeval simplicity, intimately bound up with earth and mud and dust. Along the wall was a sort of running ledge covered with a crazy variety of objects: cardboard houses, paper flowers, clumsy drawings and bead work. 'These are the work of children who have studied here, and some of them have a special significance: presented to me by the outgoing children or the very special effort of a child. They are the trophies of this school. I consider them a real source of joy. For instance, the very first work of a child has some peculiar value. I don't know if others understand that there is anything in it at all ... you will understand it better if I say look at that green paper boat. Can you guess who has made it? Your daughter on the very first day she came here, she finished it within an hour.' I felt thrilled. Beside a parrot cut out of a cardboard picture and an inkpot made of paper, this green boat stood. I went over and picked it up. My little Leela in relation to an outside world, making her own mark on it: I was filled with pride and satisfaction. 'It is a whaler with a knife-edge at the keel!' I cried in joy. He jumped out of his seat: 'That's what I say. See how lovely it is!' The sight of it filled him with a mystic ecstasy. 'She is a grand child. So are the other children. The first work of almost every child is here and the other works go into the general hall.' The walls were hung with different pictures, tigers and lions and trees drawn with childish hands. He swept his hands about and declared: 'Every one of these is children's work. They are the real gods on earth.' He stopped before each picture and enjoyed the thrill of it anew. He had done away with table and chair. In a corner he had a seat for visitors. 'This will do for a school. We are a poor country, and we can do without luxuries. Why do we want anything more than a shed and a few mats and open air? This is not a cold country for all the heavy furniture and elaborate buildings. This has cost me just fifty rupees, and I had three such built. But we have not much use for them, most of our time being spent outside, under the tree ...'

'Many people think,' I said, 'that you can't have a school unless you have invested a few thousand in building and furniture.'

'It is all mere copying,' he replied. 'Multiply your expenses, and look to the Government for support, and sell your soul to the Government for the grant. This is the history of our educational movement. And another thing. What a fuss they have learnt to make of sports! As if colleges and schools were gymnasia, the main business of which is to turn out sturdy idiots. When I think of all the pampering and sentimentality of sports and games!' He shuddered. 'The main business of an educational institution is to shape the mind and character and of course games have their value. Why worship sports, and the eleven stalwart idiots who bring in a shield or a cup? It is all a curse, copying, copying, copying. We could as well have been born monkeys to justify our powers of imitation.'

'Yes,' I said. 'In our college Brown forgoes even his club to see a match; loses himself in excitement, congratulates the team and shakes hands, and gives no end of liberties to the tournament players and even sends them on tour,' I said, catching the infection of his mood.

'And do you know, they not only get a lot more touring and tiffin than the others. They are even made to pass examinations! And this sort of thing is supposed to make our people modern and vigorous ...' He laughed, but the excitement was too much for him, and he subsided into a fit of coughing.

'I'm sorry,' he said. 'Sit down, sit down. I wanted to show you the stories I've made ...' He pulled out a box and brought out a big bundle of brown paper: huge pages covered with letters as well as figures cut out and pasted. 'This is a new method which I find fascinating,' he said. 'I invent a story, write it down in words, and illustrate it with pictures cut out of illustrated books and papers and pasted at the appropriate places, for instance this,' he threw down ten volumes, 'is a pretty long story of a bison and a tiger in the forest ... just glance through it.' Every page had a figure or two; the illustrations ran along with the story.

'They are almost real you know,' he said as I gazed on the pictures. 'Just watch, I'll show you how it works.' He stood in the doorway and announced: 'Story! Story!' The children who had been playing about, stopped, looked at him and came running in, uttering shrieks of joy.

They sat around their master. When they subsided into silence he opened the large album and said looking at it: 'This is the story of a tiger and his friend the jungle buffalo, called Bison. It happened in Mempi Forest. Who can tell me where Mempi Forest is?' There followed a discussion among the children and one girl said pointing at the doorway: 'There, near the mountains, am I right?'

'Right, right,' he said. 'There are a lot of jungles there. See here.' All the children leaned over each other's shoulders and fixed their eyes on the top of the album where a perfect jungle had been made with the help of dry tinted grass pasted together. 'These are all bamboo jungles, full of tigers, but we are only concerned with one tiger. His name is Raja. See this. There he is, a young cub.'

'He is very young,' said the children, looking at him. The album was passed round for the benefit of those sitting far off. 'What a fearful fellow!' commented a few. My daughter, sitting between two friends older than herself, refused to touch the album because of the tiger, but was quite prepared to see it if held by her neighbour. 'This little tiger was quite lonely, you know, because her mother had been taken away by hunters – bad fellows.' Thus the story of the tiger went on. The tiger came across a friend in the shape of a young bison, who protected him from a bear and other enemies. They both lived in a cave at the tail-end of Mempi Hills – great friends. The bison grew up into a thick rock-like animal, and the tiger also grew up and went out in search of prey at nights. One night a party of hunters shot at the bison and carried him off to the town. And the tiger missed his friend and his cry rang through the Mempi Forest the whole night. The tiger soon adjusted himself to a lonely existence.

The children listened in dead silence and were greatly moved when this portion was read out. They all came over to have a look at the tiger in his loneliness, and our friend, rightly guessing that they would ask for it, had procured a picture. The tiger was standing forlorn before his cave. The children uttered many cries of regret and unhappiness. 'Master, how can he live without his friend any more? I hope he is not killed by the bear!'

'No. No, that bear was disposed of by the friend before he was caught.'

'Poor bear! Let me have a look at him,' said a girl. The pages were turned back and there he was, dark and shaggy. 'He could have fought with the bison. He looks so strong,' said the girl. She was, somehow, unaccountably, on the side of the bear. 'You should not like the bear,' said another girl. 'The teacher will be angry if you like the bear ...'

'No, no, I won't be. You may like what you like,' said the teacher. This was an inducement for another child to join the ranks of bear-lovers. She said: 'I always like a bear. It has such a lot of hair. Who will comb her hair, teacher?' 'Of course, her mother,' said another child.

'Has she a mother? Poor thing, yet she was allowed to be killed by the bison. I don't like bisons. They should have more hair!'

'If you are so fond of bears, why do you listen to this story?'

'Because it's the story of a bear, of course,' replied the child.

'It isn't.'

'It is. You see the picture.'

'Master, she is looking too long at the bear. I want to see the tiger.' The teacher interfered at this stage and restored order. He whispered to me: 'The most enchanting thing among children is their quarrels. How they carry it on for its own sake, without the slightest bitterness or any memory of it later. This is how we were once, God help us: this too is what we have turned out to be!' He resumed the story. My daughter, who felt she had left me alone too long, came over and sat with her elbows resting on my lap. She whispered: 'Father, I want a tiger.'

'A real one?'

'Yes. Isn't it like a cat?' I nudged the teacher, and told him of her demand. He became very serious and said: 'You must not think of a tiger as a pet, darling. It is a very big and bad animal. I will show you a tiger when a circus comes to the town next. Meanwhile you may have a picture of a tiger. I will give you one.'

'All right, master, I will take it.'

'And you can have a real cat. I will give you a small kitten I have at home.'

She screamed with joy. 'Is it in your house?'

'Yes, yes. I will give it to you and also the picture of a tiger.'

'Father, let us go with him ...'

'Surely, surely.' The teacher looked delighted. 'Come with me ...' He went on for a few minutes more and ceased. The story would run on for a full week. He stopped because the clock struck twelve. The children wouldn't get up. The tiger had just been caught by a circus man for training. The children wanted to know more and more. 'Master, you mustn't stop. What happens to the tiger? Is he happy?' He would answer none of their questions. He ruthlessly shut his books and got up.

'We are hungry, teacher. We will go home.'

'That's why I stopped the story. Go home and come and listen to it tomorrow,' he said.

'Do they kill the tiger?' asked the child.

'No, no, he is quite safe. He will be quite all right, trust me,' said the teacher. The children, greatly pleased, ran out of the school. My daughter asked: 'Is it the same circus you promised to take me to?'

'Ah, something like it. Here too you will see a tiger,' he replied and we got up. He locked the shed and the gate and walked down with us. When we reached our house, my daughter insisted upon going with him though she was hungry. He cajoled and coaxed her to go in. But she was adamant. At which he offered to come in and wait for the girl to finish her food and then take her with him. I seated him in my study.

'This is the book I read,' the girl said placing the big catalogue in his hand. He turned over its leaves and was lost in its pictures. I took her in to dine. I told the old lady: 'There is another person for dinner today. Can you manage?'

'Oh, yes,' she said, although I knew she'd give her share of food or cook again. I invited the headmaster to sit down with me. He looked happy and at the same time uncomfortable: 'My wife at home, she will be waiting ...'

'Won't she guess you won't be in?' I asked. 'Come on.' He yielded.

It was a most delightful party. I found him more and more fascinating. He took off his coat, folded up his sleeves, and asked: 'Where is the bathroom? I should like to have a wash.' He came out of the bathroom and said (his face wet with water and hands dripping): 'Don't offer me a towel please ...'

'Then how do you dry it?'

'I just leave it alone, and it will evaporate. I never use a towel.'

'Why, fear of infection?'

'I don't know. I have never liked a towel, not even my own. Even after a bath I just keep standing till the water evaporates, and then put on my dress with the result that every day my wife creates a most fearful row outside the bathroom, because you know it takes a little time for a wholesale drying like that.'

My daughter was delighted that her teacher was dining with us. She was sitting down in her place with her silver plate in front of her, and was half-way through her rice. But when she saw her teacher she exclaimed with joy: 'I will also eat with teacher,' and tried to get up. She was, however, pressed back into her seat. She was very unhappy. 'Eat slowly, but don't get up. Eat slowly till your teacher joins us,' I said. The teacher would want some more time for himself. 'Please grant me fifteen minutes. I usually pray and meditate for fifteen minutes before dinner, the only time that I can spare. Just fifteen minutes ... Another thing that seems to upset my wife.' His wife seemed to be weighing on his mind. He muttered: 'I could have managed well as a bachelor, but they wouldn't let me alone.' There was something very appealing in the way he spoke. He spoke of himself as if it were someone else. His own life seemed to give him as much amusement as he found the company of children inspiring. I found a place for him to sit and meditate, left him alone and came away. He preferred the back courtyard facing the east. He squatted on the floor and closed his eyes and was lost in it. He was completely wrapped in his own vision for quite a long while, and then came and joined me. He did not seem to have the slightest feeling of being in a stranger's house. He conducted himself as if he were in his own house. As he came into the dining-room and took his seat on the plank next to mine he asked: 'What have you done for dinner? I hope I have not put you to great difficulty or extra trouble?'

'Oh no. Some simple fare. I hope you won't find it too bad ...' The usual courtesies were going on in the usual manner, and he said suddenly: 'Don't you think we have evolved some silly social customs? For instance ... ' Now as the old lady served us on the leaf the first course, fried brinjals, 'I am not very fond of this. But can I say so?' He gently pushed it away to a corner of the leaf: 'Please forgive me if I don't touch it. I would sooner swallow poison than eat brinjal ...' A most eccentric man. But we had almost arrived at a tacit understanding to be strictly truthful rather than formal. So I replied: 'Well, I won't apologize for it, you know. If you don't like it, it is a pity. I hope you will like something else presently ...'

'That's right. I like to speak and hear only on these lines. This is the simplicity to which all human conduct must be reduced. This is what the company of children has taught me. A fact which makes it very difficult for me to manage in an adult society. But then why should I ever try to get on with adults?' My daughter remarked: 'Our master doesn't look like himself without his coat.' He usually wore a loose, colourless coat, buttoned up to his neck. Now without it he certainly looked different. He looked rather young and slight. He seemed to put away ten years when he took off his coat. Indistinct features, greying at the temples, pouches under the red eyes. With all this there was a touch of freshness about him. My daughter asked: 'Tell me a story, teacher ...'

'No, no, we must never tell stories while eating. Only at school. What should we do at school, if we had spent all the stories at home while eating?'

After food he reclined on the mat in the hall. My daughter placed before him a plate of betel leaves and areca-nut. He chewed them with contentment. His lips became as red as his eyes. He looked very happy. The child sat nestling close to him and exhibited to him all her toys; the scores of coloured utensils, and brass miniature vessels, the rubber balls and her big doll. She carried the doll on her arm and said: 'This girl wants to come with me every day to school. She cries and shouts every day. What shall I do, master?'

He looked at the doll and said: 'Not a bad girl.' He pretended to pinch its cheeks and said: 'See how soft she is ...' My daughter was greatly pleased. She looked at the doll affectionately and said: 'She is a most lovely girl, master. But she does want to go with me to school, what shall I do?'

'Do you want to bring her or not?' She shook her head sadly. 'No master. She is a bad baby and will give a lot of trouble at the school. She will not allow me to study there. She will quarrel with everyone.' Certain inescapable anti-social characteristics of this doll seemed to sadden Leela, but she had steeled herself to a sort of resignation. So her teacher said: 'Well, why don't you lock her up in a box when you come to school?' Leela shook her head: 'That I can't do because she will die. I will lock her up in a room.'

The teacher asked: 'Do you mind if I lie down and rest a while?' He lay down and shut his eyes. My daughter insisted upon lying down beside him. Soon she was fast asleep. So was he. I went away to my room, picked up a book, lay on my camp easy-chair, and dozed.

We were all ready to start out at four in the afternoon, my daughter persistently asking for a cat.

We walked down the road. His house was in Anderson Lane, which was a furlong east of my house – a locality we had never visited. It was a street within a street, and a lane tucked away into a lane. There was every sign that the municipality had forgotten the existence of this part of the town. Yet it seemed to maintain a certain degree of sanitation, mainly with the help of the sun, wind and rain. The sun burned so severely most months that bacteria and infection turned to ashes. The place had a general clean-up when the high winds rose before the monsoon set in, and whirled into a column the paper scraps, garbage, egg-shells, and leaves; the column precipitated itself into the adjoining street, and thence to the next and so on, till, perhaps, it reached a main thoroughfare where the municipal sanitary staff worked, if they worked anywhere at all. And it was followed by a good wash-down, when the rains descended in November and December and flushed the streets, and water flowed along the roadway and joined the river.

Malgudi had earned notoriety for its municipal affairs. The management was in the hands of a council with a president, a vice-president, and ten elected members; they met on the last Saturday of every month and battled against each other. One constantly read of disputed elections, walk-outs, and no-confidence motions. Otherwise they seemed to do little by way of municipal work. However, when a distinguished visitor came to the town, the president and the members led him up the stairs of a tower in the municipal building and from there pointed out to him with great pride Sarayu cutting across the northern boundary of the town, glistening like a scimitar in moonlight.

Carpenters, tinsmiths, egg-sellers and a miscellaneous lot of artisans and traders seemed gathered in this place. The street was littered with all kinds of things – wood shavings, egg-shells, tin pieces and drying leaves. Dust was ankle deep. I wondered why my friend had selected this of all places. I was afraid to allow my daughter to walk here. I felt she would catch all kinds of dreadful diseases. Unkempt and wild-looking children rolled about in the dust, many dogs growled at us, donkeys stood at attention here and there. I offered to carry my daughter on my arm but she refused to be lifted. Her teacher said: 'Don't worry, leave her alone. This is really a healthy place for all its appearance. She will be all right, don't worry about her too much ... No harm will come to her ...' I left her alone, rather abashed, and feeling rather that I had been found out.

'Who is the Anderson of this lane?' I asked, looking at the impressive name-plate nailed on to the wall of a house.

'God knows. At least to honour the name I hope they do something for this place .... I have often tried to find out who Anderson was. But nobody seems to know. Perhaps some gentleman of the East India Company's days!'

He suddenly stopped and said: 'Now this is my house.' The tiles of the roof jutted into the street, a gutter gurgled and ran down in front of the house.

'Come on carefully, don't fall off into the gutter,' he said.

As soon as we had crossed the gutter, three children of ages between seven and ten stood in the doorway and hugged him. 'Is your mother at home?' he asked.

'No,' they replied.

'Excellent,' he said and went in. He looked relieved to hear it. 'Now, young fellows, here is a new friend, see what a fine girl she is.' The children looked at Leela with interest. Somehow this attention seemed to puzzle her. She gripped my hands tight and tried to get behind me. The children adjusted their positions so that she might still be within range. Finally she could stand it no longer. 'Let us go, father. Where is the cat?'

'Wait, wait,' I whispered. 'You must not ask for it at once. See how nice those children are.' They weren't. They looked too wild. Their hair full of mud almost matted, their dress torn and dirty, an abnormal liveliness about them. They stood relentlessly staring at my child. Their father had slipped in and now came out with a roll of mat. He spread it in the passage, between the front door and the central hall, a large part of which was an open courtyard with a well in the middle; the whole place was unspeakably wet. The hall was choked with old furniture, clothes and vessels. Beyond was a narrow kitchen, black with soot. The mat was an old, tattered, Japanese one with a girl holding a parasol painted in the centre. I and my child sat down. The three children stood around gazing. He asked: 'Where is your mother gone?'

'We don't know. We couldn't ask because she was angry you hadn't come. Why didn't you come home, father?' 'I had somewhere else to go to,' he replied lightly and tried to dismiss it from their minds. But they insisted until he said: 'You mustn't keep asking the same question.'

The eldest asked: 'Have you had food?'

'Yes.'

They looked at each other and said: 'Mother went away thinking that you wouldn't have eaten, and that you would come and ask for it.'

'Not I,' he said. 'I know your mother – well, children, you may all go away now ... or take this baby with you and play with her.' There was consternation in my daughter's face and she muttered: 'Father, don't let them call me.' He saw this and said: 'You don't want to go with them? Then don't. Now you may all leave us.' With a great shout they ran towards the street and vanished. I couldn't help asking: 'Where are they going?'

'I don't know. I can't say – perhaps to the gutter, or to some low-class den in the neighbourhood. I've no control over them. They are their mother's special care, you know.' There was a hint of a terrible domestic condition. I did not wish to pursue it. But I blundered into it. 'Don't they attend your school?'

'They!' he repeated: 'I could sooner get the Emperor's children. My school is for all the children in the world except my own.'

'Where do they study?'

'You may know better....' At this point a fat woman of about thirty-five, with sparse hair tied into a knot at the back of her head, her face shining with oil and perspiration, strode up the steps of the house. She threw a look at him and did not seem in the least to notice me sitting in the passage, though striding past us. She walked into the house, muttering: 'So you have found the way home after all!' gritting her teeth. He didn't reply but merely looked at me sadly. She stood in the doorway of the house and said: 'How long must I keep dinner waiting? Do you think I'm made of stone?'

'Nobody asked you to wait.'

'You are not to decide who should wait and who should not. You and your school! You don't know the way back from your school, I suppose.'

'Don't speak rubbish. Here is a cultured visitor, who will laugh at us.'

'Let him, what do I care? If he is big, he is a big man to you. He is not a big man to me. What do I care? Answer me first. Where were you all the time? Do you think I'm a paid watch-keeper for this house?'

I could not watch this scene any longer. I got up and said: 'We will be going.' He looked at his wife and said: 'I can't bring a gentleman to visit me without your driving him away with your fine behaviour.'

'Oh, no, it is not ...' I began.

She replied: 'Ah, what a fine sermon. I'm not going to be another woman than myself even if the king is here. What did I do to him?'

'Don't take it ...' I began, starting up. My daughter said: 'The cat. He hasn't given me the cat.' He said: 'Right. I never meant to forget.' He looked at his wife and asked: 'Where is that kitten? Is it inside?'

'I don't know,' the wife said. 'I have too much to do to be keeping count of the cats and dogs that pass this way.' He smiled at me weakly and said: 'Can't get a straight answer from her, at any time of the day! There are people in this world who have rough tongues but who are soft at heart – but this lady! I look ridiculous, speaking of my wife in this manner. But why should I not? Children have taught me to speak plainly, without the varnish of the adult world. I don't care if it strikes anyone as odd.' My daughter punctuated his narration with 'Where is the cat?' I had the feeling that I ought to run away. So I said: 'Perhaps it has gone out, he will bring it when it comes back home.' He said, 'Wait,' and went in and looked about and returned shaking his head. 'It used to be in the store behind that tin. Forgive me, baby. I will positively get you a cat soon.' My daughter looked very disappointed. So I cheered her up with a joke or two and walked out. He followed us back to our house. He seemed to feel more at home in my house than in his. He reclined in the easy-chair, pulled out a book and was soon lost in study. I looked at him in surprise. The book was a criticism of the Elizabethan dramatists, Beaumont and Fletcher. 'This is the dullest work I've read in the English language. How is it that it interests you so much?'

He lowered the book, removed his silver spectacles and said, 'I'm not reading it. If I open a book like this and allow my eyes to rest on the lines, it helps me to do a lot of private thinking. I read very few books for any other purpose. This book, for instance, has helped me to reflect deeply and earnestly on the question of family, marriage, and such other institutions.' My daughter came in and showed him a house she had made out of a matchbox. He seemed to forget all his troubles in an instant. 'Oh, what a house, what a house. The only house worth having in this world,' he added turning to me, as she went out, carrying it away with her. Her friends were at the gate calling for her, and she shouted, 'Father, I'm going to play,' and ran away and joined them. 'She seems to have had enough of adults' company since this morning,' he remarked, putting away Beaumont and Fletcher. He looked at the book and said with a smile, 'Not a line in the whole book to distract your thought – an ideal book for a contemplative turn of mind ... Not a line in it ...' He put away the book, remained silent for a moment and said: 'Did you notice how quickly that child dropped us and joined her fellows? Adult company is unfit for angels. Adults who can't even keep a promise in regard to a kitten. Helpless fools we must appear to her. What wishy-washiness!'

It was nearing six. I looked over the wall of our next house, and saw my child playing with half a dozen children. I asked: 'Come on, child, are you coming out with us for a walk?' She hesitated. Her friend suggested: 'Let us play here. Let father go out and return.' She accepted the advice and said: 'I am not coming, father, you may go.'

I and the headmaster walked down to the river-bank, sat on the sand, and watched the sunset. He told me: 'Some twenty years ago when I passed my B.A. at the university, they wanted me to take law; and then wanted to rush me into an office chair, but I resisted. I loved children and wanted to start the school. How can anyone prevent me from doing what I want? I had been hustled into a marriage which did not interest me, and I was not going to be hustled into a profession I did not care for.

'I was the only son of my father, but he said such bitter things that I left home. We had a fine house in Lawley Extension, you wouldn't believe it. I was brought up there, it is the memory of those days which is rankling in my wife's heart and has made her so bad and mad. I walked out over the question of employment; and went back home only on the day he died. And then my wife thought I would occupy that house after his death, but not I. I don't know what he has done with it. He had married a second time after my mother died and I think she and her children or his brothers must be fighting for it. I don't want that house, I have no use for it, I don't want any of his money either. But my wife expects me to be fighting for these rights. I can't enjoy these rights even if I get them, and I think it is a waste of one's precious hours of living to be engaged in a contest.'

'But your wife and children could be in better circumstances ...'

'You think so? No chance of it, my friend. She will create just those surroundings for herself even in a palace.'

'But you have not put her in a very happy locality ...'

'Perhaps not. But I chose it deliberately. It is where God resides. It is where we should live. And if we have any worth in us the place will change through our presence. But my wife does not believe in anything like it. She thinks my school a fool's idea; won't send the children there. I did my best. But it is no use. She has a right to send them where she likes. I think she sends them to the gutter and pigsty: you saw what they are like. She is an impossible type. But my only hope is that there may be a miraculous transformation some day and that she may change. We should not despair for even the worst on earth.'

'Till then don't you think you should concede to her wishes and move to a better place?'

'No. First because it is a duty for me, and secondly because she will carry the same surroundings wherever she goes. You see, the trouble is not external.'

The river flowed on against the night. I listened to him; he appeared to me a man who had strayed into a wrong world.

'How did you get this idea of a school for children?' I asked.

'The memory of my own young days. Most of us forget that grand period. But with me it has always been there. A time at which the colours of things are different, their depths greater, their magnitude greater, a most balanced and joyous condition of life; there was a natural state of joy over nothing in particular. And then our own schooling which put blinkers on to us; which persistently ruined this vision of things and made us into adults. It has always seemed to me that our teachers helped us to take a wrong turn. And I have always felt that for the future of mankind we should retain the original vision, and I'm trying a system of children's education. Just leave them alone and they will be all right. The Leave Alone System, which will make them wholesome human beings, and also help us, those who work along with them, to work off the curse of adulthood.' He was seized with a fit of coughing. He recovered from it, paused, and said: 'I will tell you a secret now. I strictly want to live according to my own plan of living and not subordinate it for anybody's sake, because the time at my disposal is very short. I know exactly when I am going to die. An astrologer, who has noted down every minute detail of my life, has fixed that for me. I know the exact hour when I shall be ... that lady will have the surprise of her life,' he said and chuckled. 'That's why I'm so patient with her.'

We walked back home. I invited him in: 'No, no, not fair. But be assured I shall make myself completely at home whenever I like. I hope you won't mind.'

'Not at all,' I replied. 'Treat this as your own home.'

'Good Lord! No. Let it always be your home,' he said with a smile and bade me good-night.

CHAPTER SEVEN

I missed my friend's sittings continuously for three or four weeks. He was ill for a few days, and then he had some work or other on hand, and then guests, all of which prevented his giving me a sitting. I went there and turned back with a feeling of disappointment, and on the fourth Wednesday I went there hoping again. There was only a garden servant to answer me. My friend had left a note behind: 'Awfully sorry. Have had to start for Trichinopoly on some urgent business, at an hour's notice. Can't say when I shall be returning, but I will write to you.' He had gone with his entire family. I asked: 'May I go and rest a while near the pond?' The servant gave me permission. I sat there on the pyol of the shrine as the evening declined. The still surface of the pond, the lotus, the evening breeze, all had a reviving effect, but the sense of disappointment was very keen within me. I shut my eyes and visualized the form of my wife. The casuarina murmured. I said aloud: 'Are you all here, can't you devise some means of communicating with me, O great spirits?' I felt ridiculous talking to myself thus. My words fell on a deep silence and died without a response – the faintest would have made me happy, but it was not there. I repeated my appeal in a low tone and felt ashamed of myself for appearing to be talking to myself. For the first time in months, I felt desolate. The awful irresponsiveness of Death overwhelmed me again. It unnerved me. All the old moods returned now. It looked as though they had been in bondage all these days and were now suddenly unleashed. I was overwhelmed.

I went home and slept badly that night. I kept asking myself: 'I have been clinging to the veriest straw, thinking that I was on land. Now the straw has snapped and I know my position. I can only drown. I'm drowned, and did not know it all these days. I was clinging to a grass blade at the brink of a well.' I went about my business next day with a heavy heart. As soon as she saw me in the morning my daughter was seized with a doubt and asked: 'Father, you are angry!' 'No, no,' I said, and with a great effort of will played with her and saw her off to school. I hated my food, I hated my work, I loathed my friends. That day I continuously lost my temper with the boys. A student in the B.A. class rose in his seat to have a doubt cleared. He was a first-class student, always serious and well-behaved: but I snapped: 'Will you sit down? I can't stand all these interruptions ...'

'But, sir ...'

'That'll do. Because you obtain more marks than your neighbours, you needn't ...' He looked crushed, and sat down. I could never forget the expression on his face, nor forgive myself for it. At the end of the period I called him aside and said: 'Well, what did you want?'

He at once mentioned his difficulty. I cleared it and added: 'Don't worry so much about these things – they are trash, we are obliged to go through and pretend that we like them, but all the time the problem of living and dying is crushing us ...' 'Yes, sir, but for the examination ...' he added. And I said: 'I'm sorry, my dear fellow, if I have been rude to you. A lot of things are weighing on my mind ...' 'I understand, sir,' he said and went away. I showed less tolerance to Gajapathy. At the quadrangle when we passed each other at the end of a day he said: 'Krishnan, I must have a word with you.' I stopped without a word and waited for him to speak. He said: 'Can I speak to you now?' I said sharply: 'Yes, why not now?' 'Here?' he asked. 'Yes, what's wrong with here?' 'You seem to be upset over something.' 'Nothing. All is perfect in the world. I'm all attention.' He took me to his room, seated me in a chair and said: 'First, I want to tell you that Brown feels we have been neglecting the history of literature. He saw the test papers of the fourth year and is disappointed. He thinks the boys will ruin themselves in the public exam.'

'Well, what are we to do?'

'He wants you to take a special period for them in the history of literature.'

'Why do they make so much of the history of literature? They have to make a history of every damned thing on earth – as if literature could not survive without some fool compiling a bogus history. If he won't mind my saying this to the boys, I will accept the special classes ...'

'Don't be frivolous,' Gajapathy said. 'Your college habits have not left you yet ...'

'Far from it. I see more clearly now between fatuities and serious work.'

He had grown more tolerant with me these days. He waited for me to finish my lecture and gave me his own advice and orders. 'All right,' I said. 'I cannot but obey you. But I will tell the boys what's sense and what is nonsense. I will tell them that they are being fed on literary garbage and that we are all the paid servants of the garbage department.'

As I was standing at the door of my house, Leela's teacher passed along the street. I saw him at a distance and tried to pretend I had not seen him and turned in. It vexed me to see people and talk to them. It was a tremendous strain. I sat in my room waiting for him to pass. But he stopped and cried 'Krishnan.' I was bound to meet him. I went to the gate and greeted him. I didn't like to call him in. So I rushed out to dispose of him in the doorway. He asked: 'Not well?'

'Quite well. I have never been in better health.'

'Coming out for a walk in the evening?'

'Sorry, I have another engagement.'

'Where is your daughter?'

'Gone out to play.' We carried on thus for a few minutes, for my part brief sentences and monosyllables.

Till late in the evening I sat alone at a corner of the river. 'A long dip in this river, or a finger poked into a snake hole – there are two thousand ways of ending this misery. But the child, the child ... She will be looked after by God, and by everyone. She is an entity. She was able to go on without her mother, and she could equally well carry on without her father. I have put by a little money for her .... Well, she will be looked after quite well – God bless her.' Far off I saw the glow of a funeral pyre over the walls of the cremation ground, and I sighed for it. It seemed to be the greatest aspiration one could have. 'Exactly where she was placed and burnt ...' I recollected her pale face, with the flies on it, and the smile on her lips, and broke down at the memory. I recovered and said to myself: 'This is also my end. Oh, God, send me to those flames at once.' I saw a picture of myself being carried there and the funeral ceremonies. And this vision seemed to give me a little peace.

Thus days followed, bleak, dreary, and unhappy days, with a load on the mind. I felt as though I had been filled with molten lead.

And then came a letter one morning from my friend, 'I'm sorry to have remained silent so long. I have been up to my ears in litigation and it looks as though all these affairs are going to take more and more of my time. But anyway, I will arrange these things and return in a few weeks. My house here is in the extension with a fine small compound, and a room all to myself, where I spend the larger part of my day in reading when I don't talk over matters with lawyers and witnesses. You see, I had to come away suddenly because an uncle of mine passed away, and there are all kinds of arrangements to be made in regard to property. He married three times and has numerous children, and you know how many complications can arise out of that!

'Anyway, my purpose in writing to you today is not to trouble you with my affairs, but a different one. I have a feeling that we might attempt an experiment while we are out of each other's reach. I want to see if we can manage a sitting – a sort of *in absentia* business. For spirit matters, space is of no account, and so there is no reason why we should not succeed. On Sunday at 4 o'clock in the evening I propose to try the experiment. So please keep yourself in your room and link up with me mentally with a request to your wife to communicate. As far as possible keep all other business from your mind. At precisely 4.30, you may consider it closed. I will send you the result of this sitting by post immediately.'

This offered me a new lease of life. Two days before me. All the weariness melted.

On Sunday I cajoled my daughter into spending her time at the school with the old lady and then shut myself in my room and lay down in my chair and closed my eyes. The clock showed two minutes to four. I stilled myself. My heart was palpitating with excitement. I had to hold my breath for a moment before it could be stilled. I opened my eyes and saw that it was four and said: 'Oh, dear wife, my friend at the other end and I have linked up. Please communicate.' I visualized my friend sitting in his room, and I fancied myself occupying a chair beside him, and my wife communicating through him. I shut my eyes and remained in a sort of half-sleep till 4.35.

Two days later the postman brought me a long envelope, as I was just starting for the college. With the books under my arm, I tore open the letter, and pulled out two long sheets of paper covered over with pencil writing. There was a covering letter from my friend.

The message read: 'It is a long time since I spoke to you through your friend. I have a feeling as if I were sitting on a wall. On one side I see your big friend. On the other side I see you, lying in your green canvas easy-chair and also trying to be present here at the same time ... Seeing you now in your old chair, as you shut your eyes and try to keep your mind still, I forget for a moment that we are in two totally different mediums of existence ...

'The most important thing I wish to warn you about is not to allow your mind to be disturbed by anything. For some days now you have allowed your mind to become gloomy and unsettled. You are not keeping very strong either. You must keep yourself in better frame ...

'We must thank your friend who has yielded to our suggestion, to try these absent sittings. I'm sure you will benefit by them. Please think yourself as being able to establish communication with us direct. You will have to prepare yourself for it. There will be a change in your state. Moreover you should not expect your friend to be troubled by you all your life. You must make yourself fit for it, and this communication will restore to you health and better nerves because of the greater harmony that comes into your life; but you must also do your bit to utilize this harmony. You must keep your body and mind in perfect condition, before you aspire to become sensitive and receptive; I have learnt a great deal after coming here; believe me if it is peace of mind you want, you cannot have it better than from us ...'

'How do I become sensitive?' I asked.

The following Sunday we again linked up at the same hour. On Monday morning the postman brought me the message: 'Don't feel sorry. It hurts me more than you can imagine. So please keep your mind free from choking thoughts. I wish to give you a picture in words.

'A weary and thirsty traveller was returning home from a long day's march. The setting sun had touched all the objects around him with a rosy magic. The birds were returning to their nests. A rumbling brook rolled along. He sat down and quenched his thirst with water. He saw a black bird sit on a thorn and whistle. A batch of white cranes flew across, tinted by the sunset. Their rhythm and their colour filled the traveller's heart with an indescribable joy. He said to himself, "Worshipping and wondering, how much life's journey is made easier for one who can see nature and God every moment!" He returned home fatigued in body, but his soul was in the rapture of a song.

'I don't know what you are going to make of this. Somehow, this picture has been haunting my soul all along: and a great inexplicable satisfaction reigns in my heart because I have communicated it to you. I have set a song to sing this to me. When I sit down and sing it, a most heavenly sunset, birds of wonderful colours, and the serenity of the brook, everything comes up palpably and we can even converse with the traveller. And the melody. It is just created out of thought, in a manner which you cannot grasp. The responses of our world are immediate and fine; you have a glimpse of it only in your striving; there your deeper mind impels you, there it is a striving; here it is an achievement. Your striving itself is proof of its reality here; to be realized when the obstructions of your state are cleared ...

'I don't know if you think I'm becoming a poet as well. I have given you many thoughts lately for writing by impressing them on your mind; you might have caught them if you had continued your old habit of occasionally writing verse. Some day I hope we shall together produce a great epic. I'm not joking. I'm in earnest. Nobody may think much of these efforts. They may appear, just as the picture of the weary traveller does, obvious or obscure to others, but certainly you will like them because they are your dear wife's efforts.'

In about ten days my friend returned to his garden and we were able to have a sitting as before. I was very happy to be back at the old seat beside the lotus pond.

After the preliminary remarks and suggestions my wife asked abruptly: 'When are you starting an attempt at your own psychic development?'

'How can I say?' I replied.

'Oh! if you do not know what you are going to do or not do, who else can?'

I felt snubbed and explained: 'I didn't mean that. I should like to be told when and what to do. I look to you for guidance!'

'Why not make a start tomorrow? Tomorrow is a day that never comes. Why not begin today as soon as you go home? Just ten minutes will be sufficient. Keep your mind free for impressions just for ten minutes. Just ten minutes of communion and relaxation. Please make the attempt and do not postpone it. You think of me by fits and starts. Sometimes for long periods you do not let your mind do anything else. I can only tell you that I am very happy here. I shall be very happy to meet you when you come over here; don't doubt me, but it is not right for you to think of passing over before the appointed time. So do not let your thoughts go in that direction. It is to prevent it that I want you regularly to bring me to your side at a stated time.'

'So you want me to think of you only at stated hours?'

'Yes, for the purpose of your complete communion with me or with anyone a degree of concentration is necessary and this can be done only with some order and plan. At other moments when you are despondent, woebegone and hopelessly in grief and think of me, I can hardly come to you, because the grief creates a barrier, and this should be avoided for both our sakes.'

'But look here,' I pleaded. 'How can I help having you as the permanent background to my thoughts? I can't help thinking of you ...'

'Just as I am thinking of you, I know you will also be thinking of me. But I want this thought to be coupled with the desire to commune with me. It is this aspect that I want to impress upon you as necessary for psychic development and free communion between us.'

'So do you wish me to check thoughts of you at all other times?'

'No, no, no. At stated hours sit for psychic development, that is, to enable me to get into touch with you directly without the intervention of the medium; this I will make possible.'

'Should I sit down with pencil and paper?'

'It is a secondary matter, pencil, paper and the rest. The most important thing is to get the mind ready and receptive, the actual form will follow automatically. Prepare your mind for this adventure. You will then know and feel my real presence. You now keep looking round to get a glimpse of me; then by and by, you will feel that I'm by your side, and it will bring real peace to your heart. Relax, be passive and think of me, and be receptive. Just ten minutes. Try.'

'Tonight?'

'Yes, tonight.'

'It may be eleven before I'm ready.'

'The time is immaterial.'

I went home singing. I felt I had picked up the key to a new world. I had never known such joy before. I felt that my duty was now to conserve all the force of my mind for this communion.

At home, the child lay awake in bed. I went in to dine, and she came over and sat on my lap as I ate. I went to bed, stroked her forehead and she soon fell asleep. I put out the light, sat down and prayed: 'I am ready.'

I looked at the clock – ten to eleven. 'My wife,' I called. I had made it all too easy in my imagination. I thought I had only to say 'be passive' to make the mind passive, 'still' to be stilled, and I would see her standing radiantly – foolish expectation. I had to struggle with my mind. I desperately cried for her. My mind seethed with ideas – irrelevant things came rushing in, college, work, evening friends, my wife's voice – in the midst of it all I struggled to keep the mind receptive. It was a desperate fight. It nearly reduced me to tears. I tried to improve matters by picking up a pencil and poising it over the paper. Beyond the scratch that I inadvertently made, there was no result. I looked at the clock. Eleven-thirty nearly. I felt exhausted. I lay down to sleep, and slept badly.

The little peace and joy I had seemed to grasp suddenly once again receded, and I became hopelessly miserable. It was as if a person lost in an abyss found a ladder, and the ladder crumbled. When I went to my friend next Wednesday, I was all anxiety for further guidance. I hoped somehow that there was a magic password which would be imparted to me, whereby I would be able to walk hand in hand with my wife. But as soon as we were ready for it, she said: 'At the last sitting I gave you advice about psychic development. Since then, I have been observing the struggle going on within you and your utter helplessness. To receive impressions from our side, the mind must be calm and unruffled. In your case, I find that thoughts of me produce just the opposite effect. I feel that it is too early and that the wound is still very raw. I think therefore you ought to postpone your attempts for some time, until you are less agitated than you are now. As it is, it does not serve the purpose I thought it would. So please do not bother now. Am I clear?' This made me more desperate. Even the ladder that I saw was removed and I was forbidden to go near it. I could almost hear her voice as she said this, slightly quivering with excitement, and with a touch of reprimand. I was in despair for a moment – but only for a moment. I became indignant. She couldn't deny me my right to attempt. I said: 'I won't stop this attempt on any account. I feel quite confident I can go on.' This had the desired effect, and she replied, 'Oh, if you are feeling confident, it is another matter. But as I watch you, I find that your mind is very unprepared. This makes communication more difficult. So I suggest that you wait for some more time. Possibly there may be a change in your outlook. Then you will derive greater benefit. I'm not saying stop it at all costs. If you feel confident, go ahead. I am only indicating the circumstances that stand in the way.' I felt very happy. And a regret seized me, as it always did, that I had perhaps been too sharp in my expression. So I felt I ought to be more considerate, and asked: 'Oh, I'm glad, so may I continue my efforts, and will you do your best still?'

'Yes, continue then. If I can give you any further assistance, I will.'

I asked testingly: 'Just to know that you are aware of my efforts, can you tell me what you saw me do on these nights?'

'I am aware and I am present, but I cannot make myself known better because of the difficulty. I have seen you every night wanting contact with me and praying for it. You had a few sheets of paper and a green-handled pencil ...'

I had over a dozen pencils in my drawer; I hadn't noticed which one I had picked up that day.

She continued: 'You put pencil to paper and hardly made a dot .... And this after trying without paper and pencil, at first. I am keen on impressing on you the fact that it will be possible for you to appreciate my presence even more than my physical presence in course of time, if the development takes place properly, that is, the necessary mental atmosphere is made available for me.'

'Can you give me some details of where you saw me sit for communion?' I asked.

'I saw you sitting on your bed. You sat up with your eyes closed. You had just begun to concentrate when a carriage passed along the street, wheels rattling and the driver singing lustily – and you gnashed your teeth and said something very rough about him.'

'I am so happy you feel the attempts I made at communication.'

'I tell you I can feel your thoughts even when you are not exactly sitting for development. Even when you just think of me anywhere and everywhere, on the road, at home, or on the riverbank when a streak of moonlight lights the water surface, and you think of me, I feel it and know your thoughts. But development is necessary for the reverse process to take place, that is, for you to feel my thoughts.'

This restored my peace of mind. 'Calm, calm,' I repeated to myself like a *mantra*. I blamed myself for not being aware of so simple a remedy. I think I sang lightly as I returned home that night. 'Be calm, my dear fellow,' I said.

Suddenly there dawned on me the meaning of her statement: 'When you see the moonlight lighting up the water surface.' Weeks ago, in my period of desolation, as I sat on the sands of Sarayu, a late moon rose in the east, and the flowing water shimmered with it. It only added to my desolation. Again, it reminded me of my wife. How often had she expressed a wish to walk along the river in moonlight, and for all the years of married life I had not been able to give her that fulfilment even once; some pointless thing postponed it every time; we never went out in the moonlight at all. And this regret tormented me when I saw moonlight on water, that night ...

At our next meeting she said: 'I still feel you have not done well. Why can't you postpone your attempt for a while?' I had been dreading this suggestion all along. Now it had come. I was not going to accept it. I said stubbornly: 'No, I feel I can still try. I find these very attempts very beneficial. I want to continue them. Will you help me as much as you can?'

'I'm very happy to hear it. Why don't you change the time from night to morning and see if it will improve matters? Not more than ten minutes. I think after a night's sleep, such sleep as you can get, the attempts in the morning will be more successful.'

'Early morning?' I asked apprehensively.

'No. After you get up and have your coffee, shut yourself in a room for ten minutes. At night your mind is not very receptive. All the day's affairs are there boiling up again and again. Sleep lulls your thoughts, and it may be you will succeed if you try then.' I shook my head. She said: 'Just try for ten days.' I was somehow very reluctant to try in daylight – there was all the hurry for school and college, the attention to the child, the shutting the door on her (she was sure to bang on it), the visitors or tradesmen who might call on me, and above all the daylight. The softness of night was essentially psychic, I felt. So I said: 'I don't usually feel very fresh in the morning. I still think night is the best ...'

'Well, get on with your attempts at night then,' she said. I was seized with a sudden fear. Suppose she said this out of despair, unable to coax me out of my obstinacy. So I asked with trepidation: 'Will you be present whatever the time?'

'I shall be present morning, noon and night. Don't worry. Just go on as usual, but with greater relaxation and ease. No harm in trying with paper and pencil too; when you feel an urge, please relax and let your hand move. If you keep a pencil, it helps concentration.'

'How will you make me feel your presence?'

'At first it will be a matter of belief – a belief in the possibility of my presence. Later on as you progress, you will know I'm there by your side. I have high hopes of making myself heard or seen, but certainly known; I shall be with you very soon.'

'I shall continue my attempts whatever happens,' I said gratefully.

'I'm trying to make matters easier and more rapid for your development. I know you sense my presence, but I feared that you might give up all attempts at communication if you did not get messages from me sufficiently early. I feared that you might then feel that your awareness of my presence was imaginary and give up the attempt for ever. That's why I wanted you to postpone rather than run the risk of losing faith ...'

I was greatly moved at hearing this: 'It is enough that I feel you are there. Don't trouble yourself to give me any sort of proof. It is not necessary.'

For a fortnight I tried to follow her instructions rigidly. I relaxed with a vengeance. I kept my mind open. I posted a sentry at the threshold of my mind to stop and turn away any intruder who might try to gain entrance. I rigorously educated my whole being, including the subconscious (where still perhaps lurked unsuspected raw grief), with the suggestion that my wife was everywhere, happy and well, and I was to think of her only with the greatest joy in mind; no cause for any sort of grief. I lay down on my bed, and then pictured her as I had known her in her best days, and centred my mind on this image without the slightest wavering for ten minutes. I felt very satisfied with my effort till on a subsequent evening she said: 'I must tell you now that your sittings for development must be even more relaxed than they are at present. Why don't you allow your mind to move round about me? Now you just picture me in your mind and do not allow your thoughts to move an inch this side or that. This rigid exercise does not help our contact. By your intense and severe thought you make almost a stone image of me in your brain. Your thoughts must give me greater scope for movement within an orbit of feelings. Your mind may now be compared to the body of a yogi who sits motionless. This is not what you seek to achieve, do you? I want you to keep your mind at these times open for my impression. What happens now is that your mind is full of your thoughts of me, which are unrelaxed, and I find it difficult to move about in your head and heart.

'The only trouble now is that your mind is rigid. Till lately I'd even greater difficulty because of your poignant sorrow. This barrier is now lifted more or less. What is still required is that you should be able to receive my thoughts. It can be done only if you do not make a stone image of me. I want you to behave just as you would if I were conversing with you. You would pay attention. Now it borders on worship. This rigidity must go and you will have better results. It takes time, but it is worth attempting.'

I had a visit from the headmaster at an unusual hour one night. I was in bed. My child had just gone to sleep. And I was preparing to sit up and attempt my daily experiment. I was about to put out the light, when there was a call for me at the gate, 'Krishnan, Krishnan.' I didn't like to be disturbed. So I kept quiet for a moment hoping that the caller might go away and I regretted I had not put out the light a minute earlier. But the call was repeated. I had to get up and go to the gate. There I saw the headmaster. 'Krishnan,' he cried on seeing me, 'forgive my intrusion at this hour. May I come in and talk to you?'

'Yes, yes,' I said, opening the gate. We sat down on the veranda steps. A ray of light fell on him from our sleeping room, and I noticed that he looked very agitated. He sat without speaking for a few minutes. A donkey brayed in a neighbouring lane; wind rustled the avenue trees. I waited for him to open his mouth and tell me his business. I felt he might be wanting a loan of money; he must be in terrible straits.

'I want to ask you ...' he began. It was at this point that the donkey brayed into the night. 'It is a good omen they say, the braying of a donkey. So my request is well-timed.'

'Go on,' I said, wondering how much he was going to want. 'Tell me what you want,' I said.

'I want you to take charge of my school, and see that it does not go to ruin,' he said. Worry seemed to have done its work on this poor man, I thought. 'All right,' I said, but added, 'but I've my college ...'

'I know it,' he said. 'But do you think you are happy in your work there?' he asked. I did not reply. It needed no reply. 'But who cares for happiness in work? One works for the money ...' said I in my sober cynicism.

'True, true,' he said. 'I cannot compel you. Please at least keep an eye on the school, and see that these children are not thrown into a hostile world ...'

'All right, all right,' I said, not wishing to offend a man mentally unsound. The light from our bedroom illuminated a part of his face. I looked at it. He had the abstraction of a mystic rather than of a maniac. I could not contain myself any longer. And so I cried, 'Tell me, what is the matter?' He smiled and said: 'This is perhaps my last day. Tomorrow, I may be no more.' His voice fluttered. 'You may remember that I had an astrologer's report with me, and I have also mentioned that my wife would get a big surprise in life; this is it. I never wanted to speak to anyone about it. But I felt I owed it to the children, not to leave the school without any arrangement for it. I hesitated the whole day, and a dozen times came up to your gate and turned away ...' I looked at him greatly puzzled: the man was talking as if he were moving to the next street .... This was too disturbing – even for me who had been educated to accept and accommodate the idea of death. He spoke on quietly: 'My astrologer has written a month-to-month report, and my life has been going on in its details like a time-table. I see it so clearly that nothing ever worries me. I give things just their value – never unduly disturb my mind over affairs; which include also my wife, who, I find, conducts herself according to the time-table.' 'What is to happen to her?' I asked, almost involuntarily.

'God knows. I only hope she won't start a litigation against my brother, over their house and property.' I sat up, thinking it over. It seemed absurd to be talking thus. 'No, no, no,' I cried. 'It can't be.'

'It is,' he persisted.

'Astrologers are not allowed to mention these things ...'

'Not my astrologer. He is not a professional predictor, but a hermit, who can see past, present, and future as one, and give everything its true value. He doesn't want you to put your head under the sand, thinking that you are unseen. Man must essentially be a creature of strength and truth. You would love him if you met him, but I don't know where he is. He came one day for alms, took a fancy to me, and sat down and dictated my life to me after a glance at my palm, and took the road again in the evening. I have never seen him since. But the few hours he was with me he charged my mind with new visions, ideas and strength. My life underwent a revolution. It was after that I left my family and home and set up the school. They jeered at us and made fun of me, but I don't mind. My life has gone on precisely as he predicted.'

'You have a duty to your wife and children,' I persisted.

'Yes, but what can I do? I shall bequeath to them the school, but would she care for it? Not she.'

'What can she do with the school? Will it give her food and shelter?'

'It ought to mean more than that if she had trained herself to view things properly,' he replied. 'I could have done so much more, if she had taken an interest. But she wouldn't even send the children. So independent a person as that, I believe, will get on whatever may happen.' I felt he could not be made to see my point, however much I might argue about it. 'Don't bother about it all,' he added. 'Leave us alone. Will you look after the school? See that it goes on at least till the present set of children leave there? Please promise.'

'I will do my best, but I have to mind my college,' I added again.

'I think my time is nearing. It is midnight, isn't it? I may not see the sunrise tomorrow.' I was greatly moved to hear him say it. I implored him: 'Don't believe all this, my friend. You will be back in the morning. Or will you sleep here in my house?'

I suggested apprehensively. He shook his head: 'It's my last night. I should like to spend it with my wife and children.'

'Shall I see you home?' I asked, hoping he wouldn't agree. I had forgotten the child when I made the offer. He brushed it aside: 'No, don't trouble yourself. I can go home quite safely. I am quite sober and sound in mind, I assure you. If you have still any doubt about me, see this paper ...' He took out of his pocket a folded piece of paper, and spread it out on his knee. He tilted it towards the light. 'Go on, read it. I took it out of the file. It is nearly the last sheet, you know,' he said with a forced laugh. 'Go on, read it aloud.' I read out with difficulty: 'This person's earthly duties over, he will pass over on this day, surrounded by his wife and children at his last moment ...' I read it, and did not know what to say about it. What does one say on such occasions?

'You are looking quite well?' I said testingly.

'I'm in perfect condition,' he said. 'But what is there to prevent anyone dying in perfect health as well as in ill-health?' he said. This was the strangest man I had ever come across. I had never known this side of the man. I felt foolish and fatuous. I had never thought that he viewed death in this manner, even theoretically. On the one or two occasions he had condoled with me on the loss of my wife, he was causal and off-hand; but I put it down to the delicacy which he might have felt. I never discussed with him my psychic efforts or experiences, thinking that it would not interest him; but now I felt like telling him about them and said: 'Do you know, I don't believe in death myself. My wife has communicated with me so often, and has given me directions for self-development.' I went on and on. He listened in silence, his head looking large in a shadow on the ground in front of us. He answered: 'Don't mistake me. It is all a matter of personal faith and conviction. But I am not interested in life after death. I have no opinion either way. There may be a continuation in other spheres, under other conditions, or there may not be. It is immaterial to me. The only reality I recognize is death. To me it is nothing more than a full stop. I have trained myself to view it with calm. Beyond it ...' He shook his head. 'In fact in my prediction, if you will turn over the page, he says something about my next birth too. I'm to be born in a Cochin village to Brahmin parents and so on ... but I don't really care for that part ...'

'When you trust so much in these predictions, you must trust in that too ...'

'But my trust is only in regard to matters of this life, not an inch beyond ... I've never looked at that page more than once. My knowledge of past, present and future, strictly pertain to this life. Beyond that I have nothing to say, because I believe I shall once again be resolved into the five elements of which I'm composed: and my intelligence and memory may not be more than what we see in air and water!'

I felt very unhappy to hear all this. I thought of my wife – all that I heard from her. Were they all self-deceptions? Was she nothing more than the mute elements, the funeral fire resolving her into vapour, unseen air, and dust? I felt sad and shaken. He said: 'This is my view. But don't let it disturb you ...' My daughter stirred in her sleep and moaned. I started up. He rose, gripped my hand, and said: 'Goodbye. If we meet once again tomorrow, don't laugh at me.' 'Oh, no,' I said. 'I shall celebrate it with a feast. I shall think you have a new life.'

I saw him off at the gate. He went away without turning his head.

I awoke earlier than usual. I was very anxious about my friend. My child was still asleep. I had a wash, drank my coffee, requested the old lady to mind the child, and went out.

At Anderson Lane my heart thumped with excitement. I gazed towards the headmaster's house. It was still half dark. A few artisans were moving about, and a few more were sleeping in front of their houses. Even this street looked soft in the morning light.

In a dozen bounds I reached the headmaster's house. The door was shut. I strained my ears to catch any sound of weeping inside. But I heard nothing except the clanging of vessels. The housewife was apparently up, and nothing untoward had happened. I took this as an encouraging sign and decided to turn back. But I changed my mind. I couldn't resist the desire to go in and see. Only the sight of him safe and talking to me would satisfy me. I knocked. His wife opened the door, and scowled on seeing me.

'What do you want?' she asked.

'Is the headmaster in?'

'No.'

'Where is he?'

'He doesn't tell me,' she said. 'Does he keep all those courtesies? Not he. He went out after dinner, and has not been in since ... Not for him such things as wife, children, home, and so on. These boys are fatherless ...' she said bitterly. I was irritated to see her in this mood, so early in the morning. I felt an admiration for the man who had stood her company for so many years. She turned to go. I felt like wringing her neck – it seemed to offer an ideal grip with her hair knotted high up. 'Why do men marry such wives?' I reflected. 'A moment, lady,' I said. 'There is a very important thing I want to tell you. Was he not here last night?'

'No. I have told you that,' she replied.

'Perhaps you will never see him again. I hope it pleases you,' I said. She could not make out what I meant. She turned, threw at me a puzzled look, and asked, with her throat going dry: 'Why?'

'Do you care enough to know?' I asked. 'It was in your hands to have made his life happier, while he lived. But now he is gone, and I hope you have a free and happy life before you now ...' She let out a shrill cry and cried, 'What has happened? What has happened?' By this time her children, dishevelled and in rags as usual, more so because just out of bed, came up rubbing their eyes and stood beside their mother. She embraced them sentimentally and sobbed. 'Oh, these are orphans today, who will feed them? They are in the streets, from this moment.' She wrung her hands and cried, 'Tell me sir, tell me, what is happening?' I told her of the prediction and his visit. 'Ah, couldn't he have confided this in me, his wife?' She broke down utterly. She collapsed on the floor and her lamentation filled the whole street, and the whole street crowded into the house. I slipped out. I began to wonder what had happened to him. I walked back home, and then saw that my child was still sleeping. My purpose was to search for him by the river, and then tell the police. I stepped out of my house and was going down the road. As I passed the school I saw him standing at the school gate. 'Ghost, ghost,' I muttered to myself. 'I never heard of a ghost being seen by morning light ...' He grinned, came towards me, and shook my hands.

'I'm not my ghost, be assured,' he said. An unusual cheerfulness had seized him. He looked rejuvenated. 'Don't look so full of questions. I can't answer them any more than you can. It simply didn't happen, that is all ... I don't know why that *Sadhu* thought fit to put my last date thus. One mistake in an otherwise perfect prediction. The first error in it, and the most agreeable ...'

'Didn't I say that it might be wrong? ...' I gripped his hand and jumped about in glee. 'I am so happy ...'

'So am I,' he said. 'You have no idea how it has been weighing me down all these years, in spite of what I might have felt and said; it was like having cancer and knowing fully when you would be finished. It was a terrible agony stretching over years. I rejoice it is over. I have no more pages to watch in my notebook. I can live free and happy.'

'But there is that thing about your next birth ...'

'Rubbish, I don't care. This life is good enough for me ...'

'You shouldn't have put such faith in that thing ... They are after all ...'

'But see here, my friend. For all these years it has been so accurate that I'd no reason to doubt its soundness; but this is the first mistake, and the last you know, for the reading stops with this, except for the next birth. I don't know what made that great hermit say this. It might be after all a test,' he said. He sighed: 'I don't know where he is. No chance of ever clearing this point with his help ...' He looked radiant.

'Didn't you go home last night?' I asked.

'No. I went up to my door, and turned back. If I had to die, I'd prefer to wait for it at the school, rather than at home.'

'But you said you wished to be with your wife and children.'

'Yes. But I felt they did not deserve it on second thoughts.'

'Go home, go home,' I said. 'The whole street is in your house. Poor lady! Her lamentations can be heard over the whole town!'

'Oh, is that so!' he cried in joy. 'What a happy piece of information! I don't care. Let her cry till she brings down the sky. I am going to treat myself as dead and my life as a new birth. You will see – I don't know if that hermit might not have meant my death, after all, in that sense ...' I implored him to go and relieve his wife and end the confusion in his street.

'Not I,' he said. 'I'm dead, I wish I could change my face somehow, so that I should not be recognized ...'

'Even by your school children?' I asked.

'Oh, no,' he said. I tried to hustle him into returning home. But he stubbornly refused. 'I have ceased to be my old self, and so don't belong to that home in Anderson Street ... It is all over. This school is my house hereafter. I will settle here ...'

'But what about them? ...'

'They can come and see me here if they like, that is all. I will give them a monthly allowance for their upkeep. That is all I am prepared to do, but not behave as a father and a husband hereafter. I didn't sleep a wink the whole night. It is a novel feeling sitting up and waiting for death .... I was wondering how it'd take me. I felt so fit and well. When I felt a little drowsy with sleep, I thought the end had come!'

After all I persuaded him to pay a visit (at least the last one) to his house. He agreed, adding: 'After all it is not given to every man to watch his own death scene ....' We walked there together. People in the street looked at him in wonder and cried: 'Here he is.' 'Yes,' he said. 'What of it?' Soon the news spread, and a great crowd poured out of his house and surged towards us. The whole of Anderson Street was there – very few tinsmiths were at their foundry, very few blacksmiths and tailors at their work. People surrounded and fired questions at him. But he refused to answer anyone. 'I can't tell you why I am alive,' he said. 'There is no explanation for it, as there is no explanation for death.' The crowd gaped at him and pressed us on all sides. 'I never imagined that I had such a large public!' he said. 'I thought I was fairly obscure!'

His wife, whom news of his arrival reached, picked herself up, her hair all over her face, swollen and tear-drenched. She looked at him, and let out a cry of relief: 'Oh, my lord, you are here! What demon thought fit to tell me ...?' She fell down and clung to his feet. His children came up and, with cries of rapture, hung on to his arms. He tried to shake himself free, but found it difficult. The crowd looked at him expectantly. He faced them and said: 'Why don't you all go away now?' They murmured something and waited for an explanation. He looked at them helplessly, with his family clinging to his feet. The crowd looked at him. He put his hand into his pocket, and took out the slip of paper, jerked it open and held it to the crowd. 'Who can read this?' A man came forward, received the slip and read it. 'Read it aloud,' the headmaster commanded; at which he read out the prophecy to the gathering, and the headmaster added, 'This is the prediction and it has not proved false. I tell you, friends, no more of this wife and family for me. You may treat me as dead or as one who has taken *Sanyasa Ashrama*.'

His wife protested and cried hoarsely. But he was adamant. He announced his decision grandly. 'She will get her money for her monthly expenses, but that is all. They will never see me here again ...' She clung to him and pleaded: 'Whatever wrong I have committed forgive me. I will be careful hereafter ...' He shook her off without a word. The children came after him. 'You may all come and see me in school later. But remember you have no father any more ...' He pushed his way through the crowd, and walked away. I followed him sheepishly. The whole business was too confusing. I didn't know what to make of it. His wife ran after us and appealed to me. I looked at her helplessly. I felt a tremendous pity for this creature now. I said: 'Headmaster, just think ...'

'Krishnan, leave me alone,' he said. 'I have a far greater work to do, and I'm going to do it. I feel such a freedom now ...' He set his face and walked off resolutely. The crowd followed us for a while, and then dissipated. His wife and children followed. 'Go back,' he said, 'create a scene if you like, it is none of my business to stop you, but don't put me in that scene, that is all, do you understand?'

Months rolled on. Life falls into ruts of routine, one day following another, expended in set activities: child, school, college, boys, walk, and self-development. This last was the most enchanting item of my life's programme. It was a perpetual excitement, ever promising some new riches in the realm of experience and understanding. I sat up at nights faithfully following the instructions she had given, keeping my mind open, and I was beginning to be aware of a slight improvement in my sensibilities. There was a real cheerfulness growing within me, memory hurt less, and I was more and more aware of vague perceptions, like a three-quarter deaf man catching the rustle of a dress of someone he loves ... That this was not a vain presumption on my part was borne out at a sitting we had about this time. Our regular Wednesday meetings were gradually given up, and we met now at unspecified intervals, once in six or seven weeks or so. Nor did I feel these days the hopeless longing for a regular sitting. My nightly contacts gave me peace. 'At first it will be a matter of belief,' I remember her saying. I clung to it fast; 'Belief, belief.' Above reason, scepticism, and even immediate failures, I clung to it. 'I do meet her when I sit down, and she is with me when I sit with my mind passive, calling her,' I repeated to myself night and day, and it wrought a curious success. Any other thought was impossible.

After a long time my friend gave me a sitting one dusk beside the lotus pond. The hour was as beautiful as ever. She started by saying: 'Have you observed one effect of your development? I can say now that you are developing quite satisfactorily. Think of about four days ago – the small hours of the night. I tried to appear and make my presence felt by you. I purposely wore the garb, which you called on a former occasion, "gorgeous" – the blue, shimmering with light interwoven. I appeared, and I tried to make my presence felt. We went out together into the garden. We walked for a while, indeed for a considerable time, and then the experience ended. You returned to bed, and went to sleep again ... You turned over and resumed your sleep, thinking that you had had a slight disturbance. If there is any chance that you remember this experience, let me assure you that it was I myself who was there with you and if you remember it, it is a sign that you are developing quite well ...'

It required no great effort to recollect this. I was overcome with great joy. I seized my friend's hand and cried: 'It is true, absolutely true. I thought it was a private dream. It wasn't. How little do we know what a dream is, how little do we understand! Yes, friend, every word of it is true. I don't remember it clearly, but I dreamt of her as standing before me with some gorgeous dress on. I greeted her, and I held her hand. We went out into the garden. That is all the dream I remember. It was not a shadow cast and created by a troubled mind, but the substance ... It was she, it was herself,' I cried.

'Ask her,' I said. 'After the dream we parted. How long did she stay with me? How often does she meet me?' It was a series of incoherent questions. I myself had no clear notion what I wanted to ask or how to ask it. I only felt the urge to ask questions ... She evidently understood whatever it was that was in my mind, and replied: 'I shall try to answer these questions of yours, but I have to do it unsatisfactorily, because of their nature. You have been in this garden house today for over two hours. Can you say you have been in the company of your friend just once, twice or thrice? The moment you call someone who is in the next room, he answers you and comes to your side if need be. I am present at your side when you sit for development and communion. At other times it is as if I were in the next room, aware of the fact of your presence, easily accessible and ready to come at your slightest behest. You may even think of the walls separating us as walls of glass.'

It was a delightful surprise for me one day, returning home from college, to receive a card from my mother, saying she was coming by the eleven o'clock bus on the following morning. I told the child immediately. But she asked: 'Who is coming with her? Is she bringing dolls?'

'Oh, yes, yes,' I said. I cancelled the walk that evening. The house needed a lot of tidying up, otherwise mother would spend her entire stay doing it. I took off my shirt, tucked up my *dhoti*, and wrapped a towel round my head, as a preparation. In the kitchen I told the old lady, 'Please polish all the vessels. My mother will be here tomorrow. You know how she views these things!' The old lady pulled down all the vessels, and the purr of her broom, sweeping the store, resounded through the house. I took a duster and a long-handled broom, and cleaned up the cornices and dusted everything, dragged the trunks about, pulled down all the books, sneezed and caught a cold which lasted a day or two. The child followed me about. She had caught the fever of activity and followed me about whining and imploring for work. I said: 'Your toy box, you have stuffed it in such a way that we cannot close it. It looks ugly in the hall with its lid thrown back agape; do something about it. Throw away all the unimportant things, and clean and arrange the things in the box. What will your grandmother say if she sees your box?'

Leela at first grumbled and demanded to be allotted some worthwhile work. But I persuaded her by dinning into her over and over again: 'What will your grandmother say if she sees your box!' Finally she realized the seriousness of the position and said: 'Yes.' She went over to her box, and as usual held it by the handle on one side and tipped the entire contents on the floor. They came down with a terrific clatter and crash – a dozen cardboard boxes, her slate, books, wooden toys and engines and motors and dolls, all crashed down in a heap on the floor. She squatted in their midst and said, 'Shall I throw away the things I don't want?'

'Yes.' She started this operation. She picked up and looked at each, and said: 'This thing is not wanted' and flung it off to another corner of the hall. This mood had caught her and cardboard boxes and all kinds of things which she cherished seemed to vex her suddenly by their presence. In a short time in another corner of the hall were heaped the bulk of her possessions. Except her school books and five wooden vessels, and a large doll, all the other things were there. I had to go on with my work in another part of the house. But when I saw what she had done, I protested. 'I tidied up this hall.' 'I will throw them in the street now,' she explained. She came over, picked up a handful, took them to the street, returned with the handful, looked wistfully at the heap and appealed: 'Father, I must put them all back in the box.'

'Why?'

'They are all important ...' she said very earnestly, looking at me fixedly. And forthwith all the toys returned to the box in the same manner as they came out – in a clattering rush.

I applied for leave in order to meet my mother. I waited at the bus stand, beyond the market square. The glare was blinding; the dust unbearable. The bus from Trichinopoly due to arrive at eleven was not showing any signs even half an hour later. I was growing impatient. The bus service people had made no provision for waiting. There was a miserable tamarind tree with sparse leaves, under which were gathered three women waiting to catch the bus, a coolie waiting for fares, as ass in the neighbourhood who could not stand the heat of the day – and a *jutka* with horse strapped to it; the *jutka* man had just brought it in so that there should be a patch of shade on the horse's snout; he seemed to feel satisfied that he had saved the horse from the heat of the sun. The *jutka* man was also waiting for the bus to arrive and provide him a fare. He waited for the bus, felt drowsy, curled up in his seat and was soon asleep. The donkey moved nearer and put his mouth into the bunch of grass thrown down on the ground for the horse to munch while the master slept. The donkey pulled out a mouthful, at which the horse stamped and neighed. The car driver woke up and flourished his whip at the donkey. And we enjoyed the whole show, although the sun baked us.

After all the bus arrived at twelve precisely. Parched and dusty, my mother wriggled herself out from among her fellow passengers. 'How is the child?' she asked getting down. It was her very first question. We put her luggage into the *jutka*, haggled with the driver, and started home. Over the rattling of the wheels she spoke – complaining about my correspondence, enquiring about the child, if the old cook was well, and how I was managing to look after the child. I was tremendously pleased: as I looked at her, warm, and throbbing with life and enquiries, it seemed to restore for a moment one's sense of security, the solid factors of life, and its warmth and interests.

My child as usual was waiting at the door, and hardly had the old lady got down from the carriage when she ran to her and was, in a moment, in her arms. I could hardly comprehend – there were so many excited changes between the grandmother and daughter. 'Granny, open your trunk, open your trunk, what have you brought for me? ...' She went on pestering even before the trunk and bed were brought in. They went in. I paid off the carriage, received the change, and followed. By that time I found there was a great argument going on between them – the little one standing on my mother's ancient trunk, and insisting upon having it opened immediately. My mother, mildly protesting, requesting to be allowed to rest for a few minutes: 'Oh, child, there's no shops in our little place. What should I bring you?' There were tears in her eyes. She cast a slight look at the room on our right in the hall, my wife's room, now empty, and touched away the tears with the tip of her fingers.

My daughter stamped on the steel trunk, and made such a row that I felt it was time for me to interfere: 'H'sh, you must learn ....' I began. But my mother stopped me: 'Don't be harsh; poor child, jump down, I'll open the trunk for you.' She muttered as she fumbled with the key and the lock: 'You used to be exactly the same: you'd cling to your father, and wouldn't let him remove even his sandals before giving you your presents.' She opened the trunk. My daughter sat on her lap and gazed into the trunk expectantly. My mother pulled out a few *saris*, a couple of towels, jackets, a horn comb, and lastly a little casket, out of which she produced a gold chain. 'I had this made for the child at the town shop when your father went there last time. He is the only goldsmith we have near at hand, though fifteen miles away ...' She slipped the chain over the child's head. 'Three sovereigns weight. How do you like it?' Leela looked down at her chest with great satisfaction. The gold chain glistened, but I was absorbed elsewhere. I was staring at the casket from which mother had taken out the chain. 'Mother, give it here!' I cried.

I examined it, measured it with my finger, held it off and scrutinized it – an ivory-worked sandalwood casket. 'Wait a minute!' I said and ran into my room. I pulled out the table drawer, turned over the pages containing my wife's messages. She had written: 'It is not a very big box – about eight or ten inches long, three inches high, and about four inches wide ... the lid of the box is not flat but slightly elevated ... It was given to me by my mother-in-law. Box of ivory and sandalwood ...' I took out a little scale and measured the box. The measurements she had given were slightly more or less by about half an inch all round. I put away the scale and read over the message again. I couldn't yet decide whether her reference was to this casket or some other. And presently I came upon a sentence, which had nearly escaped me all these days. 'The casket is mounted on short ivory legs, resembling tiger-paws.' I lifted the casket and examined its legs. The tiger-paws were there. I grew red with excitement. I clutched the pages and was about to run out to read them to my mother. But I checked myself. I'd never spoken of these to anyone so far. She might not see it as I did, she might doubt, cross-examine, feel on the whole disturbed. It meant a new habit of thinking in regard to death, all too difficult at her age, or she might think I was mad. In any case this information was too precious to part with, to make public even to a mother. I put the papers into the drawer, went back, and sat down beside my mother. I said, 'I like this box, mother, what do you keep in it?' 'All your,' she lowered her voice and muttered in my ear, so that the child should not hear, 'wife's jewels. I got this from my sister years ago. Susila used to be fond of it and had once or twice even made bold to ask for it. But somehow I didn't give it to her ... Now I keep her jewels in it. I'll give it to the child ...'

'Can I keep it with me?' I asked.

'Why do you want it? It's a jewel box ...'

'I like it, mother. I'll keep some of the child's knick-knacks in it,' I said. She gave it to me.

This discovery made me write to my father-in-law next day for the bundle of fourteen letters, which Susila had often mentioned. Four days later I received a reply. 'I have searched every nook and corner in the house and every box, but not a single letter is to be found. Perhaps they were in that lot which I saw her and her brother destroying in the fire one day when she was here last. I hope you will forgive this disappointment and not feel dejected.' In his last paragraph he wrote: 'I don't know if you are already aware of it. I have written to your father about it. I intend to make an endowment for my dear grandchild Leela to benefit her when she comes of a marriageable age.'

I went to my mother. She was sitting in the hall, combing the child's hair. She did everything with her own hands nowadays, often complaining that my neglect had made the child's tresses shorter.

'I've a letter from my father-in-law,' I began.

'Oh, has he written to you about this matter?' she said slyly pointing at the child.

'Yes – he has.'

'He wrote to your father,' she said. 'He proposes to set apart,' she indicated with her fingers six, 'for this person, to be given to her on the day of her marriage.'

'Whose marriage, mother?' the child asked.

'Somebody's marriage, child, don't listen to our talk,' she said, and continued. 'And your father also proposes to set apart a similar sum for the same purpose.'

'Oh,' I said, not knowing what to say. 'She is very lucky!'

My mother smiled cynically, 'Of course you must admire her luck.' She added, with a sigh: 'What are these? Can these things ever compensate for the absence of that one person?'

'Who is to be married, mother?' the child asked again.

'A girl in our place,' said her grandmother.

'How big is she?' asked the child. For some unknown reason she seemed to be concerned with the bulk of this bride. My mother said: 'Even if she has proved unlucky in other matters, let her at least have a well-provided future.'

My mother stayed with us for four weeks. My father's condition had improved and she could stay with us – happy days; the child bloomed with a new life, under her handling. She ceased to approach me for company or help. She stuck to her grandmother morning to night and slept on her bed at night. She bloomed in this warmth. Children need above all else the warmth of a mother's touch. Watching her now I realized with a pang that the very best I could provide was still hopelessly inadequate. And if the child had looked happy under my handling it was more out of tolerance than anything else.

On the eve of her departure mother was packing up. The child stood beside her watching and asked: 'Mother, are you going?'

'Yes, dear, yes.'

'Don't go,' she said and looked so miserable that mother said: 'Will you come with me?' Leela jumped at this suggestion. She cried: 'Give me a box, father, I want to put my things into it.' I said soothingly: 'There is time, there is time.' At which she became uncontrollable. My mother said: 'Seriously, why don't you let me take her with me?' I said: 'She will not go. She will want me too ...' Granny said: 'Your father will not come with us.'

'Oh!' said the child, 'why not?'

'He has his school to attend ...'

'But I have also my school,' Leela replied irrelevantly.

'So, you must stay and let grandmother go,' I said.

'Why will she not stay here?' the child asked. I saw that she had made up her mind to go with her grandmother. She was thrilled to hear that there were other children in the house. My sister's two children and a few others, numbering in all seven. Leela could not understand what it meant. How could there be children at home? Children were to be seen only in schools. So she asked: 'Is it a school?'

Next afternoon she was ready to start with her grandmother. I felt acute anxiety about sending her by bus. I had never been separated from her; the thought appalled me. But as I saw her bubbling over with enthusiasm I told myself: 'Don't be selfish. She must have her own life.' Her trunk of toys and her bed of clothes were there, perched upon the bus next afternoon. I had been dinning into my mother's ears instructions regarding the child. Even as the conductor blew his whistle I shouted instructions. 'Don't allow her to lean out. See that she doesn't eat too many sweets. She gets a racking cough at nights. Oil and bath every Friday, but the water must not be too hot ... She must be immediately wrapped up ... Milk, only half a tumbler ...' My mother merely smiled.

The child said: 'Father, I will write you a letter.'

The bus groaned and moved, and was soon lost in a screen of dust of its own kicking.

A few weeks later a letter arrived from my father, enclosing a scrap of paper with a scrawl on it. My father wrote: 'The enclosed letter is from your Leela. I just mentioned today that I was going to write to you, and at once she declared she had much to write to you too. I gave her my pencil and the paper, and she has written this letter.' I looked at a small slip of paper: the familiar memo pad of my father's neatly torn in half. I saw huge scrawls looking like trees or clouds and a few letters of the alphabet and at the bottom the huge word: LEELA. It was folded and on the flap was written 'To my beloved father', which was in my father's handwriting, though he tried to disguise it by writing rounded capital letters. Moreover there was his favourite ink. I looked at this communication from my daughter and felt very happy. I folded it and put it in my purse as if it were a rare document. My father's letter explained: 'You may want to know what she has written. Here is the paraphrase. She is always surrounded by a dozen children, always playing, building a castle on the pyol on which her grandfather is resting. He is spending all his time watching her and what a great joy it is. It has made him forget his illness, watching her. In the evening she goes out with her granny to the tank or the garden. She is in splendid health, eating and digesting everything that her granny gives her. A teacher comes to teach her in the afternoon. She sleeps beside her granny. I asked her if she wants her father. "Yes," she says, "let him come here," which is a very profound suggestion. I would ask you to come and spend your week-end holidays with her. After all she is only four hours off from your place. So I hope you will not allow any feeling of loneliness to oppress you ...'

I boarded the bus for the village next week-end.

I returned from the village. The house seemed unbearably dull. But I bore it. 'There is no escape from loneliness and separation ...' I told myself often. 'Wife, child, brothers, parents, friends ... We come together only to go apart again. It is one continuous movement. They move away from us as we move away from them. The law of life can't be avoided. The law comes into operation the moment we detach ourselves from our mother's womb. All struggle and misery in life is due to our attempt to arrest this law or get away from it or in allowing ourselves to be hurt by it. The fact must be recognized. A profound unmitigated loneliness is the only truth of life. All else is false. My mother got away from her parents, my sisters from our house, I and my brother away from each other, my wife was torn away from me, my daughter is going away with my mother, my father has gone away from his father, my earliest friends – where are they? They scatter apart like the droplets of a water-spray. The law of life. No sense in battling against it ...' Thus I reconciled myself to this separation with less struggle than before. I read a lot, I wrote a lot, I reflected as much as I could. I saw pictures, went out for walks, and frequently met my friend the headmaster. I spent a great deal of my time watching the children at play or hearing him narrate his stories for the children as they sat under the mango tree in the school compound. When I sat there at the threshold of his hut and watched the children, all sense of loneliness ceased to oppress, and I felt a deep joy and contentment stirring within me. I felt there was nothing more for me to demand of life. The headmaster's presence was always most soothing. He was a very happy man nowadays. His school had over two hundred pupils studying in it and he was able to spend as much as he wanted in staffing and equipping the school.

His wife and children visited him often, at least thrice in a day. He treated them kindly, although he still refused to visit them at home, and strictly forbade them to call him father or husband. His wife, a greatly chastened person now, often implored him to let her bring him his food. He firmly declined the offer, declaring: 'No, it is there that all the trouble starts. The kitchen is the deadliest arsenal a woman possesses.'

CHAPTER EIGHT

My mind was made up. I was in search of a harmonious existence and everything that disturbed that harmony was to be rigorously excluded, even my college work. One whole night I sat up in the loneliness of my house thinking it over, and before the night was out my mind was made up. I could not go on with that work; nor did I need the one hundred rupees they gave me. At first I had thought of sending in my resignation by letter to Brown, and making an end of it. I would avoid all the personal contacts, persuasions, and all the possible sentimentalities inevitable in the act of snapping familiar roots. I would send in a letter which would be a classic in its own way, and which would singe the fingers of whoever touched it. In it I was going to attack a whole century of false education. I was going to explain why I could no longer stuff Shakespeare and Elizabethan metre and Romantic poetry for the hundredth time into young minds and feed them on the dead mutton of literary analysis and theories and histories, while what they needed was lessons in the fullest use of the mind. This education had reduced us to a nation of morons; we were strangers to our own culture and camp followers of another culture, feeding on leavings and garbage.

After coffee I sat down at my table with several sheets of large paper before me. I began 'Dear Mr Brown: This is my letter of resignation. You will doubtless want to know the reasons. Here they are ...' I didn't like this. It was too breezy. I scored it out and began again. I filled three sheets, and reading it over, felt ashamed of myself. It was too theatrical and pompous for my taste. I was entangled too much in theories and platitudes and holding forth to all whom it might concern. It was like a rabid attack on all English writers, which was hardly my purpose. 'What fool could be insensible to Shakespeare's sonnets or the *Ode to the West Wind* or "A thing of beauty is a joy for ever"?'

I reflected. 'But what about examinations and critical notes? Didn't these largely take the place of literature? What about our own roots?' I thought over it deeply and felt very puzzled. I added: 'I am up against the system, the whole method and approach of a system of education which makes us morons, cultural morons, but efficient clerks for all your business and administrative offices. You must not think that I am opposed to my particular studies of authors ...' The repetition of ideas uttered a hundred times before. It looked like a rehash of an article entitled 'Problems of Higher Education', which appeared again and again in a weekend educational supplement – the yarn some 'educationist' was spinning out for ten rupees a column.

'This is not what I want to say,' I muttered to myself and tore up the letter and stuffed it into the wastepaper basket. 'There is something far deeper that I wish to say.'

I took out a small sheet of paper and wrote: 'Dear Sir, I beg to tender my resignation for personal reasons. I request you to relieve me immediately ...' I put it in an envelope.

I walked into Brown's room that afternoon with this envelope in my hand. He was in a leisurely mood sitting back in his swivel chair, reading a book. I placed the envelope before him.

'What is this? Applying for leave?' he said, a smile spreading on his aged handsome face ... 'Be seated ...' He read the letter. His face turned slightly red. He looked at me and said: 'What is the matter?' He lit a cigarette, blew out a ring of smoke and waited for my answer, looking at me with his greenish eyes. I merely replied: 'I can't go on with this work any longer, sir ...'

'Any special reason?' I remained silent. I didn't know what to say. I replied: 'I am taking up work in a children's school.' 'Oh!' he said ...'But I didn't know you had primary school training ...' he replied. I looked at him in despair; his Western mind, classifying, labelling, departmentalizing ... I merely replied: 'I am beginning a new experiment in education, with another friend.' 'Oh, that is interesting,' he replied. 'But look here, must you resign? Couldn't you keep it on as an extra interest ... We do want a lot of experimenting in education, but you could always ...' He went on suggesting it as a hobby. I replied: 'Sir, what I am doing in the college hardly seems to me work. I mug up and repeat and they mug up and repeat in examinations ... This hardly seems to me work, Mr Brown. It is a fraud I am practising for a consideration of a hundred rupees a month ... It doesn't please my innermost self ...' Thus I rambled on.

'I do not know,' he said scratching his head. 'It seems to me unfortunate. However, I wouldn't make up my mind in a hurry if I were you ...'

'I have thought it over deeply, sir,' I replied. 'My mind is made up.'

He asked: 'What does it mean to you financially?'

'About twenty-fives rupees a month ...' I replied.

'That means a cutting down ...'

'That is so. I have no use for money. I have no family. My child is being looked after by others and they have provided for her future too. I have a few savings. I have no use for a hundred rupees a month ...' Brown looked quite baffled. I added: 'Of all persons on earth, I can afford to do what seems to me work, something which satisfies my innermost aspiration. I will write poetry and live and work with children and watch their minds unfold ...'

'Quite,' he replied. 'A man like you ought to derive equal delight in teaching literature. You have done admirably as a teacher of literature ...'

I shook my head. 'I don't feel I have done anything of the kind ...'

'Do you mean to say that all those poets and dramatists have meant nothing to you?'

I was in danger of repeating the letter I had torn up. 'It is not that. I revere them. And I hope to give them to these children for their delight and enlightenment, but in a different measure and in a different manner.' I rambled on thus. I could not speak clearly. Brown bore with me patiently. Our interview lasted an hour. At the end of it he said: 'Take another week, if you like, to consider. I do wish you wouldn't leave us.' He held out his hand. I gripped his large warm palm, and walked out of the room.

* * *

They arranged a grand send-off for me. The function was timed to begin at six. I arrived five minutes earlier and was at once seized on by Sastri and Rangappa, the moving spirits of the occasion. They waited at the porch and the moment they sighted me, they dashed forward, and gripped my hand and dragged me on to the quadrangle, where they had made spectacular arrangements. The hotel man had risen to the occasion; he had tied up coloured buntings and streamers, spread his embroidered tablecloth on a dozen tables, and placed his usual gold mohur bunches on nickel vases. Porcelain cups and plates clanked somewhere. White-shirted serving boys stood respectfully on the edge of the scene. They looked at me with respectful interest. In fact everyone looked on me as a sort of awe-inspiring personality. What was there in this to make a sudden hero of me? It was very embarrassing. On the air was borne a gentle suggestion of jasmine and rose. I knew a garland was waiting for me somewhere.

I was pressed into a high-backed chair. Next to mine was another chair for Brown. On my left sat Gajapathy. All around were gathered a miscellaneous crowd of teachers and boys. Everybody kept staring at me. I felt very unhappy. I had never felt more selfconscious in all my life. Gajapathy was highly nervous and excited, and wriggled in his chair. He kept muttering, 'Why is not Brown here yet?' And constantly looked at his watch.

There was the sound of a car stopping outside. 'The Principal,' everyone muttered. The creaking of fast footsteps and Brown arrived in an evening suit. 'Even he is dressed for the occasion,' I said to myself. 'Why, why all this ceremony?' Gajapathy shot up in his seat. Sastri and Rangappa went forward to receive him.

Now we were all ready. Brown bent over to me and whispered: 'I was afraid the weather wouldn't let us see the quadrangle today.' I looked at the sky and mumbled something about the weather. Gajapathy, uninvited, joined us in the conversation. 'Rain is very unusual at this season, but strangely enough we have had it for the past two days. But today our luck is good ...'

'Yes,' Brown echoed, 'rather unusual ...' Perspiring and puffing, Rangappa moved about, and passed a signal on to the servers. There were nearly ten courses. Brown lightly touched each one of them; withdrew with quick caution from items which were over-spiced (experience born of thirty years' stay in India), put small bits of sweets into his mouth and sent them on without moving his lips. Gajapathy sat back with his fingers locked into each other, sadly looking at the plates. The other guests were talking among themselves, a merry hum pervaded the place. I asked Gajapathy: 'Why?' He shook his head sadly: 'I am a sick man, can't afford these luxuries ...' Brown looked at him without comment. He wanted to change the subject from personal ailments. He held up between his thumb and forefinger a gold-coloured sweet and said: 'This is also a variant of *jilebi*, isn't it?'

'I suppose so, sir,' replied Gajapathy. 'I think it is the stuff made of American flour, while the real *jilebi* ...'

'Ah, I'm right. I know my *jilebi* when I see it.' A smile spread round his eyes. We laughed. Rangappa, who had been observing us from his chair far off, looked at us enquiringly, and also smiled out of politeness ...

When coffee was served, Brown clutched his cup and stood up. A silence fell on the gathering: 'To the health of our guest of this evening,' he said in his deep sonorous voice. 'I don't know if it would be right to toast with coffee but we won't bother about these proprieties now ...' On behalf of the assembly he wished me all prosperity and happiness. He continued, 'I have known him, I have lost count now how many years. I remember the day he came to my room with an application for a seat in English Honours. I've seen him grow under my eyes; he has shown himself an able teacher. The boys have loved him. And I'm sure they have had reason to dread him very much as an examiner.' Some boys looked at me with a grin. 'Everywhere, under every condition, he has proved himself to be an uncompromising idealist. His constant anxiety has been to find the world good enough for his own principles of life and letters. Few men would have the courage to throw up a lucrative income and adopt one very much lower. But he has done it. Success must be measured by its profitlessness, said a French philosopher. Our college can look upon this idealist with justifiable pride. And ...' looking at me he said: 'when your institution has developed and made a mark in the world, I do hope you will allow us a small share of the gratification that you yourself feel ... Gentlemen, I'm sure you will all join me in wishing our friend all success.' He raised his cup.

I felt too disturbed to look up. My hands trembled. I sat looking down. Brown sat down. I was too moved: 'Many thanks,' I murmured. Three more speeches followed: one by Rangappa who traced our friendship to the hostel days, one by Sastri and one by an Honours boy. 'Our country needs more men like our beloved teacher who is going out today,' he said in his high-pitched tender voice. 'The national regeneration is in his hands ...' Goodwill and adulation enveloped me like thick mist. In the end I got up and said: 'Gentlemen, permit me to thank you all for your kind words. Let me assure you I'm retiring, not with a feeling of sacrifice for a national cause, but with a very selfish purpose. I'm seeking a great inner peace. I find I can't attain it unless I withdraw from the adult world and adult work into the world of children. And there, let me assure you, is a vast storehouse of peace and harmony. I have not had in mind anything more than that, and I hope you will correct your estimates accordingly. I am deeply grateful to you and to our chief for your great kindness ...' I sat down because I found my voice quivering.

Rangappa brought a heavy rose and jasmine garland and slipped it over my neck. He brought another and put it on the Principal. Applause. 'Three cheers for our guest of the evening,' somebody screamed. 'Hip! Hip ...' burst like an explosion. And then 'Three cheers for our Principal ...' On this thunderous note our evening concluded.

I was walking down our lone street late at night, enveloped in the fragrance of the jasmine and rose garland, slung on my arm. 'For whom am I carrying this jasmine home?' I asked myself. Susila would treasure a garland for two whole days, cutting up and sticking masses of it in her hair morning and evening. 'Carrying a garland to a lonely house – a dreadful job,' I told myself.

I fumbled with the key in the dark, opened the door and switched on the light. I hung up the garland on a nail and kicked up the roll of bedding. The fragrance permeated the whole house. I sprinkled a little water on the flowers to keep them fresh, put out the light and lay down to sleep.

The garland hung by the nail right over my head. The few drops of water which I sprinkled on the flowers seemed to have quickened in them a new life. Their essences came forth into the dark night as I lay in bed, bringing a new vigour with them. The atmosphere became surcharged with strange spiritual forces. Their delicate aroma filled every particle of the air, and as I let my mind float in the ecstasy, gradually perceptions and senses deepened. Oblivion crept over me like a cloud. The past, present and the future welded into one.

I had been thinking of the day's activities and meetings and associations. But they seemed to have no place now. I checked my mind. Bits of memory came floating – a gesture of Brown's, the toy house in the dentist's front room, Rangappa with a garland, and the ring of many speeches and voices – all this was gently overwhelmed and swept aside, till one's mind became clean and bare and a mere chamber of fragrance. It was a superb, noble intoxication. And I had no choice but to let my mind and memories drown in it. I softly called, 'Susila! Susila, my wife ...' with all my being. It sounded as if it were a hypnotic melody. 'My wife ... my wife, my wife ...' My mind trembled with this rhythm, I forgot myself and my own existence. I fell into a drowse, whispering, 'My wife, wife.' How long? How could I say? When I opened my eyes again she was sitting on my bed looking at me with an extraordinary smile in her eyes.

'Susila! Susila!' I cried. 'You here!' 'Yes, I'm here, have always been here.' I sat up leaning on my pillow. 'Why do you disturb yourself?' she asked.

'I am making a place for you,' I said, edging away a little. I looked her up and down and said: 'How well you look!' Her complexion had a golden glow, her eyes sparkled with a new light, her *sari* shimmered with blue interwoven with 'light' as she had termed it ...'How beautiful!' I said looking at it. 'Yes, I always wear this when I come to you. I know you like it very much,' she said. I gazed on her face. There was an overwhelming fragrance of jasmine surrounding her. 'Still jasmine-scented!' I commented.

'Oh wait,' I said and got up. I picked up the garland from the nail and returned to bed. I held it to her. 'For you as ever. I somehow feared you wouldn't take it ...' She received it with a smile, cut off a piece of it and stuck it in a curve on the back of her head. She turned her head and asked: 'Is this all right?'

'Wonderful,' I said, smelling it.

A cock crew. The first purple of the dawn came through our window, and faintly touched the walls of our room. 'Dawn!' she whispered and rose to her feet.

We stood at the window, gazing on a slender, red streak over the eastern rim of the earth. A cool breeze lapped our faces. The boundaries of our personalities suddenly dissolved. It was a moment of rare, immutable joy – a moment for which one feels grateful to Life and Death.

This book is set in BEMBO which was cut
by the punch-cutter Francesco Griffo
for the Venetian printer-publisher
Aldus Manutius in early 1495
and first used in a pamphlet
by a young scholar
named Pietro
Bembo.